LAN

D1327061

PRINCE
OF THE SPEAR

Also by David Hair

PRINCE
OF THE SPEAR
THE SUNSURGE QUARTET BOOK II

DAVID HAIR

Jo Fletcher
BOOKS

First published in Great Britain in 2018 by Jo Fletcher Books

Jo Fletcher Books
an imprint of
Quercus Editions Ltd
Carmelite House
50 Victoria Embankment
London EC4Y 0DZ

An Hachette UK company

A CIP catalogue record for this book is available
from the British Library.

HB ISBN 978 1 78429 096 2
TPB ISBN 978 1 78429 095 5
EBOOK ISBN 978 1 78429 097 9

10 9 8 7 6 5 4 3 2 1

Typeset by CC Book Production
Printed and bound in Great Britain by Clays Ltd, St Ives plc

This book is dedicated to my wife Kerry, whose love, patience, support, honesty, sense of fun and adventure get me through each day. This writing gig would be impossible without you, and I'm eternally grateful that we met and for where life has taken us. Thank you for everything.

TABLE OF CONTENTS

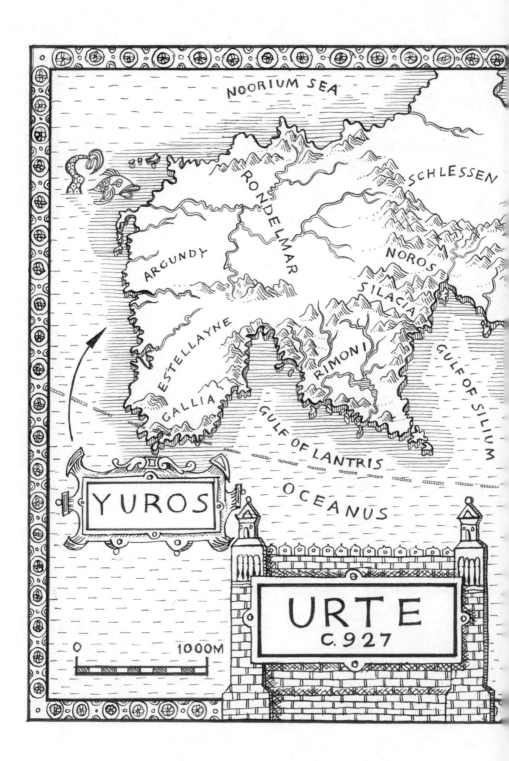

NOORIUM SEA

SCHLESSEN

RONDELMAR

ARGUNDY

NOROS

SILACIA

ESTELLAYNE

RIMONI

GULF OF SILIUM

GALLIA

GULF OF LANTRIS

OCEANUS

YUROS

URTE
C. 927

0   1000M

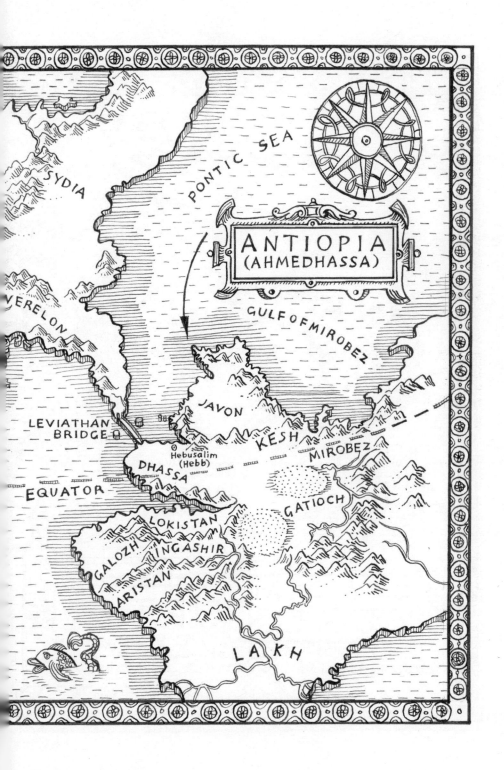

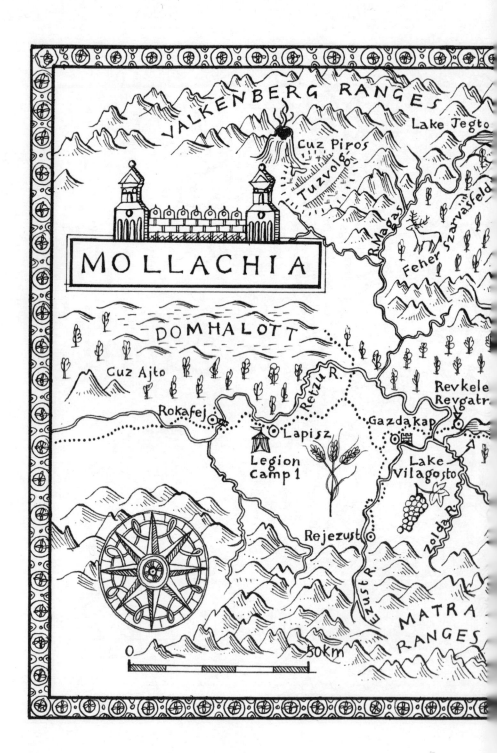

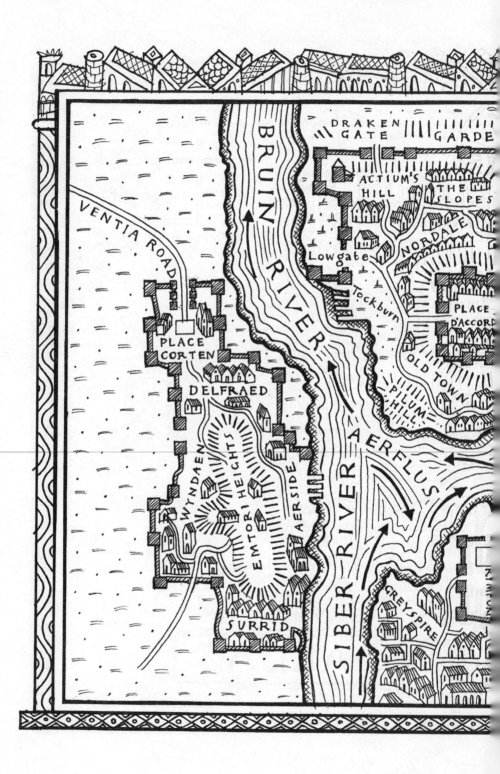

NORTH WALL

0 1 2km

6km to Finoskarre

SERTANUS PARADE

N

GRAVENHURST

Roidan Heights

OLD WALL

IMPERIAL BASTION

HIGHGRANGE

ESDALE

DAWNPORT

Roidan Heights

CLEAVE

Fisheart

KENSIDE

NORTHBANK

DELTA PIERS

BRUIN RIVER

CELESTIUM

SOUTHSIDE

Fenreach

Sharrod Fens

ac Corin

PALLAS

WHAT HAS GONE BEFORE

The Events of 930–935
(*as related in* Empress of the Fall)

In Junesse 930, Alaron Mercer and Ramita Ankesharan, co-founders of the Merozain Bhaicara, seized control of the towers of the Leviathan Bridge, saving it from destruction and using the energies roused by the Keepers to destroy the Imperial Windfleet above, killing Emperor Constant and Mater-Imperia Lucia and many more of the court's most influential mage-nobles. These deaths create a power vacuum at the very heart of the Rondian Empire.

The Church of Kore reacts faster than the remaining Pallas nobility: Grand Prelate Dominius Wurther has been entrusted with the emperor's children, Prince Cordan and Princess Coramore and he prepares to form a Regency Council in Cordan's name to secure the continuation of the Sacrecour dynasty. He doesn't suspect that his confidante, the prelate Ostevan, has other loyalties: he tips off his kinswoman, Duchess Radine Jandreux, in the northern city of Coraine, birthplace of Natia, Emperor Magnus' first wife. The Corani fell from favour after Natia's demise and Constant's ascent to power. Now their time has come again . . .

Striking quickly, Radine sends Corani mage-knights, led by Sir Solon Takwyth and the spymaster Dirklan Setallius, steal Cordan and Coramore from under the Church's nose – and more importantly, they free a woman of whom they had no knowledge, who turns out to be Lyra Vereinen, the daughter of the late Princess Natia.

Acting swiftly, the Corani plot a return to power. With their rivals paralysed by the disasters of the Third Crusade, those keeping order inside the capital – Grand Prelate Wurther and Treasurer Calan Dubrayle – are persuaded to turn their backs on the Sacrecour clan; they come to an agreement for the Corani to return to Pallas; that agreement includes the banishment of Ostevan, in revenge for his betrayal of Wurther. Duchess Radine marches her soldiers south into Pallas, where the populace, fearing a civil war, greet them with great rejoicing, aided by the faery-tale circumstances of Lyra's rescue.

But Lyra is no compliant tool to be wielded by Corani ambitions: she is a complex young woman with her own secrets; there are un-answered questions over her parentage, and she has never been trained in the gnosis, despite being a pure-blood mage. When she does finally awaken her innate magic, it's not the gnosis, but the heretical arts of pandaemancy. Worse, she has also fallen in love with her rescuer, the jaded Corani knight Ril Endarion, a highly unsuitable relationship for the woman who is to be the figurehead of the Corani cause, their queen and the new empress.

On the eve of her coronation, with Radine demanding that Lyra accept the dour and formidable Solon Takwyth as her husband, Lyra blindsides the duchess. In a secret ceremony, Ostevan, acting out of spite and knowing he is facing exile, marries Ril and Lyra. After Lyra has been crowned the following day, she openly declares her marriage before the world. Radine, Takwyth and Setallius are forced to accept her actions, and Takwyth goes into voluntary exile after he strikes Ril, the new Prince-Consort.

Despite this shaky start, the Corani are able to face down their rivals and the succession crisis appears to have been resolved. In relief, Pallas and the empire settle to deal with a new world and a new ruler.

Over the next five years, the Rondian Empire struggles on. There's civil strife in the southern regions of Rimoni and Silacia, where bandit-lords and mercenaries are fighting, but that's nothing new. The Treasury has been forced to impose heavy taxes to rebuild the finances of the empire, and vassal-states like Argundy, Estellayne and Noros are clamouring for greater autonomy, but the Corani gamble in seizing the throne appears to have paid off. Duchess Radine dies, still embittered by Lyra's betrayal, but Ril and Lyra continue to reign securely in Pallas – although the economy is wavering, there is unrest in the provinces and Lyra has had two miscarriages and remains without an heir of her blood.

In Ahmedhassa, the Sultan Salim Kabarakhi is trying to rebuild his realm with the aid of the mighty eastern mage, Rashid Mubarak. His efforts are undermined by corruption, and by the Shihadi faction, who are demanding revenge against the West, even though the Leviathan Bridge, the only link to Yuros, will remain below water and unusable until 940.

In 935, new crises are developing in East and West. A secret masked cabal, whose identities are concealed even from each other, is formed by the rogue Ordo Costruo mage Ervyn Naxius, a genius unconstrained by morality. He offers the cabal members powers beyond even those of the Merozain Bhaicara, who are Ascendants capable of utilising all sixteen facets of the gnosis. What Naxius offers is a link to an ancient super-daemon called Abraxas, and the ability to enslave others using the daemon's ichor. When Naxius proves to his cabal that they, not the daemon, will be in control, the 'Masks' join his mission to unseat every throne and make themselves rulers of a new era.

In the West, the cabal aims to supplant Empress Lyra with the pliant Prince Cordan, but to do this, they must snatch the royal children from Corani custody. They strike during the jousting tournament which was supposed to bolster Ril and Lyra's faltering rule; instead, the tourney becomes the centre of a web of intrigue. The exiled and embittered Ostevan, now a member of the Masks cabal, engineers a return to court as Lyra's confessor and soon begins to infect people with the daemon's ichor. The effects are not dissimilar – at first, at least – to the symptoms of riverreek, a seasonal illness. He uses this hidden control over other courtiers to engineer the snatching of the royal children on the last day of the tourney.

The climax of the tourney is a clash between Ril, a fine warrior for all his faults, and an 'Incognito Knight'; the victorious unknown is revealed to be Solon Takwyth, returned from exile. He begs a boon from Lyra before the entire crowd: that he be forgiven and permitted to return to Corani service, and Lyra is forced to allow this – then they receive the shocking news that the royal children have been abducted.

Meanwhile, in the East, the Masks strike a savage blow against peace: at the height of the Convocation, the religious and political event that shapes future policy, Sultan Salim is murdered by masked assassins. The only survivor of his household is Latif, his impersonator, who goes into hiding while Rashid Mubarak seizes control, and shifts policy towards war. His sons, the brutal Attam and the cunning Xoredh, advance his plans for Shihad, a holy war, against the vast and hostile nation of Lakh, to unify his new sultanate.

But Rashid is working a delicate tightrope, striving to appear just as well as strong, and he appoints his nephew, Prince Waqar, to investigate Salim's murder. Waqar is distracted by the plight of his mother Sakita, Rashid's sister: she too was attacked that same night, by Salim's marked murderers. Waqar encounters Tarita Alhani, a Javon spy, who is also investigating the murders, and they agree to collaborate. When Sakita dies, Tarita goes north, seeking clues in Hebusalim, while Waqar is sent south, into the wild, mountainous land of Lokistan, on a secret mission for Rashid.

All over the world, momentous events are taking place that may have a profound effect. In Dhassa, the Mollachian princes and mage-brothers Kyrik and Valdyr Sarkany, long held captive in the East's dehumanising breeding-houses, are reunited. It's not an amicable meeting, for Kyrik has converted to the Amteh faith and been released into the care of Godspeaker Paruq, an Eastern priest of Ahm, while Valdyr has remained staunch in his western faith. He escaped his breeding-house, but was recaptured and for the past five years has been a slave-labourer. He has been under a Rune of the Chain since he was a child, which has concealed and disarmed his gnosis.

Paruq manages to secure the brothers' release, taking them by wind-ship to Yuros and setting them down among a tribe of Sydian nomads, with whom he has been conducting missionary work. The brothers are intent on returning to Mollachia and reclaiming their inheritance, but they are captured by tax-farmers, an unhappy by-product of Empress

Lyra's efforts to fund her reign. Their dead father owed a fortune to the empire in taxes and the tax-farmers have new – draconian – laws on their side; two Rondian legions have occupied Mollachia and are busy stripping it of its wealth. One legion is under the command of Robear Delestre and his sister Sacrista, who have the tax-farming contract on behalf of their father; and the other, an Imperial legion, is commanded by Governor Ansel Inoxion. The brothers are locked up and left to die, but local freedom fighters – the legendary Vitezai Sarkanum – rescue the brothers, who agree to head up the resistance movement. Kyrik has discovered a common mythology shared by Mollachs and Sydians; he returns to the Sydian steppes to recruit aid. The price: marriage to the fiery Sydian witch Hajya. Valdyr distinguishes himself against the Rondian occupiers, despite having no gnostic powers; the Chain-rune has been removed, but he can feel nothing.

In Pallas, Naxius and his Masks are readying their follow-up attacks. Ordinary citizens, apparently suffering a particularly virulent outbreak of riverreek, are in fact possessed minions of the daemon Abraxas: they're used as shock troops in coordinated assaults on the Imperial Bastion and the Celestium, the Church of Kore's holiest site. Using secret underground tunnels, the attack penetrates all defences, ready to unveil Prince Cordan as the new emperor, and backed by the arrival of a Sacrecour army at the gates.

In the East, the new sultan's careful long-term planning reaches fulfilment. Rashid has assembled a vast windfleet capable of sailing across the skies to invade even as far as the West. The only thing preventing invasion is the Leviathan Bridge itself: if the Ordo Costruo or the Merozain Bhaicara unleash the powers of the Bridge's towers, as they did against Emperor Constant's fleet in 930, Rashid's ships would be destroyed.

During this coordinated assault on peace and order, a new variable enters play: dwyma, or pandaemancy, a heretical form of magic believed to be extinct, has only ever lain dormant. Now Fate has placed three people with the power to use it in the midst of these world-changing events. But two of them don't even suspect they have such a power . . .

In Pallas, the attacks on the Bastion and the Celestium appear to be succeeding; and the Masks look to be on the brink of seizing power – until Empress Lyra uses dwyma to destroy one of the apparently indestructible Masks. In the Celestium, a burst of light from a shrine associated with Saint Eloy, a dwymancer who supposedly abjured his powers, destroys another Mask.

In Mollachia, on a wild night on the sacred Watcher's Peak, Valdyr Sarkany receives the gift of dwyma from four ghostly Watchers and uses it to freeze a legion of Rondian solders just as they're about to defeat Kyrik and his Sydian riders. Robear Delestre perishes, but his sister Sacrista, always the better soldier, survives.

But in the East, the dark side of dwyma is revealed. Sakita Mubarak is also a dwymancer, part of a project by the Ordo Costruo to resurrect this long-extinct form of magic. Now a prisoner of the Masks and kept alive by necromancy, she uses her devastating powers to destroy Midpoint Tower, though it costs her 'life'. Arriving too late, Waqar and Tarita recover artefacts from the tower and receive some clues about the Masks – but Rashid's windfleet appears on the southern horizon, heading for Yuros, and Waqar realises that his beloved uncle may have been working with the masked assassins – he might even be behind his mother's death. He also learns that he and his estranged sister Jehana may have the same 'gift'.

It is Julsep 935, and for the first time in recorded history, the East is invading the West, which is disunited under an inexperienced empress. The Ordo Costruo and Merozain Bhaicara cannot prevent the invasion – all their energies must go into repairing the Bridge before it is washed away. And for the first time in five centuries, dwymancers are walking the lands, with unpredictable and devastating powers.

What they do may damn both East and West to aeons of suffering.

The Masquerade (Beak)

On the Primacy of Knowledge

I once deliberately infected a child with leprosy. But before you condemn, consider that from that experiment, I discovered much about the disease that led to new gnostic treatments which have eradicated the disease from civilised regions.

We're at war against barbarism, superstition and ignorance, and a general who wins a victory in battle while minimising casualties is lauded. Yet I'm being hounded by jealous peers. Yes, I suffered casualties in my research battles – but the victories I won were stunning!

ERVYN NAXIUS, DEFENCE NOTES FROM HIS TRIAL,
HEBUSALIM, 869

Lowgate Tower, Pallas, Rondelmar, Yuros
Julsep 935

Nothing reveals character more than defeat, Ervyn Naxius reflected, as he – or more particularly, his spiratus – soared invisible through the night, covering miles in seconds as it sped across northern Yuros until the Imperial capital – Pallas the Golden, the centre of the Rondian Empire for five centuries – was spread below him. She was like a massive piece of old jewellery, her gems glittering and lovely but the crevices between grimy with the detritus of ages. Pallas: a city of magnificence, excess and most of all, conspiracies. It was here that power, wealth and authority were divided up, in open court and secret backrooms. The heart of Yuros, where every vice and failing was magnified.

Mine, one day soon. Tonight was another step on that journey.

Naxius swooped down to a roofed cupola atop a disused watchtower and took on the appearance of an ancient, black-robed man – his true form. Those who awaited him were similarly attired, but each of them wore a mask of lacquered copper.

A cabal such as theirs needed anonymity, a collective identity and a certain style; he'd taken the ancient Lantric plays for his theme. He knew they were all wondering what to make of the masks he'd selected for each of them; did his choice imply a role, or suggest his interpretation of their character?

All of the above, my dear pawns.

None of them were *truly* present; like him, they had flown here in spirit-form, freed from lumpen flesh to roam the world – one of the more useful gnostic arts.

For Naxius, the journey had been long, but he was well-used to such travel and knew many ways to ease it, from ensuring his body was left in an elevated, open-air site to using drugs and lotions to aid the separation of spiratus from flesh. He touched ground, as tangible to his spiratus as to his human body, and initially ignored his three waiting acolytes, wanting to savour the view. The tower stood near Lowgate, which these days was primarily a rubbish-disposal portal, but as a spiratus lacked olfactory senses, he wasn't required to endure the stench. First, he looked east towards the Bastion, the giant rectangular edifice that dominated the city from atop Roidan Heights. From this side, the scars of his minion's failed coup, which had left the young Empress Lyra Vereinen still enthroned, were invisible.

Below the Bastion was the Aerflus, the swirling body of water formed by the confluence of two great rivers, the Bruin and the Siber. Pallas surrounded the confluence and grew fat off the river trade. The waters also divided the temporal from the spiritual: south of the river lay the giant glittering dome of the Celestium, which had also been unsuccessfully attacked, leaving the Grand Prelate Dominius Wurther still secure on the Pontifex's Curule.

Naxius was untroubled by these failures – any experiment could face unexpected setbacks. He was more interested in the cause of the reverses than the fact of them.

We thought we knew what we faced, but we found deeper defences.

Most importantly, he'd discovered that Lyra Vereinen was a pandae-mancer – or dwymancer, if you preferred the more sympathetic term for the heretical magic. Remarkably, her powers appeared to extend right into the heart of the Celestium. Furthermore, Solon Takwyth had remained loyal and saved her life when Naxius would have sworn the worthy knight hated his empress. Learning these facts had been worth the casualties.

But as he finally turned to face them, he saw his three surviving Western Masks were consumed with worry. Jest sported a diamond-patterned mask; Tear's eyes wept rubies; Angelstar's seraphic features remained austere. He knew their real identities, of course – having recruited them – but as far as he knew, they didn't yet know each other's true names.

'Brother Jest, Brother Angelstar, Sister Tear,' he greeted them. 'We spoke only days ago. What need is there now for further discourse?'

Jest responded first. 'Master, we wished to speak with you without the Easterners present.'

Ah yes, how very predictable. The whole of the West was reeling at the news that Rashid Mubarak, the new Sultan of Kesh, had crippled the Leviathan Bridge and launched an invasion of Yuros. Even now his windfleet was collecting his second wave of troops, while the first armies were preparing to depart Pontus and march west. After three bloody Yurosian Crusades, the Eastern counter-attack – their *Shihad* or holy war – was underway.

His three surviving Western minions now knew that his four Eastern Masks had been central to Rashid's plans, and clearly felt threatened.

'When we last spoke,' Naxius replied, 'you worried that the left hand of my cabal didn't know what the right hand was doing. Nevertheless, you are of the same body. Consider your own hands – they obey the brain, without consulting the other limbs. I give you far more autonomy than that. I've given you tools and pointed you at a problem: that Lyra Vereinen and Dominius Wurther – a guileless girl and a fat priest – sit on the two most powerful thrones in Koredom. You have attempted to unseat them, and failed: learn from that, and try again.'

Their Masks didn't completely hide their reactions; Jest was calm, already adapting and looking forward, and Angelstar was feigning indifference. But Tear was visibly stressed.

'Who will replace Twoface?' she demanded.

'Whomsoever I choose,' Naxius answered. 'You thought you knew who Twoface was, Sister Tear, but you were wrong and you jeopardised your anonymity. Don't make that mistake again.'

She bowed at his reprimand, but didn't look at all repentant.

'Master,' Angelstar said, 'during our attack, we infected ordinary citizens with the daemon ichor – now those people are in captivity, are they a danger to us? Can they be used to trace us?'

'A good question,' Naxius approved. 'The potency of that diluted ichor will lessen and certain things can burn it away entirely, so no, I don't anticipate it being used to trace you. Forget them. Our enemies will even now be adjusting their defences to account for such attacks, so you must find other ways to assail your foes.'

'We faced pandaemancy, which is a heresy,' Angelstar noted. 'Even an empress doesn't stand above the law. Mother Church can bring her down.'

'Indeed – but Grand Prelate Wurther owes his life to that very heresy and I think he knows that,' Naxius replied. 'If you want to drag her to the stake, you must find another man to do it.'

'Empress Lyra's garden is the nexus of her pandaemancy,' Jest said. 'Master, is there anything you, with your vast experience, can tell us about how to overcome such a place?'

'Dwyma has been considered extinct for centuries, and I too believed so, until recently,' Naxius admitted. 'But believe me, it has now become a priority for my research.'

'But the Easterners claimed that a pandaemancer serves them!'

'"Served" – past tense. She died when they damaged the Leviathan Bridge. And we have learned something: that even a dwymancer is not proof against our ichor – they can be infected and controlled, but only for a brief time before their magic rejects them. Get close to Lyra Vereinen and when the time comes, bring her to me. I wish to study her.'

Jest bowed his head obediently but Tear didn't look pleased. 'Brother Jest wishes to operate in both the Bastion and the Celestium,' she complained, 'but I dwell at the heart of the Imperial Palace. Master, please instruct Jest to confine himself to the Holy City and leave the Bastion – *and* Lyra Vereinen – to me!'

It was time to let his irritation show. 'Work together, and resolve your differences!' he ordered. 'You have *one* purpose – one *common* purpose – which is the overthrow of the empress and the grand prelate. I expect cooperation – and success.'

They bowed their heads – reluctantly, but that was to be expected; they were powerful people used to getting their own way. Creative tension was inevitable, perhaps even desirable.

'Go forth. Conquer. Through Abraxas, our chained daemon, you have access to all sixteen Gnostic Studies, and more power than any mage in history. Make it count.'

He waited until they'd bowed again, then in a flash he was gone and streaming back through the aether to his lair.

Ostevan Jandreux waited until the Master's spiratus had vanished, then turned to his fellow conspirators. 'Well, you heard the Master.'

'Aye,' said Angelstar, 'play nicely and get the job done. I'll be going south with the army, so you won't see me for some time. Best you two resolve your issues.' Then he too was gone, a streak lost in the darkness.

Tear bowed her head. 'Jest, I did truly believe that Twoface was Solon Takwyth.'

Ostevan wasn't surprised. Takwyth's face had been ruined on one side, rendering it akin to Twoface, and the exiled Corani knight had shown up just before the latest crisis. In truth, he'd thought the same as Tear – not that he'd admit that now. 'Too obvious,' he said, his tone offhand.

Tear's mask twisted into a lacquered sneer. 'Don't pretend omniscience: you were as much surprised as I! Esvald Berlond was only ever Takwyth's shadow. I believe Takwyth can still be swayed, though.'

'Really? When he all but laid down his life for Empress Lyra?'

'He lives for House Corani – but one can love Coraine and loathe Lyra Vereinen, as I do.'

A raw nerve, Ostevan noted. *Your loyalties to House Corani clearly run deep, Lady, whereas I outgrew mine years ago.* 'If you think he can be persuaded, by all means try – but don't let it spoil your aim for the true prize.'

'I won't,' Tear grated. 'And the Bastion is mine – stick to the Celestium, *Priest.*'

If she was seeking to threaten him by hinting that she knew his identity, she failed. And he had no intention of confining himself to the Holy City, not when he was so intimate with Lyra herself. After all, was he not her personal confessor?

But for now, he dissembled. 'Very well, Lady Tear. I'll deal with Wurther, and you deal with the queen.'

Or what's left of her, after I'm done . . .

Pontus, Yuros
Julsep 935

A mile south of Pontus, Beak awaited his fellow conspirators. His mask of copper and lacquer was an ugly thing, with squinting, leering eyes and the long beak-like nose which apparently gave the character his name – he couldn't comment; he'd never seen a Lantric play. Ervyn Naxius had enlisted him almost two years ago: an outer sign of a profound inner change.

Before that, 'Beak' had been a mere low-blooded mage, an overlooked scholar of the Hadishah, employed in their secret breeding-houses. Captive magi were vital in the struggle against the Rondian Crusaders and matching breeding-partners was a crucial task – but not one that brought a great deal of recognition.

But his knowledge and lust for discovery had brought him to the attention of Naxius – how the Ordo Costruo renegade had found him, he had no idea, but from that moment everything had changed. Any pretence that he must follow the Gnostic Codes had vanished, along with all supervision. He'd been given as many live subjects and resources as he needed, with a single mandate: to expand knowledge of the gnosis. Freed of both oversight and moral constraints, guided by Naxius and his incredible insights, the only limits were his own low blood and his imagination – and he and Naxius had overcome even those.

He is the Master, but I am his closest servant. I am his . . . heir. Beak licked his lips, thinking of all the delicious young men and women who'd unwillingly given their bodies and souls to his research. Everything he'd achieved was through their sacrifice, and those who were hardest to break had been the most rewarding subjects.

Apparently Beak was a nosy busybody in the Lantric Masques, the tormentor in particular of Heartface and Ironhelm, the star-crossed lovers about whom the plays revolved. How apt; he was exactly that sort – so it was rather amusing to be awaiting Ironhelm and Heartface here, overlooking the fallen city of their enemies.

They arrived separately. Despite being clad in black and wearing their masks, he was fairly certain he knew who they were. Ironhelm rode a Rondian horned horse – they called it a khurne – captured during the last Crusade. His war-helm gleamed dully in the afternoon sun.

'Sal'Ahm, Brother Ironhelm!' Beak greeted him in Keshi. Since linking with the master-daemon Abraxas, he'd become effortlessly multilingual. He wondered whether to bow, but as the *harbadab* – the 'war of manners' which governed all social interactions – instructed only the barest of greetings between socially equal strangers, he settled for touching his right hand to his forehead. 'You're early.'

Ironhelm mirrored his greeting. 'Sal'Ahm, Brother Beak. I've always believed in arriving early – it enhances the chances of catching people doing something they ought not.'

'Trust me, all is as it should be here,' Beak replied. He pointed north, where the Keshi windfleet hung about the city of Pontus. The hills were brown from lack of rainfall and the city shimmered in the heat haze. 'How fares Pontus, the newest jewel in our sultan's crown?'

Ironhelm tapped his scimitar hilt in satisfaction. 'The Rondian garrison has surrendered and the Ordo Costruo have fled their Arcanum. We've plundered the city for supplies. All wealth will be sent to Ahmedhassa.'

'And the populace?'

'The young women have been rounded up to serve the soldiers; the young men will be shipped to the Dhassan slave-mines and the rest of the slugskin peasants sent to serve the supply-camp we've established. Only the Kore priests were executed. The sultan is merciful.'

Ironhelm's voice feigned regret but Beak wasn't fooled – after three Crusades, he knew the mood of Kesh and Dhassa: the Westerners must pay. He too held that opinion.

'And the children?'

Ironhelm glanced at him curiously. 'To be taken as devshirmey and taught our ways. The blood-tax will give us many eager young soldiers who will now grow up devoted to Ahm.'

'"Give me the boy and I'll make the man",' Beak quoted.

'Indeed.' Ironhelm studied him. 'I can't place your accent, Brother?'

'I am much travelled. It's strange, isn't it, to not even know each other's station? So much of our interactions are based on social rank, but when strangers must remain strangers, the harbadab is silent.'

'If Master Naxius holds us equal, Brother, then equal we are.' Ironhelm turned as a windskiff swam into view through the shimmering haze. A single figure guided the tiller, her mask glinting. 'As is she, I suppose.'

'Sister Heartface,' Beak mused. 'Ironhelm generally woos her, does he not?'

'I don't believe the Master intends us to take these masks so literally,' Ironhelm replied calmly as they watched Heartface furl her sails, her every gesture and movement elegant. 'Greetings, Sister,' he called.

Beak studied Heartface's gait: in the first meeting, before they'd all accepted Naxius' blessing and the daemonic ichor, she'd moved awkwardly; now she flowed, her movements graceful, like a dancer. Of course, the ichor had enabled all of them to perfect themselves physically.

I care little for physique, but I fancy that to you it's everything, Heartface.

They exchanged greetings, then gazed together at conquered Pontus. They'd caused this more than anyone except Sultan Rashid himself; it was their control of the pandaemancer Sakita that had enabled the destruction of Midpoint Tower, the nexus of the powers which could have destroyed their windfleet. They had lost one of their number, though: it was at Midpoint that Felix had perished.

'What news?' Beak asked at last.

Heartface's voice was filled with satisfaction. 'It's confirmed: Rene Cardien, the Archmagus of the Ordo Costruo, died at Midpoint, as did several others of his order, and two Merozains. Those Ordo Costruo manning the other towers have locked themselves in and are threatening to burn any vessels that approach, but they're clearly pouring most of their energies into sustaining the Bridge.'

'Can they repair it?' Ironhelm asked.

'Who knows? The towers collect sunlight and convert it to gnostic energy. The seas are at their highest right now, and the forces unimaginable, but each tower has emergency reserves. The real question is whether they can sustain it long-term – that will require thousands more solarus crystals, which are incredibly hard to find and enchant. I've heard that the Merozain monks are going to their aid – including Alaron Mercer and Ramita Ankesharan.'

The absolute hatred in her voice confirmed her identity in Beak's mind; everyone knew the Merozains had cast down Alyssa Dulayne, Rashid Mubarak's *ferang* mistress.

'Would Sultan Rashid prefer the Bridge to remain intact, or not?' he wondered aloud.

'I don't know,' Heartface grumbled, clearly believing she should. 'What's important now is exploiting this situation. Are we clear on our roles?'

Ironhelm inclined his head. 'I'm with the Shihad. We're pushing west at all speed.'

'To what end?' Beak wondered. To him the invasion was a sideshow; he was more interested in what knowledge could be gained along the way.

'It's early summer and the army must reach the rich lands of the west before winter. Sultan Rashid wishes to overwinter in a large city – do you realise that in this Ahm-benighted place it *snows*, even at sea-level? No army can survive that in the open. We must take *intact* a major city by the onset of winter. After that, we can press on the following spring. I will be lending my weight to those endeavours.'

Beak couldn't resist the chance to probe. 'Then you're senior in the Shihad army?'

If a mask could scowl, Ironhelm's would have. 'Of course I am. And you, Sister Heartface?'

'I'm charged with finding the daughter of Sakita Mubarak.'

'Sakita had a daughter and a son, Jehana and Waqar,' Beak said. 'Who is assigned to Waqar?'

'Leave Waqar to me,' Ironhelm said. 'Remember, Sister Heartface, the Master wants Jehana Mubarak alive.'

'I know my orders,' Heartface sniffed. 'She fled Pontus before we arrived, but I'll find her.'

'As for me, I've been sent west,' Beak announced, 'on a secret mission for the Master himself. I leave by windskiff tonight. You won't hear from me for some time.'

The other two shared a look.

'Can we be told nothing at all?' Heartface asked.

'I'm afraid not,' he replied, thinking, *See, the Master gives the most crucial tasks to the one he trusts most. And once you've served your purposes, it'll be back to just Naxius and me, as it was before.*

1

Guardians of the Gnosis

The Gnostic Keepers

The first Keepers were giants of the gnosis – men and women like Baramitius, Sejentia and Bravius who pioneered our knowledge of what is and isn't possible. But later generations of Keepers have become mere sycophants, who see their role as less to serve the gnosis, and more to serve House Sacrecour.

ORDO COSTRUO COLLEGIATE, PONTUS, 841

Pallas, Rondelmar
Julsep 935

Everything we have is so fragile, thought Lyra Vereinen, Empress of Yuros and Queen of Rondelmar, staring out at the city spread before her like an offering. From up here on her balcony Pallas looked tranquil, but only a few days before a ravening, disease-maddened horde of her own citizens had assailed the Bastion. The maze of streets below were quiet now, and across the river the luminescent Celestium still glowed majestically.

Despite the serenity of the view, Lyra's thoughts were all of her vulnerabilities.

I've just survived a coup – and I still can't identify the Masked Cabal who led the attacks. I'm empress, but my father wasn't the emperor and I don't know who he was. I've got no heir except the child in my belly, and I have a history of miscarriages. I have no gnosis, for all I'm mage-born. But I do have a heretical form of magic called dwyma, which could see me executed. Oh, and the East have invaded Yuros.

The immensity of the challenges was overwhelming – so many people were relying on her, a convent-girl not even out of her twenties. Thousands of people had left Coraine to follow her to Pallas, even though the last time the Corani came here, they'd almost been destroyed. No matter what, she couldn't allow that to happen again.

She took no comfort from the height and thickness of the fortifications: her enemies had already been inside. The only thing that had saved her was a power she barely understood – that and the loyalty and courage of a few people.

If I gained anything, it was a clearer understanding of who I can trust.

Amidst all of the confusion a few had stood firm: her husband, Prince-Consort Ril Endarion; her spymaster Dirklan Setallius and his agents Basia de Sirou and Mort Singolo; her senior knights, Solon Takwyth and Oryn Levis, and the men they led. Some, like her confessor, Ostevan Comfateri, had proven their loyalty by standing with her.

But the Masked Cabal are still out there . . .

It was a warm, embracing summer morning in northern Rondelmar, the sort of day about which poets would wax lyrical. *Too bright for gloomy thoughts*, she decided, straightening. It helped that the curtains behind her opened and Ril emerged in his nightclothes and stood behind her, circling his arms around her distended stomach: close, and yet slightly remote.

She twisted in his arms and looked up at his lean olive face framed by fine black hair – very rare in the pale-skinned, blond north. He was half Estellan and favoured his southern parent, a stark contrast to Lyra's pale skin and honey-blonde hair. But she'd lost her heart the moment he'd burst into her room in the convent and saved her from murder: a real-life Ryneholt, rescuer of the faery Stardancer.

Reality had proven harder to live than faery tales.

Why is it that when I need him most, he always pulls away?

They'd married in a flurry of clandestine infatuation, defying the life mapped out for her by Duchess Radine Jandreux, but real happiness had been elusive. Two miscarriages hadn't helped, but there had been other shadows; his heart had older allegiances, and her journey from prisoner and nun to queen and wife was still not complete. She had never shaken the feeling that she disappointed him – and now, just when she'd thought them through the worst, something had happened during the attack that had shaken him badly.

She thought she knew what that was: one of Ril's former lovers had been revealed as a servant of the Masked Cabal and been slain before his eyes. *Perhaps it's that. He and Jenet Brunlye were together a long time . . .* But she didn't know how to ask, so all she said was, 'Did you sleep well, my love?'

'Well enough, considering. You spoke well last night,' he added. 'You sounded brave.'

She was so sick and tired of holding court, playing queen. 'I didn't feel brave.' She'd been almost petrified, wondering if any of the Masks were in the room.

'It's important to do these things, to show that you're calm, even if you aren't.'

Masking her emotions was another hard lesson life clearly wished to teach her. Ril was better at it than she was – too often she felt like she had no skin at all to protect her from the world, while Ril was sometimes all surface, his true self buried out of her reach.

Will our child take after him or me? she wondered. Now she was in her fifth month she could feel the baby moving, a magic as deep as dwyma. Thinking of her secret power, she looked over the railing to the garden below. Just a few days ago she'd been fighting for her life there. She'd had an Earth-mage repair the stairway access immediately: it was the quickest way to get to her garden, the centre of her dwyma and the key to her safety.

'Has there been any more sign of this "Aradea"?' he asked, as if he were reading her mind.

'No, but she's there, if I need her.'

On the night of the attacks – people were calling it 'Reeker Night' – she'd been saved by a presence in the garden that had taken the form of Aradea, the Fey Queen. Of course Aradea didn't exist; she was just a story, but the guardian spirit of a 'genilocus' or place of dwyma could take *any* shape. She, the daughter of pure-blood magi, had never gained the gnosis; that potential had been locked beneath a Chain-rune for almost all her life. Instead, she'd gained the dwyma – and that heresy could see her dethroned and burned at the stake.

Do my enemies now know that secret too?

But there were other more pressing things right now: the news from the East needed a reaction, which meant Ril would have to leave soon, to fight the invaders. 'Have the summons gone out to the provincial rulers?' she asked.

'Yes. The muster has begun and we'll gather in a couple of weeks to appoint the generals.'

'I wish you didn't need to lead the army.'

He sighed. 'I know – but it's going to be the largest army in Yurosian history: whoever leads it will have enormous power. It *has* to be me. You do see that, don't you?'

Lest they turn it around and march on Pallas. 'I know. At least I'll have Dirklan with me.'

'Aye,' Ril acknowledged, 'and Takwyth.'

That his former rival for her hand had been at her side instead of him at the height of the attacks – a coincidence, nothing more – clearly still rankled.

It hadn't been his fault: Ril had been too far away when the attacks began. Her faith in his loyalty was unshaken. But the court was a vicious place, full of backstabbing gossips, and no doubt the 'facts' were already being whispered about.

'Solon proved his loyalty and I trust him,' she said firmly. 'He is House Corani to the core.'

'Aye – but he thinks House Corani would be better served with him as your Prince-Consort. And he's not alone.'

That's true. But she'd seen Solon Takwyth afterwards, and the reverence on his face. He'd risked his life for hers when a more calculating man might have held back. And now they had a shared secret too: she knew that he'd been offered a place in the cabal. He could have been one of the masked assassins, but had chosen to oppose them. *I believe in him, even if Ril doesn't.*

'What are your duties today?' he asked distantly.

There was a certain irony, she thought, that she'd taken to royal duties – and council-room intrigues – more readily than he, even though he'd been raised in the court. 'I'm visiting the Reeker Night prisoners – the riverreek sufferers.' She tried not to shudder. *They spit at me and try to bite me, or they just stare with blank eyes, like reptiles lying in wait.*

'Let others visit the Reekers,' her husband advised her, but she shook her head.

'No, I have to go. They're still our people, despite what was done to them.' She squeezed his hand. 'Will I see you this afternoon? I'm free for a good two hours, if you'd like to . . .' She stroked his face, letting her expression complete the offer.

I need my husband to prove he still loves me . . . He'd not slept with her since Reeker Night.

'I can't,' Ril said, not meeting her eyes. 'We're recruiting – we lost too many good men. We need to replace them, and quickly. I'll be busy all day – probably right through evening too.' His haunted expression reminded her that he too had almost died that night. But it still wasn't like him to be so dismissive of her, despite her condition.

She bit her lip, trying to conceal the hurt, especially since he'd spent most of their married life complaining that she wasn't enthusiastic enough in bed. *Is he punishing me for rejecting him so often?* she wondered, *or is it something else?*

Then Vita, her new maid, knocked at the doors: it was time to dress and begin the day.

Lyra kissed Ril goodbye, unable to shake the feeling that sometime on Reeker Night, she'd lost him again.

Ril left the royal bedchamber, a feeling of oppressive tension following him – because he was its source. He shouldn't be distancing himself from Lyra, not right now, but he couldn't help it. There was someone else he needed more.

He found her in a secluded alcove. Behind the curtains, large windows faced north over the well-to-do areas of Gravenhurst and Nordale. Basia de Sirou was sitting on a cushioned seat, looking blankly out through the glass. Her narrow face was framed by boyishly short auburn hair and she wore her habitual riding leathers. She looked up when he slipped between the curtains and joined her on the seat.

When he put his arm around her shoulders, she sank into him with an aching sigh. 'Everything's different now, isn't it?' she murmured, her eyes searching his.

In answer, he covered her mouth with his, locking them together. The forbidden thrill, the burning need and the feeling of completeness, of having marrow in his bones again, were almost overwhelming. Even knowing he could be dethroned, exiled or even executed for this wasn't going to stop him.

How could I have been so blind when she's always been at the centre of my life?

Basia finally pulled away, and panted, 'This is *beyond* stupid—'

'I don't care. We should have done this years ago – that's the stupid part.'

When they'd been caught up in the Sacrecour strike against House Corani twenty-six years before, they'd been trapped in a collapsed well; for three intense days and nights they'd kept each other alive. Love was too inadequate a word for what they shared – but that bond had also kept them apart, both too scared to start a love affair they'd never be able to leave if it soured. But on Reeker Night, in the midst of danger, they'd finally kissed. Now there was no going back.

'We were just children in 909, Ril,' Basia said, her normally ironic voice quivering with emotion. 'We didn't know how to deal with such enormous things.'

'We're not children any more.'

'True: you're now the prince-consort and about to be father of the royal heir. I'm your queen's bodyguard and you and she are the most scrutinised people in the empire.'

He pulled her face to him and kissed her forehead. Stroking her back, he asked, 'Then what are we going to do?'

She took his hand and drew it to her heart, which was hammering as hard as his was. 'Ril darling,' she said fervently, 'we're going to be very, *very* discreet. Now take me somewhere and rukk me senseless.'

*

'How bad will it be today?' Lyra asked the lean, silver-haired man await-ing her at the guarded doors of the Bastion.

'Bad enough,' Dirklan Setallius replied, 'but they're improving every day.'

Setallius wasn't by nature a comforting presence. His silver hair covered the badly burnt half of his face and he wore a patch over a false eye. Beneath the black kid-leather glove he always wore was a false left hand made of silver and wood. Despite his grim appearance, however, Lyra felt safe with her spymaster; she confided in him almost as much as her confessor. Dirklan always made her feel that his first concern was to protect her – and as a pure-blood mage, that protection was not inconsiderable.

'Then show me,' she said, taking his arm.

He led Lyra along a dark corridor towards a square of light. This southeastern part of the mountain of stone that was the Bastion had been sealed off for use as a special prison, as the usual cells weren't equipped to deal with infectious prisoners. They emerged on to a bal-cony of shaped stone overlooking a courtyard filled with people. The stench of sweat, urine, faeces and vomit baking in the summer sun hit them first.

Lyra's stomach rebelled. 'Kore's Blood, it's no easier to breathe in here!'

'I keep telling you to bring a posy, Milady,' Setallius replied.

'How would having flowers up my nose help me perceive these improvements you've been telling me about?' She looked down at the wretched prisoners. Most were asleep in the shade; some wakeful ones were staring up at her mutely. A filthy young woman in bloodied clothes waved, and Lyra waved back, realising this was the first human reaction she'd seen on her daily visits. 'Dirklan, the smell here is *worse*, not better.'

'Milady, the smell only seems worse because today is hot – but the buckets are less used, and they're keeping their food down. There is improvement.'

Only two hundred of the thousand-strong ravening mob that had assailed the Bastion on Reeker Night had survived; all of them people who been driven insane by the seasonal riverreek disease – *or something else*. The depraved attackers had been horribly difficult to kill – only decapitation or dismembering them had stopped them. For all their ferocity, they'd mostly used teeth and nails in the fray, and anyone who fell to their bite had also been afflicted. Even her mage-knights had struggled to stop the Reekers – that was the usual nickname for those contracting the seasonal illness, but no one truly believed riverreek had caused the madness.

'You say they've not been violent since the attack, Dirklan?'

'Milady, from the moment you slew Twoface they've been direction-less.'

'So if one of these Masks reappeared, they might be stirred up again?'

'Possibly,' he admitted. 'For the first four days they'd eat only meat – and the worst of them tried to eat their fellows; those haven't improved, so we're keeping them apart. But most started to get better as soon as they were exposed to sunlight. Some of them can even talk now.'

'Do they remember what they did?' Lyra asked.

'Apparently not. We've found signs of daemonic possession, but we can't be sure.'

She thought about that, then asked, 'So there's two degrees of . . . um, infection?'

'It appears so. The dozen we've locked up below are still violent, superhumanly strong and cunning too – they feign fainting or even death, then try to bite the guards. They won't touch anything but raw meat and they speak in gibberish.'

'What about the royal children?'

Twelve-year-old Coramore had been infected, and she'd slaughtered Lyra's ladies-in-waiting. It had taken extraordinary efforts to subdue her. Her elder brother, Cordan, hadn't been affected. Now they were locked in separate rooms in Redburn Tower, on the northwest corner of the Bastion, until Lyra could work out what to do with them.

'Cordan is still frightened,' Dirklan reported, 'but he's rediscover-ing himself. Of course, as the Sacrecour emperor, that just means he's regaining his arrogance and pride – but this experience has changed him. He knows Ril saved his life and I'm hoping he's turned over a new leaf. It's Coramore I'm worried about: she's still dangerous, like all those in the dungeons. The beneficial effects of the water from your garden have worn off.'

'Should I bring more? It must be worth trying,' Lyra suggested.

He didn't look convinced. 'Whatever's inside her has unleashed her inner spite. She's not the girl you knew – and she wasn't exactly easy to love in the first place, was she?'

'I'll have more water sent regardless,' Lyra promised. 'The pool in the garden is only small, but if there are positive effects on Coramore, then give everyone here a cupful.' She stepped to the edge of the balcony; her movement drew the eyes of almost every conscious person, but she concentrated on the girl who'd waved at her. She was pallid and hollow-eyed, barely eighteen. For a moment their eyes locked – and then the girl gazed down at her hands, still smeared in blood, and it looked to Lyra as if she *saw* herself, properly saw herself, for the first time.

The girl cried out, a desolate keening that shivered through Lyra's bones.

'For Kore's sake, we must *wash* these people!' she exclaimed. 'We must remind them they're human, Dirklan! How can we expect them to recover when we pen them up like animals?'

She hurried away, on the verge of tears. *The masked ones are still out there, and they don't care what they did to these people. They'll try again and again, until we stop them.*

Once in the darkened passage she sagged against the wall, shaking. Dirklan caught her up and pulled her against his chest – it might be a breach of protocol, but she needed to be held.

It should have been Ril here to support me, she thought unhappily. *Why isn't he here?* 'What can we do?' she asked plaintively.

'We're going to heal these people, and repair the Bastion. We're going to find the Masked Cabal and kill them. And if the trail leads to Garod Sacrecour, we'll have his head too.'

'And the Easterners?'

'The army will deal with that, Milady. This is the Rondian Empire: there is no greater power. One day at a time, Lyra, we'll get through this.'

'Walls couldn't protect me,' she replied, her voice tremulous. 'They were already inside. They turned people who had no reason to hate me into killers. Nothing I cling to is solid. I'm bringing a baby into this world and I don't know who or what to trust.'

'Trust in those you love, and who love you,' the spymaster replied, his voice unusually emotional. 'There are more of us than you think.'

Ril lay on his side, staring into Basia's face, inches from his own, her breath tingling on his flushed skin. The air was heavy with their sweat and musk. The sheets had been long since tossed aside; their clothing was strewn about the chamber. Their swords were propped against the door, Basia's artificial lower legs on the floor beside his boots. It had been slightly disorienting the first time, that his lover's body ended at the knees, but he'd been around her so long it wasn't worthy of comment. Basia had proved herself entirely whole long since, and all woman much more recently. They'd been here in this dusty room in the unused guest wing all morning, making up for years of lost time.

He stroked her shoulder and nuzzled her lips, then murmured, 'So you weren't a virgin?'

She lifted an eyebrow. 'Did you honestly think I would be, darling?'

He smiled. Basia was the worldliest woman he knew. 'I just thought I'd've known—'

'One day, I might even tell you who. So, was my lack of innocence a problem?'

'Kore's Balls, no! Let someone else do the breaking in, I've always said, then I'll do the riding.' He ran his hand over her pert breasts down to her bony hips. 'Are you going to be able to carry on as Lyra's bodyguard?'

'What, you think I'll stab her in the back so I can have you for myself?'

'No, of course not! But others might wonder if you'd still be motivated to throw yourself in front of danger for her.' He sighed. 'I'm pretty sure Dirklan would take a dim view of it.'

Basia gave a small shudder. 'Don't remind me! Look, it's my job. I'm a loyal Corani and I'll still fight for her – and you.'

He encircled a nipple, still engorged, and licked it. 'I'll need to go south soon, to fight the Noories. Will you come? You could ask Dirklan to be reassigned to me.'

Basia frowned. 'It'll only make him suspicious.'

'But it'd be worth it, don't you think?' He slid his hand over her mound and cupped it, teasing her with his fingers. 'There'll just be you and me . . . and a couple of hundred thousand soldiers.'

She gave a hungry groan, grabbed his shoulder and pulled him atop her. 'Convince me,' she whispered, and drew him in for another bout.

The next morning, after another night alone, Lyra rode the Purple Path, a route specially prepared for the empress to traverse her city. The route had been secured, all other traffic stopped and people cordoned away. A Purple Path had to be organised long before she left the Bastion – it took *hours* to clear the roads and check anything overlooking the route for dangers, and mage-knights of the Imperial Guard had to be assigned to protect her. It wasn't done lightly.

When Lyra arrived in Pallas, she'd naïvely envisaged walking the streets, meeting ordinary people and learning about their lives. Dirklan had laughed. 'Lyra, you're Queen of Rondelmar and Empress of Yuros. You don't go *anywhere* without giving us days – if not weeks or even months – to prepare. You certainly won't be disrupting the lives of tens of thousands on a whim. Think of yourself as a travelling circus: we all enjoy them, but there's a time and place.'

At the time the jest had delighted her. Later, it felt like another bar on her gilded prison.

Today the Purple Path ran from the Bastion to the Keepers' Citadel on Actium's Hill. 'Tell me again about the Keepers, Dirklan,' she asked.

'They're Ascendant-magi, pledged to serve the gnosis.'

'Not the empire?'

'No, that's your job – nor do they concern themselves with religion: that's Grand Prelate Wurther's problem. They study the gnosis and pass on their discoveries to our Arcanums. They protect the Scytale of Corineus – that's the artefact used for raising ordinary magi to Ascendants. They keep record of the bloodlines and in some cases, guide dynastic marriages. They also study the enemies of the gnosis – Souldrinkers and the like.'

'Including dwymancy?'

'Of course. A dwymancer can match a hundred magi or more – from a distance, at least. They're a dangerous proposition.'

As far as they knew, Lyra was the only dwymancer to have lived in five hundred years. She suspected she was the only person who'd realised Saint Eloy, the mage-priest credited with the elimination of the dwyma, had in fact preserved it secretly, in the very bosom of the Church – and she'd also begun to suspect that there were other dwymancers out there.

'Will the Keepers know what I am just by looking at me?' she asked.

'It's doubtful. To me, your magical aura is normal, if a little featureless.'

'But if they ask me to use the gnosis, I won't be able to.'

'That's not all that unusual – many mage-women never use their powers, preferring to live normal lives. And demanding that someone prove their gnostic power is considered rude.'

'But if they knew what I am, I'd be in trouble, wouldn't I?'

'Yes,' the spymaster admitted, 'I fear so. The early magi felt threatened by the dwyma – that's why they gave it another name: dwyma – "life magic" – sounds beneficent, but pandaemancy means "the power of all daemons". We always demonise things we can't understand or control.'

'Just as I can't understand or control it.'

'You invoked it and it saved you. For now, that's enough.'

'But surely the Keepers sensed it?'

'They probably sensed *something* – I'm sure every mage in Pallas felt a surge in energies. But did they know what it was? I doubt it. Can they prove your involvement? I doubt it.'

'But what if Wurther tells the Keepers about me?'

'Then he'd be a fool, because my people tell me Wurther was about to be slain when a light from the cave of Saint Eloy blasted one of those masked assassins from their body. Dominius Wurther is many things, but he values his own skin exceedingly highly. He won't forget that.' He winked at her and added, 'I've talked to him about it, and we're of the same mind. He knows how close we all came to death, and he knows we both face the same enemies.'

Lyra changed the subject and asked, 'Did Coramore accept the water I sent this morning?'

'She did, and then vomited.'

Lyra sighed. 'We'll keep trying.' She patted her belly, and the five-month-old child growing inside her. 'What sort of world am I bringing this child into, Dirklan?'

'A dangerous one – but one worth fighting for,' the spymaster said firmly. 'One that is all the better with you in it,' he added. 'Never doubt that it's worth the fight, Lyra.'

'Is there any news from Pontus?'

'Our wind-scouts have seen mounted forces on the Imperial Road. The Eastern windfleet is vast – Milady, I hate to admit it, but I never saw this coming, or the attacks on Reeker Night. It's my duty to know these things, but I've been blindsided at every turn.'

'I'm sure no one could have done more than you – you've been under-resourced, for a start. We know the state of the Treasury – but I'll get you more men, more money.'

'That'll be appreciated,' he admitted, 'but it takes years to build up an information network. The real issue is that most of the Volsai left Pallas when we Corani arrived; most of the old Imperial Secret Service now serve Garod Sacrecour. For now I must work with what I've got.'

'Which is?'

'A few hundred informants spread over the Great Houses and a few dozen magi. It doesn't sound like much, but it's not bad. Spy networks need to be kept tight to be effective. What I lack in numbers, I make up for in knowing that my people belong to me. Garod can't say the same. He's more scared of my reach than I am of his.' He rubbed his chin tiredly. 'Unfortunately, I lost several of my people in Dupenium during this attempted insurrection.'

'Garod knew what was happening, clearly.'

'Indeed. Not all our enemies wear gaudy Lantric masks, my Queen.'

Lyra fought a feeling of helplessness. 'What can I do, Dirklan? I know I'm pregnant, but there must be *something* I can do that matters.'

He studied her with his one good eye and she thought there was pride in it. 'Milady, on Reeker Night, it wasn't the magi or knights who saved us – it was you, and the power you possess. Learn it! Some dwymancers wrote about their lives – the Church burns heretical books, but I know where to find copies, if you wish?'

She pictured herself learning dark secrets by candlelight, like a wicked witch in the Fables she'd so loved growing up ... the notion was appealing, despite that. But she was also mindful of her pregnancy. 'Will it be safe for my child to be inside me when I do that?'

'I don't know, Lyra,' Dirklan admitted. 'You're a mystery. By now, a woman pregnant to a mage should be showing signs of what we call "pregnancy manifestation" – that's when a non-mage bearing a mage-child begins to gain the gnosis herself. Sometimes it's fleeting, sometimes permanent. You're showing no such signs, and we have no records that any dwymancer ever bore a mage-child in the past. I don't know if your child will be mage, dwymancer, both or neither.' Then he met her eyes and added, 'But will your child get to have a life at all if you don't embrace this power you have?'

Put like that, it wasn't a choice at all. Feeling a new sense of resolve, she said, 'Very well, bring me your books.' *I'll become a dwymancer. Kore, be with me!*

'One other thing, Lyra,' Dirklan added, 'keep your secret close. Ril knows, Basia and Mort also, and Wurther and Wilfort, and Solon Takwyth perhaps. Ostevan clearly experienced something in his chapel. Others may suspect something because of what they saw on Reeker Night – but if anyone outside our immediate circle approaches you about it, be cautious. Draw them out if you dare, but make sure Basia or Mort or I are close by.' He met her eye. 'One *bite* could be all it takes to destroy us, Lyra.'

With that chilling thought, they finished the journey in silence. Clattering to a halt in a courtyard, he peered through the curtain. 'We've arrived, Lyra. Are you ready for this? The Keepers can be intimidating.'

'Of course,' she said, putting on her 'Queen' face.

'That's the spirit. Deny everything – that's my motto.'

She allowed Dirklan to help her from the carriage and looked up. Her first sight of their hosts caused her confidence to falter, even though only three of the mysterious order had come out to meet her. There was an intimidating aura to them, in their lined faces, their pallor and dark, centuries-old eyes that weighed and judged silently as she ascended the stairs. Robed in white and gold, with raised cowls, they leaned on long, smooth jet-black staves heeled with heavy hoops of bronze and merely inclined their heads in welcome, the barest acknowledgement.

The central of the three figures, an androgynous woman with a lined face and short grey hair, spoke first. 'I am Edetta Keeper, Majesty. Welcome to Actium's Hill.'

The experience of holding court before the mage-nobility gave Lyra the presence of mind to push aside her awe and recall her briefing notes: Edetta oversaw the Imperial Beastariums and was suspected of favouring the Sacrecours.

She and her colleagues led Lyra and Dirklan inside and into a circular auditorium. A long table in the middle of the room was encircled by banks of seats, enough for at least two hundred people, but there were only a dozen anonymously cowled Keepers seated there, in pairs or alone.

Have they no interest in me? Lyra wondered, surprised at the low attendance.

Edetta led her to the table and indicated three seats on one side. Neither of the two men already seated rose to greet her. She knew one of them and forgave the omission. Grand Prelate Dominius Wurther was obese; he seldom stood without dire need, and his rank meant he never had to. His jowls wobbled as he gulped a swallow of wine before saying unctuously, 'Greetings, Majesty. Welcome.'

'Good to see you, Dominius,' Lyra replied warmly.

The Grand Prelate traditionally had a seat on the Keepers' Council, as the Gnostic Codes and the Church had overlapping jurisdictions. She'd exchanged messages with Wurther since Reeker Night, but they'd not met in person since.

At the head of the table, a hawkish-looking man with surprisingly youthful features was studying her. 'Lord Cardoni?' Lyra guessed.

Delmar Cardoni had ascended in 907, one of the most recent magi to be given the ambrosia. The renowned Sacrecour mage-knight had been at his prime some twenty years ago . . . at the time of the 909 massacres.

'I am now Delmar Keeper-Prime,' he replied smoothly.

She'd momentarily forgotten that it was like joining the Church: a Keeper left their family name behind. But the Cardonis were from Fauvion and closely allied to the Houses of Fasterius and Sacrecour, Lyra's enemies. Mater-Imperia Lucia Fasterius herself had ratified his ascendancy.

I'm only surprised she didn't make her whole damned clan into Ascendants, she thought.

'Gendrick is Scribe of the Gnostic Code,' Edetta said, gesturing at the man on her right as they sat, 'and Farlan liaises with the Inquisition on heretical magic.'

Lyra kept her face schooled while greeting the two men, especially Farlan, but neither gave any hint that they knew what she was.

'If I may ask, wasn't the Ordo Costruo renegade Ervyn Naxius given an advisory role in the Imperial Beastariums by our late emperor?' Dirklan enquired.

'For a time – but he's not been heard of since the untimely fall of Emperor Constant,' Edetta replied dismissively. 'It's presumed he died in 930.'

'And the Beastarium adheres strictly to the Gnostic Codes? Naxius wasn't a great one for rules, I hear?'

'He had an advisory role only,' Edetta said testily. 'Now, if you don't mind, we're here to discuss these so-called "Reeker" attacks, and this unidentified "Masked Cabal". I understand they're still unknown and at large?'

'At large, yes,' Lyra put in. 'Unknown? Well, perhaps – but Duke Garod Sacrecour arrived at my gates the morning after the attack, fully ready to march in and "save the city". So perhaps he's acquainted with them?'

'He claims his spymaster warned him of an impending coup,' Delmar replied.

'He's lying,' Lyra replied. 'He was here to claim the throne, not save it!'

'An unproven supposition, and regardless, it's outside our ambit. The Keepers don't involve themselves in politics,' Edetta said loftily. 'Our concern is the nature of the attack – and the nature of the defences that thwarted it. From our vantage here, we saw two simultaneous bursts of golden light, one from the Bastion, the other from the Celestium. They were accompanied by a surge of gnostic energy. I presume everyone present saw and felt these phenomena?'

'I did indeed see and feel them,' Grand Prelate Wurther said. 'Every Reeker present was struck down, including the man in the Lantric mask who led them – Jest.'

'Did you identify his body?' Delmar asked.

'Aye. It was a lowly priest, a man called Junius.' For a moment Wurther looked like he was about to say more, but he didn't. Lyra knew he fervently believed her confessor, Ostevan, was behind the attack – and she was equally convinced that he was innocent.

'What else did you see, Grand Prelate?' Delmar pressed.

Wurther glanced at Lyra, but shook his head. 'Nothing else, Keeper-Prime. I was flat on my back with Jest's sword tickling my tonsils – not a good vantage, I fear.'

'What did those with you see, your Holiness?' Farlan asked.

'I was the only one still alive,' Wurther replied, shuddering at the memory. 'My protectors had all perished at that point. I'd been chased to the Winter Tree garden.'

'The Shrine to Saint Eloy?' Delmar and Edetta exchanged looks. 'Are you saying this was *pandaemancy*, Grand Prelate?'

'I'm not saying *anything*: I'm just telling you what I saw. It was very confusing, and I was about to die. If I'm not a terribly reliable witness, I'm sorry.'

Delmar scowled, but he had to accept the grand prelate's response. That Delmar didn't seem to know more made Lyra wonder; she'd always believed the Keepers to be all but omniscient. Now she looked at the almost-empty auditorium and thought, *Perhaps they're not snubbing me? Perhaps there's only these few left?* She'd imagined hundreds of them, a mighty power in the realm, but this place felt like the sort of home for the aged many convents maintained.

Edetta turned to her. 'From whence did the light appear in the Bastion, Majesty?'

Lyra answered honestly, because she suspected the whole of the Bastion knew. 'From the gardens beneath my suite, Keeper-Prime – but precisely where or why, I know not.'

Do they know I have a cutting from Saint Eloy's Winter Tree there?

Delmar frowned. 'Your garden?'

Evidently they don't: good. Lyra sat up, heartened. 'I'm just grateful that *something* happened, because all appeared lost, Keeper-Prime. But shouldn't we be more concerned about the nature of the attackers, not the defences?'

'Both matters concern us greatly, Milady. Neither are within our experience.'

That admission also sounded important. Lyra glanced at Setallius, then said, 'You're welcome to send people to examine the site, Keeper-Prime, and I'm sure Grand Prelate Wurther feels the same. We'll be most interested in what you find.' When Wurther agreed, she added, 'I'm told that sustained possession, both solely and en-masse, are impossible? How do you explain the attack we experienced?'

'As you know, we have also examined the survivors,' Delmar answered. 'Some fusion of disease and mind-control is likely, one feeding the other.' He shifted uncomfortably, then added, 'Queen Lyra, I feel compelled to warn you: just as your mother Natia's life was spared by the Sacrecours at our request, we demand the same for young Coramore and Cordan. These children are of the holy line of Sertain – their lives are under our protection.'

'I know that,' Lyra confirmed, 'and I'm *not* the kind of person who murders children.' She glanced away, peeved by the inference, saw Dirklan throw her a warning look and swallowed her annoyance. Tired of being questioned, she asked another of her own: 'During the attack, Coramore named the being possessing her as "Abraxas". Do the Keepers know the name?'

'We'll look into it,' Delmar answered. 'You can rely on our aid.'

'With respect,' Lyra answered, feeling the urge to vent some of her own frustrations, 'I didn't see any aid from your quarter that night,

Keeper-Prime. You say you witnessed the attacks – you must have seen how unnatural they were – and yet you did nothing but watch. What would you have done if they'd succeeded? Taken notes?'

'The attacks were over before we could react. Secular matters are not our concern.'

'But gnostic security is,' Wurther grumbled. 'You failed both the Bastion and the Celestium, Keeper-Prime. As soon as it became apparent that the attackers were using unknown gnosis, you should have intervened.'

'That was not apparent to us until afterwards,' Edetta growled. 'You have armies to protect you. Don't make us responsible for your security. Look to your own.'

The meeting broke up soon after, as if the Keepers were anxious to hustle these interlopers out of their lives. Lyra walked with Wurther to his carriage, where a handsome young Estellan with swarthy southern features awaited him. He was armed and armoured, wearing a tabard of purple with a gold dagger bisecting the tunic: a knight of the Pontifex Guard. He started towards them, but Wurther waved him away.

'My new bodyguard,' he commented. 'He took the rather eye-rolling name of "Exilium Excelsior" when he joined the Inquisition, would you believe? But unusually, he defected to the Kirkegarde soon after, so there may be hope for him. I'm told his prowess in combat is extraordinary.' Then he dropped his voice and added, 'My dear, what I said stands: the Keepers have failed the realm. You *saw*, didn't you?'

'I saw that they're all *old*. No new blood. And there are so few of them! They're the guardians of the Scytale of Corineus – why aren't there more of them?'

'I believe the answer lies in this question: who are the newest group of Ascendant-magi?'

'Do you mean the Merozain Brotherhood, in the *East*?' Lyra looked at him in puzzlement, then her mouth dropped open. 'Are you saying the Keepers have *lost* the Scytale?'

Wurther smiled grimly. 'It's treason to say so, Milady.'

'But the Scytale is vital to the empire!'

'Indeed. But there have been no new Keepers since 907. My people now believe it went to Noros, would you believe? And thence, it appears, into the East.'

She put her hand to her mouth. 'This invasion! You don't think—'

'Who knows? But there are better places to speculate about such things than the doorsteps of the Keepers.'

She gave him a fond look: they came into conflict at times, especially over Ostevan, but she had grown to genuinely like Wurther. And a more fanatical man might have denounced her. 'I'm fortunate to have you as a colleague, Dominius,' she said. 'We should talk more.'

'We should,' he agreed cautiously, 'but I can't afford to appear a patsy to you in the endless Bastion-versus-Celestium eyeballing contest. So let's be discreet. I'm reviewing security and greatly limiting those who have access to me, Majesty. I suggest you do the same.'

Then he dropped his voice and added, 'I would also ensure Ostevan Comfateri is not one of those allowed access to you.'

'I'll make my own choices about personal contacts, Grand Prelate. See you at the next Royal Council.' Lyra curtseyed awkwardly, then waddled off to rejoin Setallius for the journey back to the Bastion. She'd escaped the Keepers without giving up her secrets, but Wurther's revelation about the Scytale had left her feeling even more insecure.

Dear Kore! As if I didn't have enough to worry about.

'And at the end of the day, we give thanks to Kore,' the priest intoned, and hearing the familiar ritual words in the mouth of her closest confidante, Lyra felt some of her tension ease.

'We give thanks to Kore,' she echoed, staring up at the icon above the altar, a six-foot icon of the Sacred Heart skewered by the sacred Dagger of Corineus, symbol of divine martyrdom. She and her confessor were alone in the royal chapel, with Basia waiting outside. Surrounded by statues of seraphs gazing heavenwards, it was easy to feel herself enclosed in Kore's gentle hands. *Only the divine is eternal*, the little church was telling her. *Only your soul matters.*

She gazed up reverently as Ostevan Comfateri placed the rim of the gold chalice against her lips. She sipped the blessed wine, then he dipped his thumb in the *krism* of ash and oil and made the cross-hilt sign on her brow. 'Let the Peace of Kore enter thee,' he said, his voice gentle and soothing. They shared a long look, and she did feel that peace. On a whim she lifted her hands to him after the final blessing and let him draw her to her feet. It wasn't proper, perhaps, but their relationship ran deeper than protocol.

Her confessor was everything she thought a priest should be: charismatic, with an intense air about him. Ostevan was handsome too, with wavy dark brown hair and a courtier's goatee, and he spoke with a commanding, spine-tingling voice. Some of her ladies gossiped that he ignored the strictures of the clergy and took lovers, but Lyra had seen no evidence; she suspected it was just malicious talk. And on Reeker Night, he'd been proven to be loyal. So she had no hesitation in saying, 'Ostevan, we need to talk.'

He was all attentiveness, helping seat her on a cushioned pew and sitting as well, not quite touching. 'Of course, Milady. I'm listening.'

She'd rehearsed how to begin. 'Ostevan, I think you know that on Reeker Night a power beyond the gnosis saved us. It's something you've mentioned to me before: *dwyma*. I know now that I'm a dwymancer, Ostevan – a heretic, under Church Law. But I love Kore and I wish to serve him. I know this places you in an awkward position – can you find it in yourself to help me reconcile these things?'

She fancied her revelation was not a complete surprise, but he still looked troubled, as well he should be. 'Milady, dwyma – *pandaemancy* – died out centuries ago.'

'So people say – but I know what I felt, and it *wasn't* evil. You said it yourself that day: the power that saved me was *benevolent*. Dwyma isn't dead. I've felt it in Coraine and in the Shrine to Saint Eloy in the Celestium. I've touched it. I've been its vessel.'

Ostevan responded carefully, 'Majesty, shall we treat this conversation as an Unburdening, so that our words are also protected?' When she nodded her understanding, he went on, 'I believe the early Church was wrong to condemn dwyma. They were frightened, and lashed out when they should have embraced the dwymancers and found accord.'

She felt relief washing over her. 'Thank you,' she said. 'It's such a relief to talk about this – especially with you, because you understand the Church.'

'My belief is that everything in this world is part of Kore's plan, and therefore the dwyma is too. You're Kore's child, Lyra, and His hand is upon you.'

'Thank Kore I have you,' she exclaimed, seizing his hands, then she blushed and dropped them again. 'I'm sorry, that was improper.'

A memory hung in the air between them: of a day three months ago when she'd complained of an injured back and he'd eased it with healing-gnosis. They both knew he could have done *anything* with her that day, but he'd gone no further than any physician. Yes, boundaries had been overstepped – but in his refusal to take advantage of her naïveté, a new level of trust had also been forged between them.

'My Queen, it was nothing,' he said, but she fancied that he wasn't unmoved by her. There had been a kind of *frisson* between them since that day. It troubled her a little, but she also felt flattered that anyone could find her pretty when she was so bloated with child that even Ril was oblivious to her.

'How are you bearing up?' he asked gently.

She could have dissembled, pretended as she did with everyone else that everything was well – but Ostevan was both friend and confessor, and she badly needed *someone* to talk to about everything that was troubling her. It all came out in a rush: her fears for her unborn child; her worry that she was losing her husband's heart; that she didn't know how to be this thing they'd made her: an empress.

'Sometimes I feel like I don't know Ril at all,' she said sadly. 'I know he's fifteen years older than me, but it's more than that: there's part of him I can't ever reach. He talks so easily with his knights, and with Basia, but I feel like an outsider, even after five years.'

'It's 909,' Ostevan told her. 'Those who went through the massacre here in Pallas have a special bond; they will always gravitate towards each other.'

'They never speak of it, though—'

'They don't have to. They all went through Hel together. The rest is unspoken.'

She sighed miserably. 'You're saying I'll never be one of them?'

'Perhaps not,' Ostevan replied, 'but you have your own identity, something *they've* not been through. You, and I, we were both raised in the Church and that also leaves an imprint. If I may say so without being presumptuous, I think it's part of why you and I have a bond, my Queen.'

The thought that it wasn't a fault in her cheered her, although it also left her with an apparently insurmountable barrier to ever winning her husband's heart. 'What about you, Ostevan? Where were you in 909?'

He looked away briefly, visibly composing himself. 'I was in the Celestium. Those of us allied to the Corani were rounded up and Chained so we couldn't use our gnosis. We were kept locked up like dogs – we feared execution at any minute. But Dominius Wurther and others secured our release by reminding the Sacrecours that as clergymen, we shed our family ties on entering the Church.' He looked up and smiled sadly. 'Dominius and I were friends, once.'

'Then you must reconcile,' Lyra exclaimed.

The confessor shook his head. 'I fear he and I will never trust each other again.'

'It's tragic, the way life can divide good people from each other,' Lyra said. Ostevan looked so morose that she put her hands over his, as if she were the one dispensing comfort. 'What's to become of us, Ostevan?'

'We'll put our faith in Kore, knowing he'll provide.'

'But most magi say Kore doesn't exist – that he's a lie invented by the Blessed Three Hundred to control the empire.'

'My Queen, I am a mage and a priest and I *know* that's simply not true.'

She looked at him. She needed her faith, the rock that had been at the centre of her life until the world took her from her cloister, but questions kept arising. So she asked, 'Dirklan says the Reekers were possessed by daemons?'

'Lyra, even those magi who claim not to believe in Kore still acknowledge the existence of daemons. They are spirits who dwell in the aether and prey upon the souls of the dying, especially people of loose morals. But virtuous souls cannot be taken by daemons, Lyra: they fly on and are welcomed by the greatest soul of all – that of Kore, waiting in Paradise.'

'But how can there be daemons and no angels?' she asked plaintively. 'Where were *they*? They're supposed to protect us! Where's Kore? Why doesn't He care?'

'Of course He cares! But if angels solved all our problems, how would we *grow*, Lyra? How would we learn right and wrong and become worthy of joining their heavenly host? This life is transitory, and Paradise is for ever. What are a few moments of suffering when so long as we stay true to Kore, eternity awaits?'

Yes, she thought, *we will not suffer for ever!* 'Thank you. I needed to hear that.'

'You needed to hear truth,' he replied, kissing her hands. 'And that's why I'm here.'

2

The Domus Pontico

Solarus Crystals

Knowing that the forces beneath the oceans were too vast to permit ordinary stone to survive, the Ordo Costruo devised a means of capturing sunlight, the most powerful and consistent source of energy known, using the famed 'solarus crystal'. Too deadly for personal use, their value lies in being meshed together, when they can turn the sun's output into gnostic energy to sustain the structure. Unfortunately, the crystals are incredibly difficult to create, and very dangerous to use. Many have tried to use them for smaller tasks – as tools and weapons – but none have found a way of surviving the energies released.

PALLAS ARCANUM, 862

Pontic Sea, Yuros
Julsep 935

The wind-dhou that had borne Waqar Mubarak and his companions to Midpoint Tower in the vain pursuit of his mother now took them northwest to join the huge fleets of Keshi windships that were sweeping through the skies. The sight was jaw-dropping – and inspiring. He and his friends didn't all support the Shihad, but they all felt immense pride in this demonstration of the ingenuity and energy of their people.

It was also testament to the vision of Rashid Mubarak, Waqar's uncle and the Sultan of Kesh, the three-quarter-blood mage who'd betrayed the Ordo Costruo and engineered the defeat of the invaders during the Third Crusade. He was a legend already, but assailing Yuros, the home ground of the Western magi, was an even greater deed.

35

Whatever else he is, Uncle Rashid works miracles, Waqar thought, staring out at the windships jammed with soldiers and supplies. Jubilant men filled the skies with hymns. But Waqar couldn't ignore his own grief. *My mother died destroying Midpoint Tower, betraying an Order she loved.* A group of masked assassins had somehow turned Sakita from a loyal Ordo Costruo mage into a monster – one who could freeze every cloud in the sky and send a giant ball of ice into Midpoint. The same masked men and women had killed Sultan Salim too, clearing Rashid's path to power, and now they wanted his sister Jehana as well.

My uncle is working hand in glove with them, he admitted to himself, *or he's one of them.*

They'd come looking for him as well – he and his friends had faced one at Midpoint and had only been able to slay him – 'Felix', a man in a cat-mask – thanks to a mysterious spear they'd found in the ruins of the tower. He was pretty sure the cabal hadn't finished with him, or Jehana, wherever she was.

'What next, Waqar?' asked Fatima, breaking into his worried reverie.

'I suppose I must re-join my fleet. I am an admiral, after all . . .' Rashid had sanctioned his search for his sister, but Waqar wasn't looking forward to reporting what he'd seen and learned.

When I tell him, will I see guilt written across his face? And if I do, can I restrain myself from accusing him?

Tamir, his most perceptive friend, put a hand on his shoulder. 'What's important is staying alive, Waqar, for Jehana's sake. Bide your time until we can unmask these conspirators. When you smoke out a vipers' nest, you must kill them all at once.'

'And we *will* smoke them out,' Lukadin added. He was leaning on the spear they'd recovered. He had released its power, killing the masked man Felix, who'd appeared to be indestructible, but wielding the strange weapon had left him severely drained. He still looked sick, but he wouldn't let the spear from his grasp. 'If this spear can kill one of them, it can kill them all,' he said fiercely.

Even if it kills you too? Waqar wondered.

'It's not a burden you should take on alone,' big Baneet told Lukadin.

'The spear's mine,' Luka replied, glaring.

'It was recovered from the Ordo Costruo,' Fatima argued. 'You're just holding it—'

'If I'm holding it, it's mine!'

'Enough,' Waqar interrupted. 'If Lukadin wishes to keep it, it's his. But for Ahm's sake, please don't overuse it, Luka!' After a moment, he returned to his biggest worry. 'Where's my sister?' he asked aloud, not expecting any real answers.

'Maybe that Jhafi spy will find her?' Baneet suggested, blinking through his puffy left eye. Like all of them, he'd taken a battering from Felix; before Luka had tried the spear they'd all thought they were going to die.

They all looked eastwards. Tarita, the stroppy young Jhafi woman who'd claimed to represent the Javon crown, had left in a windskiff barely half an hour before the first of the Shihad fleet had caught them up. She was lowborn, but her gnosis was incredibly strong – and Waqar had liked her. Perhaps she could track down Jehana where they'd failed.

His mother's final words, whispered in his ear as she died, wouldn't stop echoing in his brain: '*You . . . Jehana . . . unique . . .*' And they'd just seen Sakita, risen from the grave and calling down a storm greater than even a hundred magi together could summon. The implication was obvious: he and Jehana had the same potential – but nothing in his training suggested such a thing. He was three-quarter-blooded and a talented mage, but the power his mother had displayed was beyond his imagining.

'The Ordo Costruo took Jehana and they're still hiding her,' he began.

Fatima interrupted, 'Waqar, your most immediate concern is what to tell your uncle.'

'I know – and I don't know what to say,' he admitted. He'd been shocked when Rashid had allowed him to leave his fleet and go off on a hunt for his sister on the very eve of the launch of the Shihad, but it deepened his suspicion that the man he'd idolised, who'd always treated him as a son, was neck-deep in the murder of Salim and Sakita, his own sister.

Did he hope I'd lead him straight to Jehana . . . so he can use her as he used my mother?

Somehow he had to conceal all his fears and suspicions when he next met the piercing eyes of Sultan Rashid Mubarak.

By the time Waqar's battered wind-dhou touched down outside Pontus a few hours later, the crew were exhausted, even with Fatima helping the pilot, sharing Air-gnosis to keep the vessel flying. As they landed in a sea of windcraft they saw one collision and a dozen near-misses – but despite the mayhem in the skies, an air of celebration reigned. The city of Pontus lacked anything in the way of fortification – because *no one* assailed the Rondian Empire – and now it was shrouded in smoke, most of it streaming from the tall spires of the Kore churches.

On the ground it was just as chaotic. Each hazarabam had been spread over dozens of windships and they were all trying to find each other and set up camp while their unit commanders argued over room, supplies and water. Adding to the sense of the surreal were the many ships containing camels and elephants, all snorting and harrumphing as they disembarked.

Waqar was still trying to work out where he should seek Rashid when a slender shaven-skulled man in the red feydez hat of a court eunuch hurried up. He had pale skin – and as the man prostrated himself, Waqar realised with a shock that he was wearing a periapt.

He's a mage? Dear Ahm, who would castrate a mage when we've been trying to breed as many as we can!

'Great Prince, I'm Chanadhan, a court-kalfas of the Al-Norushan,' he said in a piping voice. 'The sultan bids you attend him as soon as possible.' The scribe looked very young, but he was confident in his bearing. He wore the sunrise insignia of Al-Norushan, the 'New Dawn' order of magi comprised of many former Hadishah mage-assassins, supposedly now dedicated to peace.

'Of course,' Waqar answered, as Lukadin and Baneet wrinkled their noses in distaste at the eunuch. Waqar looked at Tamir nervously, but Rashid was a challenge he must face alone.

Chanadhan led him towards the city, through the maze of hulls, ropes and milling soldiers. The cacophony was such that they couldn't converse until they'd escaped the landing site. They climbed a gentle slope to the city walls and walked alongside a road jammed with wagons full of plunder.

'How did you come to be a kalfas?' Waqar asked.

'By accident, my Prince. In military training, when I was eight, my testicles were ruptured and became infected. They were removed to prevent the infection killing me.' Chanadhan's voice was sad, but not self-pitying. 'A place was found for me in the bureaucracy.'

'It must be awful,' Waqar said, thoughtlessly.

'Is it? I don't know, Great Prince. One knows only what one experiences; the rest is hearsay. This is my first role out of the Elimadrasa and already I have exchanged words with the Great Sultan. I'm honoured to serve as Ahm wills.'

Waqar suspected the mage-college system must have been awful for a castrated boy, but Chanadhan appeared to be at peace with his life.

They were admitted into the city – and found far worse within than outside. The streets were flooded with Keshi soldiers busy smashing their way through every door with loud enthusiasm and dragging out any Yurosi they found hiding. The noise was deafening: Yurosi women screaming, men shouting, cries of triumph, fear and pain. Waqar had seen the aftermath of sackings in the East; knowing this was revenge didn't make it any more pleasant.

They crossed a square where groups of half-naked white women were being herded towards the roads. It was clear most of them had already been raped. Corpses were piled up in alleys like refuse, and newly made slaves laboured to keep the arterial routes flowing. Godspeakers were blessing the flames consuming a church while inside, the congregation screamed in terror and agony; any who tried to escape were shot by archers. The air was filled with smoke and the noxious reek of blood and death.

The Shihad looked a lot like the Crusades.

Is this truly justice, Great Ahm?

Chanadhan led Waqar unerringly through the din to a white-walled complex patrolled by soldiers of the Sultan's Guard; now Waqar began to recognise officers and nobles. Chanadhan gestured towards the building. 'My prince, this is Domus Pontico.'

'The Ordo Costruo's Pontus headquarters?' Waqar looked up at the towers. Most were now blackened, and there was smoke lingering in the air. 'Was there fighting here?'

'No, just Rondian magi burning their administrative records before fleeing. However, the libraries were left intact.'

Someone might know where Jehana is. 'Were prisoners taken?' he asked.

'I don't know, my Prince. This way, please.' Chanadhan led him through a doorway with a bridge sigil, the emblem of the Ordo Costruo, carved into the lintel. They crossed an entrance hall and entered a long room dominated by a rosewood table big enough to seat forty. More than a hundred Keshi noblemen, all in glittering, bejewelled armour, were backslapping and crowing, but Waqar ignored them and looked around. The ceiling was a series of domes, each elaborately painted; the walls were of white marble inset with wooden panelling. At the far end, the late afternoon sun was streaming through a dome of glass, illuminating one man.

Sultan Rashid Mubarak I, 19th Emir of Halli'kut, Victor of the Third Crusade and ruler of Ahmedhassa, had his back to the room as he stood looking out over the captured city.

Waqar barely noticed Chanadhan slip away as another official scurried up. 'The Great Sultan will see you now,' he said.

The entire room stopped to watch him approach. Of course his cousins, brutish Attam and crafty Xoredh, were among the self-congratulatory gathering, determined to be present at this historic moment – but neither of them were standing with their father.

He's making all his generals wait while he speaks with me, Waqar realised as he strode through the room, his boots echoing. When he reached the entrance to the glass dome, he sank gracefully to his knees and placed his forehead to the marble, letting the coolness of the stone seep into his skull.

It was fully a minute before Rashid spoke. 'Nephew, join me.'

Nephew. So they would be speaking as family. He joined his uncle at the window overlooking the fallen city. Pontus was spacious; he had been told it only ever filled up during the Moontide, when the Leviathan Bridge was open.

'Congratulations, Uncle,' Waqar said first, devoutly hoping he sounded suitably impressed. 'This is a stunning victory.'

Rashid's vivid green eyes lit with ironic amusement. 'So I'm told, but in truth, there's been little resistance. Between Moontides there's only one legion stationed in the region: in a fortress north of here, where they watch the Sydians. We've trapped them already.'

'And this is the Ordo Costruo's palace?'

'Ai: the famous Collegiate, where they feel free to criticise the teachings of both Kore and Ahm from a safe distance.' The sultan smiled. 'No one can hide from Truth for ever.'

Or you, Waqar thought. 'Were any of the magi taken?' he asked.

'In true scholarly style, many refused to leave their research, but as most of those are in their dotage, they'll be of little use in the breeding-houses. Of the rest, those who hadn't had the sense to flee west have locked themselves in Northpoint Tower.'

'Is the Bridge irrevocably destroyed, Uncle?' Waqar asked. Whatever was left of his mother's soul would be devastated if it was.

'It's too soon to say. If the invasion goes well, I'll permit them to repair it – it will be useful as a supply-line come next Moontide. But if we're checked, I'll assail the remaining towers and bring them crashing down. In any event, I need not decide immediately.'

Waqar wondered what the Ordo Costruo and their Merozain allies would do next. Would the plight of the Bridge keep them out of the game, or would they seek revenge?

But Rashid's quicksilver mind had already moved on. 'Tell me, Nephew, were you able to find Jehana?'

Waqar mustered his concentration; they might not have drawn scimitars, but this would be a duel. 'Uncle, we couldn't find her.'

Rashid turned to face him. His expression was neutral. 'I allowed you to abandon your post on the eve of the most important military action of my reign. What happened? Did your Javonesi spy prove untrustworthy?'

'No, Uncle, but we were countered – by the masked ones who slew Salim. I think they too are hunting Jehana.'

Rashid pursed his lips. 'Why would they do that?'

'Why would they kill my mother?' Waqar countered daringly,

pushing the law of harbadab somewhat, when uncles stood higher than nephews.

'I know not,' Rashid said after a heartbeat, letting it pass. 'So, tell me everything.'

Being trapped in Rashid's emerald stare was like being a hopper-mouse before a cobra, but Waqar had rehearsed his words carefully. 'We arrived in Hebusalim and met with the Javonesi spy. She had been assailed by one of the masks – Heartface – but managed to elude her.'

'Then she is talented, this spy. What was her name again?'

'Tarita, of Ja'afar.'

'Javon is small, but they have some resource. Did she mention her master's name?'

'She called him "Qasr", but I don't know if that's his true name.' The word meant 'hawk'. He'd met Qasr in Sagostabad, but he needed not mention that. 'He didn't join us. Tarita managed to do some clever scrying which led us to believe Jehana might be right here, in Pontus, so we followed the line of the Bridge.' Admitting they'd actually been tracking his supposedly dead mother could lead the conversation into dangerous places; this was a safer version of events.

'Indeed? And what did you see?'

'A sudden storm and a *vast* explosion – Uncle, it was truly huge! Then we saw the broken tower. We moored ourselves to it – we wanted to see if there were survivors – but the seas were flowing in, flooding what was left, so we left again.'

And if you know different, he thought, *then you're* definitely *in league with the Masks.*

As uncle and nephew regarded each other in silence for a few seconds, Waqar tried to keep his face expressionless, while trying to penetrate Rashid's gaze.

How do I read that flicker of the eye, the faint lift of the eyelid, that tiny shift in his stance?

Rashid turned back to the windows. 'Where is this spy, Tarita? I wish to question her.'

'I believe she's back in Javon.'

'You let her go?'

'She was never my prisoner, and I deemed her more useful in the field.'

'Useful for *whom*? What binds her to you?'

'I'm a Prince of Kesh,' he said. 'She has a price.'

In truth, there had been several reasons to let her go, not least that she was Merozain and beyond his powers to compel – although revealing that to Rashid would certainly prejudice the sultan against her. Regardless, Waqar didn't want her interrogated by Rashid's people. She'd promised to find Jehana, and he believed she would.

There was another reason: he *liked* Tarita, though sentiment should have no place in such decisions. He admired her perky determination, her swiftness of thought – and her smile.

'I hadn't thought you so manipulative, Nephew,' Rashid observed.

'I'm learning. Court life does that,' Waqar replied wryly.

'Then well played,' the sultan said. 'The lowborn are venal by nature and that can be exploited. Only those who understand wealth are free of its lure.'

Or those whose every desire has been spoon-fed to them from birth? Waqar thought ironically. *I'm not convinced, Uncle: I've found the greediest to be those who are already obscenely rich.*

Rashid went on, 'My sister was a special woman, Nephew – not just as a mage, or as a noblewoman of the highest rank. Do you know of what I speak?'

Waqar remembered the massive ice-ball that had slammed into Midpoint, and his mother's face as it had been in his final gnostic vision of her: not dead, but young and alive – and as implacable as a serpent sculpted in steel. But that was a memory Rashid didn't know he had.

'She was my mother,' he replied. 'That's all I know.'

'She was much more than that, Waqar,' Rashid replied. 'I didn't understand that for a long time. She and I were born to different women of our father's harem. Her mother was a Vereloni mage-woman who'd never learned the gnosis; Sakita was her only child. I grew up in Halli'kut, but your mother was taken in by the Ordo Costruo at a very young age and we seldom spoke after that. She had more loyalty to the Ordo Costruo than to her own people.' His voice made it clear that this was an irredeemable crime.

'She loved us, nevertheless,' Waqar said; the harbadab permitted him to defend her memory.

Rashid waved away his objection. 'Of course – but her *higher* love was to her order. Even when I joined the Ordo Costruo myself and became a trusted member, I wasn't privy to what she and her husband were doing. But I now believe that Antonin Meiros was seeking to unlock some great power in her: yes, he who so decried the breeding-houses may well have been doing something similar himself. You and Jehana were the result of an arranged marriage – a *specially* arranged marriage.'

Waqar didn't have to feign shock. 'But Mother *never* told me of this!'

'Surely there were hints?' Rashid probed. 'Think, Nephew! Did Jehana say *anything*? Could it be something handed down the female side? Because if these masked assassins took an interest in your mother, surely they will seek your sister . . . and you.'

'There were no hints, Uncle – truly, I am as mystified as you.'

'Then I fear for you both.' The sultan's voice was heavy. 'I'll make enquiries. If we're fortunate, she's inside Northpoint Tower and I can negotiate her freedom. But Waqar, we must also now consider the possibility that you too have a hidden power. If it can serve the Shihad, then we owe it to our soldiers to unlock it.' He waited as Waqar bowed his head in acceptance, then added, 'Either way, others will take up the hunt for your sister.'

Waqar had been hoping he'd be tasked with looking for Jehana, but he knew better than to protest. 'Of course, Uncle – I place myself at your disposal.' Then, his voice carefully pitched to show a hint of boyish amazement, he asked, 'Uncle, how *did* you bring down Midpoint Tower?'

This time it was Rashid who hesitated, although if Waqar hadn't been watching for it, he'd have missed it. 'I had a person on the inside – a convert, someone who hid their loyalties for decades, awaiting just such an opportunity. They disrupted the solarus crystals and caused an explosion, sacrificing themselves for the Shihad.'

Waqar gaped, knowing this to be a total lie – but that was fine, because it was the expected reaction. 'Then that person is a hero!' he managed to exclaim. 'Who was it – do I know them?'

Rashid shook his head. 'They still have family within the Ordo Costruo, so the secret is not yet mine to reveal.'

'Then I'll pray for their soul!' Waqar said fervently, his mind racing. But now was not the time for speculation. 'Uncle, do you wish me to take control of my windfleet once more?'

'No, Nephew, I have a new assignment for you. The air is a new front in this war and we require new weapons.' He looked at Waqar the way he used to when he was just 'Uncle Rashid' giving his beloved nephew a gift. 'Do you know what I'm talking about?'

'No, Uncle.' He was genuinely mystified.

'Then I won't spoil the surprise. You'll learn soon enough. Someone will collect you – your friends may join you. Be prepared to learn – and indeed, to be amazed.'

The interview was over. Waqar bowed and backed off, then turned and hurried away. He barely noticed the eyes of the high and mighty trailing him.

He lied to me about how the tower fell – which means he does know what they did to Mother! His stomach was roiling. *So I'm right: he's either working with the Masked Ones, or he's one of them. Ahm protect me . . .*

Waqar's progress through the chaos of the landing site hadn't gone unnoticed; most of those who saw him would have dearly wished to catch his eye – but one man had crouched and hidden as the young prince passed.

That man was Latif, an archer with Piru-Satabam III, the third elephant contingent. The unit was smaller than a traditional hazarabam of a thousand men; it comprised just forty elephants with a hundred and twenty riders, and twice as many labourers to support them.

Latif hid because he knew Waqar Mubarak; he had spoken with him a few days before Sultan Salim was murdered. He knew young Chanadhan, the mage-kalfas, too – but that was when he'd been one of Sultan Salim's impersonators. To reveal himself now would be to risk death: there was no place for the impersonators of murdered rulers.

I'm just a soldier, he reminded himself. *Nothing more.*

So he busied himself doing the bidding of his new master, Ashmak, a scar-faced Keshi mage-warrior, who had command – and the power of life and death – over the elephant Rani, her keeper Sanjeep and him. He trudged on, hauling the handcart full of feed to the elephant pens. He still marvelled at the amount Rani could eat each day – four to five times the weight of a man, and even more if they had to travel far. Right now, that feed was readily available, flown in from grain silos in western Dhassa, but he wondered how long that would last as the war progressed and supply-lines became stretched. Keshi war-tales often told of mounted soldiers being forced to eat their beloved mounts. It would break old Sanjeep's heart if they were reduced to eating Rani; he'd reared his giant beast from birth.

Ahm willing, it won't come to that.

He found Sanjeep washing Rani as she drank placidly from the water trench they'd had to dig the previous day, alongside four other beasts. Their metal-tipped tusks were wrapped in cloth and their howdahs were stacked nearby.

'Where have you been, Latif?' Sanjeep called in Lakh. 'You've been hours!'

'You think it's easy?' Latif panted, in the same tongue. As 'Salim', he'd had to be fluent in many languages from the East and West. He dragged his barrow to the edge of the trench and tipped it up. 'All the elephant-ships landed north of the city – but some *matachod* sent all the feed-transporters to the *south* side! Damned fools.' He patted Rani, who stroked him with her trunk, then picked up a massive sheath of grain stalks and devoured them. She looked so gentle, he could barely imagine her in battle.

'Ai, it's a damned mess,' Sanjeep agreed. 'But think of it: we're standing on *Yurosi* soil! What a thing to tell our children, eh?'

'You have no children,' Latif snorted, 'and neither do I.' *Not any more . . .*

'Ah, but once we get our hands on some nice white-skinned yoni, we'll fatten her up, eh!' Sanjeep was in good spirits: Rani had stayed calm for the entire journey, despite being penned in the hold of a windship for almost three days. 'Ashmak says each hazarabam will have its own string of whores. They've taken thousands in the city, he says.'

'What, we're going to drag Rondian women into our beds? We'll end up with our throats slit!'

'But soldiers need whores, eh? Otherwise they drink and brawl.'

'They'll do that anyway.' Latif had seen soldiers on campaign.

'That is truth.' Sanjeep took a swig from his flask, then offered it to Latif, who shook his head. Sanjeep's fenni was the closest thing to poison he'd ever drunk.

Latif had no intention of using the unit's whores, no matter what they looked like. He was still mourning his wife. So it was with little interest that he watched a dozen women being herded into their camp. Many were taller than the Easterners around them, with white skin and pale hair, but there were others little different to their own Eastern women. What unified them was their glassy-eyed disbelief and palpable fear. They'd all been weeping, and most had torn dresses and bruised faces and limbs.

For a minute, everyone stared. Then Hazarapati Selmir strode into their midst. Latif faded into the background; he'd known the commander too, during his life as an impersonator, and was anxious to avoid him. 'Hear me,' the hazarapati shouted, 'these are the women assigned to Piru-Satabam III! No other *chotia* can touch them – *no one*, not even the Sultan Himself! But they aren't free, hear me? The army paid out for them, and you'll pay them off. The quartermaster will post the rates. Any man taking a free fuck will be flogged! *Now, get back to work!*'

Within a few days, almost everyone had spent most of their money on the women, while Latif sat on his coin and brooded. *Rashid Mubarak became sultan when my master was murdered. Who commits a murder? Nine times out of ten, it is he who benefits from it most . . .*

Gold could purchase much more than whores: maybe even an assassin who could penetrate the sultan's court.

The day of the invasion, Jehana Mubarak was buried deep underground in the Domus Pontico archives and barely heard the warning bells. When she wasn't in lectures, an anonymous figure in a bekira-shroud

47

completing her final year as a student, she was down here in mould-ering scrolls, trying to unlock her mother's legacy.

Her brother Waqar had no idea what he'd turned down when he'd chosen Rashid and court life over the Ordo Costruo – not only would he have been tutored by master magi, but he'd have learned what he *truly* was: one of only two people left alive of the handful raised by the Ordo Costruo to be both mage *and* dwymancer. But he'd chosen Rashid's court, despite their mother's repeated pleas. Perhaps if she'd been free to tell Waqar the truth, he might have been swayed – but that was too dangerous; he'd had to join of his own free will, and he hadn't.

Now Mother was dead – *murdered* – and Jehana had been moved into hiding. And even here wasn't safe: when the bells rang out, she *knew* they were summoning her.

'Are those the alarm bells, child?' called old Magister Olbedyn, shuf-fling blindly along the aisles full of old manuscripts and scrolls. 'Can you help me?'

Olbedyn, a full Rondian by blood, was descended of the original Builder-magi who'd founded the order. He was all but blind from age; she wondered if he even knew she was Keshi. The order was mixed race, but those of Eastern blood usually dwelt in Hebusalim.

'Come, Magister, this way,' she said, forcing herself to walk slowly for him, although she wanted to run as fast as she could. Other bodies detached from the shadowy aisles, bobbing mage-lights preceding them as they funnelled towards the stairs. Most wore the pale blue robes of the order; those clad in green were sentinels, their battle-magi. One of those, Sentinel Levana, a tough-looking woman with closely cropped dark hair, was hurrying towards them now.

'Hurry, Magister – that's the "imminent threat" pattern,' Levana said, in her deep voice. 'Stay with him, girl.'

That Jehana was a princess and a Mubarak was something these people were determined to ignore. At home, even a noble could be flogged for omitting her title, but here, she wasn't 'princess', just 'girl'.

Together they helped the old man up into the atrium of the Archive, where Magister Hillarie, a prim blonde woman in her forties, intercepted them. 'Student Mubarak, Sentinel Levana, come with me.'

'There's an alarm ringing, Magister,' Levana said tersely. The gulf between scholar and battle-mage was a wide one in the order; it prided itself on being a meritocracy of intellect.

'Which is why this student must come with me,' Hillarie replied. 'Student Durara will aid Magister Olbedyn. Come!' She bustled off, moving so quickly that Jehana and Levana had to trot to keep up. When she ushered them into the map room, Jehana was alarmed to find a dozen of the most senior scholars and sentinels present, attending upon Magister Vernou, the Arcanum Vice-Chancellor and second-ranked mage of the order's Pontus chapter.

'Princess Jehana, welcome,' Magister Vernou said. His voice sounded strained. 'Fellow scholars, sentinels: the Chancellor is preparing to address everyone in the great hall, but he's asked me to convene this meeting and get things underway.' His face grave, he announced, 'Overnight, Rashid Mubarak launched a thousand windships across the Pontic Sea. He preceded his attack by severely damaging Midpoint Tower, where Arch-Magus Rene Cardien died. Magister Odessa D'Ark has assumed control in Hebusalim.'

Stunned gasps and cries of grief echoed through the room; even Jehana put her hand to her heart in shock, feeling as if a long-armed afreet had just reached across the sea to seize her. *Uncle Rashid, what have you done?*

Every face turned towards her and one of the scholar-magi voices exclaimed, 'Are we bitten by those we hold to our breast?' Jehana recognised the quote, from a popular play – these scholars couldn't help themselves, even in a crisis.

Chancellor Vernou made a dismissive gesture. 'Princess Jehana's mother Sakita was slain by assassins and the princess is here for her own protection. She was as ignorant of this assault as the rest of us. Nevertheless, her position here must be considered. The sultan has demanded our surrender. He promised our complete safety – as long as we hand over Jehana to him.'

'Then that's what we must do,' Hillarie sniffed. 'Our order comes first.'

Hand me over to Uncle Rashid . . . ? Jehana felt a sudden sense of panic. Her mother had rejected Rashid's demands that she serve the Shihad

– they had quarrelled bitterly over their divided loyalties. If Rashid claimed her, he would make her serve him in any way she could.

I won't do that.

'But what of the Bridge?' someone asked, and for the moment the discussion left her. Jehana shrank against the wall as details emerged: in the early evening of the previous night, Midpoint Tower had been assailed by windships; there had been a cataclysmic explosion in the tower.

'Cut to the heart, Vernou,' Loric, an engineer-mage, growled. 'Can the Bridge hold?'

'Yes, Loric, the Bridge *can* hold – in theory. Midpoint needs immediate repairs, and all four peripheral towers will need to increase their energy feeds. Hebusalim is already flying in a support, but the problem is access. Right now, the Shihad control the air over the Pontic Sea.'

'What's Rashid's goal?' someone asked, and everyone looked suspiciously at Jehana again. Rashid Mubarak had once been a trusted member of the Ordo Costruo himself – until he betrayed the order which had nurtured and taught him.

'His message speaks of "holy war" against the Rondian Empire. He claims he brought down the tower to prevent us from "aiding our Imperial overlords" and destroying his windfleet.'

'The empire isn't our overlord!' several magi called out.

'That's not how the Keshi see it,' Levana grunted. 'Can we use Jehana as leverage?'

'My uncle doesn't care about me except as a pawn in his games,' Jehana snapped. She fervently hoped her brother Waqar remembered their familial love.

'Nevertheless, he's demanded that she's handed over,' Hillarie said. 'Why shouldn't we?'

You don't know what I am, Jehana thought.

But Vernou evidently did know. 'That's out of the question,' he said briskly. 'We look after our own. The chancellor is ordering a withdrawal to our havens in Verelon, but that's imperial territory, where Princess Jehana would face incarceration. The chancellor has given me responsibility for her safety.' He looked around the room, then said, 'Ladies, gentlemen, give me ten minutes to resolve this matter. When I return, I want to hear your evacuation plan.'

Vernou signed for Levana and Jehana to follow and led them to another room where he first turned to the sentinel. 'Levana, you were assigned to protect Jehana. I'd like you to continue that role, if you would?'

'Of course,' Levana responded, 'but where should I take her? The wilds of the northeast?'

'I've a better idea: Sunset Isle.' When Levana looked surprised, Vernou went on, 'It's out of the way, and unexpected. If you go in secret, no one will know she's there. There's enough sea around it to prevent scrying, not to mention the wards on the tower itself. And it has a solarus cluster, so it's defendable, even against a windfleet.'

Being locked up for who knew how long on a rock in the middle of the ocean? That sounded ghastly – but Jehana's opinion wasn't invited, and regardless, she couldn't think of a better alternative. In the East, the first person who recognised her would hand her over to Rashid's people, and in the West she'd be treated as an enemy. The wilds sounded even worse.

When Levana agreed, Vernou went on, 'We're preparing windships to send supplies and resources to the towers. Magister Hillarie has been assigned to Sunset Isle and you'll both join her at the last moment. You must leave in two hours, before we're cut off by the Keshi windfleet. Tell no one where you're going.'

'Yes, Magister.' Levana paused, then added, 'We should still send another ship more openly to the northeast, with someone dressed as Jehana aboard. Have them create a false trail.'

'Good thinking, Levana. I'll see to it.' Vernou turned to Jehana. 'Princess, we will protect you, I swear.'

You'll try, Jehana thought, *but you're up against Uncle Rashid. In the end, he always wins.*

As Vernou turned to leave, Levana blurted, 'How did it come to this, Chancellor? Have we been sleeping? The Bridge is *everything* to our order!'

'We're still trying to understand,' Vernou admitted. 'But the Merozains have pledged aid, and our chapter in Hebusalim hasn't – *yet* – been assailed. We'll do all we can to save the Bridge.'

Two hours later, a small, anonymous windsloop left behind the chaotic bustle of other vessels being laden with as much of the order's research and treasures as they could carry. It rose into the air and swept away on a northern trajectory – they'd change course once out of sight.

'Will they get it all away?' Jehana asked, watching the frantic activity fade into the distance.

Levana sighed. 'I doubt we have the windship capacity to remove more than a tenth of our records. Most of our older magi have elected to stay, to try to protect the records from wanton pillaging – and to plead with Rashid to keep the Arcanum and Collegiate intact.'

The Ordo Costruo set so much store in knowledge that they're prepared to risk death or incarceration rather than abandon their work . . .

Most of those aboard the sloop were openly weeping as the craft turned its prow towards the south, but Levana, solid as a tree-trunk, was glowering as she laced her wrist-braces and flexed tattooed biceps. 'Has anyone tried to scry you since this began?' she asked Jehana.

Jehana had been fending off attempts to find her for the last hour. 'They're trying right now.'

'Then get below and sit by the keel,' Levana told her. 'The energy concentration will distort your aura.'

Jehana did as she was told, conscious that everyone bristled whenever they looked at her. She barely knew any of them, but her life was now in their hands. *How many would rather just pitch me overboard?* she wondered, trying to pretend she wasn't terrified.

3

After the Storm

Dwyma

Of the handful of variants to the gnosis that emerged among the survivors of the Ascendancy of Corineus, the most troubling was dwyma. The wielder of such 'magic', rather than drawing on power native to their body, drew on residual energies present in nature, so they had both a far greater reserve of power, but also far less control. Indeed some form of consent appears to have been required from a 'guardian spirit' before a dwymancer could draw on that power.

Some dwymancers went mad. The rest were persecuted to death within a few decades.

ORDO COSTRUO ARCANUM, HEBUSALIM, 887

Feher Szarvasfeld, Mollachia
Julsep 935

'Lad, it's the strangest battlefield I've ever walked,' Dragan Zhagy murmured in Kyrik Sarkany's ear.

Kyrik couldn't claim to have seen many battlefields, but he knew what Dragan meant. This was more like the aftermath of a blizzard. If you didn't peer too hard into the ice, all you saw were the trees and bushes below the surface; you could pretend this was a frozen lake, broken only by a few tree-tops.

But it was summer, they were below the snowline and the 'frozen lake' sat atop a cliff. Not all those dark shapes below were foliage, either: there were hundreds of men down there, who'd been encased by ice in seconds.

53

My brother did this . . . My little brother, who can't even use the gnosis . . .

'What have our scouts found, Gazda?' Kyrik asked.

'More than half the Delestre legion lie dead below this ice,' Dragan replied. His title, Gazda, signified his rank as head of the Vitezai Sarkanum, a clandestine group of Mollach freedom fighters. 'The rest are in Hegikaro, Ujtabor and Banezust – fewer than two thousand men, split over three camps. Governor Inoxion's legion of Imperial Guard are in the lower valley, in Lapisz, Gazdakap and Revgatra. They're intact: five thousand men, fifteen magi.'

'What about Robear and Sacrista Delestre?'

Dragan jabbed a finger downwards. 'Robear the Red is under ice, but our scouts saw Sacrista stagger into Inoxion's camp at Revgatra yesterday.'

'Sacrista is ten times the soldier her brother was,' Kyrik muttered. He'd barely survived when they'd crossed blades during the storm. Her gnosis was stronger, but swordsmanship mattered just as much in a duel and she'd been the best he'd ever faced. 'What of our own situation?'

'Thanks to Valdyr, we've lost only a few dozen of the Vitezai, and as many of the Sydians,' Dragan replied. He peered sourly down into the ravine below, where their unlikely allies, Clan Vlpa, were massing. 'We've five thousand men all told, but if we could free Hegikaro, several thousand townsfolk could be brought to arms.'

'No, the Sydians need to join the rest of their clan and get their horses to pasture – they must continue their journey down the Magas River and into the Domhalott. This place is a wasteland now and they desperately need feed.'

'Ysh, but we've another battle to fight – we may not get a better chance to strike, lad.'

'We need to recover first – we were almost destroyed here, trapped below the cliffs. Even Valdyr doesn't seem to know what he did, or if he can do it again.'

They both turned to study Kyrik's younger brother, dark-haired where Kyrik was blond and introverted where Kyrik was open. His expression was giving away little. The brothers had spent half their lives in Kesh as prisoners of war, but they'd had very different experiences in the East: Kyrik had been taken under the wing of Godspeaker Paruq Rakinissi, a good man who'd un-Chained his gnosis and shown him the peaceful Ja'arathi version of Amteh. But Valdyr had been tortured, scarred physically and mentally, abused in the inhuman breeding-houses of the Hadishah and barred from his gnosis so long he'd not been able to unlock it since.

When they'd at last returned to Mollachia, they'd found their parents dead and their kingdom in thrall to the Delestre family, imperially appointed tax-farmers. The Delestre siblings had locked the brothers up, thrown away the keys and left them to starve to death; they were only free thanks to Dragan and the Vitezai Sarkanum.

'Sacrista had me at sword-point,' Kyrik admitted. 'Then the ice-storm struck . . . But *how*?'

'Perhaps you should just ask Valdyr?' Dragan suggested.

I wish it were that easy, Kyrik thought, but Dragan was right: he had to try. He patted Dragan's shoulder, muttered, 'Wish me luck!' and went to join his brother at the cliff-top.

'Val. How are you this morning?'

Valdyr flinched. 'I'm fine. How does Hajya fare? Will she keep her right hand?' He gestured around and added, 'I'm amazed she survived.'

Kyrik's Sydian wife Hajya had been wounded and thrown from the cliff-tops, only surviving through her gnosis. 'She's recovering, thank Kore,' Kyrik replied. 'She has her fellow Sfera to aid her, and she's strong-willed.'

Valdyr laughed dryly at that. 'Ysh, she is that.'

A few days ago, he'd not have had a kind word to say for her, Kyrik reflected. *Whatever happened, it's softened his views on the Sydians.*

The awkward conversation skidded to a halt as they both stared down at the milling horses and riders on the banks of the river below. The Vlpa had been camped there since the battle and the air now had a dung-fire pungency, but they were heading downstream tomorrow, seeking the Domhalott, where Kyrik had promised them land.

'Dragan wants us to keep attacking,' Kyrik said after a pregnant pause, 'but the Vlpa need pasture as a priority. We're not provisioned for more than a few days' ride, and Hegikaro is fifty miles from here as the crow flies – that's assuming we can pick a path through the ice.'

They both turned and squinted at the sheet-ice now covering the upper reaches of Feher Szarvasfeld. The name meant 'White Stag Land', and Kyrik had seen Valdyr and those with him riding white stags that night.

There's no use skirting around the question, he decided. 'Val, what happened that night?'

His younger brother, taller than him by an inch, and broader too, for all Kyrik was a big man, shrank into himself, and his reply was hesitant. 'I was with Dragan's men on the lower slopes of Watcher's Peak. The Delestre rode past us, cutting us off with no way to warn you of their arrival – then a white stag came . . . It wanted me to follow – I don't know how I knew that – but I did, right up Watcher's Peak.'

Watcher's Peak was the legendary mountain where the hero Zlateyr had built a stronghold, and died. Why it had a Rondian name was just part of its mystery. 'Did Dragan go with you?'

'He tried, but the stag went swiftly and I couldn't wait. When I got to the old fortress, Zlateyr himself was there, with his sister Luhti, his son Eyrik and the shaman Sidorzi.'

Kyrik raised his eyebrows. 'You saw ghosts?'

'I don't know – they felt as real as you and me. They fed me the meat of the stag . . . and then we rode to war – the storm broke over us and the stags we were riding swept down the slopes, and suddenly we were here.'

'I saw them.' Kyrik placed a hand on his forearm. 'I saw *you*.'

'Brother, you were *right*,' Valdyr breathed, 'Zlateyr really was Sydian, just like your Vlpa friends – he told me so himself. They're blood of our blood. I doubted you, and I *hated* your Vlpa. But you were right and I was wrong.'

Kyrik couldn't imagine what that had cost his brother, who equated all dark-skinned people with those who'd so abused him in Ahmedhassa. He put his arm around Valdyr's shoulder and said simply, 'Val, I'm proud of you.'

For a moment they embraced, then pulled apart awkwardly.

'You've not heard the rest,' Valdyr said. 'They told me I have something called "dwyma" – and that I can draw energy from something called the Elétfa, the Tree of Life. That storm? It came from the Elétfa.'

Kyrik had never been much of a scholar but he remembered a little from his time at the Arcanum. 'Dwyma's a dead heresy – I'm sure our tutors said it no longer existed.'

'Your tutors were wrong. Zlateyr said it unifies all living things. You know I'm a true follower of Kore – I never broke faith in all my years in Kesh. I'm *not* a heretic.'

'Then perhaps it's wrong to call it a heresy,' Kyrik suggested. 'What's a "heresy" anyway? A law made up by a group of priests.'

'Men guided by Kore!'

'No, fallible men who died centuries ago. I trust you over them.'

'But I had virtually no control over that storm – I almost killed everyone in this valley!' Valdyr looked away, then muttered, 'You don't know how close I came. It felt *so* good, to hunt and kill – I almost couldn't stop—'

'"Almost", Val. We all have "almost" moments.'

'It was a dance along a knife-edge – I could have fallen so easily . . .'

'But you *didn't*.' Kyrik put a hand on his brother's shoulder again and said earnestly, '*All* war is fought on a knife-edge: a thousand tiny decisions decide the day, one way or the other.'

'Or one big one.'

'Maybe – but the question is, could you do it again? Because we're still facing a full legion of Imperial Guard, with all their magi.'

Valdyr hesitated, then said, 'Yes, I could try to reach it again. I can feel the potential inside me still. But it's not a tool, Brother; it's not like your gnosis. I have to *ask* for this power, and if it comes, it will do what's in its nature.'

All that power, but no control? No wonder it was made a heresy . . . Kyrik rubbed at his stubble. 'But it destroyed our enemies that night.'

'Ysh, indeed! But once unleashed, control is almost impossible. When we rode, we were moved by the spirits of destruction – even great Zlateyr. Our blood was up, and we were ready to kill anything that moved.'

'So dwyma is a sledgehammer, while the gnosis is a razor.'

'If you like.' Valdyr threw him an uneasy look. 'I can't use it easily, or on demand. But I will use it, if and when I can, for our people. For Mollachia.'

Kyrik thought that through. 'I think what you've told me makes the way forward clearer. We can't go into battle, not in the lowlands where most of our people live – this gift of yours could kill as many of us as enemies.'

Valdyr looked hurt, but he couldn't disagree.

'We must proceed cautiously,' Kyrik decided. 'We'll get the Vlpa riders into the Domhalott, then we'll raid the upper valley – the remaining Delestre soldiers are trapped and weak. I'll fly to meet the rest of the tribe and bring them into Mollachia.'

'It feels like a wasted opportunity.'

'If the Rondians try to attack us, then your gift can protect us. Away from the lowlands, fewer innocent lives are at stake. Think of this as a chance to learn control, Brother.'

'Ysh; I know you're right.' Valdyr glanced towards the camp below. 'When will you leave?'

'Tomorrow. Hajya will stay – she's too weak to travel, even by skiff, and we lost the chieftain's son in the battle so you'll need someone to liaise with. So keep her close, and safe.'

Valdyr bowed his head and they clasped hands. 'Of course,' he said.

Valdyr watched his brother return to Dragan to explain his decision, then descend in kinesis-fuelled bounds to seek his wife. He envied Kyrik's easy command of the gnosis as he leaped hundreds of feet down the cliff in seconds.

Why can't I reach my gnosis? he wondered yet again, bitterly frustrated. He found a fallen log on the edge of the ice and sat listening to the wind. Dragan came and joined him, followed shortly after by Rothgar Baredge and Juergan Tirlak, senior men of the Vitezai. Rothgar, a stolid bearded man, was descended from the original people, the Yothic Stonefolk; Valdyr liked his laconic competence. Juergan, a confident shaggy-haired young man with a wild streak, was a hunter and trapper who prided himself on his physical prowess. The three of them deferred to him as their prince – but now they saw him as much more than that.

He listened as Dragan outlined Kyrik's thinking. 'But the Rondians are broken,' Juergan protested, when his gazda was done. 'This is timid!'

'No, it's sensible,' Rothgar replied. 'We must learn our weapons before we fight again.'

'Ysh,' Dragan agreed. 'Too many of our own people will die if we take ice storms into the farmlands.' He turned to Valdyr. 'Lad, you won this victory, not the Vlpa riders. Perhaps Kyrik's alliance with these people – well-intentioned, of course – was premature. If we lure Inoxion out and destroy him, we won't need the Vlpa.'

'Kyrik's committed. They're already here. And they really are our kin . . .'

'If you say so, lad. But if a man's cousins move into his home so that he's forced to sleep outside, is that right?'

'Then you should raise it with Kyrik,' Valdyr replied, though he partly agreed.

'I've tried, lad, but he's deaf to reason. And his wife has a sweeter whisper than I.'

'My dog has a sweeter whisper than you, Gazda,' Rothgar chuckled. 'Anyway, we may yet need them. We don't celebrate before the victory is won.'

That too was sensible. They fell into silence and a sense of unspoken agreement settled over them. *It isn't disloyal*, Valdyr told himself, *to not share Kyrik's dream.*

Kyrik splashed across the river and onto Neplezko Flat, where the Vlpa riders were encamped beside the Magas River. He couldn't help thinking this piece of flat, open ground would have been a slaughter-house, if Valdyr's dwyma hadn't saved them. He was still shaken at the revelation. The people of Mollachia were devoted to Kore; if his brother was branded a heretic, it would cause immense distress, and might even bring down the Inquisition upon them. And the nature of that power also concerned him. *I'm worried about his lack of control. He needs to learn that, fast.*

Acknowledging gestures of respect from the riders, Kyrik entered his hide pavilion. The air inside was stale, so he tied back the flap before going to Hajya's side. She was awake, her moon-face heavy-eyed, but her hair was damp and she was freshly washed.

'Greetings, Husband,' she murmured, her husky voice ironically formal.

'Good evening, Wife.' He knelt beside her and examined her right arm, which was strapped to the elbow. Then he looked into her eyes. For the first time in days they were sharp and alert. 'Have you eaten?' He ignored her nod and picked up the pot of stew to feed her while he told her his plans.

'So soon?' she said, when he said he'd be leaving the following day. 'I hoped we'd have more time.'

'Chief Thraan will be anxious for tidings. I've got to get your people into Mollachia somehow. Our riders were able to traverse the Sunrise Path, but I doubt the wains or herds can. We may have to assail Collistein to get in.'

'So long as the herds can enter – they're our lifeblood.' Hajya took his hand. 'I know neither of us would have chosen the other for marriage – you know we Sfera never marry; it's our duty to bear children with mage-blood for the tribe – but I'm content with you, Kyrik Sarkany.'

'And I with you,' he replied, wondering where this was going.

'It would please me to bear your child,' she told him, her face frank.

'Good,' Kyrik grinned, 'but you've got a broken wrist and severed tendons that are still rebinding—'

'Ysh – and I'm bored of lying here with nothing to do! Disrobe and join me.'

He was a little taken aback to realise she was completely in earnest. They were still working through the tangle of strangers marrying, but the discoveries had been rewarding so far, and unlike the pious Mollach women, she had no shyness. 'Are you sure it won't hurt you?'

'It's only my wrist and arm that's broken; the rest is healing . . . and I bathed earlier.' She pulled his face to hers and kissed him hungrily.

'A real lady wouldn't be so forward.'

'A real lady would bore you.'

The rest of the evening passed in a tangled blur of sweating bodies and hard-earned bliss.

'I'll miss you,' he told her as she drifted into sleep, and she murmured something fond in return. Within seconds, she was snoring. He lay back, staring up at the hide walls and listening to the camp settle, and running underneath all the human and animal sounds, the never-ending song of the Magas, and wished he didn't have to leave.

But next morning, he bade his wife and his brother farewell and rode upriver while everyone else went downstream. A few days later, he recovered his windskiff hidden near Lake Jegto and took to the skies to seek the rest of the Vlpa clan.

Revgatra, Mollachia

Sacrista Delestre bolted her door and added a locking spell for good measure, feeling like a castellan in a besieged keep.

Which is what I am, she thought angrily, as she stripped off and plunged into the barrel of hot water Governor Inoxion had ordered for her. For all she knew, the governor was watching through a peephole; he was just the sort. But the water was still wonderful, easing the bone-deep chill of this mountain kingdom.

Robear is dead. That was the inescapable fact her brain couldn't move past. Though he'd exasperated her, her twin brother was the only person who'd ever loved her; he was the only one who'd stood up for her against their tyrant father. Knowing he'd never again breeze into her room, spouting his adorable nonsense, made her eyes sting and her heart ache. Not even the thought of gutting Kyrik and Valdyr Sarkany was enough to assuage her pain.

She'd been bathing daily – once a week might be considered excessive by most, but she needed to feel *clean* after her ordeal escaping the frozen battlefield. And when she wasn't immersed in hot water, she'd spent much of the last three days since she'd staggered into this camp asleep. She knew Inoxion wanted to speak with her, but she didn't want to deal with him until she felt like herself again. *If I could put it off for ever, I would.*

But life didn't work that way. She was a woman in a man's world, and that meant dealing with brutes and bullies head-on.

It also meant knowing when to bend instead of breaking.

By the time she'd scrubbed herself clean and the scented water had soaked into her raw skin, she felt something like ready. She rose, dried herself and dressed in borrowed clothing – some village doxy's dress, she assumed, too low and loose at the front for her small breasts, too short in the skirt for her height. She laced herself in as tightly as she could, combed through her short gingery-red hair with her fingers, pinched her pale cheeks and decided she'd done all she could. It was time to go into battle again.

Governor Ansel Inoxion awaited her in his private dining room. He'd been an unseen presence since inviting her to stay in his requisitioned house near the Revgatra Ferry, although he'd sent solicitous notes wishing her a speedy recovery and inviting her to dine. She finally felt strong enough to accept.

A servant showed her in. Unsurprisingly, there were no other guests. Inoxion rose as she entered. He was already partway through a bottle of Brician merlo. The Rondian governor was a tall, balding man in his forties, with a voluptuary's red, moist lips. 'Milady Sacrista,' he exclaimed, bowing languidly. 'It gladdens me to see you up on your feet again.'

No doubt it would gladden you even more to see me on my knees.

She approximated a curtsey. 'What news from Augenheim, Milord? Has my father responded?'

'Straight to business,' Inoxion mock-approved. 'Clearly, you are recovering! But sadly, your father hasn't yet responded, either to your letter or my attempts at a gnostic calling. I'm told that he has gone north, to Pallas.' He poured her a glass of wine, which she accepted warily.

'Father's gone to Pallas? Why? He hates the place – it's full of people richer than he is.'

Inoxion laughed. 'Bending the knee is tedious, but sometimes it's necessary.'

As subtle messages go, that's not very subtle, she thought coolly.

'All the empire's power-brokers have been summoned to the capital,' Inoxion told her. 'Pontus has fallen. The empire is at war.'

Good grief, Sacrista thought, *how long have I been asleep?* 'At war? With whom?'

'The Sultan of Kesh has landed a thousand windships at Pontus. The Leviathan Bridge is destroyed, the Ordo Costruo are all dead – or so the reports say – and Empress Lyra has declared a state of war.'

Sacrista stared, her mind struggling with this completely unexpected news. Then she leaped at the obvious question. 'Are you to be recalled also, Governor?'

'When my territory is in a state of open rebellion?' Inoxion's eyes ran over her. 'That's the problem, isn't it? I'm needed in Augenheim, but I'm also needed here.'

You'll go where the profit is, Sacrista thought, trying to think this through. Was it a lifeline, or another blow to her chances of getting out of this Kore-forsaken place?

'Let's dine,' Inoxion said, pulling out a chair for her. She accepted – she needed to eat, and if the governor's company had to be borne to do so, then needs must.

A sumptuous meal was served: spit-roasted pork and root vegetables, with pickles and jellies. She wolfed it down, but Inoxion ate sparingly, sipping on his wine as he relayed the news, mostly of the Eastern invasion. 'They don't stand a chance, of course,' he concluded. 'The might of Rondelmar will crush them.'

'We lost the Third Crusade,' Sacrista replied, to annoy him – she wasn't at all concerned.

'No, "we" did not. The Sacrecours lost: a corrupt, mismanaged regime so complacent it thought it had only to send armies to be victorious, all led by a pompous ass. The "great" Kaltus Korion's reputation was undeserved. No competent commander would have failed as he did.'

Easy for you to say, five years later, Sacrista thought. What mattered to her was getting her remaining men out of this ghastly place with enough plunder to satisfy her father's rapacity, but she doubted she'd be given the chance: she and Robear were bastards and August Delestre didn't suffer failure gladly, although he was generous when it came to doling out blame.

Father gave us a legion because he trusted Robear. He never realised I have always been the better soldier. Forcing herself not to dwell on Robear, she concentrated on devouring her food while leaving the wine as untouched as possible, although she'd been craving a drink for days. When the platters were emptied, she mustered her excuses for retreating graciously – but first, she needed to know what Inoxion would do to help her men. 'So, Governor,' she started, 'you've got five thousand men in the lower valley and I have around two thousand in the upper valley, where the best mines are. How are we going to manage this rebellion?'

Inoxion took another sip of wine – his lips were now *very* red – and peered at her over his cup. 'Please, do call me Ansel. You know, Sacrista, I admire you. You're strong-willed, more than competent as a commander, you have a good head on you, and you've retained your feminine side. I think we could work well together.'

Sacrista sincerely doubted that. 'We've got about three months of production before winter closes the mines again,' she said, sticking to business. 'That's not much time to meet Father's targets and get out.'

'An exceedingly difficult task, even without this rebellion,' Inoxion mused. 'But what happened, Sacrista? My skiff-pilots have overflown the battlefield and they claim it's locked in *ice*. What happened out there?'

Inoxion's voice had become sharper, betraying fears of his own. They'd both believed they were facing a handful of embittered local renegades; he was just now realising their enemy was something else entirely.

Can I use his fear to get what I want? she wondered.

She schooled her voice into a monotone. 'Our scouts detected horsemen moving south along the Magas Gorge. We advanced, intending to trap them below us.' Their column had got strung out, but Robear had been so blasé when she'd tried to instil some urgency. 'The weather worsened, but we had the enemy trapped, so we pressed on. We made contact – we had their commander, Kyrik Sarkany, at sword-point—' Suddenly her voice choked and she reached for the wine.

'Are you distressed?' Ansel Inoxion enquired, his tones gentle, his eyes predatory.

Am I distressed? My brother's dead, *you arsehole!* She tipped the wine down her throat, then pushed the goblet away, blinking furiously. *He's a frozen corpse somewhere under the ice-sheet and I can't even bury him!*

When Inoxion took her hand, she almost punched him – but no, that would *never* do, not when she needed his help. So she forced out the rest of her tale. 'Then the storm broke over us – the worst I've ever seen. In seconds the air was thick with snow and the wind was a reaper's scythe. Day became night – even mage-light barely penetrated the darkness. You needed all your strength just to keep your flesh from petrifying. I lost *everyone!*'

She could hear the horror in her voice, but she had to complete the story. 'I hid beneath a shelf and called heat through the gnosis – that's how I escaped the worst of it. But when I did finally manage to get out, the forest was twelve feet or more deep in snow and ice, for miles around. While the Mollachs burned their dead on a pyre, I crept away.'

She didn't mention the riders in the storm who'd laughed as they slew. They'd ridden giant stags, like the Storm Kings of the Sollan faith come to life. *Surely I imagined them?* She must have: the gnosis couldn't do such things, and the Sollan gods were only myths.

With as much dignity as she could manage, she withdrew her hand. 'So, *Ansel*, it was a good thing I didn't *persuade* you to give me any of your men after all. They'd have been buried up there too.'

She had the satisfaction of watching his smugness curdle. If she'd been enough of a whore to give him what he'd wanted, she'd have had those men. So, a small point to her. But he still had the best pieces on the board, and he quickly regained his composure, if not his warmth.

'As you know, Sacrista, the Imperial Legions exist to protect imperial assets, and that must always be my priority. This kingdom is yours to tax under your tax-farming contract against the Sarkany family, but protecting the mines isn't specifically my jurisdiction.'

'But ensuring the kingdom remains an imperial vassal-state *is* your concern,' she countered. 'When the resistance to our legal tax-farming operation was just a few dissidents in the wilds, you could leave them to us. But there's an army out there, Ansel, no more than fifty miles away, at last sighting. We estimated more than five thousand riders in the gorge – we've no idea who they are or where they came from, but they're sure as Hel a threat to imperial governance.'

His leering had been replaced by cold concentration, which suited her fine. 'What is it you want, Sacrista?'

'I want your help to deal with them so that I can get on with taxing this kingdom.'

Inoxion visibly gave up whatever ambitions he'd harboured for the evening, to her relief. 'I will need to verify the numbers and nature of this invading force. I'll need a written account of what you've just told me to send to the imperocracy in Pallas. I need your dispositions, and an undertaking to support my efforts. If this territory is going to be put on a war footing, then I'll be forced to assume full control. Is that your wish, Sacrista?'

'I'll cooperate to the letter of the law, Ansel.' *And not a hair's-breadth more*, her eyes added.

Inoxion sighed, and they stood. *I'm sure you've got a back-up whore waiting for if I didn't play your game*, she thought disdainfully, but said politely, 'Goodnight, Governor. I'm going to Hegikaro tomorrow.'

The night passed quietly, as did the morning's ferry ride upstream to Hegikaro. Sacrista found the garrison locked in, fearing imminent attack, but they were expecting her and she quickly reasserted control over the town. She threw herself into her work, doubling the size of all patrols while keeping them closer to base, ceding the wilderness to their enemies. As days passed, the fragile peace held.

Despatches from Inoxion told her that he'd found the invaders and was tracking them into the Domhalott, the hills north of his position. They were *Sydians*, unbelievably – who knew what they were doing in Mollachia, or how they'd got here? Had old alliances been triggered? Either way, she was happy that was now the governor's problem.

Finally, as Julsep ended, despatches came from the wider world. Her father had still not written, but his secretary did: August Delestre had been given a senior role in the army riding to war against the Shihad and was demanding that all available tax monies be sent immediately, *'if you wish your welcome to be assured'*. Nothing was said about Robear's loss, which simply deepened her hatred.

Rukka te, Father, she thought. *I've half a mind to keep the plunder for myself and head for Becchio*. The mercenaries always needed battle-magi, and she fancied she could hold her own. If she raked in enough money, perhaps she could buy her own legion?

4

Moral Compass

Magic and Ethics

The Lex Arcanus *– the Gnostic Codes – are the laws governing use of the gnosis. From the first sign of dissent among his followers, Emperor Sertain began working upon creating a framework for control. It now fills tomes and can justify any action the Crown takes against fellow magi, even though we're all the Blessed of Corineus.*
ERVYN NAXIUS, ORDO COSTRUO, PONTUS, 828

Pallas, Rondelmar
Julsep 935

It was Darkmoon, the final week of the month when Luna hid her face – or descended into the underworld, if you preferred Sollan mythology. Lyra Vereinen believed in Kore profoundly, but she'd always loved the legend of the estranged daughter of the King Below, who visited her father in his gloomy realm for one week every month.

In the month since Reeker Night, dozens of Earth-magi had been working on the Bastion and she was able to report to her Royal Council that rebuilding was almost complete. 'How do your own repairs progress, Grand Prelate?' she asked, looking down the table at her advisors.

Dominius Wurther finished a mouthful of honey-cake with a satisfied gulp. 'Well enough, Milady, although the damage was considerable.'

'I see you've even appointed a Pontifex Guard, Dominius,' Dirklan Setallius noted. 'The first bodyguard for a grand prelate since Grand Prelate Loekryn, I believe?'

'If these people are willing to strike at me, I must take precautions,'

Wurther replied. 'Young Exilium is reputed to be a fine bladesman, exactly the sort of fellow I need at my back if we have another Reeker Night. So many dear sons of Kore were lost that night.'

'Every prelate dead or driven insane,' Calan Dubrayle mused. 'I suppose many were your own appointees?'

'Those are the *dear sons* I truly grieve,' Wurther replied dryly.

Many of the prelates had been appointed by Wurther's predecessor and he'd found them troublesome opponents. But Reeker Night was still no laughing matter to Lyra. 'Many good people were turned against their very nature that night,' she reminded them, thinking, *Ostevan would not have been so callous.*

Wurther bowed his head. 'You are our moral compass always, Milady.'

She clasped her hands over her swelling belly – *my gown needs taking out again* – and ran her eyes over the rest of the attendees. Ril was staring distracted into the middle distance, his mind clearly elsewhere. Calan Dubrayle, the dapper and diligent Treasurer, was browsing the meeting papers; grey-haired, brittle Edreu Gestatium, head of the imperocracy, was sipping coffee, and Solon Takwyth was half-turned away at the foot of the table.

He's hiding the ruined side of his face, she realised. Four years before, bandits had branded Takwyth with a red-hot Sacred Heart – but they'd not ensured he was dead, a mistake they'd paid dearly for.

This was the first council meeting Takwyth had attended since his exile – and since his friend Esvald Berlond had been revealed to be Twoface, a member of the Masked Cabal. To all appearances Berlond had been a loyal Corani – if more loyal to Takwyth than his queen.

Is anyone *above suspicion?* Lyra put aside that maddening thought, tapped the table and announced, 'Gentlemen, to business. As you know, I've summoned the peers of the realm to a war council which will begin tomorrow, to be run by two of the men I trust most in this world. One of those is my beloved husband, Ril Endarion, Knight-Commander of the Empire.'

'Phew,' Ril grinned. 'I was hoping you were talking about me.'

I do still trust you, she thought sadly, *even though I fear for our love . . .*

'The other is Sir Solon Takwyth, my loyal protector, Knight-Commander of the Corani.'

This second announcement was greeted with cautious nods; Ril and Solon had vied for her hand in marriage and their antipathy was the stuff of Pallas tavern folklore.

'A good choice,' Ril said.

'No, it isn't,' Takwyth said. 'My Queen, I'm still recovering from my injuries – I'm in no state to lead an army.' He was still walking with sticks after Reeker Night.

Lyra smiled inwardly. Takwyth could even make humility sound pompous! No one had said he'd be *leading* the army; that would be Ril.

'Solon, your advice will be invaluable when it comes to appointing our generals.'

'Thank you, my Queen, but truly, I'm not worthy,' Takwyth said, and she could hear genuine pain and remorse in his voice. 'I share some guilt over Reeker Night: I should have *known* – Esvald was my closest friend!'

'*None* of us saw it, Solon,' she replied. 'Dominius didn't see that his prelates had been corrupted—'

'To be fair, they were corrupt to start with,' Setallius commented.

'Now, now,' Wurther admonished. 'You're in a frisky mood, Dirklan.'

'Frisky? I've not been called frisky in decades.'

'That's enough,' Lyra told them, but she was pleased these deeply serious men could still be boys at times. She turned back to Takwyth. 'I trust your loyalty and judgement, Solon. None of us knew what to look for, then – we do now.'

'There are signs,' Setallius agreed, his voice sober again. 'Outward symptoms of the riverreek, plus violent tendencies and aversion to sunlight. Of course, soon the *real* riverreek will strike, which could mask another attempt to create these "Reekers". The Guild of Healers has pledged to try to suppress the illness this year – it's not been considered worthwhile before, but in the current circumstances, we should act.'

Most of the surviving Reekers were recovering now, after enforced exposure to the sun and meat-free diets supplemented by water from Lyra's garden. But the worst dozen, those who called themselves 'shepherds', continued to resist. Lyra had visited one that morning; Hanetta, a nun, had raved and spat and shrieked about the Master who would be coming for her soul. She'd almost strangled herself trying to reach Lyra, her teeth snapping like a rabid dog.

But Dirklan hadn't yet been able to learn who this Master was . . .

No one had anything fresh to say on the matter, so they moved on. The Rimoni wars rolled on interminably, but there was a new power emerging: someone calling himself the 'Lord of Rym' had declared the intention of rebuilding the ancient Rimoni capital of Rym. 'Rumour has it he has an army of daemons,' Takwyth commented, then he paused. 'What if they're Reekers too?'

More investigation was clearly needed. Setallius added it to his list.

Gestatium and Dubrayle reported on the Crown's resources and the state of the Treasury, which was worsening. 'We owe the bankers much more than we can feasibly repay,' Dubrayle admitted, 'and the noble houses are no better off. Tax income is falling and those who gambled on the Third Crusade lost heavily. Jusst & Holsen and the other major bankers are foreclosing on even the oldest houses, which is adding to the Crown debt.'

'Why?' Setallius asked.

'Because thanks to the Sacrecours, there are ancient statutes protecting the pure-blood families,' Dubrayle grumbled. 'They've never been invoked before, but suddenly we're receiving requests for alms from some of the richest men in the empire – and we're not legally allowed to refuse.'

'The Church has similar constitutional requirements to ameliorate penury,' Wurther added, looking no happier. 'In 678 some idiot grand prelate signed a guarantee of last resort to any family whose lineage includes a prelate – that's *hundreds* of families.'

Ril raised a hand. 'You're saying the Crown and the Church are underwriting the debts of the Great Houses, the richest and most powerful families in the empire? That's criminal!'

'The Sacrecours were the biggest, best-dressed gang of thieves in Koredom for five hundred years,' Dubrayle remarked. 'They've left us a labyrinth of legally enshrined privilege, much of which is only now coming to light.'

Lyra wished she understood more about money, but even she could work out that not being able to pay your servants and soldiers was the edge of a cliff to oblivion. 'What are you requesting, Treasurer? Another tax increase?'

'Majesty, we're at a tipping point,' Dubrayle replied. 'The Crown must be the only entity responsible for the administration and security of the realm – delegate it to the landowners and the empire becomes nothing more than a patchwork of petty kingdoms. We've managed this for centuries now, but if we cannot pay our debts, the breakdown of the empire begins, which means we'll be plunged into civil war – in the midst of an enemy invasion! You must raise emergency revenue, which is why I've recommended a poll-tax: one auros per head.'

'The poor can't afford it,' Setallius objected. 'An auros will keep a man in food for a month.'

'But rich men can: as you'll note in my report, I'm proposing that business owners pay on behalf of their employees, nobles for their servants and landowners for their tenants. Those who can pay will be made to.'

'That'll be a first! I can think of a hundred ways such a tax can be evaded without even trying – and a dozen ways that the poor will still be caught.'

'I'm sure I can too, but we must do *something*, Dirklan. There are no cost-cutting measures left – even the tax-farmers are failing to reach their targets. We can't afford not to do this, not if we want the empire to survive.'

'Are we still tax-farming?' Ril asked. 'I thought we were going to stop that.'

'We're reviewing it,' Dubrayle sniffed, 'but now's not the time to change policy.'

'How many rebellions against the tax-farmers are we dealing with?' Setallius asked. He had the air of a man who already knew the answer.

'Five,' Dubrayle admitted. 'The worst is in Mollachia, which appears to be in open revolt. We've got violent protest and sabotage in parts of rural Midrea, Andressea and Brevis. The local governors are moving to suppress them.'

'We're making war on our own people,' Lyra said, feeling sick inside.

'I'm no happier than you, my Queen,' Dubrayle said, 'but we're trying to prevent the disintegration of the realm.'

Gestatium, Takwyth and Wurther all voiced their agreement. Lyra looked to Ril and Dirklan. 'Is no one else concerned that we're destroying the lives of our own people?'

'I don't dispute that we need funds, Milady,' the spymaster replied. 'It just rankles that there are fortunes out there – landowners, merchants and nobles – out of our reach. We need to target the Great Houses – they're a greater danger to you than every peasant who riots when the price of bread rises.'

'That's a dangerous step,' Wurther rumbled. 'Would you punish the successful, who are blessed by Kore?'

'Those best able to look after themselves, in other words?' Setallius sniffed. 'I'll wager you that my investigations of Reeker Night will lead to a rich man's castle, not a peasant's hovel.'

Takwyth raised a hand. 'We're at war – surely we can use that fact to get what we need?'

'Grain, livestock, certainly. And making our noblemen send their fighting men south might prevent insurrection at home,' Dubrayle agreed. 'But that doesn't give us gold, and believe me, wars soak up more money than they bring in – for the Treasury at any rate. Individuals may profit from conflict. We don't.'

They all turned to look at Lyra, who'd never felt more out of her depth. With a hollow feeling forming in the pit of her stomach, she said, 'I believe we've no choice but to proceed. Let the poll-tax be ratified.'

'There'll be trouble,' Setallius warned.

'From the same peasants you just told us were no threat?' Dubrayle asked. 'Toughen up, Dirklan. You're not an outsider any more, you're a Royal Counsellor.'

'And forced to defend your missteps!'

'Gentlemen!' Lyra exclaimed. She hated conflict and the taste it left. 'These are hard times and we need to work together.' It came out more plaintively than she'd wanted, but at least they stopped snapping at each other. 'The decision is mine, and it's made.'

They all bowed their heads. Eventually Wurther said, 'This should cheer you all up. As you know, I'm having to elevate thirty-two new prelates after last month's disaster. Perhaps inspired by your Majesty, an abbess from Estellayne – Valetta, daughter of the late Prelate Rodrigo – has petitioned to have women elected.'

The men all chuckled, but Lyra thought, *Why not? If a women can be an abbess – or an empress – then surely she can be a prelate?* 'I remember Valetta – she attended upon me on the morning of my coronation. I trust you'll give her a fair hearing, Grand Prelate.'

'Fair hearing, aye, surely! If all nuns looked as she does, we'd have more priests,' Wurther chortled. 'But the prelature is for priests and there's an end to it. Nothing she demands is supported in the *Book of Kore.*'

'Other religions find room for priestesses, Grand Prelate.'

'As does ours – we call them *convents*. The pagans had priestesses, but those faiths failed, Majesty.' Wurther nudged Gestatium. 'Does the Crown employ women in senior roles? Does the army? I'm aware of many singular women, not least yourself, my Queen: but by nature most women are better suited to supportive roles.'

Am I really so singular? Lyra wondered. She just felt ignorant today, tired of being pregnant and stressed, unequal to the tasks Fate kept piling on top of her. All of a sudden it was too much.

'Gentlemen, I'm exhausted, and I believe the rest of the meeting is largely routine. Ril will take my part and I'll read and ratify your recommendations later. Please, play nicely while I'm gone.' They rose as she did, and remained standing until she'd left the chamber.

Outside the room, her bodyguard, Dirklan's protégé Basia de Sirou, was talking to Wurther's new man, the intense-looking Exilium Excelsior – or more truly, Basia was trying to converse, while the stiff young Estellan glared about him as if expecting an assault any second. Both looked up in surprise at Lyra's early exit. As they rose to their feet, Excelsior saluted formally, while Basia merely bobbed her head.

'Is everything all right, Milady?' she asked, worried.

'I need fresh air,' Lyra replied. 'Come,' she added, walking on as Basia hurried to join her.

'Lovely to meet you,' Basia called over her shoulder to Excelsior as they left, then she rolled her eyes as they turned the corner. 'I've had better conversations with stone walls. I mean, gorgeous and well-put together, but for Kore's sake, I don't think he's cracked a smile since his mother pushed him out.'

'I'm told he's very good with his sword.'

'I doubt that – he seems to regard women as sin made flesh!'

Lyra snorted, and Basia blushed furiously. 'Oh, you mean his *actual* sword! Sorry, Majesty, I've clearly spent too much time with the Joyce brothers lately.'

Lyra smiled; moments of such camaraderie were a rare luxury in her life, to be savoured. They made their way through the maze of stairs, corridors and galleries to a small courtyard where a barred archway had been carved in the image of a man with leaves for skin. The Greengate was the only other entrance to her private garden beneath the palace walls and the inner Bastion wall other than the steps descending from the royal suite above. The guard on the gate opened the iron grille and Lyra, seeking solitude, left Basia beside the roses and pushed on through the Oak Grove.

At the far end of the long, narrow garden was the place she considered its heart, a pool formed by spring water trickling over a stone pile, surrounded by tall elms and oaks. She knelt awkwardly and cupping the cool water in her hands, drank as the insects hummed about her, birds sang and sunlight shimmered through the leafy foliage above. Above her, a sapling swayed in the breeze – her five-year-old cutting from the Winter Tree, a brackenberry planted by Saint Eloy in the Celestium. She closed her eyes and emptied herself of thought.

Gradually her anxiety receded and her thoughts turned to things that *lasted*: ancient trees, the rolling river below, the far mountains. A bell-like sound chimed inside her and when she opened her eyes again, the reflection in the pool was no longer the trees and the sky but just of *her* tree – and then it too faded as a face formed in the water.

The woman had bark for skin and leaves for hair – although Lyra suspected the guardian spirit took the form of Aradea, the Fey Queen, just to please her.

Setallius had found her one of the banned books about the early dwymancers. A place where such spirits resided, like this pool, was called a 'genilocus'. She'd read that many of them mirrored the old pagan deities, like Taurhan, the Argundian war-god, and his Schlessen counterpart Minaus; the Sydian horse-gods, Amazar and Ponya; sea-gods like Osheen, Seidopus and Calascia, even a sky-being called Epyros who dwelt atop a magical tree and sounded a lot like Kore Himself.

If these beings existed before the magi, then how long has the dwyma existed – and how long have certain people been able to reach it?

'Aradea,' she greeted the genilocus.

'Leeee-raaah . . .'

A sense of oneness with the Fey Queen filled her, and as they silently communed, the world shifted and it seemed to Lyra that she'd dived into the tiny pool and sunk fathoms deep, until she burst through the sky and soared over landscapes of frigid grey peaks, dark forest glades, grimy caves and salt-encrusted coastal cliffs. She tasted snow and brine, smelled pine needles and animal musk, felt the echoes of time soak through her skin.

Then she saw a face: a young man with lank black hair and haunted eyes, a long moustache drooping from the corners of his downturned mouth. He didn't see her; he was staring out across an ice-covered forest and she sensed that he was like her, another dwymancer.

Then he was gone and somewhere else, a deep liquid bellow was echoing through the air and shaking her back to awareness . . .

. . . and she was kneeling beside her pool again. Her knees were sore and she realised the sun was no longer overhead but near the western horizon; hours had passed like minutes. An owl was watching her, and for a second she saw herself through its eyes: a blonde woman with a distended belly, kneeling in the mud like a commoner . . . with webs of light radiating from her in all directions.

Then she blinked, and she was herself again. But she felt calmer – and excited by the glimpse of that young man. *Who are you?* The thought that someone else out there could do as she did was profoundly strengthening. She lifted her face to the Winter Tree sapling and thanked the genilocus. Once more, her garden was her strength.

Somehow, I'll get through this. As long as I have this place, they can't touch me.
She thought about Ostevan's suggestion: *Kore made this world, so He also made the dwyma.* She basked in that thought, wondering if the Church might just be wrong in labelling dwyma a heresy.

I believe in Kore, and so I have to believe I am doing His will.

From the balcony of the queen's suite, Ostevan Comfateri watched the pale figure of Lyra Vereinen emerge from the Oak Grove, conversing with Basia de Sirou. The garden intrigued him. Despite the power of Abraxas coursing through him – and *because* of it – the garden was the one place he feared to tread.

What do I do about Lyra? That was the question he kept returning to. If the Keepers knew of her heresy, they'd be obliged to put her on trial – but what a waste that would be. Master Naxius wanted her for his own elaborate plans, but that too felt like a missed opportunity, when Lyra commanded a power that Naxius might just be vulnerable to.

Do I really want the Puppeteer pulling my strings for eternity?

Naxius – and Abraxas – wanted him to soil her: a few seconds of pumping ichor into her body and within minutes she'd be grovelling at his feet, her intellect crushed by the overwhelming presence of the daemon. But that would render her all but useless, according to Naxius, as the dwyma gave power only to those it accepted.

I need a better way if she's to be the weapon I require.

Naxius had shown the Masked Cabal three ways to enslave someone with Abraxas' ichor: the first was with fluid infected with daemonic ichor, which produced Reekers who were swiftly reduced to a bestial state. They were savage tools, not thinking predators, and the infection was vulnerable to sunlight and silver.

Infecting with a bite or through sex, depositing fresh ichor into the body of the victim, produced Shepherds; their will was subsumed by whoever infected them. They were autonomous, reasoning, enhanced in power but subject to a new lust for blood and depravity.

But Lyra was the most scrutinised woman in Pallas. Reeker or Shepherd, she would be discovered swiftly and the trail would inevitably lead back to him.

But there was a third way. Inside his chest, wrapped around his heart, was Naxius' brilliant creation: a construct creature which produced the ichor and formed the bridge to the daemon Abraxas. And that creature self-seeded; he already had more than a dozen of its spawn housed in his chest. Perhaps Lyra could be persuaded – or compelled – to take such a creature into herself?

But that would probably destroy her link to the dwyma too. No, I need her to serve me voluntarily, while remaining who she is. This needs old-fashioned means: I must appeal to her heart. That's it, surely . . . I need her to fall in love with me. What a victory that would be.

There was something about Lyra's earnest, winsome desire to be the faery-tale queen, virtuous and true-hearted, that made him *desperately* want to corrupt her: to make her moan in his arms as she surrendered virtue for the profane. Her weekly Unburdenings had told him much about her inner desires, needs Ril Endarion was unaware of, but she clung tightly to her notions of honour and virtue. She wouldn't be easy to win, and her current condition further inhibited that path: her concerns right now were for her child; desire was all but forgotten. It would have to be a chaste wooing, something he'd not essayed for many years.

But I'm her confessor . . . It's her soul I must conquer and the rest will follow . . .

Ril looked down from the dais in the Hall of Swords feeling more nervous than he cared to admit. He'd been Knight-Commander of the Empire for five years, but this was his biggest test yet.

He beckoned to Solon Takwyth and murmured, 'What are we calling this campaign? Is it still a *Crusade* when we're trying to free our own lands from the Noories, instead of invading theirs?'

Takwyth – who looked entirely at home on the dais – replied, 'A Crusade is a war in the service of Kore. It could be argued that the Crusades to date have actually been in service of the Sacrecours. Either way, if the queen wishes to avoid the term, we should.'

'Then I suppose we're "Defenders of Yuros" or some such?'

'I doubt it matters. Shall we begin?'

Although none of the men gathered below them wore swords or armour, the martial air was unmistakable. Lyra had the right to command the attendance of the noble families of the realm when the empire was threatened and the Great Houses, although invariably locked in unholy rivalry, were duty-bound to attend. Of course, such a summons also presented opportunities for power and influence that no one was prepared to miss.

Kurt Borodium, Duke of Argundy, a king in all but name, had arrived early. He was Lyra's cousin through her father Ainar – although in fact, she had no idea who had actually sired her. The swarthy Alexan Salinas, Duke of Canossi was accompanied by his son Elvero and a crowd of southern lords. Earls from Brevis, Andressea, Midrea and Hollenia stood alongside Governors of Noros and Verelon. The military arms of the Church were represented by Lann Wilfort, Supreme Grandmaster of the Kirkegarde, and Dravis Ryburn, Knight-Princeps of the Inquisition. Even Garod Sacrecour had turned up, with a contingent of Sacrecour-Fasterius men from Dupenium and Fauvion who were staring about belligerently.

These were the men Lyra was relying on to provide leadership and manpower. Some had little or no military experience; others were hard-bitten veterans of Crusades and domestic conflict. *But I've got to lead them*, Ril thought nervously, signalling to the trumpeter to sound a call to arms as the stragglers came in, including a young-looking man in Brician plaid.

As the last note rang out, Ril stepped to the front of the dais. 'My Lords, welcome to the Bastion. You all know why we're here: the Sultan of Kesh has landed an army at Pontus. The city has fallen. The Keshi are setting out towards Verelon and according to our airborne scouts, Sydian tribes are flocking to join their march.'

The room exploded; this last fact was hitherto unknown outside the Royal Council. There was a volley of curses aimed at the Sydian savages, while others wondered aloud why 'fellow Yurosi' would march with the Noorie invaders.

Ha! The one thing Ahmedhassans and Sydians agree on is their hatred of us. After a moment he raised his hand and cried, 'Yes, the clans are riding to war! We estimate that more than two hundred thousand nomads have joined more than half a million Ahmedhassans on the march.'

More voices clamoured, voicing opinions as facts. Ril shouted for quiet, and when he didn't get it he signed to the trumpeter again, but before he could lift the horn to his lips, Takwyth stepped forward and the room went silent instantly.

Prick, Ril thought.

'I know you men,' Takwyth told them. 'You can't see the profit in marching all the way to Verelon and you don't see the glory in fighting Eastern rabble. You think a Keshi army in Yuros is going to collapse in a few months from supply-chain issues. You think Rashid Mubarak is a fool, and it doesn't matter what we do, his army is doomed. You think that he's got no idea what he's getting himself into. Am I right?'

Murmurs of agreement filled the chamber, while Ril simmered at being upstaged. Then Takwyth barked, '*RASHID MUBARAK IS NOT A FOOL! RASHID MUBARAK IS A KORE-BEDAMNED GENIUS!*'

That got their attention. A hundred or more shocked faces stared up at them.

'It's Kore's truth!' Takwyth snarled. 'I'm not easily impressed, as I'm sure you know – but this Noorie bastard has done more than all the gods of Lantris could have: he's *broken* the Ordo Costruo and wrecked their beloved Bridge – he's built and launched a *thousand-strong* windfleet without *anyone* knowing – he's raised an army in a war-torn land and got a dozen mutual enemies marching to his beat! Rashid Mubarak is three-quarters Yurosi, three-quarters mage – yet he's the beloved ruler of a land that hates both Yurosi and magi! He defeated *two* armies we considered invincible in the Third Crusade, commanded by Echor Borodium and Kaltus Korion, the two best generals in Koredom – so damned right, the man is a genius! You think stopping him will be easy? He's going to take us to Hel!'

The Hall of Swords was silent now, all the high and mighty lords of the realm gazing intently up at Takwyth as he went on, 'So let me ask you this: who among you wants to be known as the Saviour of the Empire? Or the man who killed the Sultan of Kesh? You think there's no profit in this? Think again! There will be battle! There will be glory! There will be renown! The tales you tell your grandchildren will be of *this* war! Your names will never be forgotten! *This* is what you men were born for! *This* place, *this* time, *this* war!'

Ril could only stand and admire as Takwyth strode the stage, his ruined visage alive with fervour and energy, and for the first time he truly appreciated why men followed him so slavishly. He could also see that this exertion was costing Takwyth: the back of his tunic was already soaked in sweat and he was limping more heavily with every pace.

'Rashid Mubarak will *not* defeat himself – so someone in this room has to do it!' Takwyth tapped his own chest. 'I wish it were me – Kore's Balls, I do! But I'm barely out of death's jaws. My will is strong, but my body rebels.' He took a deep breath, then suddenly dropped his voice, a masterly move that had everyone straining not to miss a word.

'When you face a man in the lists, lances set, hurtling towards him with all the speed of a winged jousting beast, you learn his soul. I've had that privilege with many in this room. We've broken lances and faced death and maiming together in the pursuit of glory. And I'll tell you something right now: I have never faced a steadier lance than the one borne by Ril Endarion at the jousts this year!' He stepped away from Ril and pointed at him theatrically. 'This man has the soul of a warrior. *He is your commander, as he is mine.*'

With a dramatic lunge, Takwyth dropped to one knee, facing Ril. 'Where you go, Prince Endarion, Rondelmar and the Empire follows.'

Ril looked down at the injured man at his feet, struck by myriad thoughts: Takwyth had never had a kind word for him before; the man had yet again managed to remind the room who'd won that *rukking* tourney; and he *had* to learn how to dominate a room like that.

You're a dangerous man, Solon Takwyth . . . Remind me why I'm leaving you with my wife?

But this was the moment he had to step up. His mind was racing, but he forced himself to speak slowly, first holding out a hand to his rival and saying, 'Please, Lord Takwyth, stand' – he tried to sound neither apologetic nor modest – 'I too wish you could accompany us, and if the campaign is long enough, I know you'll join the fight and play your part.' Then as Takwyth rose and stepped back, he turned to the room again. 'But it falls on *us* to fight this war, my lords: our empress commands it. And this will be a war unlike any ever fought in Yuros. If it is lost, we don't just lose land or honour – we lose our entire way of life! Would you have your family forced to grovel to Ahm? Would you have Godsingers wailing from our towers? Would you have our women shrouded in black robes from head to foot? Would you have your children forced to learn Keshi and raised on the *Kalistham*?'

There was more; Setallius and Wurther had briefed him well and he remembered most of the salient points. And somewhere along the way he forgot that he was hectoring men who regarded him as an interloper, who had actively connived against him and Lyra from the start.

But others were true allies. He'd barely finished his oration when Kurt Borodium stepped forward. 'Argundy stands with her kinswoman, Lyra Vereinen, daughter of my uncle. We will proudly march beneath her banner!' proclaimed the new duke.

After that, all Ril needed was to be gracious in accepting the various pledges. Numbers would matter later, and perhaps some might overstate their aid in a bid to enhance their own prestige. But as he stepped back to accept the pledges, Solon Takwyth touched his shoulder. 'Well done, Milord,' he said quietly, a second kind word in one day.

The last to pledge was Garod Sacrecour. 'House Dupeni will furnish seven legions. My nephew Brylion will command them.' It was far less than he could have sent.

Ril glanced at Brylion, a hulking brute whom he loathed, and just about managed to look pleased – but that brought them to the subject of commanders. So far, forty-two legions had been pledged, more than two hundred thousand men. No army could travel and live off the land in larger than ten-legion groups, even well-provisioned, so they needed smaller units and differing routes.

Ril raised his voice again. 'The Northern and Central armies of Rondelmar, supported by the Church and Inquisition, will be designated the First Army, and I will command, with the aid of Lord Rolven Sulpeter.' Sulpeter might be stuffy and unimaginative, but his seniority made him the natural choice. 'The Second Army, comprising legions from Dupenium and Fauvion, will be commanded by Sir Brylion Fasterius.' Sadly, that was unavoidable. 'The Third Army from Aquillea has nominated Prince Elvero Salinas, son of the Duke of Canossi, as commander, which I endorse.' Ril had met Elvero at the jousts and liked him. 'The Fourth Army, Argundy and Hollenia, will be commanded by Prince Andreas, son of Kurt, Duke of Argundy.'

Ril acknowledged the duke, then turned to the men from the south-eastern provinces, recognisable by their Rimoni-styled plaid tunics. 'Which leads me to the Fifth Army. My lords, you've not yet given me the name of your commander—'

The Andressans, Bricians, Midreans and Noromen looked at one another uncertainly. Unlike the other armies, this one had no political unity; the semi-autonomous vassal-states were geographically widespread and ruled by governors. Finally August Delestre, the pure-blood Earl of Augenheim, raised a hand. 'My Prince, we do have a candidate: we trust your Highness will not take our nomination ill.' He turned to the young Brician who'd been last to arrive.

Ril glanced at Takwyth, who shrugged. 'And you are?' he asked the Brician.

The young man had plain but steady features framed by close-cropped blond hair. He bowed. 'My name is Seth Korion, Earl of Bres, your Highness.'

The name set a buzz around the room, while Ril thought, *The son of Kaltus Korion? What is this, an insult?*

Kaltus Korion had been a pillar of the Sacrecour regime, widely considered the greatest general of his age, but he'd perished in the Third Crusade. What made the nomination even stranger was that Korion had been notorious for crushing the Noros Revolt – and he wasn't even a native of the south; he'd purchased vast tracts of land in Bricia, using wealth gained in the first two Crusades.

Ril wondered if he was missing something. 'Why you, Earl Korion?'

'With all respect, it's because I brought twelve thousand men home across the Bridge in 930.'

Ril had heard the tale: survivors of a broken army, fighting their way home against the odds. There were enough contradictions in it that he'd thought it a fiction. 'Will the lords of Noros follow a Korion?'

A Noroman bowed and stepped to Korion's side. 'There were Noromen among the survivors the Earl brought home, Highness. He is *not* his father.'

Ril frowned at Takwyth, then turned back to Korion. 'And what qualities do you bring to the position?'

'I have experience with fighting against Easterners, Highness, and leading men in the field. I settled most of the men I brought back from the East on my estates: my two legions are the only ones in the empire with such experience. We alone escaped Shaliyah, and we fought at Ardijah and Riverdown without defeat.'

It all sounded impressive. Ril leaned towards Takwyth. 'What do you think?'

'I've heard the stories,' Takwyth whispered. 'In some he's a hero, in others a traitor who murdered his father and stole his legacy. Which is true, I don't know, but I like that he has experience and can make friends of enemies. And the name Korion alone will stiffen the backbones of the rankers.'

Ril nodded his thanks, then turned to face the room. 'Then your nomination is accepted. We have our generals: let preparations begin: *we will march in two weeks!*'

Much later, Ril sat with Setallius on his balcony. Lyra was already asleep – not that he'd been planning to see her that night. The spymaster had brought a potent whisky from Brevis, which was warming his belly nicely.

Ril took another sip, then said, 'So, Dirk, does five armies mean five sets of problems?'

'At the very least,' Setallius replied. 'It's not ideal, but I think it's the best we can do.'

'Constant had it easier during the Crusades,' Ril grumbled.

'It was different then: you were either in the Sacrecour-Fasterius cabal or you didn't count. The only dissent on the inside was over who took precedence. Our situation is far more complex: everyone knows our reach is shorter and weaker.'

'Thanks for spelling that out. I suppose Rolven Sulpeter will be sound, but our knights all think Takwyth lit the stars – and I'm also saddled with a legion of Kirkegarde and Inquisitors.'

'Watch out for Dravis Ryburn,' Setallius commented. 'That man would skin his own mother if he thought it might advance the Inquisition. And his bodyguard, Lef Yarle, is an addictive killer.'

'Charming. Then there's the Second Army: Garod's men, with that Kore-bedamned lout Brylion Fasterius leading them.'

'True – but at least your outright enemies are all under the same banner. Give them a key role, one they can't shirk, and pray that Rashid Mubarak gives them Hel.'

'I shall! At least I think we can trust Canossi's Third Army, and Elvero seems a decent sort.'

'I agree; they'll play their part, and so will the Argundians – they see Lyra as one of theirs. But they're notoriously slow marchers, so you'll need to watch that.'

'I'm more worried about this Seth Korion. I had a Fasterius courtier in my ear earlier, telling me a lot of things about Kaltus and his son – feuding, inheritance questions, mutinies . . . he told me Seth Korion betrayed the empire, that everything about him is a lie.'

'Consider the source,' Dirklan drawled. 'I've heard good things about that young man.'

'I hope you're right. The real thing that worries me is leaving Takwyth here.'

'You shouldn't. Solon holds his personal honour in very high esteem. It makes him a pompous lughead at times, but to be seen as a traitor would shame him far beyond what you or I could understand. And he's no conspirator, believe me. I've had him watched since he returned, and while he postures as if he's ready to cut you down and supplant you at any minute, he's passed up every opportunity to actually try it.'

'Is that supposed to be reassuring?'

Dirklan smiled. 'Take it as you will, Milord.' Then his face became more serious. 'You're probably aware that Basia has applied to leave her post as Lyra's bodyguard and ride as a mage-knight in the coming war?'

'She did mention it,' Ril admitted cautiously.

'Well, I'm denying that request. Her place is here, not with you in the south.'

'I suppose that's for the best.' Ril swallowed another mouthful to hide his disappointment, keeping his face expressionless. He shrugged as if it didn't matter and changed the subject. 'Did Takwyth oversell Rashid Mubarak today? I know I asked him to make sure he was presented as a genuine threat, otherwise they'll waste all their energy backstabbing me. But I've never heard him speak like that.'

'Oversell?' Dirklan shook his head. 'No, he didn't – not at all. Rashid Mubarak is every bit as dangerous as Solon painted him. You're going into a full-scale war with a military genius, not some route-march with a bit of a barney at the end.'

'I was afraid of that. Do you think the sultan has the same problems as us? I mean, needing to rely on a bunch of backstabbing arseholes?'

'With respect, he's very different to you. The men who lose his trust lose their lives.'

'I take it that wasn't supposed to be reassuring either?' Ril drawled.

'The truth seldom is.'

Lyra's last night with Ril was unfulfilling. At five months pregnant, she felt ungainly and unattractive, and he'd shown absolutely no interest in joining her in the marital bed, even though it was their last night together and they'd be apart for months. That morning she'd seen him talking to Basia and there was something in their closeness that crushed her heart.

I'm losing him in so many ways.

The irony of wanting him physically just when he'd given up on her was painful. Desire had proved to be the hardest part of her marriage – they'd managed at times, but not consistently, and she'd never understood why she didn't find sex enjoyable. But last night when she'd tried to kiss him, to draw his hands to her belly and remind him that she carried his child, he was unresponsive, holding her more like a sister than a wife. At last she just gave up. 'Promise me you'll return for the birth?' she asked, barely managing not to burst into tears.

'I'll only ever be days away,' he reassured her, one eye on the door. 'I want to be here – and unless we're mid-battle, I shall be.'

That was a little bit more reassuring, but she felt wretched when he pointedly yawned and left, then just a few minutes later Basia closed the gnostic wards on her lonely suite and bade her goodnight. 'We'll be victorious,' her bodyguard told her. 'You mustn't worry. It'll be over before you know – and your confinement too.'

Confinement – what an apt name. Lyra tried to imagine four more months of growing bigger and more uncomfortable, with no one to hold her, and all at once, the night felt utterly unbearable. 'Basia, could you send a message to Ostevan? I'd like to Unburden.'

'You prayed with him this morning, Milady,' Basia said, as if Lyra were losing her memory.

'And I wish to do so again,' Lyra snapped back. *You applied to leave my side and go south*, she thought vindictively. *With* my *husband.* But she almost immediately felt vile for thinking such a thought, especially as she had no proof of infidelity.

It might have helped if she actually disliked Basia, but she didn't. All the tales said that lovers must be free to love, and those who conspired against them were always villainous for doing so. She didn't want to be – she *wouldn't* be – cast in that role.

True peace didn't come until after Ostevan knelt with her. Together they sent their prayers up to Kore and she was able to confess her fears and her loneliness and be absolved.

'I don't know what I'd do without you, Ostevan,' she told him as he left. 'I'm so glad that you, at least, are staying here with me.'

Ril looked up as Basia de Sirou slipped through the hidden door behind the tapestry and into his bedchamber. He greeted her with a lingering kiss and pressed a goblet of wine into her hand. 'A Brician merlo – the best we have. Kore knows I need it!'

'How's the muster going?' she asked.

'Well enough. We're as ready to march as we'll ever be. It's just leaving you behind that's eating me up.' He stroked her face, admiring the definition of her high cheekbones and chiselled jaw. 'I hate having to sneak around – I want to tell the world that I've finally found you.'

'I doubt we'd have been able to hide this during the march.'

'Probably not,' Ril admitted. 'I just want this damned war over so we can leave.'

'I know – so do I. But it won't be for ever.'

They had the beginnings of a plan: once the Shihad was defeated, they would disappear – fly south to Rimoni, or even east to Pontus and then Javon. They would find somewhere where they could live together, anonymous and free.

Basia knocked back her wine and said, 'Do you mind if I loosen a few straps? The stumps ache like Hel tonight.'

He knew the routine; he helped pull off her leggings and remove the artefact-limbs, then knelt and massaged first her left stump, then the right. The sewn-up flaps were chafed and clearly painful, but he'd learned over the years how best to ease her.

She groaned sensuously at the pleasure-pain of his massage. 'Kore's Bollocks, that's better,' she sighed when he was done. 'Normally I get a break from wearing them, but it's been a full day today.' Then she grinned. 'While you're down there, darling . . .'

She spread her thighs and he lowered his mouth to her cleft. He knew that drill too now, her taste, where to lap, how firmly, how quickly, and in minutes she was quivering and clutching at him, then drawing him hungrily on top, where they moved together in a frenzy of want and need. Afterwards, they sank into the bed together, giggling like children.

'I still can't believe we've not been doing this all our lives,' he told her.

'I was as much to blame as you.' She snuggled up, suddenly all kittenish. 'You do know I'll miss you.'

'I do – and I'll make sure we win a speedy victory, and then we'll get out of here. Lyra will be better off without me and Takky can finally get the throne, and her. He's clearly got designs.'

'Takky? No, I don't think so, darling – it's that damned slimy prick of a confessor I'm leery of. I don't know why she can't see through him.'

Ril refused to dwell on that. 'Priests aren't real men. It's Takky who'll be at her. But you know, even the idea of him finally getting his arrow into Lyra's quiver doesn't bother me any more. She's like a nun between the sheets.'

'Don't be mean-spirited,' Basia scolded. 'Just because you couldn't raise any passion in her, doesn't mean she doesn't have any. It's just tied up in prayers and Unburdenings, that's all. She's still a convent girl at heart.'

Ril yawned. 'Really, I don't care: you're all that matters to me – you, and winning this damned war. I'm going to have to prove myself all over again.'

'You'll do well, my "Prince of the Spear",' Basia twinkled. 'The commoners named you right, didn't they? Look at that spear of yours: all ready for another joust!'

The next morning, Ril left Lyra on the steps of the Bastion before all of Pallas and led the Corani legions from the Place d'Accord down to the docks to begin the long march to battle.

She put on her bravest smile, trying to hide her fears, but he could see through her – and he was pretty sure she could see through him, too, but neither said a word, even when he stepped past her and hugged Basia last and longest, before riding away to war.

5

Into the West

The Third Crusade

The Third Crusade is over. It will be remembered in the East as a mighty victory and in the West as a calamity. It was the culmination of decades of misrule, hubris and tyranny by a weak-chinned despot and his infamous mother. Constant Slackjaw and Lucia Fastrukk sentenced millions to death and misery to enrich themselves. But finally they have met their ends! Now is the hour! The empire is weak! Rise up! RISE UP!

PAMPHLET CREDITED TO THE 'LORD OF RYM', RIMONI, 931

Pontus and Verelon
Augeite 935

'Prince Waqar,' said the plump woman, rising from her prostration.

Waqar and his friends, clad in riding leathers as requested, were gathered in the reception hall of a small castle near Pontus. It had been abandoned without a fight, but it had been thoroughly ransacked, the tapestries and ornaments plundered and the family portraits slashed or burned.

Waqar's friends were bright-eyed, eagerly anticipating today's promised revelations. Outside the walls, the vast camp was shrinking daily as the soldiers marched into the west. Rashid's son Attam, his brother Teileman and Faroukh Valphath, a Dhassan general, had each led a great army away and Waqar, anxiously awaiting his own orders, was feeling somewhat left behind. The camp noise grew quieter by the day, but finally here was the person they'd been told to expect.

The woman was dressed in a bekira-shroud, only her face emerging from the black robes. Her coarse features were uncharacteristically weathered by sun and wind; highborn Eastern women generally shunned the elements to preserve a youthful pallor. She was perhaps thirty, with the confident manner of the mage-born.

'I am Parena, Great Prince,' she said. 'Please follow.' She led Waqar, Tamir, Lukadin, Baneet and Fatima out of the rear gates towards a charred Kore church in the field outside. The priest had been immolated inside it.

'He refused to flee,' Lukadin said, following Waqar's gaze. 'He got what he deserved.' Luka was still holding the mysterious spear they'd recovered from Midpoint Tower; he wouldn't let it go, although he'd not tried to unlock its powers since.

'Then the priest was a brave man,' Fatima replied.

'He was a fool – and his kind did worse six years ago.'

'I know they did,' Waqar said, still nauseated.

Outside, the noise of the camp filled the distance. The skies were filled with more clouds than Waqar was used to, but at least they were benignly white. The temperatures were cool, even though this was apparently summer.

'Well?' Waqar demanded, turning to Parena.

She smiled and touched her periapt. Seconds later, Tamir pointed excitedly. 'Look!'

Six large winged bird-shapes had appeared over a line of trees, flying in a ragged vee, keening as they banked and swooped towards them. It took Waqar a moment to realise their scale, then he gasped, 'Dear Ahm, they're *huge*!'

The birds emitted piercing cries and descended, unfurling giant wings, massive talons spread to land. They were eagles, but far larger than nature intended. The five friends stared in awe as Parena strolled out and greeted the gigantic birds as if they were pets.

Her head only reached their underbellies; beaks were flashing about her face, talons as long as her arm raking the air on all sides, and Waqar worried she'd be injured, but she scolded them casually and they all settled down.

It took a few seconds for Waqar to register that they all had intricately harnessed saddles fastened behind the thick neck, ahead of the wings.

'You can *ride* these?' he called incredulously.

'I can, Great Prince, and it is the will of the Sultan, Ahm bless his name for ever, that you learn also, so that you may lead the aerial forces of the Shihad from the fore.'

Yet again his conviction that Rashid was his enemy warred with pride. Despite himself, the power and majesty of the giant birds made his heart soar. 'I'm truly honoured,' he told Parena, and his friends echoed the sentiment.

Parena beamed as she handed him a set of reins.

The next few weeks were the most intense of Waqar's life, and not easy: taking orders from a woman was a new experience, one that challenged every social reflex, especially as Parena showed no deference to rank or gender once they were in the air.

'The Rondian magi have been flying for centuries,' she lectured them. 'Windships are a fact of life for them. Constructs like these, animals altered by the gnosis, are scarcely worthy of a second glance as far as they're concerned. They create strange beasts from their mythologies: winged reptiles and mammals, creatures with claws and jaws. Compared to them, our Beastariums are like children playing with toys.'

None of that boded well, but Waqar quickly came to appreciate the wisdom of the Hadishah Animagi. Instead of trying to come up with strange beasts that matched the Rondian constructs, they'd instead relied on the perfection of nature, seeking only to enhance it. And best of all, they'd drawn on the ancient tales of Kesh to do so: the giant eagle known as the Roc was a staple of such tales, a companion of heroes.

They abandoned their comfortable beds and slept with their rocs, tending their needs – Parena told them other roc-riders raised their birds from hatchlings, so they had some catching up to do. Every day they learned more about winged flight: how to make the giant birds climb, dive and turn, and the theories of aerial warfare.

'Use fire and lightning to destroy sails and masts of windships,'

Parena told them. 'You will have the advantage of speed: even a skiff will be slower than you. In the air, speed and elevation are everything. You've learned to fight using gnostic shields, but a head-on encounter happens at such speed that that protection is partially negated – an oncoming arrow or spear can penetrate your shields because of the additional impact velocity. So you must learn not to rely on such protections. When you encounter a Rondian mage on a construct, you must outmanoeuvre your foe to strike him from below or behind.'

The training was all-encompassing, taking over every thought. At night they dreamed of flight; during the day they lived it. And after a few weeks, with the army long gone and the castle virtually empty, they were joined by two dozen more Keshi magi, each with their own rocs. There was a brotherhood amongst these sky-warriors that Waqar hadn't seen before, as if the shared experience of flight and the humbling experience of caring for their beasts eroded all normal social barriers.

But rivalries were still inevitable.

One afternoon he took his roc – he'd named her Ajniha, or Wings of Grace – into mock combat against Shameed, a breeding-house urchin who'd grown into a vicious, backstabbing brawler. The quarter-blood was the uncrowned king of the roc-riders and he could fly like no one else – and he'd been goading Waqar from the moment they'd met, as if his skill gave him immunity from repercussions. Waqar had never met anyone so blatantly hostile to authority.

Shameed's campaign to put Waqar in his place began with insulting gifts: overripe, worm-infested fruit or broken-winged sparrows, followed by pointed criticisms as he belittled Waqar's mastery of his new steed. And he never called Waqar by name, just 'Entitled One'. He cared nothing for the fact that in any other circumstance he'd have been flogged, or worse.

Baneet and Lukadin had offered to break Shameed's face, but Waqar refused; he didn't want others to fight his battles.

Waqar was a three-quarter-blood mage; he would have destroyed Shameed on the ground – but in the air, as Parena had warned, things weren't so clear-cut, and Shameed had an almost instinctive understanding with his steed.

Which is why this is madness . . .

He and Ajniha flashed into the dive as he nudged her neck with his right knee, just a touch to correct her course while he aligned the wooden pole he was carrying. *Jousting*, the Rondian knights apparently called this insane pastime of trying to smash another rider off his saddle as they flew headlong towards each another. Parena had told them it was forbidden, on pain of floggings, with no exceptions – but she was absent today, and she'd left Shameed in charge.

After a few hours, the insults weren't to be borne.

As the distance between them closed with alarming speed, Shameed's roc started weaving from side to side, forcing Waqar to constantly correct Ajniha's trajectory while he huddled behind a round wooden shield, the wind stinging his eyes and making tears run, his cloak whipping around him. Ajniha screamed a warning as they closed. All week they'd been aiming at static targets, flying deliberate near-misses to train steeds and riders for the realities of fighting in the skies, but this was different: Ajniha could sense collision, and so could Waqar. They were only yards above the ground as they came together.

As they met, Shameed completed a roll that resulted in his roc's claws raking Waqar from the saddle as he jerked his pole aside, then he was bellowing in terror and outrage as the two-foot-long talons wrapped about him; in a burst of flailing feathers and wings they were spinning and falling together.

Then Shameed's steed let go and Waqar was plummeting, winded and dazed . . . but he engaged kinesis sufficiently to slow his fall. He hit the ground without breaking anything, rolling and bouncing to a halt in the grass and mud.

He came up in a bundle of fury, striding back to the other riders, calling Ajniha with his mind. Shameed landed amidst crowing and backslapping, until Waqar shoved everyone aside and swung a fist at his rival's face.

He struck shields and all but slammed through them, slapped aside a counter – and then people from all sides were grabbing their arms and hauling them apart.

'What did the dirt taste like, Entitled One?' Shameed jeered.

'I'm sure you know, you dust-eating cretin! You nearly got yourself killed!'

'I should have known you'd be a bad loser, Entitled One.'

'I pulled out of the collision – why didn't you?'

'Because I'm no coward! What a war, that a gutless wonder gets put in charge of us.'

'Are you mad? If I'd levelled that lance, even without a spearhead, your roc would now have six feet of wood struck in its ribs. That stupid spin you tried would get you killed in a real fight!'

'You missed and lost.'

Waqar drew in a harsh breath. He'd had enough of playing the humble learner. *I might not be the best flier here, but I'm going to command us in battle – and better me than this idiot.*

He looked around the avidly listening group. 'I hope you all heard that? Shameed has had his roc since it hatched, yet he risked it like that? Idiocy! The first Rondian he meets is going to gut her – and him. He keeps telling us all he's the best, but he exposed his bird's belly and could have lost her. Parena's been telling us for weeks how to fly and fight and he broke *every rule* at the first opportunity. When you fly under my command – and you all will – I'll have none of that reckless-ness. These birds are precious to my uncle, and I'll not have you waste them or yourselves. Now get back in the air!'

Shameed had turned puce, especially as most of the fliers were nodding at Waqar's words, but he tried to reassert authority. 'I was left in charge.'

'For today – but *I* have been appointed to command the aerial fight-ing men of the Shihad for the rest of the war. So yes, you take the drills, Shameed – and do so knowing that you and everyone else here belong to me in the end. And you will start sharing the little tricks and manoeuvres you're so proud of: there will be no skill-hoarders here!'

The breeding-house boy bunched his fists. 'You can't make me.'

'I shouldn't have to.'

Waqar was conscious that the mood of the gathered riders had shifted. He suspected most still sided with Shameed – after all, the gulf between the breeding-house magi and those of noble blood was immense. But most Eastern magi were products of mating with a Rondian, either enforced or arranged, and were both valued and cursed for their gnostic powers.

Shameed's bragging and recklessness had divided their opinions, so Waqar didn't wait for the outcome; he just strode back to tend to Ajniha, his friends behind him.

There was quite a different atmosphere when Parena returned the following day: Shameed was still swift with sarcasm when Waqar or one of his friends failed to execute a new move first time, but he was now *teaching* them.

And the next time Parena was away, Waqar was left in charge.

By the middle of Septinon, after only a month of training, they began moving in the wake of the Shihad, following the massive swathe of churned earth. Getting such a perspective on the march was instructive; from above, they could see the army as the generals saw it, like markers on a map. They could easily tell the disciplined lines of Keshi and Dhassan regulars from the amorphous blobs that were their Lakh and Sydian allies. The towns were usually little touched, apart from the burnt-out Kore churches. Supply-caravans carried grain and equipment, and lines of Westerners – captured slaves destined for the mines – trudged behind, flanked by skirmish lines. But their lofty vantage hid the true costs in death and suffering. It still felt more like a game of tabula than war.

The full moon hung over the skies as they flew into a vast camp outside the Vereloni city of Thantis. It was only six weeks into the invasion and Thantis was some seven hundred miles away from Pontus; much of the 'march' had been accomplished by using the windfleet to cover vast distances. But Thantis was the first major city after Pontus. There were large fires burning within the walls and the camp was fouled by the smoky air and usual army stenches. Flaming torches guided them in to a field where they found more than a hundred construct-rocs; the squalling sounded like a giant hen-house.

Waqar sensed Ajniha's anxiety as he took her in; he'd finally bonded with the bird. Hours of one-on-one time with her, on the ground and in the skies, had honed his control until it was largely instinctive. The roc ate a huge amount, a cattle-beast every night, and like her kindred she was bad-tempered and vicious, but she had accepted Waqar as her master.

'A messenger awaits you,' the man who took Waqar's reins told him, and indicated a familiar face. Chanadhan, the court-kalfas, bowed to the ground then rose smoothly.

'What's happening here?' Waqar asked.

'The city is about to fall,' the scribe reported. 'The buildings behind the eastern gate are burning and the defence is faltering. We'll be inside tomorrow.'

'And then?'

'A sacking, like the towns we've taken already – only more people will suffer, I suppose, as they refused to surrender,' Chanadhan said, with a shudder in his voice. 'More throats to cut.'

Waqar had been spared all this so far, and he was grateful for that.

He was taken to a captured manor house, a terracotta villa in the southern Yuros style, and shown into Rashid's presence. The sultan was attended by his eldest sons, shaven-skulled and snarling Attam, and lean, cruel-mouthed Xoredh. The sultan's younger brothers, Teileman and Daarid, less impressive versions of Rashid, were also present, as was the effete Dhassan Faroukh Valphath, and a bland-looking mage-noble with a curly grey beard and bald pate introduced as Admiral Ali Neniphas, the commander of the windfleet.

Rashid quickly explained the command structure to Waqar. 'Attam, Teileman and Senapati Valphath lead the three wings of our march – each of around three hundred thousand men. They report directly to me, as does Xoredh, who controls information and supply. Admiral Neniphas and you, Waqar, as commanders of the windfleets and roc-riders respectively, report to Xoredh. Your role is scouting, and to protect us from the air.'

'Do we know where the Rondian army is?'

'No, and that's your first task.'

'There are Vereloni towns and cities ahead,' Neniphas said, pointing to a map spread across the table, 'but my windskiffs report no Rondian forces east of the Silas River.'

'It doesn't mean they're not out there,' Xoredh said, eyeing Waqar doubtfully. 'You've got hundreds of miles to cover and only around two hundred beasts at your disposal. You're going to have to work for your crust, Cousin.'

'You'll have to drive those lazy pricks hard,' Attam growled. 'And their foolish birds.'

Attam, an Earth-mage through and through, was notably prone to air-sickness. 'You're welcome to join us in the air to get an overview of the terrain,' Waqar told him.

Attam's eyes narrowed.

'You'll join the vanguard,' Xoredh told Waqar. 'They're already near Spinitius.'

'The Rondians are surely marching by now,' Rashid said, 'so we're pushing hard to get as far westward as we can before we encounter any real resistance.' He placed a hand on Daarid's shoulder – the teenager was a decade younger than Rashid, and visibly overawed by his elder brother. 'Daarid has been given a hundred thousand men to capture the Vereloni coastal cities, to prevent them harassing our rear as we push past. We can't rely on the windships to transport us in large hops henceforth; they must first bring up supplies and then be refitted for battle.'

'Our overall goal is to secure a major city inside the empire before winter,' Attam said, as if it were his idea. 'These Vereloni cities are too small, and too far from the imperial heartland to serve as a base. Our goal is Jastenberg.' He tapped the map, indicating a city in northern Noros.

Waqar did some calculations. 'My roc-riders can fly several hundred miles a day, and so can our enemies. I'll start meeting imperial mage-knights in the air within a few weeks.'

'Then I trust you've learned how to fight as well as fly,' Rashid said calmly.

After they'd dined, Rashid called Waqar aside as the others left and led him to a small garden behind the banquet hall where balmy winds stirred the lavender. The sultan looked tired, but his gaze was as piercing as ever. 'Have you had any contact from your sister Jehana?'

Waqar was already on guard, but was able to say truthfully, 'No, I haven't.'

'Neither have I,' Rashid admitted, 'but we're certain she's alive and that the Ordo Costruo are hiding her. I'm going to entrust you with a few extra relay-staves, for you to try to call her. If she's in hiding, I don't think she'll emerge for anyone but you.'

'Of course, Uncle,' Waqar agreed, his heart beating a little faster.

'Nephew, the whereabouts of one young woman, even one as beloved as Jehana, may seem a small concern compared to the command of an army as vast as this Shihad, but I promise you that I'm doing all I can. For her to be lost on this barbaric continent worries me greatly.'

The show of concern didn't fool Waqar. *If he wants Jehana, it's for his own purposes*, he reminded himself as he thanked his uncle profusely for his care.

Latif and his fellow archers saw the giant eagles silhouetted against the face of the moon as they came in to land: yet another reminder that this was a new kind of war. For the first time, such creatures were on their side.

The Rondians might have underestimated us in the past, but they never will again. He turned his thoughts to the coming day: the walls were toppling on the eastern flank, right before his unit's position, so Piru-Satabam III was preparing to go in first, to open the way for the infantry. So far all they'd done was plod across the endless plains; with good roads and no opposition they'd been making twenty to thirty miles a day. They'd passed sacked villages and seen columns of captives, but so far he'd not had to fire an arrow in battle. Seven hundred miles later, they'd been given a much-needed week of rest, which they'd spent watching Earth-magi and siege-engines battering the walls of Thantis while footmen attempted to scale the battlements. Now it was their turn.

Latif knew from his past life in Salim's court that Verelon was effectively the edge of the Rondian Empire, with few magi resident. He prayed to Ahm those had all fled, because otherwise the elephants would be tempting targets.

Next morning, with the eastern sky turning scarlet, Sanjeep roused him. 'It's time, Latif-ji. Help me with Rani.'

Rani was normally a placid beast, but they'd been training with goads, to enrage her as she charged, making her lash out with her tusks, trunk and giant feet. But she was still calm as they settled the wicker howdah on her back, fitted her bronze-tipped tusk covers and the spiked leather loops over her trunk and hung the long skirts of thick leather to protect her from arrows and spears. Alongside them, thirty-nine other beasts were going through the same ritual.

As the sun rose, Ashmak arrived with the other magi, one per elephant. Their hazarapati, Selmir, was with them, and Latif hid his face; when he'd been Salim's impersonator, he and Selmir had often clashed.

'Piru-Satabam III, form up!' Selmir shouted, and Latif scrambled up the ladder behind Sanjeep. The mahout, protected only by a leather jerkin and cap, clambered into the front of the howdah while Latif climbed to the higher castle atop the beast. A few seconds later, Ashmak floated up to join them, eschewing the ladder. The burly, scar-faced mage hooked several quivers of arrows to the inner wall of their perch. There was a growing respect among the four of them: Ashmak was a hard man, but he was gentle with Rani, and he'd fought hard to get his two crewmen the best in food and equipment. He recognised that in Sanjeep he had an able mahout, and in Latif, one of the company's best archers.

The drums reached a new crescendo and the elephants began to stride through the arrayed infantrymen towards the city. The distance shrank swiftly, then they were passing through the front line. There was still a sullen red glow behind the walls, which were already looking battered and uneven, the original smooth plaster long since smashed away. With a savage crack, the nearest catapults hurled fresh boulders, the rocks whistling high overhead, only to crash down a few seconds later. The range had been well-learned and the great chunks of rock hit hard.

The Godsingers wailed prayers, but it was to war that the elephant contingent were called. Ahead, the church bells rang, warning of another assault, and voices were raised on all sides, hoarsely sung hymns beseeching protection in this world and solace in the next.

'Do virgins really await us in Paradise?' Latif murmured. 'The poor girls . . .'

'Do this right and there'll be virgins waiting for us in this life,' Ashmak muttered. Then with a sharp cry he raised his hands and encased the howdah in pale blue light as the first volley of arrows flew from the defences. Sanjeep and Latif cowered behind the wicker as shafts cracked and broke on Ashmak's shielding. The miracle of the gnosis preserved them, though they saw one elephant career sideways, two arrows in its skull, wobbling, then collapsing onto its forelegs. Selmir, sitting on the rear beast like a shepherd driving his herd, shouted an order and Sanjeep took the long goad and jammed it into the folds of Rani's neck. Like the other beasts, she shrieked in anger and broke into a trot. The Dhassan spearmen alongside them broke into a run too, howling battle-cries as they pounded up the final slopes. As the arrows continued sleeting down, Ashmak fought to maintain his shielding. Latif saw a Vereloni archer in a spiked helm, barely sixty yards above him, loosing an arrow, then ducking back, and he started counting, feeling remarkably clear-headed amidst the turmoil. On the count of six the man reappeared, fired again and vanished.

One. Two. Three. Four . . .

Latif's arrow was nocked now and the bow drawn. 'Steady!' he called to Sanjeep and the old mahout laid a hand on Rani's neck while Ashmak used Earth-gnosis to send a torrent of broken rubble at the defenders.

. . . Five. Six.

Latif shot as the man came into sight, his mind dead to what he was doing, and the shaft flew true, striking the man through his eye-slit. He vanished soundlessly and Latif switched his aim to the next crenulation, his shot taking a man in the shoulder hard enough to spin him round. Then Rani was lumbering up the slope and Sanjeep was readying a grapple.

Two men tried to tip boiling oil on them, but Ashmak hurled them backwards with kinesis; judging by the screaming, their deadly load spilled over their fellows. Then Sanjeep's grapple flew and bit, and Latif shot the first man to try to cut the rope.

'Heave!' Sanjeep called, guiding Rani backwards until the rope was taut. A dozen more had gone up, although half were immediately cut away and another two elephants were shot, falling and crushing their crew and the footmen beneath them. The walls here were already weak from the battering they'd taken and they suddenly gave way and toppled towards them. With the pressure off, Rani stumbled and almost rolled as well, causing Sanjeep to yowl in dread, but the venerable beast regained her footing in time. The men on the walls were hurled down among the attackers; Latif saw young and old faces, men who looked little different to those assailing them, but they were all stabbed and left motionless.

Then the signal came for all-out attack, Ashmak roared, '*Go! Go!*' and Sanjeep urged Rani back up the slope. Keshi windskiffs hurtled overhead, hurling torrents of fire down inside the walls. The footmen preceding them were mown down by defending archers who suddenly appeared in the breach, but Ashmak hurled fire into them and they broke, their burning clothes lighting up the gloom like rising suns. With a ragged cheer the footmen leaped past Rani as she trudged carefully through the breach. The air was filled with choking smoke, but Latif saw enough to put three burning defenders out of their agony. Behind them, and in breaches on either side, more men and elephants were swarming through. Officers were lashing out at their men, shouting contradictory orders, jamming the alleys as fresh fires broke out everywhere. Above them, more skiffs were circling, all of them Keshi.

They reached the flat ground and while Ashmak and the other magi conferred mentally with their commander, Sanjeep made hurried repairs to the harness and Latif slithered down to seek unbroken arrows in the debris. He found only a couple, buried in fresh bodies, then saw another, jutting from the bloodstained shoulder of a fallen foe.

As he pulled it out, the body give a groan, and the dust-caked face blinked open an eye. He groaned, realising he'd have to either kill or capture the wounded defender – then he cursed when he realised that the survivor was a woman. For a long moment, their eyes met. She was young; she must have been desperate to help her city-folk, to take to the walls with a bow. But her shoulder was torn and useless, and now . . .

. . . if I reveal her, she's going to be raped and likely murdered . . . and if I

leave her, the next man to come looting will do just that. He looked up to see other men nearby, coming closer. And he'd seen the whore-slaves their unit had purchased; already most were broken of body and spirit; some were dead. *Can I condemn her to that?*

He pulled out his dagger, placing a finger to her lips to urge silence. She had a plucky, snub-nosed face, pretty in a boyish way, and blonde hair that fell from the rim of her helm. Her eyes were pleading.

Ahm on high, have mercy.

Grimly, he pushed his blade into her throat and sliced. She gurgled, then her frightened eyes emptied. *I'm sorry*, he whispered to her ghost. *Better that than you be taken alive.*

Waqar Mubarak watched the fall of Thantis from high above. The Vereloni didn't contest the skies; likely they had insufficient magi to do so. The progress of the sacking could be traced in the rising smoke tendrils that gradually engulfed the city.

Afterwards, they all descended to rejoin the camp. He sat with his friends as a column of the prettiest young women were brought into camp for the Keshi nobility to bid upon. According to the *Kalistham*, these women had brought this on themselves: they should have taken their own lives rather than accept capture. But it was hard for Waqar to see it that way, and even Lukadin looked nauseated.

The Amteh ideal for marriage was a man of twenty to wed a fourteen-year-old girl, both of them still virgins – but in Waqar's experience, that wasn't common. Like most of his male peers, his first sexual experiences had been with slave-girls, and the only non-slave he'd ever slept with was Fatima, who used her own special status as a mage to do pretty much as she liked. Sexual availability was considered part of a slave's duty and there was no shame in it – for the man. He'd never considered the inequality of the arrangement before today.

I've never forced a woman, and I never will, Waqar reminded himself. But now he found himself thinking about degrees of willingness. Chastity was unmanly, but the priests called unmarried non-virgins whores. *Is a woman who doesn't take her own life when captured truly a whore or a coward? Is she not simply surviving?*

It was time, he decided, to establish some rules for his own command. So he went among the riders, forbidding them to bid for the captured women. 'Buy time with women from the whoremongers in the camp if you wish, but I forbid you to bring a slave on campaign.' There were grumblings – and some snide remarks about Fatima and the other female fliers in his unit – but no one was foolish enough to take him on.

That night, on the eve of departure towards the Brekaellen, he took out a relay-stave and called. Jehana made no reply, but the other name he sent into the aether responded immediately.

<Tarita Alhani . . . ?>

<Prince Waqar!> Her face formed in the smoke of his brazier, bright-eyed and angular. Tarita was a native of Ja'afar, the northern kingdom populated by both Jhafi and refugees from Rimoni, but he wasn't precisely sure of her background – she appeared to occupy some middle-world between mage and maid. But he'd learned to trust her: she'd aided his hunt for Sakita, and then Jehana – and he'd kissed her, a brief, almost chaste pressing of lips that had nevertheless made his heart pump more than anyone since Fatima.

<Tarita! Where are you? Have you found Jehana?>

<I'm sorry, no,> she replied. *<I'm in Pontus right now, and I've spoken to the Ordo Costruo in Northpoint. They claim Jehana's gone – she left on the eve of the invasion.>*

Waqar burned to go and find his sister. The territory he could cover with a roc would be immense. But he feared he'd simply be leading Rashid – and therefore the Masks – straight to her. *<I wish I could help, but I've got too many eyes on me. We're going to be running into an imperial army in a few weeks. I have to leave this in your hands.>*

<I understand.>

<What's happening at the Bridge?> he asked.

<The whole of the Ordo Costruo are now working on repairing it, and they've got the Merozain Bhaicara helping them. But the repairs are going to take months, even years, and they might still lose the Bridge. I've been given leave to keep looking for Jehana, though. And tracing you-know-who.>

Waqar frowned. When they were hunting the Masks, Tarita had

found a name: *Asiv Fariddan.* <*Perhaps someone might know that name in my uncle's court?*> he suggested.

<*I don't think it's wise to ask. The masked assassins will have agents there – be very careful whom you confide in.*>

<*I will. And you also,*> he told the Jhafi girl. <*Please find Jehana, and keep her safe.*>

6

Sunset Tower

Intelligent Constructs

It quickly became apparent to me that it was possible to create constructs that were superior to humankind: stronger, faster, perhaps more intelligent. I could even imbue them with the gnosis – but that then raised the very difficult question of what place humankind would have when faced with such a rival species.

That's why the Gnostic Codes forbid such constructs.

BARAMITIUS, PALLAS, 457

Sunset Isle, Pontic Sea
Augeite–Septinon 935

After the excitement of her flight to Sunset Isle, Jehana Mubarak's life swiftly reverted to claustrophobic monotony. Because the tower was surrounded by sea, she was permitted above ground, but she was given nothing to do and all day to do it.

The small group of magi who maintained the tower were rotated every month, which left Jehana alone in the middle of hundreds of miles of ocean, with just eighteen worried men and women. There were three senior magi: the aged and testy Manon, the engineer-mage Loric and brittle Hillarie. The younger magi included two other women and nine males, and three sentinels. Jehana was excluded from the eight-hour duty shifts, which rankled because she knew they didn't trust her.

I'm a Mubarak, I'm a Keshi, and they think I'm their enemy.

In truth, she was mortified that her uncle had destroyed so much and was plunging their world back into war. If she thought it would have made any difference, she'd have gone to him and pleaded that he stop. But in Rashid's hands, she'd become just another weapon.

With no work to do, she spent her time reading the books about dwyma she'd brought from Pontus or gazing from the viewing windows high in the tower, watching the endless sea tossing and swirling far below. Levana kept an eye on her, but they had little to say to each other and eventually Levana rotated her guard duty to a junior sentinel, a handsome blond man named Tovar, who was at least good to look at – although he clearly knew it. He and the young skiff-pilot Urien became her only real companions during the following days.

'Hey, Princess,' Tovar drawled one morning as the two young men joined her at the window where she'd been gazing out like a caged bird. 'Have you seen the bowels?'

'The what?' she asked, wrinkling her nose.

'The bowels of the tower,' Urien explained. 'The engineering levels.'

'They're worth a look,' Tovar told her. 'Come on.'

She decided that one would be chaperone for the other, so she followed them down the giant spiralling stairs, a thousand-foot descent from the tip to the ground, and then deeper below the surface. Everyone else was working hard or sleeping, so they barely saw another soul. The major work here was to maintain the energy-flows through the solarus crystals, deal with repairs and maintenance and scry for incoming traffic. So far the Shihad windfleet had ignored them while passing by, following the line of the Bridge while avoiding Northpoint or Southpoint – and they were wise to do so: the energy of the solarus crystals could be used to send lethal bolts of energy into the sky for almost a hundred miles, and non-violent scholars or not, the Ordo Costruo were burning to strike back.

As they descended, Urien kept up an amiable patter, apparently at pains to ensure she knew he had no suspicions about her loyalty. 'I never met your mother, but everyone says she was the greatest weather-mage ever.'

That's because she used dwyma, not Air-gnosis, Jehana thought, but she only asked, 'Is there news from Pontus?'

'The Keshi have seized the city and the Arcanum and Collegiate,' Tovar replied. 'Everyone left behind will be enslaved or dead,' he added, as if that were academic. Though a sentinel, he had the scholarly dispassion that appeared to be the Ordo Costruo's defining characteristic.

They reached the engineering level; Sunset Tower was a giant cylinder with a hollow core that fed energy from the solarus crystal cluster down into the subterranean tunnels where giant spirals of copper wire ran underground beneath the sea to Midpoint, and then off to Northpoint and Southpoint. The flow of energy was controlled from a throne beneath the cluster manned by the senior mages in eight-hour shifts. Thick pipes of lead-sheathed copper protruded from a cylinder of thick glass in which raw energy flowed, a jagged stream of vivid blue light. The cylinder was surrounded by all manner of coils and pipes, channelling light and heat to the tower above, with various levers for regulating and adjusting the flow.

Magister Loric was gazing into the cylinder, his face lit by the blue light. The air was stale here, and smelled oddly of animal. It was dimly lit, the shadows full of unexplained lumps of machinery that occasionally rattled and clanked into motion. He glanced their way when they entered, looked twice at Jehana, but turned back to his work.

'Has the Midpoint Tower been rebuilt?' Jehana asked Urien.

Loric heard the question and snorted. 'In five days, girl? Hardly!' He pulled back on a lever, making the light dim slightly. 'In six months, ask again!'

'Then where's the energy going?'

'Right now, we're channelling it to Northpoint and Southpoint. They're feeding the Bridge from either end, pushing Earth-gnosis through the structure to preserve it. So far, we're doing enough.' The engineer's voice was proud. Then he called over his shoulder, 'What's the heat reading, Ogre?'

A giant pile of leathers moved and a cavernous voice growled, 'Five . . . three . . . eight.'

'Ahm on High!' Jehana squeaked. The voice was coming from a shape of alarming proportions, a hunched tower of muscle draped in furs: the source of the strong beast-odour.

Tovar smirked, and she realised that frightening her had been at least part of his purpose in bringing her here. Then she stifled a cry as the shape emerged into the half-light. It was probably seven feet tall, with a big belly, tree-trunk legs and arms, and a skull twice the size of a normal person. Its face, all folds of loose, wrinkled brown skin, was pitted with pockmarks. It had no beard, so she could clearly see huge teeth, and its long, stringy hair was coiled into rope-like strands. After a moment she realised that it was hunched over; it could easily add another foot to its height if it straightened.

'Sal'Ahm, Jehana Mubarak,' it rumbled, a deep masculine voice speaking Rondian. It bowed, and she realised it was performing the fourth genuflection of the harbadab. Its long-nailed hand could have encompassed her skull. 'I am Ogre.'

It recognises me. She was startled into response. 'Sal'Ahm alaykum,' she squeaked, and reached out to touch the back of Ogre's offered hand. It was leathery and warm.

'Ogre works these levels for the engineers,' Loric said, clearly amused at Jehana's surprise. 'He's the only one who can withstand the debilitating effects of the tower's energy full-time.'

'What is he?'

'Ogre is Ogre,' the giant thing replied, looking at her gravely. 'The Master made me to serve.'

She glared at Loric. 'You *made* him?'

'Not I, Princess. The Master he's referring to is Ervyn Naxius. Have you heard of him?'

'Mother's told me – the renegade.'

'Aye. When he was expelled from the order, we found he'd constructed a network of secret lairs throughout Pontus and Dhassa – we kept finding new ones, and in 922, we raided a property in Spinitius and found Ogre. It appears Naxius had been breaking just about every law in the Gnostic Code, including making intelligent constructs.'

'Master is bad man,' Ogre commented. 'Ogre is happy to be free.'

'Does Ogre live down here?' she asked Loric, not quite able to ask the creature directly.

'This is my home,' Ogre said. 'I like to watch the sun rise and set. Master never showed me.'

His words touched her. 'Then I'm happy for you, Ogre.'

Ogre genuflected and rumbled, 'Shukran, Jehana.' He retreated into the shadows again. Jehana was relieved – his sheer size was frightening, like being too close to an elephant in a parade. She gave Tovar a look of annoyance; she didn't like such surprises.

Loric gave her a tour of his domain, with Urien and Tovar chipping in as he described their work; it was undeniably impressive, but also unsettling, and a troubling thought occurred to her. 'What did you mean, about the debilitating effects of the tower's energy?'

'Prolonged exposure to this place isn't good for you: you become more prone to illness and you get jittery, like having too much coffee,' Loric answered. 'That's after a few weeks. Longer than a month, it gets worse. Two months and you're a wreck – flaky skin, lumps, brittle hair, running nose, perpetual chills.'

'But what if we're trapped here for longer than that?' she yelped.

'Don't worry, Princess,' Tovar chuckled. 'The living quarters are un-affected. It's those who sit on the throne at the top of the tower who suffer the most.'

It didn't sound overly comforting, but she had little choice in the matter. They were turning to leave when Tovar said, 'Hey, do you want to see under the ocean?'

Her eyebrows shot up. 'Yes, please.'

She followed Tovar and Urien down a long, straight corridor that she quickly realised must have been hollowed out of the island foundations. When they arrived at the end of the corridor, she stopped and stared.

A massive glass panel had been installed – how that miracle had been achieved, she had no idea – and Tovar grandly announced that it was permanently underwater. The water surged against it at a frightening speed, and sometimes debris hammered against the glass, but Urien reassured her, saying, 'The panel is virtually impregnable, Princess.'

She barely heard him as she took in the fish of all shapes and colours and sizes swimming by.

'Sometimes you see giant sea creatures,' Urien enthused, 'fish and squid as big as houses.'

'Even bigger monsters than Ogre,' Tovar put in.

'Well, I feel sorry for poor Ogre,' Jehana replied.

'Whatever – just don't get trapped in a room when he's farted!' Tovar sniggered, pinching his nose and waving at the air. 'You'll die choking.'

Jehana pointedly ignored him, turning her attention back the water, but such monsters weren't evident today and after a time they wandered back to the domestic quarters. If the young men had been trying to impress her, they'd failed – these Rondians didn't have the faintest idea what being a princess *meant* – but she appreciated the company, at least.

Once she was alone, it was back to work: official lessons might be suspended, but she badly needed to learn about the dwyma – she might not have gained the power yet, but she knew *how* to, in principle, at least: she needed to find a guardian spirit – a 'jinn' in Eastern parlance. Her mother had once spoken of a dwymancer named Amantius who'd been active in Verelon long after the others died: the man they called the '*Sea* King' and 'Lord of *Oceans*'. The names were suggestive, and gave her the encouragement to keep working.

Perhaps there is actually a jinn, all the way out here in the middle of the sea?

Pontus

Alyssa Dulayne sat staring into the globe of light she'd conjured, waiting. It was after dark now, and contact should be imminent. The Heartface mask lay beside her on the table and the air was heavy with the smoke of incense candles and human musk.

A beautiful golden-haired, pale-skinned Yurosi youth was curled up on her bed in a gnosis-induced dream. She'd released the energy that sustained her beauty in public so that she could enjoy him without distraction. Her back might be bent, her flayed spine laid bare, her scalp just scar-tissue over bone, but once she'd reduced his brain to little more than libido, the slave had given her everything she'd craved. As soon as this task was done, she had every intention of waking him for another bout; since the ruin of her body, such pleasures had been distressingly rare.

But her current task was more important than pleasure.

Where have they hidden that damned girl?

Her network of spies and agents was far smaller than when she'd been Rashid Mubarak's lover, but orders had come from on high and she'd been given the resources for her hunt.

Finally, the contact came from her chief mage, Nuqhemeel, a grey-bearded Hadishah who'd fought in secret for almost two decades and tasted defeat before the recent victories – it showed in his cautious demeanour. *<Lady?>* he called warily.

<Any trace of your quarry?> She'd dispatched several windships to various points around the Pontic Peninsula, trying to find where the Ordo Costruo had hidden Jehana. There had been rumours of a ship bearing a woman in a bekira-shroud flying north, hours before the Shihad arrived. Nuqhemeel had followed that trail to the east coast of Yuros, a forbidding wilderness.

<A windship landed here: we found a campsite, and tracks going into the coastal hills. And we found an Eastern-style brooch near the midden.>

This was the first possible contact they'd had. *<Find them!>* Alyssa commanded, then she broke that contact and started on the next. By dawn, a dozen windcraft would be converging on the place. With a satisfied sigh, she let the globe of light fade and slumped painfully. She briefly considered restoring her body to its artificial perfection, but found she couldn't be bothered; the slave-boy wouldn't notice, and anyway, he'd not live to report her ruin to anyone. He ought to be grateful that she'd given brief meaning to his pitiful existence.

She had other lines of enquiry open, including a handful of agents still within the Ordo Costruo, but none of them had shown up among the captives in Pontus. Some were still in Hebusalim; others were presumably in the towers, where communications were blocked. If she could reach them, perhaps more might be revealed . . .

But that was for another day. There was only one more duty to perform now, then the pleasures of coupling and sleep awaited. She made another call into the aether, trembling with trepidation and excitement, and Ervyn Naxius appeared in the globe of light, his lined face pale and dark-eyed.

<We may have found her, Master!> she sent. *<What are your commands?>*

*

Tarita Alhani lurked in the lee of a hedge, watching the flickering lights of the window two storeys above. She'd been here all afternoon, crouched on her haunches wielding a short-handled broom or pulling weeds from the bone-dry, ill-tended garden. No one *ever* noticed servants.

Alyssa Dulayne was nothing if not arrogantly sloppy; using the house of a captured Ordo Costruo mage as her personal lair made her easy to find, especially as she'd made little effort to hide her presence. Strong gnosis was now being worked in her suite, mostly communication spells; she could feel the expenditure of the energy like a prickling on her skin. She'd have loved to know more, but she didn't dare try to tune into it.

After ensuring she wasn't being watched, Tarita went over the wall like a frightened gecko and shrank into the shadows. She was inside the witch's lair. There were sentries – Alyssa had been given half a dozen Hadishah magi and more than thirty soldiers, a sign that she was gradually reclaiming her place in the sultan's hierarchy – and judging by the grunting and gasping emanating from her bedroom window, she was getting some practise for when she was reinstated in the sultan's bed.

Tarita grinned to herself. She'd never been averse to a tumble herself, but months undercover and then travelling meant she'd been unable to play for far too long. And now the demands of her mission were keeping her chaste.

'*Unghhh!*' Alyssa cried. She clearly believed fornication was more fun if everyone knew you were doing it.

Keep busy, Bapachod, enjoy it while you can, Tarita urged silently as she slipped to the ground-floor window. She used an unlocking spell and waited for a sentry to pass before sliding inside the small parlour. She could picture some Ordo Costruo scholar here, scribbling away. Boots sounded in the hallway – had a mage half-sensed her spell? – but no one entered, and when she poked her head around the door, she saw a man's back vanish around a corner, heading for the inner courtyard, where a windsloop was being prepared. It was simple enough to join the line of servants loading goods, pick up a bundle and take it aboard. She knelt to deposit it, pressed a copper coin through the floorboards, rose quickly and left again.

A minute later she was outside the compound as Alyssa gave vent to a series of orgasmic shrieks. *Showy bitch*, Tarita grinned as she hurried away. *I probably won't need the tracking coin – I'll just follow the sound of her screwing.*

Escaping the city again presented a few problems – women alone here were in all kinds of danger – but wrapping herself in illusions to slide past people's eyes and using mesmeric-gnosis to compel those who did actually notice her to decide they weren't interested, she managed to slink away.

She'd left her skiff in a gully two miles to the south; the Shihad was advancing northwest so there were no patrols here. But she'd still been careful, removing the mast and burying the craft in dirt and brush. Now she crawled into the concealed lean-to she'd built and lit a fire, then sent a pulsing signal aimed at her handler Capolio in Hebusalim, far across the sea. She didn't have a relay-stave but he did, enabling him to follow her signal back.

<Little Bird, are you well?> he asked as his shaven-headed face appeared in the smoke.

<I am,> she replied warmly. *<I've found the Dulayne bitch and placed a tracker-coin on one of her ships. Where she goes, I follow.>*

<Not too closely,> he warned. *<She's dangerous.>*

Tarita snorted. *<You don't need to remind me!>* She raced into an account of the events since she'd last spoken to him: after uncovering Alyssa's secret presence at the Ordo Costruo, the hunt for Sakita Mubarak and the destruction of Midpoint Tower. Then she unwrapped her trophies from the tower, holding up a silver-bladed scimitar and an old leather-bound book.

<I don't even know what metal this is,> she confessed, gripping the gnostic link and pulling his perspective to right up on the scimitar's blade. *<Do you?>*

Capolio frowned, then shook his head. *<My first guess would be argenstael,>* he replied, *<except that argenstael is very brittle and frankly, no use except for decorative weaponry.>*

<This thing broke my favourite blade,> Tarita said ruefully.

<Then I don't know,> he admitted. *<But I can tell you about that book: It's*

the Daemonicon di Naxius. *Ervyn Naxius was an Ordo Costruo renegade: he was cast from the order for gnostic experiments that violated the Codes. That was before the First Crusade, I think. Some people say he's dead.>*

<*A Daemonicon? What's that?*>

<*An address book of daemons and a diary of the interactions a wizard has with them,*> Capolio replied. <*Hold onto it – it's got value for certain people.*>

<*Felix of the Masked Cabal clearly thought so,*> Tarita noted. <*Hey, I could use some support over here.*>

Capolio gave her an apologetic look. <*I've no one to send. You know how few of us there are, and there's all manner of intrigue going on here too. Rashid's people are working actively to isolate Javon – perhaps in preparation for an invasion. I'd bring you back, but if you can find Jehana Mubarak, that could give us the leverage we need to stave off war.*>

Tarita bowed her head. <*Then I guess I'll manage,*> she sighed.

Her mandate was clear: find Jehana Mubarak and use her to get to the bottom of the Masked Cabal. Right now, Alyssa was her only lead.

She spent another rough night in the wilds, but next morning she knew precisely when Alyssa's craft rose into the air and headed north and within a few minutes, she'd loaded her few possessions and treasures onto her own skiff and set off in pursuit.

7

The Vlpa Trek

Schlessen

Schlessen is a vast land populated by hundreds of tribes which are unified only by their barbaric ways. A 'Schlessen' does not answer to that term; they call themselves by their tribal name. Only where the Rondian and Rimoni have settled in proximity does there exist a modicum of civilisation.

ANNALS OF PALLAS, 631

The Bunavian Gap
Julsep–Septinon 935

Kyrik Sarkany had been flying for a day and a night, not daring to set the craft down in hostile lands. Now he sent his skiff winging over the tree-tops of the Bunavian Gap, the only path through the ramparts of mountains bordering Schlessen, the mightiest forest in the known world. The upland trees were mostly spruce, but the lowlands were more varied, the towering pines besieged by other lesser species. Ravines and thousands of streams split the landscape. Rising smoke showed the camps of Schlessen hunter-gatherers, tribes who lived off the land. Here and there patches had been cleared for cropping, and Kyrik glimpsed occasional clusters of huts around a *langhausen*, all fenced in by wooden palisades. He followed the line of a stream south until it dissipated into fenlands – and all of a sudden the trees were behind him and grasslands stretched like a sea before him. He groaned in relief, wiping his reddened eyes. The sun was westering, dropping into thick cloud and painting them deep crimson.

'Red skies at gloaming, sets beasts a'roaming,' he quoted, hoping the old folk rhyme would hold true and he'd have fair skies on the morrow. According to his reckoning, if the Vlpa clan had managed to avoid detection on their westward trek through hostile lands, they should be nearby. Clear skies would help him find them.

For now, though, it would be enough to find a place to land and make camp and get some sleep for the first time in almost forty hours. He spied a high point with a dell behind it, below the line of the hill and out of the wind, and after circling it to ensure no one else was present, he set his craft down. He anchored it loosely, in case he needed a fast getaway, before making camp, but he'd barely finished devouring the stew before his eyes closed and he was asleep.

He woke before dawn, soaked in dew, drawn from slumber by a lowing sound that reverberated through the stones. He came awake with a jerk, stiff and cold, still heavy-eyed, and engaging his gnostic senses, crept into the lee of a rock and scanned the bluff above him. Only when he was sure there were no eyes upon him did he crawl to the ridgeline and peer below.

Dark shapes were picking their way through the fens, passing beneath his hill. Ordinary eyes would have seen no more, but engaging the gnosis, he picked out more detail. Most were Schlessen warriors with spears and fur cloaks, but there were women and children too, and huge cattle-beasts with burdens strapped to their backs. This wasn't a raiding or hunting party but a small tribe of several hundred people and as many beasts, leaving the forest for the plains, which was almost unheard of.

Perhaps the Vlpa aren't the only ones on the move, Kyrik mused, pressing lower as voices sounded close by. Two warriors, one of them a giant of a man wearing a red legion cloak, were climbing to the very ridge where he sheltered, presumably to survey the landscape. One of their great shaggy beasts was following them, tearing at the coarse grass and chewing as it trudged up the slope. Kyrik wrapped an illusion about himself, initially just a casual veil, but he was slightly startled when the red-cloaked giant, still a hundred feet away, glanced in his direction, so he wove the spell tighter to conceal even the aura of the spell.

A Schlessen mage? Is there such a thing? Unlike the Sydians, the Schlessen had never made any real effort to gain mage bloodlines, but clearly there were a few. Kyrik gripped his sword-hilt, but the two Schlessen men stopped where they were, still below the ridge. They exchanged some words in their deep, sonorous tongue, while the huge bull came and ruminated beside them, rumbling as if part of the conversation. All the while the big man looked about him as if he suspected they weren't alone.

Before they left, the Schlessen leader's eyes swept the ridge one last time, then he made an ironic salute in Kyrik's general direction as they trudged away.

Perhaps they spotted my skiff when I flew overhead yesterday?

Kyrik wondered for a moment who this group were and where they were going, then shrugged. The world was full of people and purposes; his was to find his adopted clan.

He repacked his skiff, ate a hurried meal, longing for something more than dried meat and wayfarers' bread, and set off, giving the Schlessens a wide berth as he rose into clear skies and headed towards the rising sun. Twenty-five thousand men, women and children herding thousands of horses and cattle ought not be too hard to find, but he had roughly five hundred square miles to search.

He found the Vlpa on the third day, a dirty stain on the grassland resolving into a wide trail of flattened grass and churned earth as he came closer. He followed it back west for most of that afternoon until the dark smear in the far distance became cattle, wains and trudging women flanked by horsemen. There was initial consternation when they saw him, until he was recognised; the nomads were used to their own Sfera, but white-skinned magi were still a rarity and he saw plenty of pointy-handed gestures meant to stave off the evil of his coming. Then the chief appeared, a shaggy, hulking, surprisingly shrewd man named Thraan.

'Greetings, Nacelnik Thraan,' Kyrik called.

'Welcome, Kirol Kyrik,' Thraan boomed, sweeping him into a bear-hug. 'We've been awaiting you! Torzo foresaw your arrival last night.' He indicated a frail blind man standing nearby. Around them, wains had pulled up and riders were crowding in protectively while the children intruded into every space the way only children could.

'How fares your bride?' Thraan enquired, signing to his servants for his pavilion to be erected – it wasn't far off dusk and the camp would likely have been called soon, even had Kyrik not arrived. 'Have you quickened her yet?'

Hajya had been part of the price Thraan had negotiated as part of the clan's alliance with the Mollachians. Helping the Sarkany brothers had suited Thraan well enough – his clan were under severe stress and in danger of being swallowed up by a larger tribe – but that hadn't preventing him from ensuring one of the women of his tribe would be Kyrik's queen.

'Not yet, but not for the lack of effort,' Kyrik reported, earning a guffaw. 'She would have come with me, but she's unwell, unable to travel.'

Thraan sized him up. 'Then perhaps she has quickened after all?'

Kyrik lowered his voice. 'She isn't sick, but wounded. Two weeks ago, we met the Delestre legion in battle.' Kyrik met the chieftain's eyes. 'The battle was victorious, Chief Thraan, but it came with a price. Your eldest son, Brazko, fell in battle.'

Thraan hung his head, then reasserted his public face. 'Did he die well?'

'He stood over Hajya when she was grievously wounded and defied Robear Delestre, a half-blood mage. The Delestre dared not come within reach, but slew him from afar with a spell.'

'How did my son come to be protecting another man's wife?' Thraan asked, clearly suspending judgement.

'Hajya and I fought the Delestre siblings, mage against mage, in the midst of a swirling battle. Brazko should never have intervened, but he gave his life to purchase an opportunity for others to claim the victory. He was a hero, and he did not die in vain. Robear Delestre is dead and his forces cower in their holes awaiting their end.'

It wasn't quite true, but Sydians liked that sort of talk.

'Brazko always sought to make me proud,' Thraan said. 'No father could want more.'

'His name will be remembered in Mollachia.'

'Then he made a good end, Kirol Kyrik. Tonight you will tell the tale of this victory to the men of the tribe. But first tell me all, so there are no surprises, eh?' He signed for drink and led Kyrik off towards a small rise to watch the sunset.

An hour later, Kyrik was more than a little drunk, despite his attempts to be restrained, but he felt that he'd given a good account of the battle – the tactical and strategic decisions, the chance events and the eventual outcomes. 'In the end, the storm that Hajya and I summoned saved us, freezing the unprepared lowland legionaries where they stood, while we were better prepared to ride it out,' he concluded. 'We were lucky.'

The fewer who know the truth about Valdyr's dwyma, the better.

'Luck has won many a battle, but luck is earned, we Vlpa say,' Thraan rumbled. 'A chance-met battle, in a perilous place, but together, Sydian and Mollach won the day. That is the lesson we will give my people tonight. Fill your tongue with poetry, Kirol. You must relate this news to my people as if it were an old tale of the heroes, to bring them cheer.'

'I'll give it my best,' Kyrik promised.

But before that began, a more sombre matter awaited: Hajya had given him a list of the dead clansmen, which he gave to the shaman, Missef, to read before the gathered clan. Each name brought a moan from all and a piercing wail from a woman, who would then collapse, sobbing, as her children and sisters rushed in. Soon many such clumps of grief dotted the gathering.

'What happens to the widows?' Kyrik asked Thraan.

'Their kin will take them back in. The clan is one family, Kirol; what we have belongs to all. The widows will hunger for their husbands, but they will not go hungry.'

As the tribesfolk broke into a hymn to the fallen, Kyrik reflected that it was his scheming that had led them here, far from their traditional paths, travelling into hostile lands. They'd been living in dread of disaster, worried for those men who'd ridden ahead to Mollachia and fearful for themselves. At least his tidings carried the *hope* of survival, that the gamble of this trek might yet pay off.

He felt unworthy to speak, but nonetheless, he stepped before the

sea of alien faces and forced out his opening words. Once they were
spoken, the rest came tumbling out and soon, lost in the ancient art of
story-telling, he almost forgot his audience as he painted the picture
of mountains, storms, villainous Rondians and heroic men and women of
kindred tribes, Mollach and Sydian. *Zlateyr – Zillitiya himself – rode with
us*, he told them, *rising from the grave to fight again for freedom! He rode
the storm, and even mighty magi fled before them!*

When he was done, there was a moment of utter silence. He looked
around to see tear-stained faces – young and old, warrior and wife – and
then they all punched the air and cried, '*VLPA! ZILLITIYA FORJU VLPA!*'

'ZLATEYR FOR MOLLACHIA!' he roared back.

After that, he found himself in the midst of a raging celebration.
Thraan poured his drinking horn to overflowing with the bitter ale the
horsemen brewed, and as they were clearly determined to see him drunk,
he resigned himself and was swept into the night on a wave of relief
and exultation, until everything swayed and tilted into a black hole . . .

Three days later, Kyrik rode with Thraan, nursing his head through
the glare of the sunlight, fighting off the waves of nausea. He'd gone
past swearing off drinking Sydian liquor and was now vowing to never
consume another fermented fluid in this or any other life. His stomach still rebelled at anything but water and gruel and his arse was raw
from diarrhoea, but he was gradually recovering. Now he had to turn
his mind to solving the problem they faced.

*How do I get twenty-five thousand people, with all their horses, cattle and
wains, into Mollachia?*

There were three options. The easiest path was to ride all the way
around the Matra Ranges, through the Kedron Valley, and enter Mollachia from the west. The flat lands would be easy for wain and cattle
to traverse, but there were Imperial fortresses, towns, villages and
farms at the western end of the Kedron, so avoiding detection would
be impossible – and that would mean the nightmare of taking on
Rondian legions.

The Sunrise Path, the route he'd taken five thousand riders earlier
that year, was mountainous and heavily wooded – and the territory of

at least three major Schlessen tribes. Horsemen could manage it, but taking wains and cattle into the forests would be an invitation to the whole Schlessen nation: another bad choice – and anyway, they'd end up having to abandon the wains.

That left the Collistein-Registein road, an icy, treacherous high pass, but it would be traversable until Noveleve. However, old women armed with brooms could defend Collistein. The fortress had never fallen, so that looked no better an option than the other two.

You're a mage, boy – work it out. That was what his father used to say to him before he even gained the gnosis. But no solution had come to him yet.

Then a cry went up and everyone turned to look back the way they'd come to stare at a windship in the eastern skies, heading their way. It had triangular sails: a Keshi craft.

'Kirol?' Thraan asked. They shared a look: the clan was strung out across the plains, horribly exposed. 'Should we set archers?'

'Wait a moment,' Kyrik advised, then he sent an open gnostic call in Keshi. *<Who are you?>*

Someone latched onto the call instantly and he caught a mental glimpse of a swarthy, scar-faced man at the tiller, who responded *<Kyrik Sarkany?>* Then he heard a side-comment: *<We've found them, Godspeaker.>*

A smile splashed across Kyrik's face. There was only one man with that title who'd be seeking him here. 'They're friends, Thraan: old friends to us both.'

As the windship touched down Kyrik was already striding to greet a white-bearded, gentle-faced man wearing the robes and turban of an Amteh cleric – the man who'd pulled Kyrik out of the breeding-houses. He dropped to his knees, touched his forehead to the wet grass, then rose. 'Paruq – Sal'Ahm! This is an unlooked-for gift!' There weren't enough hours in the day for Kyrik to express his gratitude to this man for past kindnesses.

Behind him, the clansfolk too sank to their knees. Godspeaker Paruq was known to them through his missionary work.

'What brings you amongst us, Master?' Kyrik asked.

Paruq gave him a fond but anxious look as the Sydians pressed closer.

'I have troubling news, my friend,' Paruq said, 'but perhaps you already know about Pontus?'

'I've not long arrived from Mollachia, where we were cut off from the outside. And here, the Vlpa have left the Wheel of Seasons. We've had no news for a long time.'

'Then what I have to say may come as a shock. Sultan Rashid has succeeded in damaging the Leviathan Bridge. He has launched an airborne invasion of Yuros.'

'*An invasion?*' Kyrik felt his jaw drop. '*Of Yuros?*'

'A thousand ships, landing more than half a million men in four waves. And the clans of Sydia have rallied to him. Pontus fell without a fight and now his armies have begun to march – and fly – west. Together they number a million. They are already sacking Verelon.'

Kyrik found himself gaping stupidly. 'I . . . I don't— Why are you here, Master?'

'To warn you,' Paruq replied, 'and to urge the Vlpa to remain neutral. But I'd not realised how hard to find they would be: we traversed the entire Sydian plains before discovering the Vlpa were no longer there.'

'Your warning is appreciated, Master – but isn't it your duty to urge them to join the Shihad?'

'No! I am Ja'arathi; we hold peace as the highest of goals. But we who speak for peace are being hounded now and my career will end in some obscure desert village, I don't doubt. This is my one chance to warn you.'

'Then I thank you . . .' Kyrik looked about, at a loss for words. He glanced up at the Keshi windship and noticed the scar-faced Air-mage at the tiller. 'Who's the new pilot?'

'Cassiphan, his name is,' Paruq replied. 'He comes recommended by my seniors, men who opposed the Shihad. But he has a militant look, does he not?'

Sinister was the word Kyrik would have used. 'How long can you stay?'

'A night, no more. Already we risk being intercepted: there are Imperial skiffs patrolling the Brekaellen and they will proliferate as the Rondian Empire musters their response.'

One night . . . and perhaps, the last time I'll ever see him . . . 'Then we must make the most of this one night,' Kyrik exclaimed.

Thraan greeted the Godspeaker with reserve. Missef the shaman and his son Groyzi vehemently opposed missionaries, but the Nacelnik welcomed Paruq to his pavilion to hear this momentous news. The Sydians had no reason to love the Rondian Empire, which had made ruinous incursions into their lands in past centuries, but in recent years they had become a valuable source of revenue, buying Sydian horses for the legions. And women of the tribes had been prostituting themselves to magi on the Imperial Road for centuries to bring the mage-blood into the clans. By contrast, the Keshi were a distant people, little more than a rumour until the recent efforts by Amteh missionaries.

Kyrik was unsurprised when the Vlpa tribesmen cheered the news of the invasion lustily, but he was pleased no one suggested actually aiding the invaders. Everyone wanted to be reunited with their men in Mollachia; all else was secondary.

After the meal, Paruq invited Kyrik to his shipboard quarters. The evening was balmy and they sat in the forecastle while the crew kept a discreet distance.

'Can this invasion succeed?' Kyrik asked.

'Define success,' Paruq said drolly. 'Will it hurt the Rondian Empire? Most likely. Will it bring back every man, woman and child lost in three Crusades? Of course not. But if Rashid doesn't overreach; if he settles for successive campaigns of gradual expansion, he could come to rule large tracts of land here. After that, it will depend what he does with the Bridge.'

'Is it repairable?'

'I have no idea. Cassiphan may know?' He signalled towards the tiller, where the Air-mage was replenishing the keel for the morning's flight.

'The Bridge will be taken, tower by tower, and then preserved or destroyed at the will of the sultan,' Cassiphan answered. His eyes had a mocking quality, as if he knew some great secret and was laughing at all those who weren't privy to it. His eyes trailed over Kyrik. 'You have a brother, yes?'

Valdyr hadn't been mentioned thus far; evidently Cassiphan had been asking questions. 'Yes. He's in Mollachia. Why do you ask?'

'Curiosity. He was once in the breeding-houses, yes? As were you? It must have left scars?'

'I'd as soon not discuss it.'

'Of course. Who wishes to revisit painful memories? And all for naught.'

All for naught? Kyrik sat up. 'What do you mean?'

'Cassiphan, you may leave,' Paruq said, his usually calm face taut with suppressed anger.

The Air-mage ignored the Godspeaker, eyeing Kyrik insolently. 'Was it impotence? Or are your balls dry, "Kirol"?' He spat, sketched a bow towards Paruq and swaggered away.

Kyrik rose, but Paruq caught his arm. 'Don't, my friend. He's ex-Hadishah and he knows the blade.'

Kyrik glowered at Cassiphan's back, his mind churning. 'What did he mean? I'm not impotent – ask my new wife!'

'Sit, and I'll explain,' Paruq said heavily. When Kyrik complied, he leaned close, his gentle face full of anxious compassion. 'Kyrik, you'll recall that I was not able to extract Valdyr from the breeding-house, yes?

'Yes. I didn't know what Valdyr had done, but—'

'Valdyr wasn't the problem. You were – you didn't quicken a women during your entire imprisonment.'

'What?' Kyrik stared. 'But—'

'They wanted to execute you; you were no use, in their eyes. But I saw an intelligent young man and suggested you might be a willing convert to Ahm. That's why they let you go.'

'You mean I'm *sterile*?'

'It's *possible*,' Paruq replied. 'As you know, the seed of the magi is thin anyway, otherwise Rashid's breeding programme would have yielded tens of thousands of magi by now. I've heard of captive male magi who have only two or three children to their name after decades, and female captives who bore fruit only after years of imprisonment. You shouldn't give up hope . . . but it is possible that you may be incapable of fathering children.'

'Kore's Blood, Paruq! This Sydian alliance is predicated on Hajya and me producing heirs—'

'Perhaps, but there were other considerations: the Vlpa need a new home, and you need warriors. And in truth, it may be for the best if you and she never bear fruit. Would your people accept a half-Sydian as your direct heir?'

'But I've always wanted children,' Kyrik exclaimed.

'Then perhaps Ahm will provide.'

'You should have told me before.'

'And destroyed your chance of gaining the alliance you need? I think not. All marriages carry a risk of infertility, and both sides needed this alliance.'

'But I could have offered Valdyr—'

'Who would not have accepted your command to marry. He is damaged inside, my friend. He needs help to become the man he was meant to be.'

Kyrik hung his head, picturing how Hajya would greet this news. 'What do I do, Paruq?'

'Blame fate,' Paruq advised, his voice sympathetic. 'Blame whatever you like. You must win your kingdom back before you can be concerned about the future. And who knows, perhaps in a year's time, she will be big in the belly and you'll look back on this conversation and laugh.'

'Please, Kore and Ahm, make it so!'

Next morning, Kyrik woke to strange news. Cassiphan had vanished – and the keel of Paruq's windship had been badly damaged, making it unflyable. Worse, Kyrik's own skiff was also gone.

His face grim, Paruq admitted, 'We scarcely know the man – one of the sentries thought he saw something large pass over him in the night: if that was your skiff, then Cassiphan was heading west.'

Strands of thought came together, not quite logical but fitting perfectly in Kyrik's mind regardless. 'He's looking for Valdyr!'

Mollachia

Valdyr Sarkany stared at the body on the altar of the tiny woodland chapel, a few miles south of Magas Gorge. Ice was melting to water and running into pools on the stone floor. In the instant of dying, it had been frozen solid – although dead for more than a month, the corpse looked as fresh as at the moment of death.

'Robear Delestre,' he said to himself: the callous bastard who'd condemned Kyrik and him to starving to death in his own family's dungeons in Hegikaro. *Was it really only a few months ago?* 'He doesn't deserve the honour of a decent burial. Leave his corpse to the wolves.'

Juergan Tirlak murmured in agreement. 'Let it rot unmarked. It's all he merits.'

'Sacrista might pay a pretty price for his body?' Nilasz Pobok suggested.

'No,' Valdyr said emphatically. 'I'll not have dealings with her.'

Valdyr glared at Robear's fleshy face, which was pouting as if death were distasteful. 'Leave it with the rest.' Hundreds of Rondian bodies were beginning to emerge as the ice melted, but many more were still encased.

'If that's your will,' Dragan agreed, 'but first there is something . . . a Vitezai tradition, one your father followed, and his before him.'

'What tradition?'

'The *ivashvee*,' Dragan replied. 'The ritual drinking of the heart-blood of your fallen enemy. The Mollach kings believed that one gained the strength of the fallen; now it is largely symbolic, a sign of the ultimate conquest.'

'I don't want that scum's blood in my mouth,' Valdyr replied, then sensing this was entirely the wrong thing to say, added quickly, 'But who would? Let his shade wail in the winds as he witnesses his own desecration.'

The looks of approval told him that was the right answer. These men were hunters – they'd all drunk warm blood from a kill in midwinter to stay alive – and they were also men of tradition.

As Dragan drew his dagger and stood over the corpse, the tiny chapel filled up; word had swiftly gone around. The gazda looked more priest than warrior as he raised his blade over the dead man's bared chest. He spoke a prayer to Kore, an old Mollach plea for the homeland, echoed by the men about him, plunged the blade into Robear's chest and opened the ribs. He cut out the heart and with bloody hands, raised the organ high, so everyone could see it, before squeezing it over a goblet that Nilasz produced from somewhere. Someone else added water.

There was something primal about the craggy old warrior and the bloody altar that made every gesture significant, weighty.

'We are the Vitezai Sarkanum,' he announced solemnly. 'Kings and rulers come and go like seasons, but we are eternal as the fires of Cuz Piros, the ghosts of Watcher's Peak and the White Stag. We are free men of Mollachia, risen from the soil to defend it: servants of Kore and of the people, pledged to defend our nation against tyrant and invader. *We are the Vitezai.*'

'*Vitezai eternalus,*' the men chorused, hands to hearts, and Valdyr copied, wondering at the fervour and the sense of iron purpose. He'd never been inducted formally into the order, and he felt a faint chill at the words about tyrants and invaders: another reminder that while he fought alongside these men and thought he had their respect and loyalty, in fact they served Dragan, their gazda, not Kyrik, their kirol.

Dragan's an uncrowned king . . . and he's a long way from approving what Kyrik is doing . . .

'Valdyr, Princeps-Mollachai, step forth,' the gazda intoned, offering the goblet.

Valdyr felt unseen eyes on him: the distant regard of Zlateyr and the Watchers, curious but not forbidding, and taking that as consent, he accepted the goblet and sipped the bitter, oily blood. It was sluggish, barely above freezing, and clotted in his throat on the way down, but he could feel silent approval filling the chapel as he handed the chalice back to the gazda.

Dragan also drank, and Nilasz too, then all the others present in turn.

Then something struck him like a bolt of light blasting through the stone walls of the chapel and transfixing him, and he was spun towards the East, where a massive swarm of flying creatures, giant crows whose wings beat in unison and made the air throb, was bearing down on them. A scar-faced man was riding the lead crow, an Easterner with pale flowing robes.

He saw Valdyr and his eyes pierced him through.

And Valdyr knew him.

A thousand dreadful memories came flooding back: the nightmare of the breeding-houses, all those dark faces and hands and bodies, slapping and prodding and teasing and laughing and sneering, being ridden by women whose names he never knew, old and young, lovely and plain, their hatred concealed from the overseers but plain when he couldn't help but meet their eyes.

But that had been only the beginning, the humiliating destruction of pride and self-worth, the erasure of innocence; that had been just a foretaste of the real horror to come. That was before *Asiv* found him.

He howled in denial as darkness closed in, riding on black pinions, calling his name: '*VALDYR? VALDYR—*'

A blow struck his face and wrenched him back to the present and he stared up at the ceiling as faces crowded above, filled with worry. Dragan bent over him – somehow he was on his back, his head was throbbing.

The gazda's hard face was softened with concern. 'Lad, lad, do you know me?'

Valdyr stared about him, bewildered and frightened, then he sat up, threw the outstretched arms aside and rose, embarrassed and angry. 'I'm fine, I'm fine, I just ... I *saw*—'

What did I see ... ?

He whirled, facing the room, scared that he would see derision on the faces of these tough, practical men. Instead, he saw anxiety ... and awe. He realised instantly that this, hard on the heels of the miracle of the ice-storm, had sealed his status as mage and prophet. Words burst from his mouth: 'Danger rides the wind from the East! They're coming here, to divide our lands and rend our souls!'

He had no more idea what his words portended than anyone present listening.

Hegikaro, Mollachia

Sacrista stared out of the window of the master suite. Hegikaro Castle was built on a promontory above the lake and the town and she could see for miles, over the dark waters of Lake Drozst, to hamlets and farms on forested slopes where the highlands rose, climbing north towards Ujtabor and Banezust, the mining towns upon which her fortunes rested. And above it all were the brooding peaks of the Arkadaly Ranges, capped in snows that crept lower each passing day. Summer was fleeting here, but the gloomy beauty of it seeped into her bones.

Behind her, her brother's room was just as he'd left it the day he rode away. She couldn't bear to sleep here, but she needed the office. The latest despatches were strewn over the desk. With a sigh she slumped into the high-backed chair, resting her head on the Sarkany Draken sigil carved into the top, and re-read the letter. Finally, her father had responded.

Half-Daughter,

it began – to August Delestre, his bastards were only ever 'halves' –

I am bitterly disappointed that you have let the family down again. Not only have you failed to deliver the required tax money, but you have allowed the situation to degenerate into revolt. You compound this by failing to cooperate with the governor in restoring the situation. I do not mention the loss of two thousand trained men, as Governor Inoxion insists that the fault lies with your brother. He believes you competent – but I am losing patience! Need I ride all the way to that pigsty of a kingdom to remind you of your duty? Take control! Ride the commoners hard! Break them! And bring me my money!
August Delestre, Earl of Augenheim

She rested her forehead on her hands, blinking away tears. No hint of regret at Robear's death; no acknowledgement of her news, that the storm that destroyed them had been gnostic, not natural. No aid. Only accusations.

Ansel Inoxion was also writing to her father, and clearly getting a more receptive ear. She doubted Inoxion's support was genuine: he just wanted to ensure that *he* controlled the situation here. He didn't want August to send reinforcements who might threaten his control, not when all he had to do was hold the river and pilfer her silver-boats as they floated by.

This whole kingdom is a trap. If I had half a brain, I'd leave. She had been contemplating escape for days. She wasn't an Air-mage; Theurgy and Sorcery were her affinities, so she'd need to ride. She'd take the Collistein Road. She could make it look official – an inspection visit – then slip away. The more she thought about it, the more it felt like the only thing she could do. Of course it wouldn't be easy; once in Becchio, she'd have to prove herself all over again. *But at least my life would be my own.*

Someone knocked. 'What?' she called, irritated at the interruption.

'Milady, you're needed.' A young squire looked in. 'I'm sorry, Milady . . . but they've recovered Milord Robear's body. It's been placed in the chapel – you need to come.'

Something in his voice warned her, whatever it was, she needed to see for herself. She wrapped a cloak about her as if it were armour, then followed the young man. *It's been in the wilds for weeks*, she warned herself. *It'll be bad. Be strong.*

The austere Kore chapel was filling up with officers and those battle-magi she had stationed here. She ignored them, focused only on the body laid before the altar. Candles had been lit, bathing Robear's face in soft gold. Tears stung her eyes as she took in his face: so peaceful, he could have been asleep. They'd wrapped him in a legion cloak, and someone had put a sword in his dead hands – it wasn't his own.

Kyrik Sarkany probably pilfered it, she thought indignantly. But mostly what she felt was relief, that his body seemed intact, no real decay set in. *It was encased in ice, I suppose. That would account for his state.*

'Who found him?' she asked, meaning to give praise.

Rafe Gabrian, her one remaining Air-mage, coughed discreetly. He was a sleek young man who fancied himself as a catch, despite being a lightweight with a blade. 'I did, Milady.' His normally supercilious expression was muted as he stepped to her side. 'I was flying reconnaissance over the battle-site when I saw movement on the ground. Four man were carrying something, but when they spotted me, they dropped it and ran off. It was your brother's body.'

'So the rebels had it? For how long?'

'It can't have been more than a day or two, Milady. The, er . . . *putrefaction* is minimal.'

'What were they doing with it?'

'I don't know.' Rafe leaned in, much closer than she normally permitted any man to get, and whispered, 'He was wrapped in a hide bag, and naked.'

The bastards . . . She thought of Kyrik Sarkany and prayed for the chance to skewer his barbarian heart. 'Naked?'

'Aye. They'd stripped him. I think they were on their way to dump the body. But there's worse, I'm sorry. Someone had cut out his heart. It wasn't in the bag.'

They cut out his heart . . .

Suddenly her chest felt like it was caving in under a crushing weight; breathing was almost impossible. Her vision swayed; she felt her legs begin to go and grabbed at Rafe's shoulder. 'Get out,' she rasped at the staring ring of men. 'All of you, get the Hel out of here!'

For a moment they all gaped, then they hurried to follow her order, some murmuring condolences, most watching her with judging eyes, as if they'd never felt grief themselves. Finally there was just Rafe Gabrian, and she had no doubt he was thinking with his groin: *Give a woman a shoulder to cry on and she's yours.*

'You get out too,' she snarled, shoving him away.

Only when she was alone did she let her grief and fury burst from her body like pus from a boil. She kept as quiet as she could as she fell to her knees, shaking, before feverishly unwrapping Robear's cloak to see for herself the gaping hole in his left breast.

Oh, Robear, what did they do to you?

When she emerged an hour later, she left her grief inside. There was no room in her heart for anything but *purpose*. What must be done, would be done. The silver meant nothing now; nor did the plunder, the family name, her own honour. *There is only you, Kyrik Sarkany. What you've done will be done to you.*

She turned to face her officers, her grief now a cold, hard thing. 'We're going to go through this valley like a hurricane,' she rasped. 'Enter every house, take anything you want, and if the people resist, punish them as you see fit. I want everything of value. *Rape this valley.* And bring me the heads of Kyrik and Valdyr Sarkany.'

8

A Taste of Power

The Forgotten Bridge

In the mid-800s, Emperor Andarius inaugurated a bridge across the Aerflus from the Rymfort in the Holy City to Fisheart in Pallas-Nord. But the project quickly ran out of money and support, especially as a permanent energy source was required to sustain it. The stumps of the foundations are a strange presence, and have attracted many urban legends. The residents of Pallas refer to it as 'The Bridge they're afraid to complete', in reference to the ongoing power struggle between the Bastion and the Celestium.

ANNALS OF PALLAS, 892

Pallas, Rondelmar
Augeite–Septinon 935

Lyra struggled up the stairs, feeling like her stomach was a boulder. Basia, augmented by kinesis, helped her to the top, but it was still a relief to reach the final step. 'Six months gone, three to go,' she panted. 'Kore's Breath, I'm *sick* of pregnancy.'

Solon Takwyth awaited them in Redburn Tower, where Cordan and Coramore Sacrecour were being housed. He led Lyra and her bodyguard to a locked door, where a guard in a tall-plumed helmet admitted them to an antechamber furnished with only a few hard wooden chairs.

Lyra groaned as she lowered herself onto one. *Would cushions be too much to ask?*

Basia and Solon took up station either side of the entry arch as a door in the far wall was opened and Cordan Sacrecour was brought through. At first there was a hopeful look on his face, then his expression fell.

He went straight to Basia, whom he liked, ignoring Lyra. 'Where's Prince Ril?'

'He's leading the army south,' Lyra replied. 'He left two weeks ago.'

Cordan pulled a sulky face. 'No one tells me anything.'

Since the attacks, there had been a profound change in Cordan's relationship with Ril: it was he who'd saved the young prince from Tear, his masked 'rescuer'. With Coramore still unwell, he'd latched onto Ril and they'd chatted happily about jousting and riding and other knightly pastimes.

He still appeared to regard Lyra as an enemy, but she was determined to gain his trust – and not just because he was still heir to the throne. 'How are you, Cordan?' she asked politely.

The young prince finally looked at her. He was fourteen now and increasingly the image of his father: a pallid youth with copper-wire hair. 'Fine. May I see Cora today?'

'I'm afraid she's still sick.'

Cordan's face fell. For all his faults, he loved his sister deeply. 'Is she getting better?'

'Perhaps. But how are you, Cordan?'

'I'm bored. I want to go back to the Arcanum. I need to learn the gnosis.'

'You have a tutor visiting, don't you?'

'He's boring. I want to see my friends.'

As far as she knew, he hadn't actually made any friends, but she was struck by a vision of this lonely, angry boy one day sitting on a throne – here, or in Fauvion – and taking out all his pent-up rage on those in his power. 'I'll see what I can do,' she promised.

There was an awkward silence, then Cordan asked, 'What news is there of the march?'

'Um, well . . .' She looked at Solon, unsure how much he should be allowed to know.

'The northern armies are marching,' he told the prince, and Cordan brightened. Solon Takwyth was a renowned warrior; even the scion of a rival House could find plenty to admire in him. 'The Corani have left Canossi, taking barges up the Sanuvo River. They'll go up the Reztu to Augenheim.'

'Why not go up the Medos and the Jaslo?' Cordan asked. 'That's much shorter!'

'A little,' Solon agreed, 'but those are swift rivers. The Reztu is slow and wide, much easier to navigate, at least until they reach Halketton, in a few weeks' time. After that they'll march into the Kedron and onwards, until they encounter the foe.'

'Has Verelon been taken?' Cordan might have been discussing a tabula square.

Lyra winced at the thought. At the last council meeting, they'd had to concede that Verelon was on its own. Even the southern armies couldn't get there in enough numbers to stop the Shihad's advance, so they wouldn't try.

The poor Vereloni . . . But what else can we do?

She rose and walked awkwardly away, leaving Solon chatting with Cordan. He was showing a softer side; he'd never been a father and she wondered if he missed that.

Basia noticed her discomfort. 'The baby, Milady?'

'I'm just tired.' None of her previous pregnancies had gone as far as this one, so she was in uncharted territory. 'I'm so exhausted – and there's still three months to go.'

'You have my sympathy. I cannot help but feel that we were created by a *male* God. You think any chap would treat another chap so badly?' Basia observed drily.

'Quite.' They shared a brief, rare moment of empathy.

After taking their leave of Cordan, they went up another level, to an even more strongly fortified door. Guards admitted them to a sitting room, where Coramore sat manacled to the floor. When she saw Lyra she tried to attack, baring her teeth and screeching, jolting the chains rigid as she strained, snarling like a rabid animal. She was all skin and bone; the manacles had twice had to be cut down so she couldn't slip them. Her wrists and ankles were gashed from the chafing, despite constant care from healer-magi. Seeing her made Lyra want to weep.

Coramore opened her mouth and a dry croak came out. '*I see the corpse in your belly still swells as it decays. Rotting meat does that, you know.*'

'Who are you?' Lyra demanded.

'*I'm everyone, Royal Slut. I'm the Sum of All.*'

The healer-magi assigned to her believed Coramore was possessed by a master-daemon, but the possession was anchored somehow, and banishing spells hadn't worked – even the Keepers had failed to cleanse her, or to control the daemon.

'What's your name? Are you Abraxas?'

'*I have ten thousand names, Royal Slut.*' The girl's face became cunning. '*Perhaps one is Natia? Would you like to speak with your mother?*'

Lyra gasped, but Solon interposed himself. 'Natia rests with Kore,' he said sternly.

Coramore's expression altered, an anxious visage, and when she spoke it was in a plaintive northern accent. '*Lyra? Daughter? Is that you? Did you live after all?*'

'Mother?' Lyra couldn't help herself – Natia had died before she ever knew her.

'*I wish I could have stayed with you, my child. I so much wanted to see you grow.*'

'Mother?' Tears welled up as Lyra reached out, despite the dangers. Solon held her back firmly. 'Her bite is still infectious, Milady.'

'*Daughter? Daughter?*'

Who's my father? Lyra almost asked, but Solon couldn't be permitted to know that Ainar Borodium wasn't. Instead she asked, 'Why, Mother?' *Why take your own life, when you had me to live for . . .*

Coramore's face became sly. '*Because I had to know what lay beyond . . .*' Then she spat at Lyra and her voice returned to her earlier vile cackle. '*I had to escape that rukking convent and the dregs of stupidity inside it!*' She squealed with laughter. '*You're not a queen, you're a lie. When they put your head on a spike, I'll be waiting to collect your bleating soul and make it mine for eternity.*'

Lyra reeled, staggered to a seat and fell into it. *That wasn't my mother . . . She's not here, she never was . . .*

Coramore turned on Solon, snarling more vitriol. '*Still longing to lift the Royal Slut's skirts, Solon? Still lusting for what you can't have?*'

Solon gestured and Coramore slowly folded into an unconscious bundle. 'I'm sorry, Majesty – I did warn you.'

None of the other Shepherds captured in Julsep had recovered either; even water from the pool in Lyra's Winter Garden alleviated their condition for only for a short time, though it had cured the ordinary Reekers. They needed new answers.

After reminding Solon that Coramore had to be kept as healthy as possible, Lyra went with Basia to the chapel. She needed someone to talk to, and who better than her Comfateri?

Solon watched Lyra and Basia leave, then conferred with the guard commander about ensuring the prisoners were given more frequent visits and better food. It hurt to be unable to do more. Then he made his way through the central courtyard towards his office in the barracks. He was limping across the square – his legs were still bad after being shattered in the fall from the royal suite a month ago – when someone called his name and he turned in surprise to see a slender, attractive woman with curling reddish-brown hair swaying towards him.

'Lady Aventour?' He'd danced with Medelie when she'd been crowned *Regna d'Amore*, Queen of Love, at the tourney earlier this year, but he hadn't seen her since.

'You sound surprised, sir.'

'It's been too long, Milady,' he replied, fumbling for courtly words. 'You've been missed.'

'Why, thank you,' she said brightly. 'I would be disappointed to be forgotten so soon. But I had some matters to attend to at home.'

Solon tilted his face so that his scarred side was hidden. 'Your family dwells west of Fauvion, yes?' Large, strategically placed estates, if he recalled correctly.

'That's right. Father is Relf Aventour, Baron of Sutherglade.' Medelie looked up at him in a way that suddenly made him realise that while he might consider himself a widower devoted only to his queen, others might see an eligible bachelor. Passing knights and courtiers were pausing to peer at the grim knight-commander and the brightly dressed young lady. She really was quite lovely, her pretty face and vivacious manner balanced by an unexpected maturity and grace.

'No man at court has forgotten the *Regna d'Amore*, I'm sure,' he replied awkwardly. 'Er, when did you return?'

'Yesterday evening. My aunty in Highgrange is hosting me.' She beamed up at him. 'This time Father has forbidden me to return home without an affianced husband.'

It had been a long time since a pretty young woman had looked at him as Medelie was. Chasing girls was a young man's pleasure, but he'd never done that, just accepted the marriage arranged by his family. Perhaps that was why her smile so undermined his composure. 'So how may I help you, Milady? An introduction, perhaps?' The court was swarming with young men and women seeking positions.

'I would never presume to be so forward,' she said, tossing her brown curls and looking up at him, her lips parted in a way that made his mouth go dry and his pulse quicken.

Dear Kore, she's beautiful . . . 'Well, er . . .' he floundered, 'I'm constantly being invited to the salons of Highgrange, though I'm not a great one for such events.'

'Nor I, but if I'm to meet a good man, I must go through the motions, mustn't I? I'm a country girl, Sir Solon: I'd really rather go riding.'

He remembered the way she'd stolen the dance from the other women and made it her own to become *Regna D'Amore*. He had no doubt that she would be a delight to anyone at a salon soirée – and that she was practised at saying exactly what people wanted to hear.

And yet, why not? He wasn't immune to feminine charms, but he'd been cautious since his return. And 'I'd really rather go riding' could be interpreted several ways . . .

'Come to my office in the barracks this evening,' he said. 'I will look through the invitations to see if any might please you.'

'Thank you, Solon,' she breathed, as if he were the only man in the world.

For the rest of the afternoon, he felt like he was.

At sunset Medelie was escorted to his office, his aide's eyes goggling as Medelie slowly pulled off her cloak to reveal a low-cut red silk dress, her creamy bosom swelling out from beneath the lacy bodice.

Solon stood, his legs feeling hollow as reeds. 'Milady—' he heard himself breathe.

She sashayed towards him slowly and curtseyed so low he saw her nipples resting in nests of lace. 'Would you like to take me to a soirée, Solon? Or shall we ride?'

'Forgive me, Comfateri, for I am a sinner.'

If only you were, my Queen, Ostevan thought, *what fun I could have with you.*

The galling thing was, it would be so easy to just take her. Lyra wasn't stupid, but she was guileless as an innocent and she had no gnostic defences. However, Dirklan Setallius or one of his agents examined her aura every night and morning and they would swiftly notice if she'd been tampered with gnostically. Lesser magi could be deceived, or veils placed over the enchantments, but Ostevan respected the spymaster too much to even try.

For now, it sufficed to imagine her in his power as he heard her Unburdening. They knelt on knee-pads at an angle so that they talked both to each other and to the life-sized wooden icon of a benevolent Corineus standing over them as if giving his blessing.

'What troubles your soul?' he asked, but instead of answering immediately, Lyra fell silent, which told him this was a significant matter, one she feared to broach even in confidence to a friend. 'Everything said in an Unburdening Room is in strict confidence,' he reminded her. 'Not even an Ecclesiastic Court can force a confessor to divulge what is said.'

As he waited for her to respond, he wondered about the absolute genius who'd first dreamed up Unburdening. *Tell us all your secrets and we promise not to tell anyone else? Brilliant! How many people have wrapped themselves in chains due to such misplaced faith?*

The wondrous part was that it answered a deep human need to be understood and forgiven. For a sensitive soul like Lyra, who blamed herself for absolutely everything that went wrong, it was immensely powerful. So he waited, swallowing his impatience.

Finally Lyra took the decision he so craved: to trust him. 'Only Duchess Radine, Dirklan Setallius and Dominius Wurther know this,' she started. 'I am Natia Sacrecour's daughter – but her husband, Ainar Borodium, wasn't my father. I was born two years after his execution.'

Ostevan stared. Physically, Lyra was her mother's image – which was why he'd never questioned the other part of her parentage. He could barely recall Ainar, other than that he'd been a blond Argundian youth, abrupt and arrogant. 'Then one of her captors . . . ?'

'We presume so.' Lyra's big eyes teared up. 'She killed herself when I was young. Dirklan said she would have hated imprisonment.'

'You could be the child of *anyone*? From Garod Sacrecour down?' he breathed, then realised he was thinking aloud. 'My Queen, I am honoured that you would share this with me. Did you merely wish to Unburden your soul, or do you require something of me?'

'It troubles me, Ostevan. I lied at my coronation, before Kore and the whole of the empire. I wonder sometimes if all our troubles are Kore punishing me for that lie.'

If you'd told the truth, you'd never have been allowed to rule, Ostevan reflected. 'Lyra, you *are* the rightful queen: you are Natia's daughter, and nothing else matters.'

'That's what the others tell me. But I hate that I must lie.'

'Kore forgives you,' Ostevan assured her. 'You must feel no guilt over this.' But behind the platitudes, his mind was racing. 'Do you actually wish to know who your father is?'

'Part of me longs to, but it's such a dangerous question.' She looked away. 'I suppose there's only two options: one of the Sacrecour knights, or a gaoler.'

Ostevan thought on that. 'There is a third option, Milady: any prisoner, however lowly, is entitled to a confessor, who is permitted to see them alone.'

Her eyes grew bigger and he could see her imagination at work, putting herself in her mother's place . . . and himself as that confessor. 'But what priest would do such a thing?' she whispered in an appalled, fascinated voice.

'One who came to love the young woman whose soul was in his keeping?' he suggested.

She swallowed, clearly thinking of their own relationship and perhaps comparing it to the emotional wasteland of her marriage. *Very soon, I'll own your heart, Lyra Vereinen.*

Then Basia de Sirou knocked and Ostevan helped Lyra rise, marvelling at how lovely she still was, even this late in her pregnancy.

As they walked to the chapel door, he mulled over what might tip the balance in his favour. She feared for her marriage; she was lonely and afraid – and Naxius himself had supplied an interesting titbit from his own research when they had last conferred. 'Corrupt the genilocus and you corrupt the dwymancer,' he'd said.

I need to accelerate things, he thought as he kissed her signet ring. *The Master wants us to attack soon. I need her in my thrall before then ...*

'My Queen, I've been thinking about our previous discussion,' he started. 'Have you considered my suggestion that Kore Himself may be the ultimate source of the dwyma?'

She nodded eagerly, her face lighting up. 'I have become convinced that you are right.'

Of course you have: the alternative is to believe yourself to be evil. 'The power of Kore protected you from Twoface, blasting the daemon from existence,' he told her. 'Perhaps you are a vessel of the Angels, Lyra: perhaps that's what the dwyma is.'

She ducked her head shyly, as he'd known she would. 'I'm just a woman,' she said reprovingly, though she flushed with embarrassed pride.

'We are all just human,' he agreed. 'It is when Kore touches us that we become more. And I can feel something special in you, Lyra. I sense you growing closer to Kore every day. I am humbled to be your guide on that path.'

She floundered, delighted, yet fearful of the sin of hubris. 'You shouldn't speak so.'

But you love that I do, don't you? he thought coolly. 'Does your understanding of the dwyma grow alongside your love of Kore?' he pressed.

'I've been reading about it, studying ... I feel that He guides me.' She looked away; such admissions must surely be heretical.

'Good. Knowledge and Truth give us strength,' he approved, 'as does love: your people love you, Lyra. All who come in contact with you sense your goodness. Everyone loves you.'

Their eyes met – all it took was a gentle mental nudge, one not even Setallius would be able to detect later – and they were gazing into each other's eyes.

'I love . . .' Blushing furiously, she looked away. 'I love Kore above all,' she stammered.

'And that is as it should be,' he approved warmly. He made a sign of blessing on her brow. 'Be at peace, dearest Queen. Kore loves you too.'

But your soul belongs to me . . .

The Celestium, Pallas

The young man in Dominius Wurther's drawing room was a dissolute drunkard and heavy gambler with two bastard daughters to his name: just another younger son wasting his life in the sure knowledge that his pure-blood mage family would bail him out of every misadventure. A larrikin and a liar with no martial skill, his only virtue was his dress sense.

In other words, Wurther thought, *he's excellent prelate material.*

'So you're telling me that if I take the vows, I'll be a prelate immediately?' Gerson Venkyle asked again, clearly not quite believing his ears. 'I don't even have to serve as a priest?'

'As I've already said,' Wurther confirmed. 'Just pass the examination and pay the fee.'

'What examination?' Venkyle asked suspiciously.

'An interview, with some very, *very* simple questions.'

'About Kore?'

'Yes, of course they'll be about Kore,' Wurther snapped. 'We're a Church, not tailors.'

Venkyle blinked. 'Well, I'm not sure.'

'Your income will treble, you'll get your own apartments in the Celestium and you'll have the chance to shape the world. There are men who'd die for such an opportunity.'

'But . . . what about girls?'

'I'm sure I have no idea what most of my prelates get up to,' Wurther said, which was as obvious a hint as he could give. 'Most of the time they live in their sinecure, where they're more or less a law unto themselves.'

'What's a "sinecure"?'

'Think of it as a barony, full of obedient people eager to serve you.' *Dear Kore, is this obvious enough for you? All I want is to know I can rely on your vote!*

'But I'm a Pallacian! I can't leave the city!'

'There are sinecures in the countryside near here.' *There are also sinecures in Rimoni*, Wurther added silently, *and I'll send you there at the first bloody opportunity, so help me! Just pledge me your obedience!*

Gerson Venkyle wrinkled his nose. 'I don't really think I want to live away from Pallas.'

It was all Wurther could do not to punch the ungrateful little snit. He terminated the interview abruptly and when he was alone, sat brooding. Filling the vacant prelates' sinecures wasn't proving as easy as he'd expected. Prelates had to be magi, of not less than half-blood, as much for their own protection as for theological reasons, and he was coming up badly short. With only a dozen new men lined up so far, he'd been reduced to approaching second and third sons of the lesser Houses, after-thoughts, by-blows and bastards – but most were no better than Gerson Venkyle.

At this rate they'd not have enough prelates to elect a successor if I died.

He was still mulling over this grim reality when a shaven-headed, skinny secretary knocked on his door and squeaked urgently, 'Your Holiness! You must come!'

'Must I?' He threw the man an angry look. 'I'm Grand Prelate – I choose what I *must* do!'

'But Holiness, you *must*—'

He sighed and rose ponderously to his feet. 'What's going on?'

'The nuns are revolting!'

'That seems a little harsh,' Wurther chuckled, to hide his momentary confusion.

'No, I mean: *they're in revolt!*'

'So I inferred,' Wurther said, waddling around his desk and choosing a crosier. 'All right, show me – and this'd better be good, or you'll be preaching in Silacia by lunchtime tomorrow.'

As they left the office, his bodyguard, the young Estellan Exilium Excelsior, stepped to his right shoulder, his helm tucked under his arm but otherwise fully accoutred for combat. The secretary scurried ahead through the darkened halls of the Celestium, beneath myriad beautifully adorned domes and ceilings, past statues of saints and past grand prelates.

'Tell me, Exilium,' Wurther said as they walked, 'why did you leave the Inquisition?'

'The Holy Inquisition is impure,' the Estellan replied crisply. 'I came to the Celestium seeking purity of service.'

'You think to find *purity* here?' Wurther clarified, trying to hide his incredulity.

'This is the heart of Koredom,' Exilium intoned. 'All true believers long to walk these halls, but few are worthy.' His demeanour was of one who saw worthiness every morning when he looked in the mirror.

'You're the sort to take your vows seriously,' Wurther commented. 'It must have been difficult to break your swearing-in oaths with the Inquisition so quickly.'

'They let me down,' Exilium said, in the same monotone. 'An oath comes with obligations. They failed.'

You could argue your way out of anything with that sort of logic, Wurther mused. *I must remember that approach at the next meeting of the Royal Council.*

As they approached the windows overlooking the plaza known as the Forum Evangelica, Wurther became aware of a high rhythmic chant that was growing in volume as they neared the courtyard – but even he wasn't prepared for the shrill wall of sound that struck him as he stepped onto the balcony.

The Forum Evangelica was full of nuns, arms raised and screeching his name: '*DOMINIUS PONTIFEX, HEAR US, HEAR US!*' Then they saw him, and a raucous cheer went up.

He stared, then looked at the secretary. 'What in Hel is going on?'

'They want . . . um . . . *things*, Holiness.'

'Do they?' Dominius looked down from the balcony, looking for familiar faces amidst this sea of women, but there were none. He might tolerate all manner of vice amongst those loyal to him, but he himself had few other than the dinner plate and the wine bottle. Women had always been a different species. 'What sorts of "things"?'

'I don't know.'

Must I do everything? The answer to that was, of course, *yes*. It was his own fault; if you had too many clever people in your retinue, they began to see you as replaceable. He looked around; so far, the loose cordon of Celestial Guard hadn't come under pressure. These nuns looked content to remain in the square, not rampage through the Celestium. But the Holy City was a place of silent reflection on the grace of Kore and this sort of racket just wouldn't do.

'Find out who their spokes . . . um, woman? . . . is and send her to me.'

Twenty minutes later he was enthroned in the lesser hall where he usually met potentially embarrassing supplicants, with a cohort of Kirkegarde around him and Exilium Excelsior at his back. After the attacks a month ago he was nervous of admitting unknowns. He glanced behind him at Mazarin Beleskey, who watched curiously. Maz was a noted gnostic scholar – and unofficially his bloodman, his chief assassin.

A delegation of three Sisters of Kore was admitted without fuss and they genuflected before him respectfully. Wurther peered at the nun leading the delegation: Valetta della Rodrigo. *You're not revolting at all*, he thought, eyeing her comely face. 'Valetta, welcome. I grieve for your family's loss.' Her father, Rodrigo Prelatus, had died on Reeker Night, either trying to protect Wurther or kill him – in the confusion no one really knew who'd done what to whom.

The dusky-faced nun genuflected again. Her face had some of that same absolute devotion to higher powers as her compatriot Exilium. Estellayne was a devout country: the source of wonderful revenues, but a lot of embarrassing fanatics too. Wurther tried to avoid the place.

'Your Holiness has an excellent memory,' Valetta said. Her face might be filled with idealism, but her voice was the low purr of a seasoned tavern girl.

'Your father was a tragic loss,' Wurther said, seeking to get behind the mask of righteous piety. 'What has so animated my dear Sisters in Kore today?'

Valetta joined her hands as if in prayer. Behind her, the other two nuns – both fleshy-faced, older Rondians – duplicated her stance. 'We've come to demand that Sisters of Kore be given equal status to men within the Church.'

'Demand' and 'Equality': two words he loathed. *Who do these trollops think they are?*

'Equal status? I don't understand,' he replied truthfully. 'Do you want concessions over the Convent Rule? Um ... nicer habits? Help me – I'm mystified.'

'Equality,' Valetta replied, as if correcting a stupid child. 'The right to be priests, to speak the liturgy, run a parish and enter the hierarchy.'

He almost laughed, but caught himself just in time when he saw that she really was serious. 'But you have your own hierarchy, Sister—'

'—which starts and ends below the rank of a common parish priest,' she retorted.

'But Corineus was a man.' That was usually enough to shut down this argument, he recalled. He recalled debates about the status of nuns in the Church College; admittedly, those had been couched as 'should nuns have a role in the mass?' and he'd never heard the argument won.

'An educated sister's devotion to Kore is the equal of a man's,' Valetta replied. 'Her understanding of scriptures is equal. An abbess has equal abilities in administration to a prelate or a crosier. Why can't we aspire to equal rank?'

'Because you're manifestly unsuited to do so. Women are made to nurture and raise children—'

Valetta pulled a pretend puzzled face. 'So those who chose the sisterhood are in fact lesser women?' she asked, knowing as well as he that scripture said the opposite, that all good women should aspire to be nuns.

Though if they did, we'd be extinct in a generation ... 'Of course not, but

147

semantics don't change nature. How safe would a woman be alone in a parish?'

'How safe is a man, untrained to the sword? Our safety lies in Kore's hands.'

'But who would respect a woman priest?'

'One who respects the word of Kore.'

'This is ridiculous. What is it you *really* want? An investigation into your father's death? Concessions regarding the retention of tithes you collect?'

'No!' Valetta exclaimed. 'We want what we've already said: *equality*.' She fixed Wurther with her large, rather captivating eyes. 'Grand Prelate, we know you're struggling to find replacements for the dead prelates, yet you're ignoring a goldmine in untapped female talent. There are abbesses with the required gnostic blood and *decades* of experience in administration and politics. Most are well-connected among the Great Houses. Think of the gratitude they would owe the reformer who allows them a place at the high table.'

Wurther stared. *Well, she's not stupid, is she?* Here he was, in something of a bind, and perhaps she was right and there were loyal votes to be purchased here. But the opportunistic gall of it was infuriating. 'I am not someone to be moved like a tabula piece, Sister! This audience is over. Your sisters will vacate the square by evening or I'll have them arrested.'

Valetta's face hardened. 'On what grounds?'

Wurther paused, because there were none, then jabbed a finger. 'Then camp there for eternity, for all I care. And at dawn when you're frozen and hungry, you'll go of your own volition.'

He rose and stomped his way out, Exilium at his shoulder. 'Women should know their place,' he fumed.

'A woman must serve Kore and her husband and their children,' Exilium said in response, quoting scriptures. 'The home and hearth of their God and husband is their rightful place, and only there will they find fulfilment.'

'Quite,' Wurther yawned. 'But these appear to want more than that, and apparently they're holier than you or me.' He studied the young guard with some amusement while waiting for Maz Beleskey to catch him up and asked, 'Are there women in your life, Exilium?'

'My family are in Estellayne, in my village. My mother is dead, but my sister looks after Papa, and I send them money when I can. I have no ties here. I have maintained my vows of chastity.'

Good grief! Wurther thought. 'Does the Celestium disappoint you, Exilium?'

'It is imperfect,' the young Estellan pronounced in his deadpan voice.

Wurther raised an eyebrow. 'Do you think perfection here on Urte is possible? Or is only Paradise perfect?' Of late he'd taken to asking his inflexible bodyguard such twisted theological questions; he took his entertainment where he could get it these days.

'I believe we must all strive for perfection. This world is a barren place sown with poor seed.'

'But is it better to burn an imperfect crop, or harvest what can be grown?'

Watching the young man's certainty collapse halfway through the act of opening his mouth was wonderfully rewarding. 'We must burn . . . er, no . . .' Exilium stammered, after a few moments' thought. 'But if something can saved . . . erm . . .'

'Something to ponder,' Wurther said, patting his shoulder. 'Ah, here's Maz. Give us some space, Exilium.' He took the scholar into a side-room; exposing Exilium's purity to the morass that was Beleskey's mind wouldn't be pretty. 'Well, Maz: is Valetta's request genuine, or an attempt to get inside our defences?'

'Well, yes or maybe no . . . that is to say . . . You know I think it is . . . Or not. A ruse, that is.' His thick owlish eyebrows were quivering as a dozen thoughts occurred to him at once, but Wurther was used to him by now. 'I believe that they believe, yes. Believers. Radicals. Dangerous.'

Wurther had that impression too. He also knew that every day nuns were abused, physically or mentally, by priests. The Church had an office for dealing with such matters – well, concealing and denying them, anyway. But he put the matter to one side for now; he had given Beleskey a far more critical mission. 'What have you learned from the surviving prelates?'

Like Lyra, he had his own small group of survivors from Reeker Night, who'd been left in Maz Beleskey's 'care'.

'Ah. Well . . . a little. That is to say, much . . .' Beleskey replied. 'There is a, *yes*, a presence . . . a possessor . . . and intriguingly, Master, it is the same presence in each: a *simultaneous possession* by one entity – never seen the like before. Rooted in blood . . . yes . . . or perhaps more accurately, *fluids*. This prevents exorcism with wizardry. And it's *highly* infectious if internalised . . . Fascinating.'

'So there's no cure?'

'Well, no . . . well, actually, yes . . . for the lesser infected, prolonged fasting and exposure to sunlight is efficacious, but for those of deeper infection – the shepherds, not the herd, you see – with them it's more embedded. We've made progress, which to say some . . . but not much.'

'What about weapons against them? Protections? Detecting them?'

'Well, and there's the thing, yes indeed. Resilient . . . very resilient . . . one can amputate a limb and they survive . . . but not the head or heart. Too crucial. One contains the intellect and the other anchors the possession. Head and heart, yes . . . Most efficient. Brilliant, yes.'

'And counter-measures?'

'Well . . . they all look sick, obviously, but it's not the riverreek, that's a mask . . . appropriately enough! Silver seems to disrupt the link to the possessing entity. Certain herbs are poisonous to them . . . though only for a time. Allium, primarily, garlic, yes . . . also aconite – wolfsbane, fleabane or monkshood – poisonous enough in its own right, but even in small doses it disrupts possession. Most fascinating. I've had to infect more prisoners from our dungeons, just to have enough subjects to study.'

There it is, Wurther thought, *the moment in every conversation when the madness behind Beleskey's scatter-brained charm is revealed.* But he had no huge objection – prisoners were expensive to keep and most were heretics anyway. At least by helping Maz Beleskey's research they would die usefully.

'Are you informing Setallius of your findings?'

Beleskey looked startled. 'Am I supposed to?' He wasn't really a sharer of information.

'At the moment, Lyra and I are working together, and your findings might keep her alive as well as me.'

'Well, I see . . . and good, of course . . . public-spirited, yes . . . but no. Which is to say, I've not reached any *conclusions*, Master. The theories remain unproven and to treat them as facts could be dangerous, and well . . . Setallius is just a cutthroat, really. No elegance. No . . . *finesse*. He doesn't even use quality poisons, you know.'

'Some would call poison a woman's weapon,' Wurther remarked. Poison was Beleskey's favoured tool.

'Oh no, no . . . an intelligent man's weapon, to be sure . . . But women only? No. No. Not really. Which is to say—'

'Which is to say, this interview is over,' Wurther interrupted. 'Very well, keep your findings between the two of us for now. But reach some conclusions, Maz! We must have counter-measures, in case these maniacs try again!'

'Of course, of course,' Beleskey replied. 'You know, whoever is behind this is a genius. Probably mad, of course, but genius is involved.'

It probably takes one to recognise the other . . . 'Do you have a name in mind?'

'Ervyn Naxius, of course. This really is his field,' Beleskey said, with a touch of awe.

'The Ordo Costruo renegade?'

'Quite, quite. If he's still alive, of course.' Beleskey made a helpless gesture, spun around as if chasing an elusive fly, then wandered out without farewell or genuflection.

Infuriating man, but valuable. Wurther nodded at Excelsior, who'd remained by the door – he presumed the young man slept, but since he'd appointed him, his guard was always to be found waiting outside. Then he pulled the door shut and shambled wearily to his desk.

We must be prepared. Our enemies will not give us long to regroup; I can feel it. He reached for the brandy.

Dawn proved Wurther's prediction about the sisters' durability wrong: they'd huddled together to sleep, and by mid-morning there were many more. They sang hymns, over and over, the sound penetrating the massive halls, echoing along normally silent corridors and into forgotten rooms. By the end of the first week, they had filled the Forum Evangelica with tents, and by then, reports were coming in of similar gatherings in every city in Koredom.

Wurther quickly became exasperated, especially when he heard that Valetta intended to petition the empress for support.

Let one damned woman have a taste of power and they all want it.

9

Refugees

Men and Beasts

The greatest sin of an Animage would be to create hybrids of men and beasts. The reasons are multitude, from the morality of carving up living men and women and turning them into half-beasts, to the dread that the resultant creature might be better equipped for survival than mankind. Yet the Pallas Animagi still cross that line, without sanction! When will the Crown – ahem – rein them in?

DUKE OSMAN BORODIUM, DUKE OF ARGUNDY, 862

Kedron Valley
Early Augeite 935

Both Paruq and Kyrik were deeply troubled by Cassiphan's disappearance and the loss of the wind-vessels, but the Vlpa clan had little option but to go on. Thraan offered the missionaries a place on the march, but Paruq declined. 'The Shihad is coming,' the Godspeaker said. 'If we walk east long enough, we will eventually meet them.' Then he added in Kyrik's ear, 'We wouldn't be welcome in your homeland, my friend.'

'But you'll be stranded in the middle of nowhere!'

'But safe in the hands of Ahm,' the Godspeaker replied.

'At least take food and horses.'

Those Paruq was happy to accept, and Thraan was generous, gifting spare mounts and pack-horses, fully supplied for the journey.

'You must avoid Rondian patrols in the Kedron and the Brekaellen,' Kyrik warned him. 'Head due east until you strike the Silas River, then follow its banks to the sea. Stick to that, and you should be safe.'

Kyrik was afraid he was seeing his beloved mentor for the last time, but he and the Vlpa had to resume their trek west. The question of their own route into Mollachia remained unresolved, and now there was another problem: they'd seen windskiffs, square-rigged legion craft, doubtless from Collistein, the nearest legion town, and there was no doubt they'd been spotted. Forces were doubtless already being deployed against them.

Kyrik was riding with Thraan and Missef, lost in thought. Kyrik and Missef had little liking for each other – the shaman invariably spoke against him in council – but he was one of the three pillars of Sydian leadership, so he was making an effort to heed the man.

As a dust cloud appeared, the Nacelnik raised an arm and his warband halted. 'What is it?' blind Torzo, behind them, asked.

'Outriders,' Kyrik answered as the men galloped in, making for Thraan.

'We've found Gyapei, in open ground,' the first scout reported. 'No more than a few hundred, with as many cattle – easy pickings!'

'Gyapei?' Kyrik asked, bemused.

'Wool-men – Schlessen,' Missef sniffed. 'When we find them in our lands, we kill them. Long ago, the Wolf Clan of the Jergathai caught a tribe of Gyapei on the plains. There are still white-haired children born to the Wolves from the hundreds of women they took that day. The corpse mound reached a span in height.'

Kyrik recalled the Schlessen migratory party he'd seen at the Bunavian Gap. 'I might have seen this group.'

'We've got them ringed in,' the second scout told Thraan excitedly. 'Your son Groyzi found them! They're on a hill, four miles from here – they're trapped.'

Thraan looked at Kyrik. 'My son burns to avenge his brother. This could be a good blooding for him.'

'There was at least one mage among the group I saw,' Kyrik warned.

'Pah!' Missef spat. 'We will pin them with arrows, decimate them, then sweep in, take their cattle and women.' He licked his lips. 'You do not know our ways, Kirol of Mollachia.'

'Schlessen tribes seldom leave the forest,' Kyrik said, speaking directly to Thraan. 'Something strange is happening here. Be cautious.'

Thraan rubbed his whiskery jowls. He picked out two men in his retinue with rested horses. 'Ride back, find Groyzi and tell him to keep the Gyapei contained, but not to attack. I wish to observe this. We will slay their men and take their cattle. Gyapei women give good sport,' he added with a cold leer.

'Does the kirol disapprove?' Missef probed, sensing Kyrik's disquiet.

'I care not what happens to these Gyapei,' Kyrik replied, not quite truthfully; he'd seen enough rape and murder for this lifetime. 'But a mage-led party is not to be taken lightly.'

'We won't,' Thraan drawled. He issued a stream of orders and his riders began to pick up pace, cantering through the wagons, exchanging banter, with neither formation nor formality. Half an hour at the canter had taken them well ahead of their wains and shortly after, they saw their goal: a hilltop crowned with Schlessen warriors forming a shield-ring around their own wains, women and cattle.

As Thraan joined them, the riders called his name, touching hands to hearts.

There was a far different mood than with those he'd fought alongside in Mollachia a few months ago. They had been staunch, brave and oddly naïve, as if fighting on foreign soil had stripped away the ugly swagger Kyrik saw here. Today was about lust, for blood and women. If he'd had the choice, he'd have ridden away, but that wasn't an option. His status was unclear here and the Vlpa would be watching him to see his mettle.

In Mollachia I'll have the final say, but for now I must support Thraan.

When they reached the front of the encircling men, Groyzi – tall, hard-faced and desperate to prove himself – demanded the right to lead the assault. Kyrik felt a deeper unease set in: the Schlessen were arrayed in strong formation, men and women lined up side by side to fight, each with a large shield and war-spear, waiting with as much discipline as any legion. Their impressive helmets were horned, but Kyrik knew most soldiers eschewed such ornamentation as the horns could too easily be used against the helmet-wearer.

Only the Bullheads wear them: the fanatical worshippers of Minaus, the Schlessen war-god.

Stranger still were the giant horned beasts which were dotted through the lines.

An Animage could induce those bulls to charge . . . His eyes sought the Schlessen commander, the red-cloaked giant he'd seen in Bunavia, who was prowling behind the ranks, no doubt exhorting courage. When he came opposite Thraan, the Schlessen stepped through his ranks and stared down the slope. He was an impressive specimen of barbarian manhood, almost seven foot tall, Kyrik estimated, with the musculature to match. He was clad in a larger-than-standard legion breastplate and a red cloak and held a massive zweihandle one-handed.

'That's the man I saw,' he told Thraan. 'He's a mage. His men have legion experience, and perhaps more than one mage. See how the cattle are positioned – a battle-mage could control them and use them to attack.'

The burly chieftain scratched his cheeks, staring up at his opposite. 'The slope is too steep for a mounted charge. Our bowmen will destroy them.'

'No!' Groyzi protested. 'Their women are in the lines – most will die in our volleys!' He spat on the ground and bared his teeth. 'What use is a dead woman?'

'We will lose more men if we take them on head to head,' Thraan growled. 'Approach on foot with our best archers – target the men, volley after volley, then rush them when they break.' His eyes strayed from the giant Schlessen to a dusky-haired, copper-skinned beauty lurking behind him. 'The black-haired woman is mine.'

Kyrik felt a sick feeling in his stomach. *These are the men I'm bringing to Mollachia? How will they see our villages and towns after a few years? Are Valdyr and Dragan right? Is this a terrible mistake?*

'We should talk to them,' he said to Thraan.

'Why?' the chief asked, his narrowed eyes suspicious.

'Because something doesn't feel right! I don't doubt we can over-whelm them, but they've got something up their sleeves. If we parley, they might reveal what that is. It could save the lives of many riders.'

He glanced at Groyzi, who was poised to argue, and added, 'It might mean getting more of the women unharmed.'

The chief's son opened his mouth, then closed it again. Missef sniffed, but said nothing against him either.

Thraan considered, then grunted approval. 'Go then, Kirol. Offer the parley. You have the sorcerer's eyes, so you'll see their traps. Give them these terms: surrender their women and beasts and return to the forests unarmed. Or we'll take everything they have.'

They all knew that no man would accept such terms.

'I'll go too,' Groyzi said immediately. 'I would hear what the kirol says to them.'

To Kyrik's carefully concealed irritation, the Nacelnik agreed, and there followed a wait as a white cloth was found and brandished. When the Schlessen chief signalled approval, Kyrik and Groyzi set off up the slope. As soon as they were out of Thraan's earshot, Kyrik turned and grasped Groyzi's arm with kinesis-strengthened grip. 'Listen, Groyzi, son of Thraan: I will speak here and you will remain silent. Understood?'

'Take your hand back or lose it, Mollach. You don't want me as an enemy.'

'No, you don't want *me* as an enemy, boy.' Kyrik let pale light bleed into his eyes to further emphasise his mage-blood. In his experience bullies like Groyzi understood only force. 'I could snap you in half or burn your face off from a hundred paces. I could break you in front of your people with my bare hands. And I will too, if you undermine me again. Think on that, and remain silent before your betters.'

The young warrior's hand compulsively strayed towards his dagger-hilt.

'Touch that, and I'll break your arm.'

Groyzi looked away. 'You put on a pretty pretence, but I see you truly now, *magus*.'

'I don't care what you *think* you see. Now, follow and keep your mouth shut.' He brazenly turned away.

'You shouldn't turn your back on me.'

'I'll always see you coming,' Kyrik answered, striding away. He looked up and saw the giant Schlessen coming to meet him, his two-handed blade now sheathed in a shoulder-scabbard. They met about two-thirds of the way up the slope and stopped ten paces apart.

Up close, the Schlessen was truly immense. He was deeply tanned, his long dirty-blond hair matted and unkempt. His clothes were dusty and sweat-stained – he looked like he'd been on the march for some time – but he was clean-shaven like a legion ranker, and surprisingly young – mid-twenties, perhaps; Valdyr's age.

'Do you speak Rondian?' Kyrik called. *I was right: that's the over-cloak of a battle-mage, and that amber pendant is surely a periapt.*

'Yar,' the Schlessen replied, the sound issuing from the back of his throat. He looked Kyrik up and down with a frank gaze that took in his Sydian dress, his Rondian straight-sword and finished at his periapt. 'You're not a Sydian.' The giant glanced at Groyzi, who looked annoyed that the conversation had begun in Rondian, a language he didn't know. 'What are you doing riding with these *Wildenschaum*?'

Barbarian scum, Kyrik translated silently. 'I'm married to one,' he replied. He noticed that many of the men and women above weren't actually Schlessen, but they all looked positively ferocious. And most of the women had skin darker even than the Sydians: Eastern women, presumably brought back during the last Moontide. *He's been a Crusader, like me.* 'I'm Kyrik Sarkany, once of Midrea IV.'

The Schlessen considered, then said, 'Fridryk Kippenegger, Pallacios XIII.'

That stirred a memory. 'Didn't they mutiny?'

'Second Crusade – before my time.'

'Not before mine: I served in the Second Crusade.'

'But not the Third?'

'No.' Kyrik wasn't about to reveal that he'd been captured in the Second Crusade. 'You must have been in the Second Army? The men who got home, under Korion the Younger.'

'Yar. Seth Korion – the Lesser Son, we called him. A good man. So, what are your *Wildenschaum* doing out here? Did they get lost chasing their tails on the Wheel of Seasons?'

'I've given them land in Mollachia.'

The Schlessen cleared an ear theatrically. 'You've *given* them land?'

'Do you not know the name Sarkany?'

'Nay.'

'I'm the rightful King of Mollachia.'

'Ah. "Rightful" usually means "currently not",' the Schlessen noted.

Kyrik smiled at that. 'Truly. A nest of Rondian tax-farmers are plundering my lands and we don't have the strength to prevent it. So I went to Sydia to secure aid.'

'And you had to marry one to get their help?' Kippenegger said.

He's not slow. 'Aye. I've got twenty-five thousand of my wife's kin nearby. Your turn – why are you out here?'

'We're going to Becchio.'

It was Kyrik's turn to lift an eyebrow: Becchio was many, *many* miles south, in old Rimoni. It had been an independent city-state for many years now, after a collective of ex-legion mercenaries expelled the Rondian governor. Men went to hire out as sword-hands.

'Bad luck you bumped into us, then.'

The Schlessen shrugged. 'If this is the day that the Bullhead calls us to his feast, so be it.'

'You've got some of your legionaries in those lines?' Kyrik guessed.

'Yar – Minaus brought us together on Crusade. We are *bruden* – brothers – and we'll die for one another. Lakh and Keshi have broken on our shields, Mollach. We faced greater odds at Riverdown and Ardijah.'

Kyrik knew the names. If these were truly men of that disastrous Crusade, it felt even crueller that they meet their end in such a way. But he could see no way of turning Thraan from his course. Groyzi would get his bloodbath. He sighed and was about to deliver Thraan's mocking 'terms' when he paused.

'You said you *were* going to Becchio?'

'A Rondian patrol from Collistein captured one of us. We're going there to get him back.'

'Have you ever seen Collistein?' Kyrik asked incredulously. *Perhaps he's a fool after all?* 'It's got walls even you can't see over the top of.'

'Even so. We've a plan to get inside.'

'A good plan?'

'I guess you'll never know.' Kippenegger drawled. He paused, as if

159

weighing something up, then looked at Groyzi. 'I want to show you something in my camp, but not your *Wildenschaum* friend.' He winked, as if he'd sensed what had passed between them earlier. 'Will you accept my guarantee of your safety?'

Kyrik hesitated. This might be genuine . . . or an attempt to secure a hostage. 'I should warn you, most of the men down there wouldn't give a damn if you took my head off right now.'

'Such is the lot of a mage among "barbarians", eh? Are you coming?'

'All right.' Kyrik told Groyzi to wait, which pleased the young bravo not at all, then followed the Schlessen back up the slope. Kippenegger's dusky-haired woman stroked his arm as he passed, the lines of hard-faced men parting to permit Kyrik in. He noted the tension, the sweat of fear, but there was no panic, just a grim sense of resignation, even among the women.

'When I returned from the Crusade, many Rondian rankers chose to follow me,' Kippenegger said proudly, 'but my tribe was not welcoming. Even though they worked hard to fit in, they were treated as outsiders. After two years, they drove us out and since then, we've been going from tribe to tribe, as *freisoldat* – mercenaries. North to south, three years of war, never welcome, losing and gaining men as we went.'

He led Kyrik into the central enclosure, where most of the cattle were. Kippenegger patted their flanks as he passed. Kyrik noted that there were polearms and battle-axes piled amongst the cattle – fall-back caches, perhaps? A curious measure.

Kippenegger led him to a huge grizzled bull with scarred flanks, weirdly sitting on its haunches, watching them approach with almost human eyes. The Schlessen warrior went to the beast, laid a big hand on its head and turned back to Kyrik. 'We both know what will happen next, Mollach: we've been caught in the open, in lands we thought empty. A sad mischance, but in life, such misfortune can be fatal. We won't go cheaply, but in the end, lives will be lost and we will feast with Minaus. But I sense you're a man of reason: someone who can be persuaded to see the bigger picture, yar? I've known men like you. To enter Mollachia, you must pass Collistein. I know how we purpose to get in: how will you manage it?'

Excellent question. Kyrik was intrigued now. 'We'll think of something.'

'For us, the Rondians will simply open the gates.'

'Really?'

'Yar. See, what they'll think they're admitting is a herd of stray cattle. But instead, they will learn that they've admitted ... *this* ...'

Kippenegger stepped away from the bull.

Kyrik stared as the muscles of the creature altered, mostly around the hind legs, but also through the torso, spine, shoulders and neck as it rose to its hind legs and stood. It was massive, fully nine foot or more from hooved feet to horned crown. As the bull stood, his fore-hooves split into slab-like fingers. He picked up a battle-axe from the grass, glared down at Kyrik and bellowed, venting a spray of wet spittle. Kyrik took three steps back before he even realised, then saw the rest of the herd rise around him and almost swallowed his tongue.

'*Constructs?*'

The giant creature before him – the old bull – belched, then gruff, massively deep words spilled from his mouth. 'The grandsons of grand-sons of constructs, Magus.'

It can talk, *for Kore's Sake!* 'But there are laws—' Kyrik gasped.

'Laws are things written *after* crimes have been committed,' the bull replied, showing a truly astounding grip of words and reason.

I shouldn't show fear, Kyrik thought wildly. 'An arrow can pierce the strongest hides.'

The giant man-bull grunted and conjured a faint shielding around himself.

It has the gnosis too ... Kore's Blood!

'This is Maegogh, chief of the Mantauri,' Kippenegger told him. 'As the fame of my Bullheads grew, many joined us – and eventually we attracted *real* bullheads.'

'We needed people to protect us,' Maegogh the Mantaur rumbled. 'I can fight any ten men, but they came in the hundreds. We sought out Fridryk's people and revealed ourselves: we pretend to be his herd and he conceals us – in turn we fight for him at need.' Something like humour entered his voice. 'At first he thought I was his god.'

'I can see why,' Kyrik admitted, his mind swirling. Creating constructs

– making new life forms using Animagery – was strictly regulated under the Gnostic Codes, but Maegogh was right, laws were written only after some terrible misuse of power. He'd heard rumours of the early Animagi making fish-men, snake-men, horse-men, wolf-men, winged men and anything else they thought could be put in service of the empire, but ordinary people had been frightened and the magi themselves had become alarmed at the notion that constructs with the gnosis might be superior to them, so laws had been made and the full weight of Church and Empire directed at controlling the Animagi. Now constructs that were anything more than superior beasts of burden, winged mounts for the military or exotic jousting beasts for mage-nobles were very rare.

But all that was secondary to his primary thought: *If they can get into Collistein . . .*

'Why would you go all the way to Collistein just to rescue one man?'

'Not a man, a Mantaur,' Kippenegger answered.

Kyrik's mind raced. 'You're afraid the Rondians will realise what they've captured and call in the Inquisition?'

'Correct,' Maegogh rumbled. 'My people are told not to reveal their true nature if captured, but this one is young: we need him back before he does something that betrays us all.'

Kippenegger turned to Kyrik. 'So you see, when your Sydian friends try to shoot us with arrows, they will encounter gnostic shielding. When they charge, they will meet a foe such as they have never encountered. And we may be only hundreds while you have thousands, but the slaughter will be so great that Minaus himself will dip his goblet in the gore. You may prevail, but your widows will outnumber your wives ere the day is done.'

He said all that with the conviction of one raised on epics of eternal quests to slay draken and rescue maidens; but despite this, Kyrik believed things would likely go exactly as he stated. *And then whatever chance I have of getting this clan into Mollachia will be gone.*

'You're right. We need to work together. But how can I convince the Vlpa that you're allies, not demons?'

'I have an idea about that too,' the Schlessen replied smugly.

*

It took some negotiation, then Kyrik re-emerged from the thicket of Schlessen spears, still dazed at what he'd seen. Groyzi was waiting impatiently, stalking beneath the eyes of the defenders like a hungry wolf. 'What took so damned long?' he snapped at Kyrik.

'Just a few details,' Kyrik said, swaggering past. He ignored all questions as they returned to the Vlpa lines, until he was in front of Thraan, with the simmering Groyzi barely able to restrain himself.

'Well?' Thraan asked.

'They've agreed to your terms,' Kyrik said.

A derisive sneer passed through the nearest riders. No warrior would ever surrender his women and beasts. Thraan looked surprised. 'That's unexpected,' he rumbled, peering hard at Kyrik. 'What's the catch?'

'They accept, provided three of our warriors can successfully butcher one of their cattle.'

That brought everyone up short, then the air exploded with laughter. But Thraan leaned forward in the saddle and gestured Kyrik closer. 'Is this a trick?'

'In a way. It's more of a demonstration,' Kyrik admitted. 'It's a bargaining position. But there's nothing to stop you agreeing, then changing your mind afterwards.'

'And if my three warriors cannot do this feat?'

'They still agree to serve you for one month, but they keep their cattle and women.'

'Their women will serve us regardless,' Groyzi snarled. 'Let's just kill the Gyapei fools and have done. We don't need this damned exhibition.'

The chieftain looked Kyrik in the eye. 'You approve this "test", don't you? Whose side are you on here?'

'Ours: this is a thing worth doing, Chief Thraan. You'll learn much.'

Thraan ruminated, then growled, 'Very well, I'll trust you. I accept: we will kill their bull for them.' He weighed up Kyrik again. 'And if I see nothing to change my mind, we will unleash our arrows and blades thereafter.' *You're on trial here too, Kirol*, his look said.

Predictably, Groyzi demanded the right to be one of the three, even though Kyrik tried to warn him not to do so, and selected two of his friends, Durvi and Orstyn, battle-hardened and capable hunters. An area on the flatland below the hill was designated.

A third of the Schlessen came down the slope and marked off one side while the Sydians enclosed the other, both sides exchanging taunts and threats. Kyrik found the atmosphere surreal. Many of the Vlpa women and children clambered onto wains and horses to see, but those closest to the Schlessen group were all heavily armed riders: it was clear that whatever happened, Thraan intended to attack immediately this display was done.

Kyrik entered the circle and explained the agreed rules to the watching Vlpa: the men would have ropes and spears. Bows weren't permitted, for fear of hitting watchers, but the spears could be thrown. If hunter or beast left the enclosed space, they would be deemed to have forfeited the contest.

Groyzi, Durvi and Orstyn entered on foot to raucous cheers; the bull – Maegogh, restored to his natural form – trotted in slowly. Kyrik felt a little ashamed, ambushing his own people like this, but it was necessary if they were to realise they weren't facing an outnumbered enemy but a powerful potential ally. Without such a demonstration, they wouldn't believe. He looked across the square at Kippenegger, they both nodded and Thraan shouted, 'Begin!'

The three Sydians fanned out with practised speed, closing in on the bull, who regarded them placidly. If any of them even saw the subtle shift of muscle in its haunches and shoulders, they didn't realise what it portended.

The three riders struck as one. Groyzi had clearly counselled them to treat the situation as a potential trick, because they showed no complacency, coordinating their attack so the bull had as little chance to avoid the thrown weapons as they could allow.

But as the spears flew, Maegogh burst into motion, hurtling forward in a lunging, climbing gait even as he rose to his hind legs. His flanks lit with pale light that dashed away the spears – one left a graze on his left flank, one missed – and one he *caught* in his left hand. The watching crowd recoiled, crying out, and some began to grasp for weapons, but Kyrik ran to the edge of the perimeter, shouting, '*Hold your weapons! Hold!*'

Maegogh gripped the caught spear by its head, reared to his full height and swept it around, taking Durvi in the shoulder with the butt-end and dashing him to the ground. Orstyn, pulling out a scimitar, tried to close with him, but the giant Mantaur backhanded him brutally across the chest, leaving him on his back gasping for air.

Groyzi backed away. 'We're betrayed!' he shrieked, as Maegogh closed in. 'Kill it!'

Maegogh advanced on his hind legs, spinning the spear in one hand, bellowing wordlessly, towering over the rider. No amount of shouting from Kyrik could keep the weapons of the riders sheathed any longer, and the watching women and children were shoved to the rear as panic threatened to break out.

Thraan spurred his horse into the arena. '*ENOUGH!*' he roared. He glared furiously at Kyrik as he interposed himself between his son and the Mantaur. '*STOP!*' He jabbed a finger at Kippenegger. 'We accept your service! Call off your beast!'

Maegogh halted and said, 'The "beast" can call itself off, herder!'

Thraan gaped, and his horse almost threw him. But he regained control and cried angrily, 'This charade is over! Vlpa, return to your tents!' He whirled on Kyrik. 'Attend me, Kirol!'

'If any other man did as you did, I'd have him torn limb from limb,' Thraan shouted, his spittle spattering Kyrik's tunic. Groyzi and Missef watched, just as enraged. Thraan's rant had begun the moment the tent flap fell closed and he was still shouting. 'You humiliate my son, who will one day be chieftain! You risk a stampede that endangers us all! You make deals behind my back and corner me into accepting them – is *this* how a Kirol of Mollachia acts?'

'You needed to see what they were,' Kyrik retorted. '*Everyone* did. I told Groyzi not to be one of the three – he wasn't hurt, or even touched. I'm sure his pride will survive – and now we have allies.'

And I have fresh enemies, he thought.

'They're *monsters*,' Missef snarled. 'You make deals with daemons!'

'I'll do whatever is required to get us into Mollachia,' Kyrik answered. 'They can get us past Collistein and into Mollachia – and *that* means a future for our people!'

'I see no good coming of this,' Thraan grumbled, but Kyrik could see he was wavering.

'But I do,' said Torzo, his voice gentler than the others. 'Kirol Kyrik has found a wondrous thing. Used correctly, he could see us safe in our new home in a matter of two months.' Then his voice took on a warning edge. 'Used wrongly, it could bring down all the weight of the Rondian Empire upon us.'

Thraan scowled, but he held the seer in high regard. 'Very well,' he said finally, 'we will proceed towards Collistein. But this is on *your* head, Kirol Kyrik. Get us into Collistein, and you'll be a hero.'

'He tricked me,' Groyzi snarled, 'and I'll have satisfaction—'

'Silence, my son,' the chief retorted. 'He gave you a chance to withdraw. When the beast rose, you faced it. Our people saw that. Your honour is intact. Now hold your peace!'

Groyzi looked far from placated, but he bowed his head. Missef whispered something in his ear and without another word, the young man stalked away.

'I'll find a way to make peace with Groyzi, I promise,' Kyrik told Thraan. 'In the meantime, we have a plan now to get into Mollachia – through Collistein. We finally have our route!'

Mollachia

The sense of impending doom engendered by his vision in the chapel stayed with Valdyr. Every night he dreamed of Asiv, and some days he found himself jumping at shadows. The new moon heralded the beginning of Augeite, the start of autumn in Mollachia. Villagers built bonfires and broached casks of oszisor, the rich malt ale. The Vitezai Sarkanum crept from the wild into outlying hamlets where the Rondians never came, to dance and sing with the locals – but in the towns, the turn-of-the-season celebrations were stamped out by the Rondian soldiers.

Governor Inoxion's Imperial Legion was still idle in the lower valley, but since Sacrista Delestre had recovered her brother's desecrated body, she'd been whipping her remaining men into action, leading incursions and torching the farms of anyone suspected of aiding the rebels.

'The people are on our side,' Dragan maintained. 'She reaches for us, but grasps only air.'

The riddle was how to proceed from here. The Vitezai ruled the wilds, but Inoxion had the lower valley and Sacrista had the upper valley and the mines, the heart and veins of the kingdom. The rebel leaders gathered at a hunting lodge on the Osiapa River, sixty miles upstream from Lake Droszt. The old lodge had grown into the landscape; even from the air, one had to know where to look to make it out. The central hall had the air of a throne room; the rosewood chairs had a tangle of wolves carved into them in a bewildering, entrancing style.

Dragan placed Valdyr at the head of the table, although he was almost the youngest present. Dragan sat at his right, with Rothgar Baredge, the laconic Stonefolk ranger, on his other side, next to Juergen Tirlak and Nilasz Pobok. On the other side of the table sat fourteen-year-old Hykkan, Thraan's fourth son, with a grey-braided Vlpa rider named Zened, and Hajya, Kyrik's wife. Hykkan was clearly on Zened's leash, and Zened was clearly in awe of Hajya. The rest of their people were now ensconced in the Domhalott.

Valdyr no longer feared Hajya, but he couldn't look at her without recalling the black-haired women of the breeding-houses. But beyond her, at the far end of the hall, Dragan's daughter Sezkia was laying out lunch, and she was everything a Mollach woman was meant to be: blonde, pretty, pink-cheeked and demure. He guessed Dragan was parading her for his eyes.

She glanced up and flashed a shy smile and he was momentarily captivated by the way all the available light in the gloomy lodge seemed to find its way into her hair and skin. There was a welcoming curve to her hips and a gentle softness to her face that hinted at a caring heart. *She's too perfect for me ... too pure.* Her radiance made the scars on his back itch and brought heat to his face. He looked away again.

'The soldiers in the taverns are saying that the East have invaded, that Pontus has fallen,' Rothgar was saying. 'An imperial army is gathering to repel the invaders.'

Valdyr wondered whether that was the true explanation for his vision and not the Vlpa migration; he had no idea what it might mean for Mollachia.

'Perhaps Inoxion and Delestre will leave?' Dragan suggested.

Rothgar shook his head. 'Not according to local gossip: they say Inoxion would rather plunder us than risk his neck against the Shihad. And Sacrista is driving her men hard to extract all she can before her contract expires.'

'Our scouts say the governor never leaves the lower valley,' Zened said. 'For now, they merely watch us. But how will Kirol Kyrik bring our people into the kingdom? Surely the way we came, your Sunrise Path, is impassable to wagons and cattle?'

'It is,' Rothgar confirmed, 'so he'll have to come in via Collistein or loop around to the south and come up the Reztu. Both ways are guarded. Can we contact him?'

They all looked at Hajya, who shook her head. 'The mountains prevent contact without relay-staves and we don't have that art. But surely the Reztu route is impossible? My husband will lead the clan through Collistein.'

'The fortress at Collistein is formidable,' Dragan said. 'We don't have the capability to attack even the lesser fortress at Registein. The kirol must make his own way – and we must continue our fight here. The most we can do is ensure that Rondian eyes are fixed firmly on the valley. The question is how.'

They all turned to look at Valdyr.

The real question, Valdyr thought, *is actually whether I can summon another storm – and is that all I can do? What are the limits – and what are the rules?*

'I know what you're asking,' he told them, 'but the answer is, I don't know. I think I must return to Watcher's Peak and see what I can learn.'

The supportive looks they all gave him lifted some of the gloom from his heart.

The rest of the meeting was about logistics: ensuring the Vlpa horses had feed enough to be ready for the next phase of operations; picking out weak points in the Delestre supply chain from the mines in Bane-zust to Ujtabor and on to Lake Droszt and the ferries; and recruitment: young Mollach men were joining them every day now, most of them simply wandering into the woods until a scout found them.

'If they can find us, so can the Rondians,' Dragan said.

'Inoxion's men are scared to come looking,' Juergan said. 'They think if they hide behind the townsfolk, we can't touch them. Sacrista is more reckless – we can isolate her men, maybe hurt her some more.'

It was a good thought to finish on. After they dined, Valdyr went out onto the balcony, feeling Sezkia watching him. He noted that his heart was beating anxiously, his skin flushed. *I've lain with hundreds of women, but none by choice.*

Dragan's hope was obvious, but Valdyr honestly didn't know if his heart could beat for *any* woman; in his final years in the breeding-houses he'd come to loathe life so much he'd become almost impotent, despite all the drugs and mesmerism the Keshi magi used to arouse him.

Asiv did that to me. The thought of lying with *anyone* was nauseating and the prospect of trying to forge an emotional connection was equally frightening, so when he heard footsteps, he didn't turn but stared at the trees as if they were more fascinating than a beautiful young woman.

This will be easier if I don't look at her.

'My lord,' Sezkia said, her voice deferential, tentative, 'would you care for some wine?' Her voice shivered through him, the hint of a melody in the timbre of her words, as if she might break into song at any moment.

My back is a mess of scars. My face is gloomy, my eyes are haunted and I never smile. I have no appetites any more. I have nothing to offer you . . . He could imagine Dragan nudging her towards him, telling her to look beyond the *ugliness* and the *coldness* and all the things that *frightened* her and instead think about thrones and a child who just *might* become a king.

'When we were young,' he murmured, 'I was the laughing child; Kyrik was the serious one, always anxious to please our father. I didn't think about serious things, because I knew Kyrik would see to them.'

'My mother says all men have a boy inside them,' Sezkia replied, with surprising assurance.

'Even your father?'

He'd meant it as a jest, because he couldn't imagine Dragan as a boy. But Sezkia didn't smile. 'I think she spoke in hope rather than certainty.' She handed him a goblet. 'It's Midrean claret.'

He accepted the cup and raised it to her in an awkward salute, no idea what to say. 'Thank you,' he managed when invention failed. She hovered, then curtseyed and vanished.

Kyrik would have said something complimentary, he chided himself.

He sighed heavily, the wine like blood in his throat. Then he heard more footfalls and his heart sank. He turned and saw Hajya, measuring her weathered, nut-brown face, greying hair and sensuous mouth. She was ten years his senior, older than Kyrik by three, and there was nothing uncertain about her.

'Kyrik told me of your power,' she said, without preamble. 'He says it's different to the gnosis: that you draw on all the spirits of the aether. That you must *persuade*, not command. It is a mighty hammer, beside which the gnosis is a dagger-blade – that's what he said. But do you require my aid in any way with it?'

'No,' he replied curtly – then he gambled on her understanding: 'But about, um . . .'

'About Sezkia?' Hajya said. 'Not very subtle, are they? They're probably afraid I'll try to interest you in one of my Sfera if they don't hurry. One brother married to a barbarian is bad enough for them, I'm sure.'

'I'm not . . . I mean to say—'

'You don't need to explain. I see you, Valdyr Sarkany: you don't want a woman – you don't want *anyone*. But they don't see that, and they will try to make you marry.'

'They fear for Mollachia if Kyrik is slain, and—'

'They fear a half-Sydian child more. I'm not blind, Valdyr. These men who huddle around Dragan fear my kind more than they fear the Rondians. All their hopes are with you now: the storm-caller, the hero-prince. To them, *you're* their future king.'

'I love my brother. I'll die before he does.'

'Don't voice such words. The gods hear them.' She gazed at him with a sympathy that made him uncomfortable. 'I'm no healer, Valdyr, but I've seen a lot of people. You fear intimacy, but intimacy will heal you.'

'But I don't know what to say to her.'

'Words will come when they're ready. That you feel you need to say anything at all reflects well on you. Many men would simply take and not give a damn whether she wanted him in return. Too many men wish to conquer bodies when they should wish to woo hearts. Those are worth much more.'

She didn't linger, to his relief. And thankfully, he was left in peace that night and permitted to find his own path to sleep.

The next morning he set out on the journey to Watcher's Peak, with Rothgar and his rangy hunting hound for company. He'd not really expected to see Sezkia again, but she joined the men farewelling him and shyly pressed a token into his hand: a copper draken pendant on a leather cord. 'For luck,' she said.

'Thank you,' he managed to stammer, and hurried away. But he did remember to turn back and raise a hand, which drew a cautious smile from her. Then, burningly conscious of the men watching, he strode away with the ranger, north and west towards the sacred mountain.

It wasn't too far, only thirty miles or so, but the terrain was hard, full of river-crossings, steep climbs and difficult slopes where shifting stone and shallow-rooted bushes made the way hazardous. Rothgar led the way; he knew the trails as well as any man. They encountered rains as cold as snow and made damp camp in a pine stand, only risking fire after dark, in a pit deep enough to hide the flames.

'Have you ever married?' Valdyr asked.

Rothgar stroked his beard thoughtfully. 'I had a wife when I was younger. Tongue like a leather strap. But she died of a fever one winter. The taverns have girls, when the need strikes, but dogs are better company. They don't mind bad smells or snoring.' He stroked the hound's back and it wagged its tail.

'But how do you talk to them?'

'Dogs?' Rothgar chuckled. 'Easy – they're good listeners!'

'No, women!'

'Ah, there's the secret. As far as I can see, you don't talk: you listen.

A woman is born with ten times more words inside her than a man: let her speak them.'

It was a strange notion, but oddly reassuring, because it implied that he didn't have to *do* anything, just *be*. But still the fear of being *exposed* roiled inside him. *What if I simply can't be with a woman any more?*

He turned his mind to his brother and told Rothgar of their lives growing up. When they were children, Kyrik had shown him so much: riding, hunting, swimming, even caving in the hills near Hegikaro. Then came the Crusade, when they'd been pulled apart – and when they were eventually reunited, neither was the same. But earlier that year, incarcerated by the Delestre siblings and Governor Inoxion, they'd found each other again in rambling confessions and memories and wordless communion as they watched each other die.

You were my hero, Kyrik. You're still who I would aspire to be, if the world let me.

'I don't want to be king,' he told Rothgar. 'I want my brother to live a long life. He's suited to it; he could lead a court or an army. I'm too ... inward-looking. I'm no ruler.'

'Then be the pillar he stands on,' Rothgar suggested. 'Be his strong right hand.'

'I like that,' Valdyr replied. *I can be the storm that you call down on our enemies, Brother.*

They tramped onwards next day, the hound questing before them, sniffing every tree and yapping happily as they made their way through the tangle of hills and woods that was Feher Szarvasfeld. By the time Watcher's Peak towered over them it was late afternoon, so they camped in the mouth of the old Rahnti Mines, whose tunnels led all the way through to the plains around Lake Jegto.

The next morning Valdyr shook hands with Rothgar and set off alone. Watcher's Peak was no place for the unwelcome; there was a reason it had been shunned for years. Within minutes of leaving the trail-marker – a stag's skull and antlers nailed to a wooden post – low clouds closed in and he found himself climbing through a shrinking world. The wind dropped; his panted breath and the crunch of his boots on the stones were the only sounds. Then something whimpered away to the left. Curious, Valdyr turned to see a dark shadow slumped against a stone, eyes glinting in the mist. As he approached, it gave a snarl. It was a male wolf, a mangy, half-mad thing. There was a long tear in its side and another on its back; blood matted the fur and its right hind leg was crooked. It lay beside a small pool; that was probably all that had been keeping it alive. The mud around the pool was thick with paw prints, mostly wolf, but also a set of cloven hooves.

There were tales of the white stags of Feher Szarvasfeld, of curses that destroyed those who hunted them. Perhaps the same curse applied to wolves? Valdyr stepped closer and the beast tried to lunge at him; heavy jaws snapped, powerful enough to break bones, but he stayed just out of reach. It was impossible not to see himself in the beast's plight: the damage and the desire to endure. He wished he had the gnosis so that he might aid it somehow, but the best he could do was to pull strips of dried meat from his food pouch and toss them to the creature. It nuzzled them suspiciously, then gulped them down.

'Better to let it die,' a chill voice called from a rock upslope, only a few yards away, and Valdyr spun, shocked that someone could get so close – but then he saw who it was and understood. Zlateyr – or Zillitiya, as the Sydians called him – was the hero who'd come to this backward mountain kingdom centuries ago and conquered it. When he'd died, Zlateyr had become as one with the land: a dwymancer whose spirit now haunted the place. He was a big man, taller even than Valdyr, who was over six foot, with broad shoulders and a lean, almost cruel face. His beard was closely trimmed and his long black hair caught up in a topknot. He had a drawn bow in his hands and his leathers were stained with sweat and blood.

'Brother Wolf came here with his pack, hunting the White Stag,' the hero noted. He glanced behind him and the mist parted, revealing the scattered corpses of a dozen or more wolves, some jutting with a single arrow to the heart, others torn by antlers. Something snorted and bellowed in the mists above. 'A hunter should know better.'

Valdyr dropped to one knee. 'My lord.'

'Rise, Valdyr. I'm not your lord, only your forebear.' The weapons vanished from Zlateyr's grasp and reformed hooked to his back. He clasped hands with Valdyr, then a dagger appeared in his hand, hilt turned towards Valdyr. 'End his suffering, if you wish.'

Valdyr took the blade and turned to the wolf. As if it sensed what had been said, it whimpered, then lifted its head and glared sullenly up at Valdyr. *I am you*, that look said.

Valdyr dropped his blade hand. 'I can't.'

'It's broken,' the hunter replied, his voice devoid of sentimentality. 'If it were to survive, it will be unable to hunt as it did. It will be outcast from other packs and die in the wilds, unless it finds its way to the lowlands and hunts sheep and chickens ... and men.'

'Can you heal it?' Valdyr asked.

Zlateyr turned his head towards him, a glint of challenge in his eyes. 'Can you?'

'My brother says dwyma can achieve big things, not small things.'

'Big things are made of small things,' Zlateyr replied.

Valdyr swallowed and stared at the wounded beast. 'But I don't even know where to start.'

'Start inside yourself,' said a gentle but strong woman's voice. Luhti, Zlateyr's sister, appeared out of the mists. The tall, full-bodied woman had a palpable sense of mystery; she reminded him of Hajya. 'You've touched the sacred Elétfa tree. Its sap runs in your veins now. Its energy is all around us, everywhere. You, the varazslo, must coax and persuade it.'

She pulled him to his knees beside the fallen wolf, which snapped at her, but its teeth closed only on air. Luhti pulled Valdyr's hand to the beast's torn flank and her voice whispered in his mind. *Lay yourself open*, she said. *Unlock yourself. The Elétfa will do the rest.*

He didn't know what she meant, but he could feel the quiet that radiated from her, the stillness within, and he tried to emulate that. *Listen to the wind*, she told him silently. *Smell the air, taste the spit in your mouth. Feel the stone through your knees and the press of your clothing on your skin. Be aware of everything ... and then remove them, one by one, until only the Elétfa remains.*

It took a long time until he could no longer feel the earth beneath him or the clothing on his back. There was neither smell, nor taste, only her hypnotic voice. Then he opened his eyes and saw a giant tree made of light, its branches becoming the roots that fed it and life streaming through its tangled branches ... *The Elétfa*, he marvelled, eyes wide ... then it was a beating heart, pulling in stale blood and sending it out again revitalised and rich with life ... just an organ, just a pump, but he followed its outward veins and found them embedded in the stone, the water, in the mist and the light above, in the insects that crawled in the crevices and the worms in the soil ... and in the wolf's torn and broken body.

Be whole.

The wolf snarled a warning, but it was just instinct and reflex. His hands, made of light, pressed into the animal's flanks and he felt something change, in the wolf – and in himself.

Done, Luhti said, *but a healed body is not a healed mind, Valdyr. You know this.*

How can I heal his mind?

You've reached the limit of what can be done, she replied. *Like yourself, this one must find his way back to what he should be.*

Then his vision cleared and suddenly the world was around him once more, the stone and the grass, the mist, the weight of clothing and flesh upon him. Luhti and Zlateyr were facing him and he envied them for being *made of life*, for all they were long dead.

The wolf was cautiously standing, stiff from having lain so long. Its hind leg was now straight and its wounds scabbed over. Idyr gaped, amazed – *I did it!* – but when he reached out, the ungrateful beast pinned back its ears and snarled, backing away. But it didn't go far.

'His name is Gricoama – Greymane. He's yours now,' Zlateyr said, 'and you're his. You've touched his soul.'

Valdyr guessed that meant more than he knew, but as he looked up at the hunter and his sister, he realised in alarm that they were now fifteen, twenty yards away, floating off without moving a muscle. 'Wait! I have to ask you—'

'You already have the answers,' Luhti called as the mists enfolded them and they vanished.

'No, wait!' He began to follow but the wolf yowled and he halted as the fog closed in, a forbidding wall of darkening grey. He'd wanted to ask so much – but somehow he knew he could walk the mists all day and night without finding Zlateyr and Luhti again.

Perhaps a few hours at a time is all they can be here? Or are the limits in me?

But Luhti said that he already had the answers. They'd placed a storm in his hands five weeks ago; they'd shown him the Elétfa. *Big things are made of small things. I can work with that.*

Sacrista Delestre, I'm coming for you . . .

The wolf named Gricoama howled, a keening wail, a warning to all his prey.

Sacrista looked up, her ears straining. From somewhere beyond the towering cliffs lining the Banezust Road, somewhere at the very edges of perception, a wolf had howled – a common enough sound here, but somehow the sound vibrated through her, making her ears thrum and her bones quiver. Then she shook off the moment, angry to be spooked by so small a thing.

Wolves? I've got worse than that to worry about! She turned back to survey the caravan they were escorting down the gorge road, the wagons laden with silver-bearing rock. Her rankers were nervous – they'd been ambushed here before, by archers from above. They were three miles north of Ujtabor now and the drivers, a mix of her men and Mollachs pressed into service, none trusting the others, were fretting. Last week one of her drivers had got too close to the edge and only just managed to leap clear; he'd blamed a Mollach driver for pushing him off the road.

She hadn't known the right of it, but she'd hung the Mollach anyway.

She'd once thought Robear wasteful for the numbers of treacherous peasants he'd executed, but she'd long since overtaken his body-count. Any family with an unaccounted-for male had their business or farm torched; if they resisted, she hung them all. *It doesn't matter what I leave behind after I've avenged Robear.*

'Milady Sacrista,' Rafe Gabrian called, cantering up and swinging his mount into step with hers, 'Governor Inoxion has come. He's waiting in the village below.'

'About rukking time,' Sacrista growled. Since she'd decided to stay to ensure Kyrik and Valdyr Sarkany dangled from the gibbet of their own castle, she'd been pestering Inoxion with demands for assistance. Finally, he was listening. She no longer cared whether she fulfilled the tax-farming contract profitably; she was here to kill two men and get out, and if that meant giving Inoxion whatever he wanted, then so be it.

'How many men has he brought with him?'

'Just a guard cohort and a couple of magi – pretty boys,' Gabrian sneered, which was rich coming from him.

'Make sure a full century of our men are present. And wake Vri Silvain to help watch Inoxion's magi.'

She let Gabrian concentrate on sending gnostic messages while she scanned the heights above. The scouts on the cliff-tops signed that all was well. She'd been getting more respect from her men since she'd started butchering the locals – although perhaps the gravity of their situation was also focusing their loyalties. They knew they needed her if they were to get out alive. *Men . . . the only things they respect are violence and fear . . .*

By the time she and Rafe reached Ujtabor, a tawdry collection of grey slate roofs and dirty streets filled with sullen mining families, her redcloaks were lining the central square, facing the governor's purple-cloaked escort. Vri Silvain, the plump Fire-mage, had been on night watch all week; he was yawning pointedly, but he saluted smartly enough when she glared at him.

Sacrista turned to greet her guest. 'Governor. A safe journey, I trust?'

'We had no trouble,' Ansel Inoxion replied, wiping sweat from his forehead. He looked unwell, which roused no pity in her. 'The rebels daren't approach my men.'

'That's because you never send them anywhere they object to. To what do I owe this visit?'

'To your request for an audience, of course. I've decided to favour you with my presence.'

'I can see that; my question was more about what finally prompted you to actually heed me?'

Inoxion smiled lazily, his eyes reptilian. 'Let's discuss that in private, Milady.'

That was hardly unexpected, but she felt stronger than him now, especially when she noted his bleary eyes and pallid skin. 'The tavern here has a private chamber and the new autumn ale is palatable.' She swung from the saddle, tossed her reins to a ranker and led the way inside, past the grovelling innkeeper.

'Your best oszisor,' she snapped. 'Two jugs, to the upper room.'

She left Rafe Gabrian and Vri Silvain with Inoxion's magi and climbed to the third floor, a room designed for eating, drinking and talking, with a dining table and comfortable leather seats. A maid followed them in with the ale, bobbed her head and left, flinching from Inoxion's eyes, which trailed over her rump as she fled.

He'll never change, Sacrista observed silently, pouring the ale and taking a cautious sip.

'You know what I want,' she told him, before he started thinking this was a social visit. 'I want at least a maniple of your men placed under my command, to help protect my mining operations. And I want—'

'Sacrista, sit down,' Inoxion interrupted coolly. 'You have bigger things to worry about than that. As you know, the empire is at war. My superior, the Governor of Midrea, is anxious: the empress has called the muster and Midrea must supply its quota.'

Sacrista fixed him with a glare. 'You told me that you're here to stay.'

'I am – but you mightn't be. I'm even now in negotiation with your father.'

'*My father?*'

'Indeed. You see, Midrea is falling short, which means your father has to supply more troops. He feels that as you're failing to enrich him, he can spare yours.'

Sacrista did sit then, with a heavy thump. '*Pull out?* But we can't – I've only got three more months before winter and the mines close!' *He's playing games with me*, she thought furiously. *This is leverage, nothing more.* 'Our contract doesn't run out until spring—'

'But your father has lost faith in you, Sacrista. Right now, the only thing keeping you here is my assurance that you will turn things around.'

'He can't do this! I've written to him every week – surely he understands my position?'

'Your father sees the situation here through *my* eyes, Sacrista. I doubt he's even read your letters. But he and I have a good understanding.'

Father's cut me loose. She felt the colour draining from her face. 'You don't understand the danger these rebels present – you'll fare no better here!'

'You overrate yourself,' Inoxion snorted. He took another mouthful of the ale, pulled a face and pushed the rest away. 'Foul stuff. How do you stand it?' He went to a satchel and pulled out a wine bottle, popped the cork with kinesis and drank from the neck. 'Listen, Milady, I know what we face here better than you. It's a *pandaemancer*: do you even know what that is?' When Sacrista shook her head, he explained, 'It's a heretical magic, stronger than a hundred magi, perhaps even a thousand.'

'It sounds like something out of a faery-tale.'

'Tell that to your brother's ghost,' Inoxion replied cruelly. 'Fortunately, I know someone who can deal with this heretic: an Ordo Costruo scholar.'

Sacrista sat up. '*Ordo Costruo?*'

'Aye. A part-Easterner, but he knows his stuff.'

'A half-Noorie?' Sacrista exclaimed. 'You're dealing with one of them? During *an invasion?*'

'The Ordo Costruo have no love for the invaders – most of the order are under siege in their own towers, watching their beloved Bridge collapse. We can trust him.'

'*Trust?* That's a high price to place on his service. Why does he care?'

'Like every good researcher, he wants a specimen.' Inoxion smirked. Finding two pewter goblets on a shelf, he filled them from his bottle and offered one to Sacrista, who waved it away. Accepting anything from him felt dirty.

'A "specimen"?' She wrinkled her nose. 'Scholars make me sick. What's his name?'

'Cassiphan.'

'How did he know to come here? How did you meet him?'

'He came here following a rumour of a deadly and unnatural ice-storm – the one that slew your brother. He sought me out as the dominant secular power here.'

'And you just welcomed a Noorie into your confidence?' Sacrista jeered.

Inoxion drained his wine and gave an odd shudder. 'Cassiphan was *persuasive*.' Then he looked at her, his eyes shadowed, and said, 'I have a proposition for you – a real proposition, Sacrista, not a game.'

A *'game'*, she thought. *Is that what you call coercing women into sex?* But she nodded for him to go on.

'Enter my service and bring your men with you. Two thousand experienced troops led by a *fine* commander is something of great value in these chaotic times, especially in a small place like this. And the silver – let's stop even pretending it's going to be sent to Augenheim. Your father has too much on his plate with the Shihad to do more than whine, and I have it on good authority that the tax-farming legislation is going to be revoked soon anyway. I'll protect you legally, while strengthening my grip on this kingdom. Together, we can wring every last drop out of this place, and after that . . . the world is a vast place, full of opportunity.'

Sacrista's immediate reaction was to dismiss him out of hand, but as he spoke, she found herself thinking that what he was suggesting could certainly be done. Without a protector, she would always be little more than her father's slave. Her current plan – to kill the Sarkanys and then run away to be a free-sword – promised nothing but an empty, brief future. But with a powerful protector, she could have so much more . . .

'I'll not be your whore,' she warned.

He raised a hand placatingly. 'Whores can be purchased everywhere. I want a partner, one I can trust: someone willing to get their hands dirty but who can also *think*. Someone tough and ruthless enough to do what must be done, and untroubled by conscience. Someone I can share ideas with, who won't go running to the Volsai afterwards, or stab me in the back. A willing subordinate, to groom and elevate as I rise. I make no secret of the fact that I find you desirable, but I'll forego pleasure for a strong business partner any day.' He gave a sly shrug. 'Who knows, you may come round to me in time?'

I don't think so, Sacrista thought, eyeing the balding, pasty-faced, frankly sick-looking governor, *but for the rest of it . . . Rukka te, Father. I'm in this for myself now.* 'All right, show me a contract.'

Inoxion gave her a hooded smile, pulled out an envelope and flourished it. 'I took the liberty of anticipating your acceptance. It's my only offer. I don't have time to negotiate.'

She took it and scanned the document. Phrases like 'mutually agreed duties' and 'full legal protection' had her nodding, and the retainer was more than she'd ever dreamed of earning, especially after years of living on whatever she and Robear could scrounge. It made her commander of the Imperial Legions stationed here in Mollachia – her own men, plus Inoxion's. It was beyond all expectation.

I could actually agree to this, she thought hungrily. 'How would we handle the transfer of leadership?' she asked.

'We'll visit each of your units and decommission them, then ask your men to re-swear to Imperial Service. That's an immediate pay-rise, the first month in advance, and those who decline can walk home to Augenheim.'

'No one will refuse,' she admitted.

He produced a quill and ink-pot from a sideboard, dashed off a signature, then presented the quill to her. 'Then do we have a deal, Lady Sacrista?'

She took a deep breath. 'Yes, we have a deal,' she said, and she signed as well. Inoxion bowed, then produced a small flask, found two liquor glasses and tipped a black fluid into them. 'A Rimoni zhambuk,' he told her. 'Smells foul, tastes divine.'

She had a policy of not drinking anything she didn't know the provenance of . . . and Inoxion was right about the smell. But she took it anyway, because when she looked Inoxion in the eyes – oddly *fascinating* eyes – she realised that she'd been wrong about him, that he was in fact a *saviour*, when she so badly needed one.

'Salut,' she toasted, a Rimoni word for a Rimoni drink, and tossed it back as he did.

A moment later she knew she was betrayed: there was no alcohol burn, nothing but foulness, and when she looked at him again his eyes had gone black, and she could see the tell-tale traces of mesmeric-gnosis swirling. *Poison*, she thought, trying to flood her system with bile as she staggered away, seeking to vomit.

Inoxion's aura boiled with cords of livid energy that sprang from his hands, far stronger than any she'd ever seen. '*Rafe*—' she tried to shout. '*Vri!*' But the sound rebounded dully from the walls and she realised that Inoxion had somehow sealed the room sonically, under her very nose.

'They're busy,' Inoxion snickered as she wrenched out her sword, trying to spit. He didn't even bother with a weapon. When she thrust her blade at him, he blurred into a neck-bending, spine-twisting evasion, laughing in her face, 'Oh Sacrista, what a time we're going to have!'

She swung; he dodged and backhanded her, moving impossibly fast and smashing her into the wall. The impact left her dazed. His eyes flashed red and a thousand voices stabbed into her brain, commanding her to *stop-lie-down-submit-give-up*. But she *refused*, shouting her denial and launching an overhead blow at his skull. His left hand shot up and caught her wrist; his right slammed into her belly.

She doubled over, retching, as he grappled with her. His left arm clamped like steel around her sword-arm wrist; with his right he took her by the throat and pinned her choking to the wall.

'You *will* be my whore, and I want a taste right now,' he rasped. 'Thanks for the soldiers.'

'Why?' she choked out as she struggled.

'Because I want to fuck you one time while you're still you,' he snarled. His left hand ripped something from her neck – her silver necklace? The touch of it seemed to pain him and he quickly dropped it. Then he smirked and slobbered over her face. 'Unwilling women are much *spicier*,' he purred, then he twisted his grip on her sword-arm and her wrist snapped.

She shrieked in white-hot agony as her blade clattered to the ground. He kicked it away while grinding her broken bones between his fingers, making her legs buckle, then he hurled her onto her back and stared down at her, not even panting, as the fluid in her belly began to burn like acid. Inoxion straddled her hips gleefully, his face a lewd parody of humanity, gripped the sides of her breastplate and wrenched, bursting the buckles and opening her armour like a clam-shell. She tried to fight one-handed, but he pinned her arm easily, tore open her under-tunic, baring her flesh, and mauled it, slobbering black saliva over her breasts. She tried to head-butt and even bite him but he only laughed and lifted his head to display teeth like a viper.

'I wouldn't be so quick to draw my blood, Sacrista. You won't like the taste.'

Dear Kore, what is he? She threw all of her strength into trying to throw him off, but he stunned her with a fist to the right eye. Her body was failing her, refusing to respond to her desperate need to fight on. Her brain fed her false hopes as she lay beneath him, petrified.

Rafe will come – or Vri. This won't happen.

Inoxion licked her belly, and her eyes were dragged down to see that her chest was turning black, veins of darkness spreading like a disease through her. A wall of voices was rising in her mind like an inexorable tide, drowning her.

'These are your last moments of freedom, Sacrista,' he told her. 'Enjoy!'

Her left arm flailed weakly above her head, but her right refused to move at all, the hand limp and twisted, every movement filled with agony. Inoxion unhurriedly unbuckled her belt, licking his drooling lips.

And her questing left hand brushed against metal . . . her silver chain – and even that touch was painful. *The silver . . . it reacts against whatever he's done to me . . . and has been done to him*, she guessed. *It's some kind of daemon-possession . . .*

Submit-give-up-surrender-yield, the wall of voices chorused as Inoxion gripped her breeches and tugged, baring his fanged teeth with a leer.

Last chance . . . She sat up in one motion, her belly muscles shrieking, but to her utter relief her body responded: she threw her left hand into a straight-arm thrust and plunged it right into his open mouth, pushing the silver chain down his throat. His teeth clamped down on her hand, his canines puncturing and injecting more of the black fluids – daemon ichor, she guessed – but then he clutched at his throat, shrieking, and rolled off her.

She rolled, flailing for her blade, and came up even as he bent and vomited up the chain.

Left-handed, but powered by all her kinesis, she swung her sword while pouring gnosis-fire into the blade, which went right through Inoxion's neck and jammed into the floor beneath, while his head bounced wetly, rolled and stopped, the eyes looking up at her as his body folded, pumping blood in dark gushes.

He didn't move, but the voices inside her head screamed and the darkness in her belly and wrist began to surge. *You're mine!* the daemon shrieked. *You're mine!*

She dropped to her knees as another debilitating spasm of weakness struck – then she grabbed the vomit-encrusted necklace, grabbed her ale tankard and doused the chain, then placed it against her stomach, wincing at the burning feeling but seeing the darkness recoil. With a fatalistic sob, she dangled it from her fingers and lowered it into her own throat, pushing with kinesis to get it inside her. The instant it struck her stomach, a sickening throb of energy wracked through her, then an explosion of white agony sent her spinning into the void.

10

Marching South

Affinity

For centuries, magi believed that no one could access all sixteen studies of the gnosis, being limited by their affinities for certain aspects, which create opposing blind spots (a Fire-mage being unable to wield Water-gnosis, for example). But now reports out of the East speak of young magi wielding all aspects of the gnosis. It's intriguing, but deeply troubling. Where have we gone wrong?

OLDRED HURGAARD, DELPH ARCANUM, 931

Southern Midrea
Septinon 935

An army on the move was a frightening thing, Ril was coming to realise, as much for the people they fought for as those they marched to face. *Five* armies was another beast entirely. He ran fingers through his long black hair, almost feeling it turning grey. The map before him showed a multitude of lines converging by river and road. What those lines didn't show was the trail of destruction left in their wake.

He looked up and said, 'Explain to me again, Knight-Princeps, how you came to burn three women in Brucken?'

Dravis Ryburn, head of the Inquisition, appeared to have no facial muscles; he never even hinted at emotions. But he clearly seethed with contempt for the godlessness of the world. 'They were witches,' he said, his flat voice remorseless.

Behind the Knight-Princeps stood his bodyguard, staring at Ril with an expression he couldn't read, but he was sure the man despised him.

The bodyguard, Lef Yarle, was said to be the best fighting man in the Church, possibly better even than Solon Takwyth himself. He was also one of the prettiest grown men Ril had ever seen, like a Lantric god brought to life: a blond Hollenian with all the arrogance of the truly beautiful and truly powerful, but with none of the Hollenians' customary earthy charm.

Ril realised Yarle's sheer presence had broken his line of thought and he dragged his eyes back to Ryburn. 'I'm a "witch", Knight-Princeps, and so are you; we use "magic"! "Witches" in the *Book of Kore* sense don't exist – and they never have! So I ask again: why did you burn these women?'

'They were not as you and I,' Dravis intoned. 'They invoked the heresy called pandaemancy to curse their neighbours.'

Ril's skin prickled. 'Pandaemancy? They were pandaemancers?' *Is this a threat against Lyra?*

Ryburn's face was, as ever, unreadable. 'They believed so.'

'But did they actually show such powers?'

'The neighbours' testimonies suggested so. With respect, Prince, you're not privy to them.'

'Maybe not – but I do know they were all landed widows! Jealousy and greed! That's all it was. Your people should have laughed this out of court! Are they really that stupid, Ryburn?'

Ryburn slowly blinked – for him a massive reaction. 'With *all* respect, Prince-Consort, the evidence was overwhelming. Our duty before Kore is to root out heresy *wherever* we find it.'

'They all confessed,' Yarle added in a musical voice. 'I questioned them myself.'

It's definitely a threat. Ril turned to the other man in the tent, Lord Rolven Sulpeter, a grey-haired, prim-looking man with an immaculate beard and austere blue eyes. He'd been reasonably efficient in keeping the Corani legions in motion. 'What do you think, Milord?'

'I think we're at war and pissing around with petty judicial matters is a waste of time,' Sulpeter replied.

'Exactly,' Ril and Ryburn chorused, then realised they'd interpreted his words in opposing ways.

'By which I mean: the Inquisition should be *riding*, not sitting in judgement on village matters,' Sulpeter clarified. 'For Kore's sake, Ryburn, tell your people to mind their own damned business. For the coming campaign, they're just soldiers, nothing more.'

'An Inquisitor is *never* just a soldier,' Ryburn sniffed. 'We're the *elite*: every man and woman is a skilled high-blood mage dedicated to protecting the spiritual wellbeing of the empire. We are the backbone of the realm.'

'You're a few thousand fanatics, Ryburn, and you can't hold back the Shihad on your own,' Ril retorted. He saw Ryburn and Yarle exchange disinterested looks as if this was boring them, but the galling thing was, unless he wanted to press charges – *against the Knight-Princeps of the Holy Inquisition!* – there was nothing else he could do. He glowered at them, but he doubted either man was remotely intimidated.

Yet another slight I must let go . . . Dear Kore, let there be a reckoning one day.

'I trust we Corani are acquitting ourselves properly?' Sulpeter asked.

Ril picked up the latest despatches. 'Seventeen desertions, five brawls resulting in serious injury to civilians, eighteen counts of theft and two buildings burned. Eight taverns ransacked. Two proven counts of rape, and another eight pending. That's just last week, Rolven, from *one* army – ours. We've got thirty-four legions on the road and another nine awaiting us in the south, and frankly, our own people are terrified of us.'

'My men leave only healed communities in their wake,' Ryburn declared.

'And the stink of burnt flesh,' Sulpeter countered. 'Prince Ril, this is inevitable: most of the conscripted soldiers have never been out of their home town, let alone left their kingdom. They see *everyone* they meet as foreign. They're new to army discipline – most of the experienced soldiers who went on Crusade in 928 never returned. But the officers will get a grip on them as the march progresses.'

'I bloody hope so,' Ril sighed. 'What is it about young men? As soon as you give them weapons and a community of strangers, they turn into thugs.'

'Their lack of godliness,' Ryburn suggested. 'My force's behaviour is exemplary.'

'Tell that to those poor women in Brucken!' Ril snapped back. 'I'm signing off dozens of restitution claims a day, with money the Treasury insist I don't have.' He looked from one man to another, then jabbed a finger at the map. 'All right, brief me – where is everyone?'

'Our legions are spread out along a twenty-mile stretch of the lower Reztu,' Sulpeter reported. 'We're making fair time, moving against the current, obviously. But the lower Reztu is gentle. The Earl of Augenheim is building docks at Brunton, a castle-town that bridges the upper river. We'll be there inside a week.'

'And the other armies?'

'The Third Army – the Aquilleans – are right behind us. The Argundian Fourth Army are further back and behind schedule.'

'Dirklan said they'd be slow,' Ril noted tiredly. 'Where are the bloody Sacrecours?'

'The Second Army under Brylion Fasterius marched across Andressea to Defonne, then took barges down the Sanuvo River, but they're well behind schedule. They claim to have been given insufficient riverboats.'

'They're shirking.'

'Fasterius has given his men leave to forage,' Sulpeter added. 'We all know what that means.'

Ril certainly did. More than half the reports of military crimes – looting, murder, vandalism, rape and abduction, were from that region. The Dupeni clans, primarily the Sacrecour-Fasterius axis, Lyra's greatest rivals, appeared to be treating Andressea as practise for the real war. He'd been bombarded with complaints from the Earl of Andressea, whose forces were too small to deal with the Sacrecours. Rule of Law was being superseded by the Law of the March: one's troops could do what they damned well liked.

'I'll write to Fasterius again,' Ril grumbled.

'You've tried that,' Dravis Ryburn noted. 'Summon him here and tell him.' He gave a cold smile. 'Let Lef and me speak to him.'

At last, a useful suggestion, Ril thought. *Dear Kore, I'd love to see Brylion worked over by these beasts ... but it'd never happen.* 'Tempting, but I'll write.' He sighed. 'These are early days. They'll pull their weight when we make contact with the enemy.' He didn't believe that any more than they did. 'What about the Fifth Army?'

'Korion's southerners are mustering in their homelands and beginning to move.' Sulpeter sniffed. 'No reports of more than cursory problems, but then, would they tell us?'

The Bricians were gathering in Bres and the Noromen near Venderon, while the Andressan and Midrean forces were still in Halketton and Augenheim respectively. Their only misdemeanours appeared to be getting into fights with the soldiers arriving from the north and west. The latest despatch from Seth Korion included a timetable of his intended route march, something none of the other armies had furnished.

'A few problems is better than hundreds, believe me,' Ril muttered. But his eyes were trailing across the map now. Equidistant between Pallas and Pontus was the River Silas, which flowed out of Schlessen and Sydia. It was a mile wide in parts. There was a bridge, and dozens of small ferry towns along its length. It didn't mark the edge of the empire, but it did mark the most obviously defendable frontier. 'From Augenheim it's more than five hundred miles to the Silas. How quickly can we get there?'

'Marching,' Sulpeter replied, 'it's ten miles a day, traditionally: five days' march a week – assuming the soldiers rest on the sixth day – means fifty miles a week, two hundred and fifty miles a month – so we'd get there in two months, at the end of Octen.'

'How fast is the Shihad travelling?'

'They have a head-start on us and our aerial scouts say they're using windships to leapfrog forward hundreds of miles at a time. And they're not all stopping to deal with the Vereloni cities; they're just deploying enough men for a siege and moving on.'

'Meaning?' Ril said impatiently.

'Meaning they'll beat us to the Silas by a good month.'

'Why aren't we doing what they are?'

'Because we don't have enough windships, and those we have are moving supplies, not men.'

'Why does our enemy have every advantage?' Ril snapped, and when no one answered, 'It's not a rhetorical question: *why?*'

'What we're doing is more efficient,' Ryburn replied. 'Men can walk; supplies can't. Rashid risks outstripping his supply-lines – that'll cost him in the end. We're better off moving more slowly and allowing time for our five armies to unite.'

The Inquisitor's analysis was somewhat comforting. 'Very well – but can we at least slow the Shihad down?' Ril tapped the point on the map marking the bridge over the Silas. 'We could start by destroying this.'

'Tell the Noromen,' Sulpeter suggested. 'They're closest.'

'No, we'll do it. I want to get the lie of the land anyway. I'll take a detachment of Corani knights by air to the river. We'd get there inside a week, flying conservatively. I'll take Earth-magi to destroy the bridge.'

'That bridge has powerful spells woven into it to keep it from being eroded away or destroyed by bandits,' Ryburn warned. 'You'll need more than a few stone-shaping spells.'

'I'll find a way to take it down,' Ril replied. 'But the armies need to move faster. Contact every commander – we must double our rate of march, which is going to require some whip-cracking. I want all mounted units to leave their infantries behind and ride hard. Right now, the Shihad have one fixed route – if we let them get too far into our lands, their options expand and we don't have the manpower to contain them.'

'Then we must fight them in the Brekaellen or the Kedron,' Sulpeter said. He tapped a point on the map east of Noros. 'There is also this place to consider – the Trachen Pass: it's a high, difficult road, but traversable. If we don't guard it, the enemy could march straight into Noros.'

'Then make sure Seth Korion is told to protect it,' Ril replied. He tapped another point on the map. 'Tell me about Mollachia. I don't like having an ongoing rebellion so close to our route.'

'The Mollachs have risen against the governor and some tax-farmers,' said Ryburn. 'It's tying up a legion that should be mustering in Augenheim.'

'We can't afford to send more men. The governor is on his own.'

'I understand the governor may actually be dead,' Sulpeter replied.

'*Dead?*' Ril rocked back on his heels. This revolt sounded serious

– but it didn't change anything: he was here to fight a war, not bail out tax-farmers. 'It's still not our problem.' He moved his finger beyond the Silas to the largest imperial fortress east of the river. 'What news from Dusheim?'

'The garrison is under siege,' Sulpeter reported, 'but the fortress is almost inaccessible. I gather the Shihad just encircled it and marched the rest of the men past. That garrison could hold out for years.'

'They may have to,' Ryburn noted, which earned him an annoyed look.

'No, they won't,' Ril said firmly. 'We're going to defeat the Shihad this year and send them packing.' He stepped away from the map and called for his aide-de-camp, Niklas Bycross. 'Round up a dozen Corani knights,' he told the young man. 'They must all have winged mounts. I want them in the air at dawn tomorrow.'

'Our scouts say the enemy also have winged constructs,' Sulpeter said.

'Good: if we meet them we'll find out if they've learned how to fly yet.' He looked at Ryburn. 'No more atrocities, Knight-Princeps. Put your "mission" aside – we're here to fight a war against the Shihad, not our own people. Dismissed, all of you.'

When they were gone – and it was a considerable relief to have the Inquisitor and his pet killer out of his presence – Ril sank into his chair and rubbed his eyes. *We're failing,* he thought. *Our armies are scattered across half the country, and in any case, we hate each other more than we hate the invader.* He poured himself a Brevian honey whisky, sinking back into his chair. Pulling out a relay-stave, he called into the aether, <Basia? Bas? Are you out there?>

Then her face appeared in his mind's eye, her voice chimed in his head and everything began to feel better.

Bres, Bricia

A brazen trumpet-blast brought the ranked redcloaks of Bricia II to attention. They were arrayed on the grounds of a vast manor outside Bres and the ground quivered as they stamped their right feet and saluted, chorusing, 'A Korion! A Korion!'

The deep masculine voices sent a shiver of pride up Seth Korion's spine as he answered the salute, then clipped along the front rank, greeting the senior officers. Many were Third Crusade veterans who'd followed him out of Hel and found a home in green Bricia. His father's estates were now a fraction of their original size as he'd gifted huge tracts to the soldiers.

'Are your men ready?' he asked a tall Vereloni pilus with a tanned face and a hint of tight black curls at the edge of his helm. It was a rhetorical question: these men were always ready.

'All present, Milord,' Pilus Lukaz replied.

Seth ran his eye down the line of Lukaz's cohort, picking out the veterans he'd inherited from Ramon Sensini: Baden, the stolid banner-man; big, genial Vidran; the aloof Harmon, possibly the best non-mage swordsman he had ever seen, and the feisty, irascible Bowe. In many ways, these men meant more to the legion than the fifteen battle-magi. They were the weathervane he trusted when ill winds blew.

'Just like old days, eh?' he remarked.

'No way, sir,' Lukaz replied. 'This time we'll give 'em a right kicking.'

'I hope so,' Seth replied fervently, and moved on, going down every line, shaking hands and learning names before returning to the steps. He raised his voice. 'Men of Bres, we've been called to war. The East has invaded, seeking revenge and conquest. We must do our duty to counter this threat. I am confident that we shall prevail, Kore Willing, but I counsel you not to underestimate our foe! They will be brave. They *believe* in their destiny. They are resourceful, and they know their trade.'

He'd seen too much over-confidence, especially among the mage-nobles, with their jingoistic belief that they faced primitive cowards, that the Shihad would be defeated by 'one good taste of Rondian steel' – and when he'd openly disagreed, he'd caught mutterings of 'defeatism'.

There's a difference between defeatism and realism. 'We will be facing magi, constructs, windships and all the panoply of war,' he went on, determined to make them see this would not be a little outing, then home for tea and medals. 'We will be facing *Rashid Mubarak*, victor of

Shaliyah, a military and political genius. He will take us to Hel and back!' Then he raised his voice, before the men grew concerned, and shouted, *'But we will triumph!'*

'Aye!' a few of the men responded involuntarily, which made him nod approvingly.

'Aye, we will triumph,' he said, 'because we're fighting for our families and our way of life. This isn't a border war: this is for *survival* – that matters more than numbers and strategy. And I tell you, this land is ours, and terrain makes the victory. They come from the desert, but this war will be fought in the green hills of Yuros. It will be fought in places we know and that will give us the edge. Place your trust in Kore and in the men around you, and we will prevail!'

The officers led the cheers; he saluted again and ordered the march to begin. They had a long way to go: through the Knebb Valley into Noros, north to Jastenberg and the Brekaellen Valley.

All over the land, similar scenes are playing out. Why does war bring us together swifter than peaceful ventures? he wondered as he dismissed the battle-magi with instructions to join their units: it would do these preening nobles good to experience the hardship of the march.

He climbed the magnificent marble stairs to his personal suite, where he found his patient-looking wife breast-feeding his child in the antechamber.

'Good speech, Husband,' she commented as he bent and kissed her cheek dutifully. 'Nice and short.'

He'd married Carmina Phyl, a half-blood healer-mage from rural Bricia, after meeting her in the Third Crusade. His father wouldn't have approved, but he was dead. His mother still didn't approve. *Only a pure-blood is good enough for a Korion*, she'd said. *A love marriage with a lesser is a wasted union.*

The irony was, Seth had never been in love with Carmina, nor she with him, but they'd both wanted *someone* – and they'd been blessed with two daughters, the youngest only recently born. Carmina was breast-feeding Gisella herself – an almost scandalous notion in high-born society – but he was happy to indulge her in all things. But it did mean that he was losing an experienced legion healer; instead, she would be running his affairs here in Bres. She'd do that diligently, he knew. 'I'll miss you,' he told her, stroking Gisella's fine hair.

'You won't have time to miss us,' she retorted. 'You'll bury yourself in work, as always.'

'It'll be busy, for sure. It already is. I've got papers a foot deep on my desk.'

'Have any of the old legion answered the call?' she asked.

'Well, lots of rankers,' he said, 'but there weren't many magi survived. Chaplain Gerdhart . . . Lanna Jureigh might come, but she's got her daughter to worry about. The others went home. But I did get a letter from Jelaska Lyndrethuse – her family legion is marching with the Argundian army.'

'I miss Lanna,' Carmina said wistfully. 'They were good days. Well, not really, but you know what I mean.'

'I do. Hopefully this war will go much better.'

'Then go and see to your work, Husband. I'll put the girls to bed. Wake me if you wish.'

Their eyes met: they had separate suites and conjugal relations were infrequent, but not unpleasant. He'd never really understood the importance others placed in sex. He didn't find women terribly interesting to talk to – even Carmina, who was a perfectly well-educated and gentle person. They had that in common: she would far rather spend her evenings with her lady-in-waiting, Prisca, than talk of matters that interested him.

'Goodnight then, my darling,' he said formally, kissed her again, then pecked Gisella's wrinkled forehead.

Once ensconced at his desk, he inked a quill, then sat back, remembering names and faces. Where was Ramon Sensini now, or Fridryk Kippenegger? Probably dead, given the lives they led. It gave him pause, thinking just how transitory life could be. In 928, when the Third Crusade marched off to war, they'd thought themselves invincible, but barely a man had made it home, even among the magi.

With a sigh, he put memories aside. An army might march on its stomach, but paper moved the food to the stomach and he had a mountain of parchments to work through.

Welcome back to the life, General . . .

Silas River, Central Yuros

Freedom, Ril thought, *finally!* To him, that meant the wind in his hair, flying southeast at the head of his mage-knights, at one with the sky. It meant leaving behind the intrigues and frustrations of the command tent and seeing his maps become real places, the rivers, forests, plains, places that were just lines and dots on parchment coming to life. Every time they landed, he heard different accents, new words. It was remarkable to finally experience the land he and Lyra ruled.

We should have done more to see our empire – a Grand Progression, like the old emperors used to do, he mused. *Then we'd understand our people better.*

He was riding Pearl, his pegasus, and that too was a joy. All his knights had winged steeds, mostly pegasi, the favoured jousting beast of the Corani, but a few rode griffons, hippogriffs or other fanciful creatures of myth, made real by the Imperial Animagi. Pearl had recovered well enough after breaking a wing in the recent tourney, but he had no intention of taking her into battle; heraldic constructs were far too valuable to be risked in warfare. But right now, he needed speed, and the reptilian venators the military used were too slow. He'd persuaded the other Great Houses to send their knights, so now there were dozens of winged units soaring southeast, intending to take and keep the skies.

Spread around him were his old friends Larik and Grylflon Joyce – he'd gifted them new mounts so they could accompany him – as well as Jorden Falquist and his younger brother Lero, Rolven's heir, Sanjen Sulpeter, the stolid Malthus Cayne, cold-eyed Jos Bortolin and half a dozen other magi who'd brought their jousting constructs on the march. Ril was enjoying this chance to reconnect with them, away from Solon Takwyth's influence.

<Where are we?> Larik Joyce asked blearily. As usual, he was hungover.

Ril pointed downwards. <*That stretch of grass you're puking on every few minutes is the Brekaellen Valley.*>

<*I'm helping it grow,*> Larik muttered.

On the maps, the Brekaellen looked featureless, but the reality was very different. The surrounding mountains were tipped in early snow, but the plains were actually countless rolling hills, undulating fields and lush pastures, home to herds of sheep and cattle, with small farming villages and towns grown up around the wayside inns dotting the Imperial Road that bisected the landscape. From up here, it looked beautiful, wide and free.

Ril stroked Pearl's neck. The clouds today were high, the sky a brilliant blue, the sun glowing and warm and they were alone in the sky – then he saw a distant flash of light far ahead and something like a falling star arced towards the ground, trailing a tail of orange light and black-grey smoke. It was miles ahead . . . but only minutes away for a windrider . . .

Someone just brought down a windskiff . . .

He signalled his knights to stay with him as he and Pearl followed the comet's tail, but inside a minute, it had hit the ground, leaving only smoke rising to mark its grave. The scouts he'd sent into the east to track the Shihad for weeks had reported Keshi windcraft.

So who just died?

They rode the winds, Pearl's wings alternately flapping and gliding. A glittering ribbon ran across their path which could only be the Silas. There were more clouds now, creating blind spots, and though he still couldn't see anyone else in the sky, his nerves were jangling.

<*We're not alone here,*> he warned them all. <*Someone brought that skiff down . . .* >

Then Jos Bortolin called, <*Look up!*>

Two dozen huge winged birds, easily large enough to bear the armed men on their backs, were circling like vultures a thousand feet above them. *So the reports are true*, Ril thought. *The Noories do have flying constructs.*

Then his heart thudded as the first of the giant birds peeled off, its shrill cry echoed as one by one, the rest followed, diving towards them . . .

11

Knights of the Air

The Draken

There was no such thing as a draken, the winged fire-breathing reptile of northern legend – until the Pallas Animagi set out to create them. Two accompanied Kaltus Korion's First Army into Kesh, and neither returned. By all accounts their main achievement was to consume more food than an entire legion. Yet no doubt the Pallas Animagi are breeding more. The waste of resources is appalling.

CALAN DUBRAYLE, IMPERIAL TREASURER, PALLAS, 932

Brekaellen Valley, Yuros
Septinon 935

As the Rondian knights emerged from the clouds a thousand feet below Waqar Mubarak's roc-riders, he felt his heartbeat surge. Finally, here was the *enemy* – not the pitiful Vereloni, outnumbered and isolated, but actual Rondian mage-knights! The desire to prove himself, to make the first kill and write his name in legend, was like hunger, thirst and lust rolled into one.

<*What are they flying?*> Fatima asked, her mental voice incredulous.

They all peered at the strange shapes of the creatures below – flying *horses*?

<*Something they summoned from Shaitan's Pit,*> Shameed sneered. <*Slow, stupid things – we'll fly rings around them!*>

Tamir was counting. <*There're only twelve, and we're above them.*>

Baneet rumbled, <*Please, Waqar, let us attack!*>

<*Ahm will grant us victory,*> Lukadin pleaded.

Waqar's mind was racing. They were out here to find the enemy armies, but the bridge behind them was important – he'd been escorting a dozen windships carrying soldiers and magi; they'd landed on both sides of the structure under the cover of night and were now securing it. If these knights arrived, they could tilt the balance.

And damn it, I want this fight too. He opened his sending to the entire flight. *<Protect your birds! Shield yourselves, body and mind – remember, these men will be stronger magi than us: higher-blood, maybe better trained – but no man can shield a well-aimed lance at the speeds we fly. Go at them, Eagles of Ahm!>*

'EL NASR AL'AHM!' Lukadin cried aloud, and the rest took up the chant as Shameed sent his roc into a shrieking dive and one by one, they all peeled off and plummeted after him.

Waqar had time for one quick private message. *<Lukadin, don't use that spear!>* The weapon they'd retrieved from Midpoint Tower was too short for aerial use; it was tucked under Luka's saddle. *<And don't lose the damned thing!>*

Luka responded angrily, *<I'll use it if I have to.>* Then their rocs folded their wings and they too dropped, the distance between them and their enemies shrinking as the Rondian knights closed up their formation, their constructs' wings beating frantically as they sought height.

We're above you and we're faster than you – Ahm is on our side!

<The leader,> Waqar called, *<that one in the gold-rimmed helm – he's mine!>* Then he aligned his lance and set his shoulder for the blow as the gap shrank to feet and seconds . . .

The Corani knights kindled gnostic fire in their lances and shielded. They'd been caught out, but Ril blared instructions into the minds of his men. *<Lads, form a wedge: I'll take the tip – climb to meet them, head on, full shielding forwards! It's a joust, boys – we don't flinch!>*

Pearl was snorting as he fed fury into her mind. The Joyce brothers closed up on his right, Malthus Cayne on his left, Jos above and Sanjen below; in seconds they'd formed an arrowhead as they climbed ponderously towards their shrieking enemies, who were coming in hard and fast, with the advantage of both altitude and numbers.

<Mage-fire!> Ril shouted, and as one he and his knights sent livid blue

bolts of energy from their lance-tips, shredding the air. Two birds were immediately blasted from the skies, their giant skulls disintegrating in the combined blasts, and others lost their nerve and zagged sideways, fouling their riders' aims and the flights of their colleagues.

Then a dark shape filled his sight, a blazing lance-tip punched through his shielding, struck his curved buckler and glanced away – while his own lance struck something and cracked. The impact almost stopped Pearl in mid-air. He saw a giant beak lash out, but his pegasus crashed her fore-hooves into the bird's skull, stunning it, and it dropped away. On all sides, collisions reverberated as beasts slammed together, the greater speed of the Keshi birds countered by the greater weight of the Corani steeds.

<*Fly!*> he shouted, and Pearl swooped for momentum, then shot forwards. He blasted mage-fire at the bellies of the next wave of Keshi birds, then he and his knights burst through into clean air. When he threw a look behind, he saw four more Keshi birds were plummeting, broken and lifeless. There was one rider-less griffon – one of the younger knights, he thought – and one pegasus was dropping earthwards, her right wing shredded, Malthus Cayne clinging to her back.

Ril shouted to Jorden Falquist to take over, then sent Pearl into a dive . . .

Waqar cursed as a torrent of light blazed from the oncoming Rondian formation and a roc careered across his path, battering Ajniha sideways and wrecking his approach, but he kept his lance forward as the Rondian knights burst into his fliers, instinctively correcting his aim as he swept underneath the man he'd sought to strike. His lance punctured the shield of a foe riding a clumsy lion-eagle thing and skewered his breastplate, but even as the man was plucked from his saddle it snapped in his grasp, which sent threw Waqar into a swirling spin. Half the straps binding him to the saddle tore loose and desperately he used kinesis to stay on her back. Then he was out the other side, terrified, exhilarated and frantically searching the skies for his friends.

He'd seen two rocs go down before contact and now he could see four more falling with torn wings or shattered skulls. As far as he could see, the only dead Rondian was the man he'd lanced, and his roc-riders were scattered across the sky while the enemy were climbing in formation.

<REGROUP!> he called. His eyes picked out Baneet and Fatima, flying together, then Tamir at the fringes. He threw his gaze about frantically. <Luka?>

<I'm here! Ahm is with us!> His friend had tossed aside his broken lance and was brandishing that cursed gnostic spear. <Fly to Paradise, brothers!>

Then Waqar saw one of the Rondian steeds spiralling slowly groundwards with a knight clinging to its back – and the gold-helmed knight he'd wanted to attack earlier was diving after him. Shameed's mental voice trumpeted in his mind, <He's mine, he's mine!> as he flashed past on an intercept course with Luka and two more roc-riders in his wake. Lukadin was waving his spear like a madman, light pulsing about the gemstone mounted behind the point.

<Luka!> Waqar shouted, then he cursed and let them go. <The rest of you, climb eastwards – get between them and the bridge and form up for another run.>

He led the remaining thirteen on an upwards spiral, swiftly overtaking the more cumbersome Rondian beasts as they ascended. Eight against fourteen; below, it was four against two. But he was remembering how the heavier Rondian beasts had made their weight count.

Can we afford another attack? But his blood was up. He'd taken the first kill. He was immortal. <Rally on me!> he shouted into his riders' minds. <We're going in again!>

Malthus Cayne was a decent man and a brave one, but he wasn't an Air-mage, and even kinesis couldn't save you if you hit terminal velocity. Ril could see that his steed was desperately trying to save itself, but the right wing was damaged; even as Ril closed in, the young knight was clinging on with one hand while working at his saddle-straps.

Then a mage-bolt hammered into Ril's rear shielding and he glanced back to see four of the giant eagles streaming after him, the lead man blazing away with mage-bolts. The rest of the airborne warriors were far above now and he was alone. *Stupid!* he berated himself as he nudged Pearl left then right, weaving as more bolts flashed by.

<*Malthus,*> he called ahead, <*hold on, I'm here!*> What he was going to do, he had no idea, but Pearl could bear two men for a short distance. After that, he'd think of something. *I'll set him down safe and send rescue – but I can't do that with those damned Keshi birds on my back.*

He banked right, presenting his side and drawing his windblade. The swords used by the knights were as long as their bodies, light and curved, perfect for slashing at an enemy as they passed – but like most knights, he'd only ever used a windblade in practice.

If I get through this, I'll write a manual, he told himself as the first three Keshi altered their flight to stay on his tail. The fourth one went straight for Malthus and he cursed, but there was nothing he could do to help right now. He hauled on Pearl's reins, losing even more speed as the enemy shrieked towards him – but this was no panicked manoeuvre: she stalled, Ril jammed his heels into her flanks and they dropped like stones. He smiled grimly as two of the birds flashed overhead, screaming curses as he fell from their reach an instant before impact. He pulled Pearl into a reverse turn as she flashed out her wings again and arced back towards Malthus; the third flier coming at him swept into pursuit.

'C'mon, Pooty-girl,' he told Pearl, *'fly!'*

But the fourth Keshi was still locked on Malthus Cayne, and Ril was too far off to intervene.

Waqar urged his charges into a line facing the Rondian mage-knights on their strange beasts, trying to keep half an eye on the fight below. One of the enemy beasts down there was clearly wounded, so it was effectively four on one. *Go, Shameed*, he thought, *get them!*

But up here things felt far less advantageous, and the mood among his fliers had changed. Their first pass had been fired by enthusiasm; they'd no idea what they were facing. Now they knew, so this was the real test: would they be able to hold their nerve and do it again? Their faces were now apprehensive, not blindly brave as before.

<*If you've lost your lance, draw your scimitar,*> he called, keeping his voice level and confident, as if this were routine, just another drill.

<You saw what they did: they'll do it again! Ahm be in your heart and on your lips: He is our strength and courage! FORWARD, NASR AL'AHM!>

As they shouted their battle-cry, the lances fell into line, the rocs shrilled and they surged towards the Rondians. Waqar kept up a stream of instructions even as he picked out his target. *<Seek the gaps in their line and go through – beware of mage-fire – be ready!>*

Baneet was on his right, leading Tamir and Fatima through. The others were converging as the Rondian wedge loomed ever closer. Gnosis energy flashed and surged ahead of him.

<SHIELD!> he roared, and an instant later his vision went from blue to purple to a red starburst as bolts struck shielding and sent them critical. To his left a war-eagle and its rider were immolated; birds and riders were screaming – then dark shapes hammered through the light – a lance-tip tore his sleeve – his scimitar slashed through shielding and struck steel – then he was through and out and shouting in terrified relief. His eyes scanned the sky and he picked out Baneet and Fatima, and then Tamir, who'd veered high; instead of using the blade, he was firing arrows that crackled uselessly against enemy shields as they wheeled and climbed again.

<Turn, climb,> he shouted, *<get above them!>*

But his eagles were in no shape to do that: another three were falling, their riders dead or dying in the saddles, and only one enemy had been unseated – and he was using Air-gnosis to hover while his winged horse swung back to reclaim him. It was now eleven against seven . . .

Then he looked below to see how Shameed and Luka were faring. Swearing wildly, he sent Ajniha into another dive . . .

Ril saw it for himself, otherwise he would not have believed it. As the Keshi eagle-rider closed in on Malthus, the young knight drew his windblade and held it behind him, gripping the saddle with his legs, straining with kinesis to control his mount's fall and give him a steady platform – which made him an easy target for the Keshi rider. With his lance jutting out, the Easterner raced for Malthus, who was almost hanging in the air, helpless—

—until he leaped—

—pushing off from his saddle, and using kinesis to take him over the eagle's head, kicked away the tip of the lance and *lunged*—

—and his blade took the Keshi in the chest and went through him. Their bodies slammed together and Malthus wrapped his legs around the dead man, clinging to him as the eagle spun and flipped. When it righted itself, Malthus hacked at the straps securing the dead man, then kicked him off. The eagle shrieked in rage and tried to peck at the enemy on its back.

Malthus, you rukking genius! Ril shouted, <*Bravo! Now get him under control!*>

He looked back at the furious faces of the two Keshi riders behind him, fending off more mage-bolts while Pearl ducked and dived across the skies, until he brought her around alongside the first Keshi. He hacked his foe's lance in half, rolled out of reach of a lunging talon and blasted off a mage-bolt at the second rider flashing past him, making the eagle flinch and turn aside, before he looked back to see Malthus still trying to master the eagle.

He's got some Animagery – he might just do this!

<*Come on, let's get out of here!*> he shouted into Malthus' mind—

—just as the fourth Keshi, the man who'd been hanging back, screamed past him, going straight for Malthus. The Keshi was howling to Ahm and hefting a war-spear, of all things, too short for use as a lance and no good for slashing. *What's the fool doing?* he wondered—

—then the spearhead blazed like the sun and a torrent of energy struck Malthus Cayne and his captured bird, the light so bright that for an instant Ril was blinded, though the searing after-image contained skeletons of a man and a giant bird.

When Ril opened his eyes, only a scatter of ash could be seen dropping to the ground.

What the Hel was that? He almost forgot to shield, until a Keshi arrow whipped past his nose. He slammed his heels into Pearl's sides and commanded, <*Ride, girl – let's get out of here!*>

Waqar realised what Lukadin was going to do an instant before it happened. He'd been grudgingly impressed by the Rondian knight's manoeuvre – then he sensed Lukadin's rage ...

<NO, LUKA!> he roared, but he might as well have shouted at the sun. A moment later a bolt seared the sky and the Rondian knight and his captured roc *ceased to be*. There was nothing but ash left of them as Lukadin's bird swept by, but Waqar saw his friend reeling in the saddle harness, his head lolling. The bird, sensing no control, began to slow, calling in confusion.

<LUKA!> Waqar urged his bird into a dive, his friends following, while the rest of his command circled in confusion, not sure what they'd seen and with no idea what to do next. The closest Rondian – the gold-helmed one – was climbing away to the west, his winged horse beating the air frantically, and the seven remaining knights were rallying to him. Thankfully, they hadn't realised the state Luka was in.

<Let them go,> he told his riders. <As long as they don't come at us again, let them go.>

He came alongside Luka, who was unconscious, and a moment later Fatima arrived and calmed Luka's bird with Animagery. Waqar took Ajniha in close and saw that somehow Luka still had the spear; he must have jammed it under a saddle-strap before losing consciousness. He wasn't sure if that was a blessing or not.

He called to Fatima, <Bring him down – we have to help him.>

Shameed ranged alongside. <What in Ahm's name was that?>

<I'll tell you later,> Waqar replied; he needed time to concoct a story. <But first we have to save Luka! Stay aloft and make sure those slugskin knights don't return – that's an order!>

Then he banished from his mind everything except saving his friend's life.

As soon as it was clear the Keshi weren't going to pursue, Ril signalled his men and took them down to one of the hundreds of hillocks that dotted the Brekaellen plains like a rash of pimples. They landed and unstrapped, all of them shaken, but full of the blood-pumping energy combat always stirred. There were a few Keshi birds following, but they kept their distance, even now they were on the ground. He looked about him, assessing the mood of his men: they'd gone into the fight as twelve; they were now nine.

'Did you see it?' he demanded as they clustered together, shaken, and bewildered.

'Aye, we saw!' Jorden Falquist exclaimed, his face pale. 'What *was* it?'

'I've seen an Ascendant Earth-mage collapse a stone building,' Larik Joyce remarked, 'but *that* was stronger! Who the rukking Hel were they? What are we up against?'

'Only one of them did it,' Jos Bortolin noted, his voice even, as if nothing remarkable had happened. 'An' he was completely laid out afterwards.'

'Some new spell?' Lero Falquist suggested. 'Some kind of all-or-nothing strike?'

'What did you see, Ril?' Larik asked. 'You were closest.'

'I saw a war-spear,' Ril said. 'That Keshi bastard was holding it like a lance, although it wasn't much longer than his body. I'm sure that's what channelled the energy.'

'Some kind of combat-focus, like a periapt and weapon combined?' Jos suggested.

'Whatever it was, poor Malthus didn't stand a bloody chance,' Gryffion Joyce growled. 'Poor bastard. It was murder, not a fight at all.'

'Aye,' the others snarled. 'It's not right, to die like that. It's not knightly.'

Ril didn't see how that mattered. 'If we had such weapons, we'd use them. I don't see you lot thinking twice about blasting some helpless sap who can't shield. I just hope it's a one-off.' He wiped his brow. 'They've got fliers this side of the Silas. How many, I wonder?'

'That might be all they have,' Jos drawled, removing his helm and rubbing at his sweat-soaked scalp. He had always been reputed to be a cold-hearted fighter; he looked to be unmoved by what they'd just been through.

'Nah, Noories come in swarms,' Larik rasped. 'I reckon they'll have lots more. Bloody quick, weren't they?'

They all nodded ruefully.

'They were *damned* fast,' Ril agreed, 'and that's a problem, but head to head, we went through them like a fist through glass. They've no idea how to fight in formation, and they've clearly *never* jousted.'

When he saw their chins lifting, he went on, 'They're fast learners, I'll give them that. A few years back they had no magi, no constructs, no windships; now they're catching up. We've been complacent, but we still have the edge, so let's make it count!' He looked around the circle. 'First contact, lads: Empire versus the Shihad, outnumbered two to one, and we inflicted more damage. Let's take heart from that while we're mourning our losses.'

'All hail the Prince of the Spear,' Larik said in an offhand voice, but there was genuine respect too. The commoners had dubbed Ril that at the jousts, and even if the other knights just rolled their eyes and grinned, he felt their spirits lift again.

'We've learned a lot here, lads,' he told them. 'Let's get back and pass it on. I don't want anyone else lost to ignorance. It's begun – we're at war now.'

Waqar paced back and forth, stamping down the tenacious grass of the plains, wishing there was more he could do, but Luka's life was in Fatima's hands now: she could use healing-gnosis and he couldn't. Right now she was simply pumping energy into Lukadin's lean frame, trying to replenish what he'd lost.

Waqar picked up the spear and examined it. The pale crystal behind the spearhead was a deep crimson, like the blood that had been running from Luka's nose when they reached him, but as he watched, the crystal faded until it was quiescent again.

The rocs were waddling about the plain a few miles west of the Silas River, as ungainly on the ground as they were graceful in the air. He'd sent Shameed with three others to fetch their fallen, while Tamir flew after the enemy; as he looked westwards he could see his friend returning.

'The Rondians stopped to talk a few miles away,' Tamir reported, when he landed. 'Then they flew off.'

'We should have pursued them,' Shameed complained. 'They would have been helpless!'

'They didn't look so helpless to me. I see eight gaps in our ranks where I once saw brave brothers and sisters,' Waqar pointed out, which quietened them all, even Shameed.

But of course Shameed was first to speak again. 'What did your friend do to kill that Rondian *matachod*? I have *never* seen the like of it!'

Everyone turned to Waqar, awaiting his answer, but he had his story ready. 'It's an experimental gnostic weapon; Lukadin volunteered to trial it,' he told them; that wasn't so far from the truth, he suspected. They'd found it in Midpoint Tower; it was the only one, so it most likely really was an experiment.

Everyone looked from the spear to Lukadin, whose nose was still bleeding, his skin ashen and his flesh so drawn the skeleton inside him was plain to see. None looked anxious to try out the spear themselves.

'Your friend is very brave,' one of the female riders commented. *Or very stupid*, her expression added.

Waqar saw post-combat shock on every face. They'd gone lance to lance with Rondian knights, the lords of the skies, and seen eight of their colleagues die in two passes. All the bravado and proud boasts that they were the equals or betters of those steel-clad veteran warriors had been proven to be idle indeed. It wasn't superior skill that had preserved them but luck, and Luka's ridiculous valour, but he had to draw something positive from this or he'd lose them.

'So, now we're *veterans*,' he began. 'We've met the enemy, and seen them abandon the fray. We've seen how they fight: in formation, each man protecting the flank of the man beside him. We've seen them blast us in the instant before combat – we'll be ready from now on. Did you note the steel shields they wear, screwed to their left shoulder? It's curved to deflect a blow and it leaves their arms free. And their beasts! They're heavy and strong – they can cripple a roc with one blow!'

They all nodded mutely, remembering the terror of impact.

'But *chod*, they were *slow*, eh? We climbed above them, we dived below them – half their speed again, don't you think? What strange creatures; at least our beautiful birds are first and foremost made to *fly*.'

'The winged horses are called a pegasus,' Tamir noted. 'I've read about them in stories from Lantris. And the lion-birds are called griffons.'

'Whatever they are, they're inferior,' Waqar declared. 'As Shameed said, we can fly rings around them.'

'But when we get close, what does that matter?' Baneet rumbled.

'One of those griffons almost took my bird's head off. We have to get close to hurt them, and when we get close, they take us apart.'

Waqar frowned; he'd wanted this conversation to be a rallying point, not a litany of their fears. But answers presented themselves. 'It's like fighting a Rondian legion: the veterans say they're good in close combat and formation fighting, but at Shaliyah we defeated them through mobility, rapid strikes and the use of archery. There are lessons for us to learn. How do we use our advantages – speed and manoeuvrability – to overcome our weaknesses?'

The girl who'd spoken earlier – she had a round face and a snub nose, more Rondian than Eastern, which wasn't uncommon among breeding-house magi – said, 'Your spear was first to slay an enemy, Prince Waqar.' She pulled her scarf from her neck and cut three thick threads from it, then tied one around his left wrist. 'My mother was from Mirobez, where archers mark their kills this way.' She stepped back and bowed mischievously. 'Sal-Ahm, *Alramh-amyr*!'

'*Prince of the Spear?*' Waqar wasn't sure he liked the name, especially as he had no intention of using this spear, nor of giving it back to Luka. 'Bashara, isn't it?'

'Ai,' she replied. She tied the second red ribbon around her own wrist. 'I shot the last who fell, in the throat.' Then she gave him the third. 'For Lukadin.'

He paused, then accepted the ribbon. 'Very well: a tradition is born. Right, we'll move when Luka is capable – Shameed, start setting up camp beside the river.'

He returned to Fatima to find Luka awake, wrapped in a blanket and looking deathly.

Waqar leaned close and murmured, 'You idiot. You almost killed yourself.'

Luka somehow mustered a wry smile. 'This is a holy war, my friend. What better way to die?'

Waqar would have hit him, if he hadn't been scared *any* blow might be fatal right now. 'What's better? I'll tell you, Luka: dying when you're seventy, surrounded by your family and friends and a hundred grandchildren – that's how I want to go, and I want you to be one of those friends, as old as me and just as blessed.'

'You can't choose your dying moment, Waqar.'

'Yes, you can – and it's called *suicide*, which was what you almost did,' he retorted. 'What did it matter if that knight got away? Nothing – no one cared if he escaped!'

'But I was so *angry*—'

Waqar put a hand on his friend's chest. 'I know – and that's why I can't let you have this spear back. I'm going to get rid of it, first opportunity.'

'*No!*' Luka's eyes bulged. 'You can't—'

'I can and I will.'

'No, you don't understand. It's mine—' He grasped Waqar's hand in his own shaking fingers and brought it to his rapidly thudding heart. 'Look at the gemstone in the spear,' he whispered.

It was pulsing red, in time with Luka's pulse. 'It's what's keeping me here,' he told Waqar. 'Take it away, and I'm dead.'

Waqar closed his eyes and blinked away fast-forming tears. Wordlessly, he pushed the weapon back into his friend's hands. *I wish we'd never found the damned thing*, he thought, though it had saved all of their lives at Midpoint Tower. 'Promise me you'll never use it again.'

Luka promised, but Waqar didn't believe him.

Late that night, Waqar walked a few hundred yards down the bank, stripped off and washed. The river was far colder than any river in Antiopia and he was shivering in seconds, but he made himself stay in so the icy water could reach into his bones and cleanse him of the terror, the images of near-death and the sickening *thud* when he'd planted his lance in the Rondian's chest.

He'd not been standing there long when he heard rustling on the grassy bank and Bashara appeared. Without a word, she languidly pulled her tunic over her head. Her breasts were high, her body shapely and the moonlight gleamed on her skin as she plunged into the water and swam out to him. Silently, she wrapped her arms around his shoulders and her legs around his hips and kissed him deeply.

'My Alramh-amyr,' she murmured, 'spear me.'

*

Latif suppressed a cynical smile as Hazarapati Selmir of Piru-Satabam III nudged his elephant to the front of the column, just ahead of Rani, but Ashmak, who had been about to lead the column forward, gave a vexed hiss. 'I want to be first across,' he muttered. 'Over there – that's the empire.'

'Half the army is already over the far side,' Latif pointed out.

'Being first in *our* unit matters. If Selmir had led the charge in battle, I'd not mind so much.'

Sanjeep nudged Rani forward, trailing Selmir's beast across the thick stone span that arched away into space. The only bridge to cross the mighty Silas River was fully a mile long.

All around them were ferries plying the waters, and the skies were full of windships – more than three hundred, according to Ashmak. Verelon had capitulated and the Shihad had reached the borders of the real empire. The Vereloni cities – really only towns by Eastern standards – were being plundered and occupied.

'They say the Rondian garrison for this bridge fled without a fight,' Ashmak said. 'They were supposed to destroy the bridge, but they didn't have the guts even for that. These Westerners have no backbone – they've only ever known victory and they don't know how to sell their lives for a higher cause.'

Latif wondered about that. 'I was at Riverdown,' he said – quietly, because Selmir was only a few yards ahead and he'd been at Riverdown too. 'We outnumbered them ten to one and still we couldn't penetrate their lines. When backs are to the wall, even the rabbit will fight.'

'Who were you, at Riverdown? You speak like a courtier at times.'

'Just an archer, son of a scribe,' Latif replied; that story had served him well.

Ashmak looked sceptical, but shrugged. 'You shoot well, and you and Sanjeep take good care of Rani. Keep your secrets; I won't ask again.'

They were halfway across when Latif noticed that Ashmak was staring fixedly at the right hind leg of the elephant in front of them. A faint flare of brownish-pink light played about his fingers momentarily and three seconds later, Selmir's beast trumpeted in distress and stumbled to a halt. As Selmir berated his mahout, Rani trudged past and into the lead.

'Poor thing tore a hamstring,' Ashmak said, grinning evilly. 'Shame; Selmir won't be first across after all.'

12

Corruption

Gnostic Trace

*Every mage's aura has a unique feeling, but the perception of it is very individual
– the sense I get of one mage will be broadly similar but slightly different to that
which another mage gets from the same person. For such reasons, gnostic trace is
an unreliable form of evidence in the Gnostic Laws.*

ARDO ACTIUM, MAGE-SCHOLAR, 748

Pallas, Rondelmar
Septinon 935

A cold autumn arrived in Pallas, but it was the news from her sprawling
realm that chilled Empress Lyra Vereinen more. *The Sacrecours ruled for
centuries. After five years I'm not sure I'll even survive a sixth . . .*

Rimoni and Silacia were a morass of conflict, mercenary legions
fighting endlessly in the ruins of the Rimoni Empire, where the mysterious Lord of Rym was apparently gaining the upper hand. The Church
was riven by crises, still without a prelature and divided over the Sisters' Crusade. Her Treasury was staggering towards bankruptcy, the
Imperocracy constantly carped about lack of resource, the merchants
complained of bad roads and banditry and the armies sent to fight the
Shihad were understrength and behind schedule.

Vita had performed her duties and gone, leaving Lyra in her nightdress and a heavy robe. The fire was finally warming her bedroom,
but her body ached from the exertions of being a seven-month-
pregnant woman in a building with a thousand stairs. She wished

she could ride a flying steed and fight, but here she was, battling her inner gloom instead.

'So much depends on you,' she told the little body inside her womb as she sat on her balcony, looking south across the Bruin River. Delivering an heir was the one big thing she could do right now: a chance to plant a banner against the disintegration that surrounded her.

She was learning remedies against despair; she closed her eyes, put her hands to her stomach until she could feel the pulse of a heartbeat within – probably imagined, but it was enough. *I'm fighting for my child, for my husband and for all who rely on me. I will be strong.* She thought of what Ostevan had told her: that her dwyma came from Kore. That was something to cling to. Her God fought at her side – surely that meant she would prevail?

Encouraged by the thought, she trudged down the stairs into her garden. The evening was still young, the western sky a glorious violet-purple hue, and the crescent moon shone brilliant above, lighting her path as she passed through the rose bowers and into the trees to her favourite bench, where she sat with a sigh of relief.

Every bird she saw, a pair of squirrels and even a small lizard, were watching her warily, and within minutes, a dozen moths were fluttering around her as well. But she quickly lost awareness of all that as she plunged her awareness into the dwyma's ghostly web of light. She'd been coming here every day, at dawn or after dusk, exploring her power, trying to ensure that when the next test came she could rise to meet it, despite her condition.

In her mind, a map had been growing, from the mountains to the north separating Rondelmar from Hollenia, west into Ventia and east to the Sacrecour lands and even into Brevis and Andressea, and south all the way to Midrea and Bricia, all linked by gossamer traces of shared awareness. Dirklan had told her that daemons lurked in the aether, just out of reach of this world – some, he said, were vast amalgams of minds, the dead and the never-alive. The web she sensed was a little like that, but *it* was very much alive, and of this world. She brushed against it and it saw her and *consented* to her presence.

More than that, she now knew that Aradea was aware of other

guardian spirits. She had the names and natures of these *genilocii* from the books Dirklan had been supplying: Saint Eloy had been associated with *Keranthor*, said to be Aradea's consort; *Epyros* was associated with the dwymancer Lanthea, and the clouds; *Urybos*, an earth-being, was linked to a dwymancer woman named Dameta, and the dwymancer Amantius was with *Seidopus* in the sea – and these were just the most-often mentioned. She felt like a child looking up at the stars, holding the hand of an adult as they named the constellations.

She touched the nodes of light in this web of stars and found a familiar one: the little garden in Coraine where the dwyma had first noticed her. She could smell the lavender there, taste the dew on the leaves and hear raindrops splashing on leaves. She moved on, finding other Winter Tree saplings: in a rain-swept churchyard in Brevis; beside a ruin in Argundy and by a lake in Ventia where the last rays of sunlight still played. Once, she touched the mind of a fox that had taken up residence in an old Sollan shrine in Aquillea and found a strange level of intelligence.

She tried again for the dark-haired man in the snowy place . . .

. . . and recoiled as if slapped.

She blinked out of her trance, her mind still frozen with that brief glimpse – a wolf's growl and then the young man, a flash of his face – then he was gone, leaving only an impression of frightened shock.

He knows even less of what he is than I do, she realised.

She tried again, this time thinking not of him but of the wise-looking grey-haired woman she'd glimpsed beside him. It took an effort, but she was certain her search wasn't *unnoticed*; she was being watched in turn, she was sure, the way the animals of her garden watched when she entered: curious but wary, unsure if she was a dangerous presence.

Hello? she called. She tried a name . . . *Lanthea?* She had been one of the four great dwymancers of the time of Saint Eloy. She'd used other names too: *Lutey? Luhti?*

She felt a sudden shift in the regard of whoever watched her, and then a distinct *closing out*; her inner vision shut down and she found herself back in her garden, dizzied from the rush of movement, followed by the shock of being still. *How did she do that?* Because it had been a *she*, she was sure. *Lanthea.*

She's watching over that young man, she realised, *just as Aradea watches over me.* That gave her some comfort, but it also raised questions, because Aradea was a genilocus, and Lanthea had been a dwymancer. Did dead dwymancers haunt their own magic?

Looking up, she realised the sky was black; at least an hour had passed and the air was growing cold. She climbed wearily back to her balcony and paused to enjoy the view. There were oil-lamps in the squares, and some buildings were lit, especially the imposing dome of the Celestium, reflected in the river.

What's that? She stared, almost sure she'd seen a dark shape flit through the rose bower and disappear into her garden, but when she stared again, there was just a bush, moving in the breeze. And she was too tired to go down again to see.

Deciding she was imagining things, she went inside, settled on her couch and opened Dirklan's book to read more about the four great dwymancers, those who'd truly mastered it and whose deaths had been accounted as the victorious end to the secret war the early magi had waged against them. Eloy had been a saint, but he died in the shadows; Dameta died, Lanthea wanished and the sea-lord Amantius had gone mad. But there had been dozens more dwymancers before the Church and the Rondian Empire moved against them. She could recount the histories almost word for word now, but there was no advice on how to *be* a dwymancer.

I'm going to have to make it up as I go along.

Sleep felt far away, so she went to her prayer-kneeler, lifted her eyes to the Sacred Heart icon and began to recite the Prayer of Safe Passage, for Ril and all her soldiers; and then the Prayer for Rest, because right now, she *really* needed to sleep . . .

Ostevan stole into the Winter Garden, keeping to the deepest shadows. It had been somewhat alarming to glimpse Lyra on the balcony above, as if somehow the garden had warned her of his intrusion, but she didn't appear to have seen him, and now she was indoors the night was his again.

He'd used illusion and kinesis to get past the guards at Greengate, but once inside he'd abandoned all use of gnosis for fear of alerting the genilocus to his presence. For a mage not using his power was like walking blindfolded, but the moon was bright and he reached his goal easily, although his unease grew with every step: the whole garden radiated energies that were the very antithesis of his daemon ichor.

This is life, and that inside me is unlife, he realised, without regret. He wished he dared to engage gnostic sight, but he was frightened to do so, instead fumbling about until he found the place where Twoface had perished, the one place that looked sickly here. There were tiny black crystals scattered among the rotting vines and grass – desiccated ichor, he realised, stripped of its potency. There were bones too.

One wrong step and I'll share the same fate. He looked up, sensing eyes on him: a pair of owls, a lizard beside the wall, a frog in the pond, mice lurking about the bower, nesting amongst the tree roots. But nothing rose against him. The books said that without a dwymancer to articulate its will, a genilocus was largely passive.

So here I am, in my enemy's inner sanctum . . . Can I damage it without sharing Twoface's fate? He feared that spreading fresh ichor would probably draw out the genilocus – and anyway, he didn't want Lyra to be infected; he wanted her to be a willing accomplice. He was here to break through her natural reserve, that sense of morality and probity that would prevent her from fully renouncing Ril Endarion and turning to him. He suspected only natural elements would produce the brew he desired, so he'd begun with a dirty brown paste from crushed poppy seed, adding his own blood after running it over silver to remove the ichor, to ensure she dreamed of him. Adding clay, he'd shaped a crude form of a pregnant woman and hardened it with Earth-gnosis and heat. Finally, he'd engaged mystic-gnosis and enchanted the figure, making it a conduit to capture, radiate and enhance a dream-sending. *Setallius would detect a direct sending, but this isn't direct . . .*

When he dropped the clay figure into Lyra's pool he felt the aether quiver for a second. That held promise; if this worked, he'd have a whole new line of attack upon his unwitting prey. He stole away back to his quarters to commence the dream-sending.

I'll be back, Lyra, every night, until you too are clay in my hand.

Halfway through her prayers, Lyra lost track of the words – and indeed, any will to pray at all. She was looking up at the Sacred Heart image when the words just drizzled away from her mouth. She fell into a strange disorienting reverie; feeling woozy, she tried to stand, but almost fell. She crawled to the bed and climbed up, wondering if she was about to be sick, but she made it to the top and lay there on her side, a little scared – but then that faded, leaving her in a waking dream that felt pleasantly real.

In her imagination, strong but gentle arms enfolded her. 'Ril?' she murmured, closing her eyes and just *pretending* that he was holding her ... but the fantasy changed and now she was kneeling before a beautiful marble seraph clad in shimmering white robes, with huge marble wings on his back. Watching in wonder, it came to life and drew her into his embrace. She sank backwards into him, his arms wrapped around her, and she felt the most wondrous floating feeling, as if he bore her in flight over the night-time world.

Lyra, the seraph whispered, his pure breath teasing her ears sensuously, *you belong with us.* The Song of the Seraphim that began at dawn on the First Day and would echo through eternity, rose around her as they spun and swooped among the stars.

It was quietly glorious, a feeling of absolute belonging, of being in one's rightful place at the centre of everything, held in secure arms and loved despite her weakness. It was perfect ...

She woke weeping for sheer joy, and then from loss, for waking broke the dream. But the warmth and safety of the experience stayed with her, sustaining her so that even alone in the darkness she felt completely safe, and free.

Lyra, the night whispered in a voice she almost knew. *Lyra, I love you.*

She couldn't remember his face, but she knew it would be gentle and somehow familiar, with a quirky and ironic smile that forgave her sins and loved her unconditionally. His eyes ... she would know them too, deep, wise orbs that saw to her soul, that always knew what she needed.

For the first time since Ril left, she didn't miss him. She wasn't alone, because she had Kore. Though it would have been lovely to have someone here now, to tell about her dream.

That feeling of euphoria was gently nudged to the back of Lyra's mind by her morning duties: the rituals of breakfasting and dressing, her spymaster's daily briefing, dispensing alms at the Queensgate, holding court, listening to the pleas of the Guildsmen for tax relief – which Calan Dubrayle told her firmly to refuse.

But finally she was able to return to her suite for her Unburdening: the highlight of her day.

'Good afternoon, Majesty,' Ostevan greeted her warmly, gesturing at the prayer-kneelers where they normally conversed, semi-concealed behind painted screens showing Easterners hunting and dancing, plunder from a previous Crusade. 'Shall we begin?'

She weighed the effort of kneeling against her exhaustion, then said, 'Let's use the couch – I'm so tired!' She signalled to Basia to withdraw, then sat beside him on the sofa, bursting to tell him of her dream but shy of sharing such an intimacy; instead, she just stared at him, beaming and feeling as silly as an infatuated girl. She found herself noticing little things: his almost perfect skin, and his fine bone-structure, accentuated by a small goatee and thin moustaches, his beautifully rippling dark brown hair. She realised that her imaginary seraph had looked like him, if he were to shave . . .

People say some of the court ladies worship *Ostevan . . . I can see why . . .* Somehow her thinking had drifted from the spiritual to something much more earthy. Her breasts were swelling uncomfortably and her nipples were sensitive – and suddenly realising she'd stuck her chest out a little, she felt her cheeks colour.

'I had the most wonderful dream,' she said, finding herself babbling. 'I dreamed a seraph statue – one of those beautiful Lantric ones, where every muscle has been perfectly rendered? – came to life and held me in his arms as he flew through the stars. It was wonderful, like a visitation.'

'Perhaps that's what it was,' Ostevan said, nodding to himself as if something he'd suspected were confirmed. 'It's known that daemons can sometimes reach into our dreams – why not the seraphim? Especially to one they have already blessed.'

She felt that magical rush again, that giddy euphoria. *Ostevan has eyes like my seraph. He sees me when no one else does . . . Why won't Ril look at me the way he does?*

'Is there anything you wish to Unburden?' he asked her.

'No, only . . . No, I feel at peace today, Ostevan, truly, I do.' *Just to be with you . . .* Then a slap of guilt struck her and she berated herself as a faithless bint, cringing at how hopelessly confused her feelings were becoming all of a sudden. 'Let's go to my garden,' she suggested, the place where her thoughts always felt more ordered.

He hesitated, probably thinking of propriety, then said, 'Of course.'

They descended the balcony stairs together, Basia de Sirou trailing discreetly behind them, and strolled through the flower beds, which were in full late summer bloom. Insects were buzzing, birds singing and the air was sultry and warm. Lyra felt sweat begin to glisten on her brow and pool in her hollows, but she revelled in the warmth.

'What do you think of the Sisters' Crusade?' she asked, wondering how she'd have reacted if the question had come up when she was in her convent – not that the Sacrecours would ever have let her leave the place.

Ostevan smiled. 'It's amusing, isn't it?'

'Is it?' she said, a little glad to find some fault with his words. 'I find their arguments compelling. Why shouldn't women have equal status to men in the Church?'

He looked taken aback, but recovered smoothly. 'I don't disagree: when I said amusing, I meant the way it's being handled, not the issue itself. Indeed, it *should* be debated. But not in this undignified way. If popular opinion is allowed to dictate policy, where will it end?'

'I suppose. I wonder what would happen if Grand Prelate Wurther were to – Kore forfend – pass away? Who would succeed him when there isn't a quorum of prelates to elect anyone?'

'Every grand prelate leaves a testimony in which they state their preferred heir. This is traditionally opened and read out during the election process, but the prelates aren't obliged to follow his will. It's only ever been done once, in the eighth century.'

'I see you've been studying the matter.'

'We're all studying our procedural texts at the moment, Majesty – but I'm excluded, regardless.'

'I do wish you and Dominius could be reconciled,' she sighed. 'You belong in high places.'

'And here I am, conversing with you. I can't think of a higher place.'

His little flattery pleased her – and then annoyed her – and then pleased her again. *Why am I so unsteady today?* She knew, though: she had touched perfection in her dream and now the imperfect world felt inadequate. What had felt transcendent while alone in the dark felt more base in the light of day. As they passed through the roses, she remembered something she'd wanted his opinion on. 'Do you know Lady Aventour?'

'Medelie Aventour? I know who she is – but she isn't one for Unburdenings and I presume she attends the church in Highgrange, so I've not really met her.'

'She's been walking out with Sir Solon Takwyth.'

Ostevan gave her a shrewd look. 'Does this worry you?'

Lyra bit her lip. *Perhaps this is a kind of jealousy, to be concerned that those devoted to my security have other relationships? Takwyth once wanted to marry me . . .* 'It would be charitable to be pleased for him, I suppose, but after Reeker Night, new faces worry me,' she confessed.

'She is young and charming, from what I hear,' Ostevan said.

'I found her less so at the Grand Tourney.' Then she mused, 'What would Sir Solon want with a woman half his age?'

'What any man wants, I imagine,' Ostevan remarked, then he looked up. 'Apologies, Majesty. It's not my place to say such a thing.'

'Sir Solon is my Knight-Commander, on whom the safety of the Bastion falls, and she seems to be a gold-mining chit. He should be able to see through her.'

'We're all blind to some things, Milady.'

They'd both turned to glance at Basia de Sirou before she realised what he was implying.

Or confirming. Her heart clenched and she felt a flash of sullen anger, blended with sadness that her husband could be happier with someone else, mingled with pity for all of them.

Dear Kore, is my confessor the only person I can wholly trust? A thought occurred to her, that Ostevan more than anyone else might appreciate the gifts this garden gave. 'I want to show you something,' she said, excited and pleased when he looked mystified, and she led him eagerly to the Oak Grove. The Comfateri was looking about him apprehensively, which restored some of her equilibrium.

This is my *place*, she thought as she led him to her pool. *My chapel.* She frowned; it looked a little murky, but she scooped some water into the wooden cup she kept there and turned to her confessor. 'Ostevan, try some of this. I believe that Aradea herself purifies it.'

The irony that Lyra, drugged up on poppy dreams, was inadvertently offering him a cup of destruction wasn't lost on Ostevan. His little experiment was working too damned well – so now he must accept, or risk losing her burgeoning affection.

Great men will risk everything, went the old quote – some Rimoni general who'd risen to be emperor had used it as the title of his self-congratulatory memoir. Still, Ostevan agreed; those words had been on his mind when he'd risked all for Lyra in 930, and they were again today.

His heart was still thudding as he took the cup.

Lyra had been emotionally all over the place this morning, veering between flirtatious and reproving; she'd voiced jealousies and insecurities she'd never before mentioned – and now this. He considered – and discarded – an excuse; that would have repercussions, especially with Basia de Sirou an interested observer: there would certainly be a visit shortly thereafter from Setallius. He could be forced into the open too soon and lose everything.

I have to pass this little test ... Twoface had perished in this place, destroyed by the same forces Lyra held in that cup. Cautiously, Ostevan damped down the link to Abraxas until it was just a faint whisper and prepared to act. He was aware of Basia nearby, and Lyra was watching him with her big eyes. She was so ripe for the plucking, perhaps just a kiss away – but she wasn't ready yet, and she wouldn't be, unless he drank and lived.

He gave himself over to fate, took the cup and drained it.

Then he laughed inwardly, because the mixture of drugs and blood he'd poured into the pool had been enough to remove the purity that would have endangered him.

It's just water now ... spiritually harmless. He handed the empty cup with a smile. 'Very efficacious, Milady. You are blessed to have such a pure spring to yourself. I'm honoured that you would share something so precious with me.'

Pleasure suffused her face, and something deeper as she gazed up at him, her head tilted upwards like an offering. Had Basia not been there, it would have been so easy ... And she knew it, and knew he knew, and she didn't look away.

The trust is total now. The rest will follow.

The Celestium, Pallas

There is a quiet place inside us all where time doesn't exist, or so Exilium Excelsior's blade-master at the Arcanum in Estellayne always said. He'd been trying to impart the need to be calm, to be in repose, even in the heat of action. *Only when we're in that silent place do we see all that we need to, to survive moment to moment.*

When Exilium had found that place inside himself it had been a breakthrough moment.

In those days he had gone by his birth-name, Carlo Quesada of Grafitè in Estellan, third son of a particularly devout mage-knight. He was physically gifted, but prone to panic, in combat and in life, thrashing about madly and hurting himself and all around him. But when he finally managed to divorce himself from that rising tide of rage and fury, that calm place changed not just his ability to fight, but everything else. He'd learned to use the gnosis with utmost efficiency, discovering himself to be a trance-mage, who could juggle many spells at once. He'd learned to meditate in prayer, to sleep on his feet and go for days

222

with minimal rest. His awareness of all around him had increased tenfold. That quiet place was the best place he knew, and he could take it wherever he went.

'Ah, Exilium,' Grand Prelate Dominius Wurther rumbled, emerging from his office with Chaplain Ennis, who scurried off on some errand. 'Have you eaten?'

'It isn't midday, Holiness. I eat only at midday.'

The grand prelate gave him a pitying look. 'Admirable, I suppose. Come, I have a meeting.'

Unusually, he led him down a long, shadowy corridor which, as far as Exilium knew, led only to the servants' quarters. But the grand prelate took a turning which wound through crypts, empty courtyards and deserted promenades stuffed with dusty relics.

'How are you settling in?' the grand prelate asked as they traversed a darkened hall.

Exilium was surprised to be asked; his father maintained the feelings of inferiors were beneath a man of rank – and anyway, emotions were confusing. People were too variable – Exilium had never understood them. It was one of the attractions of the Church, that everyone would think the same way. As it turned out, though, priests argued worse than fishwives.

'Well, Holiness,' he said dutifully.

'Made a few friends, I hope?'

Exilium frowned, unable to tell if the grand prelate was mocking him or taking a genuine interest. 'I don't make friends. It would interfere with my duties.'

'We all need friends, Exilium.'

'Only our duty to Kore matters,' Exilium replied. 'All else is unnecessary.'

That amiably lugubrious face looked perplexed. 'Kore made us social animals, Exilium: we cannot exist without each other. Even insects create hives.'

'With respect, I disagree,' Exilium replied stolidly.

'But what do we do anything for, if not for friendship? No man can triumph alone. We must band together to survive and thrive. Men need each other. And women, too.' The grand prelate nudged him as if they were drunks at a bar. 'There wouldn't be much of a species without women, eh?'

'I've always thought that regrettable,' Exilium said uncomfortably. To his intense embarrassment, his boss roared with laughter. He tried to work out why. *Oh my Lord, does he think I'm a froci now?* 'I respect all women, of course,' he stammered, 'and I *adore* my sister!'

He only laughed more. 'You're the soul of an Estellan, Exilium.'

'Holiness, if my views displease you, there are other men who could perform my duties—'

'But none of them would be *you*,' he interrupted. 'You're beyond price. And you love your family and respect others. These are the base values of a good man.'

Am I being mocked again, or appreciated? Exilium had never been able to tell. Faces, bodies, tones and words were such a puzzle. 'I do my best.'

'I'm sure you do, but you should make friends among my staff. We have only two eyes and two hands. We need others if we are to be strong and fulfil our duties.'

That at least made some sense. 'I will endeavour to befriend other men,' he promised.

'Buy a round of drinks.'

'I don't drink. Intoxicants are a pernicious evil.'

'Of course they are ... but sometimes we have to pretend to like them, to make friends.' The grand prelate winked. 'You don't think I actually *enjoy* all this food and wine, do you? No, my consumption is purely for conviviality's sake.' He laughed again, then pointed to an unlit stair going down below ground. 'Now, I have a meeting in there. Please await me here.'

Exilium looked around doubtfully. They'd ended up in a somewhat derelict part of the Celestium, where old mausoleums and libraries sat alongside each other: burial grounds for books and bones. 'Here, Holiness?' he said uncertainly.

'Here. Don't worry, the man I'm meeting likes to lurk in such places, but he is a valuable member of the clergy.' He patted his arm again. 'Take a seat; I may be some time.'

It wasn't Exilium's place to question, so he bowed and sat on a stone bench beneath a broken statue of a seraph, watching the grand prelate huffing and puffing down the stairs.

In the Inquisition he'd thought to find spiritual brothers and sisters, but mostly what he'd found were fragments of virtue, thinly spread among a group of brilliant but cruel, avaricious and *worldly* mage-knights too bent on temporal domination to realise that true freedom was spiritual. The journey outwards came from turning one's eyes within. That's why he'd sought service in the one place where perfection surely must exist, and he'd risen quickly in the Celestium too – but even here, imperfection was the norm, venality and corruption just as prevalent.

But he was learning to steel himself against it, resolved to reach the heart of this holy place – which had, quite unexpectedly, led him to be given the sacred task of protecting the holiest man on Urte.

And now I wonder if he is just as sinful as the Inquisition . . . He'd seen gluttony, avarice and jealousy, heard lies and glimpsed other, deeper sins – and the grand prelate tolerated it, even *used* it, he was coming to realise. Although the richness and splendour of the buildings and monuments made his heart soar at the glory of Kore, the stench of sin tainted everything.

No wonder the holiest of the Estellan saints were all hermits. One day, he'd take that path too – but for now, he was not yet shorn of human ties, and his father and sister depended on the money he sent back to Grafitè. *Duty elevates,* said the *Book of Kore. Duty gives meaning.*

There has *to be some meaning,* he told himself. *Somehow, life has to make sense.*

'Well?' Dominius Wurther rumbled from the shadows, and Friar Deshard turned as if caught unawares, though Wurther was quite certain he'd detected him entering the vault. The grand prelate waddled to an old sarcophagus where food and drink had been laid out and sniffed the wine. 'Hmmm, a Silacian achantia. You must try it, Deshard.'

'I have an ale and that'll do me fine,' Deshard sniffed. 'I'm from Tockburn: we ain't fine topers like you.' He glanced towards the stairs. 'Where's your new shadow?'

'Young Exilium? Upstairs, with instructions to keep his eyes open and his ears shut.'

'You're the first grand prelate since Loekryn to need a personal guard,' Deshard noted. 'Why is that?'

'Because none of them did anything worth getting killed over. They were just caretakers in purple cloth. The Lord of Hel himself wouldn't have objected to anything they ever did.'

'Whereas the Dark One sees you as a genuine threat, I'm sure.'

'My enemies would say he sees me as competition,' Wurther chuckled.

Deshard smirked, then asked, 'So, what's troubling your Worship-fulness?'

'What isn't? I've only got seventeen prelates, which is eight shy of a quorum, and I can practically feel the crossbows aimed at my back. Beleskey's not found these Masks and neither have you. Ostevan Jan-dreux is still whispering in Lyra's pretty little ears, and I've got Valetta della Rodrigo and her safian wolfpack on my doorstep, demanding to be treated as "equals", whatever the Hel that means.'

'To be fair,' Deshard tutted, 'I doubt more than a tenth of the sisters are saffies. That's the usual count in any place where you lock a bunch of women up together for too long without a man.' He pulled a wry grin. 'Or if you lock up men with men, for that matter – want to guess at the number of frocio in the clergy?'

'It was a figure of speech, and no, I don't! I don't care what they do in their cloisters; I just want them to bugger off back to them.' Wur-ther drained his goblet and poured more. 'The question I set you was this: why is everyone turning me down? I've got thirty-two prelates' sinecures and I can't fill half of them!'

'Because everyone sees them as a death warrant,' Deshard replied. 'You didn't need me to tell you that.'

'But are my candidates being actively warned off accepting?'

'I don't think so. The fact of it is, people believe you're doomed, and your little empress too. They think the Sacrecours will be back in charge by year's end and don't want to be on the wrong side of the bloodletting.'

'But I worked hand-in-glove with the Sacrecours when they were in power – I'll still be here when Lyra Vereinen and her fool husband are just headstones.'

'You crowned her, so your fates are entwined – I've heard a Sacrecour agent say exactly that.'

'It's got that bad?'

'The riots will start soon in the poorer quarters,' Deshard predicted. 'The soldiers are all off at war and Dubrayle's tax-farmers are facing open resistance – most of them are pocketing everything they can and sending nothing north anyway. It's been a complete disaster, but Dubrayle can't see it, and neither can Lyra. Lovely girl and all, but she's no more a ruler than I am. She's too nice. You need to be a villain in this game, present company included. All it's going to take is a flashpoint and the empire will fly apart, mark my words.'

Wurther would have liked to disagree, but sadly, he feared Deshard was right. 'But Garod Sacrecour . . . ?'

Deshard snorted. 'That cunni? He's one option. But there's another fella who could unite everyone against Garod, given the chance.'

'Takwyth.'

'Aye. He should've had the throne in 930. His time's not just come, it's overdue. You need to get chummy with him, Worshipfulness, because he'll be emperor one day soon.'

Wurther sighed heavily. Lyra had been a gamble, but perhaps it was time to cut his losses. 'Perhaps you're right. Takky could well be the coming man.'

'Unless you're planning on uniting the two thrones yourself?' Deshard enquired. 'It's been centuries since we had a real Pontifex. Did all those nuns shouting "Dominius Pontifex" get you excited?'

'The last man to voice that old dream was Ostevan,' Wurther told Deshard reprovingly, 'so don't you start. I don't believe in much, but I do support the separation of Church and Crown – for survival purposes.'

Deshard gave him a wry grin. 'Then best you bed down with Solon Takwyth, before someone else does.'

Highgrange, Pallas

'Oh Solon, oh Milord – yes! Yes – yes! Oh Sweet Kore, *yes!*'

Medelie Aventour's gasps were both music and goad to Solon's ears, driving him on in another frenzied bout, their bodies battering at each other, her fingers raking his back. He could feel release coming; he'd been fighting to hold it back, to spend more time in this state of near-ecstasy, but when she went into rapture beneath him, arching her back, her breasts pressed heavenwards in the most intoxicating way, her face wild with anguished pleasure, that took him over the edge. Quivering uncontrollably as he flooded her, they sank into the softness of the mattress, dazed in the aftermath of passion.

'Kore's Blood, you do me well,' Medelie panted. 'I swear I almost fainted.'

He gasped for breath, trying to imprint this moment for all time. His marriage had *never* been like this. *Is this still my life?* he wondered. Her darkened boudoir was heavy with candles scented with rich oils; they didn't quite mask the musky smells of fresh sweat and bodily fluids, but he didn't care – he adored those smells too. The intoxication of learning her mysteries captivated him. *Medelie Aventour, with your hair of midnight, eyes of fire, lips of wine: a poem made flesh, here in my arms.*

'Every man should experience such joy,' he said, losing himself in her eyes.

'The joy of bedding me?' she asked, her eyes teasing. 'That's just for you, my dearest.'

'No, I meant this feeling of . . . *everything* . . . pleasure and fulfilment and oneness . . .' He struggled to find the right words. Sexual union with his deceased wife had been unfulfilling from the first moment; she'd claimed it hurt and humiliated her. Inevitably, there had been no children. But making love to Medelie – that was heart-stopping. She hadn't been a virgin; her ease with her sexuality had, he was certain, helped them find this glorious rapport.

'Is this feeling you describe anything like love?' she suggested archly.

Love? Perhaps that's what it is? He felt so swept up in her that he couldn't tell if this was just infatuation. 'I only know that I've never felt this way before.' When she stroked the good side of his face, he seized her hand and placed it against his branded cheek. 'Does this trouble you?'

'No, never. I see you as you truly are.'

'Those scars are how I truly am.'

'No. You're perfect, Solon. You always have been.' She pulled his face down to her breasts, like a mother cradling a child. 'I've always loved you.'

'You barely know me,' he snorted, making no effort to move away. 'We've only just met.'

'You think so – but I believe that I've known you all my life. You're the best of men. It should be you on the throne, not that upstart Ril Endarion.'

That made him go still. He'd spoken such words himself, many times, and others had said them to him. Yes, he knew he was the better man, and that Lyra Vereinen had been stolen from him – but this wasn't the right time for such thoughts. 'I've learned to bide my time,' he replied at last, and added, 'And were I Prince-Consort, I wouldn't be here in your bed.'

'Who knows? I would still have come to court.'

'And I would be a devoted husband to my wife.'

'Then let us celebrate that things are as they are. Thank Kore for my faithful knight!' she added, and when he suddenly frowned, she asked, 'What is it?'

'That's just what old Radine Jandreux used to say to me.'

She giggled. 'Were you bedding her too, "Faithful Knight"?'

'No! She was twice my age and as prim an old biddy as you'd ever meet.'

Medelie pulled an odd face. 'I thought you Corani revered her?'

'Revere? I suppose we did. She was our duchess, and as shrewd as they come. She put all her life into House Corani. Without her, there would be no Lyra Vereinen. Radine was bitter, though, when Endarion took Lyra behind her back. It killed her in the end.'

'She had every right to be angry,' Medelie said, with surprising heat.

She stroked his shoulder. 'Solon, should aught happen to the upstart, you mustn't let opportunity slip through your fingers. You should have had her in 930; everyone knows this. The empire needs you.'

He sat up, a little uneasy. 'I hadn't thought you so political – nor so eager to push me off onto another woman.' He looked into her bewitching eyes. 'Are you tiring of me already?'

'Oh, no,' she replied with a giggle, 'I want you all for myself. But sometimes personal ambitions have to be sacrificed for the greater good.'

That struck him as a surprisingly worldly view for a young woman, but then she leaned in and kissed his scarred face and was his young lover again. 'Do you have any energy left?' she purred. 'Because I do . . .'

He let her pull him down into the softness of her yielding body.

And afterwards, he dreamed of a throne.

13

Collistein Castle

Prepared Ground

It is a truism that in a trial of strength, defensive gnosis tends to defeat offensive gnosis. This is because an attack, by its nature, leaves the caster like an arrow fired from a bow. The defender has a shield they can strengthen, while the attacker loses contact with his weapon when it's discharged, so it can't be further empowered. The other advantage of defence is the ability to prepare the ground: there are spells that can weaken an anticipated attack, provided one knows of the attack in advance. As always, knowing one's enemy is the key.

MAGISTER JOSIH ORTYNA, ESTELLAN BATTLE-MAGE, 838

Collistein, Matra Ranges
Septinon 935

Url Rudman, Battle-mage Secundus of Midrea VII, was a puzzled man. Two weeks ago, a wide patrol had caught one of the shaggy red cattle-beasts the Brevians called rufines, wandering alone on the Kedron Plains. Quite apart from the fact that rufines had never been seen in these parts, this one was a bull-calf, which meant there should be more of them: but he was still surprised by the sight at his gates: a whole damned herd of rufines, grazing the killing field in front of Collistein's gates as placidly as if it were a farmer's paddock.

'What do you think, sir?' asked Laine. The aide was one of those well-connected young mage-nobles with a glittering future, thanks to his knowledge of etiquette and military theory, for all he barely knew which end of a javelin to point at the enemy. One of the few joys of

Rudman's military life was outranking morons like him, at least for a time. Doubtless he was a future general.

'Damned if I know,' Rudman admitted. 'But there's enough beef down there to see us through winter and to spare.'

'I weep to think of it,' Laine agreed enthusiastically. 'Push garlic and rosemary into the flesh and baste as they turn the spit-roast . . . divine.' He licked pink lips.

'Does sound good.' Rudman glanced up at the watchtower, where his tribune was already drunk. The decision was his, but opening the gates was no small matter. The fortress guarded the road to the pass and the city of Collistein, built on a plateau above and left; a travel-ler could bypass the city but must still traverse a number of arched passages and courtyards designed to be death-traps to the unwelcome. Collistein had never fallen, though in truth, the only attacks had been by Schlessen tribes with no magi.

Wherever they came from, this rufine herd is now legion property, Rudman decided. 'Okay, bring them inside and take them to the west pens where we put that calf we found. They look pretty lean; we'll need to fatten them up.'

Laine sighed. 'Do we have to wait? That's a shame . . . How about testing just one?'

'Trust me, that'd be a waste,' Rudman told him sagely. 'Right now they'll be tough as old boots. Tell you what, get the cooks to broach that salted pork we've been saving. That'll give everyone a lift.' He did his best for his men. Kore knew, Collistein was a shithole of a post-ing. Empress Lyra, bless her pretty face, might think she ruled all of Yuros, but everyone knew that the empire ended here, at the edge of the Kedron.

The herding was no problem: the rufines were so compliant they walked straight in the gates of their own volition, and by then hundreds of burghers had lined the walls to watch. Novelties always brought a crowd – you never knew who or what might blow in from the lowlands.

That got Rudman's mind working. The recent news from Mollachia hadn't been good. He'd exchanged despatches with Governor Inoxion and occasionally with the Delestre siblings; but the last word he'd had, from a Mollach fur-trader with a cartload of pelts to trade, was that Robear Delestre was dead, the Sarkany brothers were free and the kingdom was in open rebellion.

He remembered the Sarkany brothers. He'd picked them up as a favour to Sacrista Delestre, thinking she might let him lift her skirts, but no such bloody luck. She'd flown off with them and that was the last he'd heard until the rumours of rebellion began. The last letter from Inoxion, six weeks ago, had requested soldiers, but Rudman's legion answered to the Governor of Noros so he'd refused. Mollachia wasn't their business.

We've got bigger things to worry about: like that giant Keshi army in Pontus, or wherever it is by now. Rudman was beginning to fear the imperial muster would take so long that he'd have a Shihad army at his gates well before the soldiers arrived. Tribune Gallius had petitioned for reinforcements, but none had been forthcoming.

He finished walking the walls, as he did every evening, then told Laine, 'Let's go and have a peek at those rufines.'

They made their way to the western pens, to find pretty much every ranker not on duty or asleep had gathered to appraise the cattle. You could always trust a soldier to have a keen eye out for his next meal. 'What did you make of the reports of a Sydian migration, sir?' Laine asked, as they admired the big shaggy beasts.

'I guess not all the savages like having those Noories arriving on their doorstep,' Rudman said. 'Our windskiff patrols have spotted a migratory tribe – they reckon twenty thousand souls, with vast numbers of cattle and horses, some forty miles southeast, but they've not moved in several days. As long as they don't come here, all's well.' Rudman removed his helmet and rubbed his balding pate. He stared at a grizzled bull rufine, noting the enormous pronged horns. 'First thing tomorrow, get the butchers to hack off all those horns,' he told Laine. 'They're a damned menace.'

The rufine studied him as if it was following every word, then it grunted, turned, lifted its tail and shat a great steaming pile of dung. 'I'll have that one's horns as a souvenir,' Rudman added.

He and Laine spent the evening dealing with the usual routines and mini-crises that were army life: a couple of rankers brawling in the east courtyard; parents from the city demanding a soldier own up – and *pay* up – for what he *allegedly* did to their daughters, and the usual stream of reports coming in from returning mounted and airborne patrols. 'Are all the scouts in?' he asked with a yawn as the third night-bell rang.

'All in, sir. Sherborne thought he spotted a group of men some six miles away, but he lost the light before he could verify. Possibly a hunting party from that Sydian tribe? Maybe a little close, do you think?'

'Perhaps those rufines belonged to the tribe and they're tracking them.'

'No brands,' Laine reminded him, 'though perhaps Sydians don't brand?'

'Best we play safe, then: double the watch, walls *and* gate. It's probably nothing, but it's time we got this fortress ready for action in any case. The Noories will soon be here, mark my words.'

Rudman dismissed Laine and headed for the legate's tower. As secundus he was a military man, but the commanding tribune was always a political appointment and Rudman had been dealing with a succession of them throughout his career: powerful magi with no fucking idea how to run a legion who got bored, had hare-brained ideas and were generally the bane of his life. Fortunately, Tribune Gallius drank heroically, which made him pretty easy to control. By now he'd be too sozzled to comprehend anything he was told, so Rudman just tucked a written report under his door.

Within the hour he was dozing towards sleep, thankful to be out of his armour, listening to the rain as it began to strike his shutters. *Kore-bedamned place. Pity any bastard who's out there tonight.* He snuffed out the candle and closed his eyes . . .

. . . until he jerked out of a dream of wading through cowshit by a grinding noise that rumbled through the stonework, a familiar sound that, momentarily, he couldn't place. Then he swore and sat up, gesturing towards the candle, which burst into light.

Some stupid prick is opening the main gate! He threw on his tunic, buckled his sword belt, pulled on boots, slammed his helm on his head and stumbled out into the corridor, rubbing sleep from his eyes. The pounding rain was a distant roar; the torches flared, contorted by the myriad draughts that made the keep such a deeply unpleasant place to live.

How often do they have to be told? Unless it's Corineus Himself, that gate stays closed until sunrise! He stormed down the stairs – and then a bell began clanging frantically and he swore and stopped: his armour was upstairs and it would take four or five minutes of fiddling until he was properly harnessed. He decided others could do any necessary scrapping: his job was to give orders, not stand in the front line.

A pair of guards were below, peering anxiously into the darkness and rain. 'Sir! What's happening?' one asked – *Drafer? Yeah, that was it.*

'Dunno, Drafer, just got here. Hold your position.' Rudman splashed down the stairs, cursing the worn, slippery footing, and hurried to the gates. He could dimly hear a right old cacophony from the pens: those damned rufines, bellowing and lowing, and there was a constant thudding, a bit like hammer-blows on wood . . . then men's voices cried out in shock and pain, coming from the same direction.

He wavered, wondering, *Is there a stampede?* He looked around to see armed and armoured men spilling from every doorway. *The gates or the pens?* he wondered, and chose the gates – but there was a tremendous roar, three men pounded through the archway leading to the cattle pens – and a rufine bull speared them, plunging those lethal horns into their backs, goring them with what must surely have been *accidental* precision. Two more bulls followed behind it, tossing their heads and glowering at the surrounding men.

'*Kore's Balls!*' Rudman looked for a pilus and roared, 'Kill those beasts, Pilus – we'll roast the damn things for dinner!'

But the gate was still opening; he could hear the grinding gears, and now the warning bells were ringing. He cursed and left the cohort commander to deal with the animals while he ran to the gates: a stampede was containable, but the gates were the key to the fortress. He found soldiers ahead of him, but they were milling about under shelter while arrows sleeted down from the covered walkways on the battlements.

Shit – someone's already seized the outer walls . . . He cast about for a battle-mage and found a young lordling near the arch, blasting mage-bolts at the archers. 'Petraville! What's happening?'

Petraville spun, saw who it was and blanched. 'I don't know!' the pretty boy squeaked.

'It's your fucking watch – it's your bloody *business* to know!' Rudman bellowed, then he seized the boy's shoulders and pitched his voice as *calm and in control*. 'Take a breath, lad, and tell me what you saw.'

'I didn't see anything,' the young mage whined, flinching as another volley of arrows tore through the curtain of rain, into the tunnel mouth. They ricocheted wildly before slapping against Rudman and Petraville's gnostic shields amidst a shower of sparks. Rudman grabbed the nearest spent arrow and examined the fletching. *Steppe-turkeys.* That meant Sydians.

'Who saw something?' he demanded, looking about the frightened men pinned in the tunnel. Behind him he could hear those damned bulls roaring and men shouting in alarm.

'The gates were opened from within,' a tall, lean serjant told him coolly. *Thank Kore for serjants!* 'It all kicked off after a pair of those bulls wandered down from the pens.'

'The *rufine* bulls?'

'Aye,' the serjant growled, 'we saw 'em from the gatehouse. I sent Nikels down to see what was what, but he din' come back. I took a few men down: we found Nikels with 'is head stoved in – and we was locked outta the wheelhouse and some prick was raising the gates. We tried to break in, but once the gates were up half a foot, there was archers on the ground, firing up at us. I lost four men, Secundus, so we got outta there damned quick and retreated here to take a stand.'

This is a coordinated raid, Rudman realised with horror. No one should have been able to get near them, not without triggering the gnostic alarms outside the walls. 'It has to be that Sydian tribe – they've got fucking Sfera!' He whirled on Petraville. 'Drop the portcullis on this tunnel, then get your men to the inner walls. We need archers up there – every one you can find. The main gate's going to open in a moment, then they'll be in, in numbers.'

Petraville nodded frantically, trying to act like he could handle this. If he did, well, there was a soldier in him after all, but somehow

Rudman doubted that. But the serjant was already ordering men to the mid-tunnel portcullis and the fire-holes in the roof. 'I'll take the battlements above,' Rudman told them. 'Get some archers up there. We've got to hold the inner walls.'

He was halfway to the steps leading up to the battlements when more of his rankers poured into the courtyard, howling in panic, and to his intense alarm, he saw they were fleeing giant figures with horned helmets who were hacking gleefully with big-bladed weapons – *halberds*?

Are they Schlessen? Have our enemies united? And how the fuck did they get inside? 'Hold this tunnel!' he roared. 'Drop the portcullis!'

Suddenly the grinding from the main gate ceased and with a whooping cry, a volley of arrows seared directly into the tunnel. The serjant he was counting on was the first to take an arrow, straight through the eye; as he folded, more men dropped and the rest fled for cover. Petraville's shields were flashing red as Sydian battle-cries filled the main courtyard; dark shapes started swarming through the outer gates.

'Drop the portcullis, *now*!' he shouted, then spun as a bull bellowed behind him and a man at least eight feet tall – *impossible, surely?* – crunched the blade of his halberd into a ranker. Rudman blasted mage-fire at the giant's head – and to his utter astonishment, the bolt exploded across shields. Then his foe dropped his head and charged into the tunnel full of men. At the last second Rudman realised that no shield was going to stop him and hurled himself into the stairway as a rufine bull ploughed past like a runaway wagon, knocking men aside like infants. He slammed the door and bolted it, then rested his head on the wall, groaning. There was a tear in his nightshirt and he realised he'd lost his helmet – he'd forgotten to strap it on.

Fucking compose yourself . . . He had to hold the inner wall – if they hadn't already lost it. He raced up the stairs while trying to reach Gallius with his mind. But the *damned sot* was unconscious, so he pounded on, leading with his blade as he burst from the upper door and onto the battlements. A man in a hide cloak turned to face him, a longsword in his hand, blond hair flashing in the lightning. He looked soaked, but fire crackled in his hands and in an instant Rudman was locked in a mage-duel. As they exchanged thrusts and parries, Rudman was forced to defend; without armour he was vulnerable. Dead redcloaks were scattered about, but thankfully this enemy mage was alone – no, there was one other, a big horned shape at the far end, battering some poor ranker over the edge.

They've used magi to get inside and sweep the walls ahead of the alarm being raised. This assault had been executed with real precision and that scared him. But he was holding his own in this duel: he was a quarter-blood and he estimated that this blond bastard was too. But he couldn't afford to get bogged down in single combat while confusion reigned.

So he feinted a lunge, then hurled himself backwards into the rear courtyard, spiralling on kinesis and a touch of Air-gnosis, and landed amidst scattered bodies and one speared rufine lying on its side. He looked up and saw that his opponent hadn't followed.

Then something rumbled behind him and he turned back—

—and stared upwards—

—at some kind of beast from Lantric myth ... a *Mantaur*? It was ten foot tall and massively built, and it was holding a wagon axle in its huge hands. He barely had time to register its presence when the damned thing swung, a blow that surely no shield could stop. He hurled himself flat and the metal cylinder whistled past his skull near enough that he felt the breeze, but then he was inside the Mantaur's guard, lunging upwards ...

... as its foot lashed out, a single hoof the size of a sledgehammer, which slammed into his chest. He felt ribs break, the air rushed from his mouth and he flew backwards, hit the inner walls and bounced, pitched onto his face and everything faded out in an airless gasp and a swallow of blood that clogged his throat ...

Rudman coughed blood and woke up in a small room to find a reed stuck in his throat and a sour-faced Sydian girl sucking blood up the tube and spitting it into a bowl. Beside her, an old Sydian man, hands lit by pale light, had peeled back the skin of Rudman's chest and was manipulating the broken ribs.

Seeing his own chest opened up was sufficiently nightmarish to send him straight back down into darkness.

When he woke again, it was morning and his chest was strapped so tight he could barely breathe. He felt battered as an old boot, but his airways were clear. He realised instantly that his gnosis was bound with a Chain-rune and he was tied hand and foot to a cot in the inner guardhouse. A Sydian rider beside the door called to someone, and the blond man he'd fought the previous night strode in.

This time Rudman recognised him. 'You're Kyrik Sarkany,' he wheezed.

'And you're Url Rudman.' The tall Mollach prince – or king, if he'd been crowned by now – glared down at him. 'You handed me over to Sacrista Delestre.'

'Jus' doin' my job,' Rudman panted.

'To deliver the rightful heirs to Mollachia's throne to tax-farmers, knowing it's in their interests to kill us? That's not *your job*, Secundus Rudman. That's conspiracy to murder.'

'No!' Rudman protested, although Sarkany was absolutely right.

'But before we consider that,' the Mollach went on, 'I'm going to ask you to handle some negotiations for me. Your commander – Gallius, is it? – broke his leg trying to run away last night . . . he's not a lot of use anyway, I deem, so you're temporarily commanding officer of this garrison. Your surviving men have either escaped into the city or surrendered. We're holding more than three hundred in the stock-pens.'

Damn Gallius and his useless coterie of fops and upstarts. Rudman gritted his teeth and managed, 'You've invaded imperial lands, Sarkany. A serious mistake.'

'"Invaded"?' Kyrik Sarkany snorted. 'More like "passing through" – I'm guiding a Sydian clan to Mollachia. We now hold your fortress, of course, but we don't intend to assault the main city; we just want to pass beneath its walls without being shot at. My proposal is this: we will be given free passage through the fortress, past the city – oh, and past Registein too – all the way to Mollachia. Or we'll hang you and the other prisoners and sack the city.'

Rudman measured Sarkany. He'd seemed a naïvely friendly man, not the mass-hanging sort . . . *But I sent him and his brother to be murdered by the Delestres and now he's fallen in with Sydians and Schlessens and Mantaurs – constructs, surely? So who knows what he'd do now?*

'What d'you want me to do?'

'Accompany my parley to whoever's in charge of the city's defence: the mayor, or whoever. He'll outrank you, but defer in military matters – which this most certainly is. You can order his men to stand down and let us pass.'

'I'm in enemy hands – he doesn't have to do a thing I say.'

'But he will, won't he? You're the real leader here. It's your own fiefdom, more or less.'

'Hardly. What were our losses?'

'Only about a hundred dead – the rest fled or surrendered. We did have to kill four of your battle-magi, and we captured three more, as well as you and Tribune Gallius.'

So we still have three and a half thousand men inside, and six battle-magi . . . But those magi were second-rate fools, men who'd not do anything they didn't have to. *And we don't really know what we're facing.* 'Where in Hel did you find those man-beasts, Sarkany? The Inquisition are going to be all over you when those get reported, you know that.'

'What man-beasts?' Kyrik asked blithely. 'Just stampeding cattle, that's all.'

'I know what I saw.'

Kyrik leaned over him. 'Listen carefully, Rudman, because I've still half a mind to hang you when this is done. You saw *cattle*, and a few big Schlessen warriors in furs and horned helmets. That's all *anyone* saw. Understood?'

There's a hardness to him that definitely wasn't there a few months ago. What did that Delestre bitch do to them?

'All right,' Rudman said, knowing when to bend, so as not to be broken. 'Have it your way.'

Ujtabor, Mollachia

'Milady?'

Uh . . . ?

'Milady Sacrista?'

Who? Oh! He means me . . .

No, you're not her: you're us, you're us, you belong to us . . . you belong to Abraxas . . .

Sacrista Delestre blinked herself awake, struggling against the throbbing in her skull. Gradually the vicious snarling and whining inside her brain receded and the awful vision, a nightmare of a wall of flesh with a million eyes and ten thousand bloody mouths, all babbling and screeching at her, faded. Then images of Inoxion rose instead, and she relived the horror of watching that ghastly ichor crawling through her body. Her stomach clenched and she rolled over and vomited off the side of her cot.

'There, Milady, there . . .' Gren Francolin, her legion healer, mercifully tipped water down her throat so she could hawk and spit her throat free of bile.

'Inoxion,' she croaked, shaking as the memories hit her like fists . . . *Daemonic possession, and ichor – someone brought* ichor *into this world . . .* But she was still herself, and Inoxion had said she wouldn't be.

'Governor Inoxion is dead, Milady.' Francolin peered at her. 'Do you recall?'

'He tried to force me.' She looked up in sudden fright, shaking. 'He *is* dead, yes?'

'Oh, yes,' Francolin said, 'decapitated and burned.'

Thank Kore . . . 'What happened?' she managed to ask, still spitting to clear her mouth of that foul taste. 'Am I badly injured?'

'Magister Gabrian will tell you. He's been waiting day and night for you to wake.'

'*Day and night?*'

'You've been unconscious a week and more, Milady. It's Septinon now.'

'*Kore's Blood!*' she rasped. 'But it can't be—' It felt like only minutes.

'You must have taken a blow to the head during the . . . erm . . . assault.'

She clutched at his hand. 'Francolin, what's *wrong* with me?'

He swallowed, then he put on the healer's mask: gravely sympathetic, but detached. 'Milady, you've been beaten and your left wrist was broken – I've put it in a splint and it's healing nicely. But you wouldn't wake, not until now.' His face told her that something had happened that he considered significant.

'What is it?' she demanded.

'You passed . . . erm . . . this, Milady,' he said hesitantly, dangling her silver chain. 'Your own necklace . . . I don't know if you knew you'd swallowed it . . . ?'

She snatched it and pressed it to her breast. *Did the silver save me, or keep me unconscious . . . ? Or both?* 'I don't recall,' she lied, looking about her and realising this was the inn where she'd been attacked. 'I only recall . . . *oh, dear Kore . . .*'

'You were brave, Milady,' Francolin said, 'but we have always known you had that quality.'

If I was so damned brave, why did I freeze up when he—? She hugged herself tightly, trying not to think, but her memories of Inoxion remained nauseatingly vivid.

'If you have the strength, Magister Gabrian is waiting. He can tell you more.' At her nod, Francolin took the vomit-soaked cloths and left.

When Rafe Gabrian entered, he was showing uncharacteristic deference. She was still a little surprised no one had slit her throat. If they'd been nursing her back to health, then they were scared enough to think they needed her – or perhaps they'd found that contract . . . ?

She let Rafe mumble platitudes, then stopped him. 'What happened that day?'

Rafe shuddered. 'We were downstairs in the taproom – me and Vri Silvain – with Inoxion's men, and those imperial pricks were lording it, telling us that you were already on your knees gobbling cock – begging pardon, Milady, but you asked. We were right pissed off, but there was something about them, something – well, *not right*.'

They must have been like Inoxion: he must have infected them too. Sacrista couldn't stop herself shuddering, and when she met Rafe's eyes, there was a moment of real empathy. *Yes, we were both frightened that day . . .*

'At first there was no sound from the room where you and Inoxion were,' Rafe went on, 'then suddenly Inoxion cried out – and the thing is, his pet magi screamed too, at exactly the same moment, yowling like stuck pigs, even though no one had touched them. Their eyes went black and they changed, like mad things – but they couldn't throw off the pain. So we stabbed them, and still they didn't drop – so we decapitated them. By the time we got to you, you'd passed out, so Vri tended you while I flew down to Hegikaro and brought back Francolin. He didn't want to risk moving you, then the weather closed in and so . . . well, here we are.'

'And the imperials?'

'We cut down Inoxion's rankers and burned them too. We've written out an adfidus too, blaming Inoxion and his men for everything, in case this goes "legal".'

She was impressed they'd created a sworn document? They knew full well that the empire wouldn't be at all happy at the death of a governor in office, but it also showed surprising initiative. 'Have the governor's people in the lower valley been in contact?'

'They sent a man when Inoxion didn't report in; we showed him the contract and the adfidus – and you – and sent him on his way. Nothing since, except a note to say that they've written to the Governor of Midrea for guidance.'

'You showed the governor's man my condition?'

'You were crying out in your sleep and your veins had turned black all over your body. That convinced him more than anything that we'd not made it up.' Rafe met her gaze again and this time there wasn't empathy but horror. 'Are you *recovered*, Milady?'

Or do we have to kill you too? his eyes asked.

If she closed her eyes, she could still hear the whisperings, and they weren't getting any quieter. 'I'm fine,' she lied. 'What's been happening since that day?'

'Rukk all.' His expression was still guarded. 'Early snows have closed the Banezust mines and the forest is full of wolves. We've holed up here in Ujtabor.'

'The mines are closed?' She pushed her fingers backwards through her hair – it was greasy, and longer than she liked. She must look ghastly if Rafe could be alone with her and not leer. 'Shit, we *need* those mines.' She remembered that Kore-bedamned storm. *Did the Sarkanys summon this cold spell too? Pandaemancy, Inoxion said.*

243

'Another thing,' Rafe said, and now he sounded fearful. 'The wolves in the woods? They're not natural. Our rankers won't leave the village, or go out at night.'

Normally she'd have wanted to be up and working, but she felt utterly wretched. And knowing the ichor was still crawling through her body was sapping her strength even more. 'I must rest – send Francolin back, will you? And Rafe? Well done.'

As he saluted, she reflected that those two words might have been the first praise she'd ever uttered. Oddly, it left her feeling a little better – but then the babble inside her soul rose again. She wrapped the silver necklace around her throat, then found her coin purse, pulled out six silver coins and swallowed them for good measure. Somehow, it helped.

It's the silver, she thought before falling back into sleep, *it did save me . . .*

Not saved, Abraxas taunted. *The hooks are too deep. But enjoy dancing on my line . . .*

Valdyr stroked Gricoama's fur as they huddled together on a ridge overlooking the small mining town of Ujtabor. Smoke rose from every chimney and hung above the slate-roofed wooden buildings in the still morning air. Sacrista Delestre's men were keeping the villagers confined; they guarded the wooden palisade. They'd kept these mighty Rondian magi penned up and frightened for three weeks now.

'We can get inside at need,' Rothgar Baredge was telling him now. 'There's a stream near the palisade the women use to get fresh water that can be approached through the woods. Yesterday a woman I know told me the Delestre witch is still badly ill. She's not been seen since the night she killed the governor.'

Valdyr wondered what it all meant: that their enemies had fallen out was a boon from Kore, but what it presaged was anyone's guess. 'And what about Banezust?'

'It's much the same up there: the Rondians have sealed off the town, but as the roads are iced up, they're stranded, and they're running low on food.'

'And the Air-mage's windskiff?'

'It's still in the village below us.'

Valdyr smiled grimly at that. With the Elétfa a pillar of light in his mind and Luhti's voice to guide him, he'd been summoning storms over these uplands. He felt a powerful sense of connection to his land: his voice was the wind, his hands the frost. The weather and the Vitezai Sarkanum had combined to place a noose around the Delestre legion, which they were tightening steadily, trapping the Rondians in the villages and closing the mines.

Gricoama glimpsed a redcloak sentry making his rounds and growled; the wolf had become a vicious stalker of the unwary. 'Hush,' Valdyr told him, 'you'll get your chance again. The Sydians will be here soon, then we'll have the numbers to attack.' He clapped Rothgar's shoulder. 'I've seen enough. Let's go.'

Valdyr, the ranger and the wolf made their way through the frost-encrusted woods, moving carefully by habit, even though the Rondians had given up patrolling outside the walls, thanks to Gricoama and his new pack, a coterie of furred killers.

When they reached the limestone caves, their current base, Rothgar went to meet the scouts, leaving Valdyr to find Dragan. As he entered the next cave, he saw a flash of blonde hair; Sezkia Zhagy heard him and rose from shelling dried beans.

'Good morning, Milord,' she called, smiling at him.

Whether or not Sezkia genuinely liked him, he couldn't say, but her gentleness was softening his unease. 'Good morning,' he replied, tongue-tied as always, but it was becoming easier to breathe around her. They'd been conversing daily, just a few awkward words, but it was a start as he dipped a toe back into the deep waters of human contact.

And Gricoama liked her; she'd won him over with bits of meat and gentle petting. 'He's so beautiful,' she exclaimed, dropping to one knee and hugging the beast, which was probably heavier than she was. 'My father won't be long. Please, be at ease.'

'He's half-wild. You must be careful,' Valdyr warned as she rubbed the wolf's ears. When Gricoama scented blood, he was deadly – the mess he'd made of the redcloaks he'd ambushed was testimony to that, although he'd also come away with a few wounds. 'Mind his new scars,' he warned.

'Scars give dignity,' she replied, her eye straying to him. She knew about his back, of course – anyone who'd seen him washing in the river knew. She appeared not to care.

She stood and faced him, and momentarily he was unable to breathe. 'You have a fine moustache: a good pelt,' she said, then blushed.

That was high praise in Mollachia; a man was *meant* to be hairy: it implied virility, but Valdyr preferred a clean-shaven chin. When he added a beard to his long black hair and his moustache, which was long enough to droop at the corners in a manly way, he looked too much like his father.

'Sezkia,' he asked carefully, 'has your father instructed you to talk to me?'

'He did,' she said with a smile, 'but he also said I could stop whenever I wished.'

'I would not wish for the pretence of liking,' he warned.

'There's no pretence in me. I have one life and Kore will judge my conduct in it. I'm fortunate: my father permits me to refuse suitors I dislike. But I'm pleased to speak with you.'

A suitor – is that what I am? 'There's a big difference between *not disliked* and *liked* – I'm not easy company, I know that. I can't make people laugh. I don't have lively tales. I fear my company is a trial for others.'

'It isn't – and I trust mine is not to you?'

'No, never.' *Well, no more than any other woman would be*, he added silently.

'Then I'm content. I have girlfriends who make me laugh when I need laughter. There are other things I look for in a man: strength, faithfulness and honour, so that I know he will treat me as a husband should. I don't want someone like Juergan Tirlak, who kisses a girl, then leaves her for the next. Jests and tales are just wind. A woman of Mollachia needs a rock.'

He nibbled at his lower lip nervously, because this conversation had begun to feel portentous. 'I'll have words with Juergan about his behaviour.'

'The fathers of Mollachia will thank you for that,' she said, with the trace of a smile.

They fell silent, staring at each other, and he had a strange urge to tell her of the breeding-houses, to admit that he wasn't strong, but brittle and very afraid. But he didn't want to scare her away.

Then Gricoama growled; footsteps sounded, and someone was whistling an old folk song.

'My Prince,' Dragan called as Gricoama bounded up to him. The gazda avoided a half-meant bite and stroked the wolf's head. 'Gricoama guards my daughter better than I do,' he chuckled.

'Sezkia is safe with me,' Valdyr said. 'Rothgar says the Sydians are only a few days away?'

'Ysh. Hajya sends birds to me every few days – they've notes tied to their legs. Damnedest thing.' He gestured impatiently to Sezkia, who curtseyed and hurried away. 'Damned girl thinks she can listen in on every conversation I have.' He leaned close to Valdyr. 'One of our men on the north side has a vantage on the square – he says the Rondian windskiff has been hauled out.'

'We should wake and arm everyone,' Valdyr answered. 'There might be an opportunity.'

'You're growing into your boots, lad,' Dragan approved. 'I'll get the lads ready to attack, if the chance presents.'

Moments later, Valdyr and Gricoama were running for the north watch-point, arriving in time to see at least a dozen redcloaks in the central square, and crowds of watching villagers a few hundred yards below. He also glimpsed Dragan's Vitezai seeking vantage points and taking up position around the village. He'd been thinking for days about the possibilities of using lightning here, but hadn't for fear of harming the villagers. But an airborne skiff was another matter . . . The question was whether he could be ready in time?

Banishing all else from his mind, he sought the touch of the Elétfa. It responded, drawing his awareness into a web of shifting energies that blotted out everything else as he began pulling the clouds down from the peaks in huge waves.

'I can't wait any more,' Sacrista slurred. Gren Francolin shot her a worried look: they had only one operational skiff and Rafe Gabrian was their only Air-mage. But she *really* needed to be in Hegikaro, where they would have access to fresh herbs and medical supplies, and she needed Francolin with her; his healer-knowledge was vital if she was going to beat this thing inside her. But that meant leaving Vri Silvain here alone: one mage to protect a hundred men – or more likely, to perish with them.

She was losing ground. She'd awakened only two days ago, but she couldn't sleep any more for screaming the rafters down, dreaming of Robear begging her to join him in death. Francolin was running out of the poppy drug that gave oblivion, her only surcease.

'Rafe will come back with as many magi as I can spare,' she croaked as she tottered past Vri, clinging to Francolin's arm. 'You won't have to hold out for more than a day.'

He gave her a sick look. '*A day*? We won't hold for an hour.'

'Threaten to kill the villagers if they attack,' she rasped. 'It's the only language these pigs understand.' She couldn't spare him more attention than that; just walking was Hel. She felt utterly drained, although all she'd been doing was collecting bedsores. Fighting this insidious possession was draining her reservoirs of power like a leak in a rusty bucket.

When she reached the skiff, Rafe had the keel thrumming with energy. Thunder was rolling above and menacing clouds were pouring in from the north: if they were to have any chance of getting out, it had to be now.

'Milady!' a ranker called, 'you can't leave!'

'Silence!' his centurion snapped.

The men knew their plight as well as she did: just a hundred rankers, trapped twenty frozen miles from safety. She should've been making plans for them, but couldn't think coherently.

Francolin climbed in beside her. All around them, villagers were staring at them, their eyes filled with hate.

Blame your rukking king! she wanted to scream. *If he'd paid his bloody taxes I wouldn't be here! Blame Lyra Vereinen and her insatiable greed! Blame my Kore-bedamned father!*

Rafe hauled on the ropes, the sails billowed and he took his place behind the mast. Drawing on the gnosis in the keel, the small vessel lifted into the air, five feet up, then ten, rocking as the breeze took it. The soldiers audibly groaned; the villagers watched balefully in silence.

In the woods, a wolf yowled.

Dear Kore, this place will be running with blood by sunset.

As the craft turned south, she clenched her silver chain, praying to a god she'd never believed in to get her home. Then thunder cracked directly above and the sky blazed with light.

Some part of her saw what was coming and she tried to scream a warning, even as she hurled herself over the edge and into the void . . .

14

A Witch's Grave

Wytchcraft

*When the magi first appeared, one of the great prejudices they had to overcome
was that the common folk thought them to be 'wytches' who'd gained their magic
through service to Lucian, the Lord of Hel. Only the adoption of the Church of
Kore, equating the magi with the seraphs as Kore's representatives on Urte, finally
overcame this.*

GOLFYN, RENEGADE PRIEST, PALLAS, 671

Ujtabor, Mollachia, Yuros
Septinon 935

In Valdyr's mind, the Elétfa was a blazing branch in his hand as he
stepped to the edge of the look-out. Ujtabor lay below, the palisade only
two hundred yards away, and the windskiff carrying three Rondians
was rising into the air . . .

He raised a hand and pointed and the dwyma articulated his will: a
sudden *crack* of thunder exploded overhead and a vivid bar of incandescent light jagged from the clouds and hammered into the windskiff, an
instant after something fell from it. It exploded in a burst of fire and
force. Beside him, Gricoama snarled, poised to bound down the slope.

In the town, soldiers and villagers alike cried in alarm as burning
splinters and bloody, charred body parts rained down on them. Then
from the woods came ragged shouts as Dragan Zhagy led his men into
Ujtabor.

Kore Willing, they've lost at least two magi, Valdyr thought, seeking his next target. His perceptions, enhanced to what felt like omniscience, focused on the shape he'd seen fall from the skiff, which had landed on a tiled roof and was lying there, apparently stunned: a woman with short pale hair.

Sacrista! He raised his hand again.

Sacrista struck the tiles hard. Although her shields managed to prevent broken bones, she was badly winded and gasping for breath, her ears ringing, as around her debris rained down. The same force that had destroyed the skiff had hurled her to the ground like a discarded doll. Above her, the skies were still boiling as lightning went jagging through the thunderheads.

The pandaemancer is here!

She was barely in control, fighting to hear herself think above the wall of voices inside her skull, but her will to live was indomitable and even as the lightning cracked again, she rolled and dropped into an alley. She landed badly, sprawling in the frozen muck, and an instant later lightning blazed into the hovel and it too burst into flame. She recoiled from a throbbing wave of energy that discharged into the ground – but somehow, it illuminated what awaited her: the sickening, constantly morphing quagmire of aetheric flesh, limbs dripping with phantasmal gore, that was Abraxas, hovering in the aether, jaws open.

She staggered to the end of the alley—

—and into chaos. Rafe Gabrian and Gren Francolin were now just *charred meat* and the soldiers she'd tried to leave behind were scattering, all discipline gone, as the villagers produced knives and pitchforks and started surrounding and slaughtering the rankers. Then a wave of rebels poured over the palisades.

A village-wife saw Sacrista and shouted, pointing her out to any who might hear. Sacrista charred the woman's face with a mage-bolt, then tried to run while Abraxas burbled and shrieked inside her brain, feeding her energy, shrieking at her to *unleash*. The daemon fed her power and she blazed fire, driving back her foes, but still they came on, warily circling her, their faces blurring as she twisted this way and that – and all the while the voices of the daemon snarled and gibbered inside her, urging her to *rip* and *rend* and *kill* and *kill* and *kill* until she was safe . . .

She leaped at the nearest man, slashing about her as the Mollachs closed in, killing one, then another, but there were too many blades to track and her shields began to fray. She tried to leap over them with kinesis, but a blade stabbed her right calf and instead she cartwheeled and slammed face-first into the muck again. A spearhead burst through the skeins of light encasing her and pierced her back, just above the hips, right beside the spine, and she lost all feeling in her legs. A knee rammed into her back, someone's full weight driving air from her lungs and pinning her to the mud. A blade stung her throat.

Then the knife was withdrawn – and the hilt smashed down on the back of her head. Light burst through her skull, but the darkness inside gobbled it up, and her with it.

Valdyr entered the village to find the victory theirs and their Rondian enemies in his hands. Dragan joined him and they mutely clasped hands. 'The other mage took about thirty men, broke out the southern gate and made a run for it,' Dragan grumbled. 'We let them go – they can tell their fellows in Hegikaro of yet another defeat.'

When they reached the square, the crowds parted to reveal an unconscious woman sprawled in the mud: Sacrista Delestre, battered and bloody, clad only in a nightdress. She looked like a dying thing, somehow desiccated. It wasn't *natural*, and everyone felt it.

'Kore has delivered our enemy to us,' Juergan Tirlak shouted. 'Praise to Him Above!' His cry was echoed by the gathered Vitezai and the villagers.

'Aye, He has,' Dragan murmured to Valdyr, 'but she's a mage: we can't keep her subdued forever. Let her speak and she'll have us kissing her feet. We must put her to death.'

'You're right,' Valdyr agreed; he'd sleep all the better if this coldheart was in the grave – but the hatred he saw on every face as they stared at the fallen Sacrista chilled even him. 'How?' he asked, but he already knew the answer.

The four most feared monsters in Mollachia had *specific* methods of disposal: a *draken* must have its carcase burned and the ashes scattered into running water. The *vrulpa*, half man, half beast, must be beheaded. An undead *strigoi* must be impaled on a stake – and a *strega-witch* must be staked into her grave.

'The situation demands Mollachian justice, my Prince.' Dragan's face was iron: an example must be made of Sacrista Delestre – for being foreign, for all the Mollachians she'd tortured and slaughtered, for her brother's sins, and Inoxion's too, even for being a female mage-warrior, an offence to the natural order. 'Our people will expect – nay, they will *demand* – a fitting death.'

'But . . . a *witch's* grave? It's barbaric.'

'That is how evil is fought,' Dragan told him. 'Fire with fire, my Prince!'

Valdyr felt sick, but the craving for vengeance was writ clear, and not just on Dragan's face. He could not reject it, so he swallowed and steeled himself. 'She and Robear walled Kyrik and me up and left us to starve to death.' He was speaking as much for his own benefit as Dragan's. 'She plundered our kingdom and hung scores of innocents. Her men have committed every crime known to man. She deserves death.' All of which was easy to say, but as prince he'd be expected to lead the execution.

Their eyes met. 'I can do it,' Valdyr muttered, not sure if he could.

Dragan nodded in grim approval, then cried to the crowd, 'By the marks on her and the witchery she conjures, I declare this woman a *strega!*' He turned to the village priest. 'Pater, do you concur?'

'Ysh! The Church concurs!' the priest shouted. 'She has sucked the silver from our soil and the blood from our veins! Her evil is evident!'

As the crowd roared in agreement, he saw the noise was bringing Sacrista round. Valdyr swallowed. *Better you never waken*, he thought. 'Bring sweetlae,' he ordered. 'We must drug her before she regains use of her gnosis.'

While an apothecary fetched the stupefying herb, Dragan gave the order, 'Prepare a witch's grave!'

Sacrista awoke, clinging to the edge of a cliff called sanity. An amorphous thing full of snapping teeth and burning eyes waited in the precipice yawning below her. Its voice was a storm, its grasping append-ages reached ever closer. But she still clung to a semblance of self, rooted in her suffering flesh.

I'm still me . . .

She wasn't wholly herself, though. There was a milky, bittersweet taste in her mouth and a floating feeling. Her eyes flew open and she saw a tall young man with black hair and a big, drooping moustache that accentuated the sadness of his gaze. 'Valdyr Sarkany?' she groaned. She reached for mesmeric-gnosis to capture his mind and—

—nothing happened. Her spell failed in a haze of jumbled thought. She recognised the sensation at once; it was like the one time she'd let Robear give her poppy.

They've drugged me. Well, at least it's keeping the pain at bay. But her brain was too scrambled for more. She tried to orientate herself and real-ised she was in a miner's hovel. Her nightshift was muddy and torn, barely covering her, but there was no sense that she'd been abused. But her legs . . .

I can't feel my legs, she realised, with growing horror.

The pitiless faces all round her told her the rest. *I'm going to die.*

Ignorant people thought that when they died, a seraph came to take them to Kore's Paradise, but she was a mage; she knew the reality. You got one life, then you dissipated from a coherent being to mindless energy and spent an unknowable period as a spirit – if you were lucky. Those whose death attracted the notice of a daemon instead fell into that being's maw and suffered for the rest of eternity. She knew the name of he who awaited her: *Abraxas*. His blood was inside her already: she couldn't escape him. She would be his *for ever*.

Tears formed at the corners of her eyes as she realised, *Only this thin silver chain around my neck is keeping the horror at bay . . . I mustn't die with this taint inside me . . .*

'Please,' she whispered, looking up at Valdyr; his was the only face with even a modicum of pity, 'please, don't kill me – do whatever you want to me, but *please*, don't let me die.'

He held her gaze for a moment, then said, 'The decision is made.'

If she told him she'd be condemned to eternity in Hel, he'd call it justice.

And I deserve some kind of justice, I know that. I've committed all manner of 'legal' crimes in my father's name. But do I deserve an eternity of suffering in a daemon's maw? Dear Kore, I know I'm a sinner, but the world *made me do it . . .* She felt panic lurking in the shadows and knew it would soon take her . . . shortly before Abraxas did.

Then a hard-faced veteran stepped in front of Valdyr; his eyes were full of cold hatred and she could guess who it was by that alone: Dragan Zhagy, the head of the rebels who called themselves the Vitezai Sarkanum.

'Do you know the tradition of a witch's grave?' he asked. 'It is known that a *strega* will always rise again, so to protect the living she is staked in the grave, so her body *cannot* leave.'

Sacrista felt her bowels loosen. 'But I'm not a witch – I'm a *mage*, you know that—'

'All I know has been handed down from my forefathers, *strega*.'

She tried to call past him to Valdyr Sarkany, 'I spoke on your behalf – I told them to kill you swiftly – it was Robear and Inoxion who walled you in – *it wasn't me!*'

'But they're already dead,' Dragan replied, 'and there's just you to answer for their sins.'

This isn't happening – it isn't real – it's a dream . . . But she knew that wasn't true: she was going to die and she would be one with that horrific creature for ever. *Unless . . .* 'Please,' she begged, 'when I die you must dissipate my soul! There's a daemon waiting for me—'

'You'll still be alive when the coffin closes, *strega*,' Dragan replied emotionlessly.

'No! *No!*' She fought the tears that flooded her eyes. There was no mercy on their faces. 'Then please, grant me this: leave me my silver chain. It was a gift from my brother. *Please!* I beg you!'

Dragan considered, then shook his head. 'Why should we?'

'No, *please!*' She was babbling now. 'The silver – it poisons the daemon! The silver poisons the daemon! You must—'

The craggy Mollach seized her face and snarled, 'Shut your face or

I'll break it.' He clamped a hand over her lips as she tried to scream, then someone forced more of the sweet-tasting drug into her mouth as she fought.

He met her gaze one last time. 'I'll see you again when you wake, Delestre: in your grave.'

She tried to rise and fight, but her body betrayed her, the milky fluid washing her back into the nightmare of the precipice with the beast waiting below with open maw and grasping limbs.

The preparations took some time, as the stony ground was frozen solid. Valdyr took Gricoama to the south road, ostensibly to be sure that no counter-attack was coming, but mostly just to clear his head and steel his mind to the grisly reality of what was to come. He'd never seen it done before; his mother had refused to let her sons attend executions, the only argument with her husband she'd won.

It's barbaric, he thought, *but who am I to stand against the will of the people?*

Dragan found him about two hours before sunset. 'We're ready, my Prince,' he said solemnly, drawing out an envelope. 'We found this among her effects: it's a contract making Sacrista Delestre Chief Legate to Governor Inoxion and putting her in charge of the Imperial Legion – a curious appointment, when she's supposedly commanding her father's legion, ysh?'

It *was* curious. Valdyr glanced at it, but the legalese meant nothing to him. 'Kyrik can read such things properly, and he's smart enough to know how to best use it.'

Dragan nodded in agreement and pocketed the envelope again. During the silent walk back into town, Valdyr's mind was fixed on the ordeal to come.

At the glade at the edge of the cemetery where the burial would take place they found several hundred Mollachs gathered to bear witness. Valdyr followed Dragan to the wide, deep grave, big enough for a man to stand beside a coffin. Next to the wooden box lying agape beside the hole was a three-foot wooden stake and a mallet.

Valdyr felt as if every eye was on him. He was the prince of these people, but his face was unknown to most; this would be their first impression of him. A true Mollach was meant to have the stomach to do these things. His legs were trembling, but he took a deep breath and cast his mind back to the slave-gangs and the awful things he'd done just to live.

I can do this.

'Bring out the prisoner.' His voice was steady.

The glade fell silent as two men brought Sacrista Delestre out. She was groggy, but coming round: a *strega* had to be awake as the fatal blows were struck. There was a risk she'd be able to reach the gnosis, but drugs and pain appeared to have mastered her. As she hung in the rough grasp of the hunters, her legs dragging limply, Valdyr felt a rush of pity – until he remembered the slow horror of seeing his coming death in the reflection of his brother's dying eyes.

Dragan turned to the crowd. He spoke first in Mollach, and then in Rondian. 'Sacrista Delestre, you are guilty of tyranny, theft against the people of Mollachia and the attempted murder of Kyrik and Valdyr Sarkany, Mollachia's rightful princes. You are guilty of witchcraft: summoning magical familiars and the use of magic. Under our ancient laws, you are a *strega* and must die in a witch's grave.'

She was trying to look brave but something in her was broken; it was a quivering girl hanging there, not a hardened battle-mage. 'Just kill . . . Please . . .'

Valdyr would happily have drawn his dagger and ended her, for pity's sake, but that would never be forgiven. *Punishments must be cruel to frighten the sinful into repentance*, the *Book of Kore* taught. *The faithful must remain steadfast. There can be no pity for the witch.*

'Place her in the coffin,' Dragan ordered.

Sacrista sobbed as they laid her on her back in the box, then bolted curved metal straps over her ankles, wrists and neck so that she couldn't move. She strained, trying to asphyxiate herself, but Valdyr knew from bitter experience that the body always overruled the mind.

As they lowered the coffin into the grave she looked up at him, mute with terror. There was no hiding from what came next. It was worse than going into battle. *She was a pitiless killer*, he reprimanded himself when his limbs locked, *and I must be the same.* But there was a bigger thing going on here: Dragan and many others didn't share Kyrik's vision of the new Mollachia, and saw in him someone who would uphold the old ways. If he refused this, they might both be swept away. *I'm damned either way . . .*

Feeling like a condemned man himself, he followed Dragan down into the grave.

Only when Dragan hefted the stake and placed it over her solar plexus did Sacrista appear to truly understand what was going to be done to her. As the wooden point pressed through the cloth over her stomach and gouged her skin, she screamed, '*No! You can't – I'll be damned!*'

So will I, Valdyr thought wretchedly. *So will I . . .*

'May Kore have mercy on you,' he said, ritual words to hide behind. 'May you never rise again.' He ignored her pleading eyes and lined up the mallet.

Then something inside her recognised him and her eyes focused. '*Asiv is coming for you*,' she whispered. '*Asiv is here.*'

A spasm of denial ran through him – whatever else she might say, he couldn't hear. He dropped the mallet and fell backwards against the side of the hole. Dragan, glaring at him, snatched up the hammer and slammed it down onto the wooden spike. It punched through the wall of muscle, past the spine and out again, through the wooden box itself and into the earth beneath. Sacrista's final scream became a gurgling bubble of blood as her whole body spasmed, then she sagged, staring up at him, her agony-glazed pupils following him still.

He almost missed the next moment – but he *felt* it . . . A kind of smoke formed around her jaw, and something like a bloody mouth full of teeth opened in the air, though no one else reacted. But Luhti's voice whispered something and her breath blew away the smoke from Sacrista's mouth. The daemonic maw howled in fury and loss, but these visions faded and Valdyr turned away, dazed, splattered in her blood, knowing he'd take this moment to his own grave. But he also knew that somehow, the dwyma had interpreted his unspoken wish for mercy and given Sacrista a peace she barely deserved.

That helped him deal with the horror he'd helped commit. And the dread of hearing that name: *Asiv . . .*

Dragan embraced him to cover his ashen face, and whispered, 'It's all right, lad, I've got you. It was too much in one so young. My mistake.' He didn't sound apologetic; his tone and face were grimly satisfied, and faintly superior, as if he recognised and scorned Valdyr's hesitations. Then he asked, 'Who's Asiv?'

Valdyr shook his head – *I can't talk about it* – took the proffered hand and dragged himself out of the grave, then staggered away as Nilasz and Juergan leaped down and nailed the coffin lid closed. Once they too were clear, stones rained down on the coffin. But all Valdyr saw was the dread on Sacrista's face. He felt like more of a monster than she'd ever been. He fell to his knees, embracing Gricoama, clinging to him as if to his brother as her final words echoed in his brain, draining the marrow from his bones.

Asiv is coming for you. Asiv is here.

Collistein, Kedron Valley

Kyrik stared across the short divide separating the legion fortress from the inner city, where the remaining legionaries and some ten thousand townsfolk cowered in fear. Thraan, and the Schlessen thane, Fridryk Kippenegger – who thankfully preferred the far more pronounceable 'Kip' – stood beside him.

'Will the Rondians hold to the arrangement, do you think?' Kyrik wondered.

Thraan looked like he'd really rather they didn't. 'My riders are poised to rain fire down on them.' He meant it, too: they'd spent the week creating a stock of fire-arrows while waiting for the main body of the tribe to arrive. Tribune Gallius and Secundus Rudman were still locked up; Legate Gallius was a pure-blood and Kyrik couldn't fully Chain his gnosis so they were keeping him drunk on Sydian liquor instead. The other captured magi were all quarter-bloods or less – this clearly wasn't a prestigious legion posting.

'Rudman was very insistent that the mayor obey the terms,' Kip chuckled.

They shared a laugh, then Thraan said, 'Thane Kip, we have a proposition for you.'

The big Schlessen battle-mage appeared to have already guessed, but he let them voice their plan. 'We've been thinking that there are few places in the world where your people – especially your Mantauri – might find the haven you need,' Kyrik began. 'I think Mollachia might be one of them, and you're already on the doorstep. If you summered at Lake Jegto and wintered on the Osiapa, you'd have a hard life, but a fair one, especially with supplies from the lower valley. What do you say?'

Normally there was no love lost between Sydians and Schlessens, but Kyrik fancied that Thraan saw something of Brazko, his dead son, in the giant barbarian; they'd been drinking together a lot, and had started developing a relationship. And of course, the Mantauri could make a huge difference in the battles to come.

'In all honesty,' Kyrik went on, 'I can't see how a group like yours could cross Imperial lands without being destroyed.'

'My intent was to go to Silacia,' Kip said musingly. 'There's a man I know there, a greasy rodent with a lying tongue.'

'Are you going to rip the little prick's balls off?' Thraan guffawed.

'What? No, nothing like that,' Kip replied, with a startled laugh. 'He's an old war comrade; he owns a mercenary legion. I was going to ask him for a job.' Then he looked from Kyrik to Thraan. They'd been extolling the virtues of Mollachia for the past couple of days, emphasising the wilderness, the backwoods and the pastures used by only deer and mountain goats; the large tracts of unclaimed land where herds could forage untroubled.

'I will put it to my people, and to Maegogh,' he said, earning a clap on the back from Thraan.

Inside the hour, they had their answer: the Bullheads would come to Mollachia.

Kyrik afforded himself a moment of doubt: *Dear Kore, between Sydian pagans, Schlessen and Rondian mercenaries and intelligent constructs, what kind of kingdom am I building?* But then he gave thanks for his new – and *deadly* – allies.

*

The following day they started out on the high road towards Registein. They took the Tribune Gallius, Secundus Rudman and three of their battle-magi with them to deter pursuit, but the mayor seemed little inclined to double-cross them and the garrison did nothing more threatening than to line the walls and stare goggle-eyed at them as they passed.

When they left the Rondian magi beneath the fortress no one pursued them.

Thraan sent scouts ahead while Kyrik rode to the edge of the cliff, wishing he had enough clairvoyance to let Valdyr and Hajya know of their imminent arrival. The weather cleared just as they reached Tulkan's Spur; a promontory from which they they could see all the way to where the rosy sunset glinted off Lake Droszt and even as far as Lake Vilagosto, midway down the valley. Thin plumes of smoke rose from distant chimneys; the pines were so dark they were almost black. Wolves howled in the deep distance.

Kyrik was entranced, and so too were the Sydians and Schlessens as everyone gathered on the spur to catch their first look at this promised sanctuary. Some were weeping, although whether from joy or loss, he couldn't tell. It reminded him again what a monumental thing it was for these people to leave their former lives behind.

Thank you, Kore, for guiding our steps. And thank you, Zlateyr-Zillitiya: we're walking in your footsteps.

Then his mind turned to the people who awaited him below. He was aching to see Hajya again, and frightened his absence might have dulled her passion for him, although his was still urgent. But he had to broach the subject of his possible infertility, and how he would do that, he didn't know.

Valdyr was down there too. Had he learned anything further of dwyma? Or to be more gentle to himself? Perhaps Sezkia had melted his heart? More worryingly, was Cassiphan here?

Thraan and Kip strode through the crowd and the Nacelnik slapped his shoulder. 'We've done it, Kirol Kyrik — it's a miracle!' The two men who'd fought hardest for this moment shared a satisfied smile.

It is a miracle, Kyrik decided, *but we might need a few more before too long.*

15

Breakthrough

Thaumaturgy: Water

What power hath water? Behold the sea!

BOOK OF KORE

Sunset Isle, Pontic Sea
Septinon 935

Magister Manon's voice rose above the chatter. 'Could I have everyone's attention, please?' he called, and the noise gradually subsided. Almost everyone living in the giant cylinder of Sunset Tower was present in the meeting room – one of the few rooms with a window. It might be several feet thick but it was crystal-clear, and it revealed a darkening sky and massive waves hammering the island beneath them.

Ahm on High, they look awful, Jehana thought, studying the three senior magi. Manon in particular was haggard, his breath coming in wheezing gulps. Hillarie, who usually took pains to look perfect, was dark-eyed and dishevelled, and Loric's sharp tongue had become vague, his manner distracted. Under ordinary circumstances a relieving ship would have been here by now, but it was well overdue and rumours were circulating.

'We've reached a critical point in our care for the tower,' Manon announced. 'The Shihad has captured the windship bringing us supplies and replacement personnel. Arch-Magus Ventrou is protesting, but the Shihadi governor in Pontus refuses to hear him.'

'How could they get captured?' growled Geryn, the senior sentinel.

'The Shihad have warships; we have only lightweight supply ships,' Manon replied.

'We should blast them from the skies,' Tovar called out brashly.

'They know not to come into range after Northpoint took one of theirs down last month,' Loric replied. 'All the other towers are in the same situation. Even the Merozains helping repair Midpoint are trapped there.'

The babble of conversation rose again until Manon lifted a hand for silence. 'We don't know how long our custody of Sunset Tower will last, but the energy levels required to sustain the Bridge are increasing and we senior magi can't sustain the effort unaided. We need your help.'

'Who's on the solarus-throne now?' Urien asked, looking around.

'Sentinel Levana is taking this shift,' Hillarie replied, 'and from today, *everyone* will learn how to manage the solarus-throne. We must share the load wider, so that all of you, scholar, student or sentinel, will spend at least two hours a day controlling the energy flows, either on the throne or below ground.'

'At the moment Ogre has the controls below,' Loric noted. 'I know some of you doubt him, but he's proven himself reliable – and anyway, his old master is dead.'

'We don't know that Naxius is dead,' Sentinel Geryn interjected. 'I met a Merozain who believed Naxius survived the Third Crusade.'

'There,' Hillarie exclaimed, 'I told you that *creature* shouldn't be permitted to carry out crucial functions.' She glared at Loric, clearly reopening an old argument.

'I tell you, he's trustworthy,' Loric retorted.

'Who knows what back doors someone like Naxius might have into its brain? That *creature* should've been put down, not kept in one of our most critical sites!'

'Ogre is a *he*, not an *it*,' Loric snapped back.

'He's a monster, inside and out!'

'He's an innocent, damaged by what he saw. Have you even been inside his mind?'

'I have no need to: I *know* what he is,' Hillarie shouted.

Loric sneered, 'That's why you've always been a second-rate scholar, Hillarie – you only look at evidence if it fits your hypothesis.'

Hillarie rose to her feet. 'Second-rate? Retract that, you . . . you *toy-maker!*'

The junior scholars stared at this rare display of discord while Manon struggled to make them hear him. 'Enough!' he finally got out, '*both* of you! We must be *united* if we are to do our duty here. On this matter, I support Loric. Now, sit, and let us continue!'

Jehana exchanged glances with Urien and Tovar, remembering her own slightly alarming encounter with the giant creature. *What if Hillarie's right?* she wondered.

'I have made a roster. Everyone will participate in maintaining the energy flows,' Manon went on, 'and Hillarie, Loric or I will oversee each of you until you've mastered the controls and gained the necessary skills. I apologise in advance – this will not be pleasant, but it's necessary.'

Hillarie pointed at Jehana. 'Obviously our "guest" is not part of this arrangement.'

Everyone looked at Jehana, who felt a flash of outrage. 'What do you mean?'

'You're a *Mubarak*,' Loric said dryly. 'Even your mother was never permitted to work the towers, *Princess*.'

Jehana looked about her and saw renewed hostility on almost every face. Manon, Tovar and Urien were the only exceptions. 'The decision isn't a statement of mistrust,' Manon said, 'but safety. If you sit on the throne, those on the other thrones will become aware of you. Sultan Rashid may still have spies amongst us – although not in this tower, I'm sure – but the risk is too great. You will have duties, Jehana; you'll play your part.'

Put like that, it made sense, but Jehana *hated* the glares from all sides. 'You'll give trust to an illegal construct before you trust the daughter of one of your greatest magi,' she said, her voice cracking. 'Well, you don't have my trust either!' She rose and walked, head high, from the room.

The next few weeks on Sunset Isle passed in an air of unreality. Jehana felt like a pariah, given duties she was sure had been chosen specifically to humiliate her: dirt-caste chores like cleaning and scullery work. No one talked to her except Tovar and Urien, but through them she learned that Shihad windships were blockading the towers. So far, none had got close enough for anyone to feel they had to divert energy from the Bridge to defend themselves, but everyone's nerves were frayed.

While her tasks were menial, what really humiliated her was the mistrust, and not even Levana was sympathetic. She tried to continue her research when chores were done, but she'd soon exhausted all her books, which left her with a lot of time on her hands. She spent hours staring out through the underwater glass window, watching the water bubble and swirl . . .

. . . and trying to call to something she wasn't even sure was there.

One day as she sat facing the glass, not really seeing, just being alone and miserable, a squid as long as her body glided by – and appeared to *look right at her*. She was instantly reminded of an illustration of a squid-headed god worshipped by Vereloni coastal tribes.

Seidopus . . . She'd whispered the name – and the squid returned a moment later.

A week had passed and nothing similar had happened, but she was *convinced* it would. *Perhaps I've been locked up here too long*, she thought. *Perhaps I'm going mad.*

The dwymancer Amantius had fled to the coast of Verelon, where the villagers harvested the tidal flats for fish and whatever else the receding water left behind each day; there were *blood sacrifices* there, the Inquisitors had reported. Some of the tribes had called the dwy-mancer *Seidopus*, equating him to their old pre-Sollan gods. He'd had wives, each taking the name *Calascia* – sometimes that was the name Jehana called with her mind.

She tried other names as well, of the famous dwymancers and the jinn they'd bonded with, like Aradea, Epyros and Urybos, but it was only when she called to Seidopus that she felt the sea was really listening.

But this wasn't enough, and she knew it. Her mother had told her that to bond with a genilocus, you had to *find* it and in a very real way, join yourself to it – and the form of that bonding depended on the genilocus itself.

I have to get outside somehow . . .

But she knew Magister Manon, the only one who knew her secret power, would *never* let her leave, even if the Shihadi blockade didn't have them hemmed in. And she was no Air-mage – but Urien was, and he was one of the few sympathetic people here. She cultivated him as carefully as she could, working up to asking for his help.

She also began lurking about the two exits to the outside world: the docking platform halfway up the tower, which had been locked since the crisis began, and the grand double-doored front entrance, sealed airtight against the highest tides which often enveloped the island and left the top of the tower sticking up like a finger rising from the waves. She wasn't sure what she was seeking, but she prayed an idea would come.

Then everything changed.

The Pontic Peninsular

Alyssa was beginning to suspect that she'd been led astray. Nuqhemeel's Hadishah, currently scouring the eastern coast of Yuros, had used hounds, winged beasts and scrying, but they'd found no real sign that Jehana Mubarak had ever been there. Eventually she decided it was a false trail and brought her people back to Pontus.

'Do you know who I am?' she demanded of the Amteh Scriptualist who'd been entrusted with the captured Ordo Costruo scholars. The two dozen old and infirm magi had remained in the Domus Pontico because they couldn't bear to leave the only home they'd ever known, and they'd wished to plead for the contents of their library.

'Of course I know, Great Lady,' the Scriptualist replied, a bead of sweat running from his right temple.

'Then do as I ask, Scriptualist Ghazel: give me access to the scholars.'

'But the scholars have been promised clemency by Sultan Rashid himself,' Ghazel whimpered. 'He knew many by name. To those who accepted Runes of the Chain to quell their gnosis, he gave his clemency. They are permitted to remain and catalogue the books unmolested.'

Rip his throat out, Abraxas muttered into her skull, and it was tempting. But there were other Shihad magi and scholars present and her authority here was disputable. 'I wish only to speak to them, Scriptualist Ghazel. My mission comes from the sultan himself, may Ahm bless and keep him.' She pushed her face closer and added, 'You know how close he and I are.'

Ghazel probably knew she'd been discarded, but he wasn't stupid enough to say so. 'Their safety is my responsibility,' he replied obstinately.

He had a reputation for zeal, but everyone had a need, and she could sense his. *I know you want to read the wisdom of the Ordo Costruo for yourself.* 'I wish only to speak to them about a matter important to the sultan and vital to the Shihad.' She bent closer to his ear. 'Godspeaker Beyrami and the Shihadi fanatics would burn these captives on pyres made of their own books if they knew what was happening here. Do you want that, Ghazel?'

He bit his lip, finally wavering. 'I was a Builder-mage myself,' she reminded him. 'I would no more wish Beyrami to torch this place than you – but I *must* see your captives.'

Actually, I don't give a shit about these wretched old parchments, she thought. *Just get out of my rukking way.*

At last the Scriptualist caved in. 'Very well, I'll have them assembled.' He chased away the servants and assembled the old dribblers, half-senile wrinkled men and women Alyssa remembered from her youth. It was something of a joy to parade her perfect body before them, her lush blonde tresses tumbling over her bared shoulders; she was almost twitching with the urge to snarl like a lioness as she stopped in front of the one she despised most. Olbedyn would always sanctimoniously explain her misdemeanours, as if she'd not known exactly what she was doing – and then take a switch to her buttocks. She'd hated him then, but now it just made her feel nostalgic.

'Dear Olbedyn,' she said. 'Remember me?'

'We remember you, Alyssa Dulayne,' Olbedyn croaked, his voice as rheumy as his eyes.

Every one of these old fools believes their precious mind is too vital to humankind for their safety to be jeopardised. Before anyone could even blink, she'd conjured a switch, the very sort he'd used to abuse her with, and lashed him across his proud face. He reeled and fell at her feet, while others cried out in outrage.

'Lady Alyssa!' Ghazel shouted, 'you mustn't—'

She locked unseen fingers around his throat, lifting him off the ground with a gesture and watched him choke, unable to break her grip. 'I'll do what the Hel I like,' she told him, and the rest of the room. The Eastern magi all tensed, clearly wondering if taking her on would be heroic or exceedingly stupid, but none of them moved. She let Ghazel drop gasping to the floor and nudged Olbedyn with the switch. 'Tell me where to find Jehana Mubarak, Magister.'

Olbedyn looked up at her: he was senior enough to be privy to such information, and despite his doddering appearance, sharp enough to have followed events. She raised the switch again—

— and some old biddy had the temerity to seize her arm and shout, 'Don't you touch him, you wicked—'

She spun and drove the switch into the old girl's eye, deep enough to blind. Blood burst from the wound and the old woman howled as she dropped to her knees. Some made strangled protests, but still no one dared intervene.

One of the other women came to Olbedyn's side. *Naria*, Alyssa recalled; the old fools had been sweet on each other for decades.

Alyssa raised the bloody rod in her hand. 'Perhaps you can persuade Olbedyn to speak, dear?'

'Don't hurt her!' Olbedyn croaked.

'Then where's the girl?' She locked eyes with him as she moved the switch to point at Naria's right eye. 'Why sacrifice someone so dear for an Eastern princess, Olbedyn? What's she to any of you?' She bent over and silenced the air around them so no one else would hear what he said.

'Sunset Isle,' Olbedyn groaned. 'Please . . .'

Ahh, Alyssa thought, followed by a surge of temper, *of course! No need to cross through the advancing Shihadi fleet, and they can blast whoever approaches out of the sky. I should have thought of it sooner!*

Irritated at being outmanoeuvred, she pushed the switch through

Naria's eye and straight into her brain until it exploded through the back of her skull in a searing wet hiss. The old woman dropped silently as Olbedyn yowled in horror. As everyone else recoiled, Alyssa relished the betrayal in his eyes.

'That's for all you did to me as a child, you pervert,' she rasped, letting the room think he was the monster when he'd been nothing but an ineffectual fool. With a jerk of kinesis, she broke his neck and he folded over the body of the woman he loved. She felt his mind die. His soul gushed from his body, seeking Naria's.

Opening her mind's eye and engaging Necromancy, she found the two faint puffs of energy, saw two souls become one—

—and inhaled them, feeling their essence turn to energy inside her: a beautiful surge of pure vitality that had her trembling in ecstasy for a few delicious moments.

She turned to Ghazel and saw that he'd comprehended what she'd done. Souldrinking was one of the greatest heresies of all. His eyes were terrified, his body petrified, like a cornered deer.

<If you dare impede me, or inform anyone of this, you'll share their fate,> she told him silently. <Now clean up.>

She stalked from the room and promptly forgot him. The hunt is on!

Within hours, Nuqhemeel's windships had swept in to pick her up and minutes later, they were streaming south on conjured winds, straight for Sunset Isle.

16

Tabula-mio

Tabula and Rebellion

Tabula has become a byword for plotting – when someone declares that he is 'taking up tabula', they're really announcing themselves politically. Emperor Celestin, Sertain's son, is said to have taken up the game a few months prior to his father's death, after his impatient demands for his father to step aside weren't met. The cry of 'Tabula-mio!' – 'My Table' – signifying that the game (or table) is won, is often used when a confrontation is resolved, either triumphantly by the victor or grudgingly by the loser.

ORDO COSTRUO ARCANUM, HEBUSALIM, 873

Pallas, Rondelmar
Septinon 935

Solon gazed down at the woman in his arms, wondering where infatuation ended and love began, for he was beginning to think there should have been some warning that if he went any further, his heart would cease to be his own.

'Medelie, Medelie,' he murmured, 'where were you hiding all my life?'

'Where have I been?' she answered, looking up at him, their sweaty-slick bodies pressed together. 'Watching and waiting for you, Solon, but it took me this long to reach you.'

He'd never much cared for his rooms in the Bastion a level below the royal suites. The furniture and décor were overly fussy; it was like living in a mausoleum. But since he'd moved Medelie in, it had become Paradise.

Am I really doing this? Me? The man who sneered when others became so infatuated that they lost sight of their careers? Am I really spending all my time tangled in the limbs of a beauty half my age? In rational moments, when duty took him away, he found himself holding his breath, sure he'd dreamed this joy and scared to wake. But when they were together, he would do *anything* to please her.

It wasn't just the lovemaking, although that was intense and joyous, as likely to end in laughter as passionate symbiosis. Her mercurial nature endlessly intrigued him: she could go from playful girlishness to stately dignity – and her political knowledge and insight astounded him, as did her memories of times before she was born. 'I keep my ears open,' she would laugh when he asked how she knew of this or that. 'You old men are always talking of the past.'

When he asked why she would want an *old man* like him, she told him seriously, 'Young men have nothing but youth. I've always preferred fully formed men. And an older man can do *everything* a young one can – especially magi like you.'

And Dear Kore, she was beautiful: as perfect as if she'd been sculpted. He knew of many female magi who used morphic-gnosis to try to achieve physical perfection, and they did, for a short time, but he had detected no evidence that she did so. No, Medelie was all natural perfection, a goddess of love, truly his *Regna d'Amore*, to have and to hold.

She showed no repulsion over his scarred face, and his injuries worried her not at all. 'You'll heal,' she'd say, 'and we've plenty of time'. But she still refused to marry him. He asked every day now. It had become a game.

'Marry me,' he ordered, as if she were a subordinate. He'd tried begging, pleading, bribery, even during lovemaking, and nothing had worked so far, but he was far from discouraged.

'Are you emperor yet?' That was her price: she would only marry an emperor. She said it was a joke, but there was serious resolve beneath it. 'Ril Endarion won't survive the war,' she'd predicted. 'The queen will need a new husband, the one she should have married in 930. You.' They both knew even that wouldn't make him emperor – not unless Lyra then died.

She reached out and stroked the scarred side of his face. 'You've been scratching at the brand again,' she chided.

'It itches some days.' Though in truth, the itch was to his pride. He'd never been pretty, but he'd been handsome enough; being with her made the ugliness worse. 'Do you know, the man who attacked the queen wore a Lantric mask: Twoface, the betrayer.'

She looked up at him curiously. 'You fought him.'

'Aye, and almost died. I've never encountered a fighter like him, and I pray I never do again. But the thing is, one of his associates thought I was him! Because of these scars, I suppose. That tells me that these Masks don't know each other's identity.'

'Should you be telling me this?' she asked, stroking his other cheek. 'Solon, it's a coincidence, I'm sure.'

'Masks are cowardice,' he growled. 'People who hide their identities for shame at their deeds? I despise them.'

'Oh, I don't know. I think we all wear masks. We put on our public face for the world. We put on a happy face for those we love.'

'Are you telling me that you're wearing a mask now?'

'A strumpet's mask?' she giggled. 'Perhaps. I'm a different person with you than anyone else. That's the licence that love gives us: to trust another so much we reveal our deepest selves.'

He kissed her and asked, 'Is it love, then?'

'To me, it's always been love. I'm waiting for you to realise.'

'I do love you,' he thought, then realised he'd spoken aloud and that it was true.

She looked almost triumphant, but asked, 'Are you sure? Have you been in love before?'

'No ... My wife – well, our hearts never touched, and our bodies seldom either. Not like us.'

'And no one else ever touched your heart?'

'Never.'

'I've heard,' she said, almost slyly, 'that old Radine Jandreux was very fond of you.'

'If she was, she was too much the lady to let it show. And she was two decades my senior—'

'As you are mine!'

'Aye, but that's different,' he exclaimed. 'You didn't know Radine.'

'What would you have done if she'd summoned you to her chamber? I'm sure she wanted to.'

'Radine wasn't like that. We called her "The Prune".'

Her face darkened. '"The Prune"?'

'It's a dried fruit, from the East. They're wrinkled and sour, like an old woman's skin.'

Medelie shoved at him. 'That's disgusting.'

'It was just a nickname – no one would ever have said it to her face.'

'So you think that excuses calling people names behind their backs?'

'I daresay I'm called worse behind mine. What does it matter? We all respected her.' A thought struck him. 'Here, you're not her illegitimate daughter or something, are you?'

'No, I'm not.' She sat up, her knees to her chest. 'So men only love youth and beauty, do they? Old women are just things to laugh at.'

He sat up too, facing her and trying to impart all the sincerity of his heart. 'I should be the one worrying about being abandoned when I'm old, darling, not you!' He put a hand on her knee. 'I've always believed in love, but until now I've not known it. Looks, age, status, wealth – they're just distractions. Love is what happens when two souls meet.' He'd never said such things before, would have laughed at the suggestion – but he was *willing* her to believe him.

Then he saw that she was weeping and he pulled her into his arms, kissed her and held her. Amidst all of the tumult going inside his own head, he almost didn't hear what she whispered in his ear: 'I *have* been hiding a secret, my love. My name isn't Medelie, it's *Radine*. I came back for you – and I will never leave again.'

His whole body went rigid, and for a moment he felt that he was the only solid thing in this world; that everything else could fade and tear at any moment.

'You've gone so quiet,' said Medelie – *no, Radine*. 'Are you so very appalled?'

He stared at the gorgeous young body laid before him, her beautiful sculpted face, nothing like the old Radine, and was momentarily lost for words. And then he saw it: the resemblance that had nagged at him without him realising. The facial structure, and the eyes – especially those, deep windows to a soul he finally recognised.

Dear Lord . . . it really is my duchess . . .

'Milady, I am your servant!' he blurted, floundering for some way to convey his reverence and his shock, too appalled to even want to begin to deal with what this meant.

She threw herself back into his arms, naked and clinging, her face upturned, *those eyes* boring into his. 'I don't want you to serve me, Solon,' she replied. 'I want you to love me – and to make me your queen.'

Lyra's nights were taking on a strange rhythm. The powerful, intense dreams she'd been having since that first one with the seraph had been evolving. Most nights she still experienced the beautiful, euphoric experience of being wrapped in angelic arms and flying through the stars, but now they were just the precursors to something deeper and more disturbing.

There were four of them: *daemon dreams*, Ostevan called them when she described them, and each one was harrowing. Every night, Vita and Basia would help her undress and see her to bed, snuff the lights and leave her alone. 'Sleep well,' they would wish her – but those good wishes had no power against this strange cycle. It might begin in the seraph's arms, but she couldn't stay in that dream; sometime around midnight she would invariably awaken and fear would set in, a certainty that as soon as she closed her eyes, she'd have another of *those* nights. She'd lie awake, trying not to sleep, but invariably she'd fail and fall.

Each nightmare was as bad as the others. In the *beast dream* she was an animal of some kind, one which bit the heads off mice and lizards in her garden. The blood in her mouth made her drunk and hysterical. These always concluded the same way: she would catch a glimpse of herself, long-fanged and bloody-chinned, reflected in her pool under a scarlet moon . . . which had a masked face etched into it, a blank Lantric mask, which was slowly removed . . .

Then there was the *fury dream*, which always felt horribly real. She stood like a giantess atop Redburn Tower, feeling a rising tide of rage until she was shrieking imprecations at the *scum* below her. A storm would rise at her command and she'd send lightning bolts, blizzards and tornados into the buildings and people below, while the Aerflus rose and flooded the city before freezing, until in the end there was only her alive in a frozen wasteland, sitting atop the Bastion and staring across at the Celestium . . . where a masked giant perched, wearing a blank mask . . .

In the *ruling dream* she held court and the supplicants before her were all guilty: sinful, snivelling creatures she despised. She would hammer down her sceptre and demand they be punished, and men in black leathers, like hooded butchers, would come forth with bloody iron implements of pain, and no matter how she then protested that no, she'd never intended this, she had to watch, screaming in unison with the victims as they were subjected to bloody brutality. The worst of these were when it was Ril and Basia dragged before her and condemned for adultery, and she had to watch as they were dismembered.

And last, there was the *lust dream*, which always began with her kneeling on an Unburdening stool, praying for Absolution to the beautiful ivory seraph statuette of her pure dream – but instead of Absolution, the urge to pleasure herself would strike her and she would disrobe lewdly, delighting in the desecration. Then the seraph statue would come to life and grasp her from behind, and she'd press herself back into him, feeling his tool probing her as he mauled her breasts painfully. In her dream, she revelled in it, even as the coupling which began as pleasure, turned her into some kind of grunting beast, as she twisted her face to try to see behind her angelic lover's blank Lantric mask . . .

She always woke before the face was revealed.

I have to tell Dirklan, she resolved finally.

She skirted around the most embarrassing details, but Setallius assured her that while dream-sendings could be mystic-gnosis, she was warded against such things.

'Your dreams are your own, Lyra,' he said. 'You're just anxious. They'll pass.'

It wasn't what she wanted to hear, and didn't answer her needs. Only Ostevan could do that.

Ostevan Comfateri paused at Lyra's door, awaiting for the signal to enter. Of late, access to the queen had become more guarded. He could guess why: every night he'd been placing new clay figures in her garden-pool, each mixed with opium and whatever mix of blood and other ingredients he'd decided on, working the clay figure of Lyra into different poses to channel the energy. Dream-spells weren't needed as Lyra's sensitivity and the dwyma itself did the rest. She was visibly coming apart at the seams.

It had become a game, experimenting with some fresh ingredient like animal blood or hair taken from a prisoner, and she'd dutifully report the result to him next morning during her Unburdening. He could scarcely keep from laughing aloud in delight at her lurid confessions.

It was the third week of Septinon already, and he was brimming with energy. Lyra, on the other hand, was almost asleep in her chair when Vita showed him in; the maid blushed when he smiled flirtatiously at her, as naïve as her mistress.

'Good morning, Majesty,' he said, sitting opposite Lyra, conscious of Basia in the corner. *I could crush them both in half a second.* But caution was needed still; it would be weeks yet before he and Tear were to strike, so there was no need to act precipitously. 'Did you sleep well last night? You look tired.'

'I'm exhausted,' Lyra confessed.

'You dreamed?' he enquired, keeping his voice casual. 'Well, if a friendly ear is needed . . . ?'

She eyed him uncomfortably, which was understandable. *I passed her little water test and she trusts me . . . but the dreams keep coming and they frighten her, and she's ashamed of them . . .*

'Milady, I'm your confessor. Whatever you tell me is sacrosanct,' he said soothingly. 'If it helps, perhaps come down to the chapel instead? The booth there is comfortable, and Kore's house will help ease your soul.'

She perked up a little. 'I think I will. I'm so sick of this room.'

He and Basia helped Lyra down the many flights to his chapel on the ground level, a long walk for a heavily pregnant woman, and she wasn't as steady on her feet as usual. Then Basia went to the refectory – since he'd passed Lyra's unsubtle 'test', the wooden-legged woman had been noticeably more relaxed about leaving him with her charge.

The royal chapel wasn't a public chapel, so he wasn't obliged to keep it open day and night. The gnostic lamps illuminated as they went inside, revealing the carven sarcophagi and statuary and the sacred heart above the altar. He and Lyra genuflected together before he helped her to the Unburdening Room. He pulled the curtains closed, sealing out the world, then settled beside Lyra, his heart racing a little . . .

We're utterly alone . . . The planned strike against Wurther was still more than a month away; arrangements were proceeding apace. *When I strike, Dom, you'll be defenceless.* But his desire to secure Lyra before Naxius could claim her required him to act soon . . . and it required a situation just like this. *Perhaps this is the day . . . ?*

He knew everything about her now, from her burgeoning political confidence to her continued emotional immaturity, the legacy of twenty years in a convent. He knew her marriage was slowly falling apart, that Ril Endarion had never known how to unlock her desires – and thanks to the blend of dreams and nightmares he was sending her, she was unravelling.

But the process was not yet complete. She *depended* on him, but he needed more than that.

'So, Milady,' he said as they settled, kneeling side by side before the small shrine to Corineus the Judge, 'you had another nightmare – was it a new dream, or one you've had before?'

Lyra cast an anxious look around her as if concerned, even here, that she could be overheard. She had the air of one who was more than half asleep, thanks to the opium and the lack of sleep. 'I can't really . . .' she slurred.

'Milady,' he reminded her, 'we're alone in the house of Kore. Pretend I'm not here, if that helps. Speak to Him Above. Trust in Kore.'

Of course that was exactly the right thing to say, because it bypassed her guilt and appealed to her devout nature. 'I'm sorry,' she groaned, 'you're right, of course. And I do need to talk about this.' As the words spilled from her, her face and voice filled with exhausted anxiety.

He listened sympathetically, inwardly gleeful as she confirmed his nightly game was a roaring success. Last night he'd layered all the ingredients into his clay figurine: the beast dream that filled her with blood-hunger; the fury and judgement dreams where she lashed out at those who'd wronged her, and then all the petty dross of humanity, and finally the lust dream that drove her to her knees with guilty needs.

She's a puppet on my strings, he thought. His own desire was mounting, but that would never do; what passed between them had to be chaste or she would slip through his fingers. He managed to keep his voice calm. 'You mustn't be embarrassed, Lyra. We all have dark imaginings at times. Better we examine them in dream than in real life, don't you think?'

'But why would I dream these things? I'm not an angry person. I'm not a cruel person. And I certainly don't dream of such . . . *sordid* acts.'

Oh, but you do, he thought, keeping his face schooled. *I feed you the stimulants, but what you see comes from your own brain, my dear Lyra.* 'Fear brings out many responses in our subconscious, Milady.' He patted her hand, then dropped his in easy reach. 'I know you're scared that your husband has been unfaithful – such emotions often become fear or anger, or even desire for another in retaliation for being put through the anguish of doubt.'

Her mouth formed an 'O'. Clearly the concept of revenge-sex hadn't entered her mind – but it was there now. 'Some mornings I can't tell the difference between waking and dreaming,' she admitted. 'I have whole conversations that I'm not sure are real. My body feels like it's been stolen – and I feel so fat and ugly.' Then she sighed, as she always did, and said, 'The bad times will pass, Ril will return and all will be well.'

That wretched mantra was the stumbling point for all his schemes. Even exhausted and disoriented as she was, disenchanted with her marriage and her life, she would not cast it all away. She was willing to be the martyr, because she believed Kore wanted it of her.

He needed to convince her otherwise. His plan was risky, but Lyra's soul had to be won, for the rest of her to follow.

'Lyra, you're not ugly,' he reassured her, 'you're beautiful and perfect, as desirable now as at any time in your life. Don't let anyone say otherwise.' He pitched his voice as earnest, and smiled inwardly as he saw his words soak into her like water into a desert, and gratitude bloomed. 'Milady, there's something I want to show you. Do you remember you asked where the seraphim were? And why they don't intervene in our world?'

'I remember,' she said uncertainly.

'Pray with me,' he offered, reaching out both hands to her, palms upward.

Tentatively she returned the gesture and they clasped, a contact that made Abraxas, waiting inside him, rear up. He soothed the daemon's eternal hunger, then cleared his mind and opened it to the aether, whilst touching hers, just enough to show her what he sensed, without leaving a trace for Dirklan Setallius or Basia de Sirou to find.

'*Barachiel*,' he called softly, with voice and mind, '*Barachiel.*'

Of course Lyra recognised the name: Barachiel was one of the seven great seraphim who governed Paradise, according to the *Book of Kore*.

Gently, he enfolded her senses into his. 'Don't be afraid – I'll protect you, if you trust me?'

Of course she trusted him: he'd been working on that ever since his return from exile. Setallius had trained her to protect her mind, but she relinquished the controls passively. He didn't need to warp her values or her memories in any way, not when the real Lyra was so close to being his anyway. This last little trick should do the rest.

'Barachiel, come to us and greet your daughter, Lyra Vereinen.'

They both felt it: the sudden gleaming of light in the aether, accompanied by a beautiful harmonic chanting that slowly swelled into their ears. He saw the way her eyes went round, then tears began to spill. The joy on her face was so intense he was moved himself, and a slow smile began to spread over his face too.

'*Blessed Be!*' a resonant voice boomed in their minds, and they were both embraced in a warm glow of approval and love. '*Thou and thou are my instruments on Urte – let thy union bring peace to all.*' Then that sense of *presence* enveloped them again, even more powerfully, so that for a few moments they were bathed in light, real light projected from the aether as the seraphic chorus soared. Then it faded and their normal senses took over once more.

Lyra's lips were moving soundlessly, her face alight with happiness and wonder.

Amazing what a little parlour trick can achieve, Ostevan thought smugly. Of course it had all been Abraxas: the warmth, the chanting . . . daemons could be quite versatile when they weren't slavering after fresh blood.

'How do other magi not know?' she whispered.

'Many would misuse such knowledge,' he replied, reprovingly, 'but the truly faithful know. We keep the secret.' He placed his hands over hers and said solemnly, 'As must you, my Queen.'

'Of course,' she said, still awestruck, then she looked up at him with utter reverence. 'Thank you, thank you so much. This is the happiest moment of my life.' Then her mind finally overtook her senses and her jaw dropped.

'The seraph . . . he said "*thy union*" – what does that mean? I'm already married . . . and you – you're a *priest!*'

Her big eyes locked on his, their faces close enough that he could feel her breath on his skin and her perfume filled his nostrils. She was stunned, perhaps even appalled, but there was no pulling away, indeed, she was leaning *into* him.

You're on the hook, my Queen. Shall I reel you in?

Am I dreaming this or awake? Lyra wondered as her mind whirled over that brief glimpse of the eternal. It had been everything she'd dreamed it would be, and had left her in a joyous stupor, unable to think clearly. In fact, she'd felt woozy all day, ever since waking with the lust dream still replaying in her brain. All day, voices had been too loud; everything moved slowly, and odd things caught and held her attention . . . like Ostevan's hands, which were carving shapes in the air as he moved them over hers, trailing stardust.

He conjured a seraph for me – Barachiel blessed us both! Surely my confessor is a holy man . . . a sacred being . . .

She remembered his hands on her aching back three months ago, and the wonderful surcease they'd brought. He'd touched her breasts that day too, because her nipples had been painful . . . *That was all right, wasn't it? It wasn't a sin, to make pain go away? Barachiel blessed him, so it had to have been all right!* Her nipples went hard at the memory, and she *ached* for him to touch them again.

She suddenly realised she was talking. '. . . and you're a priest!'

Oh, but you're also a man! And Barachiel said 'thy union'!

Her skin was suddenly dripping perspiration; her bones felt hollow. The whole world had shifted in that brief glimpse of the eternal and suddenly her path was clear before her. One of the seraphim had *commanded* that she put Ril aside and marry Ostevan! The unthinkable, something that would have been a sin, a transgression beyond the pale, was now a *divine command.*

Kore knows I no longer love Ril . . . and Ostevan has been so kind. She could even picture lying with him . . . *I've fantasised about it at times,* she admitted to herself, *pictured his hands touching me late at night sometimes, these lonely months.* Her face went crimson at the memory, but she couldn't look away.

'Milady, I'm as shocked as you are,' he said slowly. 'You're a married woman and my calling . . .' But he took her hands, still staring at her face. 'You know I care for you, Lyra – as deeply as I love Kore Himself.'

The touch of his fingers reassured her, told her she was in *good hands.* Then her baby kicked her bladder and she gasped, pulling his hands to her stomach. *Good hands . . . I want his hands . . .* For a moment his features froze; she could see the patterns in his irises and felt a dreadful urge to kiss him.

'My baby . . .' she gasped, but it was just an excuse to make him *touch* her. 'Can you feel it?'

Slowly, trailing light, Ostevan's long right hand moved to the stretched fabric of her belly and traced the swell of her body from her swollen breasts until it settled on her stomach and she felt the child within wriggling. They shared the moment of wonder – one she hadn't had with Ril or anyone else for months – feeling the life within her stir. In some ways it was like that moment when Barachiel touched her.

'Do you feel it?' she asked.

DAVID HAIR

'I do, my Queen,' he said warmly, and she knew he meant more than just the baby's movement. He went to remove his hand, but she held it there while her heart hammered.

'Why am I having such wonderful and terrible dreams?' she begged, certain that only he could help her, and trying to distract him from any impulse to let her go. A man who spoke to angels could do anything. And that hand felt *glorious* on her belly.

'Milady, you're a dwymancer: your awareness transcends your body. I believe that when you dream, your awareness travels the aether, too bright and brilliant to be assailed. You leave your body and seek the seraphim. Sometimes you find them, and your dreams are beatific – but sometimes the daemons find you and they try to tear you down – they find the chinks in your armour where you are weak. Those are your nightmares.'

'But I don't want to hurt anyone . . . Not even Ril and Basia . . .'

Forgive those who transgress against you, the Book of Kore *says.*

'Even though they have betrayed you and committed adultery?'

Somehow she'd gone from supposition to certainty on that question. 'I don't hate them – and I'm not a vengeful person. I'm angry, yes: Ril has given me a child and now he's pulling away. But love is blind, Ostevan, so how can I blame them for falling in love with each other? Especially when I don't love him any more either . . .' Her voice trailed off.

Dear Kore, I've said it . . . And it's true. I don't love Ril any more . . . Then she felt a tremor of panic and looked away from him to the statue of Corineus Justiciar, his stern face condemning some dreadful sin. She flinched and looked back at Ostevan's gentler visage. Unreality pervaded everything, words were tumbling unchecked from her subconscious to her tongue. 'Is the sexual dream part of my yearnings too?' she asked, 'or are daemons playing with my mind?' *Because, dear Kore, I want you right now . . . as the seraph commands . . .*

'Lyra, the chinks the daemons find in us are always self-made,' Ostevan responded, his face inches from hers. 'If you dream of making love, it's because you crave intimacy . . . and if the intimacy you crave is not with your husband, that doesn't mean it's for someone specific.

The seraph could be an idealisation, a dream lover, when reality has let you down.'

'Or it could be a real man,' she said, fearful that he didn't understand. *I love you, you, you.*

'It could be a real man,' he admitted, his hands still pressed to her belly, his mouth so close.

'Is sex a sin, then?' she breathed, her whole body throbbing with a sudden rush of *wanting.*

'No, but adultery is,' he replied, speaking the words her heart knew. They shared an incredibly intense look and she realised that he knew exactly what was churning inside her mind. *Adultery is a sin, and we are both good people, raised in the Church. But the lovemaking of a wedded couple is pure and good . . .*

'My marriage is over,' she said with utter certainty. Her heart was thudding so hard she thought her ribs would crack. 'I have to set Ril free . . . and myself. We both deserve better.'

'That's a huge decision,' Ostevan said, and she loved him for not leaping in to claim her.

He doesn't need to.

'I'm going to have my marriage ended and choose another husband. Ril has committed adultery, but I can't have him executed; I'll offer him exile. And then I'll be free.' She raised Ostevan's hands to her lips and kissed them. 'You do understand, don't you? I'll be free to love where my heart desires.'

Ostevan cupped his beautiful hands around her face and pulled her mouth to his as the whole universe chimed and rang. His mouth tasted of plums, his soft whiskers teased her cheeks and she had to fight not to drag him onto her as wet heat rose in her loins. That he wanted her was just as clear as he groaned into her mouth, his body against hers burning hot. But that would be too soon, something to be ashamed of, and she wanted everything to be pure this time.

'I love you,' she breathed, reluctantly pulling away. 'I think I've loved you for months and not realised. You're the only one who knows me.'

And you can summon angels!

'I love you too, Lyra,' he replied, and she could have danced at his words. 'But we mustn't commit the very sin we both condemn in others,' he went on seriously, and she adored that his virtue was as strong as hers. 'If we wish to be together, we must go about it with decency and dignity, or we risk tearing apart your reign.'

'I do want us to be together,' she said, the words tumbling from her mouth. 'It's truly what I want! You do feel the same, Ostevan, don't you?' She clutched at her heart. 'Dear Kore, I'm asking you to renounce the Church!' Panic seized her. 'I can't ask that of you, I can't expect—'

'You don't have to ask, Lyra,' he interrupted gently. 'I would do anything for you – even that. And Barachiel himself wills it . . . I never thought to get so wonderful a commandment.'

She seized him and kissed him again, fiercely, then gushed, 'Oh Ostevan, I feel giddy and silly and happy and . . . Oh Kore! I've not felt this way since, since—'

Since the night I married Ril . . . That sudden thought made her suddenly chill. *I have to be sure I'm not dreaming this. I have to sit and be still for a while on my own . . .*

'Are you all right?' he asked, and she knew he understood what she was thinking.

He's a mage – I'm probably an open book to him. 'Yes, yes, I'm just . . . I need to be alone, just to think, that's all. To take it all in.'

'Second thoughts already?' he enquired, with a whiff of irony.

'No, no – never! I just need to collect my thoughts, and work out how to proceed, who to tell . . .' Her brain careered off on a tangent as she listed them in her head: *My counsellors, of course, and Basia – oh Kore, Basia! And how do I tell Ril?* She realised she was beginning to hyperventilate and had to clutch Ostevan's hand and concentrate on breathing. 'I need my garden,' she panted. 'I need to be alone and think this through.'

'I'd as soon never let you leave my side again,' he said, making her smile, 'but that's clearly impossible. Of course, go and collect your thoughts – then come back to me and we'll work this out together.'

She squeezed his hands, feeling euphoric. This, finally, was how love was meant to be: this feeling of communing with a man who understood and wanted to share her burdens. *Oh Ril, why did we never reach this point together?* The thought brought surprisingly little pain, as if he were already in her past.

'If I kiss you again, I'll never leave,' she giggled. 'As it is, I think I'll float to my garden.'

Letting go of his hands was the hardest part, and then there was the first step away. She took her time, walking backwards from pew to pew, beaming back at him, until finally she blew a kiss and slipped through the door.

Outside, Basia looked at her critically. 'Are you all right? You look flushed.'

Flushed . . . Dear Kore, I feel like my life has been turned upside down! 'I'm fine,' Lyra managed. 'I just need to sit . . . and some cool water from my fountain, I think,' she added as if she'd only just thought of it. She seized Basia's arm, realising that she felt no anger towards her any more. 'Thank you for your service,' she babbled.

'Milady?'

Oh Kore, she probably thinks I'm dismissing her . . . which I will, but not yet . . .

'I don't thank you enough,' she said quickly. 'Come, let's go. I need water – I need to think!'

Ostevan kept his composure until Lyra had left, her face filled with dazed adoration. Then he sank to his knees on the stone floor, his mind racing . . . *Will she go through with this? Have I won her heart – and gained my weapon against Naxius?*

The taste of her mouth still lingered on his; he recalled with a shudder that first moment they'd kissed, and inside him Abraxas had howled for him to *bite and rend and rip and tear.* He still couldn't quite believe he hadn't. Somehow his survival instincts had won out; he'd left his prize intact.

I was touching her before I knew it, and then . . . Despite all his preparation, that moment of physical contact had almost overpowered him; he so nearly wrecked all his schemes for a moment of gratification. *I wanted to charm her, certainly . . . but how did I not take her and rukk her senseless?* It was terrifying, how close he'd come.

Gradually though, a slow smile spread across his face as he recalled each delicious moment – her yielding heart, the tremulous first kiss, her passion rising. There were depths there, places Ril Endarion had clearly never gone. She had desires she barely admitted to herself.

And I have a few of my own, Lyra . . . It's down to her now, he thought as he went to the altar, poured sacred wine into the chalice and drained it. *If she is truly convinced, then I've won. Ril Endarion will be gone and I'll be the next prince-consort . . . and finally able to move against Naxius, leaving me in control of all that power . . .*

If she wavered, then his position was in jeopardy. He had his emergency bag ready in case he needed to run, but as he replayed their encounter over and over, the more secure he felt. *She doesn't have it in her to not obey a seraph!* That she could fall for such an old ploy was almost laughable, but then, she had no gnostic training. *She clearly doesn't realise that no one has ever found a trace of the least angel of Kore in centuries of trying . . . They just don't exist.*

He'd crack her façade of piety and faithfulness, and her burgeoning martyrdom. She was his now. *Crozier takes queen, and becomes king. Tabula-mio! The game is mine.*

17

Guilt and Retribution

Thaumaturgy: Air

I'm the storm wind, rolling in from the mountains, blasting the backwaters and scouring the streets of the foetid cities. I'm freedom, riding the air, and I'll always be above you.

POL LYCEN, FUGITIVE MAGE, HOLLENIA, 741

What goes up will most certainly fall. Hard.

FYLLARA, IMPERIAL OWLS, HOLLENIA, 742

Pallas, Rondelmar
Septinon 935

Lyra felt like she was floating as she made her way through the Bastion to the Greengate. She barely noticed Basia behind her; she was wholly caught up in how wonderful the last half hour had been, how terrifyingly, joyously life-changing. *I've been so lonely and unhappy, and Kore saw that and sent me a gift: His seraph touched me . . . and sent me a new man to love . . .*

The path ahead would be difficult, she knew. She'd have to issue a writ against Ril, accusing him of adultery – of which he was surely guilty – and hope he went quietly to avoid a public trial and the inevitable scandal. And then she would have to assert her right to choose a successor – *Ostevan!* – when her counsellors and court would surely expect Solon Takwyth.

Barachiel has shown me what Kore wants. Surely through His will it will happen. She drifted weightlessly past the guardsmen at Greengate, euphoria still suffusing her very being. The long narrow garden opened before her: first the flower beds, then the Rose Bower. As Basia followed on her awkward false legs, Lyra thought of what must come. *I have to confront her, tell her of my intentions, so that she can go to Ril. I wish them happiness together, I truly do – somewhere beyond the empire.*

But first, she desperately needed a cool drink of water, to help order her thoughts.

Then a rose vine inexplicably broke free from its trestle and lashed sideways – she didn't even see it coming, just felt the sudden jagged pain as her cheek was ripped open by a thorn. She squealed in fright and staggered – she would have fallen, had Basia not caught her with kinesis.

'Lyra? Are you all right?'

'Yes – *no!*' Lyra shrank as the rose vine quivered, but it was just swaying in the gentle breeze as if nothing had happened. She brushed the back of her hand against her cheek and it came away bloodied. 'I think it just tore loose of its trestle, that's all.' But she didn't believe that, not here, not for a second.

She looked about her, trying to reach the place in her where the green coil of energy lay: the touch of the dwyma. It was hard, harder than it had been when she was still trying to learn how, and when she broke through, there was no enfolding embrace, just a sense of watchful hostility.

'What's wrong with my garden?'

'Milady?' Basia was looking about her as if assessing threats in a crowd.

Lyra hadn't realised she'd spoken aloud. 'Nothing . . . I just . . .' She felt strangely scared: this was her haven, but it felt like it had been turned against her. She wondered if some enemy had stolen in while she was absent. 'Let's go to the pool – I can work out what's wrong there.'

They went cautiously now as Lyra's happiness turned to confused hurt and a sense of violation. *This is my sanctuary!* But the sense of wrongness didn't dissipate as they passed through the Rose Bower and into the Oak Grove bordering the fountain pool. It got worse: birds shrieked and took to the air, a polecat stopped in the path and snarled before flashing away and a wasp began to buzz menacingly about her until Basia's hand flashed with light and the insect crackled and fell lifeless to the grass.

'Lyra, should I summon the guards?' Basia asked, pulling at her sleeve. 'What if there's an enemy ahead?'

An enemy who can turn my own dwyma place against me? Is that possible?

But what little she knew was that dwymancers *served* – so how could two dwymancers ever be pitched against each other when they both served the same thing? She rejected the notion – and then a frightening thought struck her: *What if the dwyma really is evil and it's sensed the touch of Barachiel on me? What if it's reacting against that?*

'We have to go on,' she breathed. 'I have to know.'

'Know what?' Basia drew her long, thin-bladed sword. 'Lyra, what do you need to know?'

Lyra didn't answer. A sudden gust of wind whooshed through the oaks, making the undergrowth billow. Leaves slapped at her face and body and she stumbled through into the glade – then the wind fell again, as if it had never been.

As they entered the small glade, Lyra saw the waters of her pool were churning as if something large was swirling to the surface; bubbles released a noxious odour.

'*Aradea?*' she called aloud, reaching for her guardian spirit, properly scared now.

A crow shrieked from the branches of a border-elm as the wind rose again, making her stagger. Basia shouted and tugged at her sleeves, trying to draw her away, but a face was forming on the curtain of vines on the mossy wall: the face of Aradea, hissing with hostility – *and fear.*

Daemon, a voice hissed in Lyra's mind, paralysing her – and the fountain water bubbled furiously as sludge rose to the surface: dark grey-black muck that surged up onto the grass before her. As she stared at the mud, she saw there were figures in it: clay figures . . .

'Milady, we should leave,' Basia pleaded.

'No,' Lyra said, walking to the edge of the pool. Groaning, she dropped to one knee, almost gagging on the sickly reek of corruption that rose from the sludge. Steeling herself, she reached in and pulled out a clay figure. It was small, only a few inches tall, and crudely formed, but it was recognisably a naked pregnant woman – only with a rat-skull instead of a head.

It's meant to be me . . .

She pulled out another, and another. Some had enraged faces, others were in lewd postures, legs apart, with twigs penetrating the space between. But the most lifelike was two figures joined together: a winged seraph coupling with a pregnant woman from behind.

Her chest gave a massive thump and her throat tightened so that she was scarcely able to breathe. For a panicky few seconds she thought her heart was failing. *This is where my nightmares come from – not from inside my head, but from here . . .*

She turned and managed, 'Basia, help me!'

Basia took the clay figurine and helped Lyra to her feet. When Two-face had assailed her in this garden, it had been as if nature itself had risen against him – and they were pretty sure he'd been daemon-possessed. Aradea herself had appeared and reduced the daemon-knight to a smear on the earth. What was happening today was akin to that, if nowhere near as intense.

Aradea feels threatened by something . . . is it something in me?

But that made no sense, because *an angel* had touched her, not a daemon . . . *Hadn't it?*

But who'd planted these things in her pool?

'Can you tell anything from this?' she asked.

Basia concentrated, holding up one of the sludge-coated figurines between two fingers, while her right hand conjured light around the filthy object. As her lips moved silently, Lyra waited, keenly aware of the unseen Aradea seething with anger. She was terrified that rage would be unleashed upon her, or Basia.

Gnosis leaves a trace, and so do other things. A mage can unravel those traces . . .

'Well?' she asked, and in the sick pit of her gut, she wondered if she already knew the answer.

A pale glow like starlight radiated from Basia's hands, forming a nimbus about the figure. She hunched over it like a poised snake, her face painted eerily by the light, and fleeting images began to appear: a dead mouse, its neck broken; a sparrow, coated in blood; a red flower—

—*a poppy*, Lyra realised. 'Oh Kore,' she breathed, 'someone's poisoned my dwyma place.' *A genilocus is corruptible*, she realised. *My place of strength is also my vulnerability*. It was a terrifying thought.

Then Basia stiffened – and they both heard and felt what came next: a black seeping ooze that bled upwards into the light and vanished, bringing with it a voice with a thousand mouths, hissing hatred, then sliding into nothing.

'Abraxas,' Lyra breathed, remembering that voice coming from Coramore's mouth.

'Tell me you've never drunk from this pool while it's been tainted,' Basia breathed.

'It's never been like this,' Lyra replied, feeling nauseous. 'The water was always clear.'

Basia intensified her efforts and the nimbus of light brightened, like the last flicker of an oil-lamp before it fades ... and it had one last secret to reveal.

'*Kore's Balls*,' Basia swore, 'Ostevan – you *bastard*!'

Despite the momentous shift in his relationship with Lyra and the prospects it opened up, Ostevan Comfateri still had duties, including the afternoon mass in the Royal Chapel, which – he'd realised in sudden alarm – was due to start ten minutes after Lyra wafted out of the room, blowing him kisses.

The taste of her lips still on his, he robed for the service, his mind still racing: he needed to marginalise Takwyth, lest the Knight-Champion pluck her from his grasp. Some kind of scandal, perhaps, maybe over his new lover, Medelie Aventour?

And Wurther, the fat slug, will vehemently oppose me until the day I push a blade through his bloated heart ...

Somehow he managed to maintain his usual serene façade as the small group of worshippers filed in – there were never many at the afternoon service. He led them in the opening hymn, 'Rest Thine Heart in Kore', but his mind was elsewhere, fantasising about everything he would do when the prince's throne was his . . . and then the Pontifex's Curule as well . . . He would become the first *true* Pontifex, ruler of Church and State, since Sertain's time.

He felt like a demi-god as he stood before the altar, raising the ritual dagger and cup, calling down the blessings of Kore on their gathering and basking in the chanted responses. *This worship is of me*, he told himself. *I'm a more real god than any of these sheep will ever encounter.*

He took up the chalice to begin the blessing of the sacrament when he felt the aether quiver; there was a sudden rush of force and every hair on his body stood on end—

—Ostevan . . .

Lyra's stomach clenched and she felt acid surge up her throat. Gagging, she bent and retched. *Ostevan did this – the dreams came from his workings – he's poisoned my genilocus . . .*

The dreams had been to torment her and drive her into the hands of someone she trusted – the only person she confided fully in – and that meant the seraph Barachiel was a lie! She'd been blind to it, but Aradea had perceived the truth. Which meant that *everything* she'd thought and felt in that transcendent half-hour with Ostevan had been a cruel, manipulative trap . . .

I kissed him and told him I loved him, and all the while he was laughing at me . . .

She could still feel his hands on her face and her belly, as if they'd stained her skin. She retched again, spat burning sourness from her mouth. Then anger came, rage at having her emotions violated, and she felt the fury dream come to life inside her waking skull.

He took away my self-control and used me. He made me his puppet.

Her fingers curled into claws.

I'm going to rip his head off.

'ARADEA!' she roared, like one of the Furies of Lantric myth, 'COME TO ME!'

There was a sudden rushing of air through the trees and she felt herself engulfed in a cloud of leaves that spun and formed about her, but she didn't give a thought to that. All her being was concentrated on becoming one with Aradea. Her vision changed and Basia became just a blur of pale light beside her, of no consequence. She saw the taint in the pool and shouted, '*BE CLEAN!*' and it was, but that was just a passing thing. What mattered was her enemy . . .

He's that *way.*

Lyra stalked through the darkened garden towards the inner walls, reaching ahead of herself and behind, her instincts finding something deep, completely beyond her perceptions, and she hauled on those pent-up forces, felt subterranean rocks bigger than houses shift and grind, then the earth audibly rumbled like thunder beneath her feet, the ground shook and she staggered as stone cracked and distant voices cried out, but she didn't care, because Ostevan's voice wasn't one of them. She shouted wordlessly, pointing forward, and the curtain wall shook, cracked and collapsed, and behind it she saw another wall go down, and then a roof beyond it. She heard panicky men, shrieking women, and felt the aether tremble.

'*OSTEVAN! WHERE ARE YOU?*'

She strode through the tumbled walls and then stopped, because where the Royal Chapel should have been was a forty-yard-wide sinkhole and the entire chapel had fallen into it, the ancient stonework collapsed, beautiful stained-glass windows shattered, old tombs and sarcophagi smashed open. At the rim was a gaggle of churchgoers, staring, aghast. Many were covered in dust and cowering beneath gnostic shields. Spilled lamp-oil caught fire and flames roared up the annexe walls, but she quelled them with a thought as she spun about her, raging still.

'*OSTEVAN!*'

The betrayal – her *mortification* – threatened to rip her apart. She wanted to destroy something – *anything*. A glowing pale thing caught her eye, right at the rim of the sinkhole, a man with a gold flame-handled knife in his heart. She gathered her might to crush it—

—and realised it was an icon of Corineus, *her Saviour*, and she realised just how far she'd strayed outside herself. And this was the *Royal Chapel* – although she might hate the man who'd made it his lair, this was a holy place.

Those thoughts were *just* enough to bring her back to her senses.

She regained herself fully and pulled something from her face – a mask, made of leaves, with a thatch of twigs that had been tangled in her hair. It was like the Leaf-Man face – there was one carved into a broken fountain base in the pond of her garden, and also above Greengate: an age-old symbol of the pagan Sollans. Her dress was covered in leaves too, green and brown and gold; they started dropping off, leaving the pale fabric stained. She could still feel the echo of that verdant power throbbing through her, immensely powerful.

The members of the congregation were staring at her in mute horror. But Ostevan was already gone.

The Masquerade (Tear)

The Lantric Masques

The Lantric masquerade is a form of entertainment steeped in history and symbolism. The cast of eight characters is unchanging and the plot always revolves around the romantic misadventures of the lovers, Heartface and Ironhelm. There's no script, and performances might contain any or all of the sacred, the spiritual, the comedic and the profane. All human nature can be found in these dramas.

PHILO ANSOPOULOS, HISTORIAN, 780

Pallas, Rondelmar
Octen 935

In the autumn of 932, Ervyn Naxius came to Radine Jandreux, Duchess of Coraine, as she lay dying. It was long after midnight and the healers were all asleep, but Radine had been unable to find rest, as cancers ate her body and bitterness corroded her soul.

All her life Radine had laboured for House Corani and the Jandreux family. She'd manoeuvred her niece Alitia into marriage with a Sacrecour prince who'd become emperor and she'd taken the Corani to Pallas, usurping control of the Imperial Court from Lucia Fasterius and the Sacrecours: the greatest triumph of her life – or so she thought, until, in 909, the world had turned against her. The Sacrecour counter-strike engineered by that *monster* Lucia had cost Radine everything but her life, leaving so many friends dead, and the survivors so *damaged*. Her own husband had been one of those, crushed by shame, mocked and forced to grovel until he took his own life.

After that, the twenty-one years she should have been living like a queen in Pallas had been about revenge. She'd worked with the new generation – brave men like her wonderful Solon Takwyth and clever men like Dirklan Setallius – to repair Corani power. She'd endured privation, intrigue, danger and despair as she put aside the Radine she wanted to be and instead became a remorseless instrument for vengeance.

Then in 930 the miracle happened: Lucia and Constant Sacrecour perished and she found Alitia's granddaughter Lyra and put her on the throne. It should have been perfect – but Ril Endarion and Ostevan Prelatus ruined *everything*: one stole Lyra's heart, and the other made it legal.

Her beloved Solon should have taken Lyra and become emperor in all but name. Only he had the strength to ensure there wouldn't be another 909. Instead, he'd been banished, leaving her great plans in tatters. *They ignored me. They plotted behind my back. They laughed at me. They're not true Corani, and they will pay.*

Naxius was the answer to all her prayers: the gift of eternal youth and the chance to destroy these false Corani and restore the true, *rightful* rulers: *Solon and me.* She'd have done *anything* for such a chance. Naxius' offer – the vile necessities it entailed – was no price to pay at all but *reward* for her life of dedication.

Finding a comely young heiress, killing her and taking her identity, was child's play. She had not only her own knowledge and experience, but the wisdom of a millennia-old daemon to guide her. Naxius had proved truthful: she did control the daemon link, and she'd gained all that he'd promised: eternal youth and beauty, Ascendant-strength gnosis and full autonomy over the daemon. The Master had delivered, and she respected him utterly for that. Sometimes the urge to wallow in pleasures she'd once have called sordid were irresistible, but that no longer troubled her – indeed, she gloried in it. What mattered was Solon, and the throne. And revenge.

And now, as Medelie Aventour, she waited in a darkened room for the Master. The aether rippled and she donned the Lantric mask of Tear, a sorrowful woman crying ruby tears. Radine wasn't altogether happy about that – she was through with tragedy.

The spiratus of Ervyn Naxius appeared before her: the Puppeteer's mask was a clever, commanding visage with a mouth caught somewhere between a smile and a sneer. The mask moved when he spoke. 'Tear,' the old mage said warmly, 'how are you enjoying your second youth?'

'Much more than my first one! To be young and free – what more could one want?' She looked about expectantly, then asked, 'Will Brother Jest be joining us?'

'Not tonight. He is deeply embroiled in Church business, or so he claims. And Angelstar remains in the south, with the army.'

Good, Radine thought. *I didn't want them here anyway.* Jest was supposed to be planning the capture of the Holy City, but as she prepared to claim the Bastion she kept tripping over his handiwork. They'd worked closely together in the first attempted coup, using the ichor to turn a horde of stupid commoners into Reekers, the shock troops who'd very nearly slain Lyra and Wurther – but failure was failure. One learned the lessons and moved on; she'd come to terms with that long ago.

'We're close to readiness in the Bastion,' she reported. 'The power-brokers here can feel that Lyra's grip is weak, just one disaster from losing control of the empire. I've called together the conspirators – we'll be meeting in a few days. But Jest is meddling in my affairs. I need you to warn him again to stay away from the Bastion.'

Naxius' ironic mask gave nothing away, but when he replied, his voice was mild. 'So long as you and he deliver what I require, the degree to which you act in concert doesn't concern me. You get the Bastion, but where the Church is concerned, you must defer to Jest.'

'But there's one clergyman I *must* deal with myself – and Ostevan Comfateri dwells within the Bastion.'

Naxius gave her an intent look. 'Have you not heard? The confessor has just been implicated in a plot against the empress. He's fled – the Royal Chapel was destroyed when they moved against him.'

Radine blinked. '*Really?*' She'd sensed a ripple in the aether earlier, but she'd been in an important meeting and unable to investigate. Now she wasn't sure whether to celebrate or curse. 'What did that damned confessor do?'

'Setallius is putting it about that Ostevan was involved in Reeker Night,' Naxius told her, 'but I suspect the truth is simpler: he was offering more than just Absolution to our good queen.'

Radine put her hand to her mouth. *'Lyra and Ostevan?* Sweet Kore, what a scandal. *Delicious!'*

'Make what use you like of it, but be discreet. Don't tip your hand too early.'

'Oh, I can be patient,' she assured him. 'I may look youthful now, but I have the wisdom of my years.' She kissed his phantom hand in gratitude. 'We shall strike in the last week of Octen, just as you requested, Master, and this time, nothing and no one will stop us.'

18

The Wounds of Betrayal

Unburdening and Absolution

One of the Great Sacraments of our Faith is Unburdening and Absolution – the confessing of sin and its divine forgiveness. All men stray – indeed, Paradise would be empty were our God not of a forgiving disposition. But some sins are unforgivable and for ever abhorrent to Kore.

CANDELIUS CROZIER, PALLAS, 594

Pallas, Yuros
Septinon–Octen 935

It was evening before Lyra was ready to deal with people again. After the *incident* in the Royal Chapel she'd been utterly drained; Basia and Dirklan had helped her upstairs to her bed, where she'd slept the afternoon away. She'd dreamed, but they'd been the sort of squalid, vivid, frightening nightmares one would expect after unleashing violent magic for the first time in her life. She woke feeling scarcely the better for the rest.

When she felt she could face people, she rose and dressed herself. Dirklan and Basia were waiting in her sitting room. Dirklan examined her minutely, taking her blood as well as reading her aura, before declaring that she was clear of taint: no daemon ichor, and no residual enchantments. 'But Ostevan slipped through these same tests,' he muttered. 'I didn't like him overly, but I believed him true to our cause.'

'We all trusted him,' Lyra said, choking. Her heart was like an open wound.

'You say Ostevan was poisoning the pool in your garden, and through it, your own dwyma-powers, Majesty?' Dirklan asked. 'I don't understand the dwyma enough to know how that was achieved.'

Lyra would happily have said nothing, but that would be cowardice, and disrespectful of her protectors. She needed these two people above all others if she was to endure, and if that meant baring her soul, so be it. 'You know I've been plagued by nightmares,' she told them. 'You told me they weren't caused by a mage because the wards around me would detect and repulse them.'

'We detected no gnostic sendings,' Dirklan confirmed.

'That's why we thought it was my own imaginings,' Lyra said. 'Now we know better.' She hung her head, then asked, 'Dirklan, tell me the worst: how bad is the damage to the Royal Chapel? Was anyone hurt?'

Exposing Ostevan's perfidy had seen Lyra consumed by rage for the first time in her life – she couldn't believe what she'd done in the heat of the moment. Somehow, she'd found a hollow chamber beneath the Royal Chapel and shattered the ground, and the building had tumbled into the newly formed sinkhole. The buttresses between her garden and the chapel, both critical to the defences of the Bastion, had been breached.

Worse yet, there had been people inside the church.

'Majesty, we got lucky,' Dirklan told her. 'The congregation was small, and there were two Earth-magi – they recognised when the ground became unstable and that was warning enough to get everyone out. There were broken limbs from falling debris, but no one died. But of course, the old chapel is ruined.'

Lyra closed her stinging eyes. 'Dear Kore – I could have killed so many people!'

The ancient dwymancers went mad, the histories said. Their powers were too great and they'd had to be hunted down. They'd been condemned as heretics and killed by the Church and the Crown. *I'm a danger to everyone near me.*

'And Ostevan?' she asked.

'Gone,' Dirklan told her. 'We've had Earth-magi of the Imperial Guard

going through the rubble, but there's no sign of him, other than this.'
He lifted a small travel bag from the floor and emptied it on the table:
a purse heavy with coin, a change of clothes, a plain dagger – and a
Lantric mask.

Lyra clutched her breast, her heart hammering. '*Jest? He was Jest?*'

'So it would appear,' the spymaster replied.

Basia, beside him, was white as a ghost. 'What passed between you?'
she demanded. 'You came out of his chapel like a young maiden who'd
just had her first kiss. What did you and he do?'

'Nothing,' Lyra moaned, wanting to deny it all – but these were her
protectors and they couldn't function if she lied to them. 'We kissed,'
she admitted, tears beginning to stream down her face.

*I've been played for a fool. I am a fool – and because of my stupidity, people
are hurt and a precious church is now a ruin.*

'You *kissed* him?' Basia spat.

Dirklan touched her arm. 'Lyra was under the influence of some
kind of spell,' he reminded her. 'The blame for this lies entirely with
Ostevan.'

Basia glared at Lyra; clearly that excuse didn't mollify her – but her
unexpected condemnation roused Lyra's temper. 'Don't look at me
like that,' she snarled. 'It's not like you've never kissed someone you
shouldn't, is it?'

Her bodyguard went scarlet, her lips thinning, but she kept her
mouth shut.

'Tell me what happened,' Dirklan said quietly.

Lyra looked away from Basia's judging eyes and stared into the
middle distance, trying to work out where to start. 'Dirklan, you gave
me a book about the history of the dwymancers, remember? There
was a chapter about Amantius and a genilocus called Seidopus. The
villagers made blood sacrifices to Seidopus and the Inquisitors believed
that drove Amantius mad.'

'Which implies that a genilocus can be corrupted,' Dirklan said,
looking worried. 'It also means Ostevan knew that. You say he kissed
you, but he must have wanted more than kisses? Are you willing to
tell us *everything* that passed between you?'

It was all so humiliating that speaking of it was the last thing Lyra wanted, but she steeled herself. She *really* needed to *unburden*, and that irony wasn't lost on her.

'During today's Unburdening with Ostevan, I felt so strange – I'd dreamed . . .' She coloured, but pressed on. 'The dreams I told you about – I had a sexual dream – I couldn't get it out of my head. Ostevan was so attentive . . . but I felt in control, then.'

Lyra bit her lip, thinking how wonderful the world had seemed when Ostevan's lies were intact. 'We talked about angels and he told me he could prove to me that they were real. He summoned Barachiel, one of the seraphs of Paradise.'

'The old "angel summoning" ruse?' Basia sneered. 'And you *believed* him?'

'Basia!' Dirklan was angry now. 'Do I need to remind you that Lyra hasn't had the benefit of an Arcanum education?'

He took Lyra's hand, but she pulled it away. It was too soon since Ostevan had held her to let another in. 'I believed him,' she admitted, glaring hotly at Basia, 'because I knew no different.' Then she bowed her head and, struggling to keep from disintegrating into tears, went on. 'Barachiel told us that we were blessed, that Kore desired our union – that I was to put Ril aside and marry Ostevan.'

Basia snorted in disgust – and Dirklan rounded on her, his seldom-seen temper flaring. 'Basia, you will listen respectfully or you will leave!'

A frosty silence settled on the room.

'I was overwhelmed,' Lyra whispered. 'I felt addled – I couldn't think.'

'If we're right about the poisoning of your genilocus affecting your dreams, that would be the opium,' Dirklan said pointedly. 'In all like-lihood, you *weren't* yourself.'

'Then what happened?' Basia asked, her voice surly.

Lyra hung her head. 'What do you think? I'd just been touched by a seraph and told to marry another man – someone I liked and trusted. I was . . . *enraptured*.'

'You're already married,' Basia reminded her unnecessarily.

Lyra blinked away the stinging tears and glared at her bodyguard.

Feeling wretched, loathing herself, she said, 'We all know that my marriage has not been happy for a long time.' She shifted her hands to her belly. 'I am carrying Ril's child, but he hasn't made love to me since Reeker Night – or even shared my bed. I'm supposedly the most desired women in Koredom and yet every night since Junesse I have been alone and scared, wondering where my husband is – and with whom.' She looked pointedly, miserably, at Basia. 'You know more of where my husband spent his nights than I do.'

Her bodyguard scowled, but she looked away and didn't reply.

'In all those months, I've had only one confidante who understands what it is to be me: a priest who was willing to listen to a former nun trapped in a gilded cage. I drank in his every word. I have bared my soul to him. I have even fantasied of him – but never more than that; *I am no adulteress* – until I thought Kore Himself had spoken, that he'd taken pity on me and answered my prayers for love.'

She looked at Dirklan, pleading for him to understand. 'No, I wasn't thinking clearly. Yes, I am a foolish woman who knows nothing of gnosis and too little of dwyma. *But I thought it was real.* I believed, and I kissed him, and Kore knows, if he'd pressed me I'd have lain with him then and there. Now I know he was playing with me. My heart has been ripped in two.'

She fell silent, unable to go on.

Basia shifted uncomfortably, but Dirklan sat utterly motionless, until finally he spoke. 'I think it is telling, all the things Ostevan did and *didn't* do. He had you in his power – and he'd won your affection. The Masked Cabal are the source of the Reeker affliction, so he could have infected you, however that's done – but he didn't. He had you alone and willing and he could have seduced you. He didn't. He could have killed you or kidnapped you and we'd have been none the wiser until too late. He didn't do that either. Instead, he extracted a promise of marriage.'

Basia stirred. 'He wants Lyra alive, for now at least. He knew we'd detect any infection, so he refrained from infecting her. He wants a willing alliance, at least initially. He wants power with legitimacy, with his true nature undiscovered.'

303

'Yes, to all of those points. And don't forget: Lyra, a dwymancer, is pregnant to Ril, a mage – this will be the first known birth of a child to a mage and a dwymancer – Ostevan may have wanted her intact to see the result.'

'Intact but under his "charms",' Basia sniffed, 'whatever they are.'

Lyra's hackles rose, but Dirklan put a hand on her arm, calming her. 'It's certainly a very different tactic; Reeker Night was all-out assault. And this time he was operating inside the Bastion, not the Celestium.'

'They tried violence; now they're using subterfuge.'

'Indeed. I hope this setback has bought us a little more time. In the meantime, we must effect repairs and improve security.' Dirklan looked at Basia. 'Leave us, please. I need to talk to the queen alone.'

Basia scowled, but left without protest.

Lyra sagged into her chair. 'Dirklan, you will see those injured are properly cared for, won't you? And the Earth-magi who saved the congregation? They're heroes. I want them rewarded.' Then she remembered how everyone had stared as she burst in. 'Do they all know what I am now?'

'News is already spreading that Ostevan was involved in Reeker Night and that the earthquake was his doing as he sought to escape. Some of the congregation have been talking, but no one appears to suspect the truth. Many have said openly that they were inspired to see their queen using her gnosis in defence of the realm. The damage to our fortifications is serious, but repairable. The real damage is to our credibility: there was already talk about how close you and Ostevan were.'

Lyra winced. 'I suppose that's out of our hands.'

'I'm afraid so.' He looked at her sympathetically. 'Lyra, my remit is your security, but if you need someone to talk to, I hope you feel that you can confide in me.'

'I thought I could trust Ostevan,' Lyra replied. *I thought I loved him . . .* 'Before today, I would have trusted him more than anyone else in the kingdom.'

Dirklan pulled a wry face. 'No one else would have, Lyra – yes, I know he passed our security checks, and we all thought him loyal to the Corani and to you, but everyone knows ambition drives him. You knew none of us wanted him on the Imperial Council, despite his apparent loyalty. Once a snake, always a snake.'

'Are you always this wise after the event?' Lyra shot back bitterly, then she looked away. 'I'm sorry, I just feel so let down – by myself, and everyone else. Now everyone's paying for my stupidity.'

'He fooled all of us, Lyra, not just you.' Dirklan paused, then asked, 'What else does Ostevan know about you?'

Lyra shuddered. 'He knows everything: that my marriage is unhappy, that I'm not a real mage – that I'm not really Ainar Borodium's daughter. *Everything*.'

'He knows you're not Ainar's child?' Dirklan looked pained. 'That's unfortunate. But it's deniable.' Then he looked at her sadly. 'Is your marriage really so unhappy?'

Lyra looked at him hopelessly. 'Yes, I'm really that unhappy.' She swallowed – the last person she'd confessed all her secrets to had just betrayed her. But she'd trusted Dirklan Setallius from the first, even though she'd never used him for emotional support. But she had to be able to confide in *someone* . . . 'After my first miscarriage, all our happiness just – well, leaked away, really. Ril always wanted more than I am. He's a man of the world and I'm just a convent girl.'

'I thought it was a love marriage?'

'It was an *infatuation* marriage,' she admitted. 'He was my hero – the man who rescued me from certain death. But I couldn't be the kind of wife he wanted. At first he was excited by the idea of teaching me about life and love. But the truth is, I bore him . . .' She hung her head and whispered wretchedly, 'It's all my fault.'

'It's most certainly *not* your fault,' Dirklan countered. 'Marriage is a wonderful thing, but it's not easy. It requires persistence and tolerance and all manner of other virtues, and even then a mismatched couple – which perhaps you are – can never be truly happy. If your marriage is failing, there are two at fault.' He glanced at the Sacred Heart icon on her dresser. 'I've always found the refusal of the Church to dissolve unhappy marriages to be cruel. They say children need parents, but I say children need *happy* parents. A good stepfather is better by far than a bad true-father.' He looked at her appraisingly. 'Do you think your marriage can be repaired?'

Lyra shrank into her chair, thinking hard. *Could it work? When Ril comes back from the war, when our child is born and this Masked Cabal are all dead, could love win through? Or can I live without love? Perhaps love just complicates marriages?*

'I think we can function as couple in public together,' she said stonily. 'As long as we provide the appearance of stability, for the sake of the empire – and our child – I'm sure we can manage.'

'But I would wish more for you, my Queen. I would wish you happy.'

'I don't feel that I'll ever be happy again.'

The spymaster looked at her gravely. 'Lyra, I have no idea how Ostevan defeated my tests, but his gnostic skill clearly exceeds mine and I fear that no matter what security arrangements we make, we'll not be able to stop him when he chooses to strike next.'

'Then I must become something he can't swallow,' Lyra said fiercely. 'I think he's afraid of the dwyma – he did nothing to counter me; he just ran. So I must learn it.'

'Do that,' Dirklan approved. 'And Lyra, you must put this behind you and carry on. Ostevan has no hold over you unless you grant him one.'

Right now, thinking of the confessor just made her sick with loathing. 'I wouldn't give him water if he was dying at my feet,' she growled.

'Good.' He rose to go, then hesitated. 'Lyra, this is twice I've let you down – Reeker Night, and now this. I hope I still have your confidence, but I would understand if you wished for another to lead the Volsai.'

Lyra was shocked. Shaking her head, she said, 'No! No, Dirklan, I trust you absolutely. If what happened with Ostevan wasn't my fault, it certainly wasn't yours.' She deployed his own advice. 'Put this behind you and carry on.'

'Thank you for your trust,' he said earnestly. 'At least one enemy has been unmasked. So let's see who else we can drag into the light, yes?'

As if those confessions weren't hard enough, the next morning Basia arrived with her scrying bowl for Lyra's weekly gnostic contact with Ril. The silence between the two women was painful as the bodyguard set up the dish on its tripod and triggered the heat and steam to aid both contact and clarity of vision.

'*Husband?*' Lyra blurted awkwardly as the smoke rising from the brazier took on colour and shape and his face appeared. He looked fit and strong, if tired, and she felt knives of guilt stab her.

Basia poured more energy into the link, then stepped away to give them the illusion of privacy. Her presence forced Lyra to pretend composure.

'Lyra!' Ril replied, his voice echoing through the link. 'I can see your face! You look . . . um . . . are you well?'

No, I'm mortified with shame and I want to die, Lyra thought. But all she said was, 'I'm tired. The baby inside me gives me no rest. I can't sleep.'

That was true enough, but it was guilt that had wrecked her sleep as she went over and over the encounter with Ostevan, trying to understand how much had been the drug and how much the real her, her naked desires pulled into the light. The only thing she did know was that right now, she would go on pretending all was well, until she was certain all danger to her and her unborn child was past.

After that, imagination failed her. *If I must be a martyr for my marriage, I will.*

'How do you fare?' she asked, directing the conversation into neutral territory.

'Well enough,' Ril answered, though he didn't sound sincere as he rattled into an update of the army's situation. She hardly listened, instead just clung to his voice. Finally Basia muttered that the gnostic link couldn't be maintained much longer – and still Lyra could find nothing to say that wasn't fraught and painful.

'We need to say goodbye.' Lyra choked out the words, the strain of keeping up this façade too much. 'Come home – our baby will be born soon!'

Ril mistook her sobs for fear and chirruped with false cheer, 'I will, once we've saved the empire! Don't worry, I'll be back soon.' He paused, then said, all innocence, 'Please give Basia my regards.'

Abruptly, she stood. 'Why don't you tell her yourself?' She turned to Basia, glared wordlessly and stomped away. She shut herself in the privy and holding her distended belly, sat there shaking, feeling utterly miserable.

Only when she was certain that Ril and Basia must have finished talking did she wipe her face and tease her hair back into shape. When she emerged, Basia's angular face turned towards her uncertainly. She opened her mouth – then closed it again, and Lyra realised that her bodyguard was just as confused and uncertain as she was.

That gave her the confidence to speak. 'Basia, when I said to Ostevan that I would put Ril aside, I was deluded by opium and false visions. I will *not* put my husband aside. My marriage will endure, for the sake of my child, and for the empire.' She glared at her bodyguard. 'Are you still sworn to serve and protect me?'

'Yes, Majesty,' Basia said stiffly.

'Good. Then come with me – I must inspect the damage to the Royal Chapel and consult with the engineers over rebuilding it.'

There, she thought. *Perhaps you deserve a little suffering too . . .*

After overseeing the drilling of the younger battle-magi of the Imperial Guard·on the tourney fields outside the city, Solon Takwyth directed his personal carriage to a tavern in Esdale where the highborn drank. It was mid-afternoon. He downed a pint with a couple of older knights, then at the appointed hour made his excuses and left via the back door. A shuttered carriage awaited; when he climbed inside, Medelie's token – an unremarkable lace square – lay on the seat.

He closed the door behind him, tapped on the roof and surrendered himself to fate.

As best he could tell, the carriage went northeast, leaving the maze that was Esdale and entering well-to-do Gravenhurst. The driver pulled into a cul-de-sac off the main road, stopped and rapped thrice on the roof.

This isn't treason, Takwyth told himself as he stepped down from the conveyance. *Not yet, anyway.*

He was at the back of a three-storey house set within a walled garden. A man in a hooded cassock led him inside and upstairs, which surprised him a little – secret meetings were usually below ground, to prevent unwanted scrying – but he could sense strong wards encasing the building.

Medelie was waiting for him at the top of the stairs. She greeted him with a brief but stirring kiss and he was struck again at the thought that Medelie Aventour and Radine Jandreux, two women he would have called opposites, were the same being.

My vibrant young lover is an old woman the world believes long-dead . . .

The *how* had been glossed over – she'd hinted at the Keepers and ambrosia and he hadn't pried. 'Is everyone here?' he asked.

'Most of them. The rest are on the way,' she answered. 'Thank you for coming.'

'I would do anything for you.'

'I'll hold you to that later.' She put her arm in his and murmured in his ear, 'Do you want to hear some delicious gossip? Ostevan was rukking the queen – and now he's been forced to flee!' She giggled wickedly. 'I must admit I didn't think our prissy little queen's fanny ever got the wets – but I suppose all nuns fantasise about priests.'

Solon kept his expression neutral. 'I heard he'd been implicated in the Reeker Night attacks?'

'That's just a cover-up,' Medelie snickered. 'They were screwing in the chapel – and her seven months pregnant! Though of course Ostevan was never one to miss the chance to lift a woman's skirts! I wonder how long it was going on?' Then she gasped. 'Perhaps the child in her belly is *his*?'

The very notion left Solon queasy, but they'd arrived at the door of the meeting room, so he gave her a warning look before escorting her into a small gathering of some of the most influential people in the empire, hovering around a long table covered in glasses, decanters and platters of bite-sized delicacies.

'Welcome, Sir Solon,' said a small, intent-looking clergyman. 'I am Ennis, and this is my house.'

Dominius Wurther's own secretary! Solon hid his shock behind a cough. 'Thank you for the invitation. Does your involvement signal the approval of the grand prelate for this venture?'

Ennis gave him a careful look. 'I wouldn't mention it in the Royal Council.'

'Enough said,' Solon told the diminutive mage-priest.

The next man to greet him was even more exalted. 'Welcome, Solon,' said Edreu Gestatium, head of the Imperocracy. 'It's a pleasure to see you here.'

The bureaucrat fawned over Medelie, while Solon turned to a well-built man clad in fine lacy velvets of maroon and gold with flowing brown locks and a rakish countenance. Solon knew him by reputation only: Jean Benoit was the Merchants' Guildmaster and possibly the richest man in Creation.

'It's an honour to greet our finest knight,' Benoit said grandly. 'I trust your wounds improve, Lord Takwyth?'

'I'll soon be fully recovered, thank you.' Healing-gnosis was slowly mending the hip shattered while defending the queen; he was close to regaining full movement.

'I recommend rhythmic hip exercises,' Benoit chuckled, running his eyes over Medelie's body. 'The more regular the better, eh.'

'He'll be recovered in no time,' Medelie purred, before asking Benoit about guild affairs, while Solon turned to greet the only other woman in the room. She wasn't someone he knew, and in any event, her face shimmered, morphic-gnosis concealing her true face. Her altered visage was blandly anonymous, like a mask made of flesh. She wore a black, high-necked dress and no distinguishing jewellery.

'Lord Takwyth,' she said, her voice ageless. 'I'm glad you're here – I hate wasted journeys and there would have been little point coming if you hadn't.'

'Might I ask your name, and who you represent?'

'You may call me "Selene". Chaplain Ennis knows who I am. Let that suffice.'

Selene was an ill-omened name – the sister-lover who'd murdered Corineus – and Solon didn't like what it implied, or that she alone was permitted anonymity. But he took his seat beside Medelie as the meeting began.

Do any of them know my lover's true identity? He was still stunned that he was bedding a century-old dowager in the body of a twenty-year-old, one who disported herself as if every repressed desire from her former life had to be fulfilled immediately. But once the meeting began, Medelie was all Radine, if you knew how to see it: clinical, insightful and fixed of purpose.

After formal introductions, Ennis spoke first. 'My lords, thank you for coming. It's not easy for public figures to gather privately so I appreciate the efforts you've all taken. I want to state first that this is *not* a conspiracy. We're loyal Rondians all, drawn together by concern for our empire. We see the problems, but we also know that it's easy for a criticism to be quoted out of context and made to look like treason. We are gathered here to speak freely, without fear of reprisals.'

'Assuming we can trust this company,' Selene put in dryly. 'But I endorse Chaplain Ennis' words. We need a forum where concerns may be raised. The empress is vulnerable, we all see that. She's never carried to term and still may not. Her husband has gone to war, with all those inherent dangers. If something happens to either of them, the empire would be destabilised. What is required is a *contingency* plan, in case something were to happen to our royal couple.'

'A plan that doesn't involve House Sacrecour regaining power,' Medelie said, in a voice that was *all* Radine.

Don't they see it? Solon wondered. *Some of these men knew her for years.* But context was everything: they all *knew* that Radine was dead.

'There are no factions here,' Gestatium replied. 'I don't care who is emperor, so long as the bureaucracy is well-funded and the empire survives intact.'

'Mother Church is deeply concerned at the weakness in the Bastion,' Ennis stated. 'Yet our grand prelate wraps his reign more closely to Lyra Vereinen with each passing day. And with his prelates massacred on Reeker Night, he seeks now to fill their ranks with sycophants. I represent an alternative: clergymen who wish to see us cleansed of the corruption Wurther wallows in. Many are currently in exile, but retain strong influence, both in the vassal-states and here in Pallas.'

'Likewise, the Merchants' Guild is disturbed that the regime uses measures that are unfavourable to trade. In her desperation to restore Crown coffers, the empress allows Treasurer Dubrayle to run amok. To put it frankly, she and Dubrayle are bad for business and we want them gone.'

'And I think it's clear that if there is a succession crisis, the answer is *not* Cordan Sacrecour,' Selene drawled. 'We don't want a fourteen-year-old boy, we need *experienced* hands.' She looked pointedly at Solon.

They all did.

Solon glanced at Medelie – *Radine* – realising this was his moment to put up or walk away. They'd discussed it, but he was still nervous. *If I don't say the right things now, this is over before it begins.*

'Ladies, gentlemen,' he said, speaking firmly, 'I hear and understand. I'm Knight-Commander of the Royal Household. The knights of Coraine are primarily loyal to me. I understand leadership – I spent twenty years serving the Duchess of Coraine' – he made sure not to look at Medelie – 'and I learned all there is to know of balancing a realm's needs for wealth, stability and strength. But I'm not merely a parochial Northerner. I spent five years in exile and I have travelled the empire from one end to the other. I understand how we are perceived, both inside and outside our borders, and I've got the scars' – he touched the marred left side of his face ruefully – 'to prove it. The one thing the empire gives our people, the thing they crave more than all else, is *stability*, which provides prosperity for those capable of profiting from it. Instability brings only ruin. If I'm forced to take control of this empire, stability will be my byword, above and beyond family, factions and other loyalties.'

Chaplain Ennis was the first to speak. 'Well said. Rondelmar needs to rise beyond regional rivalries.'

'Then I'm your man.'

'I believe you,' Selene responded. She looked around the room. 'So, are we agreed that should the need arise, Sir Solon is our cause?'

There was a murmur of agreement and Solon bowed his head in thanks.

'Good,' Ennis said. 'Now, I think we all realise there is no representative of the Treasury here.' He looked at Gestatium. 'Do you see that as your purview in any regime change?'

'Dubrayle will be first on the block,' the bureaucrat replied. 'He's failed the realm. The Crown is in penury and the empire destabilised by his tax-farming cronies.'

'Those tax-farmers should be second on the block,' Jean Benoit added. 'Along with all the internal tariff and toll barriers – they're crippling trade. Dubrayle has raised these fourfold and my people are suffering. Restore such measures to pre-Vereinen levels and you'll see the money flow again.'

'Into the purses of your Guild, at the least,' Medelie said dryly.

Benoit lifted his nose. 'My dear young lady, when the traders and merchants are flourishing, the empire is awash with gold. We are the conduit for all the wealth that flows into the realm. My Guild, not the Treasury, has always been the true measure of prosperity in Rondelmar.'

'My father taught me that true wealth lies in the land.'

'An outdated notion.'

'We've more urgent concerns than economic theory,' Gestatium grouched. 'The sort of crises that will trigger a regime change – the death of the queen, her child or the prince-consort – could happen any day, so we must be prepared. Reliable men must be placed in key positions, standing ready to act immediately to promote and back Lord Takwyth's authority. They need to be present in the forces fighting the Shihad as well as bureaucrats, courtiers, highborn magi and clergymen here in Pallas. We here are in a position to effect this, but we must work swiftly.'

Solon raised a hand. 'You speak of crises, but only one of those would trigger a succession crisis: if Lyra herself dies. The death of Ril Endarion or of their unborn child would not be legitimate grounds for dethroning her.'

'The death of the prince-consort would leave the queen unmarried – we will compel her to marry you,' Medelie replied, making eyebrows lift around the table.

'I rather had the impression you wanted to be the next Lady Takwyth yourself?' Benoit observed.

'I want what the realm needs: Solon as our ruler,' Medelie said. 'As for the convent girl . . .' She pulled a sly face that suggested she saw Lyra as no competition.

'If need be, we can depose her through legal channels,' Ennis said, with the air of someone who knows something others don't.

'Under what grounds?' Solon asked, genuinely surprised.

'There are ancient laws that could be invoked.'

'Then invoke them now,' Jean Benoit suggested.

'But we're not yet in a state of crisis,' the chaplain replied. 'It's a fall-back strategy. All I can say at this stage is this: *there will be a crisis.* Prepare for it now – because we will need to be ready, and ready soon.'

Those around the table looked at him expectantly, but he refused to say more. The rest of the meeting was spent creating a programme, with the goal of being ready by the end of Octen when, according to Ennis, the armies of the Shihad and the empire would clash. It was less than a month, but everyone had their own networks, and the ability to move swiftly when necessary.

As the meeting concluded and they all rose to leave, Solon turned to Ennis. 'Chaplain, you're the grand prelate's secretary, someone he trusts more than anyone. You have a good life, thanks to Wurther – so what's broken your faith in him?'

The chaplain looked down at the table, then admitted, 'That's a fair question. Are you worried this is all some elaborate ruse to lure you to the gallows?'

The expressions around the table told Solon they'd all been thinking exactly that.

'One word,' Ennis said. '*Neglect.* I'm still his chaplain and secretary, five years after helping him secure Lyra's throne, a betrayal of my own Sacrecour kin. That kinship doesn't matter overly – it was just a ticket to high office – but I did expect a prelature in reward. However, like all those Wurther values, he wants me exactly where he put me, to serve him. He believes luxury – fine things, good food and wine – is reward enough, because to him it is. But I want more – and I've been promised it.'

By whom? Solon wondered, but decided not to ask.

They parted with little further conversation, other than Medelie filling everyone's ears with her rumours of Lyra and Ostevan Comfateri's supposed intimacy. Solon left with a final lingering glance at

'Selene', whose morphic disguise hadn't frayed in two hours of meeting, an impressive feat. He joined Medelie in her carriage, admiring the way she carried herself – stiff-backed and close-lipped, exactly as Radine had been. It made her look regal.

'What did Ennis mean?' he wondered. 'If there is some legitimate way that Lyra can be deposed, that's a threat to the Corani in and of itself.'

'I know what he meant. Solon, are you ready for a shock?' She licked her lips, enjoying her revelation. 'Lyra isn't the rightful queen.'

Whatever he'd expected, that wasn't it. *'What do you mean?'*

'When we put her on the throne, those in the know – me, Setallius and Wurther – hid one crucial fact: *Lyra isn't Ainar Borodium's child.* She's Natia's, yes, but Lyra wasn't born a few months after the coup, as we've been telling everyone; she was born two years later. She's not twenty-six: she's twenty-four. She's not the legitimate heir – she's a bastard.'

That rocked Solon backwards. 'But—'

'Exactly. We lied so that a Corani – well, a part-Corani, at least – could be placed on the throne. Without her, we had no legitimate claim; with her, everything became possible. But now she's a liability – she has to go.'

'Kore's Blood! Does Lyra know?'

'She does,' Medelie replied. 'Presumably, her real father also knows – but we don't know who that is.'

He wiped his brow, trying to think. 'She *is* Natia's child – she's virtually her mother's image – but not that cretin Ainar . . . so the father has to be a Sacrecour! Natia was their prisoner—'

'Exactly. But think: whoever knows – and it could be any number of men who had access to a vulnerable, beautiful young Corani princess – has sat on that knowledge for many years, which tells me they're estranged from Garod and his cronies.'

'Kore's Balls, this is a complex situation. So who is our rightful ruler?'

'Well, *she* is: Magnus made Natia his heir ahead of Constant,' Medelie reminded him. 'Hold to that fact! But a case could be made either way if the facts ever came out. We *cannot* allow that.'

'Then what do we do?'

'For now, we wait. As you gathered from Ennis, Wurther will be silenced soon, and good riddance.' She drew her finger across her throat, the gesture chilling. 'The old hog has ruled too long already.' Then, sliding across to his side of the carriage, she started nuzzling his face and reaching for his belt. 'That's enough talk, lover.'

He caught her hand. 'After all that, I'm not in the mood.'

'Ah, but I *love* these conspiracies,' she purred. 'They make me *wet*.'

'Medelie . . . Radine . . . I don't think—'

'Then don't think at all . . . *feel*.'

He stared into her determined face, then with a sigh, let her hand loose again. With a triumphant little smile, she unfastened his buckle. 'I've been given a second chance,' she said. 'You mustn't deny me anything, *ever*.'

19

Breaking the Blockade

Hermetic Magic

Ardo Actium describes Hermetic gnosis as Manipulation of the Unseen to affect the Tangible: living energies that can only be sensed intuitively are used to make visible and tangible changes to the natural world, including our own bodies. Thus a Hermetic mage might be a healer, or a shapeshifter, or control the flora and fauna, depending upon their affinities.

ORDO COSTRUO ARCANUM, PONTUS

Sunset Isle, Pontic Sea
Octen 935

Her chores done for the day, Jehana Mubarak wandered like a ghost about Sunset Tower, seeking a way out. Her sense of entrapment had grown over the past week, and the resentment of her was more pronounced every day. But she was developing a thick skin. Now her footsteps took her to the engineering chamber beneath the ground level of the tower and she stood for a while, watching the handsome young sentinel Tovar, under Magister Loric's guidance, manipulating the energy flows, until he glanced up at her and winked. Everyone inside the tower was labouring to keep the gnostic energy flowing via the links to Southpoint and Northpoint into the Leviathan Bridge – everyone except her.

I just clean things, like a dirt-caste menial.

There was little news: only the Ordo Costruo communicated with them, and with so many listening Keshi magi circling the towers, those

317

communications were minimal. No relief ships had arrived; although they still had plenty of water and wine, grain and preserved foods, everything was now being rationed.

'Remember, Tovar,' Loric was saying, 'you're looking for paler or deeper hues in the four spirals. Reduce the settings when you see darker blues or purples, but increase them when the colours grow pale.' The mage-engineer coughed into a cloth, then started speaking again, but Jehana had moved past and into the tunnel leading to the Oceanarium.

She smelled a musky scent as she padded along and wrinkled her nose; it was no surprise to find the giant shaggy form of the construct-creature, Ogre, staring out into the waters intently. She stopped, shocked, watching light bleeding from his fingers.

Ahm on High, he has the gnosis! she thought in alarm. The Gnostic Codes forbade any construct to have human intelligence, let alone the gnosis – he was twice the abomination. *Why didn't they destroy him?*

The massive creature turned his big, misshapen skull towards her. His eyes gleamed in the darkness, pale like opals. Instinctively she shielded, although the energy in his fingers had already dissipated. She still felt threatened: his immense strength was clear in his bulging arms and squat legs, his huge clawed feet, his big chest and belly. Three or four big broken teeth jutted through his lips like tusks. When he saw her, she was sure that some surge of violence ran through him, like the currents of energy Loric and Tovar were working on – but when he spoke, his tones were gentle enough.

'Princess Jehana,' he rumbled. 'Sal'Ahm.'

'What were you doing?' she demanded, and he flinched guiltily.

'Watching the sea,' he answered. 'There are many shoals today. Levana will cast nets soon. Fish good, mmm?'

She'd come here to be alone . . . and to explore her tenuous connection to the dwyma, to drop the name 'Seidopus' into the ocean and see if anything responded. She most certainly didn't want Ogre here – he smelled, and he scared her. 'I want to be alone.'

'As you wish,' he intoned in his cavernous voice and rose. His bulk and power were alarming, but he shambled away. *What if he was calling to someone?* she wondered. *What if that man they fear – Naxius? – is in contact with him?*

She used Air-gnosis to remove Ogre's smell, then sat cross-legged before the window and *reached* . . .

Seidopus, she called, and the schools of fish outside intensified their movements. She felt an odd sensation as a particular gold and silver fish swam near, batting itself against the glass, then went flashing away, only to return, again and again, until she lost herself in the task . . .

'What are you doing?'

She spun her head and saw Tovar leaning against the door. 'Nothing! Just watching the sea.' She was struck that she'd reacted to being caught out exactly as Ogre had, which made her flinch guiltily.

'Sure, Princess,' Tovar said. 'What's a Seidopus?'

Jehana coloured. 'A type of sea creature,' she lied. 'I could ask what you're doing here too?'

Tovar looked tired – working on the tower was taking it out of everyone, she'd noticed – but there was a calculated air to him today, as if she were goods being appraised for sale in a market. Men weren't supposed to look at a princess that way, even fine-looking ones like him, with his blond hair and well-formed features. But all he said was, 'Just looking for company, Princess!' as he sauntered up and sat beside her, too close for propriety. 'I'm too tired to sleep and my brain's fizzing. You'd know what it was like if you were doing your bit.'

'That's not my fault—'

'Sure, but a princess doesn't work anyway, right?'

She went to rise, snapping, 'Well, I see I can't win.'

He grabbed her arm. 'Sorry,' he exclaimed, suddenly contrite. 'Look, I apologise, okay? I'm just tired and bored and sick of this damned place.'

She tried to pull his hand away but he resisted – and then he leaned in and kissed her on the mouth. The audacity made her brain freeze, so that she didn't pull away—

—and then he was on her, mashing his lips to hers, trying to push his tongue between, and she was so shocked she hurled him away with kinesis. Her almost pure-blood strength had him flailing across the room and slamming into the wall. He tried to rise and then flopped, clutching his shoulder.

'Don't you touch me!' she snarled.

'Sorry . . . I just . . .' Then his eyes narrowed. 'I thought you wanted it, with all those come-hither glances.'

'*What?*'

'I've seen the way you look at me. It was clear what you wanted – well, I thought so, anyway.'

'I've *never* encouraged you!'

'Oh, I think you have. Everyone is saying so.'

'They're *what?*' She rose to her full height, her fingers now blazing with gnosis-light, ready to blast him as frustration welled up, so strongly she barely recognised herself. 'You're *nothing* to me, you pig – I am a *Mubarak!*'

She ran, shaking with anger, back up the stairs to the massive foyer, enraged by what Tovar had thought he could get away with. The knife-edge of an unprotected woman's life, something she'd always been spared, suddenly felt very real to her.

But as she reached the main foyer, she stopped to stare – for once, the main doors were open and Levana and Geryn, the two senior sentinels, were hauling in a net full of wriggling, gasping fish. Jehana, a Water-mage, found watching the fish perish distressing and was about to leave them to it, when a sudden flash of gold amid the silvery-blue caught her eye.

She reached into the slippery pile, grasping with fingers and kinesis, and extracted a gold and silver fish, suddenly certain it was the one she'd glimpsed below. In an instant she had surrounded it with a sphere of salt water, drawn from the seawater on the floor, to preserve its life. The sentinels ignored her as she turned and ran.

She'd seen a fish tank in one of the lounges. She hurtled into the chamber, almost bowling over the plump young scholar Simonia, and threw the rescued fish into the tank, where it thrashed about for a moment, almost knocking itself out on the glass, and then began to swim normally amid a dozen or so brightly coloured companions, a more exotic species.

'What are you doing?' Simonia asked.

Jehana was wondering that herself. 'It's mine,' she said. 'No one else touches it.'

Simonia threw her a puzzled, scornful look. 'Whatever you say, Princess.'

She was still wondering what had compelled her actions when suddenly the tower filled with alarm bells. The racket had everyone, asleep or on duty, scrambling – and just like in Pontus, Jehana immediately feared the worst: that whoever was hunting her had found her. She and Simonia were halfway to the meeting hall, a level above the foyer, when a sound came that sent a thrill of fear rippling through her.

A booming blow rattled the locked and bolted main doors and a woman's voice rang out, gnostically projected through the barrier: '*LET ME IN!*'

The destination of Tarita Alhani's Hadishah enemies was swiftly apparent once their windfleet left the Pontic Peninsular on a southerly bearing: Sunset Isle was the only thing out in that direction. *If Jehana's at Sunset Tower, I have to get there first*, she thought, and turned her mind to how she could get there ahead of Alyssa and her minions.

Her lightweight skiff gave her a slight advantage, but she wasn't a navigator and although Sunset Tower had a beacon, it wouldn't be hard to miss in the thousands of square miles of featureless ocean.

And the Tower will be watching, and as the ships close in, they'll react.

If she was to be any use at all to Jehana, she had to get inside without being spotted by Alyssa's fleet or mistaken for an enemy by the Tower and blasted from the skies. She picked up speed in the bitterly cold air as below her, the ocean sculpted vast mountains that continually collapsed and reformed. According to her tracker coin, she was drawing level with Alyssa's fleet, somewhere on her left; it was time to start tacking southeast to cut in front. She knew no one on Sunset Isle, but somehow she had to let them know she was coming, and that she was a friend.

As she began to veer westwards, seeking to fly out of sight of

Alyssa's vessels and overtake them, she sent, *<Sunset Isle? Sunset Isle? Please respond.>*

A moment later, a powerful mind fastened on hers and Alyssa snarled, *<You?>*

Tarita slammed up her mental shields, pulled fresh wind to her sails and lowered the prow as other minds also sought to latch onto hers. Mental hooks and claws were reaching but she slapped them away and hurtling onwards, strained her eyes for the beacon of light she sought – and the enemy ships she must evade.

Alyssa stood on the fore-deck, her mind's eye wide open as she sent her mind arrowing after that damned Merozain girl. *She's* still *stalking me? Unbelievable!*

Around her the windship crew worked feverishly to extract more speed, while each windsloop launched a pair of skiffs manned by her best Air-magi. She'd called ahead to those ships already blockading Sunset Tower and a dozen roc-fliers were streaming in from the east. She opened up her mind and addressed every mind that could hear.

<There's a skiff tailing us – the pilot's a Jhafi spy. Find her, hem her in and then all attack at once – take her alive if you can.>

She didn't tell them Tarita was a Merozain. The Merozain Bhaicara had taken on an aura of invincibility in the five years since they'd first emerged and she didn't want her fighters half-defeated by fear before battle. What she really wanted was for them to slow the girl down so that she could finish her off herself.

Nuqhemeel joined her. Stroking his unkempt beard, he asked, 'What in Ahm's name is a Jhafi doing here?'

'Meddling,' she replied. The last time she'd seen this girl, she'd been in Hebusalim, asking awkward questions about the Masked Cabal and the death of Sakita Mubarak. Alyssa had tried to silence her there, but instead of the easy kill she'd expected, Tarita had proven formidable and resourceful – even when caught between Alyssa and the revenant of Sakita Mubarak.

I know I can defeat her, but I'd rather someone else took the risk . . .

Her presence wasn't a coincidence, Alyssa decided. 'Contact all my captains,' she told Nuqhemeel. 'Tell them to search for a tracking talisman on their vessel – you'll find it if you listen for an aetheric pulse.'

Nuqhemeel bowed and withdrew, returning soon afterward bouncing a coin up and down in his hand. 'Great Lady, here's the tracking talisman.'

Alyssa took it, then sent it spinning away into the sea. 'Tell your men I'll give the girl's weight in gold to the one who brings her down, and double that if you can take her alive.'

Scrawny runt that she is, it'll be a cheap reward . . .

A few minutes later, the first excited shout came through the aether. <There she is! I see her!>

Inside five minutes, the first Keshi skiffs had appeared in the slate-grey skies, angling to head Tarita off as her skiff skimmed the waves – and there were more ahead, swirling above like gnats . . . then a point of light winked into view on the eastern horizon: the Sunset Isle beacon.

There were no low clouds to conceal her, so Tarita stayed just above the turbulent ocean waves as the attackers closed in on her course. The excitement of the chase was building inside her. *All right, let's see how good you all are . . .*

She tacked south-southwest, arcing away from the point of interception, deliberately slowing to confuse their estimates of the interception point. As they loomed closer, she saw that each craft had two magi, one to fly and one to fight – but that would make them slower . . .

Right, let's go!

She called a torrent of wind just as the Hadishah windskiffs reached the edge of bowshot range and her craft surged forward, her keel cutting like a blade through the wave that rose beneath her. She shot through their cordon even as it closed, leaving the Keshi firing impotent arrows as they fell into her wake. For several minutes she whooshed along, ignoring the hopeful long-range mage-bolts dashing harmlessly off her shields, veering through the troughs – then another enemy vessel swooped in and sent a fireball into her sails. She shielded in time, then blasted the archer in the front and swerved away.

Then a giant eagle – one of the new 'rocs' the entire East was marvelling at – came shrieking in, its Keshi mage-rider blazing away at her. She shielded again as she hauled the tiller sideways, leaning away from the tack as the roc skimmed past her masthead, its rider whooping. More loomed above her – then she engulfed the lead bird in her own fireball and the rest scattered. No one was yahooing any more. She stopped the next to come at her with a punch of kinesis that sent the stunned bird tumbling into the waves, then a ballista spear raked the air behind her and she looked up to see a Keshi windsloop turning across her bows. The sides were lined with archers, all with bowstrings taut—

—then a bolt of light from Sunset Tower ripped the sky in half, the windsloop burst apart and Tarita was weaving through the debris while pursuing skiffs and eagle-riders shot in all directions like startled sparrows. She broke into clear air, put her bow down and aimed for the Tower, calling to them in Rondian, *<Sunset Tower, let me in! I'm from Javon! Let me in!>*

A moment later a male voice filled her head: *<Turn aside, Javonesi!>*

Tarita cursed, then realised she had a better call on their friendship. *<I'm a Merozain!>* she responded as more giant eagles caught her up, clearly deeming themselves too small and swift to be targeted by the tower – and perhaps they were, because the next bolt missed entirely, but at least it wasn't aimed at her. She fended more mage-bolts and tried Animagery to target the minds of the eagles, but they were too well-bonded with their masters. Another torrent of energy struck her shields, turning them momentarily scarlet.

Then another bolt from the tower ripped through the swarming eagles and they broke away again, shrieking as they went. The island was close now, the tower climbing halfway into the sky. Behind her the Keshi fleet swung away, giving up the pursuit, and as she powered onwards, she was praying that lethal bolt of light wouldn't now be unleashed on her.

It wasn't, and she landed on the island, which was barely half a mile wide, right before the giant doors to the tower. She strode to the doors and hammered on them, shouting: '*LET ME IN!*' Then she turned away, listening to the aether. She could almost taste Alyssa Dulayne's frustration. But there were more than thirty Keshi windsloops circling the horizon – getting out was going to be a Hel of a lot harder than getting in.

The doors swung open and she was swept inside by two very competent-looking Ordo Costruo sentinels who circled her warily, then politely asked for her scimitar and periapt. She surrendered both while her eyes roamed the large curved foyer, then latched onto a slender Keshi girl with a proud demeanour and aristocratic features very similar to Waqar Mubarak's.

Found you, Jehana, she thought triumphantly as they exchanged stares.

The female sentinel was examining the scimitar curiously. 'What metal is this?'

Tarita actually had no idea. It had been recovered from Midpoint Tower, along with a spear and a book; Waqar had given it to her in thanks for her aid, a princely gift. But if she told the woman that, the Ordo Costruo would reclaim it.

'It's a new Eastern alloy,' she lied brazenly.

The sentinel grunted in an unladylike way, turning over the blade suspiciously.

Then a brittle-looking Rondian woman stepped between them, demanding identification. Tarita showed her palms and bowed formally, as a Merozain would. 'Sal'Ahm. I am Tarita Alhani of the Merozain Bhaicara.'

'I am Magister Hillarie. What proof do you have of your identity?' the woman demanded. She looked tired and frustrated, and quite ready to take it all out on the intruder before her.

'That won't be necessary,' a new voice intruded, and an old man with a querulous face appeared.

'Magister Manon,' she said, bowing again. Capolio had once introduced them in Hebusalim.

'She is who she says,' Manon told Hillarie, who didn't look best pleased at having her prey snatched away. 'Sal'Ahm, Tarita. What are you doing here?'

'It's a long story,' she warned him, 'and it involves Jehana Mubarak.'

*

An hour after the mysterious young woman had arrived in her battered skiff, Jehana was summoned to the council room just beneath the solarus-throne chamber. All three of the senior magi and Geryn, the ranking sentinel, were present to meet the newcomer.

Jehana's eyes went instantly to the young Merozain. She was small, even for an Eastern woman, and looked barely twenty, but she had a worldly air, as if she'd been through much. Despite a voluptuous chest, she was skinny, her lean face almost birdlike. She wore a scimitar and her periapt glinted at her throat – they'd evidently determined she was trustworthy and returned them. Freshly washed and clad in clean clothing, she positively bristled with energy.

By contrast, the Ordo Costruo Magisters looked exhausted. Only Geryn was outwardly refreshed, stroking his beard as he watched Tarita curiously. Manon introduced the two Eastern women and Jehana bowed cautiously – the harbadab was silent on how one greeted foreign mage-spies, although she was likely low-caste, judging from her sun-darkened skin. Tarita responded in kind.

'Why don't you tell us how you came to be here?' Manon asked Tarita. 'I'd like to hear the whole story.'

'It began when I was sent to Sagostabad for the Convocation,' Tarita replied; she spoke tersely, clearly used to giving briefings to superiors. 'I witnessed the attack upon Sultan Salim and the poisoning of Magister Sakita, Jehana's mother.'

Jehana gasped. 'You saw who did it?'

'I saw people in Lantric masks committing murder. I aided your brother Waqar in pursuing them.'

Jehana's heart leaped. 'You met my brother?'

Tarita smiled pertly. 'A nice boy.'

'He's a prince of the royal family—'

'And yet still a nice boy,' Tarita smirked. 'And a good kisser.'

Irritating bint, Jehana thought, but she was desperate for news of Waqar. 'How does he fare?'

'He's heartbroken at the loss of his mother, and he misses you. It was he who commanded me to find you.'

'Why?' *Is she here on behalf of Javon, or Waqar . . . or Rashid?*

'Because he's frightened for you,' Tarita replied. 'His friends and I slew one of the Masked Cabal, a man in a cat-mask, Felix – it was he who killed your mother. We also deduced the identity of two other members, and determined one of their goals was capturing you.'

Jehana put a hand to her heart as the four Ordo Costruo magi looked her way. 'Do you know why?' she asked, though she could guess. *They know about my capacity for the dwyma . . .*

Tarita's steady gaze told Jehana that she did know, but wasn't going to say so here.

'I am a member of the royal family,' she said aloud.

'That must be it,' Tarita agreed. 'Waqar wants his sister to be safe.'

I wish I believed that . . . But Waqar dances to Rashid's tune now.

The chamber fell silent and Jehana looked away, staring through the windows. Sunset was coming and the western skies were turning crimson. She listened while the Ordo Costruo magi asked Tarita about the world outside, but all she could think of was her brother. She pictured his face, wishing he was here so she could hug him, ask him what lay in his heart and his head.

Then the chamber door opened and Tovar hurried in and whispered in Geryn's ear. The sentinel sat upright immediately. 'We have received a gnostic sending from the Hadishah fleet. They are demanding to speak to whoever is in charge.'

They all turned to Magister Manon, who hunched as if his already stooped shoulders were bearing even more pressure. Then he straightened and said, 'Let us go to the solarus-throne and show them how we negotiate with aggressors.'

The magister gestured for Jehana and Tarita to follow as well, and as they all hurried up the stairs the Jhafi girl remarked, 'You must all have magnificent buttocks, thanks to these stairs!' which made Hillarie glare and the men smirk.

In the solarus-throne chamber, Levana relinquished the chair to Manon. Jehana, not allowed up here before, looked around the circular chamber with interest. The roof, thick darkened glass, formed a protective dome directly beneath a giant glowing cluster of solarus crystals. What looked like pillars on the outside walls were actually conduits for energy, running from the crystals above to the hollow cylinder below the floor and all the way down to the engineering chamber and the massive wires that fed the Bridge a thousand feet below. The energy of the Bridge was harnessed from the throne, and could be used to empower gnosis beyond the strength of even a thousand pure-blood or Ascendant magi.

Manon sent out a pulse of energy to signal his presence and added, 'I'm here.'

A woman replied languidly, 'Dear Manon, how nice to hear your voice again.'

Manon stiffened. 'Alyssa Dulayne?'

'The same,' the woman's voice tinkled. 'Restored to health and with a fleet of windships at my command. Look out of your window and count them, old friend.'

'I'm no friend of yours.'

'Oh Manon,' Alyssa laughed, 'I'd not be so swift to disavow me, were I you – or Hillarie, Loric and all the rest. After all, I'm the person who'll determine who lives and dies in there.'

'You'll determine *nothing*, Alyssa,' Manon retorted, though he was clearly alarmed that Alyssa knew who else was present. 'Attempt an attack and we'll blast you from the skies. This tower is impregnable.'

'Midpoint Tower wasn't impregnable, Manon, and nor are you immune to starvation, or to the debilitating effects of tending the tower. Time is on my side, old friend. There'll be no relief, no rescue, just a slow wasting, until I walk in unopposed and drag you all away. Unless you hand over Jehana Mubarak.'

Everyone inhaled sharply, and Jehana felt all eyes turn her way.

'Truly, I have no interest in seeing Sunset Isle fall,' Alyssa went on. 'All I want is that girl. Oh, and the head of the Merozain bint would be a fine additional gift – for that, I'll even resupply you.'

'Why should I believe you?' Manon demanded.

'Why shouldn't you? Honestly, if my Master wished the Bridge destroyed, it would already be rubble.'

'Which master is that, Heartface?' Tarita called, joining her voice to the link.

Heartface! Jehana thought. *Is Tarita saying that Alyssa helped kill my mother and the sultan?*

Alyssa seemed momentarily taken aback, then she laughed. 'Wrong again, little spy. The master I refer to is Sultan Rashid Mubarak, ruler of Ahmedhassa, victor of the Third Crusade and conqueror of the West. He values the Bridge as I do – as a fine conveyance for resupplying his armies in six years' time. But he wants his niece back. He values family above all things.'

As the chamber fell silent again, Jehana was still keenly aware of the eyes on her. *Who am I to these scholars compared to their precious Bridge? Or their lives?*

'You'll already be rationing, I'm sure,' Alyssa taunted. 'And illnesses will be setting in. How long can you hold out? And why bother? Give me the girl and this blockade ends.'

Hillarie would gladly let her go, and probably Loric too. Only Tarita looked adamantly opposed to surrendering her. Her heart sank as Manon visibly wavered . . .

Then the old magus straightened and rasped, 'Who are you to dictate to us, treacherous whore? Come closer and I'll rip you from the skies.' He broke the contact and rose, his face filled with fury. 'I never liked that bitch and I'll be damned if I give her a single thing she might want.'

Jehana felt like cheering, but the rebellious looks in Hillarie and Loric's eyes told her that the matter was far from closed.

20

A New Form of Warfare

The Rimoni Empire: Military Organisation

The conquering Rondians copied the Rimoni military model, right down to the terminology and tactics of the legion. To this, over time, they added battle-magi and other tactical and technological developments such as archery, windskiffs and cavalry. A Rimoni legate from the year 300 would recognise much of what he saw in a Year 900 Rondian army.

ANNALS OF PALLAS, 907

The Brekaellen Valley
Octen 935

Waqar nudged his roc's neck with his left knee as his flight of birds circled above a trio of Rondian skiffs. Ajniha responded with practised grace. Mental communication flashed between the roc-riders as Waqar split them into four trios and assigned the approach sequence.

They were learning so much every day, of how to fly and fight, and their clothing, harnesses and weapons were constantly evolving. They'd discovered glass could protect the eyes and allow one to see while flying at high speed, so now they all wore glass discs set in padded leather thongs to keep the rushing air from their eye-sockets. Armour was virtually useless against a lance and the steel could get deathly cold – despite being nearer the sun, higher altitudes were freezing – so they all flew in supple, close-fitting fur-lined garments now. And they'd adopted curved bucklers strapped to their left shoulders, like the Rondian knights wore, to deflect lance-heads.

330

Rocs could stay aloft for hours just by gliding and riding air currents, but the giant birds were fragile. Shielding one's beast was hard, and most magi couldn't effectively protect the belly, so getting beneath a foe often brought reward. Archery and speed won victories; going head to head with Rondian knights brought death.

And then there was the sun: it could blind you, so you mustn't look at it: but you could hide in it if you were clever in your positioning. Right now, their shadows were mingling with those of the Rondian skiffs below and their quarry appeared to be unaware of Waqar's band.

<Stay high and attack the sail first,> he reminded them. He glanced at Lukadin. This was his first flight since the day he'd wielded the mysterious spear. His friend looked to be recovered, but he still refused to relinquish the weapon. <Come in on the second wave, Lukadin – follow Shameed's lead. Ahmaal – your flight is in third; Tamir, keep your trio high and cover us.>

Then Waqar sent Ajniha into an exhilarating dive, with Bashara and a new man called Indrakh at his wing-tips. As they plummeted towards their foes he kindled gnosis on his spear-head, then balanced it on his shoulder. They'd discovered that a heavy javelin, hurled at close range with the momentum of flight, could be as lethal as a Rondian lance.

Down they swooped, the distance shrinking fast. The heraldry on the sail became clearer and now he could see the man in front of the mast, fiddling with something bolted to the hull. Then their shadows fell across the skiff, the man's head jerked round and Waqar recognised what the man was doing . . .

'Evade!' he shouted, kicking Ajniha's right flank and slapping the top of the left wing beside the shoulder, sending the roc into a spiralling dive away from the skiff. His sudden move took his two comrades by surprise, and Bashara reacted swiftly, spinning onto his tail-feathers.

But Indrakh didn't move so quickly—

—as with a crack, the mechanism in the fore-deck of the skiff discharged: a mounted crossbow that sent its gnostically-charged shaft plunging through Indrakh's shielding and took his bird in the eye, stopping it dead in the air – then the giant eagle's skull imploded in a blaze of blue light and it plummeted.

'*Indrakh!*' Waqar shouted, hauling Ajniha out of her spin as the struggling warrior tried desperately to get free of his straps in the midst
of a vertiginous spin. Above him he sensed Shameed's second wing
wheeling away as a second fiery crossbow bolt blazed an arc through
the formation, but all his focus was on Indrakh. At full falling speed,
even kinesis couldn't save you – and Indrakh wasn't an Air-mage.

Indrakh finally pulled free, but he was still too far away for Waqar
to reach. He tried to get closer to grab him with kinesis, but Bashara
shouted a warning even as Indrakh shrieked and fell from reach and
Waqar twisted in the harness to see a dozen huge shapes dropping
towards them: the big winged lizards the Rondians called venators. They
were bigger than rocs and twice as heavy, much slower but durable –
and if you let their big jaws snap closed on your bird, you were doomed.

Indrakh was spinning earthwards and there was nothing Waqar could
do – and at the end of a long day, the last thing his tired rocs needed
was a fight. With a curse, he called his fliers in and they sped away,
leaving the ponderous venators behind.

The wind from the east was rising and it would be a long haul to get
back to camp in the remaining daylight. Below them the plains went
on and on, but he could see dark lines cut in the swathe of green: the
fork in the Imperial Road, running northwest towards Kedron and due
west to Trachen Pass. Sydian horsemen were already galloping ahead
of the main host to seize the fork.

They pulled well clear of the incoming Rondian venators, annoyed
to be letting the skiffs get away – but they'd learned better than to go
up against the Rondian knights in an even scrap if they could avoid it.
Such skirmishes were still frequent, though, and so was loss and death.

But soon enough they were bantering as if nothing had happened.
Indrakh wasn't mentioned: the dead were gone. Life was wonderful up
here in the skies, but it was brief.

They found the army vanguard and their support people an hour
before sunset. There were a few burns and scratches from the brief
combat but most were unhurt and able to see to their mounts themselves. A passing band of Dhassan cavalry stared at the giant birds,
but the warriors of the Shihad was growing used to such sights now.

As the servants erected tents and lit cooking fires, Waqar's comrades joined him at the water wagon, drinking and reliving the encounter with the skiffs.

'Crossbows,' Lukadin was snorting, 'a coward's weapon!'

'I told you they'd do something of the sort,' Tamir replied. 'They had to.'

'We made them do it,' Fatima noted. 'After last week, they had to react.'

Six days ago, they'd found a six-skiff patrol and harried and harassed the enemy craft from a distance until all six were burning and immobile, then closed in and slaughtered the pilots. To kill six enemy magi without reply had been a massive coup and went some way to redressing their own losses. They'd yet to see the gold-crowned rider and his knights again, but some of Waqar's other flights had and those encounters hadn't gone well.

Bashara joined them, looking angry. Like all the female fliers, she now wore fitted leathers and disdained the bekira-shroud. Waqar's fliers understood, but many others didn't: 'Some damned Godspeaker just told me I was "a disgrace to the Amteh",' she snarled.

Waqar felt his hackles rise. 'Why? For how you dress again?'

'Of course, for how I dress! Too bad that my veil would drag me from the saddle, or that I'm risking my life against Rondian knights every day! All he could think was that I'm "inflaming Ahm's warriors with unholy lust".'

'We're back in camp now,' Lukadin noted. 'You could put your bekira-shroud on here.' He looked at Fatima and the other women fliers. 'You all could.'

'What's that so-expressive Rimoni phrase? "*Rukka-te, arsehole*",' Bashara shot back. 'I'm too damned hot to put a shroud on. I hate them!' She stuck out her chest. 'Would you rather look at these, or a tent?'

'It's for your own protection,' Lukadin countered. 'Men who see a woman's flesh lose all control.'

'So *we* have to cover up because of *your* lack of morals? My sword and my gnosis are my protection and those spineless worms will find that out if they try to push me around again.'

'They're holy men,' Lukadin snapped. 'Waqar, shut your woman's mouth for her!'

'I'm not "his woman". I don't *belong* to anyone!' Bashara yelled, while Waqar threw Luka an angry look. Then Fatima stepped between them before they came to blows again. This sort of thing was becoming a nightly event in camp now: Bashara versus Lukadin, fighting over whatever religious stricture Bashara had taken umbrage against that day. Waqar found himself torn down the middle: Lukadin was his life-long friend and he would die for him – but he could be a pious prig at times, and he was definitely getting worse.

'Luka, expecting Fatima, Bashara and the other women fliers to fight as front-line warriors and still behave like traditional Amteh maidens is ridiculous,' he told him. 'It's just not practical.'

'Would you say so if you weren't riding her tail?'

Keeping his temper was an effort. 'You know me better than that, Luka.'

'I thought I did,' Luka snarled – then he bowed his head and raised an apologetic hand. 'Sorry, I don't want to fight – but you're wrong: she should wear a bekira-shroud when she can.'

Waqar put up a hand for silence because he'd had enough bickering for today, and Lukadin was visibly unwell. *It's the damned spear*, he thought. They were all afraid for him, but Lukadin refused to even discuss surrendering the weapon. As for Bashara, he liked her and certainly enjoyed bedding her, but she had years of catching up to do before she meant as much to him as Fatima, Luka, Tamir and Baneet.

'I'll talk to the Godspeakers again,' he said. 'Last week they wanted all our women sent to the rear – a fifth of our fliers! Before that they wanted only male healers, because it was immoral for a female to touch a wounded man! Next week it'll be something else. You know what they're like.'

'If we're not the people of Ahm, who are we?' Lukadin muttered.

Before Waqar could respond, Tamir nudged him and pointed to a distinctive wind-dhou coming in to land. 'That's Prince Xoredh's vessel.'

'I'd better go and welcome him,' Waqar sighed. 'See you after the meal – I'm assuming I'll have to dine with the prick.'

He did indeed have to eat with Xoredh, who arrived with a swarm of officials who constantly whispered in his ear. A pavilion was swiftly erected, and meat set roasting – the army was devouring the Sydian herds in vast quantities. Xoredh had arak too, and opium, which Waqar declined. He also had a gorgeous white girl, clad in a lace shift that concealed nothing, kneeling at his feet. Her skin was bruised and she flinched constantly.

'So you've sighted the enemy ground forces, I hear?' Xoredh asked, his eyes hooded as he sucked on a hookah. He appeared to be able to consume immense amounts of the drug without dimming his faculties.

'We found them four days ago and have been tracking them since, Cousin. They're on the Imperial Road, twenty miles east of a place called Collistein Junction.'

'Well done, Cousin,' Xoredh said condescendingly. 'Our advance guard will reach the fork in the road to Trachen Pass tomorrow. I've sent thirty thousand men. They march only at night and set concealed camps. Father hopes to fool the enemy into believing we're ignoring that route.'

'Trachen Pass is fortified,' Waqar noted. 'We overflew it two days ago. The fortress there overlooks a single-file approach. You'd do better to ignore it.'

Xoredh shrugged. 'Any man the enemy sends to Trachen is one we won't face in the real battle.' He tapped the map. 'Two hundred and fifty miles between us and the enemy. Both forces are moving twenty miles a day or so, so the gap between us shrinks by forty miles a day. At that rate, we'll encounter them in seven days.'

'But that's just the advance guards,' Waqar commented. 'Cavalry only. My patrols haven't seen enemy infantry yet, so that puts them no closer than Jastenberg – and our main body is still crossing the Silas. That's four hundred miles between us, and infantry can only cover ten miles a day: so twenty days until a full-scale battle – assuming either side will risk it.'

Xoredh considered. 'Then we'll encounter them somewhere in the Brekaellen Valley. Does the terrain change overly as we go north?'

'Not really. It's all low hills, flatlands and bogs. Some of the rises might be defensible, but most of it is flat, open terrain, which will suit us.'

335

'What would you know of such things, Cousin, from safe up there in the sky?' Xoredh sniffed.

Whenever they had to interact, at some point Xoredh simply ran out of respect and felt compelled to belittle him. 'We're the eyes of the army, Cousin.'

'You're the tits of the army,' Xoredh retorted, then he snapped, 'Show me this spear of yours. The one that can destroy a mage-knight with one blast.'

Someone told him about Lukadin's spear? 'You're misinformed,' Waqar lied. 'I think not.'

Waqar felt his heart thudding. Rashid's sons had always been the terror of his life: Attam was a brutal bully and Xoredh a cruel torturer. This evening's had been the most cordial conversation they'd ever had. He should have known it wouldn't last. 'Perhaps your spies have misunderstood something.'

'My father the sultan put me in charge of information: I'll make him aware if you obstruct me.'

'I'm not. You're simply wrong.' Waqar stood. 'Goodnight, Cousin.'

'I've not dismissed you.'

'Wasn't this a family meal?' Waqar retorted. 'I don't require dismissal.' He rose and strode from the pavilion, his cousin's snickering trailing him out.

Before seeking his own bed, he warned Lukadin of Xoredh's interest.

The elephants of Piru-Satabam III plodded on and on, down a road that never ended, in the middle of a miles-long column of marching soldiers. Some were singing hymns or folk songs, but most marched silently to the beat of the drums. In just under four months the elephants had trudged from Pontus to the Brekaellen, an average of twenty miles a day. Seven of the forty had died, three in battle and four on the road, but replacements had been flown in on windships.

'It's getting colder,' Ashmak noted, pulling his blanket closer around him; the howdah offered little in the way of shelter.

'Ai,' Latif agreed, 'and it's not winter yet.'

They shared a silent, eloquent look and lapsed back into silence.

They'd been together so long now, they'd run out of things to talk about. They'd recounted their pasts – although Latif's was mostly invented – and places they'd been. The countryside held no interest and topics ranging from religion to women, food and drink, jokes and anecdotes, had all been exhausted. Mostly they dozed, like Sanjeep on the lower platform, while Rani the elephant just walked on. Rain lashed them at times and the wind, which had started as a warm southerly breeze, was now a blustery northerly. They just wanted to *arrive* somewhere and *stop*.

I had no idea soldiering was so damned boring, Latif thought. *How do they all stay sane?* He then mentally amended that to, *No wonder soldiers go insane.*

But the landscape *was* changing, gradually. The Brekaellen Valley was a flat expanse, but up close it was threaded with streams, riddled with pools and bogs, dotted with hills and covered in vast fields of bush and heather and small woods. There were herds of wild deer and kine and all manner of small animals – hares, rabbits, foxes and other unknown creatures. Wolfpacks hunted the plains – bigger and more formidable than Ahmedhassan jackals, but not big enough to try their teeth on the huge army, which drove all living things away.

The sky above teemed with a new kind of life: flying vessels of all sizes, as well as the new winged beasts. Latif was amazed at how well-prepared Rashid Mubarak was for this war, with his fleets of windships and flocks of giant birds. A strange new kind of battle was being fought up there, one they glimpsed from time to time in the shape of a distant streak of flame as a windskiff went down, or dots whirling far above. Sometimes they found the wreckage – sheared-off wooden planking, or the shattered bodies of a roc or a Rondian venator. During the Crusades, the Rondians had owned the skies – now they were being contested.

Rashid, you've worked miracles. Then Latif remembered the masked assassins and his butchered wife and son. *I'll see you dead, regardless.*

Another couple of hours slid by and Rani topped a rise and reached up with her trunk to nudge Sanjeep awake. They'd reached another supply-dump. The amount of coordinated effort that went into getting an army anywhere was incredible; errors could leave thousands of men without fresh food and water for days on end – and such errors were not uncommon.

'Finally,' Ashmak sighed. 'I'd murder for a beef shank.' It was a pleasant fantasy; the best they'd get would be some kind of mash and flatbread.

'Or fruit,' Latif muttered. 'Oh, *melons*.' He could almost taste the sweet nectar.

'My wife's daal,' Sanjeep put in, before chuckling sadly, 'or my wife's melons.' The joke would have been funnier if they hadn't heard it a hundred times already. And if his wife were not long-dead.

They plodded into camp, following the other elephants towards the feed wagons. The raw stench of the latrine trenches hit them first, followed by the clamour of the camp. Selmir, their hazarapati, was bawling at a harried supplies officer when someone cried out in alarm and a nearby grain wagon exploded in flames.

Suddenly the sky above them was filled with giant swooping beasts and a blaze of flame shot from a man on the back of a winged lizard, igniting another wagon. Two screaming labourers, their robes in flames, leaped to the ground. One rolled to smother the flames but the other blundered into a group of men and was instantly gutted by a spear. Archers appeared and useless shafts flew in all directions.

'Rani!' Sanjeep was calling, amazingly calm in the face of chaos. 'Stand, Rani!'

Latif and Ashmak strung their own bows and nocked arrows. More flying beasts were searing in and Latif saw a winged horse, pearly-white and beautiful despite its unnatural form, gliding through the rising smoke. Its rider, a knight armoured and gold-crowned, blazed mage-bolts into the archers. '*That one!*' Latif shouted.

Ashmak counted out loud, '*Wahid, athnyn, thlath!*' and released, Latif firing his own arrow a deliberate instant later. They'd learned to aim ahead of the speeding target so Ashmak's gnostic-infused shaft could strike shields and momentarily fuse them, allowing Latif's a chance to punch through, even though it wasn't magically empowered. They shot well together: Ashmak's arrow exploded and fused the shields and Latif's struck the knight—

—and glanced off his armour. The knight spun in alarm, then he and his mount were out of range.

'*Chod!*' Latif swore.

'Good shot, Brother,' Ashmak growled. 'Unlucky.'

'I was aiming for the damned horse,' Latif snarled, nocking another arrow as one of the venators turned their way. Someone had noted Ashmak's blazing arrow. 'Watch out!'

'Hold, Rani!' Sanjeep shouted, keeping the elephant stable to help the archers. The venator dived at them, shields battering aside a storm of arrows, then a ball of fire erupted from the rider.

'*Tajaanu-hai!*' Ashmak shouted, scarlet shields billowing before them. Flames boiled around their safe cocoon, but the air still filled with stinging, skin-blistering heat. Latif had released his arrow an instant before the venator's claws caught in their howdah. Bamboo snapped, cloth tore and Rani lurched sideways and almost rolled. Latif expected to be crushed, but the elephant staggered and regained her balance as the venator flapped away.

'They're coming in again!' someone shouted as the smoke blew clear. The venator who'd raked them had soared away, unharmed, and was turning back. An eagle-headed winged lion flapped by, dropping the archer it had clutched in its claws; the creature screamed as the two bloody pieces fell to the ground.

'Archers,' Selmir was shouting, '*form up!*' But a hundred other orders were being bellowed, adding to the confusion.

Latif ignored his commander and pointed at the venator. 'He's coming back!'

Ashmak conjured light at his fingertips. 'He's a Fire-mage,' he said, 'so I'll have to protect us – it's your shot.' Then he reached across and touched Latif's arrowhead, making it briefly flare. 'It's not so effective if I'm not shooting it, but who knows?'

A strange calm settled on them as the enemy venators began another run. Rani was oblivious to all around her and Latif settled himself, trusting in Ashmak's skills, and his own. Then the enemy hurtled in, blasting with lightning and fire, as arrows rose to meet them in a hissing storm, several glowing with gnosis-light. Shielding crackled, most arrows shattered, a few punched through but most glanced off the thick hide of the reptiles. Jaws snapped, claws raked and deadly spells tore the air.

All the while, Latif and Ashmak kept their gaze on *their* venator, making straight for them. *He knows we've a mage aboard. He's ready for us . . .*

Then it was on them again, and the mage-knight riding loosed a bolt of flame that washed around Ashmak's shielding in another hair-crisping wave of heat. As its dark bulk swept overhead, the rush of air from its passing making even Rani stagger, Latif fired straight up into the beast's belly.

Then the creature ploughed into the elephant behind them, battering it to the ground. Its tail lashed Rani and she staggered, struck a fallen wagon and almost toppled. Straps burst and the howdah slipped sideways. Latif was hurled clear, hit the ground and rolled. Sanjeep clung on grimly, while Ashmak struck the ground in a burst of sparks and came erect, then bounded towards the downed venator.

An armoured knight rose from the wreckage of bodies, rising into the air – and three arrows immediately hammered his shields. He stopped rising, but his shields reformed as he torched a group of archers, tracing a wheel of fire about himself. Ashmak fired and his arrow deflected harmlessly, then the next wave of Rondian knights swept overhead, and another of the great lizards plucked the Rondian away in its claws and then they were all rising. Ashmak fired again but missed, while Latif ran to Sanjeep and helped him calm Rani. His familiar voice won through and she subsided. The broken howdah was still tangled around her.

Then someone shouted, '*Aiiee!*' and everyone looked upwards to see a dozen roc-riders sweeping in, mage-light stabbing at the Rondian knights and their beasts. They shouted in hope as the Keshi fliers struck the Rondian formation from above at thrice their speed. Javelins sleeted into the Rondians and five of the reptiles stalled in flight, then smashed into the ground before their riders could get free. In seconds spearmen were covering the fallen men and beasts and stabbing, roaring triumphantly.

But the remaining Rondian knights were rising, their shields vivid and their counter-strikes direct and deadly, as if in extremity they were dredging out their best. *Pure-bloods*, Latif realised. *Elite mage-nobles.* He saw the crowned pegasus-rider again, leading his knights in a searing, gnosis-assisted climb, and the Keshi rocs, reeling from the greater fire-power of their enemies, let them go. In minutes the Rondians were dots on the northern horizon. The rocs circled overhead protectively.

'That venator was your kill, Latif!' Ashmak crowed. 'Ahm guides your aim, my friend! Go to Selmir and claim the bounty!'

'Not me,' Latif replied. The last thing he needed was Selmir taking notice of him. 'Someone else made the kill – my shot missed.' Ashmak raised his eyebrows, but he knew Latif well enough by now not to press the point.

The camp was in ferment as officers tried to regain order and get the fires put out. There was wreckage everywhere and the air was filled with black smoke and the wails of the injured. But the men were exhilarated at the sight of their own flying magi driving off the much-vaunted enemy.

I've just seen the future: winged magi striking from above without warning, Latif thought. *A new kind of war.* He badly missed Salim, and imagined how they would have discussed this, pulling it apart to look at it from all sides before calling in Rashid and deciding on their counter-strategy. *But Salim is dead, and Rashid Mubarak can go to Hel. Let him work it out for himself.*

21

Mobilising Forces

Tax-Farming

It was the Rimoni who first developed tax-farming: after their term in office, consuls would be rewarded with a colony for one year, and the right to tax it. It was up to them how they extracted the largesse, and most did so in brutal ways. It was an ignoble practice which I hope the Rondian Empire never returns to.

BLAYDEN MALCOTTO, IMPERIAL TREASURER 861–868,

MEMOIRS, 872

Gosberg, near Jastenberg, Noros
Octen 935

Gosberg lay on the Jastenberg-Knebb road in northern Norostein. There'd been a battle there in the early months of the Noros Revolt in 909, a Noros victory, but the town had later been abandoned uncontested. General Kaltus Korion had used it as a base during his bloody Knebb campaign.

The Imperial Legions had recruitment quotas, and one thankless Imperial facultor had been given the task of enlisting men in a place where the empire was still deeply loathed. 'Duty demands that you join the fight!' the portly official declared to the passers-by in the town square, eliciting reactions from stony-faced hostility to heckling and abuse. 'It is time to repay our beloved empress for her protection! Two hundred men must enlist by sunset, or the town falls under Imperial interdict – and we'll conscript three hundred!'

The armies of the empress were even now on the march into the

Kedron Valley – or malingering in Midrea, in the case of the Sacrecour forces – but many of the Noros legions were under-strength – harvest was a bad time for rural men to leave their lands. The recruiters had been ranting all afternoon; some were stridently patriotic, some East-hating veterans, while others preached from the *Book of Kore* about slaying the heathen and bringing the light of Truth to the dark races.

It still wasn't going well.

Ari Frankel looked around, assessing the crowd, awaiting the opportunity to say his piece. He'd spoken most days as he'd made his way south, but only in villages off the beaten path. He was no recruiter and had no interest in the war; his own mission was quite different. It wasn't easy, balancing his personal crusade with not being arrested for sedition, but he could no longer stay silent. Ari *lived* for the moments when upturned faces drank in his words and momentarily shared his vision: that was when he felt truly alive.

As a legion tribune finished a limp attempt at rabble-rousing, Ari saw his opening: he leaped onto the top step to the tavern and shouted, 'People of Gosberg, I have something to say about freedom!'

As dozens of faces swung to face him, he felt the familiar thrills of trepidation and exhilaration. 'What do *you* want?' a few demanded, but they were quickly drowned out by his followers; a dozen ragged men who began shouting 'ARI! ARI!'

Ari had once been a priest. Because he could read and write, he'd been sent north to the Rymfort in Pallas and ordained as a friar in the Inquisition – specifically, a Book-Burner; his task was to root out heretical texts. But he'd fallen in love with his enemies, especially the forbidden heresy of *suffragium*, or governance by the will of the people, expressed by vote; it had, all unexpected, lit a fire in him.

He could be locked up for advocating suffragium, though, so he had to sneak up on the topic. 'Isn't it wonderful that we have the freedom to march under our own banners again, after twenty years?' he shouted, blending in with the jingoistic nonsense the recruiters had been spouting. 'It's wonderful to see the Silver Hawk of the Sixth!'

'What's it to you?' someone yelled.

'A source of pride!' Ari cried. 'What a great realm we are part of, different peoples united under one empire!' He saw the facultor relax, presuming Ari was just an opportunist imperialist with a bent for ranting. 'Is it not wonderful,' he went on, 'that one can walk from Pallas to Norostein and hear only the Rondian language? I've heard imperial officials declare that all local dialects should be eradicated!'

Noros itself had four regional dialects: Gosberg children spoke both Knebbish and Rondian, and his own accent spoke of Jastenberg. As his words sank in, the crowd became attentive, realising that something interesting, maybe even subversive, was happening here.

'The other great thing about this empire is that everyone you meet pays exactly the same taxes to Empress Lyra, Kore bless her!' Ari winked at the nearest man, and added, mock-intimate, 'Regional excises, tolls and tributes notwithstanding, eh?'

The man spat. 'Aye, we 'ave a few o' them. More'n they pay in Pallas, I warrant.'

'And you'd be right! But I'm sure all that money is well-used!' Ari declared. 'The roads speak for themselves . . .'

That brought grunts and wry looks. Everyone knew the empire taxed the vassal-states harder than Rondelmar, but the Treasury, which had been virtually bankrupted by the Third Crusade, had let the provincial roads deteriorate alarmingly.

'I also find it a great comfort to know that all Church tithes go straight to Dominius Wurther's platter – I surely wouldn't be able to sleep were it otherwise!'

By now everyone had caught the sarcasm. You couldn't walk a mile in rural Noros without coming across corn-kings and other tokens of the Sollan faith, reverently created to bless the harvests. The Church of Kore might have been pre-eminent for five centuries, but many still invoked the Sollan deities who held sway over the harvests.

'For myself,' Ari told them, as if confessing a secret, 'I'm glad that all local authority is crushed, for what need does an empire have of local rulers? All authority comes from her Majesty in Pallas – and I rejoice! You should hearken to the facultor, for he is Pallas-appointed and above us all.'

The said facultor was now staring sourly at Ari while an aide muttered in his ear.

'What need is there for a Noroman to speak at all, when we have our king to speak for us?' Ari shouted, knowing that the muzzling of the Noros king since the Revolt was a source of anger. 'Noromen don't need tongues, just ears,' Ari added, deliberately quoting a phrase beloved by the current governor.

'What're you saying, boy?' a brawny farmer growled.

'I'm saying that *you*, my good man, are nothing and nobody – and nor am I. We have no say in the running of this empire. We can't choose our tribune – and why should we? We're not bureaucrats, so we wouldn't even know who to bribe!' He picked another surly face at random. 'And you sir, probably don't even realise that the money you earn here is better and more wisely spent in Pallas—'

The man bunched his fist, not at Ari but at the skies. 'Rukking Pallacians!'

The facultor's voice rang out. 'I don't like your tone, speaker.'

'My tone? Damnable days, I *must* work on my tone!' Ari said theatrically. 'I'm just a poor man like you, Facultor: living hand to mouth. Why should I be permitted a voice at all? But you see, it rankles: because we're all of Frandian blood, aren't we? Rondians, Midreans, Bricians, Noromen and the rest – we're *Frandians* – and that makes us better than, say, *Rimoni*, doesn't it?'

'Damned right,' a few chorused, but most were perplexed by this turn in his argument.

Ari whirled on them. 'Then why did the poorest, least of men in the *Rimoni* Empire have more say about who ruled them and how than we in the *Rondian* Empire? Do you know that the Rimoni used to *vote* their tribunes into office? They even used to vote for their consuls, one-year-term rulers. "No kings in Rimoni" they used to say. *Suffragium*, it's called: one man, one vote – and the least man in Rimoni had one vote! How many have you got?'

Near silence greeted that mini-tirade: not rejection, but an intense scrutiny of his words. This was a land where the lack of independence burned deeper than elsewhere. The Noros Revolt had begun here only twenty-two years ago.

'The officials of the Rondian Empire are appointed by Kore Himself!' the facultor shouted, his face puce, hands on hips. 'Our God chooses us.'

'And he chose you rightly,' Ari answered, all irreverence now, '*absolutely* the right man. I dare say he came down from the Heavens to your very door and handed you your chain of office personally?'

That got a few more snickers from the crowd. The facultor turned a deeper shade of purple. 'You have no right to impugn me!'

'I haven't, Sir Facultor. Point out my falsehoods and I'll retract them, gladly.'

Silence descended as the facultor wavered ... then the hour bell starting ringing – and that was important, because the facultor was now off-duty and suddenly this obnoxious, slippery speaker was someone else's problem. The official, looking more than happy for that to be the case, shouted a few admonishments, to try to look like he was in charge, then hurried away while the crowd yelled abuse at his back.

Then, as always, people crowded in, calling, 'Mister! Can we buy you a beer?'

Next morning, the seed sown, Ari Frankel and his friends moved on to Meiburg, the next town on the Jastenberg road, and another chance to explore the beauty of an idea called freedom.

Collistein Junction, Kedron Valley

Ril Endarion led his fliers into their latest camp, near the junction of the Imperial and Collistein Roads, his mind racing in the aftermath of combat. Each time they met the Keshi rocs, they learned something new; he was seething at this latest lesson.

We thought the skies were empty when we hit that supply-camp.

But rocs could fly so much higher than they could – right up among the clouds, where venator blood became dangerously sluggish. He'd taken his flight into the attack on the enemy supply-camp thinking they faced only ground-troops, and they'd been hammered from above:

eight beasts lost, and worse, five knights. If they'd not had stronger gnosis, they could all have died.

We were beaten today: out-thought and out-flown. And I know whose damned fault it was!

He landed, strode over to Jorden Falquist and punched him in the helm with his gauntleted fist, sending the younger knight sprawling onto his backside. It wasn't gentlemanly, but Ril didn't care. 'I told you to stay aloft and watch for the enemy – but you followed us in, you damned fool!'

Jorden's eyes blazed. 'A Falquist does not get left in reserve—'

'You'll do as you're damned well told or I'll send you home,' Ril snarled. '*Five men are dead* – and that's on you, because of your negligence!'

Falquist glared up at him sullenly, but didn't respond. As the other knights gathered, Ril saw he wasn't the only one with bunched fists.

'I thought we were alone up there,' Jorden admitted. 'I thought I was safe to go in.'

'No, you didn't "think" – you were just caught up with your glory-hunting,' Ril railed. He fumed over him a moment longer, ensuring the point was made then he offered Falquist a hand. 'Get up,' he said, and when the other man grudgingly accepted his aid, hauled him upright. 'Five men of ancient houses – including one pure-blood line – have been lost to us today. We *cannot* afford that. The strength of our legions is in their discipline, but we mage-knights clearly don't share that virtue. The enemy only has to dangle a target and we roar in like bulls in an Estellayne arena! We *all* need to learn to follow orders and watch our backs!'

They took his tirade sourly – knights weren't used to being berated – but they knew he was right. 'We're too damned slow, is half the problem,' Larik complained. 'You'd think our Animagi might've realised that *birds* fly better than bloody lizards and horses!'

'Lessons will be learned, I assure you,' Ril told them. He'd spent an hour the previous day shouting at the head of the Pallas Beastarium via relay-stave, making that exact point. 'But it'll be months before any giant birds reach adulthood, even if they use the gnosis to accelerate growth, so we have to make do with what we've got. Yes, our pegasi, griffons and venators are slow, and they can't fly like the enemy birds – but they can carry fully armoured men, and they themselves can fight. We've got to use our advantages and nullify our disadvantages, because if we don't win in the air, we lose on the ground.'

In the past, the skies had been uncontested. Flying mage-knights had been able to break up enemy units with impunity, with massed archery presenting the only real danger – until Rashid Mubarak's first fielded a few windskiffs during the last Crusade. That they were now being out-flown by the Easterners was galling.

They debated a few ideas – some good, most not – then Larik and Gryff Joyce followed Ril to his pavilion. 'There'll be battle soon, and armour and firepower will be worth more than speed,' Gryff said, as they broached the wine. 'Those Noorie pricks can't just fly away mid-spat.'

'Velocity by weight by angle,' Larik agreed, the old jousting maxim. 'We'll carry the day when it matters, Ril.'

'We have to.' Ril spotted his aide and called, 'What news from home, Niklas?'

'A few despatches, Milord,' Bycross said, 'and a letter from the queen.'

Ril felt the usual pang of worry: was all well, or had another crisis prompted the missive? Most magi found the whole concept of writing anachronistic – the gnosis provided instant visual and aural contact – but letters did have their place: they provided a permanent record, something to refer back to. He also suspected Lyra preferred the more impersonal and one-way nature of writing.

He tore the envelope open while Gryff and Larik made themselves comfortable.

Lyra had written in her formal manner,

My Dear Husband,

All is well here. Our child continues to thrive within me and gives me no peace. It is only a month, perhaps two, now, until I must face the birthing bed. A son, I'm sure, as he kicks me with gusto and frequency. I cannot wait to look him in the face and see your likeness therein.

Ril blinked away a sudden rush of guilt that he wasn't there.

I have distressing news: we have discovered Ostevan Comfateri was linked to the attacks on Reeker Night, as you suspected. Unfortunately he has eluded capture.

Ril swore under his breath. He'd been convinced Ostevan was guilty, and frustrated that no evidence had been found. Lyra's simple sentence hinted at far more unsaid: she'd been far too close to her confessor for his liking. It was a relief to know that worm was no longer in her life, but he hoped they caught him quickly.

The City has grown quiet since you left, with so many men gone to fight for our freedom. There has been no sign of the troubles of Junesse reigniting. Dirklan has me closely protected.

That gave Ril little reassurance. The masked assassins were still out there.

The crisis in the Celestium rumbles on. I have sympathy with Valetta and her Sisters, although I deplore their timing. Poor Dominius is terribly stressed, but he is assembling a quorum of new prelates to be sworn in.

Ril had never seen 'poor Dominius' Wurther as a real ally, and he found the whole 'Sisters' Crusade' hilarious.

Valetta is not the only opportunist. I've been shown some very insolent pamphlets printed in Noros, naming me 'tyrant' and calling for my overthrow. They speak of some ancient practice called 'Suffragium'. I've never heard of it! As you're in Noros, perhaps you can have someone look into it?

He lifted his head from the page and asked, 'Niklas, do you know of any pamphlets originating from Noros? Something called "suffragium" – is it heresy or treason?'

'It could be either,' Bycross replied. 'Suffragium was an old form of government through elected rulers: it evolved in Lantris before they fell to the Rimoni, who then adopted the practice for two centuries, until the reign of the first Rimoni emperor. The premise, that all men are inherently equal, was declared heretical by Mother Church in 411 – Kore chooses our rulers, Milord, not the people.'

Ril rolled his eyes. To him, Kore was no more than a pleasing tale to keep the commons in line: men with swords chose rulers. 'Lantric, you say?' That reminded him uncomfortably of the Masked Cabal.

'Indeed. You could go either way on it, Milord: heresy, because it contravenes the Church's edict, but also treason, because it undermines the ruler's right to rule.'

Ordinarily, he'd have been happy to have someone else worry about it, but Dravis Ryburn's Inquisition's heavy-handed progress through the south was leaving a trail of bodies tortured and executed in the name of religious purity. Ril was sick of them.

'We've got bigger issues to deal with, but I don't want Ryburn marching in and burning everyone. Tell him he can investigate, but anyone they arrest must be sent to Setallius *intact*.'

Bycross bowed. 'I'll draft the order, Prince.'

Ril stalked to the table, waving Gryff and Larik over. Bycross had diligently marked the maps with the positions of the five Imperial armies, according to latest despatches, and the positions of the enemy, from the reports of the aerial scouts.

'How is it that we Corani, having the furthest to travel, are the most advanced?' he asked rhetorically.

Gryff stated the obvious. 'Because the other bastards are stalling.'

'The Sacrecours are still north of Jastenberg,' Larik complained. 'Even the Aquilleans and Argundians are ahead of Garod's men now.'

Ril pulled a face. At this point his armies were in no shape to run into the Shihad, which was advancing in well-coordinated order – the fact he was having to personally lead raids on supply-camps was testament to just how stretched his forces were. Brylion Fasterius ignored his orders, while Elvero Salinas and Andreas Borodium swore to be at his side any day, but missed every deadline.

'What about the southern army?' he asked. Seth Korion's Bricians, Midreans and Noromen were still scattered over the region; they hadn't even unified yet.

'Either he's got them superbly synchronised, or he's procrastinating like the rest,' Gryff said. 'The Korions were deep in Sacrecour pockets – his father Kaltus was on Emperor Constant's Imperial Council.'

Dear Kore, is anyone truly on my side? Ril wondered.

The evening passed calculating distances and logistics, working out where they could move men and supplies to safely without leaving them at the mercy of Keshi fliers. The emerging picture wasn't a good one. 'If we keep running to meet them, House Corani is going to end up facing the whole Shihad on our own,' Ril summarised. 'We have to slow down and pull everyone together.'

'Then let's stop where we are,' Gryff said. 'The further we move, the more excuses you give the stragglers. There's nothing out here anyway so you might as well just pick a spot.'

'A defensible spot, because you can count on being outnumbered,' Larik added. 'We need a narrow battlefront, and whatever advantages we can find.'

They were right: the headlong rush to pin the enemy down somewhere far from civilisation had failed; they had to choose the battleground before Rashid chose it for him. All at once Ril felt utterly unready, completely inadequate for the task. *It should be Takwyth here, not me.*

But Takwyth was still healing, and sending for him now would be tantamount to Ril admitting that he wasn't worthy of command. *I'd never survive the war, win or lose.* So he took a deep breath and made his best guess at the right thing to do. 'We'll fight *here*: this junction, where the Imperial Road meets the road from Collistein. Contact all units – we rally to the junction. Inform the other generals that I expect them here in two weeks or they'll find their appointments revoked.'

Which is all very well, Ril thought, *but I'm in their hands, and they all know it.*

Once he was alone, he poured himself a whisky and drew out his scrying bowl. He didn't have to wait for long. As the fourth night-bell sounded, light shifted in the steam and Basia's face appeared. He gazed at her angular face, drinking in the sight.

<Good evening, Lover,> he breathed. *<Kore's Blood, I wish you were here . . . >*

Jastenberg, Noros

After Meiburg came Veisen, and then it was the big city: Jastenberg, the crossroads of the southern empire – but by then, a new thing was driving Ari Frankel's quest, a miracle that was neither religious or gnostic: *woodcut printing.* Ari had been persuaded by a patron to put his ideas on paper and now his pamphlet on suffragium was being nailed up in squares all over Aquillea and Midrea, alongside crude drawings portraying lewd images of the latest gossip from Pallas – apparently the lily-white Empress Lyra had been screwing her confessor. Ari didn't care if it was true; it painted the empress as untrustworthy and that was grist for his mill.

His closest followers; sarcastic, unruly Neif, pious Lothar and big, muscular Bek, were handing out the pamphlets here in Jastenberg. They'd accompanied him when Ari had left the Book-Burners, certain he wouldn't be able to manage without them.

'You got most of your ideas from me anyway,' Neif had said.

Lothar had told him, 'Someone needs to remind you of the love of Kore.'

Bek had just hugged him.

Dozens of the pamphlets were now pasted to walls here in Cuimbrae Square, an open space around a well where the Butchers' Guild held sway; they were covered with suffragium slogans, along with crude, inflammatory line-drawings depicting the hypocrisy of the empress and the grand prelate. A good-sized crowd was here, listening to a dull itinerant preacher; Ari waited with his mind churning over his choicest themes. The preacher finished to a smattering of lukewarm applause.

Time to light some fires, Ari told himself. *Time to burn!*

Neif took to the stage. He was wild of hair, drank too much, thought himself the true genius and came to fisticuffs with someone on a daily basis, but he knew how to create an entrance. 'People of Jasten-berg,' he bellowed, 'you've heard of my friend already! His words are made of *flames*, Good People! You've heard of his legendary pamphlet on the power of suffragium – if you haven't, see me after – but for now, I'm *enraptured* to introduce to you the Voice of the People . . . ARI FRANKEL!'

The rush of adrenalin as Ari stepped onto the makeshift stage was wine in his mouth; this place was now the centre of Creation. 'Thank you for your welcome, Jastenberg! My name is Ari Frankel, and if that name sounds local, it's because I was *born* here: this is my home – one I've dearly missed on my travels.'

Ha! Missed like one misses a burned-off wart, he thought, then pushed on. 'Does it feel to you some days like you have no control over your world? That no matter how hard you work, the powers that be are going to take it all away? They'll just tax it all away – they'll impose tolls on the roads, like brigands – they'll commandeer your goods and produce for their armies – they'll tithe you for the right to pray?'

These were keenly felt complaints here, in the path of so many armies. The governor was besieged with tales of looting in the name of war, and a myriad associated crimes. So the crowd was right with him, if wary of the soldiers loitering at the fringes.

'We can petition our lords and masters and ask them nicely to stop fleecing us – but do they ever listen?'

'Like Hel,' a few voices muttered.

'Exactly,' he said, 'like Hel! Because as far as they're concerned, our voices are less than the cawing of crows!'

He led them through tales of mass protests that had changed the thinking of rulers in the past, reminded them that when people banded together, they were stronger than when they were alone. It was a delicate dance in a time of war, but speaking about the past wasn't illegal – yet. 'A wise man once wrote a book, *Res Publica – The Kingdom of the People* – which taught that nations are stronger when leaders are chosen by the people, to serve the people. When was the last time we *chose* a leader? When was the last time we had a leader who served those he leads?'

'Kore chose our rulers,' a devout soul shouted back. 'He gave them the gnosis.'

'He gave magi the gnosis,' Ari agreed – it was heresy not to – but then he added, 'but His purpose remains unknown. Read *Disputations: Chapter VI!* And pay attention: *nowhere* does it say that only magi have the divine right to rule.'

That caused a murmur, but he pulled out a Kore icon, a Sacred Heart, and kissed it. 'I've been a lay priest: I love Kore with all my heart. But is a man with the gnosis a more virtuous man than one without? We all know of magi outlaws – the Kaden Rats, the most infamous criminals in history, are magi. The gnosis is a gift, but like all gifts, Kore judges us by how we use our gifts – read *Revelatory Visions: Chapter II.*'

Then Ari happened to glance to the back of the square – and flinched: there were two black-and-white-cloaked Inquisitors listening. But the people nearer to him were murmuring encouragement; even most of the soldiers were nodding – he *couldn't* stop now. 'I'm not here to say that all magi or rulers are evil, but there is such a thing as a bad ruler, or a bad law – shouldn't we the people have the right to be rid of them without recourse to force? Why should a man be able to give his secular authority to his child, unearned? Why should only he decide the laws? Let the people – all of us together, strong and powerful – decide!'

And that, he thought as he waved and shook his fist, *is as close as I can come legally to what I really want to say.* 'Kore bless us all!' he shouted, then leaped down, seized the nearest hands and started pumping them as Bek and Lothar closed in.

The Inquisitors were shouldering their way through the crowd.

'Let's go,' he hissed in Neif's ear, and in seconds they were pelting down an alley, the sounds of the crowds fading into the distance, his mind already questing ahead, planning his next speech.

22

A New Kingdom

Marriage

Consider dowry: ostensibly a gift from a father to his daughter, so that should her husband die, she will have some wealth to fall back on. In reality, it goes straight into the coffers of the groom's family. What widow has ever lived off her dowry? The bride's family are paying for someone to take their daughter off their hands.

My point is that even institutions that are supposed to protect women, in fact serve only men.

ABBESS LYNDEA GRANGE, AQUILLEA, 840

Hegikaro, Mollachia
Octen 935

Valdyr Sarkany was staring out the window at the lake, burnished silver by the cloudy skies, almost perfectly still as the winds had dropped to nothing. He'd peered from this same window as a child: this was his father's keep, *home*, Hegikaro Castle retaken bloodlessly after the remnants of the Delestre legion fled.

He'd been a boy when he left, still without the gnosis. *Now I'm what: A heretic? Or a hero?*

Either way, he was home. The Imperial Legion was still in the lower valley, but Governor Inoxion's death had left its captains paralysed, while the Delestre legion was disintegrating as the men deserted and fled west. The tax-farming had been abandoned: Mollachia was now destitute – and almost free.

But Valdyr couldn't celebrate, for he kept hearing Sacrista Delestre's

355

dying words: that Asiv Fariddan, his tormentor in Kesh, was *here*. Just thinking of the Keshi scholar was enough to make his legs tremble. *She must have been possessed by some evil spirit – how else would she even know about him?*

Someone knocked at the door. 'Prince Valdyr, your brother's allies are here.'

I know, Valdyr thought. *I just wish they weren't.* He flinched guiltily at the thought, but couldn't retract it. Kyrik had arrived with another twenty-five thousand Sydians, and Valdyr knew that many in Mollachia weren't happy.

I love you, Kyrik, but your people do not *want this alliance.*

All the most influential men in Hegikaro had approached him since his return, from Earl Radeska to Pater Kostyn; they all believed Kyrik had recklessly imported one enemy for another. And he couldn't dismiss their concerns, even though he understood Kyrik's decisions. He too worried that the alliance with the Sydians of Clan Vlpa could be a recipe for disaster, especially with the kingdom on its knees. Dragan Zhagy had been saying things like 'our own people must come first' and calling Kyrik a 'naïve idealist', and when Dragan spoke, people listened.

However, Valdyr knew his duty: he must back his elder brother – his kirol – so he belted on his sword and made ready to lead the welcome party. At the doorway, the wolf Gricoama yawned, but remained curled up – the animal knew he wasn't wanted in a crowd. He was still more wild beast than companion.

'I'd rather go hunting,' Valdyr admitted, and the wolf growled in agreement.

He descended into the Great Hall, remembering his own arrival a few days ago, when the news came that the Delestre men had fled the castle and the town. There had been unconstrained joy that day as every man, woman and child in the city emerged to greet the Vitezai Sarkanum. They'd treated him and Dragan as heroes. When he'd entered the Great Hall, where his father and his grandfather had held court, people had wept. It was a heady feeling when all he'd known since he'd left as a nine-year-old was slavery and abuse.

'Is everything ready?' he asked the Gazda of the Vitezai Sarkanum at the doors. 'Do the guards know to only admit the kirol and his retinue?'

'They know.' Dragan caught Valdyr's shoulder and whispered, 'I know it's only protocol, but your brother isn't kirol yet. He's not yet crowned.'

'He will be,' Valdyr said, wondering what the gazda meant.

'I know, but until he's crowned, his title is Crown Prince. History is listening today, Valdyr.' Then he waved his daughter forward. 'Sezkia, you look lovely today.'

Dragan wasn't exaggerating. Sezkia Zhagy was a beautiful young woman, today dressed in a close-fitting, richly embroidered blue velvet dress, her hair caught up in a tall three-cornered Rondian hennin trailing a lace veil. Her mouth was a rosebud.

'Good wishes on this blessed day, my lord,' she murmured, looking up at Valdyr with shining eyes.

Dear Kore, she's lovely . . . And his, if he wanted her. That'd been made clear. But his dreams were still haunted by Asiv Fariddan and any notion of intimacy was still nightmarish. 'You look, um . . . very fine,' he mumbled, unable to meet her gaze.

Sezkia curtseyed, and the gazda frowned at his odd reaction, but the doors were swinging open and they joined the chief burghers on the steps to await Kyrik. Petty functionaries crowded in, bombarding Valdyr with questions: Is the order of ceremonies confirmed? Does Kyrik know he must await Pater Kostyn's blessing before ascending the steps? Would Kyrik's 'consort' understand the words? Would these Sydians know their place?

As to that, Valdyr had no idea.

The castle sat above Hegikaro on a jagged promontory, overlooking the lake. Thin cheers were rising from the narrow streets leading up to the fortress as riders appeared at the gates. Kyrik's big frame and blond mane were unmistakable as he led the procession of mounted Sydians through the press.

Kyrik's wife Hajya was riding alongside him. She'd made some concession to her new life: she'd shed her steppes leathers for a plain Mollach smock-dress and her mane of thick hair was tied back and constrained by a headscarf. But she was the only Sydian who'd changed

357

attire. Behind her, Nacelnik Thraan was a brooding tower of suspicion, eyeing the archers above as if expecting shafts to fly. The shaman Missef looked even less at ease, glowering about him as if he thought this all a trap, just like the dozen warriors who followed.

They'll never belong here, Valdyr worried, *and they'll never leave.*

Pater Kostyn, the Kore head-priest, indicated that Valdyr should descend with him to greet the newcomers as they dismounted, and finally Valdyr's brother stood before him again. He longed to seize him and hug him tight, but this wasn't just a reunion – Kyrik was the exiled heir, returning to claim the vacant throne. Many of those in the crowd had never even seen him before; he'd been a youth when he left nineteen years ago. And there were protocols that must be followed, so the brothers contented themselves with just looking at each other, suppressing their grins.

Pater Kostyn, clad in his full regalia, all stark white and blood-red, raised his hands and intoned a blessing in ancient Rimoni, his deep baritone voice echoing across the crowd, before crying out, 'Crown Prince Kyrik Sarkany, son of the lamented Kirol Elgren, welcome back to the kingdom that is yours, by right of birth and before the eyes of Kore! Welcome to your new subjects, the Vlpa clan of Sydia! Praise and thanks be unto Kore, God of Victory!'

'Praise to Kore!' everyone chorused in response – except the Vlpa men, something that the Mollachs all noticed. *Is it Ahm they worship now, or will they cling to their old gods?* Valdyr wondered.

The junior priests raised their censors, filling the air with a pungent pine-infused smoke, and finally – *finally!* – Valdyr was able to embrace his brother. Despite all his misgivings, for a moment Valdyr was a boy again and Kyrik his hero, even though he was now the taller and stronger of the siblings.

'Val – dear Kore, it's good to see you,' Kyrik enthused. 'And you've retaken Hegikaro – I'm so proud!'

Valdyr drank in his brother's handsome face and open features. He was wearing a princely circlet and looked regal: at thirty-four years old, he looked like a man who'd explored the East, seen deserts, mountains, oceans and plains and Ahmedhassan courts and palaces. But he'd also been a prisoner in the breeding-houses and that showed on his face too. Despite that, Kyrik always saw the best in people, a virtue – or weakness – Valdyr knew he didn't share.

'All was done in your name,' Valdyr said.

'But it was your victory, Val,' Kyrik insisted. 'I hope everyone knows that.'

Valdyr nodded reluctantly. *They do know: that's also a problem.* The burghers of Hegikaro credited him and Dragan with this victory – and they did not understand why their Crown Prince had brought in these foreigners. 'We're still facing a full legion in the lower valley,' he murmured. 'This is far from won. The Vlpa will get their chance to prove their worth.'

'I know,' Kyrik replied. 'Oh – and I must tell you of our other new allies – you won't believe your eyes.'

That didn't sound good either, but Valdyr pretended to be pleased, thinking, *I have to set an example.* He turned to Hajya. 'Sister,' he greeted her, loud enough for the word to carry, and kissed her hand. He went to lead her up the steps, but she baulked.

'Wait,' she murmured as Kyrik gestured and the shaman Missef stepped from the clump of Sydians and planted a carved stave in front of him, some kind of religious icon, Valdyr guessed, with beast faces etched into it. He issued a sudden, fierce cry, making everyone recoil, except for Kyrik and the Sydians. Hajya gripped Valdyr's arm and put her mouth to his ear. 'He invokes the gods of our people, to join us in this new land,' she whispered.

Does it have to be so . . . grotesque? Valdyr thought as Missef first crouched on his haunches and keened like a fox, then launched into several minutes of caterwauling, growling, chest-beating and foot-stamping, a rhythmless dance full of ear-splitting cries that was arousing nervous reactions among the watching Mollachs. He saw more than one woman mouth the word 'animal'.

Dear Kore, Brother, what were you thinking, to let him do this?

Mercifully, Missef finished his dance, then knelt and offered his stave to Kyrik. 'He gives the Gods' blessing to the new king,' Hajya said loudly, 'in token of friendship and loyalty.'

Afterwards the Sydian warriors greeted their shaman with a palm laid on his heart, clearly moved, but everyone else just stared; this alien rite in their heartland was too much to bear. Kyrik, clearly sensing the atmosphere, strode up the steps and turned to face the crowd, to try to rekindle the earlier air of celebration. 'My Lords and Ladies, people of Hegikaro, I thank you! I had thought to lay siege to my home, but the victory is won: Hegikaro, you are *free!*'

That roused some cheers, but Valdyr suspected the shaman's display had them wondering if they might yet be besieged. *They think we've exchanged one enemy for another*, Valdyr thought. *I hope they're wrong . . .*

'But the struggle is not over,' Kyrik shouted. 'There is still a battle to be fought, to free the lower valley. An Imperial Legion – five thousand rankers – awaits us, but we can win! We have the manpower and the magi, thanks to our allies of Clan Vlpa!'

If Kyrik had expected cheers at this, he was badly disappointed. His words echoed around a silent throng.

'We will have need of *every* man,' he went on doggedly. 'We need the courage of the men of Mollach, handed down from Zlateyr the Archer to the people of Mollachia *and* Sydia. We are kindred peoples and today we celebrate that kinship and lay the groundwork for building a stronger, *independent* Mollachia!'

Those words finally raised cheers: throwing off the shackles of Pallas was a long-held dream. Dangling that possibility showed Kyrik understood that much at least.

That was smart, Brother. But you should still have left these barbarians in the wild.

Now Valdyr offered Hajya his arm, to walk her up the steps. She didn't look comfortable in the full-length dress, but he could have told her that her days in hunting leathers were gone. *You wanted the marriage and here's the price*, he thought. *Mollach queens don't hunt, Hajya. They embroider and breed.*

But what he said was, 'This is your home now.'

She looked up at the stone keep. 'It seems a cold place to raise children.'

'It's where Kyrik and I were born,' he replied, leading her up the stairs, Thraan and his riders following. On all sides the well-to-do of Hegikaro wrinkled their noses when they thought no one saw as they followed Kyrik into the dining hall and took their seats for the feast. Musicians sawed on rebecs and shook hand-drums fitted with chimes, playing the folk music of the mountains.

This is a mistake too, Valdyr thought, seeing the way the Sydians ripped at the food with fingers and teeth and flicked their waste to the floor. *They don't even understand cutlery.* As the Mollach gentry whispered behind their hands, Valdyr felt his brother's hopes that this feast might bring them together shrivelling by the minute. Finally Kyrik had enough; he clapped his hands for silence, surprising the musicians, who stopped with a discordant screech of bow on strings. Someone tittered, but Valdyr shot them a warning look that silenced them dead. *I might disagree with my brother, but I'll not see him mocked.*

Kyrik looked dispirited as he spoke. 'Friends, thank you for your attendance, but the time has come for me to show my wife her new home. I especially thank Nacelnik Thraan and his people for gracing us with their presence, as they will again.' He raised the carved staff Missef had given him. 'I am honoured by their gift, and what it signifies. I hope and pray for the day when our two peoples are one.'

From their faces it was clear the Mollach gentry had no such wish.

The volume rose as the Sydians quit the hall moments after Kyrik led Hajya upstairs: the Mollachs were eager to discuss what they'd seen. Many threw glances Valdyr's way, clearly trying to assess his reaction. Then Dragan appeared beside him, and murmured, 'There will soon be a meeting of concerned citizens, my Prince: people worried about the future of our kingdom. I wondered if you wished to attend?'

The request reverberated in Valdyr's brain. *What's Dragan asking?* he wondered. *For me to take sides against my own brother? Or to pretend I am while spying for my brother? And where does he stand?*

He decided; 'I'll attend – but Kyrik is still my brother, and my king.'

'Ysh,' Dragan replied. 'And you are still his heir.'

'That was awful,' Hajya said, and she wasn't wrong.

Kyrik turned from the window to face his wife, overawed by the fact that this was his father's castle, his father's kingdom, and this was his father's bed that he was about to lie upon. *If he was here, he'd take a stick to me.*

'Hajya, the first meeting was always going to be difficult.'

'*Difficult?* They were laughing at us behind their hands. "Primitives" – that's what I heard them call us.'

'It was hard for them: they've never met Sydians before. They'll get used to you.'

Hajya gave him a hard look. 'You know better than that. Even the Rondians aren't so alien to them as we are. And they don't think they need us now anyway, not now your "hero brother" has already won the day.'

'We *will* need your people and they'll realise it soon enough.'

Her dark face had a way of looking like stone or tree-bark when she was angry, as she was tonight. She wasn't beautiful in any conventional way, but she fascinated him: her moon-like face, her wide lips and big, passionate eyes, the tangle of her black hair and her lush, lithe body that could take anything a man gave. 'I have no regrets,' he told her. 'Especially about you and me.'

'Don't try to charm me! There was one woman with fingernails two inches long who told me I had "labourer's hands".' Hajya looked at her fingers, deep brown and leathery. 'She held her breath when I was near so she didn't have to breathe where I'd exhaled. And she wasn't the only one.'

Kyrik pulled her against him. 'Hajya, I know it's hard, but what we achieve will secure the future of the Vlpa and Mollachia. It's worth it, I promise.'

'Fool.'

She'd ridden hard to reach him, but they'd been reunited only an hour or so before they'd entered Hegikaro. This was their first moment alone. He tugged at her scarf and loosened her thick tresses, then tilted her head upwards so he could see her eyes. 'I promise you'll be happy here, in my home. And I don't want to talk any more.'

He kissed her, savouring her longed-for taste. For a moment she resisted, then they were wrenching at clothes, baring flesh as he tumbled her onto the bed, her brown skin sharp against the white covers, dragging his body free of leggings and landing atop her, kissing her again, writhing against her as his already rigid phallus sought her cleft and then he was in and riding her, their eyes locked as everything in his world came down to this one thing that took him and possessed him until he was crying out, helpless as it felt like his entire body expended itself into her.

After a minute of panting and nuzzling, she chuckled. 'Not much restraint there, my husband.'

'I've missed you, every moment of every day and night.'

She gave an earthy sigh. 'I missed you too. I didn't give up my life in the Sfera for chastity and loneliness.'

'I didn't like it either. Three months without you – or anyone else, I hasten to add.'

She raised a faintly surprised eyebrow. 'You're Kirol – if you'd asked for a woman, one would have been given – any woman in the Sfera would have gladly taken you, for a start – yours is a valuable bloodline.'

He felt a little hurt at that. 'It never occurred to me – we're *married* . . .'

'You can still strengthen the tribe. The mage-blood is a clan's strength.' She pulled a face. 'I wouldn't mind . . . so long as you didn't enjoy it too much.'

But I'm sterile, he thought miserably, the shadow of that awful revelation returning in full. But that was the last thing he wanted to speak of. She'd had too traumatic a day as it was, and so had he. 'There's no one I desire but you,' he told her. 'I'd have failed with anyone else.'

'Ha! You lie prettily.' She looked up at him teasingly. 'I'm *dark* and *primitive*, with *labourer's hands* and my teeth are yellow and I have stretchmarks and belly fat. You could do much better.'

'You're wise, passionate and strong, and I'm not worthy of you.'

She snorted. 'True, but I like you anyway. You have a way, Husband, of nobly shaming the world into seeing things your way. I like that trait, but not all will bend to your will. Some will resist, and they won't fight as fairly as you.'

'I know. But forcing people to accept my decisions won't work. They have to see the value in them – which means our two peoples must free

the lower valley together. Only then will we truly become one people.'
He stroked her weathered face and added, 'What you and I show the
world is also vital. Seeing us as husband and wife will show them it's
possible for two to be one.'

'Are you going to invite them all in to watch us, then?' she asked
archly. 'I thought you Kore-worshippers were against that sort of
thing?'

'You know what I mean! If you and I can embody the union of our
people, we'll begin the process.'

Her face softened. 'You have big dreams. I like that.'

'I swear, Hajya, I would fight every man in the valley to make this
work.'

'You may have to, Husband.'

23

The Princess and the Fey Queen

Hermetic: Healing

Some believe that any condition can be cured by healing-gnosis, but sadly this isn't so. Most of us mage-healers don't even understand what we do – we fumble around trying to restore a feeling of 'rightness' to a part of the body that feels 'wrong'. Our ignorance humbles us.

RHEA FARRINTON, NOROS HEALER-MAGE, JASTENBERG, 766

Pallas, Rondelmar, Yuros
Octen 935

The Bastion is like a tree in autumn, Lyra reflected, *shedding people like leaves until it's stark and bare.*

As winter approached, most courtiers had returned to their country estates to oversee the end of the harvest. The Sacrecour emperors used to make a grand procession through the kingdom, to remind all imperial subjects who ruled their lives – and to escape the frozen north. House Korion owned a massive palace outside Bres, where the Sacrecours were wont to repair for the Winter Court. But House Corani had no such alliances, so Lyra never left Pallas; in any case, she was heavily pregnant and frightened to leave. Ostevan and the Masked Cabal were out there somewhere, so Dirklan and Oryn Levis had increased her security: guardsmen dogged her steps and Basia slept on a couch at the foot of her bed. She was never alone, but even then, the only place she felt safe was her garden.

This blustery autumn morning, with the sun barely up, the air was chill and the dew was lying heavy on lawns covered in fallen leaves. Lyra was shivering at the cold, her child was battering her insides and everything felt like a trial. She clambered slowly down the stairs on Dirklan's arm, Basia trailing behind them.

'Just two months to go,' she groaned. 'He's kicking me to pieces.'

'"He"?' Dirklan enquired.

'Domara says so: he'll have dark hair and fair skin, she says.' But she hadn't come here to brood. 'Basia, please fetch Cordan and Coramore. It's time to begin.' Time to begin her plan to combat the ongoing misery of the Reeker shepherds they still held.

As Dirklan sat next to her on the bench to wait, she said, 'Did you know that none of the women I've asked to attend on me as ladies-in-waiting have agreed? They've all made polite excuses, then vanished to their husbands' estates.'

'To be fair, Majesty, they can't be entirely blamed for that,' Dirklan replied. 'Many are simply afraid.'

It was true that her last ladies-in-waiting had all died horribly on Reeker Night. 'I know. It's just ... I feel so lonely,' she blurted. Then she hung her head, because loneliness had contributed to her *fall* and she was still plagued with guilt, despite the knowledge that Ostevan had been manipulating her all along. *How much of me was willing?* she kept asking herself. *Surely it wasn't all the opium ...*

'Some of the women still here must be agreeable?' Dirklan asked.

'They're all wives of merchants and courtiers, with the souls of magpies.'

Dirklan smiled at that. 'What of young Medelie Aventour?'

'I do not like that young woman. And she's chasing Solon Takwyth.'

'She does wear her ambition on her sleeve,' Dirklan admitted. 'I'm worried she'll infect our good Knight-Commander with the same affliction.'

'I doubt that would take much. Is there news from the army?'

'Despatches say the pace is picking up; battle will be joined soon. In the meantime, Ril's mage-knights are scouring the enemy fliers from the skies. It's just like the jousts, Ril writes.'

Even knowing that Ril was a tourney champion didn't comfort Lyra in the slightest. Recalling mid-air collisions and adding pointed spear-heads to the equation just made her stomach churn all the more.

'What do those remaining at court gossip of?' she asked, dreading to know.

He gave her a sympathetic look. 'I'm sorry, but the story that your child is Ostevan's continues to spread. There have been pamphlets printed – it's this new woodcut printing. They're crude, not fit for your eyes, my Queen.'

She closed her eyes, dying a little more inside. Every time she held court now, she could feel the scorn, even though she'd done no more than kiss her faithless confessor whilst in a drugged haze.

If I were a man would they be so contemptuous? she wondered futilely.

Then Basia reappeared at the Greengate with Mort Singolo, the giant bald warrior nicknamed the Axeman; he was followed by a full cohort of twenty Imperial Guards, escorting two smaller cloaked and hooded figures who were being led by the hand.

'Good morning, my Queen,' Mort called.

'Good morning. You had no problems, I hope?'

'None, Milady. They're both quiet – and they haven't had the chance to interact.'

Dirklan waved the two prisoners forward, then untied the taller one's hood. Cordan Sacrecour's face was white, his eyes huge with unshed tears. He glared at Lyra. 'What's happening? What are you going to do to me?' Then he noticed the other hooded shape. '*Cora?*'

'She can't hear you,' Basia said. 'I've blocked her hearing. Don't worry, Cordan, we're here to help her.'

Cordan didn't believe her. 'Are you going to chop our heads off?'

'Never!' Lyra exclaimed. 'We have no wish to hurt you – and you're both protected by an interdict from the Keepers, regardless.' She put her hands on his shoulders. 'Cordan, I'm *not* your enemy. One day, our Houses will need to bury our ill-will. Let's start today.'

Cordan looked towards his sister. 'You've not let me see her since that horrible Reeker Night,' he grizzled. 'Not even once, so that I knew she was alive!'

'I'm sorry – there were reasons. She's not been well.'

Something in the way she said it finally struck home and he winced. 'Do you mean like those . . . people?'

'Yes,' Lyra said sympathetically, 'just like that.'

Cordan bit his lip, determined not to cry in front of these Corani men. On Reeker Night he'd been paraded before the court by the Masked Cabal and he'd seen the Reekers up close.

'What do you mean about helping Cora?' he asked.

'We're going to take you both deeper into the garden – just Dirklan, Mort, Basia and me. Once we're in there, I'm going to give her a drink that I hope will help her. It's just water – but it's special. She's had it before, but not inside the garden.'

'*Water?*'

'Magic water.'

'There's no such thing as magic,' Cordan sniffed. 'It's the peasants' word for things they don't understand.'

'You'll see.' Lyra signalled and Mort took Coramore's shoulders and guided her through the Rose Bower. The remaining knights and guards looked uncomfortable to be left behind, but Lyra fancied they were relieved too: no doubt her garden had developed an eerie reputation of late.

Cordan tried to take his sister's hand, but Mort blocked him. 'No, boy. Not a good idea. Follow me.'

Lyra led them to the pool, where the Winter Tree sapling flourished. Beside her, Dirklan and his fellow magi were watchful. Cordan was puzzled and scared, but Coramore, unable to see or hear, was still quiet.

'Take off her hood and release the spells,' Lyra said to Mort. 'She needs to see that Cordan is unharmed.'

'Be ready for anything,' Dirklan advised. 'She may become violent once her senses engage with this place.' He turned to Cordan. 'This may distress her, Cordan, but please remember – she is *not herself* right now.'

The prince swallowed, but he nodded to show he understood.

Mort removed Coramore's hood and released the spells and her eyes fell open. For a moment she was petrified by fear, then she saw Cordan. '*Brother!*' She strained against her bindings and Mort's grip, trying to go to him.

'Cora!' Cordan replied, looking at Lyra imploringly. 'Please, can I—'

Then Coramore's face changed: her eyes rolled, then darkened, and she pulled back her lips to expose her teeth. Her voice dropped to a vile rasp. 'Why, it's the Bed-wetter! Still pissing yourself, you spineless turd?'

'*Cora?*'

'Cordan, don't listen,' Lyra warned. 'It's *not* Coramore speaking.'

Coramore turned on her. 'Shut up, *Queen Miscarriage*. My brother is no business of yours, you insipid, sanctimonious heifer. Why don't you go and fuck a priest?'

Lyra forced herself not to react. Mort's grip tightened on Coramore's shoulders as she strained against him

'What's your name, daemon?' Dirklan asked.

'Go to Hel, One-Eye. Another 909 is coming and you're powerless to prevent it—'

'Try us and see,' Basia retorted.

'Oh, I shall, Cripple,' Coramore snickered. 'I could almost pity you, but you're so good at pitying yourself I can't be bothered.'

Basia's face hardened. 'Talk all you like – at least I have a life, daemon.'

'I have a million lives, Twig-legs. I'll be there when you die to gobble up your soul. It'll be very, very soon.' The girl gave a ghastly, choking laugh that ended in a savage attempt to plunge her teeth into Mort's hand, but he clamped her skull with kinesis, grimacing at the effort.

'Stop her talking, please,' Cordan pleaded. 'I don't like it.'

Dirklan looked at Lyra and she nodded, feeling dreadful. The Volsai raised his hands and gnosis-light flared, making Coramore gurgle. The sound of her voice grew muffled as her tongue sealed to the bottom of her mouth. Her eyes blazed, but only a furious snorting came out.

Cordan was weeping, and this time he didn't pull away when Lyra put a hand on his shoulder. 'Come with me. I think I can help her, but she needs to see you do it so she knows it's safe.'

He nodded mutely.

'Brave boy.'

As she led him to the pool he looked up curiously at the Winter Tree sapling, which alone in the stark garden was covered in bright pink blossoms, then at the Leaf-Man face carved into the broken fountain.

'This is the old garden,' he said in a puzzled voice. 'I used to play here with Cora when we were little.' He looked up at Lyra and dropped his voice. 'What's wrong with her?'

'She's possessed,' Lyra said bluntly. Softening the truth wouldn't help. 'But I'm told it's not a normal possession, so to end it we're trying something different.' She bent painfully and filled a clay cup with water while in her mind she called to the dwyma. As it responded she felt a renewed sense of wholesomeness. Leaves stirred in a gentle breeze and from amid the elms an owl hooted, a low and mournful sound. She raised the cup into the air. 'Lady Aradea,' she called, 'bless this cup.'

'Aradea's a faery-tale – she doesn't exist,' Cordan said, looking around fearfully.

Lyra didn't respond; she was caught up in the warm rush of Aradea's touch as the unseen presence enfolded and sustained her. The notes of the water-drops in the fountain changed, resonating to a secret song. The Leaf-Man's eyes were open, watching her solemnly.

Lyra presented the cup to Cordan. 'Please, drink.'

Cordan took the cup in trembling fingers. She doubted anyone here had been really aware of her communion with the genilocus, but Cordan had clearly sensed something strange. He took a sip and frowned. 'It's just water.'

'To you, yes,' Lyra said quietly. She topped up the cup and went to Coramore.

The girl's demeanour became fearful. 'No!' she screeched, 'take it away!'

'You know what to do,' Lyra said to Mort and Basia.

While her bodyguard restrained Cordan, just in case, Mort gripped the girl's head with kinesis, then pinched her nose – and after a horrid struggle, her lips finally parted. Lyra tipped the full cup of water into Coramore's mouth and Dirklan clamped it shut before she could spit it out again. For a few seconds she resisted, but Dirklan was stroking her throat and at last she convulsed and gulped it all down. She fell to her knees and then onto her side, but they kept hold of her until they were sure she'd not try to vomit everything straight back up.

Cordan had stopped struggling and was watching, gnawing on his knuckles. Lyra pulled him against her side and turned her face into her shoulder. 'This water helped save her life on Reeker Night,' she murmured. 'I hope this time it might purge her completely.'

Together they watched Coramore twitching, then she curled into a foetal position – until, with an awful moan, her back arched and she vented a gush of liquid from her bowels that stained her dress and filled the air with a vile stench.

'Is she going to die?' Cordan cried. 'Cora? *Sister?*'

Lyra held him back. 'Wait.' She glanced at Dirklan. She could feel something building, almost as if there was too much air in the garden. Her eardrums popped and her skin trembled. Coramore was lying on the ground, writhing and whimpering as if in a bad dream—

—and then vines shot from the undergrowth, enveloping the girl. Cordan cried out as his sister screamed, but the vines moved with frightening speed and hauled her up into the tree. She was out of reach before Dirklan, Mort and Basia, combat veterans all, had even managed to draw their weapons.

They could see Coramore enmeshed in the tangle of vines. Something hissed inside Lyra's skull and she warned them, '*Put your blades away!* She doesn't like them.'

The three Volsai looked at each other, then wordlessly sheathed their weapons.

'What's happening?' Cordan whispered.

'I don't know,' Lyra answered, but she didn't sense violence, only a silent struggle as Coramore hung splayed in the vines, her skin chafed and bleeding from the rough handling, her mouth working silently – and then dozens of tendrils plunged into her skin and she howled as her veins bulged and turned black. The vines pulsed, and now Lyra could see that they were sucking dark fluids from her body . . .

. . . and in a few seconds it was over.

The vines that had pierced Coramore withered and died, collapsing like dead serpents and crumbling, while the thicker cords sagged and loosened. Mort caught the girl with kinesis as she fell and laid her gently on the ground.

'She's alive,' the Axeman panted in relief after checking her over.

Then Coramore coughed and her eyes opened. Her skin was covered with small bleeding holes; she was shaking and looked terrified. 'Cordan!' she wailed, and her brother flew to her arms.

Lyra was profoundly shaken, but hopeful. 'Burn those,' she told Dirklan, pointing at the withered vines that had leached the princess. The Sacrecour children were staring at each other intensely as they whispered, glancing at her occasionally. Then they finally gripped hands and came towards her.

'Am I safe now?' Coramore asked, her voice tentative, as if she was scared to hope. 'Is the *beast* gone?'

'The beast?' Basia asked.

'*Abraxas,*' Coramore whispered. 'That was its name. It came when the masked woman *bit* me.'

Lyra looked at Dirklan, wondering whether she could trust this. *Is she really cured – or exorcised? – or is this still the daemon speaking?* Then Coramore plunged to her knees and seized Lyra's hand, and it took all her fortitude not to snatch it away.

But the princess was only kissing her hand, and now Cordan was kneeling too, and pressing his lips to her other hand.

'You brought Cora back,' he said, his face amazed. 'You used *magic* and brought her back.'

'I hope so,' she said. 'Let's see if it lasts.'

'Abraxas has gone,' Coramore said, her voice thick with emotion. 'I'm *sure* of it.'

Cordan touched Lyra's hand to his forehead, an old gesture of fealty. 'I don't know how to thank you,' he said stiffly.

'You don't have to,' Lyra replied. 'You're still my heir, if anything happens to my child. And we're *family*.' She hugged them, feeling kinship for the first time.

After such an ordeal, it felt awful to have to send the two children back to Redburn Tower, but they needed to ensure Coramore really was permanently freed of possession – and of course, they were still potential targets for her enemies. Lyra promised she would move them to the royal suite as soon as they were certain the possession had been truly broken.

Mort and the guardsmen escorted them out, leaving her with Dirklan and Basia, who were gazing at her with awe.

'The very best healers couldn't help her,' Dirklan said. 'Not even the Keepers.'

'It was *heresy*,' Basia reminded them. 'If she really is cured, there are going to be a lot of questions. I don't know how we can answer them all.'

They shared a worried look, and all at once, Lyra felt exhausted. Even the climb back to her apartment felt beyond her. So she sat down with Dirklan on a bench while Basia hovered nearby.

'I'm sorry to bring this up when you've only just solved one major problem,' Dirklan said quietly, 'but I've learned of a new conspiracy against you. Some members are known, but if we move too soon, some may evade us. Are you comfortable with me just maintaining surveillance at present?'

'I trust your judgement, Dirklan. Act as you see fit.' She took his hand and asked, 'How many more of these Reeker shepherds do we have locked up?'

'There are six left,' Dirklan replied.

'Then make preparations to bring the rest here, one a day. If Coramore can be saved, so can the rest of them.'

She thought she saw pride in her spymaster's eyes as he bowed over her hand, kissed her signet and hurried away.

We can beat this, she thought. *And we'll beat you too, Ostevan, wherever you are.*

Escaping those who hunted him had been easy enough. Ostevan Jandreux had all sixteen of the gnostic studies at his disposal and the power of an Ascendant; he'd changed shape and appearance within seconds of sensing the explosion of power in the Queen's Garden. He'd effortlessly brushed off the attempts to scry him, and the one thing he really feared – that Lyra might somehow bring the dwyma to bear against him – never materialised.

For all that, it was a bitter defeat.

To be torn from the heart of the Bastion, where he'd laired like a fox in a henhouse, was galling. To have come so close to tasting Lyra's succulent body and soul, only for her to be pulled from his jaws, was beyond frustrating. And to know that his ambitions of ruling both Bastion and Celestium had been ruined was devastating.

Worst of all: he had to tell the Master.

After a few days in hiding, castigating himself for his stupidity and trying to think up excuses that might save his neck, he'd finally worked up the courage to contact Naxius. He chose an abandoned shepherd's rick on the Eastern Road, twelve miles out of Pallas, to make his confession. Running or lying wasn't an option, not when Abraxas was inside him. He needed Absolution – an irony that was bitter to the taste.

'Master,' he breathed, kneeling as a dark shape blurred from the skies and took form in the shadowy meadow.

Ervyn Naxius was here in spiratus form; his physical body could be anywhere in Yuros. He chose to appear masked as the Puppeteer, but his eyes remained the same: ancient and callous. 'Ostevan,' he replied, looking down, 'you've been hiding from me – I had to hear secondhand that Ostevan Comfateri had fled after being unmasked as a conspirator against the queen.'

Ostevan hung his head. 'I overstepped and betrayed myself.'

He knew better than to resist when the Master's fingers gripped his hair, accepting the pain as his due.

'In what way did you overstep?' Naxius snarled.

'I tried to drive a wedge between Lyra and Ril Endarion so that she would instead fall in love with me. But she realised somehow, and I was unmasked.'

'Is she infected with the ichor?'

'No,' Ostevan admitted, wincing.

The Master was most definitely not pleased. 'Why not?'

'Because it was too soon and the infection couldn't have been concealed.'

'Then why did you go near her at all?'

Because I couldn't help myself. 'It was a mistake.'

'You're admitting that you've jeopardised everything we're working towards – to achieve *what*? To persuade her to yield willingly what you could as easily have taken by force? I am *perplexed*, Ostevan.'

Ostevan took a deep, deep breath, knowing he could die here if he chose the wrong words. 'Yes, I wanted her to yield willingly,' he started. He dared to look up, because he needed Naxius to believe this, to believe that all this was misguided cruelty and not an attempt to gain a weapon against him. 'Corrupting the innocent is more gratifying to me than rape.'

Naxius' mouth twitched. 'I see . . . But it was still folly.' His spiratus-hands seized Ostevan's skull in such a way that snapping his neck would be effortless.

'Yes, it was folly.' Ostevan closed his eyes. *This is it . . . This is the end . . .* Except it wouldn't be, because in the aether, Abraxas waited.

Naxius laughed, the sound like a snake hissing. 'So, the cunning priest is brought to his knees by his own cleverness. I see your mind, Ostevan. You sought to control the queen while also seizing the Celestium, leaving poor, hardworking Sister Tear with nothing. Not only that, but you withheld infecting Lyra not for fear of revelation, but for fear of damaging her link to the dwyma – because you hope one day to tame her and make her your weapon. Am I wrong?'

Denial was pointless. 'No, Master.'

'I admire your ambition, Priest, and your imagination. But these things have occurred to me already. Daemons and dwyma are inimical: they cannot coexist – as Brother Twoface found, the dwyma is one of very few things that can destroy us.'

'But the Easterners boasted of using the dwyma to destroy Midpoint Tower—'

'They infected a dwymancer,' Naxius replied, 'but from then on, they had only a small window of opportunity before the dwyma recognised what had been done and rejected her. I want the queen infected or dead: there's no other way, *fool*.'

Ostevan closed his eyes again and surrendered to the inevitable as Abraxas snarled and jabbered threats in his head. *The Master sees through me . . . I'm doomed . . .*

But to his amazed relief, Naxius dropped his hands, and stepped away. 'I will spare you for now, Brother Jest. You have erred, but you still have value.'

'Thank you, Master,' Ostevan croaked.

'Take the Celestium and your error will be expunged,' Naxius rasped. 'Fail, and you know the price.'

'You are merciful—'

'Merciful? No, I'm practical. Time is running short and I wish this matter resolved, so that we may move on to the conquest of all Yuros. Get inside the Celestium and bring down the grand prelate.'

'And the queen?' Ostevan asked, keeping his face submissive.

Naxius' voice filled with malice. 'Leave her to me.'

24

Father to Son

Noros

*Noros is a country of primarily Frandian peoples who settled there during the east-
ward migrations of their kind. They made peace with both Rimoni and Rondelmar
and only ever rebelled in the ill-advised Revolt of 909–910. That the Revolt lasted
as long as it did can be attributed partially to the tenacity of the Noros resistance,
but primarily to the inability of the Rondians to take it seriously.*

Ordo Costruo Collegiate, Pontus, 922

Jastenberg, Noros
Octen 935

Ari Frankel stared at the weathered door. There was little to distinguish
it from hundreds of others, but for the chipped green paint and the
weathered *Sol et Lune* symbol on the lintel. The damp, muddy alley was
a hundred or so yards west of Cuimbrae Square, in south Jastenberg,
and he'd not walked down it for eleven years. This was the house where
he'd been born and raised.

'Are you sure you want to do this?' Neif asked.

'They're my parents,' he replied. 'I have to.'

'To quote one Ari Frankel: "My parents are the sort of ignorant bigots
I speak against". Date: yesterday.'

'I was drunk at the time.'

'Why are you here?' Lothar asked. 'If it's to abuse the people who
birthed, raised, clothed, fed and educated you well enough to despise
them, it's an unworthy purpose.' The towering Bek nodded in support.

'Father would applaud if the Inquisition locked me up,' Ari admitted. 'And Mother thinks that dew is formed of Kore's tears. But I miss her cooking.'

They all looked at each other doubtfully as Ari rapped on the door. It opened a few seconds later to reveal a scruffy man with several days' growth on his chin and a shock of thin grey hair not really covering a sunburned pate. 'What'n Hel d'you—' he began, then he stared. '*Ari?*'

Ari raised both arms, thinking his father might maybe hug him, but Cuthmann Frankel made no move other than to shout, 'Magga!' over his shoulder, then ask gruffly, 'What d'ye want, boy?'

'Just ... um, just visiting, Father,' Ari replied, dropping his arms. 'I'm passing through Jastenberg and—'

'Yer nae in uniform, ah see,' Cuthmann said. '*Magga!*'

A woman in a dirty smock and apron appeared, red-faced and sweating from the kitchen. She looked anxiously at the visitors, then saw Ari and shrieked, '*Boy?*'

'Um, Mother ...'

She burst into tears and Ari tentatively stepped forward and put his arms around her, which made her cry all the harder.

'We en't got food for ye and yer friends,' Cuthmann said, his voice stony.

'We've brought some,' Bek answered, proffering the bag they'd purchased earlier.

Cuthmann wavered, clearly wondering if he could accept it and then tell them all to piss off, then he stepped back. 'S'pose ye should come in, then.' He led them into the kitchen and sat heavily in one of the three chairs, while Magga tipped out the produce and muttered to herself as she grabbed pans and a knife. 'What're ye doing 'ere?' Cuthmann demanded, picking up his tankard and finishing what smelled like weak ale. 'Ain't got a spare drop,' he added.

'Oh, that's all right, we brought our own,' Neif said dryly, pulling out bottles of a better brew.

Cuthmann looked sour until Neif pushed one in his direction.

'Obliged,' he muttered. 'So, you was sayin', boy?'

'I've been speaking in the squares for two weeks,' Ari said, vaguely surprised his father didn't know, then he reminded himself that in his family, square-speakers were considered parasites and vermin.

'Have ye?' Cuthmann considered. 'What about?'

'Society,' Ari replied, playing it safe.

'Ye should be with the feckin' army,' Cuthmann grumbled. 'Ye all should be.' He looked at Bek, the tallest of them. 'Specially ye, ye big lug.'

'We're lay priests, Father,' Ari replied, though that hadn't been true for a while.

'Thought ye were workin' up north?'

'We were. But . . . um . . . we were sent here.'

'It's lovely that you're back,' Magga chirped. 'If you want your old room—'

'—ye can't feckin' 'ave it,' Cuthmann interrupted. 'It's rented, to a fellah what pays actual *coin*, an' 'as a proper *job* – workin' for *me*. Doin' the job *ye* should be doin'.'

'Father, I'm not suited to being a tanner—'

'"I'm not suited to be a tanner, la-de-rukking-dah",' Cuthmann sneered. 'Me 'ands is all soft and precious an' I ain't cut out for real work. So I runned off an' became a feckin' "lay priest", whatever the Hel that is!'

'It means we're unordained,' Lothar said, unwisely, 'but we're apprenticed—'

'Apprentice feckin' priests,' Cuthmann snorted. 'Unpaid layabouts, more like.'

'It takes *coin* to be a priest, and *exams*,' Neif sniffed.

Mostly coin, Ari reflected, *which is why none of us got ordained.*

'Not just any riff-raff can do it,' Lothar added, *really* unwisely.

'Well, good thing me layabout son en't riff-raff, eh?' Cuthmann jeered. 'I wanted a son to work me bus'ness, so's I can rest as befits me age. But Kore saw fit to give me a lily-handed get.'

Why, Ari thought, *did I bother coming here?*

The evening passed awkwardly. Bek helped Magga cook – although Cuthmann told him not to; 'It's wimmin's work, big 'un.' – while Ari tried to explain himself.

'I'm taking time away from the stress of the Church to preach, Father.'

'Stress? *Stress?* Ye don' know what stress is, ye pansified runt. Stress is nay 'avin' food enough f'table! Stress is 'avin' Tafter's thugs at yer door demandin' protection money one day an' Holdson's boys the next. Stress is pissin' blood when ye know yer got nain to take over t'bus'ness and protect yer ma if'n ye drop dead!'

That really did sound horribly stressful. 'You have blood in your urine, Father?'

'Aye, me "you-rine" runs red some days – usually after a session on Kapp's home brew.'

'Dear Kore, is Kapp still alive?'

'Nae, it's 'is son what brews now. He's a shifty prick, but at least he took over his pa's bus'ness, eh?'

Serving the meal brought some respite, and Magga joined them, though apart from telling Ari that he looked like her brother Kennet, who'd died when he was twelve, she had little to say. Cuthmann hogged the conversation, complaining bitterly about the taxes and tolls that were destroying any profit in his business.

'Local mayor and guilds all protest, but Guv'nor down in Norostein don' give a shit,' he grumbled, 'an' now them army boys comin' through 'as made it worse. Ev'rythin' costs more an' folks got men billeted on 'em what eats their grub an' don' pay. Young wimmun 'ave t'carry knives, an' still some's been forced, an' there's a whole lot more silly doxies 'ave lifted they skirts willingly an' be knocked up now, life ruined afore it's even started.'

'Have you got a baby yet, dear?' Magga asked.

'Mother, I'm not married. I'm a *priest*.'

'Oh, yes . . .'

Cuthmann Frankel had been a legionary during the Noros Revolt; he was a survivor of the Lukazan campaign, captured during the infamous surrender of General Vult. 'Ye lads should join t'army,' he repeated. 'They actually *pays* folk – might make a man o' ye. Word is, they's about to collide wi' 'em Noorie bastards in the Brek'len. Be a swag o' plunder. Them darkie princes is rich as senators, I 'ear.'

Bek was making a show of being interested, but Neif and Lothar went into a meditative trance as he went on, 'Gen'ral Robler, now 'e was a real gen'ral, not like yer nance Ril Endarion. "Prince-Consort", fer feck's sake! He's got his legions strung out from Augenheim to Collistein while the Noories burn Verelon unopposed. You mark these words – 'e's headin' for a feckin' disaster.'

Ari wouldn't have given a jot for his father's views, but everyone was saying much the same. 'We're the Rondian Empire, Father. Our legions are unbeatable.'

'The Hel they are! The Noros Revolt showed 'em that! An' we're not bloody Rondians, either: we're *Noromen*, an' ye should know better'n to forget it.'

They finally escaped after another sustained and tearful hug with Magga. It was almost pitch-black out; three bells had already rung. They picked their way through the maze of alleys back to the Gate Road and headed back towards the centre.

Jastenberg, built at the crossroads of the Noros Kingsway and the Imperial Road that stretched all the way to Pontus, had long outgrown the city walls. Even this late the thoroughfares were packed with soldiers, burghers, traders and whores. The Second Army led by Brylion Fasterius and the Sacrecours had arrived in town; they were two hundred miles from the Collistein junction and had no chance of arriving before battle was joined. They were quite prepared to break the skulls of anyone foolish enough to point this out. There had been armed clashes with the Noromen garrison already. The streets were throbbing with supressed violence.

'You're right, Ari,' Neif said as they neared the rough tavern where they'd been staying, 'you were begat by ignorant commoners.'

'Salt o' the earth,' Bek defended them, when he saw that Ari wouldn't.

'Are you sure he's your father?' Neif asked. 'Leaving aside that you've got his nose.'

Ari was contemplating a scathing retort when a pair of soldiers stepped in their way and stopped. They were Inquisition Guard. 'Ari Frankel?' asked the taller of the pair, a middle-aged man solid as stone.

Neif, terrified of torture, quaked and jerked a thumb at Ari. 'He's Frankel.'

Ari couldn't really blame him. 'What is it?' he asked. 'What's the problem?'

A man in brown robes detached from the wall. He lowered his cowl to reveal a smooth face with tonsured grey hair and a full-lipped mouth. 'The problem, Frankel, is you.'

Seeing his former Book-Burners master was an unpleasant shock. 'Assessor Albroch – what a surprise!'

Hanzi Albroch wrinkled his nose. 'To you, maybe, but I've had my eye on you for some time, Frankel. I've heard you, railing against "the infamous corruption of Mother Church", and quoting forbidden texts as you do. I think you've supped too deeply at poisoned wells.'

Ari felt his blood go cold. 'The problems I speak of aren't heresy,' he replied. 'Illiterate priests – sinecures purchased by bribery – indulgences and remittances from sin sold like market produce. Land confiscations on trumped-up theological charges, witch-finders and illegal trials: those aren't heresies, they're crimes!'

'Ah, but I recognise the phrases you utter: quotes from Diophanius and Ceterus and others, "clean" phrases cherry-plucked from *heretical* texts. Did you keep copies of banned books, "Brother" Frankel?'

'No, of course not,' Frankel lied, hoping he'd hidden his copy of *Res Publica* well enough, because he wouldn't have put it past Albroch to have already ransacked his room. 'I just have a good memory.'

'Are you sure?'

'Quite sure,' Ari snapped. 'And I've resigned from the Hereticists, as have my friends. Unless you have specific charges, you can't lay a finger on us.'

'What an ivory tower you do live in, Frankel,' Albroch chuckled.

Ari never even saw the first blow coming, but suddenly the side of his head exploded and he was hammered sideways into Lothar. His ears were already numb when, an instant later, a mailed fist hit his belly and he snapped over at the waist like the closing of a flip-knife – then his meal came up in a gush as he struck the muddy street.

'Hey!' Neif said, backing away.

Lothar bent over Ari, while Bek interposed himself. 'Get out of the way, or I'll cut your fucking throat,' the Inquisition man snarled, poking a knife under Bek's chin.

'Unghh . . . unghh,' Ari croaked, trying to warn Bek not to move.

'Consider this a warning, Frankel,' Assessor Albroch said. 'I don't give them out lightly, but you did good work once.' He bent over Ari. 'I hear you're planning to speak tomorrow in Braiser's Lane? Don't keep that appointment, Frankel – not if you wish to keep your teeth.'

Albroch and his men sauntered off and within a few seconds Ari found himself crowded about by well-wishers, all explaining that *If they'd only realised sooner* or *If they hadn't only just arrived*, they most certainly would have shown those brutes a thing or two.

'So, are you going to speak tomorrow?' Neif asked when they finally got back to their room in the tavern, after they'd checked that their books were still well-hidden.

'What do you think?' Ari replied. He'd been working on his most ambitious speech yet, a furious denouncement of the Inquisition's current campaign of terror. The encounter with Albroch had redoubled his ardour.

'That you'd have to be suicidal,' Neif said. 'Forget it, let's get out of here.'

'But there're some stout lads following us,' Lothar argued. That he, normally the cautious one, was willing to stay puzzled Ari, although it was true that Lothar *despised* Albroch.

'You think they'll stand up to a bunch of Quizzies?' Neif sneered.

'There are people who believe in what Ari says,' Lothar retorted. 'Truth frightens the evil man, but liberates the virtuous,' he added, quoting the *Book of Kore*.

'And it's fatal to the unarmed,' Neif drawled. 'We don't need to put our necks on the line here.'

'We could go south – or wait until the army moves on?' Bek suggested.

'If they ever do,' Ari replied, still angry and scared. 'Albroch's a churchman – how dare he stoop to violence? He can't bully us and get away with it.'

'He *did* get away with it,' Neif pointed out.

'I want to speak tomorrow!'

'Of course you do – but *don't*, Ari! We've got pamphlets being produced in a dozen towns – something big is starting. We're getting some real donations now, from men who don't like the Church or the Crown. Don't sacrifice a strong start. It's *only* Jastenberg—'

'It's my *home*. They threatened me in my own home!'

'Aye: it was Albroch – it's what he does. Let it pass.'

But the more they told Ari to stop, the less inclined he was to listen, until finally Neif threw up his hands and stomped away.

It was left to Bek to give him some closing advice. 'If you're going to do it, make sure you've got an escape route ready.'

'PEOPLE OF JASTENBERG!' Ari Frankel roared, gazing from his barrel over the sea of faces crammed cheek to jowl in the square at the head of Braiser's Lane. 'WELCOME TO A MOVEMENT OF THE PEOPLE! WELCOME TO THE DAWN OF SUFFRAGIUM IN THE RONDIAN EMPIRE!'

A ragged cheer greeted him from forty or fifty ragged young men near the front; he picked out faces familiar from previous rants. They'd just heard that the soldiers and Inquisitors had marched that morning to Collistein Junction. The relief had him jumping out of his skin.

'You think our leaders are set in stone? You think nothing can change them?' He jabbed a finger skywards. 'Not my words, but those of a Lantric scholar, six hundred years ago, railing against the tyrannical might of the Rimoni Empire: he *despaired* that such a mighty behemoth could ever be brought low, little knowing that *in his lifetime* the magi of Pallas would rise up and destroy the Rimoni stranglehold—'

'One tyranny for another!' someone shouted from near the front, brave in a crowd. *Seditious words.* That was the line Ari had to stay the right side of. He could see uniforms at the edge of the gathering. But there was an irresistible energy to the sweat and heat and upturned faces, straining eyes and ears to hear something – *anything* – that might change their lives.

'What is suffragium?' a man shouted – likely someone Neif had primed.

'You are,' Ari shouted back. 'You are the People, those who will vote for every ruler and every law – join this movement and you will gain *suffrage*: the right to vote for your chosen leaders! *You the People are Suffragium.*'

'The Sufferers?' a few echoed, mangling the word, and Ari felt a momentary flicker of irritation – and then his brain caught fire. 'Yes: you are the Sufferers: those who must endure the rule of despots and tyrants! *You are the Sufferers!*'

'Aye,' they roared back, as the term took root, '*Aye!*'

The Sufferers . . . why not? Sometimes spontaneous things work best.

'Surely voting for a leader is better than dying to get rid of one?' Ari shouted. 'Because Kore knows, they're all out to get each other – why do Dupeni hate Corani and all the rest, if they're *all* the chosen of Kore? Why can't our poor empress – *Kore Bless her name* – sleep secure in the loyalty of Garod Sacrecour?'

'Backstabbing cock-tugger!' another man bellowed, because this was Noros and it was fine to criticise Garod, especially when his soldiers had left that morning.

'Ask any honest mage – *if you can find one* – about the gnosis, and he'll tell you it's a *tool* he's been born with,' Ari went on. 'So I ask this: does a *tool* give a man the right to *rule*?' The innuendo got a broad laugh and he went on, warming to his theme. 'Does the sword make a man a better ruler, or just a better killer? "Cast down the warlord, for he is not fit to rule", says Chapter Seven, Book Nine of the *Book of Kore*. *What's the difference between a battle-mage and a warlord?* "Give weapons to our protectors, and counsel to our leaders" – Chapter Twenty-Four, Book Two. Kore sees our protectors as *different people* from our rulers – but the Pallas magi don't!'

He caught his breath, letting the crowd digest that. *These aren't easy concepts*, he reminded himself. *Let them think it through.* He took a slurp of ale from Neif's flask, then turned back to the gathering.

'The *Book of Kore* also says: "Put aside the plough of your birth and find the path Kore has made for you". Think on that: Kore *wishes* us to find our *destiny*, guided by *His* principles. "Be virtuous, and learn your own strengths", His book says. Find the life you're best suited to, using your gifts to serve others, and you'll find happiness and peace. If you love the soil, till the soil, for you'll till it better than a man who doesn't love the soil. If you love to weave, then weave, for you'll master it with your love. If you love children, nurture our children, and they will be better people for your love. So it follows that if you're born with the vision and skill to lead a community, then you're better suited to do so than some privileged prince with a sword of gnostic fire. Have our magi overlords brought us peace and prosperity? I think you, the people of Noros, know the answer.'

'*AYE! NOROS FOR EVER!*'

Take that, Albroch, he thought fiercely. Looking across the crowds, hundreds of men and a fair few women, packed into the square, he glimpsed armoured men at the rear – but the very air was alive with inspiration. The first battle of the Noros Revolt had been fought just seven miles from here.

'Remember the Battle of Jastenfeldt-Nord?' he shouted, 'and Morbenholt Forest? The Blackstand – Lukhazan and Knebb – these are the names that live in our memories, the places where our kin sought a dream: the places where all the platitudes that Pallas gave us, promising to rule with justice, were revealed as lies . . .'

He was in full flow now, making eye-contact with the most enthusiastic below him, hands waving as if he could conjure visions to match his words. Caution was forgotten; there was only *truth*.

'They tell us the Treasury is empty – but does Pallas suffer? The Hel it does! It's we who suffer: *we the Sufferers* – it's us who must march in their armies – we can't even cross a culvert without paying a toll . . . but do the dukes and earls go without? Does our empress and the priests she's bedding? Who chose them as our rulers? No one – they stole that privilege from the people they pretended to liberate.'

There were guards moving in now, and Neif and Lothar were looking panicked. Bek was glancing anxiously towards the alley behind them. A good two-thirds of the crowd were roaring in support, punching the air at each point; but plenty were shouting him down, invoking Kore, shouting praise of the empress. This was a spark away from a riot.

And a riot might give him his only chance of evading arrest . . .

'FREEDOM,' he hollered. 'Let us set our own taxes – and spend them here – let a Noroman lead us, not a foreign empress – let us choose our ruler, and his successor too: *that* is the essence of suffragium, choosing your destiny – choosing your masters and making them accountable: *FREEDOM!'*

'*LONG LIVE THE SUFFERERS*,' Neif shouted over him, and then everyone was crying out the phrase.

A guard tried to break through the people packed in the front, but someone punched the helmeted man in the face and the spark became a fire. A facultor from the governor's office ordered a cohort forward, but there was nowhere for the crowd to go. Hands seized at the hafts of the guardsmen's halberds; onions and fruit snatched from stalls flew through the air as women screamed and men shouted.

Across the square, Hanzi Albroch fixed Ari with a stare, then clamped a hand around his own throat, his message clear: *You'll hang.* Then Ari's barrel was knocked over, he fell into Bek's grasp and was hauled backwards. A rough hand clamped on his shoulder. He looked up and froze. '*Father?*'

Cuthmann Frankel's unkempt hair was wet with spilled ale, but his eyes were steady. 'That what ye think, boy?'

'Yes, Father.'

Cuthmann shook his head, as if mystified. 'I'm a tanner, me, like me Pa. Ain't never wanted else . . . Nae like ye.' Behind them, the crowd shoved, held at bay only by Bek's tree-trunk legs and arms. 'Doin' aught else en't in me. Like bein' a tanner en't in ye, I see.' He put his mouth to Ari's ear. 'Best ye run, son.' Then he turned and waded into the press, shouting, '*Noros voor de mensen! Noros voor de vrij!*'

Neif collared Ari, shouting, 'Let's get the Hel out of here—'

'No – no, let me stop this!' Ari shoved his friend away and clambered onto a hitching rail close to a wall. He caught his balance, then he yelled, 'STOP – *STOP!*' It was insane enough to make as few of the brawling crowd stop hitting each other, though they kept jostling. Ari thrust a finger at the Noros Governor's facultor. 'You! Are you a Noroman?'

The man's eyes bulged. 'Aye, and proud of it—'

'Then tell your men to stop attacking other Noromen!'

'Then get your rabble out of their way!'

So Ari shouted, '*LET THESE GOOD MEN THROUGH! THEY'RE JUST DOING THEIR JOB!*' The crowd looked startled, and even his own father was looking at him like he'd gone mad – although that was a more or less familiar expression. 'I mean it,' Ari shouted, 'let them through: mine is not the only voice that should be heard here – let the good *imperocrat* persuade us of his beliefs; let him explain his loyalty to the empress so we can bow down before it.'

Ari jumped down from the hitching rail – landing before a guardsman with a bleeding nose and a furious expression. 'Ari Frankel,' he said, offering his hand.

The guardsman balled his fist, but the facultor grabbed his arm and glared at Ari. He was a florid man, with greying hair and plastered in sweat. 'Enough of that. You're under arrest for inciting rebellion against the empress.'

'I don't recognise her authority. This is Noros.'

'Well, I recognise it, and that's what matters, shit-stirrer.' He picked two soldiers. 'Take him.'

Ari's supporters closed in, fending off the soldiers, and the tension levels shot back up. 'No, wait,' Ari said, 'tell us why you support the empress, and I'll come quietly, Facultor . . . ?'

'Barien Fletter – and I don't have to tell you anything.'

'No, you don't *have* to, but you could.'

Fletter looked about worriedly, realising that the violence might be far from over. Then his natural belligerence kicked in. 'All right: you might mean well, but there's gonna be blood, so I'm shutting your blathering gob before it gets someone killed.'

'So you're *protecting* us all from the empress?'

'I'm protecting us all from you!'

Ari ignored that. 'So your job is to prevent Noromen from criticising foreign tyrants?'

'People die in rebellions, imbecile – you might remember we tried it, and look where it got us—'

'Better to have never tried, eh?' Ari snarked.

'I'm not saying that.' Fletter jabbed a finger under Ari's nose. 'I fought, I did my bit. I came back to a burnt-out house and found my wife had gone off with a Brician trader. We're not going through that again.'

There was a murmur from those listening – of recognition, if not support.

'I agree, why should we?' Ari said. 'Why should we have to? An unwanted ruler should step aside, not trample their subjects! If a ruler must enforce their reign with violence, where is their right to rule?'

'Aye,' his supporters shouted, bunching in closer, and more pushing broke out.

'Noros has a king,' Fletter answered, his homely face uncertain now.

'An emasculated puppet since the Revolt,' Neif sniffed from somewhere behind Ari. 'He can't even name an heir. When he dies, the governor gains the rest of the king's authorities and becomes Duke of Noros.'

Which was true, and caused more rumblings of anger in the gathering.

'That's the way the world is,' Fletter shouted, 'laws are laws. If they change, I'll enforce the new ones. Listen, I get it: there's a lot of anger, and I feel it too, but when you're locked up with lions, you don't goad them.'

'Mustn't upset those Rondian lions,' Ari said, deliberately snide.

'That's it – I've had enough of you, disturbing the peace, inciting a riot: you're under arrest—'

'That's not good enough, Facultor Fletter,' a new voice said. They all turned as Assessor Albroch's two Inquisition men shoved the town guardsmen aside and the assessor came forward. 'You have *under-charged* him.'

Fletter's jaw came out. 'Back off, Albroch.'

'I will not. This fine fellow is a heretic, like the scum he attracts.'

Those words washed over the angry crowd like pepper-dust, and many growled in displeasure. But to Ari's surprise, Fletter wasn't cowed. 'Laws are my concerns; sins are yours, Assessor. He's *my* prisoner.'

'I heard heresy,' Albroch persisted. 'That makes him mine.'

'I didn't hear heresy at all,' Fletter replied. 'You're entitled to petition the governor for his custody, but while he's my prisoner, he's none of your business. Come back when you've got the right paperwork.'

'Are you protecting a heretic, Fletter?' Albroch asked, in menacing tones.

'Are you threatening me?'

'I'm offering you the chance to avoid wrecking your career. You appear to consider yourself a realist, so I'll tell you of a greater reality.' Albroch stabbed a finger at Ari. 'This *whoreson* is at the heart of a movement whose ideas are being propagated across the south by pamphleteers and rebels. Ideas can take on a life of their own, Facultor. Men he's never met are speaking of insurrection and rebellion and this "suffragium" nonsense – all because of *his* words. While real men are marching to war, he's dividing us against each other.'

'Then petition the governor.'

Albroch scowled. The Noros Governor's office was infamously slow, and apt to favour Crown over Church. 'Listen, Fletter, he is a heretic because I say so – and I claim him now, so hand him over.'

'No.'

Albroch stared and Ari feared the worst – then the assessor turned away.

And Cuthmann Frankel's fist crunched into his nose.

Albroch staggered, his legs buckled and he fell in the mud, blood gushing. 'That *whoreson*,' Cuthmann said, glaring, 'is *my* son. An' me wife's name is nae to be slandered by shit like ye.' Then all the pent-up aggression exploded: Ari's followers laid into the guards and the guards went for the two Inquisition men, and Fletter roared for order—

—as Neif grabbed Ari's arm and wrenched him backwards. 'Now – let's get the fuck out of here!'

They got about twenty paces before a fresh contingent of City Guard burst in from a side street, cutting off them from Lothar and Bek. The guardsmen, deciding anyone running was guilty of *something*, thrust weapons in their faces, then they were grabbed, slammed into the mud and had knees placed into their backs. Ari heard his father swearing amid the roar of the mêlée, then Fletter was bending over him.

'As I was saying,' Fletter drawled, 'you're under arrest, and the charge sheet is getting longer by the second.' Then he grimaced and added, 'We'd better get you behind bars, for your own good.'

They were hauled through the streets and hurled into a lock-up near Robler's Gate, with a dozen drunks and a sneak-thief. The stench of alcohol and piss filled the air; there was barely room to sit and no chance of rest.

Ari and Neif didn't see daylight for another five days.

25

The Dying Tree

Sorcery: Clairvoyance

If knowledge is power, then there is a case for claiming that Clairvoyance, the gath-
ering of information through the spirits of the aether, is the most powerful form of
the gnosis. If you can observe your enemy, then you have a tremendous advantage.
Most magi are therefore constantly vigilant against such observation.

ARDO ACTIUM, MAGE-SCHOLAR, BRES, 518

Pallas, Rondelmar
Octen 935

Cordan Sacrecour was wrapped up in his game, moving battalions of
lead soldiers, both Rondian and Keshi, into position on the large table
that filled one room in the suite he and Coramore were now sharing
in Redburn Tower. Most of the Keshis had chipped paint and broken
limbs, as he had a habit of throwing them at the wall when they 'died'.

'Prince Ril's windriders have cleansed the skies and our cavalry
charges – we sweep in from the right and left – the sultan runs, the
craven coward – but Prince Ril's on him in a flash! He skewers him
– *victory!*'

Coramore watched fondly, amused at the earnest stupidity of boys.
Today she wore a lacy dress of pale green and white, and her ginger
tresses had been teased into ringlets. She felt clean and pure and
almost happy.

But the months of having that dreadful presence in her mind had
left scars, both visible and unseen, from the episodes of self-harm as

the daemon tortured her, revelling in the pain, to the sordid, disgusting things it had forced her to do – eating horrible things, abusing her captors, instigating lusts she'd not been ready for. But Abraxas was gone: really, truly gone, and each day she felt a little more removed from his shadow.

'Is Uncle Brylion in this battle?' she called to her brother from the sofa. 'You never have him do anything.'

The queen had sent knight figures for all the heroes of the Five Armies, their colours and heraldry intricately replicated. But the Dupeni figures were at the rear of Cordan's battle-lines, and as far as Coramore could see, untouched.

'He's not even at the battle,' Cordan replied, his voice sullen with shame.

Queen Lyra – or Solon Takwyth if she was busy – visited them every day to give them news and keep them company. Yesterday, Sir Solon had confirmed that the battle in the Kedron would soon begin, but the Dupeni army had failed to arrive in time. 'The truth is, your Uncle Garod believes he can overthrow Queen Lyra more easily if everyone else fights the Noories while his men hide behind the lines,' the Knight-Commander had told them.

Neither of the children wanted to believe that, but it did sound horribly true.

After Lyra had risked her own life to heal her, it also felt shameful. When Coramore was younger she'd thought such trickery clever, but now she thought it dirty and vile, the sort of thing *Abraxas* would have enjoyed. Both of them were increasingly confused, torn between family loyalties and moral debts, right and wrong horribly twisted. 'I have a new way of deciding things,' she said. 'If the daemon would have liked it, I don't.'

'You shouldn't think about *it*.'

'I try not to,' Coramore replied, 'but sometimes bad words come out. You know I don't mean them, don't you?' She took a deep breath and asked the question that was troubling her. 'What will happen to us now, Cordi?'

'I'm going to be a Knight-Commander, like Sir Solon – I'll lead armies into battle and save the West.' Cordan had gone from resenting Solon Takwyth to idolising him.

For her part, Coramore saw him as a tragic figure, with his scarred face and his history. He'd almost died protecting the queen, and that was something she could respect. And she fancied he was mellowing. One of the maids said he was in love, but she couldn't imagine him reading poetry and wandering through bowers singing, which was apparently what lovers did.

'Well, I still want to be queen,' she told her brother, 'but I'm only twelve. There's plenty of time.'

Neither of us said we want to be emperor and empress, she suddenly realised – but that felt right in her heart, because that was Ril and Lyra's role. And wouldn't Abraxas just hate it if they ruled *for ever*?

Infiltrating the Celestium wasn't hard when most of the doors stood ajar, thanks to the thousands of nuns protesting in the Forum Evangelica. Ostevan ghosted through the vast complex undetected at will. The Sisters' Crusade had grown beyond recognition: Valetta's nuns were like an army of occupation, complete with ranks, divisions and supplies, and all eyes were on it. Donors sent in food; waste was tipped into the Aerflus and swept away. There was constant song and prayer, and the inner circle of holy women harangued the gathered crowds for hours on end. They'd even set up a tribunal for hearing complaints and had started putting guards and priests on trial – theoretically, at least – for alleged sins against women.

Ostevan could imagine Dominius Wurther's outrage, especially as many powerful people were enjoying his discomfort. Some noblewoman publicly supported the cause, and Valetta had read aloud the empress' messages of support, which made Ostevan laugh. *Bravo, Lyra! Drive a wedge between you and Wurther, just when you need him most.*

When he was grand prelate, he'd have these foolish bints swept into the river with their garbage, but for now, he had a baser purpose. With security in a mess, coming and going in secret had never been simpler, especially for someone like him. He picked a cloudy night, just after sunset, and altered his features to appear female; that was all he needed to slip through a door behind the kitchens Valetta's horde had commandeered and enter the main sanctuary.

In seconds he was a man again, Wilbur, a mage-scholar in the Scriptorium, small-built and blond this time, nothing like his true face. The remains of the real Wilbur had been disposed of in the Aerflus.

Even the doors that stealth and disguise couldn't open were no match for Ascendant strength and Abraxas; he could feel the murmur of the daemon's thousand voices as he crept through the sanctified halls, marvelling avariciously at the incredible wealth in tapestries, plate, relics, paintings and carpets.

He bypassed the Cathedral of the Sacred Heart, where the bones of Corineus were kept in a casket of gold and glass, and entered a hall that ended in a locked wooden door. He ducked from sight as a familiar monk stalked past; Mazarin Beleskey was Wurther's foremost blood-man. He'd been experimenting on captured Reekers and was quite as mad and dangerous as Naxius himself.

I wonder if they know each other?

Ostevan put that thought aside; now the real work began. The heavy door before him was gnostically locked with a kinesis-enchantment that froze the locking mechanism, bound the door edges to the frame and reinforced the door itself. The pure-blood mage who'd set it, one of Wurther's senior staff, would become aware if it was attached without guile. Ostevan had the strength to break that binding, but he had no desire to be discovered – but he had shown Abraxas the spell some days ago, and the daemon, really a conglomeration of thousands of minds, had been seeking out the spell's weak points. Now Ostevan touched the door handle and Abraxas showed him where and how to *push*. A pulse of energy rippled through the enchantment and the spell was unbalanced, pulled fractionally out of shape, enough to allow him to open the door without alerting the mage who'd set it. As he intended to come here again, he left the spell unbalanced: the door would look locked, even to gnostic sight, but in fact, anyone could now open it.

He slipped through and scanned the large triangular garden in front of him. It surrounded an earthen mound several times his height and topped by a brackenberry; even though it was autumn, it was in full blossom. This was the original Winter Tree.

The walled garden was deserted; no one ever came here. It was tucked in behind the cathedral dome but open to the rain-swept sky – although only an idiot would have tried to fly in, for the air above was well warded. There was an opening in the mound that led to a cave and the shrine of Saint Eloy, the man who'd convinced the last dwymancers to lay down their power, or so the story went.

The Master wanted Lyra infected or dead, but the fact that he'd sent Ostevan here told him that he preferred the former.

And now we know how to corrupt her . . .

Ostevan climbed to the foot of the Winter Tree; the otherwise ordinary-looking brackenberry's twisted branches were clad in small, thick leaves of deep emerald and encrusted in blossoms. It wasn't particularly impressive; the trunk was only a couple of feet wide and the canopy was thin.

There's a sapling of this tree in at least three dozen church gardens throughout Rondelmar, from Coraine to Dupenium in the north, through Canossi and Klief to the Aquillean cities in the south, and all places between. And in Lyra's garden in the Bastion . . . and who knows how many in the wilds?

The question of *why* intrigued him; it suggested a deliberately created web of power. *Which Naxius seems to be content to preserve . . .* It all intrigued him, but right now he had to follow orders and await his chance.

He pulled out his dagger and began gouging a hole in the dirt at the foot of the tree. Earth-gnosis would have been faster, but he didn't know what reaction using spells might engender – what had happened to Twoface on Reeker Night still worried him.

Naxius maintains that without a dwymancer to channel the site's power, the genilocus is unable to protect itself – but I notice he didn't come himself.

When the hole was ready, Ostevan opened his mouth and spat a vile-smelling gobbet of filthy daemonic ichor into the hole. He'd long given up caring that such stuff was present in his body. *After all,* he reasoned, *when you're a demigod, who cares how your power is sustained?*

If Lyra's garden could be poisoned by means as simple as opium and blood, what might a daemon's ichor achieve? *Corruption, my Queen. Your realm is full of it* . . .

The dream began innocently enough: Lyra was floating through clouds with the lines of Ril's latest letter running through her mind: 'We soar over the plains, using low cloud for cover, seeking the enemy fliers. It's a magical game of hide and seek, with moments of poetic savagery. But the real joy is the flying.'

Lyra's dreaming mind conjured wide expanses and brooding mountains and she soared over them, filled with a quiet joy. She was weightless, revelling in being unencumbered by her pregnant body. The sky was her father, holding her in his unseen hand; the earth was her mother, a living, growing thing that went on for ever. Every lake reflected her face as she flew above; the mountains were carven images of people she knew: Ril and Dirklan and Basia and Solon and so many others . . .

Then an unexpected voice intruded – *Lyra, come to me! Come to the Winter Tree! We* need *you!* – and a face appeared in the waters of the lake: an old man with a visage made for smiling and laughter. His head was tonsured and he wore a Sacred Heart. She'd never seen him before . . . but in her dream she knew him.

Saint Eloy? she responded. *Eloy?*

The Winter Tree – come to the Winter Tree!

Her sense of place suddenly blinked and she found herself behind the cathedral of the Celestium, in the Winter Garden – and immediately she sensed a blight, a darkness in the roots of the plants, lurking in the crawling creatures that writhed through the dirt. She recoiled in revulsion, then the voice made a final call, echoing from the underground chamber where the saint's bones lay unburied.

Lyra, come to me!

Then the tree branches became limbs: fingers and hands and fleshy tentacles with bony hooks that reached for her, growing and growing, filling the skies as she shot into the sky. A vast hand with long, dirty nails blocked out the sky as a toothy maw opened in its palm to engulf her—

—and then it was Basia's hands, shaking her awake, the bodyguard's narrow face taut with worry. 'Lyra – wake up! It's just another night-mare. It's only a bad dream.'

Lyra came to herself lying in wet sheets, her distended belly rippling as the baby squirmed and kicked. The oil-lamp beside the bed made the shadows dance like that awful hand.

'Another nightmare?' Lyra asked. 'You said "another"?'

Basia gave her a worried look. 'It's the third time it's happened to-night.'

Lyra put a hand to her heart and another to her belly. Her first instinct was that Ostevan had found another way to reach her – but it didn't feel the same . . .

That was Saint Eloy, I'm sure of it, calling to me in my dreams – and then that other thing came . . . Memory gave it a name: Abraxas.

'Tell Dirklan I need to see him,' she told Basia. 'I have to go to the Winter Tree – I think it's dying!'

The second meeting of Medelie's conspirators was again in Chaplain Ennis' house in Gravenhurst, with the same attendees. None had been idle in the meantime: messages had come and gone, with Ennis the go-between, and tentative plans had been agreed in a series of secret one-on-one meetings.

Solon Takwyth looked around the table: Jean Benoit was full of rest-less energy and Edreu Gestatium was anxious, but the woman 'Selene' affected cool detachment.

'Will we be meeting any of the exiled prelates today?' Medelie asked Ennis.

'Not yet, but they send their support,' Ennis replied, handing around a handful of promissory notes. 'As you can see, they have sent funds, a sign of their active support.' They were sizable enough sums to make even Benoit raise his eyebrows. 'We won't lack for a war-chest.'

'Then let's move to practicalities,' Gestatium proposed. 'What's our situation?'

'Very simply, a crisis will occur in the coming weeks: the Prince-Consort will die in battle, or the queen will die in childbirth, with her child. Or both.'

'You know this because you'll be *causing* these events?' Takwyth asked.

'Let's just say that we have reliable information on the matter, Knight-Commander,' Ennis replied.

Evasive to the last, Solon thought, but all he said was, 'Fair enough.'

'Once the news breaks, we must move before Setallius can react,' Ennis went on. 'Will the remaining knights and the Palace Guard obey you if you move against the queen, Lord Takwyth?'

'They will. Oryn Levis has always been devoted to me, and the men have faith in my judgement. If I tell them we need to seize control, they'll do it.'

'Good – and what of the royal children? They must also be your purview, Lord Solon: only you and Setallius have the required access to Redburn Tower.'

'I would have thought them best kept exactly where they are?' Solon replied.

'Not if we wish others to bear the blame for their unfortunate demise,' Ennis replied. 'You must discreetly retrieve them and hand them over to Lady Selene. She will do the rest.'

Solon looked at Selene. 'You? I don't even know who you are – and yet you expect me to give you the only two people around whom a credible revolt could be formed?' He glanced around the table, seeing he had the support of Medelie, Gestatium and Benoit.

'It's necessary, Lord Takwyth,' Selene said, 'that I take the children.'

'Do you know the true identity of this "Selene"?' Solon asked Ennis, his gaze fixed on the woman, who returned his stare with impassive calm.

'I do, and the secrecy is necessary.'

Solon remained unconvinced. 'Murdering children, even by proxy, is not the start a new regime requires. Cordan and Coramore Sacrecour are daggers at Lyra's throat and will become the same to me. The Sacrecours killed Corani children in 909. I deplore that. Those children will remain my prisoners.'

'No: they will be given to me,' Selene said, in a forbidding voice.

'But how will I know you won't use them against me yourself?'

'You don't.'

<I don't like this,> Solon told Medelie silently. <I won't be her puppet.>

<I don't like it either, lover. But when you're emperor, you'll have weapons you don't have now.>

No one appeared willing to budge and he wanted this coup to go ahead. Unwillingly, he gestured his acquiescence. 'Very well. I'll hand them to Selene.'

'Excellent,' Gestatium said. 'I'll secure the bureaucracy and arrest the Treasurer.'

'And I'll reassure the guilds and ensure continuity of supply to the city,' Benoit added. 'I'll also ensure that the bankers extend emergency credit to the Crown to tide us through the crisis.'

'Then my croziers and prelates will issue proclamations in support of Lord Takwyth,' Ennis concluded, 'and after that, the throne is yours, Lord Solon. Marry Lyra and take the throne, or do away with her. Either suits me.'

'The tattle about her affair with Ostevan is spreading,' Medelie chortled, 'and the common herd are turning against her. Chop off her head and start afresh. The Argundians might object, given her lineage, but they don't have the reach to oppose us.' She shared a look with Solon and silently added, <Once we let it slip that she's not Ainar's child, they'll abandon her anyway.>

With their roles settled, discussion turned to the triggering of the crisis. 'We have men watching the Crown Prince. One is particularly well-placed; he'll ensure he doesn't survive.'

'An assassin?' Solon asked, managing to keep his voice neutral.

'Jasper Vendroot's most highly placed informant,' Ennis said, with considerable satisfaction, dropping a name into Solon's mind, clearly aiming to impress him.

Solon was suitably impressed.

'Through the gnosis, we'll know almost instantly, certainly ahead of anyone else in Pallas,' Ennis went on. 'We'll still need to move swiftly to secure our targets.'

'As far as the queen is concerned, who knows what such a shock will do to her?' Selene commented. 'Plans are afoot to ensure that if the assassins fail, her own demise is triggered.' She glanced at Mede-lie. 'New blood may be beneficial – you and Lord Solon would make a most becoming royal couple.'

'As I said at the previous meeting, I place the stability of the realm ahead of personal ambitions,' Medelie replied, while Solon wondered, *Can she even have children? Is that behind this willingness to stand aside? And how long can whatever she has done to cheat death sustain her?*

During the journey back to Medelie's house in Highgrange, Solon couldn't get a nauseating image out of his mind, of making love to her as she disintegrated into a rotting corpse. He was grateful that a mage could bolster performance, because the images left him a long way from desirous of her that night; somehow, he managed, and as they disentangled from each other she purred appreciatively.

'Do you think the people at the meeting are who we all think?' she asked once she'd recovered.

'Unlike your good self?'

'Obviously,' she giggled. 'No, I meant . . . Solon, if you suspected . . . no, if you *knew* . . . that Selene was really Tear, the masked woman from Reeker Night, would you refuse to work with her?'

Solon looked away, troubled. 'The Masked Cabal infected innocents with some kind of mass possession and set them loose on the Bastion and the Celestium. We lost dozens of men and women of House Corani and hundreds of burghers had their lives destroyed. And they did it all to free Cordan Sacrecour.'

'Yes, but Tear claimed she was merely using Cordan and Coramore to lure in Garod and destroy him. She wanted Corani rule to continue, just as long as it wasn't Lyra and Ril. Isn't that exactly what we're doing?'

He hesitated, thinking, *Kore's Balls, I hate conspiracies.* But here he was, immersed up to his eyeballs in one. 'Yes, but the methods they used were evil.'

'What is "evil"?' she asked, seriously. 'Letting fools ruin this glorious empire, or sacrificing a few for the future of millions? The means don't matter, Solon, provided the goal is right and true.'

He rolled on his side to face her. 'So you think that Selene is really Tear?'

'I'm saying that it doesn't matter to me if she is, and nor should it to you if you wish to be emperor.' She stroked his cheek. 'You do want this, don't you, darling?'

'Yes, of course I do.' He hardened his gaze. 'You're right, it doesn't matter how we bring Lyra down, as long as it's done.'

26

Across the Table

Theurgy: Mysticism

What the healer is to the body, the mystic is to the mind. They can bring sanity to the lost and peace to the troubled. But they can do so much more, and that is the problem. If our minds are our final refuge, the castle and sanctuary inside ourselves, would you let a stranger tend the well?

GRAVUS MYLLATON, MEMOIRS, FAUVION, 722

Hegikaro, Mollachia
Octen 935

The tension in the air as they entered the throne room hit Kyrik like a slap to the face. The divisions weren't hard to see: all the Mollachs on his right, all the Vlpa to his left, hostility crackling across the pitted wooden table.

Kyrik glanced sideways at Hajya, today dressed in a Mollach dress of red and white, her unruly hair tamed into a coif; her face was as disturbed as his own. He placed her to his right, quite deliberately seating her at the head of the Mollach side. Valdyr, who'd been standing behind that seat, give him an unreadable glance, then shuffled sideways, forcing the other men to do the same. Dragan Zhagy represented the Vitezai Sarkanum as its gazda with Rothgar Baredge his second, Pater Kostyn represented the Church of Kore and Tabias Nanski, Mayor of Hegikaro, spoke for the people – or at least those of wealth.

Opposite them were the Vlpa's Nacelnik Thraan and his shaman Missef, the blind seer Torzo and Thraan's eldest surviving sons Groyzi and Hykkan. Kyrik had still not had the opportunity to make his peace with Groyzi and the rider wasn't hiding his dislike. Hykkan, at fourteen, would blindly follow his father's lead.

And at the end of the table Fridryk Kippenegger, the massive Schlessen, was drinking and looking utterly at ease, as if he'd not even noticed the tension – but when Kyrik looked at him, he just might have winked.

Kyrik settled into his father's throne, a tall carved wooden seat which made no allowances for comfort, and began the meeting. 'Friends, we're gathered today to plan our campaign to expel the Imperial Legion from the lower valley. May Kore bless our purpose,' he added, glancing at Pater Kostyn, then nodding to Missef and adding, 'and so too the gods of the Vlpa.'

He'd warned them both earlier that he'd not elevate one over the other but give both their due and now neither was happy: Pater Kostyn scowled at the reference to the Vlpa's pagan gods, while Missef was clearly unhappy to have his own deities mentioned second.

'Minaus blesses us also,' Kip put in, unhelpfully. 'He likes a good war.'

'I welcome you all to table,' Kyrik went on, ignoring the interjection, 'and I thank you for the vital contributions you've made to date. Mollach and Vlpa are one people, sundered by time and distance. Our common ancestor, Zlateyr the Archer, won this land many generations ago. He is remembered here, as on the plains, as a unifying leader, and it is in his name that we will conquer, regaining that which he won for us: our freedom.'

'Praise to Zillitiya,' Missef murmured provocatively.

Kyrik shot the man a warning look, then glanced at Valdyr. 'When we defeated the Delestre legion my brother had a dream-vision of Zlateyr, or "Zillitiya", which guided his gnosis. Truly, our ancestor is with us.'

He was careful to emphasise the word 'gnosis'. If he called it dwyma, Kostyn would doubtless be duty-bound to arrest Valdyr as a heretic.

'It is not the custom for the kirola to attend a council of war,' Kostyn said, eyeing Hajya distantly.

'My Queen is here as head of the Sfera,' Kyrik replied. 'We face *magi*, Pater Kostyn: prayers won't suffice.' He turned to Dragan. 'What's our condition, Gazda?'

'The Vitezai are strong, but we're a small irregular force,' Dragan replied, clearly uncomfortable about confessing the fighting strength of his people in front of the Vlpa. 'The Delestres confiscated your family armoury, but we have hidden weapons, plus our hunting bows. I believe we can field five thousand Mollachs from the upper valley, and more will join us in the lower valley as we advance.'

Kyrik watched Thraan and Groyzi absorb numbers that must sound surprisingly low to them. 'Clan Vlpa has twelve thousand riders, battle-hardened and fully equipped,' the big Nacelnik boasted. 'We can bear the brunt of the fighting.'

'It will be our victory,' Groyzi couldn't help but add.

'With Minaus' blessing,' Kip put in, *very* unhelpfully.

Groyzi glared at Kip, who ignored him, burped and swigged more ale. The Mollachs just looked at each other in confusion.

'I'm sorry, who are you again?' the mayor demanded of the big Schlessen.

'The *freisoldat* who opened the doors of Collistein,' Kip replied, raising his tankard. 'Skol!'

'Thane Kippenegger commands a small but immensely powerful unit,' Kyrik told the room. 'His people will be crucial in the struggle against the Rondians.' He silenced Nanski with a glare, then looked at Dragan. 'What do we face, Gazda?'

'An Imperial legion: five thousand men with fifteen magi. The legion commander, Legate Cavan Galrani, assumed control after the governor died.'

The mayor had contacts in the lower valley. 'Galrani is petitioning Augenheim for aid, but so far he's been denied – the Shihad's getting close and that's taking priority.'

'Is there any news of that?' Rothgar asked.

'The armies are expected to clash in the Kedron in a few days' time.'

'This is close, ysh?' Hajya said. 'If the Shihad takes Collistein, they could come here?'

Everyone went silent at that and Kyrik realised they'd all been so caught up in events here that they'd been ignoring the outside world. But Hajya was right, the Shihad could affect them directly. 'Collistein has never been taken – we only drove them from the guardhouse for a while.'

'Those fools won't be able to withstand a real assault,' Kip rumbled.

'Probably,' he conceded, 'and if Collistein falls, so will Registein.'

'I'm told hundreds of thousands of Sydian riders are riding with the Shihad,' Pater Kostyn put in. 'Perhaps the Nacelnik could explain his own people's stance?'

Thraan returned his unfriendly stare like for like. 'Missionaries of the Amteh came amongst us several times: generous men, with gifts of steel and trinkets to beguile our womenfolk. They were less arrogant than the priests of Kore so we found less reason to drive them away. But the gods of the Vlpa do not number Ahm in their ranks.'

'You drove away missionaries of *Kore* but not Ahm?' Kostyn emphasised.

'We mount the heads of Kore missionaries and leave their carcases for the wolves,' Missef replied with sullen malice, and Groyzi chuckled at the memory, baring his yellowed teeth.

'Past times,' Kyrik said placatingly.

'Two summers past,' Groyzi agreed.

'The priests of Kore were brutal when they came to Mollachia,' Rothgar stated. He was Stonefolk, not Mollach. 'But we are here to discuss a military campaign.'

'Well said,' Kip put in, raising his tankard. 'Let's talk about killing Rondians.'

'As long as it's clear that we're all on the same side,' Nanski said. 'But what would we do if the Shihad comes here, Kirol Kyrik?'

'We're Mollachs,' Kyrik replied firmly. 'We resist *all* invaders.'

'Mollachia for the Mollachs,' Nanski said slyly.

'Mollachia for those for whom Mollachia is home, from the eldest bloodlines to the newest,' Kyrik replied sharply. 'Stonefolk, Mollach, Vlpa, even Schlessen: all those whom I as Kirol welcome. We in this room are *allies*, my lords – get used to it!'

For a moment he feared his bluntness might lose them, but Kip stood. 'I'm with you, Kirol Kyrik – and you, Kirolyna Hajya!' He rather spoiled the moment by draining his ale and belching loudly.

'Hear, hear,' Rothgar added, with a somewhat self-righteous glare about the table – but then, his ancestors looked on Zlateyr not as a hero but a conqueror.

Between them, Kip and Rothgar more or less shamed the rest into doing the same and finally they were able to return to the matter at hand.

'Half of my men are here in Hegikaro,' Thraan told them, 'and the rest are in the Domhalott – which my people are calling the Dry Hills. The pastures are less than you promised, Kirol Kyrik,' he added with a glower.

'It's been a poor season,' Kyrik said. 'I warned you the Domhalott was marginal, and I do not control the weather. We'll get you feed, but perhaps you should consider culling the herds to suit your new environment?'

There were looks of consternation among the Vlpa and Thraan put a hand on Groyzi's arm to forestall an angry outburst. Even Hajya was troubled.

'Win the war and these problems will solve themselves,' Kip interjected sagely. 'So, can we get back to talking of battle?'

'Yes, let's,' Dragan agreed. 'Rothgar, where are the Rondians now?'

'They're in the legion camp outside Lapisz.'

'True warriors don't hide behind walls,' Groyzi sniffed.

'Perhaps not, but good soldiers do,' Kyrik replied, trying to forestall another round of sniping.

'They will remain encamped,' Torzo suddenly put in. The blind Sydian's head swivelled as if, despite the cloth around his eyes, he could see them all. 'They fear to stay, fear to leave. They are alone.'

'Then we have time,' Dragan said thoughtfully. 'How quickly can we march?'

'My people are always ready to fight!' Groyzi declared.

'By which my son means three weeks,' Thraan growled. 'I must inform my riders in the Domhalott, then take them into the lowlands to besiege this legion camp.'

'About the same for us,' Dragan agreed. 'The Vitezai are ready, but organising any militia takes time.'

'What about the gnosis?' Hajya asked. 'The Sfera are not battle-magi.

Do you wish us to split our resources between the clan and the Vitezai?'

That brought the table to silence again. The Mollachs had just two magi, Kyrik and Valdyr, while the Sfera numbered more than thirty, although all were low-blooded and many had never used their powers in battle. To expect them to defeat fifteen legion battle-magi was a tall order, but they could at least distract and occupy them while the rest tried to make numbers count.

'What about these "Bullheads"?' Dragan asked, looking at Kip.

'We're a secret,' Kip replied, winking and raising his refilled tankard. Kyrik had offered his people, Schlessen and Mantaur, lands at the head-waters of the Osiapa and most were already encamped there. 'Point us at the redcloaks when the time comes and you won't be disappointed.'

Everyone looked at Kyrik, who signed his satisfaction. He could see that annoyed the Mollachs, but he said no more about Kip's people.

The questions turned to Valdyr. 'Can you aid us, Prince?' Dragan asked formally.

'I'll do what I can,' said Valdyr; it wasn't much of an answer, but he couldn't promise more when he still knew so little about his power.

Kyrik tapped the map. 'We must advance on the Rondians carefully, always leaving them a retreat. If we corner them, they'll fight harder – and perhaps be reinforced.'

'You're too timid,' Groyzi growled. 'Father, we should encircle them—'

Kyrik slapped the table, interrupting him. 'Nacelnik Thraan commands the Vlpa, but *I* am Kirol in Mollachia: it is *my* decision where and how we fight. We'll muster in three weeks, during Darkmoon, then ride west as one army. In the meantime, Hajya and I will be crowned and we will renew our marriage vows before Kore. With our rule legitimised and blessed, we will go to face the Rondians.' He stood, and those around the table were forced to do likewise. 'Go forth, my friends, muster and arm our peoples. There is much to be done.'

He took Hajya's arm and left the room, feeling the simmering ill-will and tension abate just a fraction as the men dispersed in little groups. He noticed Kippenegger left with Thraan.

Kyrik held a finger to his lips and led Hajya to a gallery overlooking the main doors, to watch who left with whom. 'Does Groyzi reflect the mood of your riders?' he asked quietly as they watched the Vlpa depart, arguing among themselves.

'Many of them,' she replied. 'New beginnings are always difficult. We have to relearn how to feed our beasts, how to hunt in these new lands. The weather is different, the land is different, the plants and beasts are different. And then there's the problem of how to interact with your people. Every day brings new challenges. But our people trust Thraan. They might listen to Groyzi and agree with his complaints, but not with his solutions.'

'Which are?'

'To plunder Mollachia, then return home.'

'Then best he changes his views or he'll never take Thraan's place as Nacelnik.'

They watched the Mollach men emerge, Dragan and Nanski flanking a morose Valdyr, speaking in low voices. Kostyn was clearly trying to make a point with Rothgar, who didn't look convinced.

'I like that one,' Hajya commented. 'He listens more than he talks.'

'The Stonefolk keep their heads down here. It's been hundreds of years, but most will still tell you that the Mollachs are invaders. I worry that Clan Vlpa will still be outsiders generations from now.'

'We'll bring them all together, Husband,' Hajya replied, her voice a mix of optimism and determination.

He looked at her. The demure clothing and headdress of a Mollach wife couldn't conceal her origins. 'I liked you better in leathers,' he confessed, 'with your hair down and your legs bare.'

She returned his appraisal. 'I liked you in plain leathers also, with the wind in your hair and no crown to crease your brow. You laughed from the heart then.' She stroked his arm and added, 'We will make beautiful babies, I believe.'

I need to tell her . . .

But Paruq had said that maybe the gods would provide – and right now, there were too many other things to worry about. So he let the moment pass, hiding his unease with a kiss. 'When will you bleed next?'

'Early in the new month. I'll be fertile when you plough me on our coronation night.' She smiled up at him fondly. 'I had grown weary of child-bearing, but I think with you, my enthusiasm might be rekindled.'

'We respect the kirol, but he is wrong on this matter,' the mayor said, jabbing the table for emphasis. Around the room, people murmured in agreement. 'He should never have brought those nomads here.'

'They're savages,' a Vitezai fighter named Bedescan shouted. 'Have you been close to one? Kore's Balls, they stink! It's like being in a pig pen. I don't think they wash at all.'

'I hear they fornicate in the open,' the innkeeper Meglyn added, who was hosting the meeting in a private room in his tavern. Others chimed in with their own anecdotes and opinions on Sydians: *They worship horses; they steal anything not nailed down!; they're here to slaughter us, not the Rondians*, and on it went, and Valdyr listened with a sinking feeling in his guts.

He was supposedly here incognito, but they all knew who the cowled man at Dragan's side was – half the room had kissed his signet ring when they entered and the rest had bowed. The talk was becoming more and more inflammatory and he could feel himself being forced towards a terrible choice.

In the three days since Kyrik's war council most of the Sydians had departed for Domhalott and the Bullheads had headed off for the Osiapa headwaters. Dragan was overseeing the muster of the citizens' militia. During the day everyone pitched in, bringing together equipment and food, repairing gear, collecting stores – but at night in the taverns, far from Kyrik's ears, the talk wasn't of killing Rondians but of their unwanted allies.

'The Sarkany has made a mistake and that's the heart of it,' Grigor Radeska, son of the Earl of Lapisz, said loudly, making Valdyr bridle; the Radeskas and the Sarkanys had been rivals for generations. 'He overestimated the strength of the Rondians and underestimated the good people of Mollachia – but then, what do you expect of a man who's grown up breeding Noories for the Shihad?' Grigor threw Valdyr a look, daring him to take umbrage and reveal himself officially.

'Don't react,' Dragan murmured. 'You'll learn more by listening than throwing punches, my Prince.'

With difficulty, Valdyr kept his temper. Golden-haired Grigor had a reputation as a swordsman and a stealer of hearts, but he fancied a broken nose might deflate his ego.

'Kyrik should never have wed that Sydian whore,' someone at the back called out.

'He's bewitched,' suggested a priest, probably one of Pater Kostyn's people. 'I hear she's been bedded by half the tribe. Kyrik should have married your Sezkia, Dragan.'

'My Sezkia has her eyes on another man,' Dragan replied. 'One who will sire good Mollach sons.'

They all heard Dragan's implicit message: that Sezkia and Valdyr would soon be wed. 'To Sezkia's husband, whomever he might be!' Bedescan called, winking broadly, and everyone raised their tankards.

'You know, I'm reminded of a parable from the *Book of Kore*,' the priest remarked. 'The tale of the Good Son: a virtuous young man with a drunken elder sibling who is driving the family to ruin. Only when the younger son casts his drunken elder out is the family's prosperity restored.'

That tale wasn't often trotted out, as the laws of primogeniture were a cornerstone of Mollach life; the tacit implication that the will of the people could alter the law made it a dangerous parable.

'There are many types of drunk,' the priest went on, 'the amiable drunk, the lecherous drunk, the foolish drunk . . . and none of them should be allowed to endanger those in their care.'

He's implying Kyrik's too nice, too love-struck and too naïve to rule, Valdyr interpreted, thinking that Grigor Radeska was not the only man who deserved a fist to the face.

'The real question,' the priest concluded, 'was whether the younger brother would save his family.'

An expectant silence fell. Everyone was looking at Valdyr. 'I believe that the younger brother loved the elder one, despite everything,' he said carefully. 'A drunk can renounce liquor.'

'So long as the house is put to rights, all's well,' Dragan put in.

Valdyr bit his lip, then gave a short nod.

'The house is ablaze,' Grigor Radeska grumbled.

'Then we'll douse it,' Valdyr replied, fixing Grigor with a cold eye, all his years in a slave-gang behind his stare. It was enough to quash the young nobleman. For now.

The meeting broke up soon after and he walked home with Dragan.

'Valdyr, I know that must have been embarrassing for you,' the gazda said, 'but it's important for you to hear what real Mollachs are saying.'

Which side do you take? Valdyr wondered, but he didn't have the nerve to ask that, not of the man whom he knew many saw as a more fitting king than Kyrik or himself. When a man became gazda, he foreswore ever seeking the throne: to be Gazda of the Vitezai Sarkanum was to lead those who resist tyrants; it was inimical with kingship. But for the first time, Valdyr wondered if being gazda was enough for Dragan.

'I will try to talk to Kyrik,' he promised, 'but I need to go to Watcher's Peak before the coronation.' He'd been called by Zlateyr and Luhti, their voices filling his slumber. 'Two days there, two or three days on the mountain and two days back. I'll return before the coronation.'

'Don't tarry,' Dragan told him. 'We need you, Valdyr. The men trust you.'

The implication that they didn't trust Kyrik didn't need to be stated.

Feher Szarvasfeld, Mollachia

Valdyr left next morning. The seasons were changing: winter was coming and the nights would start to drop below freezing. They would be lucky not to end up wading through snow. But Juergan Tirlak was guiding him and he was lively company. Rounding out his companions were the cheery Bartra Feszy, taciturn Ricolai Tuun and the hunters Petr and Mikel Hulder, who were typically reserved. And Gricoama, of course, who was excited to be back in the forest.

Watcher's Peak was some fifty miles away, across rugged terrain, but they knew the best tracks, through the hills of the Osiapa headwaters and into Feher Szarvasfeld. It took three days to reach the lower slopes, near the mouth of the Rahnti Mines. The weather had been kind, although the nights were bitingly cold; frost encrusted the open slopes and the air beneath the trees was frigid, making the rocks icy and the paths up into the heights increasingly treacherous.

Juergan joked about Valdyr calling back summer for them, and he smiled. *I wish I could*, he thought as they climbed, *but the truth is, I don't know* what *I can do.*

But something was definitely changing inside him. As he approached the Peak, his dreams were becoming more intense. In them he was always a beast – usually a wolf, quite possibly inside Gricoama's head, ranging far and wide, visiting high tarns to drink, hunt, feed and mate – a disturbing experience. Other times he was a stag, coursing through the heights, or an eagle riding the updraughts, seeking prey below. He could feel the ice settle into the mountains and the headwaters begin to freeze. And at times he was sure he sensed others – far-distant presences, just glimpses . . . a pale, lovely woman in rich clothes, heavily pregnant and shadowed by a Tree-woman; and a dark presence coursing through the ocean. And all the time he could feel Luhti and Zlateyr's gaze, looking down from the heights above.

Come to us, they called. *Your eyes are opening – let us show you how to see.*

That night they camped in the mouth of the Rahnti Mines. The next morning was chill but the skies were clear as they climbed. He left Juergan and the others below the stag-skull pillar marking the trail, and in seconds, his companions were lost to sight.

Gricoama looked at him with bright, eager eyes. Then a stag's roar echoed out of the mist above, calling them home.

27

The Revolutionaries

The Noros Revolt

After being exploited to the point of penury by the empire, in 909–10, Noros finally revolted. It ended, predictably, in defeat and destruction. All self-determination was removed, the King of Noros was reduced to an imprisoned figurehead and a governor was placed in supreme authority. The Rondians believe this has removed all likelihood of future rebellion. My estimation is that it has made it inevitable.
Dirklan Setallius, Despatch to the Duke of Coraine, 920

Jastenberg, Noros
Octen 935

Ari expected his next public appearance to be before a justiciar, with a sentence to gaol or a flogging – but instead, he was taken from the cell and led to an upstairs room where half a dozen middle-aged men sat. They all looked like Noromen and instead of being introduced by real names, they were 'Master Church', 'Master Trader', 'Jonas Burgher', 'Thom Clothier', and a watchful man named as 'Master Kingsman'. Facultor Fletter – or 'Master Warden', as he was here – nodded to him.

Only the man apparently hosting the gathering clearly identified himself. 'I am Justiciar Vorn Detabrey,' said the portly man with frizzy grey hair and a pugnacious, battered face. 'What we discuss tonight will determine whether you stand trial.'

Ari gulped. 'Yes, Milord.'

'Polite now, isn't he?' Detabrey remarked. 'First and foremost, this is a gathering of citizens. Some of us are wealthy, and Master Church

414

and Master Kingsman belong to prominent organisations. We meet to exchange ideas that sometimes lead to words in the ears of certain people whose opinions matter more than ours.'

Ari was still trying to pull his thoughts from the dread of torture and execution.

Detabrey went on, 'We're neither a business nor a cause, and we are most certainly not idealists. We bear no particular animosity towards the empire – well, beyond that of any Noroman. What we're interested in is how our society might work better: stronger institutions, improved public safety, the rule of law, an end to barbarism. Public water that's fit to drink, buildings that won't fall down, guardsmen you can trust and a Justiciary that punishes the criminal and exonerates the innocent. Knowledge put to the service of the people.' He waved a hand airily. 'I could go on, but I trust you see what I mean.'

'Yes, sir.' *Mostly people like you just want to preserve their riches*, Ari thought, but this was an unexpected boon when he'd feared the worst.

'Good.' The justiciar leaned forward. 'Now, tell us about suffragium.'

All unexpectedly, this was what he'd dreamed of: the chance to put his case to men of intellect and influence. He was soon talking enthusiastically; he had to keep himself from leaping to his feet as if this were another village square.

After his initial rant, they asked probing questions: *How did the Lantrians deal with tyranny? How did they compel a corrupt magistratus to stand down? How is the military kept subordinate to the elected ruler?* and many more. Some were problems the Lantrians had never fully resolved, and of course, there had been no magi until centuries after the fall of the Lantric city states and the Rimoni Republic.

'In the end, the law has to stand above all: an agreed code by which we live, and all men must be equal before that law, whether they're a lowly beggar or a king,' Ari concluded. 'The might of the military must *only* be deployed to enforce the law or to protect the people.'

'What is the status of a king in this *res publica* of yours?' Master Kingsman asked.

He's an agent for the Noros king, Ari guessed, and answered carefully, 'The book *Res Publica* is about a society whose king dies with no issue.

It seeks to show suffragium as the means by which the succession struggle is resolved. In the story there is a "tyrant", although in Lantris, "tyrannus" actually meant a temporary ruler, someone who took control as an *emergency* measure.'

'Yes, yes, but what of kings?'

'The Lantric city states overthrew their kings and ruled by elected magistrates, a council that controlled the bureaucracy, the armies and civic institutions. No man could hold office for more than two years at a time, and never for more than six years in all. Their decisions were subject to public scrutiny by a senate of elders.'

'Noros has a king who's not a tyrant, but someone beloved by his people,' Kingsman told him.

'With respect, his role is mostly ceremonial, and it's subordinate to the governor, who is appointed by Pallas. When the king dies, all power will revert to the governor.'

'You are evading the real question: can Monarchy and suffragium coexist?'

'If there must be a king at all, I see his role as ceremonial only,' Ari replied, which made Kingsman scowl.

'Who should rule, then?' Master Clothier asked.

'The magistrati, all subject to the rule of law.'

'Bravo,' Justiciar Detabrey said, winking broadly around the group.

They all smiled, then Master Church asked, 'Where does Kore feature in your fantasy?'

He doesn't, Ari was tempted to answer, but Lothar had talked endlessly of this. 'Like the magi who adopted the Frandian god Kore for their own needs, I believe that the Church's role is to create the moral imperative. The secular laws of the Church – to not kill, steal, rape, coerce and so on – are much the same as those of the Crown. The Church should promote "godliness" as respect for the law and the rights of others, and hopefully shape the nature of the people for the better.'

Church looked no happier than Kingsman, but he indicated that he understood.

'You speak like someone who's read about people but never met them,' Jonas Burgher growled. 'People aren't "godly"; we're pissants and brawlers who do as little as possible and to Hel with the rest of 'em.'

'I've met such people, but I don't agree that they are the majority. Nothing and no one is perfect, truly, but most people will sacrifice themselves for others – their children, their families, their loved ones. Others don't, but the ideal is clearly present. That's why the law must stand above human variability.'

'But why should a drunken fart on the side of the road have as many votes as men of standing?' Master Clothier asked.

'Does he?' Ari replied. 'You are men of standing: prime candidates to be *magistrati*. Your words will influence others. I doubt the drunk's will do the same.'

'But what of the popular but evil man?' Master Church asked. 'What of the rich man who bribes the voters? What of the criminal who intimidates them? All of these people could pervert your suffragium.'

'Of course,' Ari replied, 'but in a kingdom, you need only corrupt the king. In a suffragium, there are many more you have to charm, bribe or intimidate. The more people they have to influence, the harder it is to hide the effort.' He paused, then added, 'The important thing with such corrupters of the system is to bring them down. Those who succumb to corruption, cronyism, nepotism and such like: let the law have its full way with them. Let them be ruined, never be permitted to hold office again. Let the law be vigilant and punish the corrupt.'

He looked around the room, feeling incredibly alive. These men could do more to promote suffragium than ten thousand townsfolk. *Or to quash it.* 'Justiciar Detabrey,' he said, 'you said earlier that you all wish to make things better. You didn't say perfect. If politics was the water-supply and you had rancid water and sewage in the system, you wouldn't stand around waiting for the perfect solution; you'd use the best tools and methods to hand. Suffragium is a better tool and method, even though it's not perfect. It's the best way to alleviate the suffering of the commoners.'

'The "Sufferers",' Kingsman remarked, somewhat scornfully. 'That is the lot of the poor: to suffer.'

'Should it be? Is it inevitable?' Ari asked. 'We produce enough food, cloth and wealth for everyone, if it were shared instead of hoarded by a few. Something must change, gentlemen, if the suffering is to end.'

'That sort of change will likely require a civil war,' Fletter said from the corner, the first time he'd spoken.

'The Lantric city-states were founded through war,' Ari admitted, 'and they lasted for two hundred years, a Golden Age that ended only when a vastly larger rising power – Rym – conquered them, then imitated them, until the Age of Emperors. That Golden Age was no coincidence: suffragium didn't just change how rulers were elected, it benefited all of society. By acknowledging every man equal under law, it gave permission for people to follow their dreams. Culture, law and science all flourished because ideas were encouraged, from every walk of life. The armies were strong because people believed in the state they fought to protect. Ancient Lantris was a meritocracy, a place where any man could achieve according to his talents.'

As he finished, Ari hoped to see enthusiasm stirring in at least some of these men, but instead he perceived only interest and deliberation. Perhaps that was the best he could do in one evening.

'Your passion and articulation do you credit, Master Frankel,' Detabrey said. 'Thank you for joining us. Needless to say, this is a confidential meeting and does not betoken support for your views. As to yesterday: no lives were lost, but there was considerable damage to property and many minor injuries, so I want you to leave Jastenberg. I'm not going to say don't speak publicly; I don't have that authority, but I urge you to take care. You're making enemies as swiftly as friends.'

Detabrey and Fletter escorted him to the door after the others gave reserved thanks. 'If you happen to go to Venderon, seek out Justiciar Parrow, who shares my interests in political theory,' Detabrey said. 'Fare you well.'

Fletter walked him out through a rear entrance, where he found Neif waiting. The facultor summoned a pair of City Guardsmen and accompanied them back to Ari's father's home, where he hoped for a floor to sleep on.

'Making sure I leave?' Ari asked with a wry smile.

'Making sure you leave *alive*,' Fletter replied.

The streets were quiet, but many who saw Ari gave him a furtive salute, muttering 'Long live the Sufferers!' But there was no sign of the revolutionary fire he'd seen on the streets the previous day, and there were many more soldiers around.

When they reached the little lane near Cuimbrae Square, they found a press of people with anxious faces. When they saw Ari, he heard people exclaiming, 'Dear Kore, it's him!' He looked at Neif worriedly, then began pushing through the crowd, the facultor and his men trailing him.

When a guardsman appeared and whispered urgently to Fletter, Ari began to feel afraid. He pushed through the people, ignoring Fletter's call to wait. One of his followers was guarding his parents' door, a cudgel in his hand, his face filled with anger and grief; he stepped aside wordlessly. As Ari walked into the kitchen, the stench of blood struck him like a blow.

He should have stopped then, but he couldn't.

They'd been stripped, gagged, branded, hung from the rafter beam, their feet dangling only inches above the ground, and gutted. Flies encrusted the bodies and the piles of intestines, gore and human waste lying beneath each set of dangling feet.

Ari couldn't speak out loud, so he named them in his head: *my father, Cuthmann Frankel. My mother, Magga Frankel. My friends Bek Tyner and Lothar Lansson.*

Bek was so tall his feet touched the ground, which meant he'd likely not died from the hanging but from the disembowelling. The others might have been dead before the final coup-de-grâce, but perhaps not. The gags were to prevent anyone hearing.

'Oh no . . .' Neif's voice was dulled by disbelief. 'Please Kore, *no!*' He was shaking, his usual poised, ironic face collapsing as he slumped against the wall. Ari stared, making himself *see* this, so that his nightmares would be precise and accurate.

Fletter entered, groaned, and caught Ari's shoulder. 'Let's get you outside.'

'Not yet,' Ari replied, going to his father, trying very hard to ignore the rest and see only the face. *Bulging, rolled-back eyes, mouth open, discoloured cheeks, broken veins, purple throat . . .*

'All he wanted was for his son to be a tanner, like him,' he said. 'The way *proper* sons do. Instead he got me – a man of words – and those words got him killed. Father, I'm so, *so* sorry.' Then he noticed that someone had jammed a coin in his mother's mouth as she died. *Because she's a whore: Hanzi Albroch says so . . .* He took it out and hurled it into the mud, tears streaming down his cheeks.

'Lothar was a true believer,' Neif said brokenly. 'Why would they kill him?'

'He believed in Kore's justice and peace. The men who did this didn't.'

Lothar, Bek, look what I did to us – look where my dreams led . . .

'Come on, lad,' Fletter said. 'You don't want to remember them like this.'

No, but I will, Ari thought. *Always.*

He let the guardsmen draw him outside. He ignored the onlookers, bowing his head and seething. *Hanzi Albroch, you* did *this.*

'We can't go on now,' Neif moaned. 'This is the end.'

'How right you are, Master Neif,' said a dark voice as men and women in the black and white tabards of Kore's Inquisition, helmed and armoured, entered from all sides. Hanzi Albroch looked smugly pleased with himself. 'These are the men,' he told the First Commandant. 'He's Ari Frankel, the ringleader. Arrest him.'

Fletter stepped in front of the first of the armoured men to move . . . but Albroch kindled gnosis-light, some kind of mental assault, and Fletter pitched forward onto his face. When Neif tried to run, a gauntlet slammed into his face, but Ari was paralysed in the face of such gratuitous brutality.

Then Albroch was leaning over him. 'As lead "Sufferer", Frankel, it will fall upon you to suffer most.'

28

The Wolf and the Jackal

Gnostic Studies and Personality

Magi are often lazily associated with 'typical' personality traits – the classics being 'quick-tempered Fire-mage' or 'stolid Earth-mage'. But these are mere caricatures; each mage's affinity with the gnosis is unique to them, and two Fire-magi can be as different as milk and honey.

LEPHANIUM, THE TOOLS OF MAGIC, PALLAS, 834

Mollachia
Octen 935

Kyrik woke to another bitterly cold morning, every bit of exposed skin numb. When he pulled open the bedroom curtains and looked out over the town, he saw Hegikaro was wreathed in fog and rimed with frost.

He scried for Valdyr before anything else, but Clairvoyance was a weak affinity for him and he came up with nothing. His brother should have reached Watcher's Peak by now. The wedding ceremony was still three days away, but in the wilds many things could go wrong, and he was anxious.

But preparations for the coronation and wedding were proceeding apace, despite the palpable unease of many. All he wanted was for this week to pass without flashpoints so that they could present a united front when they marched against the Rondians. The Imperial Legion had withdrawn from Revgatra and Gazdakep and was entrenched in Lapisz; they still hadn't been reinforced. His fear that they would march before he was crowned hadn't materialised, so he planned to muster his forces in Revgatra in the first week of Noveleve for battle.

But first, my pagan wedding will be blessed by Kore and I'll be crowned.

With that optimistic thought, he turned to his wife. Her sprawled body lured him back to her side and he slithered beneath the furs and on top of her, kissing her face while she feigned sleep until she opened one eye and murmured, 'Ysh,' and pulled him into her. All worry receded as they moved together, sighing and groaning until he climaxed and they fell into a long slow kiss.

'I'm impressed,' she murmured. 'I thought I'd emptied you last night.'

'I have phenomenal powers of recovery,' he grinned, stroking her face. She was *handsome*: that was the agreed word in court, not delicate and pretty, no archetypal Mollach girl with her plump lips, wide nose, pitted skin and greying hair. But she was so vividly alive. *I love her, but I have to tell her this thing that might tear us apart . . .*

To have that conversation immediately after making love felt unfair, but the rest of his day was going to be taken up with soldiering and hers with dress-fittings and ritual preparations. So he sat up, to establish at least a little distance, summoned his courage and said, 'There's something you need to know.'

She was instantly alert to his change in mood. Pulling her knees to her chest and hugging them, she asked, 'What is it?'

'Do you remember Godspeaker Paruq? He visited the trek to warn us about the Shihad. But before he left, he told me something I never knew – or even suspected. It's important to remember this was something I didn't know when we married.'

Her eyes narrowed. 'You never knew *what*?'

He swallowed, then came out with it. 'That the reason Paruq was able to have me removed from the breeding-houses was that in four years of trying, I'd never once fathered a child.'

'Mmm?' she said, and then, '*Oh.*'

'I *never* knew. But I know now, and now I'm telling you.'

Her face ran through a range of reactions, then she gave a small sob. When he reached for her, she pushed his hand away. 'Why are you telling me now?'

'Because we married believing we would have children of Mollach and Vlpa blood to unite this kingdom.'

'But if Paruq told you . . . you've known this for *months*! Why didn't you say something sooner?' Her expression went from miserable to angry. 'Because you needed us then but you don't now? Is that it?'

'No – *never!* I believe absolutely in a united and free Mollachia, with your people and mine equal parts of that vision. I believe in you – and I love you. But I was scared if I told you, I'd lose you. Not the Vlpa – *you*.'

She stared at him, her eyes wet. 'I wish I believed that.' She looked down at her body, then blurted, 'You made sure to screw me *before* telling me, I notice. You *picsaba* coward!'

'Hajya, I—'

She clambered out of the bed. 'I need to be alone.' She pulled a gown around herself and stomped out the door, not looking back, ignoring his calls.

He didn't see her all day and she didn't come to dinner or to his bed that night. The coronation was only two days away. He began to wonder if she'd be at his side at all.

Asiv Fariddan had lived most of his life with the secret jackal tattoo of the Hadishah upon his inner thigh, but he'd been both hunter and hunted: a killer whose desires were condemned even by his fellow assassins. He'd grown used to covering his tracks and ensuring those with the power to unmask his sins were misled or silenced, which required self-control, to hold onto his lusts when he had to.

Such patience stood him in good stead here in this bitterly cold forest. He was far from inured to hardship, but he could endure until the right moment came to strike. He'd spent three weeks in this Ahm-for-saken country now. The Puppeteer's awareness of the use of powerful magicks was unrivalled and he'd detected something profound here: a great expenditure of energy that was not the gnosis. *Pandaemancy*, Naxius had called it, the same power that had been harnessed to destroy Midpoint Tower. Asiv's mission was to capture that pandaemancer.

That Mollachia was the homeland of his former pet Valdyr Sarkany was a bonus; it appeared Valdyr and his brother Kyrik were leading a fight to free the kingdom from the Rondians. But Asiv moved cautiously, especially after losing Ansel Inoxion, the first man he'd enslaved.

He sniffed the air as a whiff of wood-smoke teased his nostrils and heard distant conversation and masculine laughter. He extended his senses to ensure he was alone, even taking the trouble to dissipate the steam of his breath as he waited. He stood for several minutes until he moved again, using kinesis to drift over the crust of snow, seeking the lee of a huge boulder—

—but no arrow whooshed from the trees; no one barked a challenge.

He'd learned to respect the Mollach hunters who controlled the upper valley. Though none were magi, the least of them could move like ghosts and place an arrow perfectly. An unwary mage could die from an ordinary arrow, so caution had become Asiv's byword. He was also hindered by an inability to scry his former pet, even with his extra powers; whenever he tried, a mist fell over his inner vision.

Because it's you, little Valdyr . . . you're the pandaemancer . . .

He'd caught one of the hunters a few days ago and bored through his mind, learning much of the Mollach worldview. Nilasz Pobok had some interesting knowledge and opinions about Kyrik and Valdyr Sarkany too; that information had brought him here, to the foot of the mountain the hunters called Watcher's Peak – perhaps significantly, the only Rondian place-name in this land.

He peered around the boulder and saw a small camp some hundred yards below him near a swift stream. The four men he'd trailed up the valley had been joined by four more – and one of them was the man Nilasz Pobok had revered above all others: the 'Gazda', Dragan Zhagy, a hardy-looking lupine character: the leader of the hunters.

And my next prey.

As Asiv settled in to await his chance, he shaped his canines into serpent's fangs and filled a venom sac in the top of his mouth with ichor. Twilight became night and the last slither of the moon, nearing the end of her cycle, rose late. The hunters sang jaunty songs, peasant-music that grated on Asiv's ears, especially when one man brought out a bowed instrument that screeched unpleasantly.

He drew on the gnosis for heat as the temperature plummeted. His prey were wary, but he was a hunter too, and had better weapons. He engaged mystic-gnosis to send somnambulant thoughts into the dreams of the sleepers and lethargy into the two sentries before he crept at last towards the nearest guard.

The man faltered, swaying dazedly, caught by the spell, as Asiv reared behind him, wrapped a hand over his mouth and wrenched his head sideways, then plunged his incisors into the man's throat. His prey struggled, but weakened swiftly as the ichor entered his bloodstream. Asiv enjoyed the oddly erotic discharge of ichor and the mental communion it brought, then he left the man in the final throes of succumbing and slipped in to deal with the other guard.

Some instinct must have warned the man, for he began to turn, but Asiv extended a hand and made a pattern gleam on his palm that drew and entrapped the eye, using illusion and mysticism to hypnotise his prey. He closed in, embracing the man like a lover, until teeth punctured skin and once again he shuddered with pleasure as he shot ichor through his fangs.

Moments later, both men rose, blood running from their eyes and necks, their gazes hungry but their demeanour subservient. Inside their skulls, Abraxas held their reins. They entered the silent camp. The banked fires were still flickering; the other hunters were lost in gnostic dreams. He didn't permit his new slaves to attack, for he wanted these men to be equals, Shepherds, as the Master called them, so he himself passed from man to man, spreading the ichor, until only the leader remained.

When all had succumbed, he gathered them round, crouched over the last fur-clad sleeper, nudged his mind and said, 'Wake up, Dragan Zhagy.'

Dragan thrashed awake and rolled, coming up sword in hand. The moonlight was just a sliver, the stars a frosting above, and there were men all round him: *his* men – except for the closest, a dark shadow with black hair and bronze skin and the whitest teeth. The stranger was clearly in the prime of life: powerful and agile – and utterly unconcerned to be facing a man with a sword.

Behind him, Dragan's companions were like statues, their eyes dark and their shoulders hunched. 'Kavan?' he called to the nearest man, 'Stivor? Blaz?'

No one answered, or even moved, except the dark man. 'They won't answer you,' he replied in accented Mollach. 'They're mine now.'

Dear Kore . . . Dragan looked around and saw nothing but blank hunger in the eyes of his companions, men he'd grown up with, hunted with, fought with. A wail of mourning rose inside his brain. But he also noticed that several had cast aside their Kore icons – the silver ones, not the wooden ones. Dragan's hand went to his own Sacred Heart. *Silver*, he thought, clutching at a faint tendril of hope. 'Who are you?'

'I am called Asiv.'

'What do you want?' Dragan glanced left and right. *He's a mage – he's bewitched them.* But that didn't explain the bite-marks on his men's throats.

'What do I want?' Asiv said with nonchalant arrogance. 'For you to join me, as your men have.'

'Enslaved,' Dragan spat. *I'll be damned before I submit to this piece of dung.* He drew his dagger left-handed. He'd always expected to die violently. Another gazda would be found – the order had been rebuilt from the ashes several times in its turbulent history.

'You know,' Asiv remarked, 'since I arrived I've had the chance to learn the politics of this place. You don't want Kyrik Sarkany's Sydian scum here, do you?'

'What's it to you, *Noorie*?'

'Me? I don't give a shit. And I don't care whether you live or die, apart from how it affects my goals. I want Valdyr Sarkany and you can help me, if you're willing. Or you can die.'

'Willing?' Dragan growled. 'I don't see "willing" here.'

'Not in your men,' Asiv agreed, 'no. But it could be different for you. A willing servant is more versatile than any slave. You're virtually a king here: every man and woman reveres you – far more than they do Kyrik Sarkany.'

'I'd die before I betrayed my land,' Dragan rasped, steeling himself. *One blow, up under my chin . . .*

'But hasn't Kyrik already betrayed your land? He's married a savage and brought an invading army. Aren't you *longing* to do something about that?'

It's true, Kyrik has failed us, Dragan admitted to himself, but he didn't trust Noories either. 'I'll take my own counsel on these matters. I'm no traitor to my kind.'

'But dozens of gazdas have risen against their kings,' Asiv said. 'The folk-tales your friends here grew up with now reside in my mind, Gazda – I know what you are! When a king betrays the land, it is your role to stand against him. And if you think Kyrik Sarkany hasn't betrayed you, ask him why he was removed from the Hadishah breeding-houses: because he never fathered a child! Is a man with no seed in his sac permitted the kingship here?'

Dragan felt his resolve lurch. 'You're lying.'

'I signed the paperwork myself. And I heard his patron Godspeaker tell him not three months ago.'

A man unable to father children is unfit to rule. As is one who brings enemies into the realm . . .

'Yes,' Asiv said, as if reading his mind, 'Kyrik is unfit to rule: someone that a gazda – the guardian, the kingmaker, the protector of all it means to be a Mollach – should be resisting, not helping.'

Asiv was voicing the same dark fantasy that Dragan had been imagining of late. *Yes, isn't the gazda the true ruler of Mollachia? And who better? Are we not chosen? Are we not the truest of the true?*

'I'll tell you what else is true,' Asiv went on, 'Valdyr is no better than his brother. You've noticed his reluctance to touch your beautiful daughter – I'll tell you why. In the breeding-houses only a *male* body could excite little Valdyr.'

'You're lying,' Dragan said again, but his heart lurched, because this also rang true. *Why else is the boy so damned reluctant to court my lovely Sezkia?*

'I'm not lying, Gazda. Your land would be better off without these damned Sarkanys. Their father bankrupted the kingdom to buy a mage-wife and brought the wrath of the empire down on you all. And now his two sons – a sterile fool and a catamite – have let foxes into your henhouse. Help me, and I'll make you king – the sort of king Mollachia needs right now – and I'll give you the gnosis as well.'

'You can do that?' Dragan stared, stunned. 'What do you want in return?' he asked, barely noticing his dagger hand had fallen.

'Me? All I want is Valdyr Sarkany. Decide, Gazda: the throne – or the grave?'

When Valdyr climbed Watcher's Peak to learn the dwyma, he'd envisaged standing on the mountaintop, calling storms and hurling lightning bolts like the giants of legend. Instead, he spent most of his time just sitting beside the fire with Luhti, or Lanthea, as she'd been known in the empire. At times her brother Zlateyr, his son Eyrik and the shaman Sidorzi joined them, but mostly it was just the two of them.

'Are there other dwymancers?' he asked Luhti.

'Two or three dozen. Many united under Eloy's leadership. We had a power the magi couldn't understand, so mistrust was inevitable. Eloy tried to find a middle ground and they made him a saint – then killed him. I wasn't so trusting, and I'm not easy to find.'

Learning the dwyma forced them into mental intimacy, and to Valdyr's surprise, he found himself opening up to Luhti, talking of things he was ashamed of and had never intended to reveal. Luhti was like a dream of his mother; he told her everything, about the Hel of the breeding-houses, the horrors of the chain-gangs – and he spoke of Asiv and Naxius and the very real daemons they put inside him. He even managed to find words for the abuse, and how he'd been too petrified to fight back.

'You were a child,' she told him, and he knew that, but somehow her acceptance *mattered*. 'Victims often blame themselves,' she said, 'even when the struggle is impossible. Some battles can't be won, just survived.'

'But Kore says we must forgive those who harm us,' he whispered, 'and I'm not capable of that.'

'*Kore*,' Luhti sniffed. 'Forgive, if that drains the poison from your mind, but monsters must be faced and slain. If Asiv is truly here, then rejoice, for it means your time is coming. Vengeance is nigh.'

'But he's a mage—'

'And you are a *dwymancer*. When you have become all you can be, you'll feel his tread on the soil and his scent in the air – and you will become the hunter.'

To face Asiv . . . That was both dream and nightmare, but it helped, recalling him as he truly was. The omnipotent beast who'd destroyed his innocence was only a quarter-blood mage, an ageing Keshi pederast with a paunch: less frightening than the Delestre siblings, less worthy of fear.

'He only preyed on children,' he snarled, 'the helpless—'

'Meek with the strong, and strong with the meek,' Luhti agreed. 'I know the type.' She placed her hand over his heart. 'You've been hurt, child, but you can still feel love, and you can still give it.' Then she leaned in and kissed his mouth – he baulked at first, then he let her taste him and incredibly, no bad memories arose. 'There,' she said, 'that wasn't so bad, was it?' Then she drew away and was motherly again. 'Don't let them pressure you into anything you're not ready for, Valdyr – but don't run away either. Let love find you.'

'Are you a ghost?' he asked, although he could still taste her on his lips.

'I suppose I am,' she replied. 'Many years ago, when my physical form was failing, I gave my soul to the genilocus, as did my family, and we became as one with the guardian spirit of this place, a being named Epyros. We protect it, although we had given up hope of ever finding someone new to guide into the dwyma. You are a godsend to us, Valdyr. We have been waiting for you for a very long time.'

Valdyr thought for a moment. 'Epyros . . . he's become the White Stag, hasn't he?' And when Luhti met his eyes with a small nod, he felt a burst of pride. Something happened to his face, a strange twisting of muscles he'd not used for a long time.

'Valdyr,' Luhti teased, 'did you just *smile*?'

He looked away, feeling very strange, shy and confused . . . and *happy*. To escape the moment, he asked, 'There's something else I don't understand: the tales of Zlateyr and Luhti are three centuries old, but Corineus and the first dwymancers date back more than five hundred years . . .'

'Oh, that's easily explained,' Luhti replied. 'I was Lanthea of Midrea

long before I became Luhti of the Clan Hraavu. I was one of Corineus'
disciples: I drank the ambrosia that first night – and I became a dwymancer. I fled when the Church crushed the others of my kind, all the
way to the Sydian Plains, where I rode the Wheel of Seasons for nearly
two hundred years. The empire never found me.'

'But then . . . is Zlateyr *not* your brother?'

'He is my soul-brother, the first man I taught the dwyma, but he's
not my *physical* brother. I taught him, and together we taught his son,
and Sidorzi, and many others. But only we four came west to Mollachia.'

'Why did you come here?' Valdyr wondered.

'There's a special place here. We needed to find it and protect it.'

He looked around the ice-glazed peak. 'Up here?'

'Another place – I'll show you when you're ready. Mollachia is more
than just a mountain kingdom, Valdyr – it is the heart of the dwyma.
In this place our power was forged, and it's here it can be unmade.
You must become its guardian.'

'Why me?' he asked. 'How did I come to be a dwymancer and not
a mage?'

'We've never understood the "how" and "why" of it, but you were
locked away from the gnosis before you gained it and you were exposed
to the dwyma before the gnosis awoke inside you. I believe those are
the crucial moments.'

'So when will you start teaching me?'

'That's what I'm doing,' Luhti replied. 'The better I know you, the
more power I can entrust you with. That's the big difference between
mage and dwymancer – they study, practise and learn; *we just are*. But
our powers are immense, so we must use them responsibly. That's why
an angry, damaged young man is a problem, but someone who has
overcome his anger is someone the dwyma can trust.'

'But it trusted me when we destroyed the Rondians three months ago.'

'We sensed a need and you presented yourself as a conduit. It wasn't
done without misgiving, I can assure you – but you are stronger of
mind now, and I think you're ready for more.'

She gave him a secretive smile, then pointed. 'Look, can you see that
blackened rock, a mile down the valley? Let's see what you can do . . .'

29

The Gathering Storm

The Black Histories

In 776 The Black Histories first appeared, giving a slanted view of the Rondian past, seeking to besmirch the Imperial line and undermine our unity. The Ordo Costruo are probably behind the work, which must be destroyed if ever encountered. They deny it, of course, but they're as full of lies as The Black Histories *are.*

ANNALS OF PALLAS, 843

Collistein Junction, Kedron Valley
Octen 935

The relay-stave burst into flames and Ril hurled it to the ground and stamped it to ash. The illusory image of Sir Brylion Fasterius fell apart, his scarred and brutish face fading as his voice was cut off mid-excuse. His army was still two hundred miles from the junction.

He deliberately burned out the link, Ril thought, stunned at the man's temerity. 'Clean that up,' he snapped at Niklas Bycross before stalking outside to get some fresh air. Luna was rising, a sliver in a star-spotted sky, and the camp was settling into night. He could hear the low murmur of thousands of men engaged in their evening routines. All along the low ridge where they'd taken up position was a snake of flickering camp fires, forming a southeast-facing crescent.

That confirms it, Ril thought morosely. *The Sacrecours won't be here in time, and nor will the Argundians. Instead of fifty legions, I'll have fewer than thirty: a hundred and forty thousand men to face nigh on a million.*

He wallowed in that misery, until his aide came to the tent-flap and called, 'The generals are waiting.'

'I waited on them long enough,' Ril retorted, then he sighed, clapped Bycross on the shoulder and joined his commanders. Elvero Salinas, the suave olive-skinned Prince of Canossi, Rolven Sulpeter and the studious young Brician Seth Korion, looking older than his twenty-five years, saluted casually as he entered.

I was given five armies and three have made it here. I've already failed. I went flying against the enemy when I should have been cracking whips over my own generals. He grabbed a goblet of wine and glowered at the map, a beautifully painted canvas full of gorgeous artistic detail, laden down with white markers in a line mirroring the campfires outside the tent.

'What news of our other two armies?' Korion asked.

'The Argundians are eighty miles west, on good roads,' Bycross reported. 'Our windskiff scouts report the enemy to be only ten miles south, but travelling slowly as they form up for battle.'

'The Argundians will miss the battle,' Ril said. *I thought I could count on them, Lyra being half a Borodium – not that we've given them the preference they think that deserves.* 'And the Sacrecours have only just left Jastenberg, the bastards.'

'The glory won't be theirs to share, then,' Prince Elvero said. The elegant Canossi was a picture of studied elegance. 'Do the Keshi know our deployments?'

'They know more than that, I imagine,' Ril replied. His windriders had been trying to prevent the Keshi flying scouts from overlooking their positions, but the enemy rocs, as a captured flier had named them, were better at climbing and faster, so chasing them off had proved difficult. 'Are your men in position?'

'Of course.' Elvero indicated the left-hand, northeastern end of the line of figures. 'Eight legions on firm ground, overlooking the road to Collistein. Forty thousand Canossi, Kliefmen and Aquilleans: the best of the south.'

Ril liked Elvero, who exuded the serene confidence of the born leader. With him in command, he trusted the left to hold, and take any opportunity to counter-attack. By comparison, the earnest Seth Korion appeared to be caught up in the details. 'And you, General Korion?' he asked the youngest of the generals.

'We're dug in well enough. The ridge you designated is too low, and there's swamp behind it, leaving me nowhere to place my reserves, so I moved my men back two hundred yards, to *here*. That gets us out of the fens and forces the enemy to advance through them.' Korion shifted a few of the markers backwards – which appeared to open up the right flank of his Corani forces, in the centre.

'Whose permission did you ask?' Ril demanded, looking at Sulpeter. 'Yours?'

'Aye.' The elderly Corani lord seemed in awe of the Korion name. 'The man who drew this map might be an *artist*, but he can't draw terrain.' He jabbed a finger at a beautifully rendered pool with a leaping fish in it. 'This lake isn't even there! I've pulled the units nearest General Korion's into line. There's no gap.'

Ril frowned. There was too much of this tinkering, but if Sulpeter approved, perhaps it was all right. 'What of the cavalry – are they in place?'

'Ready and eager,' Elvero replied. 'I have mine east of the Collistein Road, to prevent us being flanked in the initial phase. They'll lead the counter-attack when we go on the offensive.'

Ril nodded in approval. 'And yours, General Korion?'

He tapped a marker behind his lines. 'Here.'

This time even Sulpeter looked surprised, and Ril barely restrained himself from shouting. 'My orders were for the mounted units to be deployed to protect our flanks!'

'Well, if you'd troubled to visit our lines, *Highness*, you'd have seen that the land south of my position is all fens and bogs,' Korion said calmly. 'The Keshi won't be flanking our right unless they have horses with webbed feet and fins – while *here*, where your artist has for some reason drawn a draken, there is a corridor of dry land right opposite my centre. My intention is that as each assault breaks, we open the lines and counter-charge with the mounted men – but only until the attackers are driven back to *here*. If we go any further, our knights will come under their archers, *here*, right when their horses are blown.'

Sulpeter gave a *harrumph* of approval, but Ril was still annoyed that this dour young man appeared to be right about *everything*. 'What about when we attack?'

'That same corridor. It's the only firm ground in front of my position. Of course, that means my men will have the same problems as the enemy. But realistically, we're not going to attack *anyone*, Prince Ril. We're outnumbered, fighting on flat ground against the best archers and horsemen on Urte. We're going to cower under our shields while they fill the air with arrows, then hope there's enough of us still alive to hold a shield-wall when they charge.'

It's that defeatist attitude I hate, Ril thought. *The 'I've seen more than you' ennui. I warrant he's never even jousted.* 'There *will* be a counter-attack, General Korion,' he insisted, 'and you must be ready for that moment!'

'If it comes, certainly,' Korion said mildly, winding Ril up even more. 'Frankly, what matters is *your* role, Milord: win the skies and their ground forces won't break us. Lose the skies, and we're a long way from a defensible place.'

'Windships have never been the decisive factor in a land battle before,' Sulpeter pointed out, but Korion was shaking his head.

'They've been too few to matter before,' he countered. 'This time, both sides have fleets capable of annihilating ground troops. We must *not* lose the air.'

'We won't,' Ril insisted. 'I have eighteen triple-masted warbirds, forty two-masted sloops, two hundred skiffs and two hundred mounted mage-knights.'

'But I believe they have more ships than us – and more constructs?' Elvero commented. 'And your reports concede disadvantages in speed and climbing . . .'

'We're slower, but that won't matter in a massed battle – they can't run from this,' Ril replied, pissed off about being doubted on all sides. 'This'll be toe-to-toe, and who punches hardest. That's us.' He straightened, injecting more authority into his voice. 'Rashid will be here in no more than two days. Let's use that time wisely.'

Prince Elvero and General Korion left, but Sulpeter lingered, muttering in Ril's ear, 'Do you know Dravis Ryburn has been recalled to Pallas?'

Ril stared. 'On the eve of battle?'

'He told me there is news of a conspiracy against the grand prelate.'

Ril felt his skin go cold. Only a day ago, Dirk Setallius had sent an agent to brief him about a palace coup. Was there to be another Reeker Night just as battle was to be joined here in the Kedron Valley?

'Kore knows, Ryburn's not easy to like, but we needed him,' Ril muttered. 'What about his men?'

'His mage-knights left with him. He left the ordinary Inquisition Guards.'

'And he did this without consultation? *Rukka mio!*' Ril looked heavenwards. 'There's a conspiracy, all right: one whose aim is to destroy this army before battle even commences.' He clapped Sulpeter on the shoulder. 'Thank you for letting me know. I won't miss him, and trust me: I'll see that charges *are* laid.'

Once they'd all gone, Bycross tidied up while Ril stared at the map and wondered, *Were we right to choose here, in the middle of nowhere?* The logic had felt solid a month ago: to block the Shihad's advance at the last place where they were confined to one road. But now it felt muddled; he wished he was closer to the Argundians. Eighty miles further back, he'd have had four of his five armies, and he'd have forced Rashid to walk further too. *We'd be better dug in, better rested and have more men.*

It was increasingly clear that he *had* to win – but that victory was far from assured. There were no foreseeable second chances, not for House Corani. If he failed, it would be 909 all over again – only this time he'd have a wife and child and a lover trapped in the middle of it, while he was thousands of miles away.

'Who do you pray to, when you know that Kore is a lie?' he asked Bycross.

If Bycross was shocked at the question, he didn't show it. Most of the so-called 'divinely gifted' magi were atheists; being able to see through the façade generally destroyed faith. 'I pray anyway, Highness,' the aide answered. 'It helps me focus.'

Ril smiled tiredly, dismissed Bycross and poured himself a Brician whisky. At least he could trust *that* to deliver. Then he reached for a relay-stave and sent his call winging into the aether. In seconds, Basia's face appeared in the air in front of him.

<Lover,> he sighed, wishing he could stroke her face, *<are you free to talk?>*

<For you, darling, always.> The warm timbre of her voice made him smile for the first time in days.

The scent of victory was heavy in the air, giving energy to the sultan's commanders and fervour to the soldiers. It added spring to Waqar's step as he entered the royal pavilion, the latest scout reports in his hand. A dozen heads turned: the commanders were all assembled.

'And here he is!' Rashid said, as if Waqar's name had been on every tongue.

'Great Sultan,' Waqar replied, going down on his knees and pressing his forehead to the carpet before rising at his signal to join the circle of men seated on cushions below the throne. As well as Teileman, Attam and Xoredh and all the generals, there was a knot of Godspeakers, led by the Shihadi fanatic Ali Beyrami. Waqar had no idea what the priests knew of war, but Beyrami had been vocal throughout the invasion. *Set yourself up as the voice of God and suddenly you know everything.* Everyone else appeared to revere Beyrami, but he couldn't tell if his uncle valued the Godspeaker's counsel.

'What are your latest findings, Nephew?' Rashid asked.

Waqar consulted the maps and shifted a few of the Rondian markers around. 'The Argundians are still well behind the enemy position: as long as we fight within five days, they won't be present at the battle.'

'We're entering Darkmoon,' Xoredh said, 'a good period for covert actions.'

'I'd prefer a full moon so we could fight all day and night and break them down,' Teileman commented, as ever leaping thoughtlessly into the discussion, trying to appear worthy of his overwhelmingly successful elder brother.

'We deal with what is, not that we wish for,' Rashid reproved. 'What else have you learned, Waqar?'

'When we overfly them, we see water reflected: there's marshland in front of their lines, especially south of the road.'

Xoredh scowled; Rashid would have expected him to know this already.

If you valued my fliers, Xoredh, you might have, Waqar thought with dour satisfaction.

'They seek to restrict our lines of approach,' the sultan noted. 'Their strengths lie in close-quarters combat.'

'We'll crush them,' Attam declared. 'Weight of numbers will force the centre, then we'll split them and mop up.'

'Ahm will grant us victory,' Ali Beyrami added. 'Our cause is just and the men believe.'

If only it were that simple, Waqar thought. 'We've counted more than two hundred wind-vessels protecting the enemy army: if we can't stop the Rondian vessels from overflying us, superior numbers on the ground won't matter.'

'This time, we've got our own windfleet,' Xoredh countered, turning to the portly Admiral Neniphas, Commander of the Windfleet. 'Neniphas will win us the skies – for what it's worth,' he added with an upturned lip.

'It's worth much,' Waqar answered, not trusting Neniphas to stand up for them. 'Our rocs get more information in a single flight than cavalry scouts get in weeks. While you've been marching, we've been contesting the skies. We know our enemy.'

'What are their strengths and weaknesses?' Rashid asked, before Xoredh could renew hostilities.

'The Rondian fliers have stamina, but not our speed, which has worked to our advantage while this was a skirmish of scouts and retreating was an option.'

'*Retreating*,' Xoredh echoed. 'Running away isn't an option any more, Cousin. We'll finally see what you're made of.'

'My fliers kill enemy mage-knights every day. Our losses are proportionate and I myself have slain seven magi in combat. We won't shirk battle, Cousin.'

'No one here has anything but praise for your efforts,' Rashid said, quelling Xoredh with an iron look. 'So long as our fleet can keep the enemy windships fully engaged, preventing them from breaking up our ground forces, they'll have played their part.'

'What do we know of this Ril Endarion?' Teileman asked. 'What manner of commander is he?'

Xoredh broke in, 'He is of mixed race, which taints him in the eyes of his people. His marriage to the empress is controversial: an ill-advised love match. Despite this "love", they have no living children, although she is carrying for the third time. Rumour has it she's pregnant to another man – a priest, if that's to be believed.'

'Ahm curse her whorish womb,' Beyrami put in, with relish.

'So the Rondian prince is not respected?' Rashid said quietly.

'Not at all: an interloper who seduced a queen and yet is now a cuckold. The disarray of his armies speaks volumes of his inability to command. I predict that they'll fold swiftly.'

The generals and Godspeakers congratulated Xoredh as if he'd just won the battle, while Faroukh Valphath, the effete-looking Dhassan, offered a price of ten thousand daric on the Prince-Consort's head, a princely sum.

'We've encountered a knight-commander riding a winged horse; he has swarthy skin and wears a gold circlet,' Waqar said, raising his voice above the chatter. 'If that's the Prince-Consort, he's a valiant fighter.'

'Compared to you, perhaps,' Attam snorted. '*I'd* make short work of him.'

'You're welcome to fly with us, Cousin,' Waqar offered, knowing Attam vomited whenever he was airborne. The giant prince glared, but Waqar was no longer intimidated, especially not here.

'You think this man is Ril Endarion?' Rashid asked.

'I'm sure of it. We took a captive some days ago who described him. The Rondian mage-knights ride winged mounts in some kind of game called "joust", at which Ril Endarion excels.' Waqar had been amused to discover that he and Ril bore the same nickname: Prince of the Spear.

'*Games!*' Beyrami sneered. 'Ungodly barbarism.'

'They won him great respect,' Waqar countered. 'The two combatants ride flying constructs directly at each other at high speed, each seeking to dislodge the other with blunted lances. Men are frequently crippled, sometimes even die. We've fought this way in the skies for weeks now, using sharpened weapons, and I can attest that it requires both courage and skill.'

'Then you believe Xoredh underestimates this Yurosi prince?' Rashid asked.

Waqar looked at Xoredh. 'I do.'

This led to an angry hubbub until Rashid's voice cut through the din. 'Hearken to my nephew: he alone has not become complacent! Do you forget that we face the *Rondian Empire*? They discovered the gnosis and have fought with it for five hundred years; our first generation of magi is still young! We're the novices here, going up against the masters!'

The men had fallen silent and heads were now bowed.

'Believe in victory, certainly,' Rashid continued, 'but take nothing for granted. Do everything you can to win and Ahm will reward us. Do less, and he will avert his gaze. In three days, we give battle. Attam, you have the centre. Teileman will take the right and Valphath the left. Neniphas and Waqar will command the skies. Xoredh, you will attend on me, as my second. Go now, and order your men for the approach.'

They all abased themselves, but Waqar was surprised to be invited to remain with Attam and Xoredh. Rashid led them to a smaller tent which had been prepared for supper. He bade them sit, then looked at them sternly. 'You will cease your public points-scoring. It is time you outgrew it. You may be rivals, but you are also kin. If you think trading insults wins you plaudits with me, you're mistaken.'

His two sons bowed their heads, but Waqar left his erect. *I don't start these fights*, he told himself.

The small supper passed in quiet conversation after that – not amiable, but not antagonistic. Afterwards, Rashid dismissed his sons and once they were alone, he asked Waqar, 'Have you made contact with Jehana?'

'No, I've had no fortune there. Is there fresh news?'

'None,' Rashid replied, then he looked hard at Waqar and said, 'Some of the captured Ordo Costruo revealed something that interested me. They reported that your mother Sakita had a gift for large-scale magic

– I say "magic", not "gnosis". The Rondians call it "pandaemancy", which means "the magic of all daemons". Have you heard of it?'

Waqar had, from the Masked Cabal member Felix, but he'd never told Rashid and now he shook his head. 'No – but surely you're not implying that my mother broke the Gnostic Codes about daemons?'

'No, not at all,' Rashid answered quickly. 'The other name for this power is "dwyma", which means "life magic" – it was believed extinct, but I now learn that Sakita had this power. The man who confessed this also told me that the Ordo Costruo intended Sakita should breed a line of dwymancers – starting with you and Jehana.'

Waqar prayed his feigned confusion was good enough. 'But I don't know *anything* about this, Uncle—'

'I know you don't – I myself oversaw your education. But this man believed Jehana to be aware of her gift. She was educated away from the rest of the Arcanum for part of every day. That is another reason for finding her.'

'I'm trying,' Waqar insisted, 'but I *swear*, neither Mother nor Jehana have *ever* mentioned any of this to me!'

A new thought struck him: *If Rashid had known of this power, he would never have let Jehana return to the order . . . Unless it was to complete her training, after which he planned to reclaim her . . .* It did nothing to contradict his fear that Rashid had ties to the Masked Cabal. 'What do you wish of me, Uncle?'

'Keep trying to contact your sister, and encourage her to come out of hiding.'

'Yes, Uncle.'

'I do believe that she will soon be found – and who knows: perhaps you share her gift? So do not risk yourself recklessly in the forthcoming battle. You may be needed for far more than fighting, Waqar.'

'The coming days will decide our fate!' shouted Hazarapati Selmir, commander of Piru-Satabam III. His words carried clearly through the morning air, cutting through the distant sounds of the other units assembling for the march. Another day had dawned and they were on the move again.

'I love the way Aunty Selmir's voice cracks on the high notes,' Ashmak chuckled.

The forty elephants were arrayed in parade-ground precision on a piece of boggy flatland on the left side of the main road, waiting their turn to join the line. Beside them, dozens of supply-windships were being unloaded in the cold air. Most of the soldiers were wearing blankets as cloaks and wrapping their feet in swaddling before lashing on their sandals. Breath steamed and the sunlight glistened on the dew.

It's only autumn and already I feel like my blood is freezing, Latif thought. *What will winter be like?*

'Ready to march,' Selmir shrilled, 'off on the right and . . . ah—'

Latif and the rest of the men followed Selmir's eyes and their jaws dropped as they caught sight of giant shapes plodding along the road. At first glance it might have been another elephant unit, but on second glance, these beasts were the wrong shape, too low-slung, and longer . . . in fact, they weren't elephants at all. They had four legs and a grey-brown hide, but they looked to be armoured. Each had two giant horns protruding from a long, horse-like nose and carried a howdah on the back with a mahout and mage-and-archer combination, the same as them. But these creatures had an air of destructive menace their elephants didn't have.

'Holy Ahm . . .' Ashmak breathed, then he shouted, 'Hey, what are those ugly brutes?'

'We're Karkan-Satabam IV,' one of the newcomers responded. 'These are *karkadann*, fresh from the construct-houses: bred to war, not baggage beasts like yours, so don't get in our way!'

'Don't listen, Rani,' Sanjeep told his elephant. 'You're irreplaceable.'

Insults flew back and forth, including lurid suggestions about where the men of Karkan-Satabam IV could stick their beasts' horns, then Selmir bellowed for silence and ordered, '*Move out!*'

All day they had to plod through the shit the karkadann left, until at dusk they arrived at a camp stinking of stagnant water but buzzing with purpose; that was explained when Latif saw a line of fires flickering in the middle distance, just a few miles northwest. 'Is that the enemy?' he asked.

'Ai,' another archer replied, 'that is the Imperial Army of Rondelmar, cursed be their name.'

Latif swallowed, remembering foreign tongues, paler faces and strange manners: Seth Korion, Ramon Sensini, Jelaska Lyndrethuse and others. *Are any of them over there? Do they remember me?*

Ashmak clapped him on the shoulder. 'So, we've found them. Nervous?'

'Of course,' Latif said. 'We're going to be stuck on top of a damned elephant: what better way to scream "Target"?'

'Ai, I know. Do you want to know the secret of surviving a battle?'

'Absolutely!'

'It's to let other people do the dying, then charge just as the enemy breaks. If Selmir gets the timing right, we look like heroes. He gets it wrong and we're fucked.'

'That's very comforting.'

Ashmak chuckled. 'It's the best I can do. Let's eat, shit and sleep . . . for tomorrow we die.'

30

Asiv's Arrow

Lanthea

Of the four great dwymancers, the most elusive was Lanthea. She fled the north, ignoring the offers of sanctuary given to Eloy and his fellows, and instead led the Church a dance through Andressea and Midrea before vanishing into the forests of Schlessen. Her final fate is as yet unknown.

ANNALS OF PALLAS, 560

Feher Szarvasfeld, Mollachia
Octen 935

The barren heights of Watcher's Peak were wrapped in fog as Valdyr tramped down the slopes, his heart higher than it had ever been since a nine-year-old boy flew across the Pontic Sea to join the Second Crusade so many years ago. Gricoama bounded beside him, eager as a pup to reach the forest below.

He'd lost count of the days until that morning, when Luhti – *Lanthea* – had told him that if he wished to be at his brother's coronation, he had to leave.

I have to be present, to show my support.

His time with Luhti had settled a lot of things in his mind and now he was eager to be there, especially when he thought of Earl Radeska's poisonous meeting. He felt ashamed at not having spoken out against the bigotry, but he was glad to have seen at first-hand the attitudes he and Kyrik had to overcome.

It all starts with Dragan, he thought. The Gazda of the Vitezai Sarkanum was as respected as any king – more so by many. *If we win Dragan, the rest will follow.*

Then a shape loomed out of the fog: the old stag skull marking the path – and Valdyr paused, thinking of everything he'd done and seen these past few days: growing trees from seed, shifting stones, shaping weather. But the greatest wisdom Luhti had imparted was that the greatest dwymancers had done *almost* nothing.

Seasons come and go, she'd told him, *and not every harvest needs to be bountiful. Few droughts are catastrophes. Not all storms need be quelled.* There was a price for everything and the wisest of the wise knew when the benefit outweighed that price.

You have the patience, she'd told him. *You've been hammered into steel by life's blows. You can endure the worst and choose the moment to act. I believe in you.*

Her words filled Valdyr with optimism.

He ruffled Gricoama's fur and they jogged down the trail, breaking from the mists into a cloudy autumnal day. There was a hint of rain in the air, the ground was frosty, and patches of snow clung to the hollows. Smoke marked the position of a cooking-fire – unusually sloppy for the hunters, although the Rondians no longer patrolled here. There didn't appear to be any sentries – and everyone was cowering in the shade of rocks and trees on a day when the desire for sunlight and warmth should have been irresistible . . .

Uneasy, Valdyr reached hailing distance and called, 'They can probably see that fire from the lower valley!'

The Vitezai men huddled in their furs turned and rose as he strode into their midst. 'Juergan, Bartra, what's happening?' He glanced at Ricolai Tuun, whose expression gave nothing away. Petr and Mikel Hulder were staring at him like he was a stranger. The sixth man didn't rise at all, but remained turned away.

Only five men came with me . . .

Then he saw the faces of the men facing him clearly and stopped, remembering Sacrista Delestre and how sick she'd looked, with flaking skin and bloodshot eyes.

Kore's Blood, what's happened here?

Gricoama bared his teeth, backing up – and the last man rose, lowered his hood to reveal sumptuous oiled black hair, and turned. His face was fuller than it had been, and more youthful, any flaws erased; even his stature was bigger. But he was visibly the same man who'd destroyed his youth.

'Sal'Ahm, Valdyr,' purred Asiv Fariddan. 'It's so good to see you again.'

Hegikaro, Mollachia

'Kirolyna? Is it to your liking?'

Is it to my liking? Hajya echoed silently as she studied the wedding gown in the mirror. The truth was: she hated it. The thick, heavy fabric was impossible to walk properly in. The deathly white looked funereal to her, the lace was fussy and irritating and it all accentuated her dark complexion, which she knew the Mollachs scorned.

But who cares? This whole ceremony is a lie. 'It's fine,' she snapped. 'I'm sick of this – finish it. There will be no more of these "fittings", understood?' She ripped the half-sewn dress from her back, tearing open more seams, and hurled it at the posturing tailor. 'Just make sure I can breathe.'

She stomped to the door in her underclothes then spun, catching the clothiers rolling their eyes. For a moment she was tempted to make some dramatic display – a gnostic light or some such – to show them that she *mattered*, but they'd only end up hating her more, so she fled to the bedroom.

Kyrik was waiting for her, slumped in a seat and looking miserable. 'Aren't you supposed to be drilling the soldiers?' she snapped. She didn't want his or anyone else's company.

'I needed to see my wife.'

'Your *wife*? Are you sure you have one? I doubt Pater Kostyn believes our "pagan" ceremony was valid – I'm sure he could annul it in seconds for you. It's what everyone here wants, after all.'

'That's not true—'

'It damned well is – do you think I'm deaf, blind and stupid? Your people *despise* my clan. When we fight the Rondians, your people won't know who to kill first!'

'We knew it would take time,' Kyrik replied, his normally soothing tones aggravating her today.

'At least Thraan can take the clan into the wilds. I'm stuck in this miserable pile of stones freezing to death while men leer at me and women stick their noses in the air. Even the servants think they're my betters!'

Kyrik flinched. 'I'm sorry. I didn't expect as much . . . resistance.'

'Not "resistance", bigotry,' she corrected. 'I don't think they even see me as human. As far as your "good people" are concerned, I'm worth less than the dogs.'

'That's not true—'

'It might as well be. And anyway, what's the *point*?' She turned away, her eyes blurred, but she refused to cry. She meant to jerk away when Kyrik's arms enfolded her, but she'd ached for his embrace for days, brooding in a lonely guest room. He'd got so much *right* with her that this wrong was doubly painful.

She hunched into herself, caught between love and resentment, unwilling to admit to herself how comforting the arms around her felt.

'I should have told you sooner,' he admitted at last, 'and yes, I concede I was scared that confessing it would destroy our alliance. I'm sorry, I made a mistake. But I have *no* intention of reneging on our vows. You laugh when I say I love you, but it's true. I would do *anything* for you.'

She felt her whole chest and stomach contract at his words, because she so wanted to believe him. 'You don't even *know* me,' she told him. 'The plains are hard, and so are we. We go round and round in our seasonal circles, enduring hardship, disease, war and famine. Love is soft – it doesn't last. I've never believed in it. Men are disposable and interchangeable, not really worth engaging with – but *you* . . . you're so damned *easy* to believe in. Thraan listened; I listened. You have a way of making foolish dreams sound plausible.'

'They're more than plausible – they're essential,' he replied in *that* voice – the passionate, idealistic one that had so lulled her. 'You said it yourself: you go around and around, never looking up, living with no more purpose than ants. Dreams are what make us human, and they're the only way this world will ever become a better place.'

446

She felt that stirring inside that only he could engender in her, and she didn't want to feel it. She wanted to be clear-headed, to make hard-headed decisions, but the truth was, since meeting him, she'd felt more alive than ever before. These last two days of separation had been among the most wretched of her life.

'How can we build something permanent if there's no child to inherit?' she asked.

'There *will* be a child. I've heard healer-magi claim they can help childless couples conceive. Or we'll adopt: it's legal, and it's been done before. There is even provision in law for you to bear Valdyr's child as if it was mine.'

She swallowed at the thought of lying with grim, silent Valdyr. 'Not that. He thinks I'm dirt.'

'You're wrong – yes, he returned from the East hating all dark-skinned people, but he's changed. He knows we're kin, Mollach and Sydian – he's acknowledged it, and I believe in him.'

'You believe in everyone.'

'What's wrong with that?' he asked, nuzzling the top of her head.

'Because one day one of those people you believe in will knife you in the back.'

He stroked her hair and she *had* to turn to face him, and it felt like he saw right through her to the girl inside the woman who wanted love as fiercely as she wanted all things.

'It's going to be hard,' he murmured, 'but I promise you'll always be loved, and always be protected. We'll build a kingdom we're proud of, and hand it on to an heir we've raised, and people who share our dream.'

She closed her eyes, put her head against his chest and felt more tears coming, but they weren't angry tears and it felt good to let them flow. It was as if she were burrowing into him; it felt like a home she could remain in.

Kyrik lifted her chin. 'Is all well between us now? Or must I beg?'

Her anger splintered. 'Ysh, all is well, Husband. All is well between us.'

But the rest of the world is falling into an abyss . . .

Feher Szarvasfeld, Mollachia

Valdyr's zweihandle rasped from his shoulder-scabbard and he placed the six-foot length of steel between himself and Asiv and whatever the Vitezai had become. His eyes were locked on his old abuser as memories rushed in to steal his strength – but he held them off with memories of the past few days, and all he'd gained.

'The past has no more power than you permit it,' Luhti had told him.

I give it none. He reached for the dwyma and felt it respond, helped by Gricoama, who was also bound to that power, being with him.

'Do you know why I'm here?' Asiv drawled languidly. 'It's not for what we shared before; grown men have no interest to me. It's this intriguing power you've gained. The Master has asked me to collect you – you remember Naxius, don't you, Valdyr?'

The name sent a shudder down Valdyr's spine.

'You always were such a fascinating research project,' Asiv said, as he extended his hand and kinesis gripped both Valdyr and Gricoama, locking them immobile. 'Take them alive and unspoiled. He's got nothing that can harm us.'

The contempt in his words burned, but Valdyr strained impotently against the kinesis binding as the Vitezai men closed in, baring teeth and nails as if they'd forgotten they had weapons. They were drooling some kind of black foulness. Something in their stance and flat gaze told them that the men he knew were already gone – and then the survival instincts of the chain-gangs took over – the kill-or-die necessity of surviving when the man next to you cracked, pick-axe in hand . . .

He called to the force he'd been using to crash down lightning from the skies and it answered, streaming through him to wrench Asiv's kinesis-hold apart. His zweihandle crashed into the crook of Petr's neck and Petr crumpled. Valdyr let the momentum of the blow pull him around, sweeping the blade up and under Mikel's chin and halfway through this skull, rendering the brothers' widowed mother childless in two seconds. The blade followed through, back to point, as Ricolai Tuun tried to reach him.

Asiv stared as if too stunned to move: as if what he'd just done was impossible.

Beside him, Gricoama ducked under a raking claw, then leaped at Batra's throat. As the beast gripped and wrenched sideways, the neck audibly snapped. He came away with dark blood on his muzzle, but the wolf appeared to have taken no harm.

'Little Valdyr's learned how to fight,' Asiv mused, as if the loss of three of his pawns meant nothing. Then he made a swatting gesture and a kinesis-blow hurled Gricoama twenty yards upslope. Valdyr's heart went to his mouth as the wolf was dashed against a rock and he heard bones cracking. Gricoama tried to rise, staggered, and with a puppyish whimper of pain, pitched sideways.

Valdyr roared in defiance, raised his blade and began to launch himself at Asiv—

—but footfalls thudded behind him and he spun to find Ricolai coming at him, hands grasping. He ducked under a swinging arm and thrust, burying the zweihandle in the hunter's chest, so deep the point emerged from his back. But Ricolai barely flinched, instead trying desperately to reach him along the length of steel. In desperation, Valdyr hurled him off the blade, watched him roll down the slope and finally go still—

—then sit up. Ricolai clambered to his feet, growling, his eyes bleeding – and Petr Hulder also stood, the wound in his neck and shoulder blade crunching as he moved, black gore streaming down his chest and the stench of decay filling the air. Only Mikel stayed down.

My blade entered Mikel's brain . . .

Valdyr heard a dark chuckle and as he turned to face Asiv, a fatalistic rage set in. He was outnumbered and his foes were more – *or less?* – than human. Although his mind was calling to the dwyma, there was no lightning in the sky above and the winds would take minutes he didn't have to concentrate their force . . .

He backed towards Gricoama as Asiv's wounded slaves closed in . . . and Juergan, as yet untouched, went to Asiv's side, strung his bow and nocked an arrow.

Asiv purred, 'Now, Valdyr, my darling boy, yield and I'll make this easy . . .'

His kinesis closed in again, not so strong this time, as if feeling out Valdyr's resistance. Valdyr bowed his head, letting the grip tighten just a little while he drew in enough from the dwyma to shatter it.

'Take him unharmed,' Asiv reminded his slave-creatures, and Ricolai, Petr and Batra closed in, the air crackling with gnostic force.

Then Valdyr roared, pulsed a blast of *something* that cracked Asiv's grip, spun left and the zweihandle arced, severing Petr's head as he pirouetted. Blocking Batra's raking nails, he booted him in the mid-riff, stepping sideways as the man doubled over, then chopping down. Another head rolled. Ricolai snarled but recoiled – so he clearly had some sense of self-preservation left. Valdyr silently mourned his friends, even as he prayed that this time they'd stay down.

Behind him, Gricoama took strength from his master's defiance. He vented a piercing yowl and lurched upright. Ricolai lunged at him, Valdyr sidestepped and swung—

—and a third head rolled down the slope, the torso flopping wetly to the gravelly slope and twitching into stillness.

'I'd rather not have to hurt you,' Asiv said in that voice of disappointed impatience he'd always used when Valdyr had fought back, before he'd been completely broken, 'but if you don't drop your sword, this archer – Juergan, yes? – will put an arrow through that wolf's heart, and if that doesn't persuade you, then the next will go into your leg.'

The Juergan Valdyr knew was very capable of such a feat, and there was nothing but confident menace in the hunter's eyes now, that and total subservience to Asiv.

How has he done this? It had to be something in the darkened blood and drool, but he couldn't see how that helped him right now. *I'm sorry, Gricoama,* he thought grimly. *I didn't save you just so you could die for me. But I can't let this man take me alive, either . . .*

He stepped in front of the still dazed wolf. 'Go!' he urged it. 'Run! *Live!*'

Gricoama shook himself and lurched upright. Valdyr stepped between the wolf and Juergan's arrow, calling to the dwyma—

—but Juergan's hand flickered, an arrow blurred and buried itself in Valdyr's right thigh. He gasped, staggering as the strength in his legs emptied, and then blue light blasted from Asiv's hand and struck the hilt of the zweihandle. An agonising surge emptied Valdyr's lungs, the weapon spun from his grip and he dropped to his knees, the thud sending another wave of sickening pain through the arrow wound.

'And so easily, the mighty dwymancer is struck down,' Asiv sneered. 'It does make me wonder what value the Master sees in you.' He swaggered forward. Valdyr felt Gricoama rise again, snarling, but a punch of kinesis hurled the beast head over heels down the slope. 'Kill it,' the Keshi told Juergan.

The Vitezai man drooled dark spittle as he nocked another arrow.

Valdyr stared at his hands. They were blackened where the gnosis-blast had taken them and three of his twisted fingers had bone poking through, but he couldn't feel anything beyond his wrists, nor could he make them move. He tried to shift, but the arrow in his thigh ground against his bone and he groaned, his vision swimming. Only one thing was clear: he'd failed – and the worst nightmare of his life was rising again to pull him down. If he could have gripped his dagger he would have stabbed it through his own heart, but all he could do was look up blearily as his old captor loomed over him.

Something whipped through the air and Asiv gasped – and the kinesis-grip holding Valdyr frayed. He fell forward, caught himself on his elbows and blinked his eyes clear in time to see the Keshi stumbling sideways with an arrow in his back.

But not for long; Asiv twisted and yanked it out. He looked up the slope and following his gaze, Valdyr saw Luhti and Zlateyr beside the stag-skull marker, at the edge of the mist.

Asiv snarled and sent a mage-bolt sizzling through the air, but it struck the mist and dissipated as if striking a shield. He roared and tried again, with the same effect, then Zlateyr's arrows flew again, forcing Asiv to cower behind shielding that barely survived the shafts.

Then Eyrik appeared beside his father: his bow flashed and took Juergan in the eye even as the Vitezai man tried to change his aim. The force of the impact made Juergan's neck crack, jerking his head backwards, and he fell bonelessly.

451

In his brain: the arrow struck his brain . . .

Suddenly everything was possible again. Valdyr fumbled for his dagger, unable to feel the grip but pushing his hands to cover the hilt and making his fingers tighten. *I have to bury this in Asiv's head . . .*

But Asiv was far from down, and Eyrik make the fatal error of stepping from the mists. A mage-bolt flashed into the ghost-archer's face, blasting him backwards. As he disappeared, Luhti and Zlateyr cried aloud in pain and grief and started wavering in and out of sight, like reflections in broken glass. Valdyr fell backwards as Asiv turned his way, his left hand coming alight with blue mage-fire.

'You're coming with me,' he snarled, raising his hand to discharge another bolt – and a moment later five hundred pounds of white stag hurtled from the mist with its tines gleaming. Asiv's mage-bolt failed, his shield collapsesd and he threw himself aside, plummeting off a bank and into rocks, bones audibly shattering as he hit.

Valdyr felt his fingers tingle with returning feeling. He began to run as the stag trotted forward, snorting and stamping, closing on the stricken Keshi.

Seeing the air around Asiv swirl and his body reform, Valdyr shouted a warning, but the White Stag's blood was up and it ploughed towards Asiv, head lowered . . .

But at the point of impact, somehow Asiv flattened himself beneath the sweep of the antlers and came up, clamping onto the stag's throat and ripping, while his hands shape-shifted into claws that ripped the beast's throat.

'*No!*' Valdyr shouted, but worse was the stricken cry from up the slope, where Luhti was clutching her chest as she convulsed and fell over. When he whirled back to confront Asiv, the Keshi was hunched over the White Stag, his face buried in its neck and his whole body rippling with violet-tinged gnostic energy: Necromancy. The stag visibly withered in his grasp, desiccating in just six seconds.

Valdyr realised he was feeling something of what was afflicting Luhti, because his own heart began to labour.

Then with a shriek, the shaman Sidorzi erupted from the mists, hurtling towards Asiv with his staff raised as a weapon. The Keshi rose, dropping the pile of darkened fur and bones and conjured more death-light.

'*No, don't*—' Valdyr tried to shout again, but it was already too late: a blast of dark purple energy had struck the shaman and he flew apart, already more bone than flesh. But his sacrifice bought an instant when the Keshi's shields were weakened and Zlateyr's arrow punched through in a blaze of sparks and slammed into Asiv's face.

The Keshi staggered and fell, and Valdyr heard himself shriek in triumph – but the shaft had torn open Asiv's cheek, not entered his skull and he ripped it out, howling wordlessly as he tore his face apart. But his next blast of power sprayed harmlessly on the mists that were now boiling down the slope again. Luhti was on her knees, clearly weak, but with her arms outstretched as she beseeched the heavens.

Even as Asiv remembered Valdyr and turned his way, the fog enveloped him, and mad thoughts of charging back to slay his old tormentor died incomplete as another convulsion shook his chest. He lurched upslope and fell against Gricoama. He clutched the wolf's shoulders for support while Asiv's bawled threats receded amid impotent blasts of energy.

Agonising moments later, Valdyr and Gricoama staggered up to the two remaining dwyma-ghosts. Zlateyr was bent over the prone Luhti, his usually austere face distraught. 'Help her,' the hero demanded. 'You must save her!'

Valdyr threw a look backwards, but they were in a sea of mist and he could no longer hear Asiv. Gricoama, still wavering from the punishment he'd taken, licked at Luhti's pale face anxiously, but she was unconscious.

'I don't know how,' Valdyr replied, his voice anguished.

Zlateyr grabbed his arm. 'You must, for *she* is the genilocus now – you *must* save her! We need you, dwymancer: *you* are what gives the power here direction. You must harness it to help her.'

Valdyr felt his world coming apart. 'But my brother's getting married in three days and I must warn him—'

'If you leave here, the dwyma has no voice and will be helpless to that being out there – *your* Asiv. You brought this evil here, Sarkany: you must protect us from it.'

Valdyr glared back, wanting to lash out, wanting to run, but Luhti looked like death, and if he left her, who was to say whether there would be still a genilocus for him when he returned – if he ever did.

Dear Kore, he's right . . . Kyrik, I think you're on your own this time . . . He bowed his head at the realisation. 'All right . . . but we have to get her to shelter.'

Zlateyr squeezed his arm in thanks, then bent and picked up Luhti. Cradling her against his big chest, he climbed the slope, Valdyr on his heels, as the mist swirled and darkened. There was no sound but their pained breathing. The arrow in Valdyr's thigh was agony and his hands were still blackened and twisted. For a few dazed moments he wondered if it were possible to walk straight out of this world and into Hel . . . then he realised he was thinking of the Amteh vision of Hel: a place of ice. Just the sort of place seeing Asiv conjured in his mind.

I won't let you win, Asiv. I can't let you win . . .

31

Not a Weapon

Hermetic: Morphic-Gnosis

Who would not wish to be stronger, younger or fairer? What a gift this is! Kore is great indeed, for only He bestows such blessings!

CARLOTH CROZIER, CHURCH OF KORE, ARGUNDY, 803

Only a mage would warp the body Ahm gave him and call that a blessing.

GODSPEAKER HEJALI, SHALIYAH, 805

Sunset Isle, Pontic Sea
Octen 935

Ogre is not a weapon or a tool. Ogre is not a monster. He is a sentient being.

Ogre's mantra had been first given to him by the great Antonin Meiros himself, when he'd rescued Ogre from the secret place where Ervyn Naxius had wrought his crimes. These words had saved his life many times over, when the darkness inside became overwhelming – but despite Lord Meiros, Ogre knew deep inside that for most of his life, he had been little else than both weapon and tool. He'd been born in a vat, bred as an amalgam of man and beast, to whom Naxius gave intellect and the gnosis. The Master had made others, both beautiful and grotesque, but he was the ugliest.

'Why did you make me ugly, Master?' Ogre asked the omnipresent memory of Naxius, and the reply was always, *The better to terrify those I wish to break.* And to the question, 'Why did you make me stupid, Master?' the answer was, *The better to foster obedience.*

455

But Ogre wasn't stupid, although he'd not understood that until much later, because the only person he ever spoke with was the Master, who was a genius.

Now, from his corner in the engineering chamber, Ogre watched the young student Urien work the control levers. Ogre liked Urien. He had an enquiring mind and would make a good mage, maybe a great one. In thirty years he might even head the order. *And I'll still be here . . .*

Why did you give me such longevity, Master? Because Naxius despised having to teach new slaves. *You will live as long as I wish you to, my dear monster.*

'Why did you make me a monster, Master?' he sighed. *Because a monster is what I require . . .*

Though these debates were just memory, Ogre was certain the Master still heard him and whispered his dark poison into his brain. Some believed the Master dead, but Ogre was certain Naxius lived, and was aware of all Ogre did and desired. Evil things never died.

The magi and their students thought Ogre grotesque and pitiful. They were contemptuous of his shambling bulk and gross features. Since his rescue, his world had shrunk to just a few corridors and chambers, rooms that were seldom frequented by others. The scholars thought him tamed; they didn't know the daily struggle he endured. He'd been alive only twenty years, but he'd been born an adult and was as strong and vital as on his first day of consciousness. He'd heard intelligent men and women argue over the purpose of their lives, but he knew what he'd been created for – and he *rejected* it.

Ogre is not a weapon or a tool. Ogre is not a monster.

The darkness heard and laughed, for it knew better.

Alyssa disentangled herself from the hard-muscled male body beneath her and stretched out on the bed, revelling in the glory of being her gorgeous, irresistible self, on her journey back to greatness. She'd decided that it didn't matter that without the gnosis, she was a crippled horror, because she *had* the gnosis. It didn't matter that a ghastly daemon-vessel was wrapped around her heart, because through it, she could do *anything*.

All that mattered was that she, Alyssa Dulayne, was *glorious*.

The dazed Keshi Air-mage beside her, barely eighteen, looked like he daren't pinch himself in case he woke: that was the sort of appreciation she enjoyed. If only he'd been Rashid, the moment would have been perfect.

But he wasn't, and she sat up, irked suddenly. The things she didn't have – a throne, Rashid, recognition of her perfection – loomed over the little she did have: this tiny cabin in a warship endlessly circling Sunset Tower, a pillar of stone raised against the sky like a giant *rukka te* to nature, the gods and her.

'Get out,' she told the young Hadishah pilot, and when he started to protest, she backhanded him viciously, ripping open his cheek with her rings. For a moment he looked stupid enough to take her on – and if he had, she'd have eviscerated him and drunk his soul – but then he blanched and fled, still naked. For a moment she regretted she'd ever let him in here. *He wasn't worthy.* He didn't deserve the honour of pleasuring her.

But then she shrugged. It hadn't been about him anyway. *Everything is about me.*

She put him from her mind as she cleaned herself, then fidgeted, bored with this siege. *Two weeks!* It felt like the world was passing her by. In the Kedron Valley, the Shihad was preparing to battle the Rondian Empire – she should be there, glowing from the success of bringing Jehana Mubarak to the Master and reinstated to her true place at Rashid's side. She needed to resolve this, quickly.

The problem was, even if one of her agents was inside the tower, they couldn't contact her, nor she them: the protective wards were *immense*, sustained by the energy feeding the Bridge. And that theoretical agent probably didn't know she was out here, or that she sought Jehana Mubarak.

The impasse was driving her insane.

I have to find a way to disable the tower, otherwise any approach will see my ships blasted apart. But the universe stubbornly refused to provide, and her frustrated fury grew as the days passed.

Milady Alyssa, a voice whispered in the aether, and Alyssa was instantly alert. *Milady Alyssa, are you there?*

She knew the voice and her heart leaped: one of the snakes she'd loosed in the grass years ago, barely touching since then, except to ensure loyalty – but this one was special . . . this one, she trusted more than most.

Even knowing the sender couldn't see her, she repaired her ruined body before seizing the link and demanding, *<Where are you?>*

<Inside Sunset Tower,> he replied, and her heart pounded with excitement. *<They're finally letting everyone take turns to serve the solarus energy flows, to help the Magisters cope.>* His voice was eager. *<Tonight, it's my turn. I've only a few minutes alone, though.>*

Alyssa crowed inwardly. *<Is Jehana Mubarak still in there with you?>* she asked as the pieces began to move into place in her mind. *<Can you get us inside?>* She was almost drooling in anticipation: at last, a chance to try the plan she'd formulated during her furtive life after Rashid had turned her out, appalled by the crippled horror she'd become. She'd wormed her way into the shadow realm of Kesh's underworld, thence into the secret society of Souldrinkers; by capturing a mage who needed to feed on the souls of others to empower their gnosis, she used her training as a scholar to work out how to duplicate what they did using a combination of Necromancy, Spiritualism and Wizardry. Now she had a new aim.

I'm already a mage, and a daemon-host: how powerful will I become when I'm a dwymancer as well?

Since Tarita's arrival, Jehana's life had become even more confined. She knew there was dissent among the senior magi about what to do with her, so now she was confined to her quarters – and it was driving her mad, even though she'd been permitted to move the fish-tank into her room. She spent a good many hours staring at the gold-flecked fish she'd rescued as it circled round and round, wondering if she hadn't been completely mistaken about its significance.

She'd not been able to speak to Tarita and that chafed too. She might not be sure she could trust the Jhafi, but she was desperate for news of her brother. She was brooding on the injustices when the door opened and Simonia waddled in, carrying her evening meal. 'Put it on the table,' Jehana instructed, yawning—

—then her jaw dropped as the plump Rondian deflated, her face changed and suddenly she was a slender Ahmedhassan. Tarita winked and locked the door, then helped herself to some wine.

'What are you doing here?' Jehana exclaimed, checking the locking-wards, which were far stronger than anything she could have set herself. *She's a Merozain Ascendant*, she recalled, suddenly nervous. 'What do you want?'

'To see you, of course,' Tarita said airily. 'They're not letting me near you – Manon fobbed me off for a week with promises, and then told me flat-out to stay away. But these Ordo Costruo aren't the slickest conspirators; it just took a little time to work out their routines.' She drank, then asked, 'What is it about you and Waqar that the Masked Cabal want so badly? No, don't try to deny it. I heard it from Felix's mouth when he tried to persuade your brother to join them.'

Jehana swallowed. *They tried to enlist Waqar?* 'What did Waqar say?'

'He said "No". Then we killed Felix – his real name was Saarif Ibram. Do you know him?'

'No – but you said Alyssa Dulayne is one of them?'

'I'm certain she is. Felix said they did something to your mother – a "gift", he called it. It all got very confusing at Midpoint that night, but we – Waqar, his friends and I – were tracking your mother when the tower exploded, and after that she was gone. Felix said that you and Waqar have some power bred into you – so what is it, Princess? And don't say "royalty"!'

Can I trust her? Jehana pondered, *or can I afford not to?* Hurriedly, she told Tarita about the dwyma, and the Ordo Costruo's attempt to breed magi who could use it. 'Apparently Mother was one of four with the potential, but the other three defected to the Shihad during the Third Crusade – they created the storm that helped destroy the Rondian Army at the Battle of Shaliyah. Mother said she'd sensed them die that day.'

'Then they must have been alive as draugs – I think that's what they were at Midpoint,' Tarita replied. 'Your mother was brought back from death too. I saw her.'

Jehana's mouth flooded with bile at the very thought. *'They dared?'*

'This Masked Cabal will dare *anything*. Clearly Rashid knew about those other three, so presumably he also knew about your mother – and you and Waqar. I wonder why he let you all run around free for so long? And why he suddenly wants you so badly now?'

'I've been wondering the same,' Jehana admitted, 'I think there are two reasons: he might have been hoping we'd come to him of our own free will, so he'd not have to coerce us – and Mother died before she could tell me how to become a dwymancer, so I can't imagine Rashid knows.' She bit her lip, then added, 'Though I do know the theory, if we could get out of here . . . ?'

Tarita said slowly, 'So he let you learn, hoping to bring you back to the fold afterwards. But are the Masks doing his bidding, or is he doing theirs? Or do they just want the same things?'

'I don't know,' Jehana admitted. 'Mother was planning to awaken the dwyma in me after I'd graduated from the Arcanum this year, but when she died they rushed me to Pontus, then here. Only Manon here knows about my potential.'

'Waqar didn't appear to know anything about it when Felix told him.'

'I was only told about the dwyma when I rejoined mother in Hebusalim, after the Third Crusade. Waqar chose to stay in Hebusalim – he was in awe of Rashid.'

'I think you'll find he's past that now,' Tarita said dryly. 'While he and I sought your mother, I could see the scales dropping from his eyes. He suspects Rashid of ordering your mother's death. He's with the Shihad because he has no choice, but he loves you: that is obvious.'

That her brother was still himself was an incredible relief. 'I suppose I should thank you,' Jehana said reluctantly, then couldn't stop herself asking, 'Did you really kiss him?'

'He kissed me, actually.'

Jehana scowled. She found Tarita irritating, although she wasn't precisely sure why – her low-caste manners combined with her confident strut, maybe? She reminded Jehana of concubines she'd met: dirt-caste beauties with no understanding of what it *meant* to be noble, swanning around court trying to pretend they belonged.

But she's Merozain – how does a nobody even become a mage? 'You shouldn't set your aim so high,' she advised. 'My brother's far beyond you.'

Tarita lifted her nose. 'I've bedded Rimoni nobles and Merozain masters – there's no man so lofty that he doesn't want to get down low with a pretty girl – even a dirt-caste like me, Princess. So spare me the jealousy.'

'*Jealous?* Promiscuity is nothing to be proud of.'

'But it's fun,' Tarita drawled, then her face hardened. 'And sometimes it's all a girl can do to survive, but I expect a precious little princess never finds herself in those sorts of situations. But that's by the by: the issue is not how I bed your brother, but how we get out of here without Alyssa knowing.'

'You're assuming I'd go anywhere with you,' Jehana retorted, then realised she was being ridiculous. 'All right, yes, I do want to get out. Everyone else wants to push me around, but I want to push back harder. I want the dwyma, but that means . . . going to certain places,' she concluded evasively.

'Do you know where?'

'I think so,' Jehana said. Reading of Amantius and Seidopus had been helpful.

'Then I'll get us out,' Tarita promised. 'Oh – what are your gnostic affinities?'

'Water and Theurgy. I suppose with your Merozain training, you can do everything?'

'Sure can,' Tarita drawled, then added, 'Listen, I'd better go – Tovar's giving me a guided tour of the tower in a few minutes.'

Jehana wrinkled her nose. 'Watch out for him. He's only after one thing.'

'I'm counting on it,' Tarita replied brazenly. 'It's been months since I got nailed.' She noticed Jehana's expression and added, 'Spare me – I know more about men than you ever will.' She sashayed out, her stolen robes billowing as illusions transformed her into Simonia again.

Dirt-caste slut, Jehana thought, staring after her. But her pulse was skipping at the thought of escape.

Tovar's tour of the tower lasted three rooms – two lounges and an empty sick bay – before he slipped up behind Tarita, encircled her waist and grasped her breasts through the thin cotton chemise she wore.

461

It was *way* too soon. Despite her bravado with Jehana, she'd not completely made up her mind how far she was willing to let Tovar go. She was still persuadable as she let him fondle her, grinding his crotch against her buttock crease, willing to see if there was magic in his mouth and tongue as she twisted and offered her lips – but when she saw the ugly contempt behind his eyes and the way he averted his mouth from hers – willing to rukk her but not kiss her – she realised that she was just a tick in a box marked 'Jhafi yoni'.

'Kore's Balls, you're almost black,' he leered. 'Blackest I've had.'

'Not *had*, and nor will you,' she retorted, using kinesis as she twisted and threw him into the wall, hard. 'I'll finish this tour on my own, *pig.*' She yanked her clothing back into place while his face went from surprise to anger to exasperation.

'Come on,' he complained, 'I was kidding – I'll treat you right.'

'I don't think so,' she snapped.

Then the door opened and Hillarie peered in, calling: 'Is someone—... Oh!'

She and Tovar exchanged a look that contained a lot more than embarrassment, then Hillarie pouted, 'If you're *done*, I need something from the cabinet.'

Tarita refused to show any shame; she stalked past the older woman and slammed the door behind her, paused as a blazing row broke out, then hurried away, feeling stupid and angry with herself.

The princess was right about him . . . and me.

Tarita had been orphaned young and had grown up so wild that one of her many 'aunties' had declared that 'she had the itch' – and that *itch* had got her into bad places at times, but it had also sometimes got her what she needed. Becoming a mage had given her the personal discipline to better control her desires, and even understand them a little.

Like some orphans I've known, you're sexually needy, but you take lovers you dislike, while pushing away friends, one Merozain master had noted. *Why is that?*

Because sex ruins friendship, she'd replied – it had certainly ruined all her past friendships with men. Perhaps Waqar would be different, when she saw him again?

Rukka te, Tovar, she thought sourly, striding away.

It was still early morning, but they were sharing eight-hour shifts now, with a third of the twenty magi and students sleeping while the rest worked above and below, or maintained the wardings on the portals to the outside. As she wandered around, she tried to envisage ways of getting her skiff through Alyssa's blockade.

Perhaps there are tunnels below . . . or some way of reaching the water? A Water-mage could swim out of here, with luck . . .

She reached the engineering level unnoticed, where she found Magister Loric instructing Urien about the fittings. 'Don't – whatever you do! – try to pull these cables out.' Loric was pointing at a copper tube emerging from the central cylinder and plunging into the floor. 'There won't be enough left of you to bury.'

Urien looked suitably aghast, while Tarita wondered if Loric would deign to explain the tower's workings to her if she asked. *I doubt it,* she decided, so she stayed in the shadows, prowling between the pipes and fresh-water tanks, then stealing down to the lowest level, where she found the rock was unburnished. She wrinkled her nose at a ripe, musky smell as she moved through the dimly lit chamber between piles of mouldering cloth and rags. Then the largest mound twitched and two pale eyes opened, too far apart for a normal person.

'Who are you?' a cavernous voice rumbled.

She was genuinely shocked that someone had got so close – so much that she grasped at where her scimitar would have been – but of course it was still upstairs.

But if the Ordo Costruo permitted this being's presence, perhaps they weren't dangerous? 'I'm Tarita,' she offered.

'Ah,' the voice rumbled. 'I hear talk of Tarita.'

'Who are you?' she asked, standing a little straighter and kindling a little light on her fingers. It revealed a hunched figure, too big and wide to be a man, with leathery brown skin, immense shoulders and thighs, a thick powerful neck and a misshapen skull. The creature had an ugly, brutish face, with an undershot jaw and broken tusk-like teeth. His nose was flat, with wide nostrils; straggling hair hung to his chest and his big eyes narrowed to slits in his jowly face.

And indeed, what *are you?* she wondered.

'I am Ogre,' the thing responded. That was the word for a type of monster from Yurosi myth, which struck her as trite, and telling. She got wariness, even shyness, but there was no sense of threat, despite his monstrous appearance.

So she curtseyed like a lady and said, 'I'm pleased to meet you, Ogre.'

'No one pleased to meet Ogre,' he replied, as if he feared he was being mocked.

And maybe I was, she admitted to herself, but his perception impressed her. 'Then I'm not no one,' she said. 'Do you live down here?' She looked around, noting that although the whole place needed a good wash and airing, there was no mould and no filth. He was reclusive, perhaps, but clearly house-trained. And there had been no wards on the doors or stairs to the upper levels to keep him in.

'Ogre serves,' the giant creature rumbled. 'Made to serve.'

Made to serve. A construct . . . an illegal *construct, because they're not supposed to be able to talk.* 'I'm surprised to meet one of your kind among the Ordo Costruo—'

'Ordo Costruo shelters me,' Ogre rumbled. 'Even though I am . . . *abomination.*'

The way he said that word spoke volumes. Some renegade must have made him – and the Ordo Costruo let him live. The scholars went up a notch in her estimation. 'People have said the same about me,' she replied. '"Why give a crippled dirt-caste girl the gnosis?" they asked. Many would have let me die. But my mistress saved me.'

Ahm bless you, Alhana.

'Then you had a good mistress, Tarita. My master was a bad man.'

'You have my sympathy,' Tarita said, holding out her hand.

Ogre's eyes widened: they were a pale amber, with a haunted quality. His massive paw enfolded her hand. 'Lady Tarita,' he said in courtly fashion, like someone reciting words in a book. 'I am at your service.'

'I'm only a servant too, no lady. But we can be friends.'

'Friends?' Ogre said, clearly surprised. 'You are not an engineer. Only engineers are friends to Ogre.' He ruminated for a long time, his expressive face going through many shifts, before he said, 'I could try.'

His earnestness, incongruous with his size and appearance, was an antidote to Tovar's crassness. 'Thank you, Ogre. I wondered, if it's not too presumptuous, could you tell me about the tower? Loric is too busy.'

Ogre ruminated, then gave her a sly glance. 'Magister Loric is always busy, Tarita. Let us not disturb him.' He rose to an alarming height – around seven feet tall, despite being somewhat hunched – but he moved with surprising grace for his bulk, and courteously, ensuring she had space.

At the top of the stairs he called to Loric, 'Ogre go to Oceanarium,' while shielding her from view, then led her into a corridor. When she squeezed his hand, he gave her a troubled look, then said, 'You are safe with me, I promise.'

'I already knew that.' Up close, he just smelled a little musky. 'Very clever, Ogre.'

'No, Ogre not clever.'

'I think you underrate yourself. Please, tell me of your tower.'

As they walked, Ogre spoke with an engaging boyish enthusiasm and she sensed an innocence that was both virtue and vulnerability. He was clearly lonely, and wanted to be liked, but there were clear hints of past maltreatment; he referred to his previous master several times, always with a shudder.

Then they entered a room with an underwater window and he fell silent as she walked to the glass and stared out at the sea, lit from above by sunlight.

'Ogre,' she exclaimed, 'this is *wonderful!*' She beamed up at him, astounded.

A tremor ran through him. '*Ogre is not a weapon!*' he muttered, suddenly caught up in some inner struggle. '*Ogre is not a tool.*' For a moment she felt threatened, until he visibly suppressed it. '*Ogre is not a weapon. Ogre is not a tool.*'

'You're a good person, Ogre,' she said instinctively. 'I'm glad to have met you.'

He took a deep, deep breath and then expelled it. 'Ogre glad to meet Tarita, too. But Ogre must go now.' He looked frightened, on the edge of some trauma.

'Wait!' she called, although he barely paused, 'may I see you tomorrow?'

He hurried away, but called over his shoulder, 'If it pleases you.'

Then he was gone.

She stared, intrigued and mystified. 'It does please me,' she murmured, sending the words arrowing into his mind. She sensed boiling emotion inside him, but deliberately didn't intrude. If he had some secret shame or struggle, it was his own. She wanted to win his trust, not rake over his coals.

'Ogre is not a weapon or a tool. Ogre is not a monster.' He sat in the dark, remembering how small and delicate she was, his new friend Tarita, but good remembrances became embroiled with bad ones, as they always did: vulnerable women Master Naxius had abused, the old man riding Ogre's body, making him do things that still gave Ogre nightmares ...

Ogre is not a weapon or a tool, Antonin Meiros had declared to the tribunal. *Ogre is not a monster. He is a sentient being, a victim of Ervyn Naxius and his madness.*

They never caught the Master. He was still out there ... and still inside Ogre's head. If he closed his eyes, he could hear him, right now ...

Alyssa's mole making contact had been the crucial first step; after that, her plans evolved quickly. A week later, standing on the deck watching the distant beacon, she turned to Nuqhemeel. 'It's time. Send in the first wave.'

The Hadishah bowed, picked up his relay-stave and transmitted the message. Then he looked at her. 'Why two waves, Lady?'

Because if this goes wrong, the first wave might be obliterated. But he didn't need to know that. 'I want to measure their response, with something in reserve.'

She watched eagerly as a dozen windships detached from the encircling ring of vessels and began to arrow towards Sunset Tower. It was after midnight and all *should* be ready. Either she was betrayed – in which case some of the imbeciles and nobodies who served her would die – or she was inside and Jehana Mubarak would be hers. The men had her description – she *must* be taken alive. The rest didn't matter.

As the ships drew nearer, her heart began to beat harder – and still the tower didn't blaze into life . . .

We're in, she thought, licking her lips. *We're in . . . Jehana Mubarak, I can almost taste your soul . . .*

32

The Key to the Tower

Sorcery

Sorcery was the last of the Studies to be codified and explored, and because it deals with the spirit world of ghosts and daemonic beings, it remains on the outer edges of our understanding of the gnosis. They cast shadows upon our consciousness, but they couldn't reach us, nor we them, until the gnosis was gained. Understanding them may lead to full understanding of the human condition, why we're here, and where we're going.

IDREA NASCOULOS, *PEROPOLIS THE FALLEN*, LANTRIS, 796

Sunset Isle, Pontic Sea
Octen 935

Tovar Kestrel – he'd chosen the name at the orphanage – had never known his mother, but he'd always dreamed that she was watching over him, guiding his life from beyond the grave. Until he turned fourteen, he had no idea who she was – but in 928, just as the Third Crusade was starting, he found a letter under his pillow.

The next day he and a dozen fellow students were flown from Hebusalim to Pontus, to keep them safe – and they were lucky, for the rest, sent to a fortress later stormed by the Hadishah, had ended up in the breeding-houses. Some were still there.

Tovar carried the letter everywhere.

Nephew, I write this on behalf of your mother. She never intended to conceive and is unsuited to motherhood. Instead, you have been left to the Order. Do not let your orphan state dishearten you. Your mother will love to see you one day, and I will arrange that. In the meantime, learn well and do not be deceived by appearances. Your father is of the East, in part through blood, and entirely in allegiance. In your heart, follow his example, and one day he will be made known to you. Your loving Aunt.

It had been a huge shock – especially the revelation of his Eastern ancestry. He'd spent hours staring at mirrors, trying to see the hints of it, but although he tanned easily, his hair was pale as his skin. The Ordo Costruo magi were able to determine that he was three-quarter-blood: the child of a half-blood and a pure-blood – but their tracing spells had failed to determine who and they believed his parents dead.

He'd expected further contact, but nothing came until two years ago, when Alyssa Dulayne had entered his life, a woman as beautiful as a dream: *his aunt.* When she'd explained her true loyalties, he'd made them his too: loyalty to the East, to the blood of his father, and most of all to her, the most bewitching creature in Creation. Their kinship remained secret for now, but together, they'd mapped out his career. So well did she understand him that her decision that he become a sentinel suited his own inclinations perfectly. The protectors of the Order were the natural place for an athletic, martially inclined Ordo Costruo mage.

And he never forgot where his true loyalties lay.

'Tovar?'

He jerked back to reality, cursing himself for letting his mind wander. He was sitting on the throne of the tower itself and the crystal dome above was glowing crimson. 'Sorry, Magister Hillarie,' he said. 'The aether is busy tonight.'

And there are twelve Keshi wind-dhou approaching, unbeknownst to anyone in here but me.

'The energy is always your *first* priority,' Hillarie said waspishly, while her eyes asked, *How could you do that to me?* He wasn't overly concerned: Hillarie had been a way to amuse himself, nothing more. It was annoying that she'd walked in on him and the Noorie, but it scarcely mattered. In a few moments, nothing would matter a jot.

He glanced around the chamber. Simonia was dozing, awaiting her turn at the throne, but that was all. A third of those supposedly protecting the place were asleep, and most of the rest were exhausted.

He scanned the skies and realised that the Keshi ships were almost ready to dock. It was time to act. So he sat up, pulling a woozy face. 'Hillarie, I'm not feeling well tonight. My head is all over the place. Could you take over?'

'Your head is all over the place?' Hillarie echoed. 'Then pull yourself together!' Despite her words, she bustled in, anxious to forgive, as he knew she would. Their liaison might mean nothing to him, but she clung to it, looking at him longingly as they swapped place. As Tovar stepped off, she sidled into position, placed her palms down on the control crystals on each armrest and closed her eyes, ready to engage with the energy flows.

As Hillarie registered in shock that there were a dozen windships practically outside the window, Tovar drew his dagger and drove the blade through her right ear and into her brain. She jerked once then sagged, already dead.

Wow! That was . . . fun!

'Magister Hillarie?' Simonia squeaked from the far side of the room. 'What's wrong?' All she'd seen from her side was Hillarie appearing to faint. She looked plaintively at Tovar. 'Dear Kore – what's wrong?'

'I think she's had a seizure,' Tovar replied, putting the bloody dagger behind his back and going to meet her. 'She's bleeding from her right ear!'

Simonia gave another strangled yelp, then she closed her eyes to begin a gnostic call for aid – so he placed the bloody dagger against her left breast, over her thumping heart, and drove it in.

Simonia's eyes flew open, her jaw dropped and she wobbled. 'Tovar—?'

Better this than the breeding-houses, Simonia, he murmured into her dying mind. *You should be thanking me.*

She thudded to the floor, her bewildered face going slack. In seconds blood was pooling around her.

Tovar had heard that killing could cause a visceral bout of remorse that hit you with guilt and nausea, but instead, he was charged with adrenalin: his heart was thumping, his skin was flushed and he felt more alive than he ever had.

That was as good as sex. Then he paused and wondered, *What would it be like to do both at once?*

But that could wait: he was committed now, and that empowered him too. His weapons tutor had told them endlessly that choice could paralyse the mind. When only one course was possible, doubt faded and one was free to do what was necessary.

Tovar carelessly rolled Hillarie from the throne, the body he'd been enjoying for months already nothing to him. He took the seat again and set about opening the warded doors to the landing platform three-quarters of the way up the tower. Then he sent out another call as the first ship landed and began to disgorge men.

<*Aunty, the key is in the lock and has been turned. You are free to approach.*>

The affectionate glow of Alyssa's touch and voice across the miles filled his skull, <*Well done, Nephew. You have my gratitude. See you very soon.*>

The sound of her, the feel of her gnostic trace, filled the void in his heart where his parents should have been. *She's going to make me immortal: she promised.*

Below, on the landing platform, successive ships landed more soldiers, who opened the now-unwarded doors and entered the tower. He felt a smile crease his face – not in enmity towards those who'd raised him, but because it felt good to be at the centre of things, making things *happen*. That was what immortals did: they made decisions that elevated some and destroyed others on a whim – like the Lantric Gods.

What a glorious night – and it's only just begun.

Jehana was pacing anxiously, counting the minutes until midnight. Tarita had left her a note that evening, saying she had a plan to get them off the island without raising the alarms.

This might be a haven, but I have to get away . . .

Her last meal was also making her brain overheat: following an impulse she couldn't even explain, she'd cooked and eaten the gold-flecked fish. The meal had been unremarkable – but now, several hours on, she was feeling the same disconnected dizziness she'd had when she'd gained the gnosis as a thirteen-year-old. The edge of her sight was blurring and sounds were coming and going strangely – which was surely how she heard a scraping, rattling sound through the exterior stone walls.

Puzzled, she went to the window and looked up towards the landing platform – and to her surprise, she saw several windships silhouetted against the dark sky. *Perhaps the blockade has been broken?* she thought hopefully – then she realised that the sails on the nearest ship were *triangular*. Her heart went to her mouth: the Keshi had somehow slipped by the vigil of the solarus-throne. They were here, *for her.*

She threw a cloak over her clothes, slipped on her most comfortable sandals and belted on her purse. *Don't let them take you*, her mind kept repeating. *Don't let them take you.* She went into the circular inner corridor and tapped on Sentinel Levana's door beside the stairs.

The door was yanked open and Levana stood there, still armed and armoured, just off duty. 'What is it?' she asked tiredly.

'There's a Keshi ship on the landing platform—'

Levana's eyes bulged and then she pushed past, drawing steel. 'Lock yourself in my rooms,' she ordered, running to the bottom of the stairs and looking up.

I'm not locking myself anywhere I can't get out of, Jehana thought, casting about. *Where's Tarita?*

Then they heard shouting from the stairwell. Levana conjured shields and went running up the stairs as a man bellowed in pain. Sentinel Geryn burst from the next room, sword already drawn, saw Jehana and shouted, 'Girl, what's going on?'

'The Keshi are here – they're inside the tower!'

Geryn grabbed her shoulder. 'Get below, girl – wake the dormitories! The emergency assembly point is the ground floor – *go!*'

She obeyed and started running down the stairs while Geryn raced to join Levana, who was shielding against a torrent of fire, then countering bolts. Smoke filled the air and Jehana felt her throat dry as her vision wavered. Geryn glanced back and shouted furiously, '*Get out, girl!*'

So she hurtled down the curved stairs, as fast as she dared descend, as the energy surges above her intensified. Breathlessly, she stopped by each door and hammered, calling, 'We're under attack – we have to get to the ground level!'

A few heads poked from doors and called after her blearily, but the alarm bells had finally begun to ring, and other students took up her calls.

'*Waken! We're breached! Waken! Waken!*'

It felt hopeless – there were so few of them, and she'd glimpsed more than one ship. *We're all magi*, she tried to tell herself, but there was a vast difference between mage-scholars and mage-warriors. Down and down she went, until she emerged on the mezzanine overlooking the ground-level foyer.

Something hammered massively on the double doors, but no wards blazed to reinforce them. *All the tower's protective wards can be controlled from the throne*, she remembered being told. Another blow struck, and then another. The iron bracings twisted and timber began to splinter.

If she hesitated any longer, she'd be trapped above the lobby – so she leaped to the railings and threw herself into space as another flurry of blows crashed into the giant doors. She used kinesis to break her fall, rolled and came up, then heard a cry of shock as more students reached the mezzanine above: Urien was standing with a girl named Shae, and there was another pair behind them.

'Down here,' Jehana shouted. '*Hurry—*'

With commendable quick thinking, Urien, an Air-mage, took Shae's hand and pulled her over the rail. The other two ran, pounding down the stairs as Urien and Shae landed before Jehana – then the main doors crashed open with a kinesis-blast that sent them all sprawling. Jehana spun across the polished floor and came to a halt, looking up blearily as a salt-laden gale howled in. A dozen Keshi poured through, screaming war-cries, as she regained her feet, clutched her periapt and kindled gnosis-fire. Urien and Shae did likewise. None of them were armed.

Then with a shrill cry, a small, dark shape detached from the mezzanine and flew down to land, perfectly poised in high guard, a silvery-bladed scimitar glinting as she rose from one knee. Fire blazed in her left palm: *Tarita.*

A maelstrom of mage-bolts and spells tore into her, but the Merozain's shields flashed so bright they were opaque and she loosed a counter-attack that shattered three men in a heartbeat. Then she erupted from the sparks, blade aflame, flashing into the midst of the Hadishah, slashing and spinning. Two more went down, one dead and the other howling and clutching his belly.

Jehana saw an opening: the door to the engineering floor. She shouted to Urien and Shae, 'Here – get below!' and they all turned to run as more Hadishah charged in, drawn to Tarita, who was carving through them like a steel wind. Her aura was a rainbow, spells of all types spiking from her as she dodged, lunged and cartwheeled away, never still, never a target.

Then some of them caught sight of Jehana and one man shouted, 'There she is!'

Jehana swore and blazed at him with a mage-bolt that knocked him off his feet, then she sprinted for the downwards stairs. Shae looked panic-stricken, but Urien was surprisingly composed as he pulled her along behind.

'Get below!' Jehana shouted again, lancing another mage-bolt at an oncoming Hadishah, who must have been low-blooded because her bolt blazed straight through his shields, leaving his skull blackened to the bone. Her gorge rose, but she swallowed, hard – and battered aside a hurled dagger, then a mage-bolt.

The other two students had been cut off and were retreating back up the stairs; even more worryingly, Tarita was being engulfed. *'TARITA!'* Jehana shouted, pitching her voice to cut through the rising cacophony, *'HERE!'*

The Merozain exploded from the press: her left arm was gashed, but her blade, wreathed in purple light, was lethal. Fire exploded around her, but she erupted from the blast like a meteor, hurtling past Jehana as the flames died.

Jehana blocked another mage-bolt and slammed the door in the face of a woman Hadishah who was screaming to Ahm, then Tarita, still smouldering, burned and bleeding, laid a hand over the door and locking wards clicked into place. 'Ascendant power,' she panted. 'It'll buy us a little time.'

Jehana was appalled at the damage the Merozain had taken: jagged cuts, livid bruises and smouldering burns, as well as a suppurating hole where she'd clearly ripped an arrow from her shoulder. Her left hand was skeletal and her clothing was in sooty tatters – Jehana noticed she was in travelling clothes; clearly she had been making ready to leave. Her leather satchel must have been well-warded, because that and her weapon were the only things she had that weren't damaged.

Tarita managed a wan grin before making some sort of complicated gesture – and a wave of healing-gnosis Jehana could almost feel pulsed through her body. Many of the wounds sealed and her left hand swelled back to normal proportions.

'What happened to you?' Jehana asked.

'I used a little too much Necromancy,' Tarita drawled. 'And the fireball I cast just then didn't help.'

Jehana gasped. 'You did that to *yourself*?'

'You should see the other guys! Did anyone else make it?'

'Urien and Shae are below. And whoever's on duty down there, I guess.'

'Loric will have someone helping him,' Tarita said, then she brightened. 'And Ogre will be down here too. We might need him.'

Jehana wrinkled her nose at the memory of Ogre – and anyway, resistance felt doomed. What they needed was a way out. 'Where's your skiff?' she asked, hoping against hope it might be somewhere accessible.

'Locked up behind the entrance hall,' Tarita replied. 'Out of reach for now.'

Another thread snapped, but Jehana clung to the invincible reputation of the Merozains. She hurried after Tarita, shouting ahead so that no one would assail them as they appeared. They found Loric with Urien and Shae and the youngest sentinel, Lakyn. Having a sentinel – even an inexperienced one – was a bonus, but their plight was desperate. Jehana spotted Ogre, his giant frame hunched over the levers, his face streaked with blue and crimson swirls of light from the central glass cylinder.

Loric threw her a disgusted look. 'Is this about you, Princess? We should have surrendered you when we could.'

Tarita ignored him and asked, 'What's happening on the throne level?'

'Hillarie and Tovar were on duty above, but they aren't responding,' Loric replied. 'Manon's gone silent too, and from the erratic flow of the energy, no one is paying much attention up there. I'm having to regulate it entirely from here, and that's not sustainable. Do I take it you've sealed the door to the ground level?'

'I have,' Tarita said, 'so now would be a good time to tell us about the secret exit from the tower, made in anticipation of such a crisis.'

'If only, Noorie. If only.' Loric pointed back the way they'd come. 'That's the main entrance to the subterranean levels.' He pointed to a smaller door, opposite the corridor to the Oceanarium. 'That's a service entrance at the back of the foyer – I doubt many know of it, but it takes you back to the same place you've just left. So essentially, we're trapped.'

Tarita *tsked*, then looked around. 'So what else can we do?'

'A few things, but none of them get us out.' Loric scowled. 'We do have the capacity to destroy the Tower and everyone in it, of course . . .'

'I'm not worth that,' Jehana said quickly, her heart lurching.

'I know you're not, Princess,' Loric responded quickly.

'Could we threaten them with that destruction?' Tarita asked.

'They'd know we're bluffing,' Loric replied. 'That's Alyssa Dulayne out there. She knows what we value most.'

Everything else is secondary to the Bridge, Jehana thought.

She was about to reply when something churned inside her gut, as if someone had grasped her insides in their hands and twisted them. Her brain filled with darkness, she felt her heart swell to bursting . . . then the pain in her belly became too much, her legs folded and she crashed to the floor.

Alyssa braced with kinesis as swirling winds threatened to hurl her from the landing platform. She was followed by the latest shipload of Hadishah and soldiers, headed by Nuqhemeel, who had a professional, wary look to him. 'Find Jehana,' she told him, 'and that bitch Tarita. Take the rest alive if you can, dead if you must.'

She took the stairs to the solarus-throne, where she found her nephew, enthroned and wrestling with the controls, trying to settle the flows again after the disruption. Two bodies were lying on the floor beside the throne. Alyssa didn't know the fat girl-student, but she certainly recognised the snotty-nosed Hillarie.

'Nephew,' she called warmly, 'you've been busy.'

He waved, then resumed his workings, and she could read the swirl of colours well enough to know that they needed immediate taming. She took a moment to study her dead sister's son by Rashid's younger brother Teileman: he was a gloriously handsome boy, which was no surprise, given his lineage. There was little evidence of his Eastern heritage, unless you knew what you were looking for.

Look at him, she thought proudly. *He's grown into exactly the sort of callous, ambitious coldheart I'd hoped for.* She paced around the throne, occasionally glancing at the corpses, but mostly just admiring her reflection in the windows.

Once the crystal dome had settled back to pale blues, Tovar bounded from the throne and embraced her, exclaiming his joy in seeing her. She suspected his enthusiasm was enhanced by greed and marvelled at her own talents in corruption as she moved him to arm's length. 'It's good to finally meet you, Nephew. Your mother would be so proud.'

His blazing eyes faltered. *'Would—'*

'I'm sorry, but she's dead. Ramita Ankesharan killed her.' A lie, *almost* true.

His eyes narrowed in hatred. 'The Merozain leader? The Lakh bint?'

'Yes – she almost killed me that same day. The dirty Lakh fought like an animal.'

'I'll kill her too.'

She patted his broad shoulder approvingly. 'And I'll give you the means to do so, as I promised. But first, we have a task here. Where's Jehana Mubarak?'

'She'll have gone to the basement levels,' he replied. 'That's where we're told to retreat in emergency.'

She'd thought as much, but the ships sent to the main doors had hopefully cut off that retreat. She'd just opened her mind to contact Nuqhemeel and get his report, when Tovar boldly clutched her arm.

'You promised me a reward,' he reminded her.

So I did. She faced him again, thinking how much he reminded her of a younger self, so eager to get on, to take the quick route and gobble up everything in her path. There had been times she should have savoured more, before she became ... *this*. Perhaps he should be warned?

'Tovar, I am everything I said I was: I'm stronger than an Ascendant, with access to all of the gnosis, and in theory, I could live for ever. But I'm also partially possessed by a daemon, and if I do die, I'll be his victim until the end of time.'

'But you'll live for ever, Aunty, so the daemon doesn't matter.'

'For ever is a long, long time to stay vigilant,' she responded. *And I'm no longer entirely me*, she could have added, but that would have meant admitting it to herself. And his eyes held that certain light: a lust for power and control she knew intimately. She surprised herself when she caught his hand and said urgently, 'Nephew, the procedure will disgust you. A creature will enter your body and lodge itself around your heart, and from then on, you'll never be free of the daemon. Every thought you have, he'll be there, urging you this way or that until you're no longer sure who is driving your body. Everything you do, you'll wonder if it was him who did it instead.'

'I don't care,' he said petulantly. 'I want *everything* you have.'

She felt a momentary conflict: the desire to see what he would become against the desire to preserve him as he was now. But the latter was borne of familial ties and concerns so alien to the being she was now that she scarcely recognised them.

'How can I refuse you?' She opened the front of her dress, revealing her perfect left breast, and he reacted just the way she always wanted handsome young men to react. She drew a gnostically sharpened nail across the top and pierced herself, right though the ribcage, creating a channel for a spawn of the daemon-hybrid inside her to emerge. There were now several offspring of the mated pair Naxius had planted in her, wrapped about her heart, feeding off her blood and waiting their moment. Then she told Tovar, 'I must open your skin too.'

He swallowed, but nodded, his eyes flickering from the wound in her flesh to the breast below, down which her darkened blood ran. She called the daemon-spawn to her, a dreadful, sensual agony as it writhed into the wound. Plunging her nail into his breast, she punched an equally deep hole before pulling his body close and pressing the wounds together, skin to skin. The daemon-embryo, a thing like a spiny worm, wriggled out of her and into him.

Tovar grimaced at the pain – then he licked the blood from her fingers and kissed her, pressing his tongue deeply into her mouth as the daemon in her breast penetrated him: a wondrous unholy communion.

Gently – maternally – she lowered him to the floor and cradled him as he went through his brief surrender. He wanted this, as she had, and it took only a minute until he rose again, blood running like tears from darkened eyes. He effortlessly summoned a gnostic flame and revelled in his new might. She remembered her own such moment, and the feeling of newly won invincibility.

And yet half of the Master's Masks are dead already. The possibility of immortality is not the thing itself.

'What now, Aunty?' he said hungrily.

'We go hunting,' she replied, 'for two mudskin bints: one to capture, one to kill.'

He smirked. 'Let me do the killing.'

'You're welcome – but Jehana Mubarak is *mine*,' Alyssa told him firmly. Her tongue was already anticipating the taste of the girl's soul.

Oh yes, she surely is mine, until the end of time.

33

Lady of Oceans

Religion: Sollan

When the Rimoni conquered central Yuros, they brought with them their gods. Although they imposed Pater Sol and Mater Luna upon their subject races, they were not rigorous about proselytising their faith; there wasn't much point as, according to their tenets, only Rimoni could find salvation in their gods. Other gods were not just tolerated but often permitted a small shrine within Sollan temples.

The Rondians showed no such tolerance when they prevailed in 329. They set out to destroy all other faiths. It was a cruel thing, the Salvation of Kore.

THE BLACK HISTORIES (ANONYMOUS), 776

Sunset Isle, Pontic Sea
Octen 935

Everything was coming apart and Tarita was out of options. The Hadishah were hammering on the main door above, but her locking wards were holding – for now, at least. She'd sealed the service-stair too, although the enemy hadn't found it yet, but it was just a matter of time before they managed to break in.

I can kill a few, maybe even Alyssa, she admitted to herself, *but I can't protect those with me, and I can't win.* She was also very conscious that she bore a prize from Midpoint Tower that she'd not revealed to the Ordo Costruo – the old book in her satchel, the *Daemonicon di Naxius.* She'd had no opportunity to hand it on for examination since then, and now she feared losing it.

She looked around, assessing her remaining allies: their resistance would likely be brief, for she and Lakyn alone were armed and trained to fight. Urien and Shae were almost as small and skinny as Tarita herself, and Magister Loric was clearly no battle-mage. Ogre was an unknown – and Jehana was curled up on the floor, unwell.

'Tarita,' Ogre rumbled, 'is Princess sick?' The big construct was wielding a sledgehammer; he alone looked undaunted.

'I don't know – can one of you lot help her?' she asked the others.

'I'll do it,' Urien said quickly, and he went to kneel by Jehana.

Should we fight at all? Tarita wondered. Could she truly ask these scholars to die for an Eastern princess? Then someone hammered on the main doors and a woman's voice penetrated the barrier.

'So, who's in charge down there?'

'That's Alyssa Dulayne,' Tarita said, looking at Loric. 'I'll talk to her.'

'*You?* This is Ordo Costruo property, Merozain. *I* will speak for us.'

'Mind the energy flows, Engineer: that's *your* job. Mine is to hold that door.' The others watched, wondering if this little struggle of wills would decide their lives.

She gave the engineer her full-on stroppy Eastern bitch look. It seldom failed.

'Don't get us all killed, Merozain,' Loric muttered, looking away.

That mightn't be an option, Tarita thought, *but I'll do what I can.* She turned to her new friend. 'Ogre, come with me,' she said, and walked to the stairs.

'Is it bad for you, if we surrender?' she asked him once they were alone.

Ogre visibly quailed. 'I will die first.'

He's an illegal construct – they'll probably burn him alive . . . They shared a look of mutual agreement: if necessary, they would go down fighting. 'Whoever made you was a genius,' she remarked. 'Although he could have made you prettier.'

Ogre surprised her by winking. 'You say . . . Ogre's not pretty?' He held up his hand as if it were a hand-mirror and peered into it, as if puzzled.

She found herself laughing aloud, and her spirits lifted. 'I like you, friend Ogre. I'll not let them take you alive.'

'Nor I you, friend Tarita,' he rumbled as they reached the warded door.

She examined her spells, which were holding, before raising her voice and calling, 'Hello, Heartface! Do your friends out there know you murdered Sultan Salim?'

'You're mistaken,' Alyssa denied. 'It was the Ordo Costruo, as the sultan's investigation proved. I want to speak to Magister Loric, not you.'

'Too bad, you've got me. What is it you wish to say?' She could almost hear Alyssa gritting her teeth in annoyance.

'Very well: my people now control the entire tower, barring the chamber you're trapped inside. I acknowledge that your locking wards are strong; it could take us days to break in – but I *have* days, even weeks. I now control the solarus-throne above and can repel any rescue attempt. So, frankly, I'm more than happy to wait until you've all collapsed through lack of food and water.'

'I think help will come well before then,' Tarita replied; she might as well plant a few seeds of doubt.

'No one will come,' Alyssa replied, her voice certain. 'We'll break in, sooner or later. We'll still get Jehana, and you'll still die. But think of those with you – do they have to die too? Or these prisoners I have here – must they also be condemned?'

Tarita closed her eyes, cursing. *Of course, there will be prisoners.* She clasped Ogre's big hand again, this time for strength. 'How many?'

'Five scholars: four young men and one sweet young woman. Should they die for nothing? I'll spare them, and all with you – if you open those doors.'

Tarita felt the weight of the world settle onto her shoulders. *Ahm, help me – I truly do not know what to do!*

'You have something she wants, too,' Ogre murmured.

Tarita looked up, realising what he meant – and what it said about the brain inside his misshapen skull. 'Clever Ogre,' she approved. She turned back to the door. 'Listen, *Heartface*, we'll open the doors just after I've cut Jehana's throat.'

Alyssa fell silent and Tarita looked gratefully at Ogre. 'You are my very, *very* good friend,' she whispered.

'Tarita is Ogre's friend,' he agreed. Then a tremor ran through him and he muttered, 'Ogre is not a monster.'

'Ogre, the Ordo Costruo saw good in you, and I do too. I don't care what your old master made you do.'

He looked back at her, his expression now wretched, tormented. 'But you should, pretty Tarita. You should!' He tore his hand from hers and fled back down the stairs.

Dear Ahm, what did his maker do to him?

Alyssa's voice brought her back to the present. 'All right, Tarita. Clearly we have something of an impasse here. I'm sure you need to talk to those survivors below. I'm prepared to be flexible. How about you hand over Jehana and we just take her and go? The Tower reverts to the Ordo Costruo – and even you can flit home, little bird.'

If I thought you'd honour that . . . I don't trust you, Heartface – but here's my counter: let me leave with Jehana and a windskiff, give me an hour's start, and then we can play chasing games, away from innocent people and valuable property.'

Alyssa snorted. 'There are no *innocents*, bint. In one hour, we behead the first prisoner.'

Alyssa prowled back and forth before the line of prisoners, Tovar at her side. He'd just joined her after stabilising the solarus-throne – at night the energy flows were minimal, so it was safe to leave the throne untended for an hour or two. The five captives knelt, heads bowed, waiting to be told who would be the first to die. From time to time they stole resentful glances at her, and especially Tovar.

If you knew the monster inside us, you'd beg *for mercy*, Alyssa thought. *And it – and we – would laugh.*

The Merozain's threat to kill Jehana instead of surrendering her was interesting; Alyssa sensed it wasn't a natural thought for the girl. Tarita was clever, but not ruthless – would she carry her threat through, if the moment came? *No, I doubt it*, Alyssa thought scornfully. *Only we, the Great, are cold-hearted enough to do what must be done. That's why we triumph.*

But there was still the nagging possibility that Tarita might have the nerve, and then Alyssa would have failed her mission, which would be intolerable. It would jeopardise her rise back to power, her plan to be the only person in existence who was three-in-one: mage, dwymancer and daemon-host, a goddess in all but name.

No, I must have her alive . . .

'Aunty, will I be given a Mask?' Tovar murmured, interrupting her thoughts.

She nodded faintly, but admonished him, 'Don't speak of it in front of the men.'

Tovar bowed his head – then he said, 'Aunty, I know how to get us in.'

Everyone around her was arguing, but Jehana couldn't focus on the words through the clenching of her gut, the bile flooding her throat, the feeling that she was hallucinating all this. Everything outside her skull was delirium; nothing could get in.

Urien was trying to console the weeping Shae, Lakyn was so white he looked about to faint and the argument between Tarita and Loric was still going in circles. Tarita had told Alyssa she'd kill Jehana before she handed her over, and Jehana didn't know whether to be appalled or impressed. Ogre was so distressed by something that he'd retreated to his room below.

Clang . . . clang . . .

They all whirled: the metallic knock came from the service door. Then a frantic male voice whispered through the barrier, 'Help – help me!'

It was Tovar Kestrel's voice.

Jehana flinched. She had little liking for the young sentinel after the kiss he'd stolen – but the dilemma was immediately clear: could they let him in?

The first person to react was Shae, who broke from Urien's arms and ran to the door, her face frantic. 'Tovar? Tovar?'

Am I the only one who told him no? Jehana thought sourly. She threw a look at Tarita, who was staring at the door with similar ambivalence. *Not such a great judge of character after all, eh?*

But those thoughts just left her feeling petty. Tovar might be a creep, but he was on their side. She rose unsteadily as Loric joined Shae at the door. The engineer conjured a globe of light and scried the space on the other side of the door. 'Tovar's alone,' Loric said tersely, 'and he's wounded.'

'Oh Kore!' Shae squeaked, then she called, 'Darling – darling, are you injured?'

'Shae? Thank Kore!' Tovar gritted. 'It's not bad. I'll live.'

Loric dispelled his scrying and tried the handle – and Tarita's locking spells blazed. Shae turned on the Merozain girl and wailed, 'Let him in!'

Another surge of salty bile rose in Jehana's throat and she seized the rag she'd been forced to use and gagged into it, filling it with spittle and mucus. The air felt like water; she felt like she was choking. *That fish didn't open me to the dwyma*, she thought; *it's poisoning me—*

'Please, open the door,' Loric demanded.

'It could be a trick,' Tarita warned.

'You have to let him in,' Shae howled. 'He's hurt, you heartless Noorie bitch—'

'It's too hot in here,' Jehana heard herself interrupt. 'I need air—' She staggered away, feeling clammy and flushed at once, seeking coolness. She stumbled through an arch and realised it was the corridor to the Oceanarium. As she lurched along it, silver flashes sparked and dark motes floated in her eyes.

She'd heard some creatures couldn't be eaten because their flesh contained a hallucinogenic drug. Perhaps that accursed fish was one. She hit the wall and fell, picked herself up and staggered on and on . . . until somehow she was pressed against the glass window of the Ocean-arium and staring out into the darkness.

A shoal of gold-flecked fish outside appeared to be watching her, then they flashed away, leaving a massive bulk of black and grey covering the glass. A saucer-sized eye appeared, looking right at her.

She squeaked, and fell to her knees.

Tarita went hesitantly to the service door. She needed support, but Jehana had turned white and run away and Ogre was still below, wrest-ling with whatever demons tormented him. Someone needed to watch the doors above, so she sent Lakyn. That just left Loric, Shae and Urien, and they'd already made up their minds.

Am I hesitating because Tovar's an arsehole, or because there's a threat here?
She pressed her ear to the door. 'Tovar? This is Tarita Alhani.'

'Tarita?' he panted. 'Are you all right?'

He sounded as he should: stressed, in pain. She scried the corridor and examined his face. 'How did you get away? Weren't you on duty in the throne room?'

'Yes – or rather, I was just coming off duty. I wasn't feeling well, so I handed over to Hillarie and left just before all Hel opened up.'

It sounded credible, but a little too convenient. *If worst comes to worst I can handle him,* she decided. 'Be ready,' she told Loric, who responded with a 'Don't tell me what to do' look but still kindled shields.

She released the locking spell and pulled the door open, keeping the barrier between herself and Tovar as he groaned and rose stiffly, then stumbled through. Shae squeaked plaintively and caught him, hugging him to her, while Tarita slammed the service door shut and re-cast her locking spell. Loric began firing questions about who else might be alive, while Urien just looked hurt at seeing Shae's concern for Tovar.

'Just a moment,' Tovar was groaning, 'I need to sit down.'

'Where are you hurt?' Shae fussed, while Loric went to the medical cabinet against the wall. Tarita was watching, still on high alert, when the assault on her locking spells at the main doors abruptly renewed and Lakyn cried, 'Help!'

'Damn! I need to be at the main door,' she told them. She called to Ogre, 'Ogre – we could use your help up here,' but there was no answer from the lower chamber.

Tarita turned away, disappointed, and ran for the stairs, feeling like the only sailor left on a sinking ship.

Tovar didn't need to tell Alyssa he was inside: through Abraxas, his aunt knew instantly. Having the daemon's mind crawling through his wasn't bothering him at all. The vast, thousand-voiced Hel-mind was vocalising all the things he'd been thinking for years: he'd never been able to look at a lesser man without contempt, or a girl without lust, so having a howling beast inside him telling him what he already knew wasn't scary. It was justification.

He let Shae fuss over him – the wound was genuine, but it wasn't deep and he'd easily heal it when the time came – and took stock. The Rondian sword at his side made him better armed than anyone here. Alyssa had drawn Tarita away, as planned. Lakyn was already by the main doors. Ogre must be downstairs – not that he mattered, but Naxius would enjoy the reunion with his favourite construct.

The only question was: *Where's Jehana?* He asked Shae as she tended his wound.

Shae jerked her head disdainfully towards the Oceanarium. 'Weak stomach,' she snarked, and they shared a smirk. Loric was still fiddling in the medical cabinet and Urien looked like he was trying to muster up the gumption to do something useful.

Let's start the show . . .

'It's not looking good,' he told Shae, pretending concern.

'Oh Kore,' Shae whimpered. 'We're all going to die, aren't we?'

'It's that or the breeding-houses,' Tovar whispered. 'Which would you prefer, Shae? Years of rape, pushing out children to serve the enemy, or a quick death?'

She flinched – it had always been so easy to hurt timid little Shae – and bleated, 'I'd rather die—'

In answer, he kissed her softly, to cover her mouth and silence her, and slipped his dagger between her ribs and into her fragile heart. <*Your choice,*> he told her as she died in utter, bewildered betrayal.

Then he erupted into action, hurling Shae's corpse at Urien while whipping out his sword and going for Loric. The engineer reacted far too slowly, his shields barely formed as Tovar rammed the sword through his chest.

He pulled out the blade, Loric collapsed and Tovar turned on Urien, raising a finger to his lips. 'Call out, and you get the same.'

Urien stared, in disbelieving terror. '*Tovar? Why?*'

'Shh,' he replied, fixing Urien with . . . *Hmm, yes. Mesmerism* . . . not normally one of his strengths, but through Abraxas he could do *anything* . . .

'Get on your knees, groveller.' Tovar reached . . . and screwed up the spell.

He'd been too confident, too contemptuous of his foe – what was supposed to have rendered Urien helpless instead elicited a panicked retaliation – and the sneaky little snit was holding a spanner. As Tovar began to thrust, the tool swept round, sparked off Tovar's shields and jolted him backwards, ruining his blow.

'*Tarita*,' Urien shrieked, '*it's Tovar!*'

Furiously, Tovar thrust, but to his amazement, Urien, who'd never been more than a fair swordsman, managed to block with the spanner. Tovar's blow drove his smaller foe back, but Urien was a pure-blood and managed to parry, while hollering for help.

Stop pissing around, Abraxas snarled inside Tovar's mind. *You're fighting like your old self* – let me loose!

So fierce was that inner roar that Tovar paused, taken aback, which bought Urien another moment, another couple of yards – then Tovar let the daemon out and his world turned scarlet.

'Tovar? I *knew* it,' Tarita swore as she heard Urien's cry, and all the despair and betrayal that filled it.

'Hold this door!' she snarled at Lakyn, grabbing his hand and planting it against the barrier, her mind showing him the locking pattern. He was weaker than her, but still a pure-blood: if he could keep Alyssa Dulayne out of his head, he might hold.

Then she drew her blade and hurtled down the stairs.

Gnosis coursed through Tovar as he moved: morphic-gnosis to bulk up and strengthen his own frame, illusions to blur his outline and blade, mage-light to spear at Urien's shields and spells to paralyse his mind. He effortlessly smashed Urien's spanner aside before whirling into a sideways slash, blasting through shields and flesh. Urien folded and fell in two pieces, his torso severed at the waist.

Kore's Balls, this is glorious! Tovar exulted as Abraxas hooted inside him. *I'm fucking invincible!*

A moment later, a piece of machinery the size of a horse detached from the floor and slammed into him, overpowered his shields and crushed him. He felt bones shatter, flesh and innards pulverized. He didn't have the breath to vent his shock as the iron pipes and bulkhead tipped off him, leaving him just lying there.

'OGRE!' The construct-creature shambled out of the shadows, roaring his own name.

Tovar knew he should be dead, but he was now a portal to the aether and a being of pure energy and intellect was waiting on the other side, so no sooner was he down than he was mending and healing. His shields reformed as Ogre's mighty frame loomed over him and a sledgehammer smashed down. They held – *just* – then kinesis hurled the massive construct away.

I'm immortal! Tovar crowed. Despite the excruciating pain of being reassembled, he was already sitting up and gathering his thoughts and by the time Tarita burst from the stairway, he was standing again while Ogre was on his knees, dazed and bleeding.

Tovar summoned his blade again and faced the Merozain, grinning merrily.

Then a searing *crack* resonated down the stairs: Alyssa had broken through.

Tarita felt her locking spell come apart and realised that from here on, all that mattered was how one died. Ogre was down and the rest were dead. Her eyes flew to the Oceanarium corridor: Jehana had disappeared down there, so that was where she needed to be to make good on her threat, if she could.

But first, I've got to get past this prick.

Tovar Kestrel was covered in blood and his body was shaking and popping as joints realigned, fractures mended and muscles reformed. His eyes were black, and so was his blood: *Just like Sakita, at the end . . .*

She strengthened her shields and glanced at Ogre, who was picking himself from the floor. 'Go to Jehana, Ogre,' she called. 'You know what you must do.'

But Tovar gestured sideways and Ogre was suddenly gripped and held immobile. 'The Master is coming to reclaim you, Ogre,' Tovar mocked. He swept his hand sideways and the construct was hurled against the inner cylinder of glass. Leaving a wide, bloody smear, he slid to the floor again.

Tovar spun his sword and pointed it at her. 'Hello, Noorie,' he taunted. 'We have unfinished business, don't we?'

Behind her, she could sense Alyssa coming, amid a swarm of protectors.

She lunged at Tovar – and almost lost her head. His blade countered hers and her silver scimitar made his blade bell alarmingly, but he battered her guard aside. She bent backwards at the waist just in time to avoid his steel passing through her neck, but couldn't dodge his boot to her groin. Mercifully, her shields absorbed some of the energy, but it was still enough to drop her, howling in pain. She barely managed to roll clear of a killing thrust. Coming onto one knee, she tried to counter-attack, but Tovar's blade hammered at her again, hurling her sideways, and her head struck something that knocked her dizzy.

Her vision wavered, then his blade was teasing her throat.

Ogre dimly saw Tarita fall to her knees, then Tovar standing over her – and it blew the swirl out of his head. The Master had made him strong, resilient, able to take punishment, so he could rise from this. Ogre didn't want to see Master again, not *ever* – but Master was coming *here*, Tovar had said so, and he had to get away.

But not without his new friend.

He knew all about this tower. The engineering level had two functions. The first was to regulate the energy sent from above and send it on to the other towers, but the second was to divert some of that immense power and send it whirring through the tower itself to light the lamps, feed the ovens, the incinerator that rid them of their waste and the pump that purified their water.

He reached for the thing Loric had said he should *never* touch. Grasping the metal piping from the central glass cylinder, roaring out 'TARITA!' he wrenched, his enormous strength augmented by gnosis and desperation, and as he yanked it out, Tovar turned.

The tube he held split from the first junction crystal and pure gnostic energy arced about the room. He clung on grimly as the thick cable reared like an enraged python in his grip, until he could point the energy stream at the shadowy figure standing over Tarita. The girl flung herself sideways just as the torrent of power blasted through the young sentinel, leaving only dust, before searing the far wall and liquefying it fully three feet deep – and then the energy fizzled out. It was a tiny fraction of what the solarus crystals produced and there were many fail-safes built in to minimise accidents. Ogre quickly jammed the tube back into the floor, forcing it down to ensure it wouldn't spring loose again, even as they heard a woman on the stairs howling in anguished loss. He swept up Tarita and her silver scimitar, grabbed his sledgehammer, then clutching Tarita against his chest, he ran for the Oceanarium.

Tarita's skull and groin were throbbing painfully and for a moment she was barely able to believe that she was still alive – but she'd seen Ogre wielding a torrent of white fire that had obliterated Tovar before melting some of the solid stone walls, and that was enough for now. Cradled against his massive chest, she could feel his thudding heart. *We're in the corridor to the Oceanarium*, she thought, and then she remembered: *I have to kill Jehana.*

That she must take a life and then die herself curdled any hope this respite brought.

But she was still alive, and she'd come back from paralysis and the bleakest despair before. So she wriggled up, put her arms around Ogre's neck and kissed his rough cheek, *hard*. 'You were *magnificent*, Ogre! But put me down, I can stand now.'

His expressive face was wonderfully grateful. He carefully lowered her to the floor and handed back her sword. She wobbled a moment, then planted her feet squarely. The window chamber to the ocean was just ahead, but there were Keshi voices in the corridor behind. They didn't have long.

She secured the satchel on her back, firmed her grasp on the scimitar and turned back the way they'd come. 'Hey!' she shouted, 'Heartface! Are you there, bitch?'

The voice that replied was diamond-hard. 'I'm here.'

'You come any closer and you get what Tovar got, understand?'

Ogre raised an eyebrow and Tarita winked at him, her smile broadening when Alyssa didn't immediately respond. *She doesn't yet know what killed the treacherous prick. I think she's a little scared . . . Excellent.*

'You're trapped, Merozain,' Alyssa finally replied.

'Nice that you think so,' Tarita retorted: anything to sow more doubt, to buy a few more precious seconds. She had no plan, only a determination to go down fighting, and to make her mistress proud when she heard how her apprentice had died.

Alyssa hesitated, then called, 'The offer still stands, Tarita: your life for Jehana's.'

'I'll think it over,' Tarita replied, some of her impudence returning.

'Tell me,' Alyssa called, 'Felix went into Midpoint to retrieve three items. We know about the spear, and I'm told you have the scimitar – what of the book?'

'I used it to wipe my arse,' Tarita called back cheerily. Alyssa fell silent, but she felt her anger ripple in the aether.

She and Ogre backed away together, following the gentle curve of the passage until the pallid glow of the night-time sea of the Oceanarium filled the end of the corridor. Then they entered the chamber – and stared . . .

Seidopus, Jehana's mind sang.

Calascia, the sea called back. *Lady of Oceans.*

She knew the name: the Sea God's consort, the name of Amantius' feminine genilocus. The implication *appalled* her, but she was trapped. She'd already considered and discarded surrender. These people had killed her mother: the time had come to break through to the dwyma, or die trying.

Yes, she sent, *Seidopus, I am your Calascia: come for me – come for me now!*

The pain in her stomach was gone now, but the sense of unreality remained. There was something out there, right now, and it was *listening* to her. The whale had gone, but a giant squid had cruised by, then a massive shark, all unblinking eyes and huge triangular teeth. The whole *ocean* was watching her.

But there wasn't just stone and glass between her and the sea; there were also gnostic wards powered by the Tower itself. They were beyond any mage . . . unless the dwyma could intercede? She'd been right: the fish she'd consumed had been a gift from the genilocus and she could feel that power now – but she couldn't seem to grasp it. *Calascia*, she called, *someone – anyone! Help me – please, help me!*

She heard Tarita call her name from the doorway and waved her silent: she'd *felt* something. The glass before her wavered and she saw a woman's face: copper-skinned, with a mass of grey hair tied into a topknot. White furs were wrapped about her shoulders and white stuff – *snow?* – was swirling about her.

<Who are you, child?> she asked Jehana, and from Tarita's expression, that mental voice was filling all of their minds. The woman sounded calm and alert – but weak, as if she were ailing.

Suppressing her excitement, she replied, *<I am Jehana, daughter of Sakita.>*

<Ah, the weather-witch had a daughter. That is well. I am Luhti.>

She's Luhti – Lanthea! One of the four great dwymancers— Jehana's heart was in her mouth, but time was pressing. *<I have to find a genilocus,>* Jehana shouted. *<I have to reach Seidopus – they're closing in on us!>*

<Then reach out and offer yourself,> Luhti said calmly.

<I've tried, but nothing's happening – they're going to kill us all – help me.>

<Hush, Jehana. Listen: if you offered and were heard, then you are answered. Seidopus awaits your command.>

<What?>

<The power is there already. Believe, and use it.>

Then Luhti abruptly vanished from her mind and from the glass. Jehana felt that the woman had over-reached, and was paying the price. She was left gaping, *wondering* . . . when she needed to be *believing* . . .

They killed my beautiful Tovar – and I would have been a mother to him, Alyssa told herself. When he'd kissed her while she fed him the daemon-embryo, they'd been almost one being. It had been like embracing herself in male form: a wondrous moment, a magnification of her own glory.

And now he's gone . . . I'm going to rip their bodies into tiny pieces before I

*swallow their souls . . . or perhaps I'll send them to Abraxas? Yes, that would be
a more fitting punishment for their transgressions against me and mine.*

Hatred burned inside, tinged by fear, because she had no idea how
Tovar had died – even Abraxas could not comprehend. However, Jehana
and Tarita and the Master's abomination were all down this corridor:
one way in, no way out.

Nuqhemeel seemed to think she should be leading the way, but she
quickly disabused him of that ridiculous notion. *The way to avoid being
annihilated by some secret super-spell is never to face it.*

'Send in the weakest first,' she told him. 'We'll wear them down,
draw their sting. And remember: I *must* have Jehana Mubarak alive.'

Nuqhemeel's face and voice were carefully non-judgemental as he
gave the orders – and just as damned well, or she'd have made him
lead the charge.

'Take the princess alive,' he told them. 'Ahm is with you, always.'

Until the moment you die.

Obediently, the first dozen men bowed to her and entered the corridor.

'They're coming,' Tarita called to Jehana. 'Luhti said you can do it – so
what are you rukking well waiting for?'

Ogre surprised her by rumbling, 'Tarita, ugly words make us ugly.'

She swallowed a retort, suddenly ashamed. Then she threw him a
wry look. 'Do you swear a whole lot, then?'

He laughed – actually *laughed* – and the rolling, gut-deep mirth shook
his belly. She felt a wave of pure pleasure at having given him that gift.
She squeezed his hand again. 'Whatever else happens, I am pleased to
have met you, Ogre. I wish I could know you longer.'

When he met her eyes this time, there was still that secret pain,
but he visibly repelled it. 'Ogre pleased to meet pretty Tarita too. I
wish . . . many things.'

Then they heard boots in the corridor, hidden by the curved approach.
'Get on with it, Princess!' Tarita urged, then she looked up at Ogre again.
The corridor was twelve feet wide, just enough for one small woman
and one large construct to fight side by side. 'No one gets past,' she said.

'No one.'

The first Hadishah tore around the corner, blazing mage-bolts as they came, scimitar blades gleaming with energy to tear through shielding. Tarita didn't know how strong Ogre was gnostically, but he shielded well as she returned fire, lancing her Ascendant-strength bolts to cut down the first attackers in a maelstrom. But the rest came on, doggedly shielding as they approached.

When they clashed, there would be too many blades to shield. Then they would fall. *Pain is brief*, she told herself, *and afterwards . . . who knows?*

The power is there already. Believe, and use it.

Luhti's words mocked Jehana as her brain grappled with all the complexities: how could she get out of here without destroying them all? How did one simply *command* a genilocus – and what could one do? The tales spoke of the dwyma being *immense*, but this place was so small: one room, and three delicate lives to preserve.

I don't know what to do, she moaned inwardly, and when she looked through the glass, all she saw now was the empty sea, without even the fish still present.

The first blades crashed together, Tarita parried and hurled the man backwards, then blocked another blow from the flank, while Ogre, beside her, bellowed and roared, spittle spraying as he brutalised anyone in reach, taking awful punishment in return. She saw a spear rake his side and an arrow slam into his shoulder and heard him bellowing in pain as he lifted one man and hurled him bodily at another. With each passing moment his rage grew, his gnostic aura blazing like an incandescent bar of light. He roared and thrashed about, his sheer ferocity a danger as he kept lunging forward when they needed to defend.

Berserk rage, she realised. *He has that in him* . . . But there was nothing she could do to quell it, and she wasn't even sure she should. She was almost at that point herself, on the edge of that desperation of *kill or be killed*. She sensed Alyssa's gloating as she lashed out again and again with naked fire and death-light to pierce the bodies of the men still pressing forward. The corridor was choked with dead, but she and Ogre were giving ground, right to the mouth of the chamber.

Last toss of the dice . . .

'Ogre,' Tarita screamed, 'behind me—'

Somehow her call penetrated his red rage, but she still had to waste a precious moment on a kinetic push to get herself in front before she launched all she could: a torrent of coruscating energy containing all the most destructive threads of the gnosis she knew. It crashed into the Hadishah and down they went, some charred, some emptied, some torn apart . . .

She clutched Ogre's arm, reeling, almost succumbing to the void of blackness and stars inside her head—

—as Alyssa Dulayne walked into view, her heels tapping on the marble floor. She was holding an ivory rod and was apparently unperturbed by the carnage around her. 'Bravo, Tarita,' she mocked. 'I must learn that one.'

This is it, Tarita realised. What little she had left could never hold up against Alyssa – against *Heartface*. And she still hadn't killed Jehana or burned the *Daemonicon di Naxius*.

I let myself hope . . .

She stared down the wand that Alyssa extended towards her.

'*NOOO!*' Ogre raged, suddenly pulling her behind him, '*TARITA MINE!*'

Then the ground shook and everything changed as she heard the sound of cracking glass behind her.

It took all three of them a moment to digest the ramifications as Alyssa Dulayne stood there triumphantly, Ogre defiant and hopelessly brave – then she gasped, '*Ogre – run!*' and yanked him with her.

Ogre ran as his world came apart in flying glass and erupting water.

He'd spun away from the deadly blonde woman and snatched up his precious only friend, then headed for the corner: the solid stone nook *beside* the breaking window. He could see Jehana had dived to the floor under the window, safe from the glass shards slashing through the air. Then there was an ear-splitting shriek of rage from their enemy, followed by swift footfalls as she pelted away back down the corridor. And then the window exploded and the ocean rushed in.

Ogre anchored his feet and arms with Earth-gnosis. Tarita clambered up his torso and wrapped her legs around his chest and she engaged kinesis to lock them together – and stunned him when she pressed her doll-like mouth to his wide lips *and pushed air into his mouth*. The fear her intimate touch engendered almost triggered a heart seizure, until her mind wrapped around his and he felt her determined resolve steady his rising panic as they were engulfed in churning seawater.

Despite his terror, the water ripping at them and the effort he was pouring into just holding on, Ogre's brain was filled with Tarita, doing something like *kissing* him, and *embracing* him, and that had never happened before except at his master's behest . . .

. . . and Ervyn Naxius' voice was suddenly snarling into his brain, urging him to forget the peril and *rip and rend and take*, until a vortex of darkness rose in his mind, to drag him down—

—and Tarita's voice cut through the clamour and Naxius' voice was jarringly, *wonderfully*, silenced.

<Well, that was unpleasant,> she remarked conversationally, as if they were sitting at the dinner table. <It was just an old compulsion spell, Ogre: something your master left behind. But it's gone now. Just breathe . . . everything is going to be fine.>

After that, the torrent was merely water, and he had the strength to hold on. His grip never faltered, and neither did her kiss and the flow of air.

As the ocean flooded in, Jehana locked herself to the stone and let it pass over her until the water began to stabilise. She should have drowned, but her lungs, which had been labouring since she ate the golden fish, had clearly been preparing for this very moment, for *breathing water*. She stared down at her hands, which were suddenly webbed, and when she touched her throat, gill-slits opened.

Even her eyes could see clearly down here.

As the water current lessened enough to move, she dared to pull herself away from the floor. Swimming like a fish, she went to Ogre, a pillar braced against the wall, with Tarita hugging close and breathing into his mouth, a kiss of life indeed. She tapped Tarita's leg and pointing upwards, sent, <Come with me.>

Tarita pulled away from Ogre, leaving a bubble clinging to his lips. *<He's got one minute of air so we have to reach the surface fast.>*

<That'll be enough.> Jehana swam through the broken window and shot upwards, carried by the currents that broke against the island until they struck the surface and burst through it, surfacing into roaring winds and giant waves right beneath the cliffs of Sunset Island. A dozen Hadishah windships were still circling above.

'We'll never escape them,' Tarita shouted, 'not trapped in the middle of the ocean.' She still had the satchel and scimitar and was determined not to lose either.

Ogre broke the surface beside her, thrashing about him wildly, real panic on his big, inhuman face. Then he saw Tarita and his face transformed, to determination . . . and adoration.

Dear Ahm, Jehana thought, *what did she do to him?*

Then they were all swamped by another wave and had to kick for the surface again. Tarita was shouting for her as Ogre flailed desperately.

Then a massive whale breached, only fifty yards away, sending another great wash of salt-filled water churning over them, and they all shouted: Tarita and Ogre in alarm, Jehana in wonder.

Seidopus heard me – this is from him!

'Don't worry,' she told them as the giant creature slowed, then rose beneath her so that she could seat herself on its broad back. She called down, 'Come on, climb up!'

Tarita's eyes went round with amazement, to Jehana's absolute delight. 'I am the Lady of Oceans!' she shouted jubilantly.

34

Into Battle

Pregnancy and the Gnosis

The discovery that a woman could gain a weakened form of the gnosis by bearing a child to a mage has long outraged Kore theologians. Of all the many hilarious interpretations that have been attached to pregnancy manifestation, as it is called, my favourite is that a man's penis is an instrument of divine blessing.

GINA FOULOS, LANTRIC SCHOLAR, 843

The Bastion, Pallas
Octen 935

There was no escaping the sense that battle was breaking out on every front, but right now, Lyra's mind was focused entirely on childbirth. 'You're going into battle soon too,' women kept telling her, 'just like our brave men in the Kedron Valley.' Wherever she went, they enquired after her wellbeing, patted her distended stomach and wished her good fortune for the birthing. '*Oh, only two weeks to go,*' they would simper when she told them, and then warn her that first babies were often early – or usually late – and everyone had different advice.

One in five women die in labour. Even mage-women die in childbirth.

The impending battle at Collistein Junction was also preying on her mind. Both she and Basia were bags of nerves, and knowing it was over the same man was a strange feeling, like a complicated dance of competitive anxiety.

But she faced another struggle as well: her nightmares were now

499

unrelenting. They were different from when Ostevan was polluting her garden; these dreams had a wider sweep but were less intimate, dealing in wholesale destruction, or showing her hordes of daemonic creatures rampaging through Rondelmar. They left her exhausted, and not even Dirklan's strongest wards could keep them at bay.

She was increasingly sure they were being channelled through the original Winter Tree in Saint Eloy's shrine behind the Celestium: she often dreamed of the saint pleading for aid, and was resolved to go there and do what she could – but it wasn't something she could do lightly. The grand prelate might suspect or even know her secret, but he couldn't give even tacit support for heresy; any misstep there could see them both in the hands of the Keepers or the Inquisition.

Dirklan had finally secured agreement for a clandestine visit to the Celestium, but she had to do it before it was too late: she was experiencing mild contractions every day now – her body making ready for birthing, Domara said. As far as she was concerned, it was just more discomfort, pain and worry.

It was a huge relief when Basia brought word from her spymaster that morning. 'We have our way into the Celestium, Milady. There's a certain sister in Valetta's entourage who deals with pregnant unwed women: we're to go as supplicants and she'll show you into the Celestium, where Wurther will meet you and take you to the shrine of Saint Eloy.'

'Who'll be with me?' Lyra asked.

'I will, and a few others.'

'Not Dirklan?' Lyra asked. She felt her throat tighten. 'Is this other conspiracy he's mentioned about to strike also?'

'Perhaps,' Basia replied evasively. 'Are you sure you can do this?'

'Domara says I still have two weeks to go,' Lyra replied. 'As long as I don't have to do anything physically strenuous, I'll be all right.'

'But do you *really* have to go there?' Basia asked.

'Yes, absolutely. I think everything might depend on it.'

'*Everything?*' Basia looked sceptical.

'Do you remember what I did to the Royal Chapel?'

Basia's face changed. The mage-engineers said it could take years to rebuild it, so in the meantime an old auditorium had been converted for use, but Lyra hadn't found a new confessor – or even looked for one.

'The early dwymancers went mad and froze, flooded or burned whole villages,' Lyra went on. 'I hadn't thought that could happen to me, but I can feel the possibility now. The Winter Tree is polluted and I have to cleanse it, before it's too late.' She pursed her lips, then said, 'A powerful dwymancer could raze this city. So make the preparations. I have to do this or something awful will happen. I can *feel* it.'

Basia rose and touched her heart formally. Lyra watched her as she left, envying her slender figure and her casual, worldly grace. *No wonder Ril prefers her.*

'Basia,' she called after her, not really sure why.

'Yes?'

They looked at each other silently for a moment, while a dozen phrases from insults to pleas to meaningless nothings crowded Lyra's mouth. Finally she said, 'The *Book of Kore* says that the greatest virtue is love. What do you think?'

Basia frowned, understandably puzzled. 'Life is too complicated for simplistic aphorisms like that, Majesty. And so is love.'

Lyra laid a hand on her copy of the *Book*, on the table beside her. 'I'm starting to think so too,' she admitted. 'You see, Ostevan didn't just destroy my self-respect. He took my faith in the Church too – perhaps even my belief in Kore. I can't read this book any more without feeling doubt. It was the tiller of my life, and now I don't know how to steer.' She met her bodyguard's eyes and asked, 'How do you live without faith?'

'I do have faith, Majesty,' Basia replied. 'I believe in the good intentions of the people I care about and who care about me. I believe in the basic decency of ordinary people, that they are capable of extraordinary generosity and kindness, with or without a big book of propaganda to tell them how.'

'Is there another book I should be reading?'

Basia snorted. 'The *Kalistham*, perhaps? We might all be needing a copy of that if things go badly down south.' Then she laughed. 'The

Church burn the books they don't like, Majesty. They don't like competition. May I go?'

We were almost friends once, Lyra thought sadly, *and I miss that. But you screwed my husband* . . . 'Yes, you may go.'

By an imposing deeply carved and heavily gilded door deep inside the Celestium, Exilium Excelsior, Pontifex Guard, stood to attention, utterly immobile, contemplating the empty corridor outside Wurther's office. Outside, the sliver of moon barely illuminated the night skies; inside, he was lit by a pool of lamplight. A passer-by might have taken him for a statue, but he'd not once lost track of everything going on around him and his inner landscape was fully alive.

He stirred from his reverie when Chaplain Ennis scurried through the doors, clearly late for whatever he had scheduled after his meeting with the grand prelate. Exilium scanned the chaplain's aura for anything amiss, then stepped through the door and asked, 'Are you expecting anyone else, Holiness?'

Wurther, eyeing a stack of new papers wearily, looked up and yawned. 'No, Exilium, I've had enough for the day. I'll sleep in here,' he added, indicating the informal bedroom behind the office where he often slept when traversing the half-mile of corridors to his own suite was too onerous. 'Ward the doors, then sleep in the guardroom outside.'

Exilium bowed and did as he was bid. He triggered the wards – the spells had been laid down centuries ago and were massively strong – before going to the sparsely furnished guardroom. Wurther hadn't lied when he'd said the role of Pontifex Guard would take over his entire existence.

He opened the door—

—and froze in the doorway at the sight of a man standing in the middle of the room, unarmoured, but wearing a sword in a richly tooled scabbard. He had a flat face and cold eyes; his thin moustache was perfectly trimmed. He had no chain of office, but Exilium knew him. Protocol demanded that he kneel, but protocol didn't explain why Dravis Ryburn, Knight-Princeps of the Holy Inquisition, was in his chamber.

'My Lord?' he said respectfully.

Ryburn showed his palms. 'Excelsior. Don't be alarmed. I'm here to talk.'

There were strict protocols over the coming and going of the Inquisition. Their domain was the southern wing of the Rymfort, where Ryburn was virtually king – but to enter the Celestium required Wurther's blessing, and for him to have got this far required a great many formalities.

Or for certain men – like Chaplain Ennis, for example – to look aside.

Exilium felt another presence and half-turned, keeping Ryburn in sight. As expected, he saw Lef Yarle, Ryburn's bodyguard. His eyes were crawling over Exilium's face.

Exilium re-entered his quiet place to escape the confusion of the moment. He scanned for further threats, but these two were alone – and two of the most dangerous men in Koredom. 'How may I serve?' he asked cautiously.

Ryburn measured him with his grey eyes, then said, 'You left the Inquisition because it was "imperfect". Now you're here. Have you found the perfection you seek?'

Exilium considered, thinking of all he'd seen, then replied, 'I'm still looking.'

'I suspect you'll still be looking when you're an old man. I see a lot of myself in you, Excelsior. I too am a seeker after perfection, and I chafe at the failings of lesser men. I would that every man in my service had your skills, your faith and your high standards. Unfortunately, people like us are rare.'

'We can all be better than we are,' Exilium replied. *What does he want?*

'True, but if the Church required the high standards you set yourself, I'd have an Inquisition of three – Yarle, me and you.' He tapped the walls, adding, 'And this place, this "Holy City", would be empty.'

Exilium waited, sensing some kind of offer pending.

'The Holy Inquisition needs its own Enquiry into its failings,' Ryburn said. 'We need men whose vision and faith are clear to burn away the chaff and reach the purity of will and devotion that our mission requires. The entire Rymfort and Celestium need to endure the cleansing fire of Kore. Do you agree?'

'Of course,' Exilium replied: that had been plain to him from the moment he joined the Inquisition. He glanced again at Yarle, who continued to stare with his unnerving reptilian eyes. There were threads of light running between the Knight-Princeps and his bodyguard that spoke of an almost symbiotic relationship: it was clear Ryburn wouldn't even have to speak or gesture to instruct Yarle to strike.

They're frocio, he realised. Part of him was appalled, but he threw that reaction into his quiet space before it could be seen.

'My cleansing fire will burn soon,' Ryburn went on. 'The torch is almost lit. But for it to be effective, I require men like you, Excelsior. I want you at my left hand. Return to us: we are your true calling. Men of absolutes like you and me belong in the Inquisition. Standards have slipped. Help me to make the Inquisition great again.'

Isn't this what I've always wanted? he asked himself. *Isn't that the shining ideal I saw when I joined the Inquisition – and why I left? This man understands that . . . and he understands me.*

'What would I have to do?' he asked.

'Leave Wurther, for a start.'

'But I have sworn before Kore to protect him, for so long as he lives—'

'It's a job, Excelsior. There are always ways to leave a job. I believe your answer just cited one.'

Exilium wondered why he hadn't seen that coming. 'But I have sworn my service.'

'You have family,' Yarle murmured. He had drifted in behind Exilium. It would be a shocking breach of protocol to turn away, so he was forced to endure Ryburn's man breathing down his neck. 'You send them money. Your sister's name is Felissa, and she cares for your widowed father Enari, in a small cottage – a cabana, yes – near the square in . . . Grafitè village, yes.' Yarle's breath was minty and he wore an effeminate perfume. 'They would be *devastated* if they found that their son, their brother, had not listened when the Inquisition called his name.'

They're threatening my father and my sister . . . and if I defy them, we'll all die, without meaning. Life must *have meaning . . .*

He bowed his head. 'I am yours to command.'

The next day dawned under steely skies, high cloud but no threat of rain in Pallas. A cold wind was blowing in from the north. 'Before the end of the day,' Medelie Aventour said grandly, 'the city will be ours.' She looked down over the walls to the river and the Celestium. 'Finally.'

She was dressed as if for a coronation, her auburn hair immaculate, her gown lustrous. But no matter how young and lovely she appeared, Solon Takwyth only saw Radine Jandreux.

The last few days had flown in a blur of complicated preparations as they placed men in strategic positions around the palace and the city, moving carefully to avoid arousing suspicion. Fortunately, people like Oryn Levis were blindly devoted to him and obeyed unquestioningly. The city was in a high state of tension anyway, with the first battle against the Shihad about to commence, which was a fine pretext for putting armed men at crucial crossroads. But doubts plagued him, especially since Medelie's hints that Selene might be Tear. *Are we just puppets of the Masked Cabal?*

Part of him longed to be at Collistein Junction. His wounds were almost healed, although his hip still felt tight and he knew he'd lost much stamina and flexibility. A nagging part of him feared that his best years as a front-line mage-knight were gone. To no longer be the best? What would that feel like? And what came next? *I have no children: if I die, who would truly mourn me?* He glanced at Medelie. *Only you.*

'Solon, darling, relax,' she said, catching his grim look.

'How do we know everyone's ready?' he asked.

'We don't. We trust, and we play our own parts. In the end, that's all we can do.'

He reached into a pouch and pulled out two necklaces, almost identical: heavy gold chains with a disc-pendant embossed with a pegasus, the symbol of House Corani. One pegasus was male, the other female. 'I had them made for us,' he told her, offering her the female pendant.

Her eyes went wide, greedily drinking in the border of emeralds and diamonds, then she brushed her lips against his. 'Solon, darling, they're *perfect*.' She slipped the chain over her head as he did the same. 'Let them be a pledge between us.'

The pieces were moving into position. Ennis' watchers were hovering close to the prince-consort, ready to make damn sure Ril Endarion didn't survive the coming battle. The secretary would know within seconds; his signal would mark the beginning of their coup.

Ennis hints that they have someone inside Wurther's circle: he will issue a proclamation, signed by his shadow-prelates, to reassure the populace. Jean Benoit will go to the banks to stabilise Crown finances while Gestatium arrests Dubrayle. Medelie and I go to Redburn Tower, secure the Sacrecour children and give them to Selene, then I go to the barracks and announce that I'm taking emergency command. I arrest Setallius on some pretext. We gain Lyra's compliance by threatening to expose her parentage. From then on, we're in control.

It was direct and within their abilities, but it all hinged on the news from Collistein Junction. 'What's the mood of the city?' he asked Medelie. 'Are the people anxious?'

'Highgrange is calm. My manservant tells me that Esdale is tense – they're all soldier families down there. No one expects defeat, though: the taverns are preparing to celebrate victory.'

'From what I hear, it will be a close-run thing.'

'They're Noories, darling. *We* are the Rondian Empire.'

'I know . . .' He looked up at the sky. 'I should be there.'

'No, you *must* be here. Rolven Sulpeter will hold our men together when Endarion falls.'

'Ril Endarion is no general, but he can fight. He may survive.'

'And if he does, we have other trigger-points: a small nudge of the gnosis and Lyra will miscarry. This *is* going to happen, I assure you.' She stroked the scarred side of his face. 'I've been waiting a long time to see you take that throne, dearest Solon. It's been the mission of my life.'

She lifted her mouth to his and he kissed her, although he felt more like pacing than passion. Then he felt a pulse of energy awaken the relay-stave on the table. As he placed his hand on it, Medelie followed suit.

Chaplain Ennis' voice crackled in their heads. *<Battle is about to be joined in the Kedron. Report in, please.>*

Edreu Gestatium responded instantly. *<Standing by in the Chancellery.>*

<We're ready,> Jean Benoit drawled.

<Already in position,> Selene's cool voice chimed in.

<Ready to go,> Solon said.

They all waited . . . and then came an anxious female voice, one Solon didn't know. <*The Queen . . . She's supposed to be in her suite, but the maid just got a look inside and she's not there!*>

Solon felt his eyes go round as curses scorched the aether. He looked at Medelie. 'Perhaps she's in labour?'

'If she were in labour the bells would be tolling,' Medelie muttered in his ear. She essayed a scrying, but of course, Setallius' people had her warded. Medelie grabbed a cloak. 'I'll find the little bitch. She's not dropping from sight now.'

They broke the connection and Medelie hurried through the doorway. All he, the man of action, could do was sit and wait . . .

Dear Kore, I hate conspiracies!

Lyra winced and clutched at her huge, stretched belly as the river ferry slipped its moorings and bobbed out into the river. The baby was awake and squirming. 'Sweet Aradea, I want my body back,' she murmured, then realised guiltily that she'd prayed not to her god but to her genilocus.

She'd gone to her garden first thing and kindled her link to the dwyma; now she was consciously keeping it intact, though she wasn't sure how far she could go from her garden and still be able to use her power. *I should have tried this earlier*, she berated herself. *I should already know these things.* But so far the link was holding, although it was giving her a headache and making her vision swim and blur. She could see better when she closed her eyes . . .

. . . *and looked into Aradea's leafy visage and tawny eyes. She also glimpsed the young man with the sorrowful face she'd seen before. A whale streamed through rough waves with a copper-skinned girl on its back.* Every time she communed, there was an increase to her reach and her awareness. Some of them were living souls, she sensed, and others were more like ghosts, revenants of the dwyma.

Strengthened, she opened her eyes again and scanned the ferry through the thumping in her head. Everything was too bright, but she could see Basia's people, a Ventian couple dressed as pilgrims, grey-haired despite their youth, a Ventian trait.

Lyra had protested when she'd been given a nun's habit to wear beneath her robes, 'But I'm pregnant – *nuns* don't get pregnant!'

'Ha!' Basia had sniffed. 'You'll see.'

Her bodyguard, sitting beside her, was clad in men's clothing and looked quite at ease. 'Getting into the Forum Evangelica should be easy,' she told Lyra as the ferryman caught the swirling currents of the Bruin and the boat surged forward. 'Just don't forget: I'm Jessen Chandler, a candle-maker from Coraine. You're my sister Lyssa: you took the veil, but found herself in trouble.'

Big trouble, if you don't go to sleep, Lyra told the wriggling lump in her belly.

They had all day. Dirklan had shut the royal suite to visitors and cancelled her appointments, claiming she was unwell. He'd remained in the Bastion to monitor the other threat – another worry Lyra really didn't want to dwell on.

The Celestium's dome grew larger as they plied their course across the river while behind her, the Bastion rose grim and grey on Roidan Heights, towering above the sea of slate-tiled roofs. To the west, the stumps of the Forgotten Bridge jutted from promontories on both sides of the river. Emperor Andarius, her grandfather's father, had run out of money for the project seventy years ago, leaving the broken stone arches emerging from a tangle of vines as eerie remnants forever reaching for each other. On certain nights, the common folk said, phantoms would walk across the non-existent bridge.

As they bobbed across the river, Lyra caught snatches of conversation, little fragments that captured some of the city's anxieties, and her own.

'—I hear the Dupeni are still in Midrea, drinking the cellars dry—'

'—and what's wrong with nuns being—'

'—we're outnumbered, but our magi—'

'—she was sleeping with her confessor, him what ran off! So whose child—'

Then they were riding a surge into the Southside Docks and the Rymfort and Celestium were towering above the buildings clustered on the waterfront. Their gleaming white marble looked far removed from the damp grime of the docks, as if gods truly had fashioned them on high, then placed them amid the dross of humanity.

She kept her cowl up as they disembarked and clinging to Basia's wiry arm, joined the throng running the gauntlet of beggars, food-sellers and relic-purveyors. There was a strange atmosphere of piety and avarice, the joy of the faithful juxtaposed with the naked greed of those trying to peddle their wares.

Distant chants filled the air as Lyra waddled along the Pilgrims' Path, feeling crushed by exhaustion, pregnancy and her crippling headache. Basia supported her with subtle strength as they climbed the gentle slope and through the giant gates guarded by Kirkegarde sentries into a huge courtyard.

The Forum Evangelica was one of several squares enclosed by wings of the Celestium housing administrative offices and barracks and priestly dormitories as well as treasury, chapels, museums and cat-acombs for the dead. Ahead of them rose the roofed colonnades of the Memorium, where statues of past grand prelates were bedecked like shrines with votive candles and fresh flowers. Inside the Forum there were thousands of women in brown, blue, black or white, habits of many different orders, raising their voices in praise of Kore. Tents edged the square and cooking-fires sent clouds of smoke streaming into the steely skies. Lines of women carried buckets to and from the river; others lugged handcarts laden with supplies.

'Wurther won't allow traders into the Forum Evangelica and he's sealed off all but one well,' Basia pointed out. 'The sisters must bring their supplies up from the docks and get water from Southside. Some pilgrims are helping them, but there are thugs who rob those who don't go in packs.'

'Wurther hasn't reported this to the Royal Council,' Lyra noted.

'Of course he hasn't: this is *his* kingdom.' Basia led the way through the crowds towards a postern gate on the western wing of the Memorium. 'A previous grand prelate permitted an office for dealing with issues raised by convents – abuse of nuns by priests, unwanted pregnancies, that sort of thing. It's always swamped and has no authority, of course, but it's become Valetta's headquarters. Come.'

This was a whole ugly side to the Church that Lyra shied away from. She'd been raised in a convent and had always believed everything was pious and wholesome. *When things are normal again, I'm going to ask Wurther some awkward questions*, she resolved. But first she had to get through today.

The postern gate had a plaque above it: *Officia Femina*. When Basia showed papers and asked for Sister Pettara, the harried woman behind the desk looked up, then gestured them into the waiting room inside – where more than three dozen pregnant women, all in habits, were already seated. Lyra sat clumsily beside a sniffling, pallid girl with ginger hair who looked at Lyra pityingly. The woman next to her – her mother, maybe – asked when she was due, but a name was called and they got up and shuffled away through the inner door before Lyra had a chance to respond.

She turned to Basia. *We're about to go into danger*, she thought, *and I want there to be peace between us.* But that required some frank questions. She'd been working up the courage to ask them and now was finally the time. 'Basia,' she asked quietly, 'are you and Ril lovers?'

Basia blinked, clearly shocked that Lyra would be so direct, then she stuck out her pointy chin. 'Yes.' The look on her face was fatalistic. 'He loves me as I love him; more than the child's love you gave him.'

I could have her hung for this, Lyra thought, to remind herself that she had the upper hand. But Basia had risked her life for her, and Ril loved her – and so did Dirklan, albeit as a father. She waited for anger, but it didn't come, even though the adultery was now truly fact. All she felt was sadness that her marriage was really over. She still needed Ril, though, to be a father to his child, to be the sword that defended her, to be someone to cling to when she felt weak.

But I do want him to be happy . . .

'When he returns,' she said quietly, 'we will rearrange the royal suite and the duty schedules so that you don't need to sneak around.'

Basia's eyes softened and she bowed her head. 'Your Majesty is merciful.'

All the things Lyra was surrendering threatened to crush her, and for a minute all she could do was breathe. Then she managed to whisper, 'I just want my husband to be happy, and I can't do that myself.' Then tears were spilling from her eyes and she sagged over her stomach and sobbed farewell to a dream of a faery-tale love.

Around her, thirty other disgraced pregnant women who probably didn't even have a husband to give away sat buried in their own far greater plights.

I'm privileged. I have no right to be miserable. But dear Kore, sometimes I just want to die. Aradea caressed her mind like a promise that better things could yet be, and in this world, Basia drew her into her arms and held her. Although her husband's lover was the last person she wanted comforting her, it did help. She sobbed until Basia's sleeve was soaked, until she was finally able to straighten and wipe her eyes.

'Thank you for your honesty,' she whispered. Then she drew on all she'd learned from the council table and the crises she'd survived and added, 'So long as he is free to carry out his public duties and be a father to our child, I will turn a blind eye.'

'The world will never know, I swear.' Then Basia bit her lip and added, 'I'm sorry for condemning you for what Ostevan did. I was wrong.'

Wordlessly, Lyra hugged her again, an odd feeling of kinship overtaking her. 'I think you and I will come through this. Like sisters,' she added hopefully.

Basia's face turned stony. 'I don't think so, Majesty, not when you hold life and death over me. But I swear I'll serve as best I can.' She turned away, visibly shaking.

Lyra felt as if she'd been slapped. *Of course, I'm the queen*, she berated herself sarcastically, *and even if I wish to forget it, no one else will.*

The rest of their wait passed in painful silence while her head throbbed and her vision swirled. She felt strangely amorphous, as if she wasn't really in her body but floating unseen above it. Every sound in the room reached her, every aroma, sweet and foul. 'I'm really not well,' she thought blearily, but they'd come too far to turn back now. She sensed this was her last chance to save the Winter Tree.

Then a severe-looking woman with an Argundian accent bustled in, peered at them and said, 'Master Chandler . . . and your sister?' When they nodded she took them through to a small, dank office. She had tired, sunken eyes and her blonde hair was shot with white, although she was probably only thirty. 'I'm Sister Pettara, Majesty,' she said, once the door closed behind them. 'Welcome.'

The door opened again and the two Ventians entered and made flourishing bows.

'Milady, this is Rhune, and Sarunia,' said Basia. Dirklan's spies were male and female versions of each other, their angular features tanned, their grey curls identically styled. Both shrugged off cloaks to reveal shortswords, daggers and quivers of arrows belted to their waist. They pulled strings from their belt-pouches, Rhune separated his walking stick into two pieces, which they quickly strung into bows.

'Rhune and Sarunia have served Dirklan for a dozen years,' Basia added. 'Don't let their baby faces fool you: they're very experienced agents.' She turned to Sister Pettara. 'Are we ready?'

'Yes, but we need to wait a few minutes. At midday the virago will speak in the Forum Evangelica – the corridors are always empty at that time: it'll make our passage easier.'

The three Volsai looked frustrated at the wait, but Lyra was grateful for the few minutes' rest. She felt permanently tired now.

'What's a virago?' Basia asked.

'It's the new title for Sister Valetta,' Pettara replied, 'from the Rimoni word meaning "Exemplary Woman".'

'Something new for me to aspire to,' Basia quipped.

Lyra asked Pettara, 'When does Wurther swear in his new prelates?'

'Tomorrow, Majesty. Tonight the candidates stand vigil, much like your crowning, then tomorrow they'll take their vows – followed, of course, by a banquet.'

'Taking oaths and kneeling takes a lot of energy, I'm sure,' Basia remarked.

'Is the grand prelate listening to your grievances?' Lyra asked Pettara.

'Hardly – he laughs at us!' Pettara looked up. 'We've all been grateful for your Majesty's messages of support.'

'I wish I could do more, and I will, if it can be done without provoking unnecessary conflict between Church and Crown.'

Encouraged, Pettara spoke of their numbers and the difficulties in getting such simple things as food and water and blankets. 'At the moment the only reason we get anything at all is through donations carried in by pilgrims. With winter coming on, fuel for fire will become an issue. Most of the sisters are sleeping beneath blankets in the Forum. Sickness is breaking out – trembles, rotskin . . . perhaps even riverreek, though I hesitate to say it.'

'Are you certain it's just the riverreek?'

'We've not forgotten Reeker Night, Majesty. Some of the sisterhood are magi, myself included. We believe we're dealing with it.'

'We can send supplies. It's shameful that Dominius is starving his sisters.'

Just then the bells tolled six times, to mark midday. Pettara rose, opened the inner door and exchanged low words with another nun, then said, 'It's time, Majesty.'

She handed Lyra and her escorts over to a tall knight Lyra had met at court: Lann Wilfort, the Kirkegarde Supreme Grandmaster, had the reputation of a pragmatist. He wasted no time hurrying Lyra's group through the maze-like corridors. Finally, Lyra saw the bulky silhouette of Dominius Wurther, waiting beside a guarded doorway, one of two entrances to the Winter Garden. His stony-faced Estellan bodyguard was with him, watching hawkishly. The grand prelate was in heavy scarlet robes and carrying a long crosier with a large, gleaming crystal in the crook of the head – it looked more weapon than symbol.

While everyone else knelt before the rulers of Bastion and Celestium, Wurther took Lyra's arm. 'Aren't these conspiracies fun? I love sneaking around, don't you?' he grinned, looking her up and down. 'The habit becomes you, Milady. How does it feel to wear it again?'

'It's not a life I miss,' Lyra replied. She was finding the garb brought back memories she'd been happy to forget, and she was longing to shed it. And her headache was getting worse, not better.

Wurther noticed. 'Majesty, you're as pale as a ghost. You should be in bed.'

She gritted her teeth and clutched his arm. 'I have to do this.'

'Then let's begin,' Wurther said, gesturing for the guards to open the doors. He led her to the threshold, and murmured in her ear, 'I wish I could do more to help.'

He meant it, Lyra realised as she thanked him. Gazing through the doors apprehensively, she felt vulnerable and cumbersome, a sitting target for any kind of threat, though none was apparent.

The shrine was much as she remembered: a poorly grassed triangle roughly an acre in size, enclosed on two sides by high walls. The third was formed by the cathedral itself, a curved bank of stained-glass windows glowing faintly from the candles within. There were a dozen Kirkegarde soldiers on each wall, and a trio of skiffs circled above.

In the centre of the space was a small man-made hill, like a burial barrow for an ancient Frandian chieftain. An opening notching the base led to the subterranean cave where Saint Eloy had once lived and where his remains lay, with some of his fellow repentant dwymancers. The walls were lined with amber, she remembered.

I drank a droplet of liquid amber, and something opened up my head . . .

Then her eyes went to the top of the mound, to the Winter Tree, which was covered in leaves and dark berries despite the oncoming winter. Like her own sapling, the tree withered in spring and summer, blossoming in autumn and winter. It brought a lump to her throat.

Apart from the Winter Tree, the rest of the garden was autumnal. The grass was sparse and the spindly border trees against the two walls had piles of dead leaves around them. A light drizzle began to fall, and from the far wall a crow cawed. Wurther muttered something about carrion-birds, but Lyra could feel Aradea inside her, wary but unafraid.

'I had a vision of Saint Eloy,' Lyra told Wurther. 'He said that there is some kind of magical corruption here that I must heal. I know this must be a tricky theological issue for you. Do you wish to wait outside?'

'The less I know the better,' Wurther replied, then he dropped his voice. 'On Reeker Night, a golden light from the shrine destroyed the masked man, "Jest" – supposedly Junius, but I now suspect he was a puppet, a mask within a mask, if you will, for Ostevan. When that golden light shone, I saw a face in it: yours, Lyra.'

She put her hand to her mouth. 'Then you knew what I was even then?'

'You saved my life, so whatever Church Law says, I owe you that.' He lifted her hand to his lips and kissed it, his lugubrious face showing rare concern. 'If aught goes wrong, I have two dozen mage-knights stationed around the walls and inside the rear of the cathedral. Call, and we will respond.'

Wurther patted the arm of his young Estellan guardsman, who turned to Basia. 'How will a crippled woman keep the empress safe?' Excelsior asked bluntly. Clearly he regarded Basia's gender to be as big a weakness as her lost lower legs.

'With my feminine wiles,' Basia told him, sharing a sly wink with Wurther, then joining Lyra as the two men withdrew. 'I think that Estellan needs a good spanking,' she remarked, which made Lyra smile.

That moment of levity lifted Lyra enough that she was able to turn from the sanctuary of the open doors without feeling like she'd been thrown into a pool full of ravenous eels. Hearing them boom closed still sent a tremor through her, but she took heart from the number of men on the walls around them, and the calm assurance as the Volsai took up position nearby. She looked around her, taking stock: they were south of the cathedral, with the man-made Lac Corin on the other side of the nearest wall. More importantly, she could still feel her connection to Aradea, and that was massively reassuring, even exhilarating. *I thought my powers confined to my garden, but I can leave my haven without losing them.*

Heartened, she told Basia, 'Wait here,' then turned to face the Winter Tree mound. Pulling off her headdress, she let her blonde locks tumble about her shoulders. Her headache still pounded, a swelling inside her skull as if something was about to burst through her crown, and her vision was too bright and too slow; every time she turned her head, the light seemed to smear. But she put that aside and silently called, *I'm here*, to the garden's genilocus.

Despite the verdant presence of Aradea inside her, the atmosphere in the garden remained deathly, and she grimaced as a writhing brown centipede as long as her hand wriggled through the dead leaves at her feet. She smelled rat droppings and felt the eyes of vermin in shadowy holes at the base of the walls. But the Winter Tree still glowed with life, which gave her hope. She hauled her outsized belly up the mound, each step forcing a painful exhalation from her lips. At the top she had to bend over, panting, until she got her breath back and could look properly.

The vivid green of the leaves shone in her sight, and the purplish glow of the berries were a balm to the tainted decay that surrounded her. She began to feel reassured – until she opened herself to the natural energies of the genilocus and her unease returned tenfold.

Dear Kore, the whole tree *is sick* . . .

The bloom of life she'd seen was real, but it was polished skin on a rotten apple. The tree was fighting for its life, its very roots mired in the *wrongness*. She nudged the ground, breaking the crust of the earth, and a foul stench like faeces and vomit immediately struck her as black, viscous fluid oozed out. She tried another place, recoiling in disgust as a dead crow was uncovered, the stench of rotting meat adding to the taint in the air. Black maggots writhed in the rotting flesh. She put a hand to her mouth to stop from vomiting and adding to the detritus. It was much worse than what had been done to her pool.

It's the same black fluid the Reekers had inside them. Reluctantly, painfully, she dropped to her knees and stretched her fingers over the gash in the soil while she reached with the dwyma. A faint light coalesced in her hand and pulsed – then the black fluid sizzled and dried to dust. But it was only a small area, and more of the reeking ooze immediately welled up.

Can I fight this? Can I cleanse it? Her heart thudded. *I have to – but how?*

The cathedral bells rang out, a gentle chime marking the half-hour. The morning was passing. In the Forum Evangelica, Valetta would be speaking about equality before Kore, and far to the south, battle was probably joined. It was time her own struggle commenced.

She climbed to her feet shakily, looking at the tree again. Close up, she could see the purplish-red berries were rotten. She clambered back to the base of the mound and told Basia, 'I have to look below.'

The bodyguard didn't look at all happy. 'I'll go first.'

'No,' Lyra said, certain that a mage wouldn't be safe down there, 'just wait here.' She found an oil-lamp and a tinderbox at the entrance, which made things a little easier. The steps and walls were smooth and gold, from the amber sap that had seeped down over the centuries from the tree above. She felt as if she were encased in a hollow drop of honey.

Wurther had once told her this amber could be used to make dying easier, which wasn't a comforting thought.

The cave was as she remembered it: a fire-pit in the centre of a small round chamber. The skeleton wrapped in mouldering monastic robes, which had alarmed her on her first visit here, was still propped against the wall.

She knelt beside the fire-pit, taking the weight off her feet, grateful her child was now sleeping, and reached inside, feeding the spark of dwyma despite the venom and disease permeating the air. As her link to Aradea came alive again, she sensed the latent power of the shrine: it dwarfed her garden like an oak towering over a sprig of grass . . . but the tree was diseased.

If only I'd come here earlier, she thought, but 'if only' was no use now. She clutched her Sacred Heart icon and prayed aloud, 'Dear Kore, I don't believe my gift is heresy – it's part of your Creation. This desecration must bring you pain too. Please, show me how to cleanse it.'

Lyra wasn't sure what she expected, but what she got was silence, and whether that was an absence or listening, she couldn't tell. She turned to the old skeleton lying propped against the far wall. 'Saint Eloy, you spoke to me before. Here I am.'

The word 'Eloy' awakened something: she immediately felt the air move, a wind that touched her skin without rippling her robes, and then she realised the amber was moving, seeping like liquid honey and coalescing around the old bones.

She sucked in her breath, unsure whether to rejoice or to run screaming, but she covered her belly protectively and watched. The amber flowing like molten gold was streaked with ash and dirt and all the detritus of the earth – twigs and leaves and worm casings and old insect carapaces – as it formed into a kind of flesh. It might have taken minutes or hours; Lyra was so enthralled that she didn't notice.

Then the body turned eyeless sockets towards her as a film of amber skin crawled over the skull, hair grew from the scalp, the mouth sprouted teeth and the eyes filled with dark fluid.

'Lyra,' the dead man said, 'you've come!'

*

Sister Valetta della Rodrigo stepped to the front of the balcony overlooking the Forum Evangelica and looked down on thousands of women, mostly. What had begun as a protest was turning into an empire-wide movement. An atmosphere of unreality reigned: that mere women could make the great of the empire pay heed. The fear that soldiers would brutally suppress their protests had given way to belief in the power of courage and truth.

The man watching her, two levels above and seventy yards to her left, drew further into the shadows and studied the enthralled crowd as Virago Valetta spoke.

'All we want is equality,' Valetta cried, her voice resonating over the square. 'All we want is to give our lives to Kore as fully as men do: equality before Kore!'

'*EQUALITY*,' the throng below her cried. '*VIRAGO VALETTA!*'

Equality, the watcher sneered internally. *What is that?*

But the crowd soaked up her pleas: that nuns deserved the same education, the same ranks, the same status as priests. Female clergy should be permitted to perform every piece of ritual, the daily Rites of Reverence, Unburdening, Marital, Child-blessing and Funerary rites – the lot.

In Valetta's mouth, such demands – although they contradicted many direct teachings of the *Book of Kore* – became just and reasonable. She'd grown in power as an orator as she honed her message and the core group, those most known for their zeal and clarity of mind, had sharpened their own skills of persuasion, reaching out to powerful women, especially female magi who'd fought their own battles to be treated as equals. More and more were embracing Valetta's mission.

'Sisters, I need your support,' Valetta called as she moved towards her conclusion. 'The day has come for us to make our points more forcibly. This evening, Grand Prelate Wurther begins inaugurating his new prelates, to replace those brothers, my father included, lost to us on Reeker Night.'

That male clergy could wed was a quirk of the Estellan branch of the Church: a throwback to when the missionaries of Kore were prepared to compromise to get their way. But Valetta's father would have been horrified by his daughter's movement – and highly amused at the pressure it placed on Wurther.

'We're not permitted to join the prelature, despite many of us being highly qualified,' Valetta shouted, 'but I think we should join their vigil anyway!'

The crowd below cheered hungrily; there were some very angry young women below who were desperate to do more than just sing and pray. Many had been unwillingly placed with the Church in the first place and they longed to batter down the walls confining their lives.

'Join us, Sisters – and Brothers too: the East Gate leads to the Gardens of Reflection, and beyond those the Prelature, where Wurther's cronies are gathering – let's see what scraps they throw us from their table!'

Valetta had been building towards this declaration for days now and as she spoke the words, they unleashed a surge of activity. She and her inner circle descended from the steps to deafening cheers, hugs and weeping and kissed hems. As the massive gathering began to move, runners attached to the Prelate's Guard were already sprinting ahead to give warning.

Above it all, the hooded watcher observed the mass of women surging towards the Gardens of Reflection with detached amusement. As Valetta's coterie of insiders left the speaking platform, he slipped back inside the giant building and into a small sitting room. A few moments later a nun opened the door, slid through and closed it.

'They're leaving, Magister Ostevan,' Sister Pettara said. 'And the Queen is with Wurther at the Shrine of Saint Eloy.'

Ostevan Jandreux bared his perfect teeth. 'Thank you, Sister. What of the Master?'

'Master Naxius awaits the queen.'

Ostevan hid his discomfort; he was still annoyed that Naxius was stepping in to take away *his* prize – but until he could find a way to surpass him, what the Puppeteer wanted, he got. He had to give his full attention to completing this coup: Wurther and Wilfort had a lot of powerful magi protecting Lyra, and they now knew how to fight Reekers. But Naxius himself would be present, and they had other resources . . .

'Wurther and Lyra are in the same place, and vulnerable,' he told

Pettara. 'You've done well and earned your reward. The Master keeps his promises, and so do I. Come, let us begin.'

Pettara kissed his ring hand, her eyes avid. She was not yet infected, drawn into his service instead by the promise of the Ascendancy. *And if I could actually grant you that, I might*, he reflected, before mentally shrugging. *Sometimes life disappoints even the best of us, Sister.*

They left the balcony together and strode through the deserted corridors towards the cathedral. The demon-spawn coiled about his heart stirred, sensing his rising excitement. Finally he emerged into a gallery and stopped Pettara, then crept silently to the edge and looked down.

Dominius Wurther and Lann Wilfort were below, in the rear atrium of the giant building, protected by Exilium Excelsior and a dozen mage-knights of the Kirkegarde. Beyond them were the doors that led to the Winter Garden . . . *And that's where I'll find you, my Queen. I still intend that you be mine . . .*

Ostevan reached inside his robes and unhooked his Jest mask. When he placed it against his face, it adhered like a second skin. Then he lifted his hood, pulled on gauntlets and unsheathed his longsword.

<*Master,*> he sent, <*I am in place, and ready.*>

The Bastion

Three miles north across the Aerflús, Solon Takwyth sat fretting in his Bastion apartment as the sun reached its zenith somewhere behind thickening grey clouds and intermittent drizzle. He was still linked to Chaplain Ennis, who was relaying reports from the battlefield. The sun rose two hours earlier in the Kedron than in Pallas: the fight was about to commence. Solon's nerves tightened with each passing moment, until even he, Knight-Commander of Coraine, veteran of the Southern Wars and survivor of 909, could scarcely bear it.

Then the doors to his suite swung open and Medelie Aventour stormed in, fuming. 'Lyra's vanished.'

Solon stood. 'Then why hasn't the alarm been raised?'

'Because Setallius' people are covering her absence. I saw Mort Singolo loitering, picking his nails calm as you like. And Basia de Sirou's gone too. Something's moving. I don't like this.' She put her hands to her head, her frayed nerves obvious.

'Should we abort?' Solon asked.

She looked appalled. 'No! Solon, we must be bold – victory is for the brave. This thing has its own momentum now. If Setallius has got wind of it and concealed the queen, then we must move regardless. Let her hide: if we hold the Bastion, we've already won—'

'But the crisis we're awaiting hasn't come.'

'Then we must make it – *we* must be the crisis! We must—'

As if fate and destiny were real things, the relay-stave hummed and they both grabbed it. Ennis' voice crackled into their brains. <*The prince is dead! I repeat: RIL ENDARION IS DEAD! Our time has come!*>

'Praise be: it's begun! The day of days—'

Medelie was exultant. She seized him, pulling his head to hers. She tasted of triumph now. Her eyes bright, she cried fervently, 'I love you!' as if that were the most pressing matter of all. Clutching the pendant he'd gifted her, she raised it to her lips and kissing it, declaring, 'I've *always* loved you, and I'll love you for ever!' Then she hurried from the room.

Solon was alone. He pulled out a coin, flipped and caught it, dithering ... *deciding* ... Then he ignited a pre-prepared gnostic link and sent, <*Dirk, it's begun.*>

He pocketed it again and hurried after Medelie, and together they strode through the palace towards Redburn Tower.

35

The Battle of Collistein Junction

Master-General Kaltus Korion

Before and during the Third Crusade, no name meant 'victory' more than that of Kaltus Korion, who crushed the Noros Revolt, brought the Argundians to heel and won victory after victory in the East. His death and the collapse of his army have never been adequately explained. His heir, Seth, is regarded by some as a hero, by others as a traitor. I urge my fellow senators to demand a full report!

SENATOR GULFI BRAEBRUCK, BRICIAN SENATE, 932

Collistein Junction, Kedron Valley
Octen 935

Ril paced while a plain-faced woman in nun's robes gorged on boiled eggs and bread. Between them was a man strapped to a chair, naked but for his small-clothes. Ril hadn't had the stomach to watch, let alone eat afterwards, as the woman had been interrogating him for the last half-hour. She'd battered him, broken fingers and ripped out nails until she'd extracted what she needed.

'I'm not sure I understand,' Ril asked the woman, who wasn't actually a nun but a Volsai agent named Veritia. 'You want the signal that *I'm dead* to be sent?'

'Absolutely,' Veritia replied between mouthfuls. She'd arrived yesterday, bearing word from Dirklan Setallius that a Pallas cabal planned to seize power once he'd been assassinated.

Ril was still in shock from learning the name of the cabal's agent in his inner circle. 'But Lyra will think I'm dead – and she's about to give birth any moment!'

'She'll be told the truth,' Veritia assured him.

He scowled, turning back to the man tied to the chair. 'This is a dirty business.'

'It is, but you get used to it,' Veritia agreed blithely. 'Dirklan's got a man risking his life on the inside and we're set to pounce. To net everyone, we need them to think you're dead.'

'But I've got to lead the army into battle in a few minutes.' He was armoured, but he'd not yet donned his distinctive helmet with its coronet.

'I know. If I had my way we'd dress you up as a corpse and let some mutton-headed knight take your place, in case the cabal realise what we're doing.'

'I'm one of those mutton-headed knights myself.'

'No, you're not, my Prince,' Veritia told him. 'You're perceptive enough to let this man send his signal.'

Ril turned to face his prisoner. Looking at his aide-de-camp, asked, 'Why, Niklas?' He was genuinely mystified. He'd thought they were friends – and the Bycross family were Corani through and through. 'Didn't I pay you enough?'

Bycross gave him a resigned look. 'Money ... nothing ... with it,' he slurred, through broken teeth and cut lips. 'Wa ... promithed ... morthality ...'

Ril looked at Veritia. 'He was promised mortality?'

'*Imm*ortality,' Veritia corrected. 'Pure-blood magi are always a sucker for that line.' She pushed her plate aside and joined him, frowning as she fingered her blades.

In the end, the key to breaking the man hadn't been the extreme pain she'd inflicted, but sparing Bycross a public trial, which would have ensured his family's disgrace and penury. Now they knew everything the aide knew: Ril was supposed to be assassinated while being armed for battle, then Bycross himself would deliver the message to Pallas. Permitting him to send that signal anyway meant letting him use his gnosis, which was a risk – he might just be fanatical enough to throw away his life and his family's honour to give the conspirators warning.

'Will you give the signal?' Veritia demanded.

Bycross looked up at him blearily. 'You . . . promith . . . No 'prithals . . .'

'None,' Ril agreed. 'Your family will be safe. You have my word.'

Bycross nodded. His family was related to the Jandreux family; they'd been critical of Lyra in court, but had been mollified by their talented son's rapid elevation.

'Well then . . .' Veritia placed a dagger against the prisoner's left eyeball. 'Even the hint of an attempt to warn them and you'll be killed and your family made examples of. And don't think there'll be mercy from the empress, for Lyra will never even know.'

The aide bowed his head. 'I won't . . . anything.'

Ril removed the Chain-rune and handed Bycross a relay-stave. In a moment, the message had gone: <*The prince is dead. May Kore be with you.*>

Ril took back the stave, then looked away as Veritia rammed her blade into the young man's brain. He jerked once, then went limp, held upright only by his bindings.

'I'll dump his corpse on the battlefield,' the Volsai told him. 'You go and win the battle, Milord.'

Ril was relieved to leave and seek enemies who fought the same way he did.

Ten minutes later, still unsettled, Ril stood peering through a spyglass, his identity concealed by an anonymous legion cloak. He was just one of dozens of observers positioned near the centre where the banners were arrayed – where he was supposed to be.

But Bycross might have comrades, so I need to be dead a while longer.

The Third Army of Aquilleans under Prince Elvero Salinas were arrayed to his left; the Corani held the centre and the Fifth Army led by Seth Korion were to his right in the southwest. The plans were laid, the pieces moving. Though his forces still felt disjointed, he hoped to bridge that disunity by sitting above it in his mighty triple-masted warbird while Rolven Sulpeter commanded the Corani ground forces.

It's in the air where this will be decided, Ril thought, *the culmination of months of fighting.* He lowered the spyglass and asked, 'What are the Noories doing?' The entire Shihad army, after much wailing, had turned their backs to face southeast, away from the Imperial Army. 'Is it some kind of insult?' he asked an Brician observer.

'They're praying – they always face towards Hebusalim when they pray.'

'It's a shame they're out of arrow-range.' Ril looked behind to his flagship, tethered alongside dozens of other large windships. The lighter craft were already airborne, the windriders circling high above them all. Then a pair of cloaked figures, Rolven Sulpeter and his aide, joined them.

'Why all this cloak-and-conspiracy?' Sulpeter demanded. 'I'd expected you to join me on the hilltop.'

'I know, but you'll need to hold things together a while longer,' Ril told him. He bent his head to the old general's ear. 'Someone tried to kill me, so I'm keeping a low profile just now, to see if we can lure out his accomplices back in Pallas.'

Sulpeter was shocked. 'Dear Kore! You're saying these conspirators tried to murder you on the morning of a battle to protect the empire?'

'That's the sort of people we're up against, Rolven,' Ril said tersely. 'So I need to remain incognito for the next half an hour or so, while Setallius rounds up people in Pallas. They're emerging right now to claim power.'

Dear Kore, keep Lyra and my child safe . . . and Basia.

The old Corani noble's expression was deeply troubled. 'I weep for Rondelmar, Milord. I pray the miscreants are caught and punished as they deserve.'

'As do I. You'll take command here and I'll be in the air – all anyone will see is yet another observer on the flagship. The Shihad will come hardest along the road – right down your throat, Rolven – *you've got to hold.* If the others are breached, we can pull in our flanks, but *you* must not be broken.'

'We'll hold, I swear it,' Sulpeter vowed. As they shook hands, he said fervently, 'Kore watch over you, my Prince. I know we don't see eye to eye, but no one can fault your courage, or your love for the queen.'

He met Ril's eyes. 'I do not believe the lies about infidelity, my Prince – about you or the empress.'

'Thank you,' Ril said fervently. *Although some of the 'lies' are true . . .*

He turned and ran for the flagship, a three-masted warbird called the *Philemon* sporting fore and aft castles, four giant ballistae and a fighting force of sixty archers and three battle-magi, including the pilot, and captained by the much-admired Jaklyn Dace. Ril would rather have been flying Pearl, but his pegasus was stabled below-decks. She could be launched from a side-hatch if needed.

Jacklyn Dace, a rakish-looking man with a certain scruffy charm, sauntered over. The ship was flying Imperial colours, but not Ril's personal banner, to give the impression that he wasn't present – pretty feeble as security measures went, but unless Bycross had co-conspirators aboard, Ril should be able to discreetly direct operations until battle was joined and everyone was distracted.

'Is all well, Captain?' Ril asked.

Dace, instructed not to bow or salute, gave a loose shrug and murmured, 'Ready to give them a good kicking, Milord. Let's get underway.' He gestured and the *Philemon* rose sluggishly on light winds – but that would change soon: a dozen Air-magi had instructions on the wind patterns Ril required, including a stout nor'wester to give a tailwind for his forces and blow the enemy backwards. Their sails filled as they climbed towards where the eighteen warbirds forming the backbone of his fleet waited in line. When he looked down, the battlefield was laid before him like pieces in a tabula game.

No, they're men, and they are about to risk their lives . . .

He could still hear the sounds of the army: trumpets braying and drums thundering as the men marched into place. The Noories were singing, hymns presumably, and forming up in great seething masses so many men deep that it made his own lines look horribly thin. It was hard to believe that his army was, despite the non-arrival of the Argundians and the Dupeni, one of the largest ever assembled by the empire; it looked tiny before the sea of Ahmedhassans.

By what factor do they outnumber us? he wondered. *Four to one? Five to one?*

And now the enemy windships were swirling upwards too, the distinctive triangular sails gaudily coloured and the rocs rising like swarms of gulls. *How do Noories fly?* went the jest; *like a rock!* – but the joke wasn't funny any more, not for those who'd seen them flash by, leaving death behind.

Captain Dace took the *Philemon* into the middle of the line of warbirds just as the enemy skirmishers and archers poured forward, spilling like a dirty stain over the pale brown plains. Even from up here the fens stank, but he could see the shape of them, and the way the Keshi on Seth Korion's flank were having to work their way around the deepest pools.

That prick has the best position, after all, Ril thought sourly. *Bloody Korions . . .*

Then the aether shivered, the clouds begin to swirl and the wind changed, just as he'd ordered – but a few seconds later, he felt a counter-pulse from the south: the Ahmedhassan Air-magi were retaliating. He held his breath, confident the pure-blood magi of the empire could win such a joust. And it appeared they had, because the wind behind his fleet began to pick up and his craft surged towards the enemy lines, a first wave to make initial contact and the second to slam into the enemy craft while they were still licking their wounds. Like Dace, the other captains began hoisting more sails. He could feel the deck vibrating beneath his feet as they ploughed through the air, moving faster and faster.

'Lead the first wave forward and engage enemy ships,' Ril ordered. 'Advance!'

<Alramh-amyr,> Bashara called to Waqar, <the enemy ships are coming!>

Waqar, stuck aboard his flagship when he really wanted to be flying his roc, looked up at his fliers, riding the thermals high above. <I see them – follow Shameed.> Then in more intimate tones, <Stay safe.>

Bashara laughed shrilly. <Safety is dull – see you in Paradise or the Pit, my lover!> She broke the contact as he sent her, Lukadin, Baneet, Fatima, Tamir and the rest a silent blessing.

The winds were rising, blowing from the northwest, as they had predicted. The Rondian magi were too strong: his fliers would face headwinds all day.

'Climb, climb,' the captain was exhorting his crews, seeking to maximise their one advantage. 'Shift it – get above them before they reach us!'

But thanks to the prevailing wind, the early initiative was with the Rondians. Suddenly the two fleets were within range of the ballistae and Waqar realised the headwind and superior Air-gnosis of the enemy meant the Rondians were above them, presenting the solid underside of their hulls as they fired down at the exposed Keshi sails and decks.

The carnage began.

The ballistae mounted on the fore castles cracked, sending thick shafts into sails and decks, where they burst into explosive flame. Arrows sleeted down, a continuous rain as the Rondian archers rotated positions, new men replacing those needing to reload. Worse still were the heaviest Rondian vessels, who started driving their hulls deliberately into the rigging of the craft beneath them, smashing masts, then hacking their way free, leaving the Keshi craft becalmed, on fire and dropping out of the sky.

Waqar's craft avoided such a fate by just a few feet as he blasted upwards with Fire-gnosis; the Rondians' hull showed no sign of his efforts except for a scorch mark. Then they were past and facing the aft-deck ballistae: more shafts, more arrows, another great gout of fire, thankfully snuffed out by one of his magi. His craft lurched and came about, seeking to climb above their foe.

Then his shields shredded and he whirled in time to see a six-foot spear impale the man beside him from chest to groin. He was pinned upright to the deck, arms and head dropping limply – it could as easily have been him!

'*Ahm on high,*' he gasped, then gestured, ripping both spear and man from the deck and sending them spinning away before the sight broke the crew's spirits. 'Climb,' he cried, '*climb!*'

All about, he saw his windships foundering. Some were ablaze, others had their masts and sails wrecked. A few had managed to get close enough to a Rondian vessel to hurl grappling hooks, but their sorties were just being hacked apart. When he looked down, they were right above the Shihad front line, where Rashid had launched the first assault along the main road.

His vessel managed to climb above the Rondian second wave as it came in – but many of his fleet weren't so fortunate. And now the Rondians' first wave was turning – at least that nor'westerly was hampering them now as they sought to re-engage. And high above, dozens of duels had broken out as his rocs went up against venators, mounted archers pitting their skills against lancers. The sky-battle swiftly lost any shape or pattern as each sought the enemy, skiffs fighting skiffs in one huge, bewildering mass.

Waqar tore his eyes from the fight, grasped a relay-stave and shouted, <*Now – strike now!*>

From out of the north came his reserve fleet: the biggest and most cumbersome of the transport vessels, refitted with steel rams and stripped of all superfluous weight. Anticipating the wind direction the Rondians would choose, he'd sent them out of sight the day before, to lurk in the shadow of the Matra Ranges until they were needed. Now they swept in on the Rondians' own tailwind, with plenty of height.

Paradise awaits you, brothers, he whispered as they began their run . . .

War always threw up some fresh horror. Seth Korion wondered what today's would be. The sky was already a chaotic mess of swooping windships and fliers, stretching all the way along the front. He had a man detailed to warn them if anything looked set to crash down on their heads, but otherwise he ignored what was going on above, instead fixing his eyes on the enemy soldiers attempting to march through the swamp towards his position. With some satisfaction he noticed their advance was punctuated by shrieks as the traps his magi had left took their toll, but those were soon exhausted and the Keshi archers began to deploy some two hundred yards from his own lines. His men were standing beside their big square shields – damnable things to lug all the way from Bricia, but now they'd be grateful.

'*Crouch*,' the legates shouted, echoed by first the centurions, then the five pilii, and every man dropped to one knee and raised his shield over his head. They also had the protection of the dirt ramparts he'd made them dig. In contrast, on the left Prince Elvero hadn't bothered with earthworks, because it might impede his counter-charge. So he said.

Seth sniffed. *If we actually get to counter-charge, I'll kiss Elvero's arse myself.*

'Are we in range?' Chaplain Gerdhart asked. He sounded nervous, even though he was a mage and a Third Crusade veteran.

'I doubt it.'

'Permission to cover up, sir?' Pilus Lukaz asked with *casual* concern. 'Precautionary, an' all.'

'Of course.'

His guard cohort went down on one knee and lifted their shields, except Baden, the stolid bannerman, who remained standing, but raised his shield to cover his face and torso. The banner flew above his head in the stiff breeze.

'Remember Riverdown?' he heard Bowe remark. 'Sky went black, heh.'

Seth remembered it well. Now the Keshi archers raised their bows, orders rang out to turn the skies black again and he watched the first volley land safely short of his position. Then he signalled, and just a few paces in front of where the Keshi archers were standing, men coated in mud and covered in grass-coloured cloaks erupted from foot-deep manholes and ploughed straight into the middle of the shocked archers, their shortswords stabbing brutally. For a full minute they rampaged, cutting down archers who were barely aware they were endangered – then whistles rang out, his men spun around and sprinted like Hel for their own lines. Their backs were exposed, but the Keshi were in a complete tither and more were running than shooting.

Minor victories, Seth thought, but his men crowed and cheered as if the battle were already won.

It was another half an hour before the Keshi came through the fens and lined up again, this time sending skirmishers forward to ensure there were no more surprises. After that, the archers began in earnest while spearmen mustered behind. Beyond them big, dark shapes loomed up out of the haze. Seth groaned at the sight of the war-elephants: there were clearly a lot of them, and according to reports, every one carried a mage.

*

Ril walked to the fore castle. It was time to take a hand. He drew his sword and extended it towards a Keshi skiff that had drifted too close after losing its sails. Ril sent a mage-bolt stabbing through the pilot's shields and he fell. Without him, the keel quickly bled out its energy and the skiff went plummeting into an enemy formation below, where it smashed and came apart like a broken toy.

They'd begun well, but things were far from decided. Rondian war-birds were better armed and more robust than anything the Keshi had – they were like flying castles, impregnable and death-dealing – but there were so damned *many* of the Noorie, with more and more ships filling the air. It was fast becoming a war of attrition, and Ril could feel the early advantage he'd won evaporating.

We need to do something decisive, he realised. 'Where's the enemy flagship?' he asked an aide, who pointed to his right. Through the midge-cloud of skiffs, rocs and venators they could see the largest of the Keshi fleet, packed with archers, a mass of magi deflecting arrows and spears and quelling gnosis-attacks. Ril called to Captain Dace, 'There's the enemy flagship – take us in!'

The captain bellowed and the *Philemon* turned into the heart of the fray.

On the ground, the Keshi archers were in full flow, sending volley after volley cutting through the sky and striking Sulpeter's lines. It was too soon to tell how effective they were. Their own bowmen were concealed still; there were just too many enemies to match volley for volley. He watched for a moment, horribly aware that Corani men were dying down there, then returned his attention to the skies. He scanned the enemy flagship, seeking the enemy commander . . . surely the dark-haired man with the coronet around his helmet?

Right, time to show the colours . . . He pulled out his own coronet and jammed it onto his helm, then shouted, 'Run out my banner!' In moments, the purple and gold pennant emblazoned with a crown and pegasus was streaming behind them and a massive cheer went up from the crew.

Then someone screamed a warning as a dark shape suddenly grew above them, falling out of the sky.

*

Waqar almost forgot to breathe as the enemy flagship – a massive vessel, beyond *anything* he could deploy – churned through the embattled skies towards his own craft. A purple banner now flew from its stern, and there was a crowned figure standing in the prow.

It's Ril Endarion, the 'Prince of the Spear' . . . He grasped his relay-stave and steadied his breath. *This is it!*

Then his big transporter ships appeared, flying unnoticed out of the north, coming in above and behind the enemy, just as he'd planned. They were using their altitude, and the Rondians' own conjured tailwind, to power their dive . . . straight at the Rondian warbirds—

The transports had been fitted with metal rams, as large as could be installed and still fly, and they were crewed by their most fanatical men, the Shihadis Waqar generally despised. They had been ordered to aim for the enemy warbirds, to hammer into them and bring them down; their own survival was secondary to causing maximum damage. They'd been moving unnoticed into position while battle joined and everyone stopped scanning the horizon . . . and now they were here, dropping towards the Rondians, rams glinting in the dull light.

Waqar smiled grimly as the first wave struck half a dozen of the enemy ships like catapult stones, smashing into them, breaking masts and deck and hulls, locking with them . . . and then spinning earthwards in a hail of splinters and falling bodies . . . More followed, seeking targets who were now aware and trying desperately to evade. Some managed to strike home, others flashed past, the pilots seeking to arrest their dives before they ploughed into the ground. A few succeeded.

But Waqar's eyes were on the enemy flagship, which magnificently evaded the hulk attempting to ram it, then sent a torrent of magefire to set the ram-ship ablaze. He swore as the enemy craft neatly sidestepped two entangled ships . . . and swerved right into their path.

'*Lift!*' he shouted, but it was already too late; the vessels had struck each other glancing blows, flank to flank, sending everyone flying. Some fell overboard, screaming as they vanished, while Waqar clung to the rail, as the vessels crunched again and timbers splintered.

The two flagships locked together.

'*Hujum-ah!*' someone screamed – *Charge!* – and all who could scrambled to their feet and threw themselves at the enemy. Waqar hurled his spear through the body of a Rondian sailor before drawing his scimitar and running forward. He leaped onto the rail as a figure wreathed in gnostic shields appeared.

'*EL NASR AL'AHM!*' Waqar roared – *the Eagles of Ahm!* – and launched a blow. All along the rail, blades were crashing together and spells exploding, but his eyes were fixed on his enemy's blade. The two weapons clashed together – and he caught a glimpse of his foe's crowned helmet.

Ril Endarion: the Prince of the Spear.

36

The Enemy Within

Runes

The ability to store magical energy was an extraordinary step forward for magi. Hitherto, spells had been instantaneous and finite. Once energy could be stored, awaiting triggering, whole new vistas opened up. The discovery was made by Ervyn Naxius, one of many by that restless intellect, before he became so consumed with learning that he lost his moral compass.

ANTONIN MEIROS, HEBUSALIM, 898

Pallas, Rondelmar
Octen 935

Solon Takwyth's dour, tense voice faded from his head, and the Volsai commander turned to Mort Singolo. 'It's happening. Let's go.'

The other man in the room, hunchbacked Taenis Coplan, bent over a relay-stave, and said aloud and into the aether, 'The signal's been sent. Keep your quarry in sight. Don't move until we say.'

Dirklan gave him a nod of approval. 'Come with me, Taenis – but whatever you do, don't get involved.'

'No intention to, boss,' Coplan grinned toothlessly. 'I know my limits.'

They left his fifth-floor office and strode through the halls, making for Redburn Tower, his mind still tracking the coin in Takwyth's pocket.

Takwyth had taken some persuading to play along with this cabal; he was a man who fought in the open. But with key members of the cabal as yet unidentified – including Selene, who might just be *Tear* – and with Ostevan still at large, he'd agreed. It had been a huge thing to ask, for the knight-commander not just to live a lie but to feign passionate love for his old duchess, but he'd managed it somehow.

He's a Corani first, and he's loyal to Lyra, despite everything.

But how to finish this cabal? That was another matter. His Volsai weren't knights or warriors but a motley collective of magi, most of them too lowborn to be knights, too individualistic for the legions and with a morality that didn't suit even Wurther's corrupt clergy. And almost all were disfigured in some way, physically or psychologically; that seemed to come with the territory.

'Mannis,' Dirklan called to a crafty-looking redheaded man lounging against a wall as they passed, 'let's go.'

Mannis rose, hefting a crossbow, as did a pair of hard-faced Hollenian brothers and a burly Pallacian woman. Dirklan had made no efforts to keep innocents away from the potential combat zone – the stakes were too high to risk any move that might tip off their quarry – and now people started scurrying away in alarm as they came upon the Volsai.

When they reached the main staging point, an internal gallery that ran to the base of Redburn Tower, where Cordan and Coramore were kept, the muscular woman peered through a keyhole into the foyer. 'They're there: Takwyth, and that tart he's bedding – Aventour.'

'Who else, Brigeda?' Dirklan asked.

'A guardsman, the gaoler with the keys ... they're checking the passes ...' Brigeda pulled a sneering face. 'If the bloody Sacrecours knew how easy this is, they'd've stolen those brats years ago.'

'It's only easy because he's Solon Takwyth,' Dirklan pointed out. He turned to Coplan. 'Is everyone else set?'

'Tymon's team and Blaise's lot are covering the Imperocracy and the Guild Hall. Patcheart has men stationed in the barracks in case there are others we don't know about. We're all in position.'

Dirklan's brain was racing. If this worked, in the next few minutes they'd net Chaplain Ennis, Edreu Gestatium, Jean Benoit and several of their functionaries – but he wanted the big prize: Selene. *Of course, there's no way any of them will be allowed to stand public trial.*

'Tell everyone to stand by: if we go too soon, our traitor-birds will fly the nest. Patcheart can flood the area with Palace Guard when we need to, but the first few minutes are just us: two-score Volsai in four teams to take on at least one Ascendant. That may be forty against one, but we all know that's possibly not enough.'

'Cheers, Dirk,' Brigeda commented. 'I'm raring to go now.'

'I'm telling you because I don't want any heroics. Just pin them down and let numbers count. And spare Takwyth: he's my man on the inside.'

That impressed them. 'Didn't fink 'e 'ad it in 'im,' Mannis commented.

'Neither did I. And watch Medelie Aventour: she's most definitely *not* what she seems. She's a shapeshifter and she will likely try to use that. Don't be fooled, no matter what guise she pulls on or who she claims she is. *I want her dead.*'

They looked at each other, clearly wondering what he meant, then Brigeda asked, 'What about this "Selene"?'

'She's too dangerous to mess around: just kill her.'

'Marvellous,' Handred, one of the Hollenians commented. He nudged his brother Fraen. 'She's yours.'

'*Rukka te*, brother,' Fraen replied. 'Decapitate first, ask questions later.'

Brigeda put her eye back to the keyhole. 'They're in. How long do we wait?'

'No more than two minutes.' Setallius glanced at Mort Singolo. 'Remember: don't get isolated, and no heroics.' Mort already had his axe cradled in his big hands.

'Sure,' Mort said. 'You've not said, but we all know they're launching on the back of a message that Ril's dead.'

'Indeed,' Dirklan replied, then he winked. 'But Veritia's down there, and the message is false. The prince-consort is still alive.'

'Good to hear it. The queen don't deserve to be widowed.'

'What about the Sacrecour children?' Brigeda asked. 'Are they actually up there?'

'They are, with no extra guards: moving them or layering on protections would have tipped the cabal off. Takwyth will protect them, and we'll support him as quickly as possible.'

They waited in silence after that, while Brigeda kept watch at the keyhole. Then she raised a hand and hissed, 'Selene's here. She's showing the guard a token ... Now he's asked her to wait ... Do we go now?'

Dirklan shook his head. 'No. The guards know not to let anyone through except Takwyth and Aventour – the knight-commander will block the door to the stairwell behind him, so she's trapped where she is. She's ours.'

Brigeda peered through the keyhole again, then swore. 'She just killed the poor bastard – broke his rukking neck!' Her eyes bulged, as the aether shivered. 'Rukka, she's just blasted the warded doors down!'

Dirklan felt his blood chill.

'She's gone inside the tower,' Brigeda reported. 'We go now, right?'

Dirklan calculated: Takwyth and Medelie – no, *Radine* – wouldn't have reached the children yet. Covert operations hinged on the tiniest nuances ... then the coin in his pocket thrummed again, no words, but the pulse of energy told him everything.

'Takwyth's in trouble – we go, *now!*'

Brigeda opened the door and Handred and Fraen led them through, moving stealthily towards the open door, past the corpse of the guardsman on the floor.

The Celestium

Lyra, you've come ... The old saint looked horrified.

'Eloy?' she asked tremulously, clutching her stomach, her heart racing. He was taking shape before her very eyes: an old, old man, thin grey hair plastered to his scalp and his eyes a watery blue.

'You shouldn't have come here, child,' he groaned in a rusty voice. 'It's not safe!'

'I know,' she replied, 'that's why I'm here. You called to me.'

'No, not I – I've been asleep until you spoke a moment ago.'

'You said to come here,' she started, but she could see from the saint's face that they'd both reached the same sickening conclusion: this was a trap. But she couldn't run, not when she could talk face-to-face to the first great dwymancer. She seized his frail hands and threw open her senses, allowing him to reach her mind to mind. With Eloy, she plunged into the web of dwyma energies that spread across Yuros.

It fed all her senses as she soared over snow-covered mountains and southern olive groves; she could feel the winds, hear the insects and birds, taste salty air, pollen and dust and rain in a hundred places at once. It was magnificent, overpowering, wonderful.

Eloy touched her belly: her unborn child was moving in her womb, awake again. 'The miracle of life,' he murmured. 'A mage-dwymancer child . . . a true thing of wonder.' Then he gripped her hand and said, 'And of course, you are the same, through pregnancy manifestation.'

She stared. 'But . . .'

'You're feeling headaches, an upsurge perception, blurred vision probably, maybe a heightened sense of smell? You're gaining the gnosis, Lyra.'

She felt her heart swell in both hope and fear. 'But I know nothing of it—'

'Gnosis is just an extension of the will,' Eloy told her. 'All the Arcanum spells and training are just ways to control it. For now, you just need to know that if you grasp that "headache" and determine on something, your physical energies will attempt to fulfil your will.' He gripped her hand tighter and added, 'Don't do so until your child is safely delivered.'

Lyra nodded, a little stunned, but time was moving. 'Someone brought me here to cure the Winter Tree,' she told Eloy. 'Why?'

'I don't know – but it wasn't me!'

'But what is the Winter Tree?'

Eloy looked at her fearfully. 'I'll be brief, then you *must* leave. The Winter Tree is the thing I grew to be the heart of the dwyma: an Elétfa, as Lanthea would say, a Tree of Life to propagate and spread, to unify the dwyma. When we first discovered our powers, there were hundreds of thousands of different genilocii, but none with enough power to protect us when the magi turned against us. We sought to unify each small locus into a greater whole, but our work was unfinished when the Church turned on us. To avoid complete erasure, we took our own lives and entered the genilocus.'

Lyra struggled to imagine what that must have been like; she doubted she'd ever have such fortitude. 'Why hasn't the Church destroyed your shrine?' she wondered.

'I doubt they realised what it truly was. And having already recognised me as a "saint", they weren't willing to admit they'd harboured a heretic. Once I was dead, they probably thought the dwyma was too. This cave and garden were closed and for a long time, they were forgotten. It's only in the last century that it was reopened for ceremonial purposes.' Then he broke off and said, 'You must get out, Lyra. The daemon is watching this place and his minions are coming. I can feel them.'

'But perhaps I can help you—' She sensed movement and turned. Behind the translucent amber walls of the chamber, dark threads were waving, the same colour as the noxious black fluid she'd seen above.

'Too late!' Eloy cried out. 'Go – *get out*! Before you're—'

Blackened root tendrils burst through the amber walls, writhing like tentacles – and reached for them both . . .

The Bastion

Solon felt as if he were walking on eggshells as he led Medelie up the spiral stairs and into the suite Cordan and Coramore Sacrecour now shared in Redburn Tower. 'Solon!' Cordan greeted him from the table covered in toy soldiers. 'Is there news of the battle? Are we victorious?'

Coramore, reading on the window seat, called, 'Hello—' Then her eyes narrowed as she saw Medelie, with the two door guards behind her. 'What's happening?'

'No news yet,' Solon said. 'We're going for an outing,' he added cheerily, patting Cordan on the shoulder, then kneeling to draw Coramore into a hug. 'There's going to be a special surprise,' Solon said, 'so run and get dressed.'

'Special Surprise' was a warning phrase he'd given them: it meant, *lock your doors and don't come out.*

Coramore gave him a wise look far beyond her years, then like a little actress gushed excitedly, '*I'm* wearing my purple cloak!' She took Cordan's hand while her elder brother was still trying to process the words. 'Come on, Cordi!'

The two children turned to dash to their rooms – and Medelie stepped into their path. 'Fie! Have you no greeting for me?'

Cordan began to panic, but Coramore covered him smoothly. 'Not for you, you silly tart!' She darted past, and Cordan followed, looking worried. Medelie scowled, but Coramore's response had been perfect: she'd never liked Medelie before, so why would she start now?

The children clattered up the stairs and as Solon wandered back towards his lover, he glanced at the two guardsmen, both magi of the Imperial Guard who'd been briefed on who exactly was an enemy.

One locked the door to keep 'Selene' below while the other laid a mailed gauntlet on Medelie's shoulder from behind. She went rigid as Solon drew his dagger and took her other shoulder. 'Medelie Aventour,' he said to his lover, his former duchess and the woman he'd once sworn fealty to, 'I arrest you for conspiracy to commit treason.'

Dirklan told me just to kill her, but I can't do that. She's still Radine.

'Oh, no, no, Solon . . . No, no, no – all this is for you, darling. *It's all for you . . .*' Her face was stricken and she bent over as if in sudden pain. Her youthful beauty vanished, leaving only the wizened prune face of Radine Jandreux behind. The two guardsmen stared, their eyes going from her to Solon.

'Sir? I . . . Isn't that—' one stammered 'It's the old duchess . . . But she's—'

Medelie sagged, tears welling in her eyes, and although Solon was utterly resolved not to be lulled, even his combat reflexes weren't swift enough . . .

On the level below, Dirklan was entering the antechamber, a square room with two banks of windows facing north and south, laced with wards to strengthen them. All the while, his links to the other team leaders told him that the tower was now surrounded. Forty Volsai, two enemies. He wondered if they'd be enough . . .

If Selene really is Tear, what's she capable of?

His quarry, a woman in a brown hooded cloak, was standing beside the southern-facing windows and staring out towards the Celestium. He saw a severe, middle-aged visage, so bland it barely looked human.

'You are "Selene", Dirklan stated, 'a woman involved in conspiracy to commit treason.' His agents fanned out, Handred, Fraen and Brigeda levelling crossbows while Mort hefted his battle-axe. 'You're under arrest.'

The woman's eyes narrowed, perhaps the only expression the flesh-mask was capable of. 'Dirklan Setallius,' she said, as if he'd stepped onto a stage, right on cue. 'It's hard to keep a secret, isn't it?'

'Lie down on your stomach with your arms and legs spread,' he told her.

'Not my preferred position, but as it appears we've been rukked by someone, it's probably appropriate.' She scanned the room, then shook her head. 'Dirklan, you disappoint me. I would have thought you'd at least make this a challenge.'

There was no further warning, not even a flare in the aether. Even as he opened his mouth to shout a warning, she radiated a blast of kinesis that slammed them all through the air. They struck the windows opposite, saved from broken skulls and necks only by instinctive shielding. The crossbows discharged, but he was bouncing from the gnosis-reinforced glass and smashing into the floor. His nose struck stone and broke, filling his air-passages with blood as his head swam. He heard cries from the others as he reinforced his shields and rolled sideways as a mage-bolt shattered the place he'd lain.

His vision cleared and he saw the woman had cast off her cloak; now she stood before them in Keeper robes, an incandescent staff in her hands, and her true face revealed. '*Edetta!*' he gasped as his gaze swept the room. Fraen was lying against the back wall, his neck clearly broken, his legs splintered, bone protruding through flesh and cloth. Mort was picking himself up; he'd dropped his broken-shafted axe and was pulling hand-axes from his back. The glass behind where Handred had been standing had a man-sized hole in it. Brigeda was whimpering: a great shard of bloody glass protruded from her right temple and blood was flooding her eyes.

We've got more men coming, Dirklan thought; *we must buy them time . . .* 'The Keepers are supposed to be above all this – you've betrayed your order—'

'*Have* I? When the empress is a heretic and a bastard?' Edetta spat.

'When a *pandaemancer* sits on the throne, who can stand aside? *All* the Keepers are with me.'

Dear Kore, the Keepers *are rebelling?* 'So you were behind the Reeker Night attacks,' he accused her. 'You're Tear!'

'Me?' Edetta snorted. 'I think not – but I doubt she's far away.'

Mort had an axe in either hand and a bleak look on his face. With a show of fortitude that didn't surprise Dirklan in the least, Brigeda plucked the glass from her skull and drew her broadsword. 'Can we rukk this old bitch now, boss?' she gritted.

Edetta didn't even trouble to react, other than the amused look on her face – then boots hammered on the stairs below.

We sell our lives to lay a blow on her and let weight of numbers take her down, Dirklan thought. It was a shitty plan, but the best he could come up with in the circumstances. 'Last chance to surrender, Edetta.'

The Keeper laughed. 'That's just what I was going to say.'

Then the first of the Imperial Guard thundered through the door and everyone moved at once . . .

37

Breaking the Line

Thaumaturgy: Fire

It was Fire that destroyed those unfortunate legions on the day of Ascendancy. What must the Rimoni soldiers have thought, coming to arrest a group of dissidents, only to find the harmless followers of a rambling preacher spouting flames from their fingertips? Did they think their gods had turned on them?

ARDO ACTIUM, SCHOLAR, BRES, 518

Collistein Junction, Kedron Valley
Octen 935

Timbers cracking, the *Philemon*'s flanks ground against the Keshi flagship, cracking timbers as spears and arrows and grappling hooks flew from the Eastern craft, smashing against the Rondian shields or thudding into wood – and flesh.

But all Ril's attention was on the man before him, for this was a serious fight: the Keshi's gnostic shields and kinesis-strength suggested he was practically a pure-blood – *is that even possible in a Noorie?* And his technique was *flawless*. Ril recognised his face from the airborne skirmishes of the past month, before instincts took over and they parried and thrust, hurling kinesis and mage-bolts at point-blank range, their blades belling and their spells carving down lesser men beside them until they gave ground. The Keshi thrust, and Ril twisted and sought to jam his blade while he slammed another mage-bolt at his foe's face. It turned his shielding scarlet, but the Keshi had ducked and most of the bolt deflected up, punching holes in the sails above.

'Repulse boarders,' Captain Dace was bellowing. 'Cut those grapples!'

Ril's men were holding against the tide of Easterners. The ballistae thumped again, making the whole enemy craft shudder – then the Keshi was at him again and the two of them exchanged muscular blows as the two vessels scraped and crunched against each other before staggering apart, gasping.

Then with a terrifying crash the Keshi ship's mast fell, plunging sideways towards the *Philemon*, crushing men on both sides as the spars went slamming through the decks. The two vessels shook, the decks tilted and suddenly Ril's foe was ten feet below him. Flailing ropes fizzed through the air; one lashed through Ril's shielding, hurling him back across his own deck. He struck the far railing, and grabbed on.

'*Axes*,' Dace screamed, '*get clear!*'

From all directions winged riders and skiffs of both forces were converging on the flagships. Ril saw a griffon-riding knight take a spear in the back from a shrieking lancer on a roc, then the bird spun screeching away as loose rigging entangled the roc's wing and ripped it clean off. Fire and lightning flashed and a venator's skull exploded barely forty yards astern, caught by the ballista-shot from a Keshi sloop. This wasn't about duels and skill; it was nothing more than luck and mischance. But the *Philemon* was tilting, the weight of the Keshi craft dragging it down, and Dace howled again for his men to free them.

Then the grappling chains snapped and the Keshi craft broke from them. The *Philemon* tilted madly, then righted herself as Ril stumbled to the shattered railing and watched the enemy ship dropping slowly, its keel still intact but visibly leaking Air-gnosis. His erstwhile foe was on the deck, scimitar blazing: now Ril could see he wore a diamond circlet on his helm and his tabard bore the Mubarak red lion.

He's a Mubarak . . . a royal prince . . . Their eyes met: Ril threw him an ironic salute and after a moment, the Mubarak returned the gesture.

Then another volley of ballistae struck the stricken Keshi craft and the vessel burst into flame.

Waqar looked upwards as his ship foundered and dropped from the side of the Rondian flagship, the broken main mast falling away. For all the wild courage of his men, the enemy defence was too strong. Then the Rondian prince reappeared and he prepared his shields to face a mage-bolt – but instead, the man put his hand to the side of his head: a salute? The tiny gesture of honour surprised and amused him, enough that he responded in kind.

Then his whole ship shook as fire erupted, the heat washing over screaming crewmen and soldiers alike. One of the wind-sailors grabbed at him, wailing to be saved, as the vessel's keel bled power and they fell towards the ground at an alarming pace.

<Waqar,> Tamir shouted into his mind, *<here!>*

Waqar shoved the poor man away – he had no way to save him – as Tamir flashed by on his roc, leading a riderless bird behind him: Ajniha, who came squalling towards him, claws spread. He leaped into her grasp and was snatched up. He clutched her leg as she fought to deal with his weight and drag, until he managed to grab a stirrup and with a thrust of kinesis he pushed himself upwards and into the saddle.

Tamir, Lukadin, Baneet and Fatima closed around him in tight formation; he could see Bashara and Shameed and a dozen others nearby, hurtling away from the press, seeking clear air.

<Shukran, Tamir!> he called, scanning the skies. The battle was going badly: the airborne fighting was happening right above the Keshi centre and it was clear the bigger, more robust Rondian craft were more than holding their own. His ploy to ram them with his worst hulks had gained some initial surprise, but now the Rondian were taking countermeasures, sending mage-knights to set the remaining ram-ships ablaze well before they could reach their targets.

On the ground, the Shihad's advance was stalled, not least because of the air-combat debris raining down on their own men. The winds from the northwest were like a broom, sweeping everyone and everything southeast.

He supposed he should be finding a new flagship and trying to direct the battle from there, but atop Ajniha he felt invincible. And the battle was chaos anyway. So he gestured, and they banked and hurtled back into the fray . . .

*

Latif crouched beside Ashmak in the turret of Rani's howdah, admiring the well-drilled archers mechanically sending their volleys arcing towards the Rondian ranks as they picked their way forward. Swarms of Lakh spearmen clad in just robes and turbans ran alongside the elephants, splashing through the boggy maze in front of the enemy lines. They were south of the road, on the Shihad's left flank. Five minutes earlier Faroukh Valphath, the general commanding their wing, had ordered Piru-Satabam III to join the assault and now Hazarapati Selmir waved them forward with an imperious gesture.

'I see Aunty Selmir isn't leading from the front today,' Ashmak noted scornfully.

Rani was in the third rank: Sanjeep also knew when to hang back. Overhead, mostly to the north of them, the sky was an incredible sight, with hundreds of windships and flying beasts vying for mastery. Who was winning, they had no idea, but all the fighting was above Rashid's lines, which didn't seem good. Of greater concern to Latif was how to survive the next half-hour. The wicker howdah was reinforced with hide and extra padding provided by bedrolls and blankets, all soaked in water, but he suspected that was nothing to a Rondian battle-mage, and bringing down the elephants was probably going to be their foe's first priority.

'Stay low,' Ashmak advised. 'I can't shield widely, so anything from the left is your problem.'

'I know the routine,' Latif answered. 'Just make sure I don't take a mage-bolt in the back.'

Ashmak, unused to back-chat, scowled – then grinned. 'Shoot straight, my friend.'

You branded me and dragged me away to war, Latif thought, *and yet I don't hate you as you probably deserve, 'my friend'.*

'Keep us alive,' he muttered, then called, 'Sanjeep, keep your head down.'

'You don't need to tell me that,' the old Lakh said. 'I only pray Rani to be safe.'

'Form up beyond the marshes!' Selmir shouted from the rear as the forty elephants trudged onwards. In front of them, ten thousand men in ten hazarabam of Lakh spearmen prepared to rush the low earthworks of the Rondians. Latif had a flashback to the battle at the Tigrates River, the place the Rondians called Riverdown, which had also been a series of massed assaults against lightly fortified lines. They'd expected an easy victory.

Instead, we were slaughtered . . .

The elephants plodded on until they were behind the archers, who were still sending shaft after shaft over the advancing spearmen. Latif checked his own bow. He had six quivers lashed to the inside of his perch, a dozen arrows in each. It didn't look like near enough right now.

The big kettle drums began to pound as the Lakh shouted in rhythm, building up into a fervour for the charge. *Lakh fight hot, Keshi fight cold*, the old saying went, and certainly these men were working themselves up into a steaming rage, stamping their feet, roaring out responses to the challenges of their captains. Then horns bellowed and they went forward in a huge wave while the Keshi archers continued to fire over their heads, trying to pin the Rondians behind cover and minimise return fire.

At Riverdown, Latif had learned that *every* attack looks unstoppable as it's launched. As arrows sleeted down on the Rondian lines, the spearmen pushed forward, their voices rising in pitch – but then came the Rondian response.

The first wavering came as archers and crossbowmen embedded in the shield-walls loosed their shafts and bolts at close range. The weight of the Lakh advance was barely checked, then a second volley, at closer range and even more deadly, made the attackers stagger. The enemy magi struck too, pouring Fire-gnosis on their foes, and Latif saw a rainbow of light jagging out from the top of the barricades.

The Lakh charge struck the shield-wall and their triumphant roar became the shattering cacophony of men trapped in the Hel of a mêlée: death cries, bloodthirsty screams and the hammering of weapons assaulted the heavens.

Beside him, Ashmak was chewing on his beard, shuddering every few seconds as fresh bursts of gnostic energy were unleashed. 'Ahm alive, there are pure-bloods in those lines,' he groaned.

'They'll be exhausted by the time we go in,' Latif replied. *I hope.*

Three times the Lakh attack was beaten back, and each time, they regrouped at the foot of the small ridge where the Rondians were dug in before charging in again, but the legionaries in their steel and leather were easily hacking down the lightly armed skirmishers. Latif watched with growing trepidation: if the elephant phalanx went in without the enemy lines being at least a little disrupted, they'd be sitting targets.

Then the trumpets sounded the retreat and the Lakh reacted immediately, wheeling and sprinting back towards their lines while the Rondians stood and cheered. But the Keshi archers resumed their fire and it all started over again, only this time with the bodies of hundreds of Lakh piled at the foot of the shield-wall, and many more trying to limp or crawl away, or just lying in the mud screaming or begging for help.

Sanjeep hung his head over the edge of the howdah and vomited, and a few seconds later, Latif and Ashmak did the same. Rani waved her trunk around as if she was offended at such weakness.

They all looked at Selmir, who was arguing with Senapati Valphath.

'He'd better not be pleading to send us in,' Ashmak growled.

Whatever the case, more spearmen were coming forward through the marshes, and another twenty sweating, tense minutes passed as they formed up. They were Gatti, from east of Kesh, desert men with braided beards, hide-shields and long curved scimitars, little better equipped than the Lakh spearmen to break a line.

They swept in, wailing prayers, battered into the shield-wall and reeled back – and this time the Rondian lines parted during the retreat and mounted knights swept out into the broken Gatti ranks and hacked them apart so brutally that the Keshi archers resumed fire, launching volleys into their own men in the hope of taking down a few Rondian knights among them. Fewer than half the Gatti escaped the carnage, and now the space up to fifty yards from the Rondian lines were covered in the dead and dying, and the cries of agony were incessant.

'Damned cowards,' Ashmak was snarling. 'Weaklings!'

Latif had been sitting on the sultan's throne at Riverdown, listening to Salim's commanders saying the same things when the slaughter was too much to bear. 'They've got no armour,' Latif replied. 'There's no money to equip them the way the Rondians do.'

'Perhaps, but Dear Ahm, let us not be sent in behind such spear-fodder.'

Ahm – or Valphath – must have heard their prayers, because the next men sent in were Keshi, properly armoured, with conical helms and bearing long war-spears in one hand and kite-shields in the other. They looked cool-headed and purposeful, these men of the sultan's standing army, and as well-equipped as any Rondian legionary. As they passed, the orders were shouted: Piru-Satabam III would follow them in.

It's too soon, Latif thought bleakly, trading hollow-eyed stares with Ashmak and Sanjeep. *The Rondians aren't even wavering. We're being sent to die needlessly.*

Seth Korion stared down from his warhorse at his lines sixty yards away from the small hillock – the highest point in these flat fenlands – that he'd designated as his command post. He was surrounded by aides and runners who came and went, while seer-magi with relay-staves constantly updated him on the state of the battle. Lakh and Gatti had attacked and been repulsed in good order, although some of his units were showing the strain: this was the conscripts' first blooding and nothing they'd imagined about battle had ever been *this* bad, judging by the expressions of glassy-eyed horror as he rotated them out, to be replaced by fresh men from the rear.

In the skies above, the chaos continued, with craft plummeting into the ground, often straight into Keshi units below. The wind was blowing the fight steadily over Rashid's army, but everything still hung in the balance.

'Any news from the left?' he asked his Brician aide Delton, who was monitoring gnostic communications.

'Prince Elvero's using his cavalry to extend his lines as the Keshi try to flank him, but he says they're holding.'

'And *our* flank?'

'The scouts say the Keshi are *still* looking for a way through the swamp.' Delton grinned. 'Shame there isn't one.'

Seth smiled, grateful to have been given the right, where the enemy's choices were limited. But now he had to concentrate: war-elephants were advancing into position and fresh enemy soldiers were entering the staging area. He lifted his spy-glass and scanned them.

'These are fully armoured,' he noted. 'Warn the front line. Our battle-magi should target the elephants – there'll be magi on each. Bring them down.'

The Keshi resumed sending huge flights of steel-tipped, feathered death slamming into his lines, striking earthworks and shields, while his men cowered and prayed. Through the blur of falling arrows he could see the enemy infantry advancing, with the lumbering elephants in the second wave: that told him the enemy leader really didn't care if his own men were crushed; he just wanted to give the elephants a crack at the front line while the defenders were fully engaged.

His stomach tensed as the moment of impact approached – then the arrow storm ceased, his men rose and their first countering volleys butchered the leading Keshi – but still those behind came on. The volume was deafening, even at this distance, as both sides vented their fear and hatred amid the crash of steel on steel. Keshi were now hurling themselves bodily over the shield-wall, only to be spitted on spears and flung back, but whole sections were collapsing under the weight of the impact, sending men sprawling down the back of the earthworks. For a moment it looked like they couldn't possibly hold . . .

But the officers knew their work, and so did the men: the reserve lines slammed into their own rear, bracing them and cutting down any enemy who'd managed to punch through. Legion shortswords and spears shored up the breaches with brutal jabs and thrusts at men barely able to move, while the battle-magi behind the lines utilised fire and raw energy to deadly effect. But all the while, the elephants were ploughing through at the back of the enemy assault, moving faster and faster . . .

When they hit, they'll go right through us . . .

'It's time,' he told his command group of magi. 'Be ready to aid the defence.'

*

Rani's crew jounced from side to side as she trotted faster. Latif clung on grimly; no way he could shoot at such a speed. He was relieved to see Ashmak's shielding – the howdah turret was faintly limned in blue threads of light – although whether it would stand up to pure-blood Rondian battle-magi was another matter. Ahead of them the Keshi spearmen were battering at the earthworks, spears thrust over the tops of the shields, seeking the faces and throats of the enemy defenders.

'Go, Rani, go!' Sanjeep bellowed, goading his beloved beast, although he hated using the vicious prod. Rani trumpeted as they heedlessly crushed their own men in their bid to reach the Rondian line. Blood sprayed as her steel-tipped tusks ripped a way through the press, then a blast of light struck Ashmak's shields amid a volley of arrows: three of them punched straight through and stuck in the walls of the howdah. Ashmak hurled a blue mage-bolt at someone on the ramparts while Latif sent this own arrows into the Rondian ranks they were suddenly looming above: they were so close he could see the whites of enemy eyes.

Rani struck the wall of shields, thrashing her head side to side, and breaking it open alongside a huge bull-elephant, hurling men left and right. She baulked as a long war-spear jabbed into her face and screamed, an almost human sound, then arrows and javelins struck her flanks. She reared, then crunched her fore-legs down on armoured flesh.

Latif glimpsed a mage on a horse: he got lucky against the shields and shot the mount in the throat. At their feet, the second wave of Keshi infantry were bursting into the gaps, trying to break up the Rondian formation, and for a wild second it looked like they would sweep the enemy away—

—until a torrent of heat, smoke and light erupted from a knot of horsemen galloping into the fray, Ashmak's shields went scarlet and Rani's bitter scream was echoed by Sanjeep. Latif glimpsed a Rondian ranker with a war-spear darting beneath them, and a moment later Rani staggered horribly. The spear was deeply embedded in Rani's flank, and he could see another Rondian spearman moving in.

His hands blurred, his arrow transfixed the man's chest and he went down – then the first man made the mistake of looking up and Latif shot him in the left eye.

'Rani!!' Sanjeep wailed, hauling on ropes to turn his beast around. Ashmak was blazing mage-bolts at anyone close enough as they staggered behind a wall of Keshi – just before those men were engulfed by fireballs. Rani was wobbly, barely standing, and they all understood they had to get her out.

Then the squad of karkadann finally appeared, the huge horned and armoured constructs mowing their own men down in their hundreds before slamming straight through the Rondian lines: a stampede of giants. Latif howled triumphantly, but Ashmak was too busy railing at Ahm, as if he blamed God Himself for Rani's wounds. Latif put a hand on his shoulder, momentarily afraid he would leap off and join the charge.

Sanjeep had managed to turn his stricken beast back towards their own lines just as horns sounded and another wave of Rondians charged in. They were all mounted cavalry and mage-knights, and the counter-attack struck the karkadann force just as they lost momentum. The torrent of precisely aimed mage-bolts were followed by the knights' vicious lances slamming into the gigantic beasts as if this were some massively unequal joust, but one after another, the karkadanns rolled over, some with three or four lances buried in their chests. Latif's eyes pierced the smoke and flame, and he saw a golden eagle standard amid the carnage, and a rider sitting motionless beneath it, as if all that happened here did so according to his will.

Seth Korion, unhelmed, and utterly calm.

For an instant Latif was stunned at the sight of his old captor, his *friend* – but then it felt inevitable, Shaitan's trick. He looked away, his heart thudding.

'Get us out of here, Sanjeep,' he shouted. '*Go!*'

The *Philemon*, damaged but intact, was lumbering on a northeast tack while Ril had the signalmen try to regain some semblance of formation. As they pulled clear of the Keshi craft, he scanned the skies.

He'd lost perhaps a dozen ships to the ramming-craft, another cunning and vicious innovation from their enemies, but it looked like they'd inflicted far worse damage, and they'd contained the enemy fleet over their own army. At least twenty enemy ships were on fire and dropping, and as many again had already crashed. Unless the Keshi had more surprises to reveal, his fleet had the edge.

He looked down: the ground-war told an equally satisfactory tale. The lines of red-cloaked men below were still arrayed in their starting positions while corpses in dun and white were heaped before the lines.

'Prince Elvero's lines have become very stretched,' Aiken Landius, his new aide, commented; they'd put it about that Bycross was unwell to explain Landius' sudden elevation. Peering down, Ril saw that Landius was right: the Keshi cavalry trying to outflank Elvero's position had drawn the Canossi prince into matching them with his own riders. His lines did look thin, and Ril could see large knots of enemy infantry mustering at the weakest points.

'Signal Elvero to close up his lines,' Ril replied, turning back to the sky battle. Ships that were still battle-worthy were reforming in the southeast quadrant, as he'd ordered, and he could see running repairs being frantically effected, damaged sails replaced and broken timber cut away. Then a wing of windriders swooped past him and he spotted Gryff and Larik and his Corani knights. Fighting the urge to rush below, leap aboard Pearl and join them, he turned back to Landius.

'Tell the weather-magi to turn that wind around: time for the southerly!'

The pre-agreed wind-change needed only the signal; the transition happened in minutes, filling their sails while the Keshis' emptied. Caught out by the unexpected wind-shift, the Shihad fleet were left motionless in the sky.

Ril smiled grimly at Landius. 'Right, let's go back and finish the job.'

Too late, Waqar realised that they'd been outmanoeuvred – and so simply. As the Rondians reformed to the south, every Keshi ship had turned to pursue – so the sudden wind-change left them becalmed while their enemy were ready, their sails billowing as they re-joined the fray. He cursed: they'd become sitting targets.

Admiral Neniphas' voice blared in the aether, his mild voice sharpened by fear. *<Tell your windriders to engage the enemy ships – you must give us a chance to recover!>*

Rocs against warbirds? Madness! But the admiral was right; there was no choice. *<Windskiffs, roc-riders: shield the fleet,>* Waqar shouted into the aether. *<Engage the enemy vessels!>*

He took Ajniha into a sharp climb, his fellow roc-riders streaming behind as a mass of enemy venators swam into the space between the fleets, and they swung towards each other. The now-familiar game of chicken followed as they manoeuvred, lances lowered and bows aimed, trying to get close enough for an effective shot without being drawn into full contact. He took Ajniha in hard, wings furled, and they went whooshing in front of a Rondian knight. Just evading a lance that scoured his shields, he sent a gnosis-fired arrow into the belly of the foe's venator. The shaft struck home; energy erupted and blasted the beast's ribs open and it dropped, the enemy knight roaring in rage and dread as he sought to rip himself free. Lances splintered – and Shameed plummeted past, his roc intact but the young man transfixed right through his body by a broken lance.

Waqar shouted in denial, but Shameed was already gone. He sent Ajniha into a corkscrew spin that took him hurtling between two venators, evading fire and crossbow bolts.

<Aieee!> Tamir shouted, firing an arrow backwards as he zipped past, a venator on his heels. Fatima and Baneet were either side, and as they wrenched their birds into another climb, Bashara swooped in. Waqar was still looking for Lukadin when the Rondian warships, not at all distracted by their rocs, slammed into the ragged line of becalmed Keshi craft. Inside ten seconds, the sky filled with flame and burning bodies and timbers rained down once again . . .

A wail went through his head as everyone screamed their despair. His imagination was already playing out the rest of the battle in his head: the Rondian fleet would destroy theirs, then descend to target the Keshi forces, stopping high enough to be untouchable and low enough to pick their targets – and death would rain from the skies. The Shihad would disintegrate, leaving a generation of Ahmedhassan men stranded in Yuros in winter, with no way to get home.

Then he felt a surge in the aether. He knew instantly what it was.

<*Lukadin!*> he called. <*Lukadin, no!*>

38

Crowned in Blood

Scarabs

Cheating death is one of the prime ambitions of any mage, which has led to some bizarre but fruitful experiments. One example is the use of a beetle to transfer the intellect of a dying mage to a new host body. It requires necromancers and dung beetles, who some would say are practically kin anyway.

LEPHANIUM, *THE TOOLS OF MAGIC*, PALLAS, 834

Hegikaro Castle, Mollachia
Octen 935

The day of his coronation passed like treacle for Kyrik Sarkany. He'd woken at dawn, pressed against Hajya's warm body but with Valdyr's voice ringing in his head. In his dream, his brother had been shouting from a snowy hilltop, but his words were lost in winds that howled like ravenous wolves. All morning he fretted, until finally he summoned Dragan to meet him, before the gazda had to attend some traditional pre-coronation Vitezai ceremony.

Haklyn Tower, the highest point in Hegikaro Castle, overlooked the lake two hundred feet below. 'Do you have word from Watcher's Peak?' Kyrik asked as soon as Dragan appeared.

'Watcher's Peak is enclosed in fog and ice,' Dragan reported. 'All the scouts looking for Valdyr have messenger pigeons. When your brother reappears, I'll know within hours.'

They silently scanned the northern horizon, then Kyrik asked, 'Is there any news from Lapisz?'

'Nothing new. The Rondians aren't moving, and haven't been re-inforced.'

'And the people? What are they saying about my coronation?'

Dragan pulled a sour face. 'No one is happy, Kyrik, but you know that. Those who support you see it as a necessary evil. Those who don't . . . just see evil.'

'What of you, my friend?' Kyrik thought Dragan looked haggard, and uncharacteristically twitchy.

'I dislike this alliance, you know that. But I'm Gazda, and I serve my people.'

Which doesn't necessarily mean me . . . 'The honour of giving fealty first is yours, my friend, and all else you might name. If you want land or honours, they will be given. You've earned them.'

'A gazda may not accept such things,' Dragan reminded him.

'I know that, but still I thank you, with all my heart. Ask anything and it's yours.'

'You always were too generous, lad.' Dragan bowed and took his leave.

Kyrik remained on Haklyn Tower, staring from the open-topped battlements out over the frigid lake, asking the sky, 'Where are you, Brother?'

The skies had no reply.

Dragan Zhagy entered the hall to see nearly two hundred men. Earl Radeska's hunting lodge was a mile out of Hegikaro, but it was almost full, mostly with Vitezai Sarkanum. The earl was accompanied by his son Grigor and a few others of his ilk; they weren't of the order, but today, they were necessary.

As Dragan strode through their midst, his men thumped their hearts with their fists, barking out reverences, none knowing how irrevoc-ably changed their gazda was. He responded gruffly, his mind already racing ahead. When he reached the stage, he turned to face the room.

Every face was turned his way, but his eyes went first to a hooded figure standing on the small mezzanine floor at the far end, unseen by anyone but him. Dragan gave Asiv Fariddan a small nod – and froze as a smaller figure appeared beside the Keshi.

His daughter Sezkia lowered her hood.

For a moment he couldn't breathe. Asiv had *sworn* he'd not involve Sezkia – and yet here she was. She was too far away to discern details, but he thought she looked pale, maybe frightened. Asiv had clearly brought her to ensure everything went to plan.

In truth, Dragan had wondered if this gathering might be a final chance to turn the tables on the Noorie, but now he discarded the notion: Sezkia was his only child, the last living remembrance of his beloved late wife. He would find a way of prising her from Asiv's grasp later, but for now, the Keshi mage would get his wish.

He raised his hands for silence before addressing the gathering. 'Brothers, welcome! Prior to the coronation of a new king, it falls upon the Gazda of the Vitezai Sarkanum to gather the brotherhood and put one question: do we bless the new king, or do we not? For *we* are the protectors of the realm. Kings come and go, but the Vitezai Sarkanum remains. *We* are Mollachia.'

'We are Mollachia,' they echoed.

'You know the circumstances: after a long exile, Elgren Sarkany's son has returned to us. You know what he brings. We will debate that, and we will emerge united in purpose.' He lowered his arms, glanced at Asiv and Sezkia, then said, 'But first, we must acknowledge a great victory: we have defeated the Delestre legion and regained Hegikaro. In such times, it is traditional to taste the blood of our enemy. I know the battle is now weeks past, but we have pig's blood – which is appropriate, given that we fought Rondians!'

Derisive laughter filled the hall and the mood lightened.

He clapped his hands and servants entered with trays containing clay cups filled with pig's blood, all unaware it was suffused with ichor, so everyone who drank would fall to Abraxas. He waited as they accepted their cups, his eyes on Sezkia, thinking how beautiful she was, and raging that Asiv would think to threaten her. *I'll let you make me king – but my first command will be your death, Keshi.*

For now though, his men had to do this, to become as he was.

It wasn't so bad being damned, he'd decided. Quelling the thousand hate-filled voices was easy enough, and surely becoming a mage was worth the price – although he was still coming to grips with what he could and couldn't do. These men wouldn't gain anything like what he had, but once they'd done what was necessary, he could set about giving the best of them more.

Once I'm king, I'll rule, not the monster inside me, he promised.

He raised his cup and the men of the Vitezai raised theirs. 'Drink with me, brothers, to the new King of Mollachia!' They all drank, while his eyes returned to the two shadowy figures on the mezzanine.

Sezkia stepped to the fore and now he saw her clearly for the first time: a stealthy grace that was not her, and a knowing callousness in the way she held her mouth. It sucked his breath away. Slowly, proudly, she pulled down her bodice, revealing a fresh scar over her heart, just like his own.

<Father,> she sent, *<how dare you think to spare me that which you must bear?>*

No, he protested silently, feeling the blood drain from his face. *Asiv, you promised me she would be untouched!*

The Keshi's voice drooled into his mind, *<But who could resist such a sweet cherry? And look how ripe she is now: a princess of the night.>*

<You promised—>

<And I changed my mind. Who do you think rules here, Gazda? Whose kingdom do you think this is?>

Dragan closed his eyes, trembling in sudden, belated terror at what he had allowed to happen.

It was a minor miracle, but the frumpy, lacy thing the tailor had laboured on for weeks was ready. Hajya glared at it, spread across her bed. A dozen pale, pinch-faced court ladies – *how did Mollachs get to be so white, if they were once Sydians?* – tittered and gushed and reminisced about their own weddings. She'd put up with them all day, although she'd have happily thrashed them from the room hours ago.

Instead she was obliged to disrobe while they stared at her brown, well-lived-in body as if they'd never seen another woman before, passing comment on everything from the colour of her nipples to the thickness of her pubic thatch – and of course her clan tattoos.

'Did they hurt?' one idiot woman asked.

'Of course they damned well hurt,' she snarled back.

'Would Milady wish to have her armpits plucked?' a servant asked timidly.

Hajya stared. '*What?*'

'It's the fashion—'

Hajya couldn't imagine many things worse. *Plucked?* 'Don't come near me,' she told the wretch. She gestured irritably at the servants, who rushed in with silken under-gowns. She'd rejected the proffered paste to lighten her skin but given in to having her hair coiled into an elaborate pile, which was then nonsensically concealed beneath a conical ivory-white hennin. The dressing went on for ever, and all the while the scrutiny and commentary never stopped.

'Striking,' one said, when she was finally declared ready and rose to face them.

Lady Lysbet Radeska delivered the most important verdict: 'Regal.'

It was, Hajya decided, a very guarded acknowledgement. She met the tight-lipped woman's gaze and inclined her head faintly. 'Then it will do. Is it time?'

Right on cue, the bells began to ring, ten dolorous chimes, reverberating across the castle as the crowds gathered inside the courtyard below burst into a hymn.

She looked around for her one ally in the room: Torzo's Sfera daughter Korznici had arrived that morning with a small escort. She extended her arm and the girl, chief maid of honour, took it. Korznici, clad in leathers and adorned in paint, was to Hajya's eyes the most beautiful woman here.

Then three Mollach girls took up the ridiculously long train and together they began their slow procession through the castle to the church.

Kyrik had expected Valdyr to be standing with him at the altar, but he was still missing when the hour struck. Rothgar Baredge hadn't returned from the wilds either, so his escort was reduced to three men he knew only passably well: Thraan's fourth son, Hykkan, who might be big for his age but was only fourteen; Grigor Radeska, a pricklish noble from Lapisz, and the giant Schlessen Fridryk Kippenegger.

Well, who knows, I might need someone to crack skulls for me . . .

It wasn't an amiable group: Hykkan had little to say, while Grigor Radeska had too many opinions, most of which Kyrik disagreed with. And Kip was brooding, probably about his people settling into their new camp on the upper Osiapa River. He clearly wished to be there himself.

Father, what would you make of this? he wondered. *Mother, would you have been proud?* He doubted either would have been content, but there was no going back now. He checked his robe, a resplendent scarlet and gold brocade concoction encrusted with jewels, smoothed his hair and turned to his escorts.

'I don't expect we will meet trouble today but if we do, stand well clear of me: I'll be using the gnosis and mightn't have time to differentiate friend from foe. A single mage-bolt can blast a hole right through a man, you know.'

He watched that reminder sink in as Hykkan blanched. His fellow mage Kippenegger just gave a wry smile, but Grigor's eyes narrowed, knowing the remark was mostly aimed at him. *Ysh, Grigor: betray me and your corpse won't be pretty.* Then he turned and marched through the halls, scattering servants and courtiers in his rush to get this over and done with.

The packed Church of Sancta Mijkal was redolent with pine-resin incense wafting from dozens of burners, and the deepest shadows were illuminated by oil-lamps. Hajya and her ladies had to wait outside on the steps, before thousands of assessing burghers in the square; Korznici was a bundle of nerves, but oddly, that helped Hajya to stay calm. Reassuring the girl gave her little time to worry about herself. And she took strength from self-belief: she'd borne children, ridden in battle, faced magi and held her own in the council-tent of the Nacelnik. Now she would become a queen. An unexpected path, maybe, but she wasn't going to let it daunt her.

Then an attendant signalled, music rose from an organ somewhere and they filed through the antechamber, past scores of Vitezai Sarkanum men, hooded, bowed and kneeling. There was a strange air of menace to those silent figures, but she knew that they'd been crucial to winning the kingdom and she raised a hand in thanks to them. No one acknowledged her, which stung a little, but then she was turning into the central aisle as a sonorous hymn to Kore rose to greet her.

Pater Kostyn, clad in the green and yellow of new beginnings, towered above everyone from his raised dais, but she had eyes only for the blond-maned figure in scarlet and gold. The question of children remained unresolved, but her heart swelled: this man had her heart, despite everything. In the eyes of these people, she wouldn't be Kyrik's wife until this Kore blessing ceremony was done, but he was already hers.

When they see us wed and crowned, perhaps they will begin to accept us . . .

The slow walk down the aisle lasted an eternity, but finally they were at the front, and here were her people, filling the first ten aisles on the left: Nacelnik Thraan, Missef, Groyzi, even blind Torzo, and dozens of other prominent clansmen, all here to witness one of their own be made the highest-ranking woman in their new homeland. She smiled as she join Kyrik before the altar and peered through her veil at his handsome face. *Already my husband in the ways that truly matter*, she thought proudly as the final verse of the hymn rang out.

> *'Lift up thine eyes, Lift up thy soul*
> *Raise your heart to Him Above*
> *Kore my Armour, Kore my Sword—'*

As the song ended, Pater Kostyn raised his booming voice. 'Children of Kore, Children of Mollachia, we gather today in the sight of Kore to seek his blessing upon the union of a man with a woman and a king with his kingdom. Father to Son the throne passes, and for too long this kingdom has been without her rightful ruler. But today, the Kirol returns!'

'We are blessed!' the congregation responded. *'Praise to Kore!'*

Kostyn launched into his declamatory sermon on the rights of kings to be succeeded by their sons, and the blessings Kore poured on such successions. He also spoke of the power of marriage to form alliances to promulgate and reinforce peace. 'Peace is a state that Kore approves above all others,' he quoted from the *Book of Kore*. 'Let this alliance bring us Kore's blessings of tranquil prosperity. May this union be fruitful and faithful, unto and beyond death.'

You never mentioned love, Hajya thought, *but there already is.*

The answering look in Kyrik's eyes as he reached forward and lifted her veil told her that he'd heard her thought. *These veils are a stupid custom,* she thought, but it did make for a touching moment as he lifted it and saw her made up like a proper Mollach lady. Something reverent entered his eyes, lifting her heart.

'As this couple have already been wed according to Sydian custom,' Kostyn declared stiffly, 'it befalls me to bless that union and make it whole in the eyes of Kore. Hajya, daughter of Jendys of Clan Vlpa, do you accept Kore as your God and Kyrik Sarkany as your husband?'

Sneaky prick, she thought, *but Kyrik warned me you'd do this.*

'I accept Kyrik as my husband and Kore as my God,' she replied, adding silently, *just not my only god.*

Kostyn looked up at her acquiescence; then he turned to Kyrik. 'Kyrik Sarkany, son of Elgren, do you accept Kore as your God, and Hajya of Clan Vlpa as your wife?'

'I accept Kore as my God and Hajya as my wife,' he replied, his voice strong.

'Do you swear to be faithful to each other, to be fruitful and raise your children to serve Mollachia?'

'We do,' they chorused, forgiving each other the lie about fruitfulness.

'Then you may kiss and claim your bride,' Kostyn declared.

Their kiss was already a warm and familiar place and they lingered there. She'd liked his taste from the first. *<Does 'claiming' mean what I hope it does?>* she teased, mind to mind. *<I thought you slugskins didn't approve of public coupling?>*

<Sorry.> He grinned, his eyes moist. *<For now, you only get a wedding ring.>*

Kyrik's mother's ring had been recovered from Robear Delestre's treasure chest and refitted to her size – Dania had been smaller, a more delicate creature. Kyrik slipped the heavy band, studded with a crown of rubies and diamonds, onto Hajya's finger as the congregation gave them scattered applause.

'I pronounce you wed before Kore,' Kostyn proclaimed. 'And now to the coronation—'

Pater Kostyn fell silent and the congregation sucked in their breath as boots sounded in the aisle. Kyrik turned, hoping to see Valdyr, but it was Dragan Zhagy. The gazda was armoured, plate-steel encasing his torso and a chainmail kilt covering him groin to knees, and he wore his longsword strapped across his back. Kyrik was struck by how deathly pale he looked; his skin was almost glowing in the gloomy church, his iron-grey hair and moustaches only accentuating his pallor – and the blood-red of his lips.

What is this? he wondered.

The people were alarmed and Kyrik felt a thrill of fear as his brain began feeding him tactical information: all weapons had been laid at the door, except the one on Dragan's back and those carried by Kippenegger, Hykkan and Grigor – and the royal blade, the *Sabie de Kiroli*, lying on the altar ... all the Vlpa were arrayed opposite the young noblemen, Jurisc Radeska and his allies ... and through the church doors he could see ranks of cloaked and hooded Vitezai Sarkanum ...

Kyrik put a hand on Hajya's arm, in case he had to draw her behind him, and called, 'What is it, Dragan?'

The gazda's voice rang out. 'I'm here as Protector of the Realm to intervene. It appears to have slipped your mind, *Prince* Kyrik, that you were freed from the breeding-houses of Kesh because you are *sterile* – so your marriage can hardly be *fruitful*, can it? Nor can you give this kingdom an heir.'

Kyrik groaned inwardly whilst noting the reactions, from Thraan's angry snarl to the intakes of breath among the notables of Hegikaro. A man might unknowingly enter marriage sterile and be forgiven, but to know and not declare it? That was enough to annul any union. What it meant in terms of the kingship was uncharted legal territory but somehow, he didn't think Dragan was here to launch a judicial challenge. There was menace in the air, and that frightened and puzzled him. Dragan wasn't this kind of man, but right now he emanated hostility.

'Dragan, why are you raising this?' he asked, trying reason. 'Hajya knows.'

'*I* didn't know!' Thraan bellowed, 'and *I* had that right—'

'I did not know until recently,' Kyrik shouted as worried-looking men started pulling their womenfolk away from the centre aisle. 'It's *not* proven – and there are other options – we've had infertile ruling couples before!'

Dragan loosed a barking laugh that Kyrik barely recognised as his. 'Ysh – you can always ask Valdyr to get your wife with child for you – assuming he'd be willing?'

A nasty laugh ran through the side of the church where the young noblemen were mustered and what Kyrik heard in their looks and gestures shocked him. *How can they know Valdyr was abused?* Then he caught a glint of lamplight on metal as hidden weapons began to appear. *Dear Kore*, he thought, *there's going to be blood—*

He loosened his fingers and roused his inner flame of gnosis as the scent of violence filled the church. Hykkan threw a scared look towards his father; Grigor put a hand to his sword-hilt. The big Schlessen was the only one who actually looked happier; maybe Kippenegger only came to life when blood was in the air.

'*Peace! This is a* sacred *place!*' Pater Kostyn roared, but few heeded him: some of Mollachia's most savage murders had been perpetrated in churches. Fighting the urge to kindle shields, which he feared would cause everything to erupt, Kyrik came down the steps, leaving Kip, Grigor Radeska and Hykkan behind him, and confronted Dragan, ten paces away. 'Gazda, what are you trying to achieve?'

'I'm here to prevent an unconstitutional king from taking the throne,' Dragan shot back, which brought cheers from the Mollach side of the church. Thraan's Sydians drew together protectively, but they were glaring at Kyrik with undisguised contempt.

'Dragan, don't do this. We must preserve Mollachia—'

'I will preserve Mollachia,' Dragan interrupted, 'from the filth that

565

you've brought with you from the corrupt, decadent East you love so much. Did you convert to Ahm there? Is Kore still your god?'

The women, the children and the timid were streaming down the side aisles now, while armed guardsmen came in and stood alongside the Vitezai men. Kyrik saw few men who might take his side. 'Gazda,' he called, 'this is a *church*. Take your men outside. By right of birth, the throne is mine!'

Dragan chuckled darkly. 'There's an older, stronger law than primogeniture, lad: the law of the sword.'

The time for caution was clearly gone. Kyrik kindled gnosis-fire openly, something few of those present had ever seen, and the sudden fear it engendered was palpable. 'I'm a mage, Dragan, in case you've forgotten – I can take you down in an eye-blink – and I will, if you don't call off your dogs.'

'Prince Kyrik,' Dragan drawled, 'you don't know *what* I am, or *what* I can do.' He reached back over his shoulder, towards his sword-hilt.

No! Kyrik's mind screamed. *Don't do this!*

<But I want to,> Dragan sent back, straight to his brain.

Kyrik reeled. *The gnosis? He has the gnosis?*

The longsword swept from its sheath and violence exploded in the ancient Church of Sancta Mijkal.

Hajya, standing behind and above her husband on the steps of the altar, traded glances with her people as they watched the scene played out. She had been about to send to Torzo, telling them to fight their way to the altar, when she felt the weight of a forbidding stare and she looked around and caught sight of a blonde woman robed in red, leaning from the balcony of the organ loft. Sezkia Zhagy looked pale, although her lips were ruby-red. Her eyes glittered with malice – and gnosis-light, which was impossible: Kyrik's family were the only mageborn Mollachs in the kingdom.

But as Hajya met the girl's deathly stare, she couldn't mistake the hatred. Sezkia was all but drooling as she leaned forward. *By all the gods, she's rabid . . . she's blood-crazed.* She readied shields and opened her mouth to warn Kyrik, who was too far ahead for her liking. Grigor and Hykkan, flanking him, were looking sideways at each other, but the big Schlessen with the unpronounceable name had stepped away slightly, freeing his arms. Then Dragan drew his longsword in one smooth motion, the few remaining women shrieked, men roared and most of the congregation swept forward, hidden knives and shortswords whipping out.

Grigor Radeska spun and thrust his sword into young Hykkan's side before she could move; she blasted fire at him, but the young nobleman was unnaturally swift, ducking her bolt as Hykkan crumpled. Then Dragan gestured and Kyrik was thrown backwards, striking the steps in a burst of shield-sparks.

But Kyrik came up fast, shouting, 'Hajya, get to the tower!' as the gilded *Sabie de Kiroli* flew to his grasp, just in time as Dragan brought his own blade crashing down – and a concussion of kinesis hurled them apart again.

To her right, Hajya saw her clansmen attacked by a crowd of Vitezai hunters, all slashing and thrusting madly. She blasted fire at someone who tried to grab her and realised an instant later it was a junior priest, but she didn't have time to think because one of the wild-eyed noblemen had launched himself at her. The Schlessen warrior – *Kippenegger, ysh?* – drew and swung his zweihandle in one fluid motion that ended with the Mollach collapsing with a severed spinal cord. The other women attending her had already taken to their heels, but Korznici appeared beside her, spewing blue light from her fingers, crying aloud in fear and fury.

'Sferina,' Korznici shouted, 'where do we go?'

'Hold here,' she cried, 'let Thraan and Kyrik come to us—' She stopped as Grigor turned towards her, raising his sword. She'd never survive if she let him get close, so she blasted at him with Fire-gnosis, engulfing him in flame and sending him screaming into the chaos, fully ablaze.

Kippenegger hacked down another man, roaring, *'Minaus!'* as he kicked someone backwards down the steps. Metal hammered on metal – and then guardsmen were pouring through with shields, swords and pikes, and for a moment she thought they were coming to help their king—

—until the lead guardsmen reached the press around Thraan, lifted his pike high and rammed it into a Vlpa warrior.

'*Kyrik!*' she howled, desperation setting in—

—as, still ablaze, Grigor Radeska emerged from the press, as if the agony of fire meant nothing to him. He raised his blade and charged, right at her.

For Dragan Zhagy, the slow tension of the hour before the wedding had been spent enduring the jabbering of Abraxas, who was eager for the blood-letting to begin. Knowing his daughter was enduring the same was horrifying, though Sezkia herself showed no remorse – it was as if she'd always been this way.

Do we all have a monster inside? he wondered, but put that aside for another time. Blades were out and he surrendered to the raging madness of the daemon. He waded forward, sending a punishing kinesis-blow that left Kyrik staggering – but for all he was outmatched in gnostic strength, Kyrik shielded with skill and the *Sabie de Kiroli* was instantly in his hands. A moment later they were hacking at each other, their gnosis-lit blades belling as the church erupted into chaos.

The presence of the daemon was like a drug in his veins: everything was more vivid, more explosive. His possessed Vitezai surged forward and the castle guardsmen, unaware of what they were helping, offered their support. In a few minutes the Sydians were cornered by pike, spear and sword.

The scent of victory goaded Dragan on: he was the better swordsman and a stronger mage, but Kyrik had been born to the gnosis and was far more skilled. Despite this, he was steadily driving Kyrik back towards the altar, where his whore-wife was ablaze in shields, struggling to keep a burning Grigor Radeska at bay. The giant Schlessen was battering aside two and three men at a time, his immense strength making him a bulwark for the few who were still resisting the Vitezai attack.

Kill the Schlessen pig, he sent mentally to the silent Vitezai men advancing behind him. Their hoods were now lowered, revealing eyes running with blood; only a few remembered to draw weapons as they surged past him, snarling like rabid dogs.

Kyrik launched a counter-attack, trying to grip his mind with mesmerism while blazing away with mage-bolts – which would have ended the fight instantly if he'd still been human. But he wasn't, and he swatted them away, laughing.

'Kyrik,' he taunted, 'I've not even *begun* to fight.'

'You're not Dragan,' Kyrik gasped, and the notion immediately made sense of this madness. *Dragan is possessed.* He ceased his gnostic barrage, which wasn't working, and tried invoking a wizardry spell designed to cripple a possessing intellect. It should have worked, but Dragan shook it off – although that he had to shake it off was encouraging. *He really is possessed, but it might be beyond me to free him . . .*

The spell did at least buy a brief respite. Hajya, beside him now, hurled an already blazing body back into the press. Kip cut down another man, the air around him whirling with steel, and the remaining Vlpa clansmen reached them, Thraan among them. 'The Tower,' Kyrik shouted, 'pull back to the doors behind us—'

Then he turned back to Dragan, repeating the same wizardry spell with more vigour; and once again the gazda shook it off, but with difficulty.

'I wasn't expecting that,' Dragan admitted – but then his wards changed. 'You won't manage it again.' His blade blurred at Kyrik's head and Kyrik was back on the defensive again, fighting for his life.

For a few precious seconds, Hajya and Korznici held the top steps, hurling fire into the press of Vitezai men trying to rush them, while the tribesmen rallied around the two towers that were Thraan and the Schlessen. Korznici had always been a quiet girl, but she was fighting courageously, her serious face intent as if she were solving a difficult puzzle. Hajya felt a surge of pride in her.

<We can do this,> she sent. <On my shout, we break for the rear.>

Hurling a man brandishing a knife away, Korznici sent back a wordless acknowledgement, even as Torzo swayed through the press as if he weren't blind, blazing mage-fire to clear a path to his daughter's side. Hajya glimpsed Kyrik below, the air between him and Dragan thick with whirling blades and smouldering energy.

'Get ready,' she started—

—then a twelve-foot pike rammed through the press and took Torzo through the stomach. The blind mage grabbed at the shaft, choking out a cry when the pike-wielder wrenched the weapon sideways, ripping his belly open. Torzo went down in a heap, blood and intestines erupting with a hideous, wet-iron stench. His screaming daughter was hurled aside by a blurring fist smashing into her jaw.

Hajya keened in grief and rage: Dragan's daughter Sezkia was wielding the pike, and laughing gleefully – then Groyzi slammed his knife into Sezkia's side and flung her folding body into the path of a Mollach with blood around his mouth.

How can this be? Sezkia *rose* again, grinning fiendishly, her wound running with blackened blood. She swatted Hajya's mage-bolt aside and appeared on Groyzi's blindside. Hajya cried, '*Groyzi, watch out—!*'

Sezkia leaped, her teeth suddenly elongating, and buried them in Groyzi's neck as she bore him to the ground. Hajya tried again to blast her, but they were swallowed by the fighting crowds.

Hajya turned to Thraan in despair – only to watch as the Nacelnik clutched his heart and collapsed onto his face, unmoving, purple sparks rising around him. Seeing the pillar of her life pulled down so effortlessly, she almost gave up . . .

. . . but she had been born to struggle. She grabbed Kippenegger's arm and with her other hand rent the air with furious kinesis and fire, sending half a dozen Vitezai spinning backwards, wreathed in flame. Roaring defiantly, the giant warrior sent a mage-bolt down his blade and through the head of the first man who tried to fill that empty space.

'Kyrik!' Hajya shrieked, finding her husband ten yards away, in front of the dais. He was still battling Dragan, but it was clear his guard was failing. She reached out with kinesis, grabbed him and pulled him from the fray, relying on him to engage Air-gnosis in time. For a moment he flailed, then he cartwheeled and landed behind her, atop the altar itself, poised and balanced. Hajya shrieked, 'Get out, Korznici!' as the young woman rose on wobbling legs. '*Go!*'

But the young woman's dazed eyes were fixed on the wreckage of her father, although his corpse was only one of dozens in a horrific mess of bloodied, broken bodies amid the smashed remnants of the pews. A wall of Mollachs, held in check only by the threat of the gnosis, were goading themselves for another charge, knowing those in the front would die. Only four Vlpa still stood, their faces glazed with disbelief. If there was a time to run, it was now.

But the Vitezai men sensed the ending too. With a bloodcurdling yell they charged, more like beasts than men, careless of wounds and apparently impervious too. Hajya was bone-tired, but she managed a ragged burst of fire, while above and behind her Kyrik conjured wind and slammed it into them, making the entire charge stagger, while fanning her blaze. Kippenegger added his own mage-fire too, less potent than her own, but enough to drop two more men.

Then Kyrik roared for them all to run and it was every man for himself. The soldiers came on again as Dragan hurtled from the rafters, sweeping Kyrik from the altar and against the wall beyond. The last handful of non-magi defenders were cut down. From the corner of her eye, Hajya saw Kippenegger grab the still groggy Korznici, launch himself at the big mosaic window and burst through in a torrent of shattered glass. *Yes*, she thought, watching him vanish, the girl in his arms, then, *Kyrik – that way!*

Even as she gathered energy to leap, a blade snaked out and severed her right hamstring and she sprawled instead, shrieking in despair. More Vitezai closed in, but flight was now beyond her. In desperation, sacrificing judgement for strength and ferocity, Hajya unleashed Animagery: her muscles bulged, her jaw distended and her hands became claws. She raked open the throat of the first man to reach her; the second she grabbed by the shoulder while plunging her fist into his heart – straight through chainmail. Ignoring the fountaining blood, she whirled, battering aside spears, trying to reach Kyrik.

Something stabbed into her back and she staggered, lost control of her one good leg and fell. She felt a wrench and snarling, looked over her shoulder to see a man bestriding her, pulling back his dagger for the killing blow—

—until he was battered aside like a toy, and it was *Sezkia* bending over her, grinning toothily.

'Sister,' she rasped, lowering herself onto Hajya's back. The Mollach girl wrenched her head back and snapped her teeth around her throat, plunging her teeth in, crushing her windpipe.

Hajya choked on her last cry as the darkness pulled her down . . .

Through the haze of blurred vision, winded from Dragan's blows, Kyrik saw Kip snatch up Korznici and smash through the circular stained-glass window behind the altar, opening a new path to safety. But his departure removed a bastion of their defence and the remaining men quickly folded. He opened his mouth to yell at Hajya to flee, but she went down with a spear in her back. Then a big arm grabbed his collar and yanked him through a side door, even as Dragan came at him again.

'My Prince, in here!' a harsh voice bellowed, and Kyrik realised with a shock that it was Pater Kostyn. The priest was weeping with rage as he shoved the door closed and locked it before thrusting Kyrik down a short corridor. A moment later, a blow like a giant's fist shook it.

'*This is a place of Kore!*' the pater shouted. '*Respect the house of God!*'

Kyrik gripped the royal sword, trying to steady his legs and to deal with the awful image of Hajya crumpling. *Do I die here, or run?* He could think of only one reason to flee: so that he could come back and kill *everyone* who'd done this. He had his bearings: the stairs at the end of the corridor went down to the dungeons, which would be a dead end, or up Haklyn's Tower. He readied himself to run, but there was something he needed to know first.

'Did you know this was planned?' he asked Kostyn, hefting his blade.

'No!' the priest responded, tears on his face – not of fear, but fury. 'I *swear* I did *not* know!'

He's telling the truth. Kyrik grabbed Kostyn's arm and begged him, 'Run, Pater – if you stay, you'll die.'

A second blow all but smashed the door apart. Dragan roared, '*KYRIK!*' and sent a torrent of shards and splinters ripping into the priest. Kostyn collapsed, his back ripped to shreds, foot-long splinters impaling his torso through to the bone.

Shields up, Kyrik staggered to the stairs and then he *ran*, up and up, hearing the thud of feet behind him, twisting away from a mage-bolt that seared past and cracked stone, burst through another door, found a gallery he knew for a dead end, pelted to the right, through an arch, the pursuit never far behind. He struck an iron-bound door like a battering ram and burst the lock, stormed up more steps and then he was on top of Haklyn's Tower, gasping for breath in the cold, swirling air.

A storm was building, whipping at the banners and moaning through the stone battlements. Two hundred feet below, Lake Droszt was a mess of white-capped waves. Lightning jagged across the northern sky and thunder cracked above, making the stone beneath his feet shudder. He spun and slammed the door, spun locking spells and fed them with all his strength before turning away, trying to think what to do.

Fight or flight? Or something else? He was an Air-mage, but he was exhausted. If he leaped, the only direction he was going was straight down.

'Valdyr,' he shouted despairingly, into the darkened sky, 'where *are* you?'

The only response was the wind, howling like wolves – then Dragan crashed through, the door splintering, and he stepped onto the turret, twirling his blade mockingly. Kyrik faced him, his back to the void.

Hajya's dead, he thought. *There's nothing left for me here . . .*

Brother, he sent into the aether, *the kingdom is yours . . .*

Valdyr Sarkany stood alone at the edge of the fire's light and heat, staring out into the fog. Behind him, Zlateyr was tending the stricken Luhti, feeding her broth and praying to Epyros, the genilocus.

But I saw the White Stag die . . . The White Stag was Epyros . . . Valdyr turned and found Gricoama looking at him, his eyes strangely aware. In the pale light of the fire, the wolf's coat looked more white than grey, and Valdyr's eyes went round.

'*Gricoama . . . ?*'

Then an anguished cry knifed through his brain and he stared, following the direction of the sound from the south, towards Hegikaro. He took a stumbling step out into the darkness; Zlateyr called his name but he didn't stop walking into the gloom over stony ground

573

made treacherous by ice and snow until he came to a ravine right at the edge of the mist. He almost fell in, but caught himself just in time.

What was that? he wondered.

A thin female voice whispered in his ear: Luhti, although she was still unconscious back beside the fire. 'Listen to the wind, Valdyr Sarkany,' she murmured.

At first he didn't know what she meant, but as he stood there the sound of battle-cries and screaming came to his ears, and he could smell freshly spilled blood. The more he focused on it, the more real it felt. Mist writhed before him, filling the chasm.

Gricoama joined him, ghost-like in the mists, and Valdyr put a hand on his neck. Alarmingly, the wolf was a full foot taller at the shoulder, with commensurate bulk, but there was no time to dwell on that: the voice he'd heard had been his brother's.

Listen to the wind . . .

He closed his eyes and visions filled his inner sight like waking dreams: he saw fighting and murder in the royal church, Mollach against Vlpa, and then he *truly* saw: the empty-eyed stare of Vitezai men who fought with tooth and claw and could barely be killed. He saw Dragan too, not as he knew him, but as an immense shadow, smashing his blade down on Kyrik. He saw Sezkia Zhagy, a beautiful, bloody killer. It was incomprehensible . . . and he knew exactly what it meant.

Asiv has taken them all.

'Kore's Blood, *I* brought all this here!' He almost fell to his knees, but Gricoama barked angrily, as if chiding him. 'What can I do?' he wailed to the wolf.

'What is it you wish to do?' Luhti's weak voice asked.

He clenched his fists. '*Kore's Blood – I'm sixty miles away, so what can I do?*'

But still he raised his hands, mind churning, trying to find a way . . .

'Dragan,' Kyrik panted, placing his back to the abyss, 'what have you done?'

Dragan spat, and something like the real man emerged – but it was just a bitter mockery of the gazda he knew and respected. 'What have *I* done? I've seized upon a power of my own: made a bargain with

Lucian, the Lord of Hel – for *Mollachia*! Because you're not worthy, and nor is your broken brother – but *I am*—'

'But how?'

Dragan snorted. 'I see no reason to tell you.' He moved into a fighting crouch. 'Come on, Prince, let's end this.'

The way he spoke, the words he used . . . none of it was the real Dragan. Kyrik clung to that. *If I can escape, maybe I can help him.* It gave him a purpose to cling to, but his brain could barely think past the loss of Hajya.

They both moved at once. Kyrik's plan had the virtues of simplicity: he feinted an attack, then threw himself backwards and began to fall, calling on his final spark of gnosis and seeking the air . . .

But Dragan gestured at the same time and an invisible kinesis grip closed about Kyrik even as his feet left the tower. He hung there, gravity unable to pull him down, as Dragan reeled him in, his sword raised . . .

. . . while Valdyr, sixty miles away on Watcher's Peak, did the only thing he could think to do—

—and blinding white light jagged from the heavens and slammed into the pinnacle of Haklyn's Tower, striking the flag-pole and crackling through the stones. To Kyrik, it was like seeing the world split open and the light behind the sky revealed. Dragan convulsed in a staccato dance, his sword incandescent and his body blackened. The kinesis grip vanished and Kyrik was hurled into the void, shocked rigid and jerking as he plummeted. A wall of darkness hurtled towards him – the lake! – and he managed the vestiges of a gnostic shield just as he struck the water.

He crashed through the surface, plunging into the deathly cold, his body spinning over, and above him the splash was an explosion of white in the blue-green darkness, and then it all turned white. Like a curtain closing over his head, the surface froze.

Dragan Zhagy pulled his still jerking body upright and staggered to the lip of the half-destroyed tower. Below him, the entire lake was covered in ice, each wave a sculpture of still life. He scried immediately for

Kyrik, but the lakewater repelled the spell. If Kyrik lived – which was highly improbable, even for a mage – there was no sign of him. And nor should there be.

We'll fish his corpse from the lake when it thaws, he told himself.

What was more disturbing was that a dwymancer – Valdyr, or someone else? – had reached down from Watcher's Peak to do this. *That* was something to be feared.

'Well?' an Eastern voice said behind him, and he turned to see Asiv Fariddan, ten yards away and eyeing him warily. 'Is he below the ice?'

'I believe so,' Dragan replied.

'Your problem, Gazda.' Asiv looked down at the town, coated in rime and glazed by the starlight breaking through the cloud cover. The momentary storm was already over; even a dwymancer couldn't sustain something from nothing for long. 'You have much work to do: a kingdom to placate or subdue, and the Rondians are still in the lower valley.' He turned back to the north. 'I, on the other hand, will deal with the real problem: Valdyr Sarkany.'

'Can you do it?' Dragan asked.

Asiv smirked. 'Of course – anything can be done by the likes of us.' With a *whoosh* he threw himself into the air and was gone.

One day, Dragan thought, *he will face me for what he did to my innocent daughter.*

Abraxas, who was likely passing his vengeful thoughts straight to Asiv's brain, snickered and giggled in his skull, mocking his rage and grief.

But the Noorie was right: there was work to do. Dragan returned to the castle below, where his Vitezai were assembled. Now that the blood-letting was done, the castle soldiers were stacking the dead. Those not under the blood-sway of Abraxas were eying the hunters fearfully. Those burghers of Hegikaro who'd been brave enough to stay were watching too, scared and uncertain. There was a ragged cheer when he appeared, but he could taste the fear in the air.

Good. If they are afraid of me, they'll be afraid to act.

Sezkia came to his side, a new dress hugging her curves – but she looked like a hungry ghost, a *strigoi*, and moved like one too: a true hunter of the night. He mourned her even as he took her hand and kissed it.

'Where's the Sydian whore?'

'Do you mean our dear queen?' Sezkia tittered. 'Below . . . I'm going to have such fun with her.' She smirked horribly. She was nothing like the daughter he loved, but the beast inside him grinned in response.

That's what we are now, he admitted, *but at least we're together. And she's so lovely, like her mother* . . .

He kissed her forehead, then stalked to the top of the steps and looked down at the throng. Raising his sword, he roared, '*MOLLACHIA FOR THE MOLLACHS!*' until the people fearfully took up his cry.

39

Desecrated Shrine

Theurgy: Illusion

*What you see, hear, touch and taste: how much of it is real? What can you really
trust, when it comes down to it? Your senses? Your god? Your family? Don't make
me laugh, lest I weep instead!*

EMPEROR HILTIUS (ATTRIBUTED), PALLAS, 901

The Celestium, Pallas, Rondelmar
Octen 935

Lann Wilfort, Supreme Grandmaster of the Kirkegarde, went from man
to man along the crenelated walls surrounding the Shrine of Saint
Eloy, keeping them focused. Empress Lyra had gone down into the
saint's cave while her three companions stood guard at the opening.
His role was to ensure the perimeter was secure, and he was burningly
conscious that the two most important people in Koredom, the grand
prelate and the empress, were currently only a hundred yards apart,
and both were under severe threat.

As well as a full century of soldiers, he had ten battle-magi, with
another half a dozen in the three windskiffs circling above. More magi
were stationed at crossroads surrounding the Celestium, and he had
as many watching over the Sisters' Crusade. So far, apart from the
demonstrations Valetta was leading in the Forum Evangelica, the south
side of Pallas was quiet.

He paused opposite Lac Corin. The still water, despite being notoriously dirty, was dappled by the occasional rising fish. The Bruin, which

fed the man-made lake, got its name from its dirty brown flow; people joked that it was all the shit from Dupenium and Fauvion, although in truth, it was as much mud and detritus from the northern forests as effluent from the myriad farms lining the banks as it wound through Brevis and northern Rondelmar. Keeping Lac Corin from becoming clogged with weed was a long-running battle.

'What's going on, Milord?' asked Barrus Gyl, the mage-knight commanding this section of the wall. He was staring uneasily towards the shrine.

'You don't want to know,' Wilfort answered. 'Keep your eyes watching outwards, not in.' He knew a little of what was happening and had theories regarding the rest, and it all added up to heresy, which was not a good word. Like Wurther, he had no desire to be made to defend the indefensible before an Inquisition Tribunal.

'Are we expecting trouble, then?'

'You know my motto: expect trouble and you'll not be disappointed either way.'

'Unless you happen to enjoy trouble?'

'Not me.' Wilfort grinned. 'I'm all for a quiet life.' *And I should never have accepted this post.* Within the Kirkegarde, the Grandmasters were equals, a meritocracy who chose their Supreme Grandmaster for five-year terms. He'd not realised how political the role was when he accepted; he'd felt safer in battle than sharing the Rymfort with Dravis Ryburn. *Just two months to go, then I can step down and take up a provincial posting – no doubt just in time for another round of peasant revolts, knowing my luck . . .*

'Still, all looks quiet,' Barrus commented.

'Never say that,' Wilfort replied. 'It's just tempting fate.'

Which – *naturally*, Wilfort thought – was the moment the lake erupted, giant shapes surging out of the water and up the steep banks, amid a mighty spray of water.

Dominius paced back and forth behind the altar in the cathedral, his long crosier tap-tap-tapping on the stone floor. It was both vexing and a relief not to be able to see what was going on inside Eloy's shrine.

Exilium Excelsior, watching Vrayne's men, and Beleskey's above, pointed at the crystal set in the crosier head as he passed him and asked, 'What's that, Holiness?'

'You don't miss much, do you? This is my war-crozier, for times of conflict. That crystal was a gift of the Ordo Costruo, centuries ago. It's a fragment of one of their solarus crystals. It can be used as a source of energy – *if* you're suicidal.'

'I thought the energy concentration was strange,' Exilium commented, then he returned to watching the watchers.

The grand prelate's own impatience was growing, so he drifted back to the wide space before the altar and choir, where Guard Captain Vrayne was standing. 'A good day for an assassination attempt,' he commented, making Vrayne start in alarm. 'Joking,' he reassured him, walking on. *Kore's Blood, soldiers are dullards.*

He glanced up at the narrow balcony running around the domed ceiling where his bloodman Mazarin Beleskey was stationed with a cohort of crossbowmen. The scholar appeared momentarily and waved. As he withdrew again Dominius breathed a little easier. *Come on, Ostevan, try something and see where it gets you*, he thought, then chided himself for tempting fate. *What's Lyra doing out there?*

He joined Exilium again, feeling distinctly uneasy. He'd learned to listen to his gut over the years, and not just because this place bred paranoia. 'Stay alert,' he muttered to the young Estellan.

'Of course, Holiness.'

He pointed at a side door. 'If anything happens, we go that way.'

Exilium frowned. 'Shouldn't we join Beleskey's men on the mezzanine?'

'I've made a career of doing what I shouldn't,' the grand prelate replied. He touched the young man's forearm and said, 'If I've not said so before, Exilium, you're doing good work. I appreciate it.'

They heard footfalls and turned to find a dozen Sisters of Kore hurrying down the aisle. His initial alarm faded when he recognised Sister Pettara, one of Setallius' people; she'd been *his* double agent for decades. He suspected Dirklan knew. 'Sister, what's happening?'

'It's the Forum Evangelica,' Pettara replied. 'Valetta's rally is getting out of hand and the guards are being forced to keep them out of the main buildings.'

He'd been worried that Ostevan would try to use the Sisters' Crusade as a means to get inside; that this was happening at exactly the same time Queen Lyra was here was plainly no coincidence. 'Thank you, Sister,' he said, turning to Vrayne to ask him to assign men to the task—

—as the nuns erupted in shockingly unexpected, maniacal violence, hurling themselves at the unprepared guardsmen – although Pettara herself slipped to the rear, where a flicker in Dominius' peripheral vision made him spin.

A scarlet-robed shape had appeared from the same door the nuns had come through: it dropped its hood to reveal the face that had haunted his nightmares since Reeker Night.

With a savage gesture, Jest slashed the air with his right hand – and a spiratus-blade carved through Vrayne's body and aura before the man had time to shield. The guard commander gave a choked cry, his body emptied and he crashed at Wurther's feet. But other men were stepping in, Celestial Guardsmen trained to react to such an assault: blades were coming out and they were hacking at the savage women.

But only one other person truly existed here. 'Ostevan,' Dominius croaked, as Exilium tugged at his shoulder and the remaining men formed a cordon about him. Three were already down, but so too were several of the nuns.

'Dom,' the masked man replied, his voice slyly ironic. '*Sur-pri-ise!*' He lifted a hand, kinesis pulsed and Exilium and the other men protecting him froze.

The grand prelate couldn't take his eyes off his nemesis. He raised his hand, tapped his crosier to the floor where silver runes had been inscribed, and a barrier flared before him, then he signed to Maz Beleskey on the balcony above. 'Take them down!'

The crossbowmen swivelled and fired—

—and he felt every single shaft that struck home, hammering into his unsuspecting Celestial Guards, the bolts enchanted to help them punch through gnostic shielding. The wall of flesh and steel between Ostevan and him crumbled – then a bolt slammed into his shoulder, breaking his right collarbone and spinning him round. He fell to his knees with a jarring thud. Only Exilium still stood, his sword drawn but unbloodied, as the barrier began to fade.

Wurther gazed in disbelief at the wood and metal bolt jutting from his shoulder; he could feel the head inside him, and a bloody mess of burnt and torn tissue. Blood was welling out, his crosier slipped from his hand and clattered on the stone, the crystal dimming. He managed to turn his head to look up at Beleskey, standing at the rail above, a man he would have sworn he could trust.

'Maz?' he choked out, swaying, pulling in every healing spell he knew, trying to *keep . . . going . . .* But with the bolt still buried in him, he couldn't do enough, and wrenching it out would likely send him unconscious.

'I'm sorry, Dominius,' Beleskey called, 'but to work with a genius like Naxius? I really couldn't turn it down. Life's so short . . . but now I have eternity . . . which is to say, a long time . . . and there's so much to do.' He pulled a helpless face. 'Which is to say, I'm really not sorry at all.'

The nuns parted before Ostevan as he stepped to the edge of the heaped corpses of Celestial Guardsmen and poked the gnostic barrier thoughtfully. It sparkled at his probing, but the mesh of pale light held.

I'm safe . . . for a few seconds. Dominius clutched Exilium's leg, trying to breathe through the agony as Ostevan turned toward him again, leering smugly.

'Dom, my friend, you should never have sent me away. All that time in Kore-bedamned Ventia, wallowing in the muck with all those inbred peasants? How could I resist when the Master called?'

I'm going to die, Dominius thought woozily. *I'm Kore's Voice on Urte, but I'm going to die.* He looked up at Exilium, his eyes pleading for a miracle.

'Do it, Excelsior,' Jest said coolly. 'Kill him.'

Lyra and Saint Eloy were paralysed with revulsion as the root tendrils erupted through the amber walls. A fat taproot lashed out and slapped her backwards, and when she spun about, her pregnant belly like a boulder, she was cut off from Eloy. As she baulked, frightened to go forward, scared to stay, several thick, supple tendrils lashed around her and jerked her off the ground. Thrashing in their grip, her stomach felt like it was about to tear open, and she almost lost her link to Aradea. But she threw her energy back into it, and the golden glow of the chamber sparked to life again, as did a wild sense of hope in her chest—

—until a dozen more tendrils, black as the night and glistening wetly, slammed through Eloy's body and the pseudo-flesh she'd watched grow on his bones fell away. With a vicious twist, his skeleton was pulled apart and he was gone, and all the while, Lyra was being wrapped tighter in the revolting grip of the tentacle-roots holding her suspended between ceiling and ground. She felt as if she were in the belly of a beast, waiting to be digested.

'*ELOY!*' she shouted. '*BASIA!*'

The roots started pulling and prodding – then a contraction tore at her, ripping her apart from inside out, and she *shrieked*. She tried to focus on everything Midwife Domara had said about breathing, venting her lungs like bellows, trying to ignore the panic and the horror, trying to breathe through the pain as the root-tendrils tightened.

Then a dark shape swirled into being: a man in black robes wearing the Lantric Puppeteer mask. The face was both wise and mocking, and the eyes inside the mask gleamed as he floated through the writhing tree-roots to where she hung.

'Lyra Vereinen,' he said, his voice lilting. 'I've been *longing* to meet you: the Fey Queen, conjured from nothing by Radine Jandreux and set upon the throne. A pathetic, cuckolded nun. The Empress of the Fall – and a heretical dwymancer.' He cackled softly. 'I know all about you, child.'

Lyra cringed from him. 'Who are you?'

'Your new Master.' He pulled up the mask, revealing an intense, blond-haired, ageless being, too perfect to be human. 'Ostevan should have done this when he had you, but he was playing games: he thinks he can outmanoeuvre me and take my place. That's the problem with servants – they have *ambitions*. Slaves are better.'

He gestured, and a taproot rose over her like a serpent, the tip open like a worm's mouth, dripping ichor. The Puppeteer pulled open her bodice, his touch oddly insubstantial, more like kinesis than real flesh, then he gestured again.

The root flashed down and she shrieked as it punctured her flesh, right above the heart. Black fluid immediately began to discolour her skin.

'*ARADEA, HELP ME!*' she cried out, but the Puppeteer just laughed.

'The genilocus can't reach you, girl, not here where I've poisoned the Winter Tree. You've learned too little, too late. You should have been here from the start.'

'*ELOY!*' she shouted, thrashing about frantically as her chest blackened and a hideous cacophony of malicious voices filled her head. '*ARADEA!*'

But she felt nothing, as if Aradea didn't exist, and inside her head, a new chorus began: a thousand voices shrieking hatred and hunger into her brain. She had a vision of herself, scouring the world, wreaking vengeance on the magi for all their sins, boiling lakes and opening up craters to spew molten lava over burning cities.

'Once I'd infected the Winter Tree, Eloy belonged to me,' the Puppeteer said chattily. 'Without a dwymancer to fight back, this place was just an empty fortress, waiting for me to claim it.' He added malevolently, '*I* told you to come here, not Eloy – so there's no point resisting. You're already too late – *slave*.'

The thread of power she'd carefully nurtured all the way here snapped, drowning beneath the rising tide of deafening hate that was filling her senses. Her inner eye beheld a wall of eyes and mouths and tongues and limbs descending upon her to crush her and swallow her. Then something burst inside her skull and light and darkness exploded behind her eyes.

Basia stared down the curved stairs leading into the mound. Something was happening down there: she could feel movements of energy and hear muffled sounds. But Lyra had warned her not to enter.

'Milady?' she called, but no one responded. She exchanged looks with Rhune and Sarunia. 'What do you think?'

'She might be concentrating on something,' Sarunia said doubtfully. They had arrows nocked and ready, although no one was in sight. 'She said to wait here.'

'I know – but perhaps I should make sure she's all right—' She stopped abruptly, turning in alarm as a massive surge of energy-use in the aether heralded a great wash of mud and water that struck the wall between the garden and Lac Corin. It overwhelmed the defenders on the battlements and brought the heavy stone wall crashing down. The shock was too immense; all she could do was gape.

The eruption of water and mud and the figures within that wave were accompanied by a booming in the aether: heavy gnosis must have been used. Lann Wilfort groaned: the one approach to the city they'd never thought to monitor was the river, and what moved beneath the surface.

Then his brain stopped analysing and started screaming at him to *do something*.

He shielded with his full strength while hurling himself backward from the walls, moments before a dozen or more massive, low-slung reptilian forms, at least fifty feet long and probably weighing more than ten tons each, struck the stone and brought it crashing down. Out of the wall of spray, a six-feet long set of jaws snapped closed on Sir Barrus Gyl and wrenched him away, while Wilfort, still shielding madly, leaped from reach. Another of the giant creatures, which looked like giant versions of the carnivorous reptiles that infested Ahmedhassan rivers, powered over and through the rubble while broken stones rained down.

Wilfort came to his feet hurling mage-bolts. Maybe half of the magi who'd been on that wall were doing likewise, targeting both the giant reptiles and the smaller creatures riding them, some kind of snake-man construct with tails instead of legs that were slithering faster than horsemen.

'Fall back!' he shouted, then, <HELP US!> with mind and voice, to anyone that could hear.

'Do it, Excelsior. Kill him.'

Exilium was so attuned to obedience that his sword-hand almost obeyed Jest's command without the intervention of thought—

Almost.

In a semi-circle around him were half a dozen slavering nuns, clearly afflicted by the same madness that had driven men and women mad on Reeker Night – and behind them was *Jest* – Ostevan Jandreux, the former Queen's Confessor, if Wurther was correct. Beleskey's cross-bowmen were reloading. The gnostic barrier Wurther had thrown up looked like it would take only a few more direct hits before it came apart like a spiderweb.

And on the floor was Wurther's crosier.

There was no logical reason not to do as bidden and take his place at the forefront of this new conspiracy as it seized power. Ryburn had promised him a lordship and the third throne of the Inquisition round table. Ostevan was to be the new grand prelate, and would reward him handsomely as well. His fortune and future would be made, and more importantly, his family would be kept safe.

But he'd given Wurther his solemn oath, and although the grand prelate was clearly as shifty, conniving and corrupt as the worst of courtiers, his imperfections seemed less when compared with a group of people who thought nothing of intimidating, bribing, bullying, killing or simply enslaving anyone in their way: the sort of people who would threaten his father and sister, a thousand miles away.

If my father and sister must die – if I must die – then let it be serving Kore.

He stepped forward and swung his sword with surgical precision – but not at Wurther's neck, so easily in reach, nor at the drooling, reeker-mad nuns, nor even at the leering Jest.

Instead, throwing his gnostic shields forward and planting his weight firmly, anchored by kinesis, he aimed his overhand blow at the crystal set in the tip of Wurther's fallen crosier.

With a blinding, earth-shattering roar, the solarus fragment exploded. Exilium had clenched his eyes shut, which saved his vision. The explosion melted the tip of his blade and his shields were ripped apart, leaving his tunic burning and heating his armour almost to red-hot – but his kinesis-held position, on one knee in front of Wurther, kept him in place and sheltered the grand prelate from the blast. As the air turned vivid orange and white around them, they alone stood firm.

The blast ripped through the outward-facing barrier Wurther had conjured and tore the unshielded Reeker-nuns to shreds – they were gone before they even recognised the danger. For a few seconds there was no sound and nothing to see except smoke and ash filling the air, then he heard yowls of pain from the mezzanine above. He stood, repairing his shields.

Ostevan, shielded but not anchored, had been hurled across the chamber and was lying against a wall. Exilium hoped his back was broken. But on the mezzanine above, some of the crossbowmen were stirring – he could kill Ostevan or save Wurther, not both.

He seized the grand prelate by his uninjured shoulder and pulled him to his feet, supporting the man's unwieldy bulk with kinesis and propelling him towards the door Wurther had pointed out. They were almost there before the first crossbow bolts flew, slamming into his shielding and glancing aside to skid across the marble floor. He wrenched open the door and shoved the dazed Wurther through. As he blocked another bolt, his eyes were on the smouldering crimson-robed figure sprawled against the far wall.

It flopped bonelessly to the floor – then the twisted and blackened mask shifted into an expression of rage. An arm lifted towards him—

—and he slammed the door, setting wards flaring. A moment later it shook, flames limning the frame as the wards turned critical, but the door held. Exilium turned to the grey-faced Wurther. He had no healing-gnosis; his affinities were Earth and theurgy. All he could do was offer encouragement and protection. 'Hold strong, Holiness. I'll get you to safety.'

Although where safety might be, he had no idea.

A light spell revealed a darkened antechamber and a spiralling stair vanishing into the subterranean darkness. Carefully, he led the stricken grand prelate to the circular shaft and placed Wurther's hands on the rail. 'Holiness, we must go down. If we stay, we're doomed.'

As my father is doomed. As my sister is doomed. But he felt only mild regret: they were blameless and innocent: Kore would reward them in Paradise. What mattered was *honour*. He steeled himself, found that inner, silent place and prepared for what would follow. Live or die, it would be with his soul intact.

Behind him, the door rattled, and then something heavy struck it and it began to come apart.

Ostevan knew exactly how lucky he'd been. Only instinctive shielding had saved him – and even then he could have ended up paralysed or with his skull crushed. Without Abraxas, he would have perished. But wallowing in relief was pointless: he was up, he was mobile, and there was blood to shed.

Ryburn had promised the sanctimonious bodyguard had been turned – clearly he was wrong. But right now, the two people he'd thought to possess come day's end were slipping from his fingers, Wurther into whatever bolt-hole he'd prepared and Lyra into Naxius' claws.

Wurther or Lyra . . . ?

Then Lef Yarle floated down from the mezzanine, followed by two Inquisitors, and shot past him, heading for the door Wurther and the bodyguard had fled through, and that made his choice.

This is destiny. Lyra will be mine . . . I am meant *to have her . . .*

Kindling light in his hands, he ran for the doors leading to the Shrine of Saint Eloy.

The gnosis is an extension of the will, Eloy had said, and now all of Lyra's will, all her fears and hopes for her unborn child and those she cared for coalesced into one burst of rage. Even as the loathsome daemon ichor seized her and the sickening images and hideous crowing assaulted her mind, knowledge also came, from dead souls in the daemon's thrall trying to seize control of her blossoming gnosis.

With that knowledge, she shaped the power bleeding through her brain into a shaft of light that blasted like a hurled spear into the Puppeteer's spectral form before he could react. The torrent of green and golden light struck him like a hurricane. Naxius howled, wavered . . . and was gone.

He was never truly here, Lyra realised, breathing hard. *He was a spiratus . . .* She suspected that was the only reason it had worked, but the result was immediate. The tentacle-roots holding her shrivelled and died and she slipped from their grasp. As she fell to the ground, a wrenching, *pushing* feeling in her gut made her cry aloud in pain and terror. But Aradea was still with her, and the ichor began to flee her body, running out of the wound above her breast in a revolting, noxious flow that sizzled to nothing when it hit the ground.

She was still recovering when Basia called down, '*Lyra! We have to get out!*'

Lyra tried to cry, 'Basia, the baby—' but a contraction struck her like a punch to the groin and she doubled over, howling as her waters broke, flooding her legs.

Basia came tearing down the stairs, then stopped dead. '*Rukka mio,*' she groaned, 'you're in labour!' She bent down, her arms tingling with kinesis to augment her strength, and lifted Lyra as if she was a child. 'Let's get you out of here.'

As they climbed the stairs, they could hear shouting, battle-cries and inhuman yowling. 'What's happening?' Lyra whispered.

'What isn't?' Basia grunted as Rhune and Sarunia shielded them.

Barely a hundred yards away, what looked like a mountain of mud and water, thick with river weed, had levelled the curtain wall. A handful of mage-knights were hurling a torrent of gnostic energy into a seething mass of what looked like enormous reptiles of all sizes: some of the creatures were lying twisted, blackened and dead in the rubble of the riverside wall, but as many again were lashing out at the gnostic barriers the Kirkegarde magi had thrown up. Even at this distance Lyra could feel the black stares of daemons: these were *constructs*, and they were all possessed.

Basia set her down and she reached for the dwyma again, but another contraction swept through her, even stronger than before, sweeping away all coherent thought. She started inhaling and exhaling ferociously, fighting through the pain, and when she looked up again, more magi were descending on windskiffs – but the seething mass of reptile attackers was also growing, although they weren't advancing, at least for now.

The Puppeteer's been banished, she realised, *and they're directionless. We have a chance . . .*

'We've got to get her out!' Sarunia exclaimed, trying to summon help.

'No . . . let me . . .' Lyra tried to reply, still clinging to her link to Aradea . . . But another contraction ripped into her, barely thirty seconds after the last had ended, and it was torn away. *Breathe . . . breathe . . .*

Then the back doors of the cathedral broke open and a single figure emerged: a scarlet robed man in a Lantric mask: *Jest.*

'Lyra!' called Ostevan, with voice and mind. *'Stay – I'll not harm you, I swear!'*

But the queen's awareness was locked away in pain, and he realised she was in labour, fighting to bring her child into the world.

She can't fight me – I needn't fear the dwyma today . . . Then the link to Abraxas gave him something else: Naxius had been here, but he'd gone.

This moment belongs to me! Behind the mask he smiled, and set about rallying the river-monsters and sending them at the Kirkegarde so he'd have a free hand to deal with Lyra. That wasn't hard: he just channelled a brutally simple vision of purpose via Abraxas, who sent the ichor-infected snake-men and their giant reptilian mounts crashing into the Kirkegarde knights again.

The Kirkegarde threw absolutely *everything* back at them: a brilliant torrent of destructive energy, and Ostevan found himself grudgingly admiring their tenacity. He focused on their commander, Lann Wilfort, standing behind the front rank, blasting one of the last remaining giant crocodiles apart. But surely they couldn't sustain that expenditure?

Ostevan glanced at Lyra: she hadn't moved, and she was all that mattered here. The Reeker-nuns were dead and Beleskey's men were dealing with Kirkegarde drawn by the sound of combat, so he'd have to do this himself. *And I wouldn't want it any other way . . .* He began stalking toward Lyra and her guards, thinking, *Crozier destroys pawn, takes Queen . . . Tabula-mio.*

Somehow, Basia managed to blot out peripheral events and amidst the chaos and clamour, focus on what mattered: getting out. She called urgently into the aether, <*VASINGEX: TO ME!*> She slipped her arms under the semi-conscious queen and pulled her upright, shrieking again into the aether, <*VASINGEX, HURRY!*>

To their right, the river-creatures were beginning to overwhelm the line of Kirkegarde magi and soldiers. Such creatures shouldn't even exist, but for years the Imperial Beastariums had been a law unto themselves, despite being under Keeper oversight. *How did those old bastards miss these abominations?* Basia wondered – then she blanched. *Good Kore – did they know all along?*

Then she saw Jest turn their way and she gulped, remembering all she'd been told of Reeker Night.

As the red-robed masked man strode toward them across the green Sarunia asked, 'Any advice on this prick?' as she took aim.

'He's a daemon-possessed Ascendant with every gnostic affinity.'

'Wonderful,' Rhune sighed. 'We're all going to die.' He turned and kissed Sarunia on the mouth. 'I love you, Saru. See you in the Beyond.'

'I thought you were brother and sister?' Basia asked.

'Ventian villages have very small gene-pools,' Sarunia replied, entirely failing to answer the question. Then the two archers turned, their smooth, timeless faces grim with purpose, and they both loosed their arrows, which shattered on Jest's shields. Their hands blurred as they nocked more shafts.

Jest spread his arms and globes of coruscating energy burst to life around each hand, every colour of the spectrum swirling and sparkling as he conjured. The next two arrows burst on his wards impotently, and then the next. The two Ventians snarled, cast aside their bows and drew blades.

And in Basia's arms, Lyra groaned, *'Aradea . . . please . . .'*

A thunderous *crack* sounded behind them, from the Winter Tree itself. Basia whirled to see the whole tree suddenly shaking like a wakening beast. Its branches writhed and the trunk heaved and roots burst from the ground. A wave of foul air flooded over them, an ichor-reek that made them all reel, then the Winter Tree rose from the ground, walking on its major roots like some kind of tentacled beast, some of those 'limbs' having delved dozens of feet into the earth. A shrieking sound rose from it, and blackened ichor gushed through the bark, as if it were purging itself.

Basia gaped, and even Jest halted, his mobile, lacquered visage wide-eyed in astonishment. Basia looked down at Lyra to see if she was doing this, and maybe she was, somehow, but she looked barely conscious.

Every step the tree-beast took made the ground shudder. It strode past them and bore down on Ostevan, lashing out with roots and branches, filling the air with howling and making half of the water-reptiles scatter.

As windskiffs came swooping in to aid Wilfort's defenders, Basia looked up, and when she finally saw a dark-winged shape appear, plummeting earthwards, she dared to hope. <*VASINGEX, HERE!*>

But the seething balls of energy in Jest's hands crackled and seethed: he extended his hands and that energy tore into the tree-beast even as it lashed out at him. Basia saw branches immolate even as verdant light burst from the genilocus – *for what else could it be?* – and speared toward the Mask.

The two powers burst over each other, filling the air with smoke, with noise, with concussions and explosions that made the air throb. She couldn't see Jest any more, but she could hear him roaring in fierce exertion.

The genilocus slew Twoface . . . it can slay him too . . .

Then at last Vasingex swept overhead. The wyvern, a product of the Corani Beastarium, was horse-sized, with leathery wings twelve feet long. His tail lashed viciously about as he opened his jaws and sent flames gushing, torching three snake-men that had burst from the fray beside the wall and were coming towards them. Yowling, the creatures staggered and fell, shrilling in agony. Then the wyvern landed, smoke billowing as he stoked more fire inside his gut.

'*What the fuck?*' Sarunia swore, staring at the beast.

'My birthday treat from Dirk,' Basia crowed.

'It breathes *fire*,' Rhune shouted, 'but it's a *wyvern*! Wyverns don't breathe fire!'

'Wyverns are *mythological*, lackwit,' Basia said. 'He's a *construct* – he can do whatever's bred into him!' Cradling Lyra, she used kinesis to lift herself into the empty saddle on the wyvern's back. 'Grab on behind the wing-joint – and don't let go! If you've got Air-gnosis, use it, otherwise this won't be much of an escape!'

Lyra was moaning, her eyes closed. Basia threw a glance back at the fray, her heart in her mouth as the Kirkegarde line collapsed – but a few windskiffs were there, hauling men aboard. And then she saw the tree-creature burst into flame, its movements becoming the thrashing convulsions of the dying, and her hopes failed with it. Wilfort was being dragged into a skiff, covered in blood, but most of his men were down – and then Jest's blackened form stepped through the burning wreckage of the Winter Tree and his masked visage turned their way again.

'*Vasingex*,' she cried, '*go!*'

The wyvern leaped into the air, mere feet ahead of a searing mage-bolt, then his wings thudded, jerking them skywards, with Rhune clinging to one flank and Sarunia the other, while Basia locked Lyra to her and prayed. They used kinesis to hold tight and all of them added thrust in whichever way they could, and the battle in the garden fell away. She heard Jest snarl and saw him raise his hand.

Then the Mask's mind closed on her own, seeking to break her control over the wyvern – but such links were well-forged, and now spell-range was also a factor: for all Jest's power, she and Vasingex repulsed him. He tried again with mystic-gnosis, but she effortlessly brushed off an assault upon her self-worth, designed to paralyse her with shame at her lost limbs and guilt over her love for Ril – she'd come to terms with the former years ago, and felt absolutely no remorse about the latter. Then they broke from his reach, leaving just a howl of thwarted rage echoing in the aether.

<Domara,> she hollered into the aether as they soared north over the Bruin, towards the Bastion, <Midwife Domara, the queen is in labour – we're coming in!>

Exilium had no idea how deep the spiral stairs went, but the stone walls were dry and the air musty. He kept his gnostic light small, just enough to show the steps in front of them. He heard the door above shatter and a voice snapping orders, but only one set of boots followed them, as far as he could tell – then something fell past them and landed lightly some thirty yards below.

He sensed more than heard someone else following – perhaps catching the sound of clothing flapping in the rush of air – and moving without thought, trusting his instincts, he leaped to the rail, anchored his feet with kinesis, and with light flaring on his blade, he swung . . .

The broken-tipped blade slashed through barely-there shields, jarred as it caught in metal, then flesh, and swept through – and two pieces hammered into the stone floor below, bouncing with a wet, metallic clatter.

Someone below couldn't suppress a taut, female cry of shock.

Exilium leaped after the bisected corpse, landed beside the spreading pool of blood and turned. He'd dropped into one end of a chamber, but only the near end was lit. He stepped over the armoured torso of the man he'd struck down. A dark shape had backed against the wall.

'Holiness, can you manage?' Exilium called to Wurther, not taking his eye from the living foe. A woman . . . He hated that.

'I'll manage, lad,' the grand prelate responded through gritted teeth, from above. 'Do what you must.'

He had to be swift – there was someone else coming down the stairs – so he went in fast, shielding the first mage-bolt that hammered into him, although it almost smashed him off his feet. His adversary was a pure-blood, his superior in power; but he'd fought them in the practise arena and skill mattered just as much.

He danced in, steel belled on steel and he lashed out with his left hand, punching against shields that barely gave. He glimpsed a blonde woman's face and that gave him a momentary qualm – slaying women violated his personal code of honour – but there was no choice, not when her fist flared with fire and she slammed it into his face at point-blank range. His shields held, defraying the heat and destructive energies, while he hacked back at her, his broken-tipped sword crashing into hers. As he shoved up and out, forcing her defences open, his left hand whipped out his dagger and drove it low, through the chainmail skirt protecting her legs and into her thigh before ripping it up upwards. She shrieked in his face, her blue eyes round with shock – and he punched his sword through her mouth and out the back of her skull, where it struck the stone wall and broke again, jarring his wrist. He dropped the hilt as she slid down the wall, grabbed her sword before it hit the ground and wiped his dagger on her leg. He sheathed it, breathing hard but clearheaded.

A woman of theirs for my sister's life, he told himself. It still didn't feel equal.

Dominius Wurther shuffled painfully to the bottom of the steps, but someone else was hammering down the staircase. He caught the grand prelate's arm, helping him keep his balance on the stone floor which was slick with the blood of the two Inquisitors. He widened his wards to cover them both, although it made the shielding dangerously thin. Then someone reached the bottom of the stairs, still in shadow.

A voice snaked out: 'Excelsior, you've condemned your father and sister.'

'Not I, Lef Yarle: I have but done my duty. The consequences are yours.'

'Walk on,' Wurther murmured, clearly in pain, 'just a little further . . .'

As far as Exilium could see they were trapped in a room with no furnishings, nothing on the walls, just a silver circle at the far end etched into the wall – a Wizardry circle, perhaps? Wurther had led him to a dead end.

He placed himself in front of the grand prelate and they backed from the stairs as Yarle emerged, shielded and wary. The Inquisitor put up his visor, revealing narrowed, calculating eyes. He stepped over the bodies of his fallen comrades, advancing like a stalking cat.

'We'll not simply kill your family, of course,' Yarle purred. 'We'll put them to torment, ruin them. Then we'll run ichor into their veins and make them serve us.'

The image of his father and beloved sister in the hands of the Inquisition torturers made Exilium's blood run cold, and the thought of them as Reekers was sickening, but still he refused to flinch, or to be drawn into retaliation as Yarle came on.

Exilium raised the blade he'd taken from the woman – too light for his taste – and banished his anger and worry to his silent place. Behind him, Wurther was groaning at each step, but he was almost at the end of the room.

If I'm to die, let it be with honour . . . So Exilium went to meet Yarle, who closed the gap between them in a blur. They hammered blows at each other, whirlwinds of destruction. Yarle was all about speed, his weapon never still, flashing and probing, stabbing and slashing with a sight-defying rhythm. But in his quiet place, Exilium observed that he planted his feet *so* when he thrust, and *so* when he parried and *so* when he darted left or right. Although illusion blurred Yarle's blade and each blow was augmented by pure-blood strength, he could see enough to block, to counter and to buy time.

Every so often blue fire burst from Yarle's left hand, almost blasting his shields apart, or a pincer of kinesis almost snared him, or a stab of mental energies ripped at the walls of his quiet place: those were the moments when he had to reel away – the moments when he almost lost everything. Then Yarle blasted a hole in the plate protecting his torso, the metal gouging his flank and ripping skin; moments later a scouring sword-tip just missed his eye, leaving a cut in his eyebrow that dripped blood. The Inquisitor was getting closer . . .

Exilium felt himself losing a duel for the first time since the Arcanum. He wasn't the inferior bladesman, but Yarle had the clear edge in gnosis and that was going to decide it. Every blow he launched was immensely powerful, and every time he shoved with kinesis, Exilium had to give ground or be sent sprawling. His shields turned pale crimson as the strain increased.

The end roared closer as Yarle caught his shoulder with a thrust, and as Exilium lurched, the Inquisitor leaped like a dancer, spinning and crashing his blade sideways at Exilium's waist, a blow that could have cut him fully in half – if somehow he hadn't blocked. Gnosis-fire exploded between them and his borrowed blade flew apart, shards of steel spinning everywhere. He staggered at the weight of the blow but still managed a kinesis-punch that shoved Yarle back, buying time to draw his dagger.

A broad smile crossed the Inquisitor's: there was only one winner now.

Then Wurther's voice rang out, shouting in Runic. Something gripped Exilium's collar and he found himself flying backwards, spinning across the stone floor, over silver lines into the Wizardry circle as blue light sprang upwards in a warding that encircled them. He struck Wurther, eliciting a grunt from the grand prelate, and pulled himself up to see Yarle launching himself bodily at the warding.

Light flashed, the Inquisitor crashed backwards and sprawled on the stone floor.

Exilium tried a mage-bolt, but it died in the wards, so he concentrated on getting his breath back. Wiping the blood from his left eye and panting, dagger still in hand, he readied himself. He could see Wurther using pale healing-gnosis on his own wounds, but he still looked weak and dazed.

Yarle climbed to his feet. After tentatively probing the circle, he backed away before raising his blade in ironic salute. 'Well, I think we know how that would have ended, Excelsior. I am the better man. Not that there was any doubt.'

'Only the stronger mage,' Exilium replied. He could see no other way out.

'That's the same thing, Estellan,' Yarle smirked. 'Stronger, more effective. *Better.* And without the handicap of your retarded emotional responses. Frankly, I've seen statues with more humanity than you. Any other man would have done our bidding, for his sister's sake, if not his own. But you . . . ?' He sniggered. 'And where did it get you? A moment's respite, and nowhere to run.'

Even in his quiet place, that stung. Exilium opened his mouth to retort, but Wurther's hand clamped his shoulder. 'Well, this has been dramatic,' the old clergyman wheezed, 'but we've got places to go.'

'You're not going anywhere, you fat imbecile,' Yarle snarled. 'My Master will be here shortly and he'll break your little circle. You're still going to Hel.'

'Perhaps,' Wurther agreed amiably, 'but not today.' He stamped his foot and the stone inside the protective circle began to slowly drop beneath the floor. Yarle's handsome face contorted into absolute rage as his prey dropped lower, and then he was gone as they gently passed through the floor into darkness.

'You're still going to die – both of you, and everyone you love!' the Inquisitor shrieked after them, sending fire washing ineffectually over the protective circle wards. 'The Celestium belongs to us now!'

Exilium stared at Wurther's pain-lined face. 'Is he right?'

'Almost certainly,' Wurther said grimly. 'Ostevan wouldn't have moved so boldly if he wasn't sure he had everything covered this time. And the queen is just outside this building, nine months pregnant and guarded by only three magi. We're rukked, lad – but while there's life, there's hope.'

The descending stone circle stopped with a heavy thud, making Wurther wince and clutch Exilium's arm. He gestured and a torch spluttered to life on the wall, illuminating a narrow tunnel that vanished into the gloom. 'Come on, we've a fair way to go before we're safe.'

Exilium looked up at the circle of light above, where Yarle still raged out of sight before helping him off the circular slab. As the stone began to rise again, he peered down the passageway. 'Where does this go?'

'All the way to a little church in Kenside,' Wurther said smugly.

'But you told the queen all the tunnels between Southside and Pallas-Nord had been sealed . . . ?'

'I lied. You'll find I do that sometimes.' Wurther gripped Exilium's arm again and added, 'Lad, you're a creature of black and white, but this is a world of greys. It pays to embrace that, sometimes. To use it.' Then he grimaced. 'I gather from what that mincing arse-licker said that you've placed your family in jeopardy?'

'They said they'd kill them if I didn't help assassinate you.'

Wurther winced. 'You'd sacrifice your kin for *me* . . . ?'

'I gave you my word. I value my immortal soul. My sister and father will be taken up to Paradise.'

Wurther stared, then shook his head. 'The *Book of Kore*, eh . . . stronger than swords.' Then he asked, faintly bewildered, 'So if you knew of this threat, why didn't you say something? To me, or Setallius, or *anyone*, really?'

'Because I hadn't decided – not until that moment,' Exilium confessed. Anything else would have been a lie.

'Sweet Kore, you're a strange man. I appreciate your final choice, and for admitting the dilemma.'

'Truth is the greatest of all weapons,' Exilium said, before remembering that it was Wurther's lies that were leading them to safety. 'Eventually,' he mumbled.

'I'm sure you're right – but let's get going, eh? A strong Earth-mage could get into this tunnel in half an hour and I'm not the speediest man alive at the best of times.'

He laid an arm across Exilium's shoulder and the young Estellan braced himself, then helped the holiest man on Urte towards safety – although both knew that if the Celestium had been stormed, the Bastion itself might offer no refuge either.

The Bastion

The blast of energy from Edetta Keeper was as powerful as any Dirklan had ever felt. An Ascendant was said to be four times as strong in raw power as a pure-blood, and Keepers were usually raised to the Ascendancy after a lifetime of honing their craft.

All Dirklan could do was shield and pray. Through the veil of blue light encasing him, he could see and feel the blast: it filled the whole room, surging towards his Volsai and the hapless guardsmen. The first men were completely incinerated, those behind reduced to roasted skeletons. The entire wall of gnosis-strengthened glass blew out in a great roar, followed by Brigeda, who was hurled through the broken window, trailing a comet-tail of sparks and fire.

As he and Mort were battered against the side-wall, his shields turned critical and began to fray. He couldn't see much – the chamber was awash in smoke – but someone cried, '*Charge!*' away to his left and booted feet burst in from the side-door. That showed incredible courage, given what they'd just seen. Through the smoke, blue lances of fire crackled and danced, burning onto his retinas.

Dirklan tried to climb to his feet, but Mort pushed him flat again. A man screamed, then another, and Edetta called out in a sing-song voice, 'Too few men, Dirklan!'

Then Mort grabbed his shoulder, hauled him backwards through the door and slammed it shut. The Axeman's bearded face loomed over him. 'That was rukking Edetta Keeper!'

'I know,' Dirklan groaned. '*I know.*'

A Keeper working against the empress? It sounded impossible, even now. *Are all of them in it? Are we really so alone?* He cursed his lack of numbers, but it would have been impossible to conceal more. A balance had been struck between risk of detection and risk of being overpowered. *And I got it wrong, again . . .*

But done was done. Now he had to find other solutions.

'What do we do, Dirk?' Mort asked.

When in doubt, panic, he thought. 'Raise the alarm and turn out the guard. Bring in windships and seal off the tower from above and below.'

Mort grimaced and rose, bawling orders while Dirklan threw his senses towards the fight upstairs. Edetta still stood, and by the time his reinforcements arrived, she, Medelie and the children would be long gone. Only one hope remained.

Solon, are you still with us? It's all down to you.

Radine twisted in Solon's grasp, a bony spur spurting from her elbow through the fabric of her dress. She slammed it into the eye of the man holding her; it went in with a wet sound and the man reeled and fell, blood welling from his eye-socket. He was dead before he clattered on the floor and for an instant Solon was stunned into immobility.

That hesitation cost the other guard his life too. Shocked at the appearance of the old duchess emerging from the flesh of the youthful beauty, his hands dropped away. Radine's fingernail was suddenly a foot long; she lunged like a fencer, sending it through his shields and armour to pierce his heart in a blaze of gnosis. His eyes went wide, then emptied. Two seconds, two mage-warriors dead, leaving Solon facing a nightmare of his own making.

Radine's skin was as grey as her hair. Her eyes were black as her bloody hands reached towards him. 'Now look what you made me do,' she accused him. 'After all I've given you, Solon – after everything I did for you.'

'Setallius knows,' he told her, drawing his sword and levelling it at her. 'He's only a floor below us . . . *Tear.*'

A bleak look crossed Radine's face, then she shrugged. 'Yes, I'm Tear – but I'm Radine, and Medelie too . . . and I love you, Solon. I want to be with you, for ever.'

Though she was only a foot from the tip of his blade, Solon could sense shields as powerful as those Twoface had thrown up – and Twoface had nearly killed him on Reeker Night. She was far beyond him in power, and she knew it too.

'Forget Lyra,' Radine pleaded. 'She's failing, and dragging us all down – you *must* take her place, Solon.'

She paused as the tower shook to an almighty crash, followed by a sensation like wind on skin – powerful gnostic energy, emanating from directly below. *Dirklan?* he thought, hope flaring, but Radine didn't look in the least perturbed.

'That's Selene, darling – or as you might know her better: Edetta Keeper. Yes, even the Keepers have turned against Lyra. Her reign ends tonight.' She reached out her hands to him, her voice beseeching, and her face changing again, a smooth transition back to Medelie in all her youthful loveliness. 'Solon, *think*: Lyra's doomed. The forces aligned against her are too great. But together, we can bring back stability. Forget this moment of doubt – pretend it never happened.'

He bowed his head. 'Must I become like you . . . ?'

'Why wouldn't you want to, darling? I'm all-powerful!'

He lowered his blade until the tip was on the floor. Below, more gnostic energy surges scorched the aether, then they heard the distinct clip of a woman's shoes on the stairs. Dirklan Setallius wouldn't be coming to his rescue.

His options narrowed again, until all that was left was this . . .

He fell to his knees, releasing his sword so that it clattered on the stone floor, and bowed his head. 'You're right,' he said in a dazed voice. '*I yield.*'

Not all of the preparations for dealing with the cabal's attack were getting people into the right place undetected. There were also the gnostic defences.

Instantaneous spells *altered* something: a mage-bolt or a kinetic push were a split-second discharge of energy to leave the world changed. But *enchantment* – energy trapped inside a spell, permanently active or waiting to be triggered – endured. Even the aura could be concealed, if cunningly set.

The antechamber where Solon knelt contained one such enchant-ment designed to be released when a certain phrase was spoken. It was simple, and brutal: four steel discs, each one two feet in diame-ter and razor-sharp, were embedded in the stonework, positioned at about waist-height for a tall man. And a fragment of each had been set in the pegasus pendant Solon had given Radine, who was in the act of reaching for Solon when the four discs erupted from the stone-work, seeking that pendant. They carved through her so swiftly and powerfully that her shields were rendered useless: one instant she was looking down at him, then a ribbon of red carved through her chest and her body came apart in a spray of blood as the discs struck the opposite walls.

She hit the floor in two pieces.

Then she snarled, and he gaped as tendons erupted from her hips and stomach, her upper and lower spine seeking to reunite, while her mouth twisted into a sneer. *<YOU IDIOT,>* her mind snarled, as a nimbus of darkness formed about her—

Instinctively he pulled his blade back to his hand and swung, hacking through her neck, severing the spinal column and sending her head rolling across the stone floor. Black blood poured from the stump as her eyes *finally* emptied.

The footsteps on the stairs below halted . . . and then came on. Selene, he presumed. He took a final look at the wreckage of the woman he'd revered more than anyone in his life, not knowing if he could ever recover from this. Then he ran for the upwards stairs, slammed and warded the door behind him. He locked the upper door too, and found the royal children in Coramore's bedroom, clutching their bags. They looked at him, scared, noting the blood on his clothing and his drawn sword.

'What's happening?' Coramore demanded. 'Where's Lady Aventour?'

'She was a traitor, and now she's dead,' Solon panted, unwilling to even think of all that meant. His heart was blasted to ash. He was functioning on will alone.

'I thought she was your friend,' Cordan whimpered.

'I was pretending, to find out who she worked with,' Solon answered.

With a great roar of sound and energy, the lower stairway door crashed open. 'Oh, children?' a woman called, her voice carrying up the stairs, a mockery of concern. 'Where are you?'

<Dirklan?> Solon called into the aether.

<Solon? Rukka mio! It's Edetta Keeper! Hold on – we're only a couple of minutes behind you! We just have to get her wards down!>

Solon looked about him. At the far end of the corridor was a final flight of steps to the roof – where Dirklan was supposed to have men stationed . . .

Edetta knocked on the door he'd just locked. 'Cordan? Coramore?'

Solon put a finger to his lips and pointed to the door to the roof. Then they froze as that door-handle turned – but the wards kept it locked. 'Who's there?' he called.

'A friend,' replied a male voice, brittle with age.

An enemy, Solon thought bleakly. He knew the men stationed above. He put a hand on Coramore's shoulder. 'Be brave, both of you. Can you do that?'

'I'm brave,' Cordan said immediately, in a frightened voice. His sister just nodded.

They're not bad kids. I almost like them. Solon planted his blade-point down and knelt, looking the two Sacrecour heirs in the eyes. Is it my duty to kill them now, before they fall into our enemies' hands? Perhaps it is, but I can't do that.

'Cordan, Coramore, I want you to remember Reeker Night, when Lyra and Ril saved your lives. They had no reason to do that, but such deeds are what makes them who they are. That's why I serve them. They're not perfect, but they try to do the right thing. By contrast, your own family want to turn you into people like Tear.'

Both children remembered Tear from Reeker Night. 'We're not like her,' they chorused fearfully.

Fists struck both doors. 'Children!' Edetta called.

'Lyra could have had you both killed any time this past five years,' Solon told them. 'But she hasn't, because it would have been evil. You owe her your lives.'

Both nodded, their eyes welling with tears. Behind him, at precisely the same instant, both stairwell doors splintered and fell open. The children went rigid as Solon rose calmly, lifting his sword to point-guard.

Edetta Keeper stepped through the lower door as Delmar, Keeper-Prime, came from the upper one. Edetta held a staff and Delmar a drawn sword. They murmured in satisfaction when they saw the children unharmed.

'Well, Solon,' Delmar said, 'thank you for keeping the children safe for us.'

'I'm surprised it was you who betrayed us,' Edetta commented. 'I didn't think you had the imagination to lie.'

'Once I was inside your cabal, I had to stay the course,' he said calmly. 'I hated it, but it had to be done.'

'Bravo,' Edetta mocked. 'But you should have killed these brats.'

'I would never do that,' Solon replied, as the children cringed. 'I believe in them.'

'It's a shame and a waste,' Delmar Keeper-Prime commented. 'You'd have made a good puppet-emperor.'

'I'm no man's puppet.'

'If you say so. Surrender the children and we may let you live.'

Solon weighed their words while his senses strained for signs that aid was coming – but there were none. The wardings that encased Delmar and Edetta blocked all awareness of the outside world.

He took a deep breath, then nudged the shoulders of the children. 'Go to them.'

'But . . .' Cordan began, bewildered, but Coramore, understanding, took her brother's hand and pulled him forward. Edetta scooped them into her grasp, smiling coldly.

'Your Uncle Garod will be so pleased to see you both,' she exclaimed, tousling their ginger hair, then pulling them towards the upper door. She looked at Delmar Keeper-Prime, who hadn't moved. 'Are you coming?'

'I have unfinished business,' Delmar replied. 'It won't take long.'

He and Edetta exchanged a look, and then she and the children were gone, leaving Solon alone with the leader of the Keepers.

'You know, I was accounted the greatest warrior of the age,' Delmar said conversationally, 'but you and I never crossed blades – not even in 909, when I slaughtered your kind and sent the Corani cowering back to their holes.'

'In 909 you slew good men and women in their beds, then murdered students and citizens,' Solon replied evenly. 'I was only twenty-three and I was forced to lead the retreat. If you'd had the guts to come near me I'd have butchered you, as I did many other Sacrecour and Fasterius toadies that day.'

Their eyes met. The Keeper-Prime's were utterly dispassionate. 'I'm going to send a message to your empress: your head, to prove that I'm still the master, "Takky".' He brought his sword up to guard and kindled his shields. 'Shall we?'

Solon raised his own blade – then a wave of Ascendant-strength gnostic force struck him, hammering him backwards. He slammed into a cot, which came apart, struck the walls and bounced, fought for footing and parried, blocked and ducked as blows rained down on him, ripping at his shields. Sparks flew as steel and gnostic auras collided. Delmar was a shadow within his own shields, a faint glimpse of bared teeth and eyes like hail-stones. It was all Solon could do to weather the storm.

But defence held the advantage over attack and a mage's shield could defeat an energy bolt of equivalent power. Solon had always been an aggressive fighter – but while Delmar's gnosis outmatched his, the man was at least ten years past his prime and had spent several decades as an administrator and politician, not a warrior-mage.

I have to outlast him.

Inside a minute, Delmar was gasping for air, pouring his energy into trying to smash through Solon's defences. Solon couldn't respond to the din of shouted gnostic calls filling the aether; all his awareness was on the blade before him and the comet-tails of gnostic energy trailing it as his foe drove him steadily back.

Then with a deft twist and snaking thrust, Delmar's longsword slashed through Solon's shielding and armour to plunge into his midriff. Solon gasped in agony as Delmar ripped his blade free, his legs wobbling in shock as they parted.

'First blood, Takwyth,' Delmar panted, twirling his blade.

'This isn't a duel, Sacrecour,' Solon gritted out.

Then Edetta's mental voice filled their minds, calling, <*Delmar, come!*>

At the same instant, Solon heard Setallius shout '*SOLON?*' from the stairwell.

He chanced a lunge, hoping Delmar was distracted – but the Keeper-Prime swayed away and suddenly his defences were open again.

The Keeper's sword came through them, taking Solon in the right shoulder and spinning him round – then he slammed a double-handed blow into Solon's blade, right by the hilt, and the steel shattered, jarring Solon's hand horribly and leaving him holding just a jagged stump of metal. He staggered, falling sideways, and Delmar's blade followed him round, aiming for his head to end the fight – all he could do was twist away, howling as the blade plunged into his collarbone, and he crashed forward as his legs gave way – even as he thrust his own six inches of broken steel into Delmar's face, through his eye and into his brain.

They collapsed together, the Keeper-Prime dead already and Solon not far behind as the fall drove his foe's sword deeper. His vision was wavering, his head ringing and blood pumping from his shoulder.

<*Delmar!*> Edetta called impatiently again.

<*He's not coming,*> Solon managed to answer, then the pain dragged him down.

Dirklan took the stairs at a run, Mort Singolo on his heels, the remainder of his Volsai following. They burst into the top chamber and his heart leaped to his mouth. There was no sign of the Sacrecour children, and Delmar Keeper-Prime and Solon Takwyth were lying entangled in a growing pool of blood.

He feared the worst until Takwyth shifted slightly, groaning as blood pumped through the fingers he had clasped over his left shoulder. Already kindling healing-gnosis, Dirklan ran to his side and set about doing whatever he could to keep Takwyth alive.

'It was Delmar and Edetta . . .' Takwyth groaned. 'Edetta took the children – Delmar wanted . . . to prove a point. He was . . . *damned* good . . .'

'He was an Ascendant – no one but you would have lasted ten seconds.' Examining the Knight-Commander's head, Dirklan added, 'You were the only one to emerge from 909 without a mess of scars. Good to see you're catching up.'

'Rukk you, One-Eye,' Takwyth slurred, then slumped sideways, his eyes closing as the healing-gnosis took both pain and awareness away.

Dirklan stared at him, marvelling that the man he'd always regarded as an intellectual lump of stone had managed to get inside and betray such a deadly group – especially when that had entailed getting so close to the woman they'd both served loyally for so many decades. He'd used Fire-gnosis to destroy Radine's body so that no one else, not even his agents, would know who'd been behind this latest plot – most of Coraine still believed their duchess was a saint. No need to destroy that legacy.

Mort called down from the roof and Dirklan relinquished Takwyth to one of the healer-mages who'd bustled in and went to join the Axeman on the battlements. There were a dozen corpses, the hapless soldiers they'd stationed here. They'd believed the Keepers allies when they'd arrived: more lives betrayed and lost.

Mort was pointing east at a giant winged creature flapping away. A flotilla of windcraft were following it, but wings were swifter than sails. 'We won't catch it,' he remarked. 'A draken?'

'Aye,' Mort replied, 'a huge fucker. I hate constructs. Should be a bloody heresy.'

'I don't disagree.' Dirklan linked to the rings he'd given the children, confirming the worst. 'Edetta Keeper has the children. They're flying straight for Dupenium.'

'Then it's civil war,' Mort muttered. 'The empire is going to destroy itself.' He wiped his sweaty pate, then asked, 'Has Basia reported? Where's the queen?'

'That,' Setallius said grimly, 'is a damned good question.'

Lyra lay wrapped in blankets, holding her sleeping son and staring up at the sky through the tangle of trees. Calm now reigned in her garden. Domara was preparing her suite for her, but for now she was content to lie here, where she felt safe.

Before her, keeping her warm, was the first fire Lyra had ever lit here, from dead branches that Aradea had gifted. The genilocus was a presence here, weakened from its exertions at the Celestium, but watching, vigilant and protective.

The Winter Tree is dead ... what will that do to all of its progeny? Lyra wondered, but it was too soon to know. And right now, she was too exhausted to care. It was enough just to be here with her protectors, spiritual and physical, and her newborn son.

The infant stirred in his sleep and she returned her gaze to his tiny, composed face. He had a few wisps of fine black hair, his father's stamp. He'd fed from her breast for the first time, a domestic miracle amid all the tumult.

I'm a mother. I have a son.

A wave of exhaustion carried her down into a cocoon of dreams, in which she floated in warm water on a river that wound through time. Ril was with her, stroking his son's head and laughing for pure happiness ...

But when she woke, it was to a silent room.

Hours had fled: she was in her own suite and it was daylight outside. Dirklan Setallius was seated beside the bed, his lined face slack with exhaustion. But when she moved he sat up, looked at her gravely with his good eye and took her hand.

'Lyra, are you strong enough for tidings from Collistein Junction?'

40

Prince of the Spear

Solarus Crystals

The gnosis is energy, and the amount of energy a mage can control is an equation between blood-purity and skill, and the periapts they use. But solarus crystals change that equation, because they don't just enhance the energy transfer, as a periapt does, but multiply it. This makes them incredibly useful, but also exceedingly dangerous.

ANTONIN MEIROS, CONSTRUCTION PROPOSAL IV, PONTUS, 702

Collistein Junction, Kedron Valley
Octen 935

For a few crucial minutes everything went exactly as planned. As the south wind drove his ships back into the heart of the lighter-weight, becalmed vessels, Ril watched the destruction of the Keshi windfleet begin. From the fore castle of the *Philemon* he saw his ships raking the decks of vessels below them, while their prows sheared off masts and sails. The Eastern fleet was at their mercy; in the first minutes of contact some forty Keshi vessels were dashed from the air.

Rondian roars of triumph rose above Keshi despair. Rocs flashed in to try to protect the bigger ships, but that forced them into close contact with the heavier, better-armoured Rondian knights and their venators and invariably, the Rondian fliers emerged victorious.

Ril raised a triumphant fist towards Captain Dace: victory was in reach.

Then lightning crashed in the corner of his eye, the aether rippled and he spun to see livid energy engulf a Pallacian warbird. Hundreds of voices cried out in terror as the empowered keel exploded, sending burning timbers ripping through the skies in all directions. Skiffs and windriders of both sides were struck, and dozens of larger craft caught fire.

The *Philemon* floundered as the air throbbed; then a few seconds later that dreadful light blazed again and another Rondian warbird exploded, this one much closer.

His mind flashed to a memory of the gnostic lance that had slain Malthus Cayne, and that showed him where to look: at the small wing of roc-riders streaming past the blast. One of them was trailing gnostic sparks.

'There!' he shouted, '*there!*' He pointed as the rocs swung towards his vessel.

Another flash, and the windship beside the *Philemon* exploded. Ril threw himself aside, trying to dodge the burning splinters tearing through the air and ripping at his shielding while the shredded sails were wreathed in flames. When he looked around again, the captain and half the crew had been mown down by the lethal splinters, and many others had been hurled overboard. He was momentarily petrified by grief and fright – then he remembered Pearl, tied up below.

Using kinesis, he hurled himself at the hatch, even as the *Philemon* lurched and began to drop slowly. The pilot was fighting the damage, but if their keel exploded, they were all doomed – and at any moment that damned spear might strike them.

He staggered down the stairs and found the crew panicking. His heart wrenched, but he had to be in the air – the ships were sitting ducks to this new weapon. The *Philemon* began to drop faster, flames licking the sides and smoke pouring in as he burst into the hold where Pearl was housed. The aether was alive with cries of mages shouting, <*The flagship's hit – she's going down!*>

He smashed open the hatch and cool fresh air rushed in as he severed Pearl's ropes, crying, 'Come on, Pooty-girl!' Exerting Animagery, he persuaded her to move, hauling her to the open hatch. The *Philemon* tipped further; she glimpsed an escape and surged forward and Ril hurled himself onto her back just as she erupted from the side of the ship, spinning free, her wings unfurling . . .

With scant yards to spare they righted, screaming over the top of the massed Keshi below and into a climb. Moments later, the *Philemon* smashed into the ground and burst apart. The air battle was turning again, Ril saw instantly: their advantage was gone and in the last minute he'd lost four warbirds. More than that, momentum had shifted: the battle hung in the balance.

For a moment, it occurred to him that he had too much to live for: that a general should be at the rear. His wife and his lover needed him, and so did his unborn child – then he glimpsed the roc-rider wielding this Hel-weapon. Raging, he urged Pearl upwards in pursuit, and as he did, his Corani knights found and surrounded him.

<*There!*> he shouted with voice and mind, jabbing a finger towards the swarm of giant eagles. <*There he is! Kill him!*>

The knights spurred their beasts into the climb even as that deadly energy ripped through the aether again, leaving another warbird shattered and wreathed in flame – then the roc-riders saw them, turned and flashed into a dive, lances lowered, coming right at them.

<*Luka – no!*> Waqar howled, but he wasn't listening. And for all his heart was tearing in two at what Lukadin was doing to himself, his brain was applauding: his friend had turned the battle, saved them from disaster and perhaps even won the day. But at what cost? Lukadin was reeling in the saddle from the succession of blasts, which had probably exceeded even his expectations.

He couldn't lose his friend. <*Luka – that's enough!*>

Lukadin just waved the spear drunkenly before releasing another, weaker bolt into another Rondian ship, barely enough to light the sails.

<*No, that's enough – you've turned the tide – now you're killing yourself!*>

He saw the Rondian mage-knights appear below, urging their beasts into a steep climb – coming for Luka. *They're beneath us, climbing into the wind, so we've got every advantage.* Then he spotted the white winged horse of the enemy prince: fate had given him another chance at Ril Endarion. More than that, perhaps if they killed the enemy commander, Luka might stop using that accursed spear.

<*Bashara – Baneet – all of you: set lances and dive!*>

He led forty or more rocs and their riders in the charge as the two dozen knights rose to meet them – then he saw that Luka was with them and his heart went to his mouth. *<No, Luka – pull out!>*

But his friend wasn't listening; he'd couched the spear as if it were a lance. Waqar tried to swing across his nose to stop him, but only succeeded in dashing Ajniha's wings against Bashara's bird, almost entangling them. Bashara shrieked at him and spurred her roc away, getting between him and his target so all he could do was watch as his riders slammed into the enemy . . .

Velocity by weight by angle – but only one of those three factors counted in their favour as Ril's knights met the diving Keshi eagles, and it wasn't enough. Straining in a hopeless climb, there was almost nothing behind their blows, and the Keshi riders picked their spots, many using lances because they could see that their enemies were incapable of dealing a blow sufficient to penetrate their shields.

In a split-second, the cream of the Corani mage-knights were dead. Gryff and Larik Joyce took spears in their chests and were torn from their venators. They dropped from the sky even as Jorden Falquist's head was separated from his neck by a giant Keshi swinging a seven-foot scimitar. Fiery arrows exploded into the exposed bellies of dozens of venators and pegasi.

Ril, heartsick, sent Pearl into a sudden dip, flashing beneath the Keshi who'd picked him out and thrusting upwards with his lance, which plunged through the roc's chest and into the rider, impaling them groin to chest. The lance was torn away and the giant eagle spun earthwards, bird and rider already stone-dead.

He flashed by a Keshi whose bird had been fouled from the line, and swung about when he realised it was the Mubarak prince . . . then he caught sight of his true quarry, the Keshi with the deadly spear, blazing towards Sanjen Sulpeter and blasting him to nothing. Ril's brain was screaming that he was probably the only one of his knights left, but the need to strike down this deadly enemy overruled all other thought.

<Endarion!> he shouted. *<Endarion for Coraine! Endarion for the Vereinen!>*

and sent Pearl into a shrieking dive as the enemy swam into his path, the deadly lance swinging his way.

Waqar heard Bashara's death-cry as the lance pierced her bird and her and fury and grief ignited inside him. The Rondian prince's winged horse shot past him before he was even aware, but he quickly swung into pursuit. Ril Endarion was hurtling towards Lukadin, but all that emanated from Luka was a song, a hymn to Ahm, resounding through the aether as he gathered his resources for another blast of energy.

<No, Luka – watch out!>

Baneet and Fatima were turning far below and Tamir was converging on them, but he already knew it was too late. As Endarion's pegasus descended on Lukadin's bird, the spear flashed again—

Ril was driven by desperation, but he hadn't stopped *thinking*. That spear would incinerate him – but only if it struck. As they flashed towards each other, he touched his heel to Pearl's flank, sending her into a well-rehearsed manoeuvre; she veered aside just as the weapon pulsed and the murderous bolt blasted at him . . .

. . . and passed his shoulder without a touch.

He corrected his trajectory as his prey filled his sight: the young man's face was ashen, his hands blackened and he looked like a corpse already – then Ril swung his longsword and took the Keshi's head. The blazing gnostic spear spun into the air while the dead Keshi's torso slumped and his bird flew on.

Ril took Pearl into a spiralling descent, searching . . . and . . . *there!*

He reached out with kinesis even as he urged Pearl into an interception path.

A dozen Keshi eagles followed him down . . .

Waqar howled as Luka died, but he stayed on the Rondian's tail, urging Ajniha into the dive. The Rondian prince was closing in on the spear as it spun earthwards; he could feel the aether crackling as he engaged kinesis, trying to pull it in.

If he gets it, we're doomed . . .

<*On!*> he urged Ajniha, drawing his scimitar. With a mental gesture, he loosened the straps of his harness and as the distance closed, he lifted his feet from the stirrups, seeking purchase on the sides of the saddle . . .

Ril *reached* and the spear stopped falling and jerked towards him. Pearl had levelled out, perilously close to the battlefield below – and an instant later, his right gauntlet was gripping the haft and the crystal set in the spear-head was blazing into life as his aura engaged with it . . .

Kore's Blood, what the Hel is this thing?

Then a shadow fell on him . . .

Waqar leaped from Ajniha's back even as the Rondian prince caught the spear and it blazed into life.

First his blade slammed into Ril Endarion's back, piercing shielding and armour and out through his chest, then Waqar struck him bodily and they were both knocked almost senseless. The winged horse dropped like a stone, wings flailing, as Waqar clung to the Rondian. The glowing spear spun away.

Then Baneet swept in, the spear flashed sideways into his grip and he kicked his roc into a climb, brandishing the weapon as the gem flared back to life.

The Rondian gave a gasp, blood gushed from his mouth and he gasped, '*Basia*—' or some other word Waqar didn't know. The white horse beat its wings desperately and her hooves slammed into the turf, mere yards away from a body of men, and then it was galloping, carried along by momentum. The Rondian was strapped on, but the impact tore Waqar free and he went over the horse's tail, barely avoiding having his skull crushed by a flailing hoof, then he struck the ground. He rolled to a standstill, utterly dazed, as a cloud of men ran in, hurling futile spears at the pegasus bearing its stricken rider. The beast was rising again and in seconds they were gone, flapping away.

The soldiers were Lakh, and they were capering madly as they hauled Waqar upright, clapping him on the back and shouting excitedly. He knew a little Lakh, but their demeanour told him more: they were not just advancing ... *they were winning.*

Then a livid bolt tore the skies and another Rondian warbird erupted in flames.

Dear Ahm, Baneet – not you too ...

There was a shining light glowing in Ril's mind as the world faded to grey around him. A woman he loved, an angular woman with spiky hair and an awkward grace, was walking on long, beautiful legs across the sky towards him, smiling, reaching down to cup him in her hands, calling his name.

Someone else called also from behind him and he turned to see a wan, blonde girl – one he'd tried to love, but somehow, despite the faery-tale way they'd met, it had never quite taken. He waved her farewell, and she vanished.

Basia, he whispered as he fell into his true love's arms and knew no more ...

Seth Korion's line had held, despite the elephants and the massive horned creatures. A combination of Animagery and brutal fighting had sent the enemy beasts reeling back and his forces were frantically trying to reset and reinforce when the sky-battle above them changed for the worse.

He'd known the windfleet's planned manoeuvres, drawing away to the north, the prearranged wind-change and the devastating sweep back down the battle-lines to crush the Keshi fleet as it hung immobile in the air, and for a few minutes it looked like it had worked. He prepared himself for the victorious windfleet to begin to attack the enemy ground forces, enabling his men to advance. *Perhaps I'll be kissing Prince Elvero's arse after all*, he thought wryly, remembering his earlier doubts.

Then came those dreadful bursts of energy that tore apart the Rondian windcraft, ship after ship. The only thing that Seth had seen that surpassed that power were the mighty blasts that had erupted from Midpoint Tower in 930 and destroyed the Imperial Windfleet. Emperor Constant had died that day, alongside most of his court, who'd been there to witness the destruction of the Bridge. These blasts might not be as large or destructive, but they had the same characteristics. Again and again, the vivid white light flashed through the Rondian vessels, and suddenly the entire fleet was falling, burning or trying to escape.

Another craft struck the ground in flames, and his aide Delton groaned. 'Oh Kore, that was the *Philemon* – the prince is dead!'

Nope, looks like it's Elvero who'll be puckering up . . . Seth spared a brief thought for Ril Endarion, who'd seemed a decent man, then cleared his mind of sentiment. 'Ready the lines,' he told Delton. 'They'll come for us next. And tell the baggage caravan to harness the horses. This may quickly become a fighting withdrawal.' He gave the man a firm salute and Delton responded in kind, clearly shaken but anchored by Seth's apparent calm.

If the rest of this lot stay cool too, we might get out of this . . . Then for a moment, Seth allowed himself to think about that well-remembered face, glimpsed in the midst of battle. *Latif, was that truly you?*

Or another impersonator . . . ?

To the north, the skies began to thin, the remaining vessels staggering apart like drunks in a barroom brawl. Dozens were fleeing northeast, but all of the craft clustered over the Rondian centre had triangular sails, and they were descending to archery range over the Corani legions.

Seth turned to his officers to order the retreat when a winged horse came skittering in from the east and glided towards him, its rider slumped in the saddle. It landed at the canter and one of the aides caught the harness and stopped the beast.

By the time Seth reached the pegasus, the rider had been cut from the saddle and was laid out on the ground. He had some skill as a mage-healer and went right into the press to kneel beside the fallen knight. As he'd suspected, it was Ril Endarion. There was a dreadful wound in his chest, but that was the lesser one; the hole in his back was worse.

'Is he breathing?' someone asked.

Seth placed a hand to the man's chest, then shook his head. 'He's gone,' he said, dazed. He looked at the faithful pegasus, staring into its wild eyes as it snorted and shook its head, clearly grieving. No sooner had he pulled loose the tack and harness, than the winged beast gave a dreadful cry, galloped a few feet, its wings thudding, then rose into the air. Shrilling in sorrow and loss, it headed west. For a moment its shape was silhouetted in the sunset, then a fresh trumpet call grabbed Seth's attention and pulled him back to the present: the Keshi were massing again, and they couldn't possibly face another attack: if they didn't disengage now, they would be engulfed as the centre collapsed.

'Bring the body,' he ordered. 'We have to get out of here.' He turned to Delton and added, 'One day I'll get to advance instead of retreat, but it won't be today.'

EPILOGUE

Wind from the South

The Darkest Hour

Many like to speak of a darkest hour, a time when all seems lost. It is vital in that moment to hang on to hope, because that's the rope by which you'll climb from the mire. Do not let it go, because regaining it is the hardest task of all.

ANTONIN MEIROS, ORDO COSTRUO, HEBUSALIM, 889

Pallas, Rondelmar
Octen 935

Lyra waited in an antechamber to the throne room. Around her, guardsmen fidgeted and attendants fussed. In the mirror, her reflection was ghostly, her skin and hair made even paler by her black mourning clothes, her eyes red-rimmed: an angry ghost, quivering with suppressed rage.

Was it only a day since the attack at Saint Eloy's shrine, since she'd given birth? It felt like so much longer: Ril was dead and their army had been defeated. She was still pale from blood-loss and exhaustion, shaky on her feet and moving in a state of unreality – but the demands of state permitted no rest.

Dominius Wurther joined her: cast from his stronghold, he was a grand prelate in exile. He moved stiffly, his shoulder strapped, and he was leaning heavily on the arm of Exilium Excelsior. Apparently the grim young Estellan had saved Wurther, at considerable personal cost. Valetta stood next to them with her most trusted sisters, those women who'd got her out when madness descended on the Celestium.

Dirklan Setallius was there too, his face spectral. Behind him, all armoured and grim of face, was a pallid, stricken Basia de Sirou, Mort Singolo and Oryn Levis. Midwife Domara, carrying Lyra's baby son wrapped in black swaddling, brought up the rear.

Trumpets blared, the double doors were flung open and Oryn led Lyra into the court, a sea of black: black for loss, black for defeat.

My poor boy's going to grow up with no colour in his life.

As she passed through the crowd, she could sense the fear: the Coraine and Pallas nobility were shivering in the aftermath of the devastating news, wondering what the future held. Was this to be 909 all over again? Would the Sacrecours sweep back into Pallas and butcher their rivals and any who had aided them? Could she, their empress, save them from the Sacrecours – or even the Shihad?

Is this the end of our civilisation?

Lyra reached the throne and sat. There was no need to ask for silence: the six hundred people packed into the hall were all straining to hear her. She'd been rehearsing this speech with Dirklan all night, drilling the words into her brain. Now they came out, high and brittle, her voice like broken glass.

'My Lords and Ladies, I thank you for being here with me to share our grief on this dark day. You have suffered loss, as have I. So many have died: the best of us. Eastern invaders have defeated our armies in the Kedron and they now march on Noros and Midrea. Rondelmar stands threatened from *without*.'

The crowd murmured in dismay, but her eyes were so full of unshed tears she could barely see them.

'And here in the North, Garod Sacrecour has paraded Prince Cordan, a fourteen-year-old boy, and declared rebellion. The Keepers, sworn to preserve the gnosis, have sided with him. In the Celestium, our beloved friend Dominius Wurther has been usurped by one in whom we once trusted. Rondelmar is threatened from *within*.'

The reaction to this was angrier – and fearful.

Lyra bit her lower lip to stop it trembling, and went on, 'When Garod paraded those children, he said, "The reign of Lyra Vereinen has failed. *She is a merely a woman, weak by nature.* She is widowed, penniless, betrayed by her counsellors, at odds with the Church and out of touch with her people's plight. Her armies are defeated in battle. Only House Sacrecour, your proven, traditional and rightful rulers, can pull the empire back from the precipice. March with us on Pallas and let us place Cordan Sacrecour on the throne he was born to sit, and let us rid the world of Lyra Vereinen and the scum who cling to her skirts. Let it be 909 again!"'

The fear those words drove into the hearts of those before her was clear. Dirklan hadn't wanted her to repeat them, but she'd wanted *everyone* to know what that *bastard* was threatening.

'*That* is what we face' – her voice was stronger now – 'a man who, during an invasion by a foreign power, plots the massacre of his *own kind*. A man who would rather kill Rondians than Ahmedhassan *invaders*. A man who would butcher Kore-worshippers while the *Amteh* take our realm. A venal, backstabbing criminal without conscience or grace: a man who withheld his own men from battle, not just in cowardice, but in calculation: trying to steal the right to rule you through a boy. A *hateful* man who plots with assassins and cabalists: a blight upon this world.'

'*Aye,*' many called, '*death to the Sacrecours! Death to Garod!*'

While she didn't exactly disagree with the sentiment, she waited until they had quietened, and then cried, 'No! Not "Death to this or that"! Say rather: *life*! For the Corani, and for all who fight to save our way of life! I do not believe that every man and woman in Dupenium and Fauvion share Garod's evil. I pray they will see the light and turn against him.'

There was much to say; she moved on. 'We now know the man behind the Masked Cabal who assailed us on Reeker Night: he calls himself the "Puppeteer" because that's what he thinks we all are: his puppets, dancing when he pulls our strings. But we know his true name: *Ervyn Naxius*.' She heard gasps, and genuine fear: Naxius had been a bogeyman for decades now, the Ordo Costruo's renegade genius, the man who rejected morality. 'We will find him, and we will end his threat. The affairs of state are not the preserve of shadowy cabals – they are the concern of every man and woman, and they must be played out in the light of public scrutiny.' She bunched her fists, in full flow now as anger swept her along. 'Naxius and Garod think we're *weak*, but we are *strong*: we are strong in courage and fortitude – strong in faith – strong in the need to protect our children!'

She gestured, and Domara handed over her son. Lifting him up, she cried, 'We will *not* surrender to the forces arrayed against us. We do *not* give up that which is ours without a fight. *Solon Takwyth* does not yield! *Dirklan Setallius* does not yield! *I DO NOT YIELD!*' She bit her lip as Takwyth's name raised the greatest cheer: it was always Solon they trusted. But she ignored that, shouting, 'It is said that *in adversity, character is revealed.* We will show our character: of the highest order. We will *not surrender* to the forces arrayed against us!'

The ferment rose and the child began to sniffle. 'We have endured crippling losses, but House Corani endures. My son' – she hoisted him up again – 'Prince Rildan Vereinen, will be emperor after me and he will have a million fathers: every man of our Rondian Empire, sworn to serve and protect him!'

She stared out across the sea of faces and shouted, '*KORE BLESS RONDELMAR – KORE SEND US VICTORY!*'

She held Rildan close as the court thundered their support. Who knew if they would be so supportive in days to come: the Ahmedhassans were coming, the Sacrecours were coming and Ostevan held the Celestium – and he had one hand around her soul. She could barely conceive how they would prevail against such powerful enemies.

But inside her was a network of warmth and shared strength: from Aradea and the dwyma; from Luhti, lying beside a fire on top of a mountain with a tall scarred man beside her, and a young black-haired Eastern girl riding a sea-beast. They were like her. They were kindred: dwymancers. Life-magi.

I'm not alone any more, she told her enemies. *You'll never find me alone again.*

Collistein Junction, Kedron Valley

Waqar Mubarak knelt beside the small row of mounds, thinking about this strange custom of burial. The Keshi cremated their dead, speeding the soul to Paradise, but this was Yuros, and they didn't have the fuel to spare. The ordinary soldiers were being thrown into mass graves, Rondian and Keshi bodies entwined. The worms wouldn't mind which was which.

But he'd insisted on his windriders being honoured – Lukadin, his head found and reunited with his body; Bashara; Shameed, and dozens of his men. The idea that they might lie unmarked was utterly repugnant to him.

Sal'Ahm, Shameed: you died in the air, where you loved to be.

Sal'Ahm, Bashara: you were a warrior-spirit; I will miss your passion.

Sal'Ahm, Lukadin: you gave up your life to save the Shihad, the cause that meant everything to you. You were the fire in our hearts and you blazed across the skies. I'll never forget you.

He rose, Fatima, Tamir and Baneet with him. That cursed spear was cradled in Baneet's arm – just like Luka, he wouldn't let it out of his sight now.

The battlefield reeked of blood and smoke and those damnable marshes. The Battle of the Kedron was a glorious victory: they'd driven the enemy armies from the field; only the loss of daylight had stopped a rout. Senapati Valphath's left wing had been checked by the Rondian right; that force was retreating in good order – but the Rondian centre and left had been routed.

A horseman joined them: Sultan Rashid, alone, to Waqar's surprise, given that Rashid was seldom without a retinue these days. Waqar's friends made obeisance, then Rashid waved them away.

'Well done, Nephew,' he said grandly. 'You won the skies for us. This victory will be claimed by many, but I know whose actions were decisive.' His gaze drifted from Lukadin's grave to Baneet. 'The spear: what is it?'

'A weapon that kills the wielder.' Waqar dared to meet his uncle's eyes. 'With it, the lowliest mage could destroy a mighty mage, and all with him. In this battle, it was wielded by one who placed your Shihad at the centre of his life. I'll never cease to mourn him.'

Rashid's emerald eyes glinted. 'Not a weapon to be used lightly.'

'It won't be.'

'If I demanded it, Nephew, you would hand it to me.'

'It belongs to Baneet now, so you'd have to ask him,' Waqar replied. 'But you can depend on his loyalty.'

Rashid considered that, then made a resigned gesture. 'Then let him keep and protect it. I am impressed by the loyalty of your friends, Nephew. It's a valuable skill, to engender such feelings in others.'

'I'm fortunate to have true friends. What happens next, Uncle?'

'Next, we march with all speed. We must capture a major city to shelter our people – Jastenberg is the nearest and best choice.' Rashid put a hand on Waqar's shoulder. 'It is winter that frightens me, not the enemy soldiers. And therefore I have a request.'

Waqar bowed his head. 'What is your command, Great Sultan?'

'We know you have an untapped power, Waqar,' Rashid said. 'If you consent to learn it, you could hold back winter itself. If ill-chance besets us and we're unable to secure shelter over winter, we will need that power.' He lifted Waqar's chin and asked, 'Nephew, are you willing to try to gain the dwyma?'

Waqar swallowed, staring out of the battlefield and remembering the fallen, all the men this war had already destroyed. *But if we fail to capture a city before winter, every man in this army could perish . . .*

He bowed his head dutifully. 'I am yours to command.'

Mollachia

Kyrik huddled in the sewage system beneath Hegikaro Castle. He was shivering with cold, but he was alive.

When the lake froze over his head, moments after he slammed into the water, he'd had just enough air and strength to seek the one safe place he knew: an old pipe, once used to transport the castle's waste into the lake. It was close enough that he'd reached it half a minute after going into the water and managed to find the will to pull himself along to a tiny alcove where workmen used to shelter when unblocking the foul pipe, before his father had had a bigger, better system built. It was still filled with debris, but the top layer was dry enough to burn for heat. And always, there were rats, which meant food. That meant hope.

He would deal with the grief of losing Hajya, and so many others. He couldn't understand how Dragan could have done this, but he had to go on: to escape, and then do what was needed to put a monster in its grave.

The Celestium, Pallas

Ostevan Jandreux paced outside the locked Prelature, ignoring Beleskey and a dozen ichor-infected Celestial Guard. After a long night, the Celestium had been secured by the Inquisition's new Reeker Guards, courtesy of Angelstar. Now he controlled the Holy City, he was rounding up senior priests, clerical staff and soldiers and was systemically infecting them with the ichor.

He'd been careful not to spread the infection too widely, to confine it to the Holy City: Greyspire, Southside and Fenreach were untouched, which was crucial; he still needed to mask his nature, for now. Pallas was the heart of the empire, but barely a tenth of the population of Rondelmar dwelled here. Those in the wider realm needed to believe that he was a worthy ruler of the Celestium.

He took a moment to reflect on how near it had all come to disaster: Lyra's genilocus had channelled its power through the Winter Tree – quite possibly the same powers that had destroyed Twoface. He suspected that only the ichor in the tree's system had weakened it enough that he'd defeated it. Victory had been won, but it could have gone dreadfully wrong.

I'll not take her lightly again . . .

A side-door opened to admit a cowled man in black robes, his large frame bulked out by armour, followed by a similarly shrouded figure with a gloved hand resting on his sword-hilt. The larger of the pair pulled back his cowl, revealing the austere mask of Angelstar.

'Ah, Knight-Princeps,' Ostevan said warmly, but neither approached closer than half a dozen paces.

Dravis Ryburn removed his mask, while Lef Yarle scanned the room. Ostevan had enough protectors that if treachery was intended, it would be a blood – *or rather, ichor* – bath. Perhaps it would come to that soon, but for now their causes were aligned.

'Congratulations, Holiness,' Ryburn said neutrally. 'The grand prelate's robes suit you.' He smiled ironically. 'You've had them taken in rather drastically.'

'I have. A shame he escaped you,' Ostevan replied. 'You told me that Estellan idiot would play his part?'

'Exilium Excelsior has signed his family's death warrants,' Ryburn growled. 'His father and sister will be seized. They will be brought here and we will make an example of them all.'

'What's wrong with the man, that he would sacrifice his kin for a fat fool like Wurther?'

'Some foolish attachment to "duty", I imagine. Has the Master made contact?'

'He has,' Ostevan replied. Minutes after being hurled from the shrine of Saint Eloy, Naxius had spoken to him via relay-stave to warn Ostevan that speaking of his momentary discomfort was forbidden.

Don't worry, 'Master', your little setback is my most cherished secret, Ostevan mused, and that brought his mind back to the empress. *Somehow I have to master you, Lyra – as my lover, or my slave . . .*

Didn't all the old dwymancers go insane? I wonder why? Whatever it took, he was determined to have her: with gnosis and dwyma at his command, his reign would eclipse even that of Sertain Sacrecour. But his daydreaming was interrupted by a signal pulsing into his head. He bowed to Ryburn, threw open the doors and entered the Prelature. Inside, thirty-two new prelates awaited, their infection wounds still clear on their bodies.

Their blank, black eyes watched as he went straight to the throne and placed the mitre on his own head. No sense in messing around with ceremony. *Let's just get this done.* Then he turned to face the room. Ryburn and Yarle, lurking beside the doors, didn't look especially pleased at his new rank, but they applauded politely.

Two of us ruling the Holy City is one too many, Ostevan thought as he made a gesture of blessing over the room.

'Behold the Voice of Kore,' the prelates chorused. 'Hail, Ostevan Pontifex!'

'I am both Emperor and High Priest,' he told them. 'I will reign a thousand thousand years.'

THE SUNSURGE QUARTET
continues with book 3:
HEARTS OF ICE

ACKNOWLEDGEMENTS

A big thanks again to Jo Fletcher for her ongoing support for this series and the world we've created. Its creation couldn't have been placed in better hands. Much appreciation too, to the rest of the team at JFB/ Quercus, especially Molly Powell, Sam Bradbury, Emily Faccini for the maps, Patrick Carpenter and Paul Young for the cover, and all involved.

Thanks again to the test-reader team: Kerry Greig, Paul Linton, Heather Adams (also my agent, with her husband Mike Bryan) and Catherine Mayo. As always, the concoction tastes better after you've added your seasoning.

The biggest thanks is reserved for Kerry, my wonderful wife, for putting up with a husband whose work never leaves him alone – or is that the other way around?

Lots of love to my children Brendan and Melissa, my parents Cliff and Biddy, and all my friends, especially Mark, Felix and Stefania, Raj, Andrew and Brenda, and to the friends we've made in Bangkok, especially Karl and Kathryn (and Max!), Mark and Jeannie, Greg and Layla, and Rawleston and Christine.

Appreciation to Wittertainment, NPR All Songs Considered and Guardian Football Weekly for being sterling company on my morning run, and much appreciation to James Mitchell for the Moontide Wikia: http:// the-moontide-quartet.wikia.com/wiki/The_Moontide_Quartet_Wikia

Hello to Jason Isaacs.

David Hair
Bangkok, 2017